The Great Gate

Titles by Scott Marcy

Novels

The Seventh Age
The Great Gate
Elven Born

Strange World Survivor Series

Surviving Eden: Episode 1
Game of Shadows: Surviving Eden – Episode 2
Into the Storm: Surviving Eden – Episode 3

The Great Gate

By

Scott Marcy

For my mother, father, and God. Their love, patience, and guidance made this book possible.

Eden
and the land of
Asgard

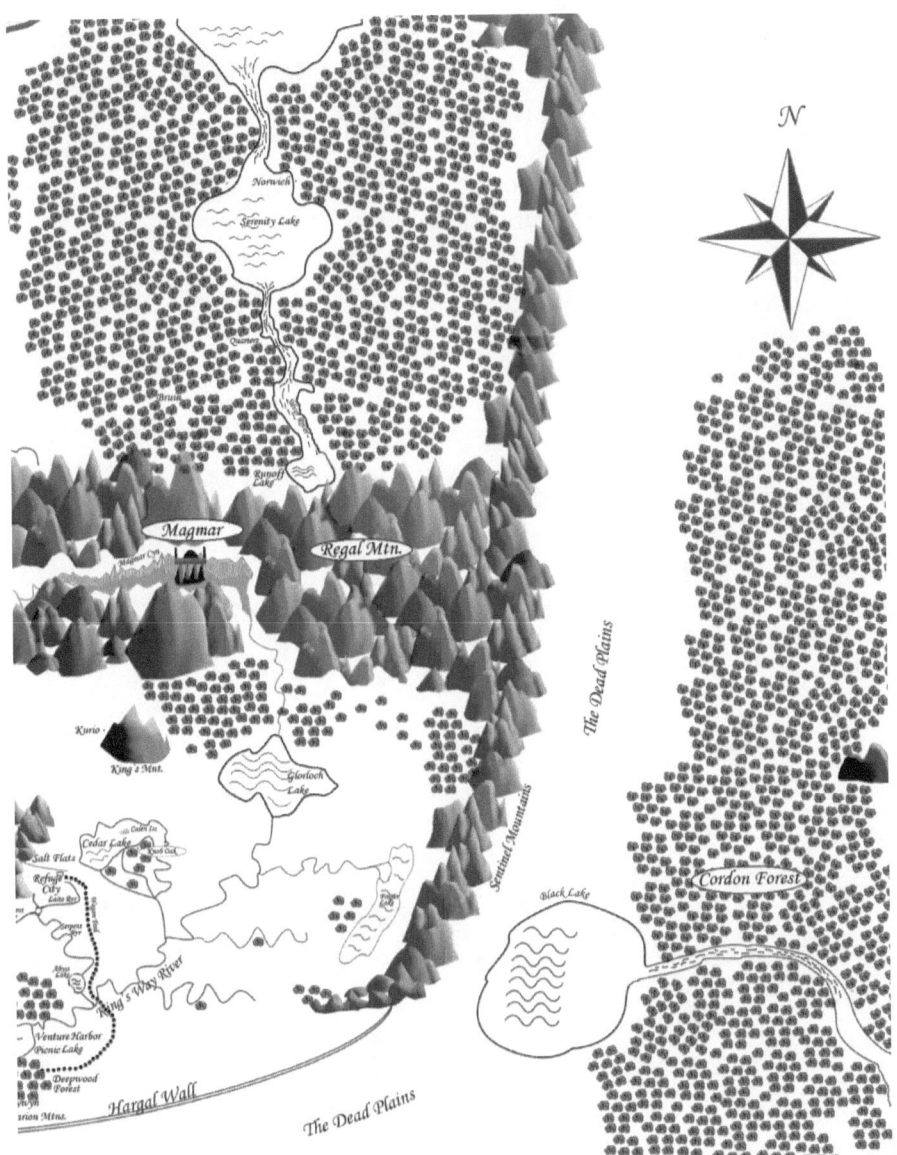

N

Norwich

Serenity Lake

Runoff Lake

Magmar

Magmar Cyn.

Regal Mtn.

The Dead Plains

Kurio

King's Mnt.

Glorloch Lake

Cedar Lake

Court In

Salt Flats

Old Oak

Refuge City

Lake Red

Serpent Spine

Sentinel Mountains

Cordon Forest

Black Lake

After Lake

King's Way River

Venture Harbor

Picnic Lake

Deepwood Forest

Hargal Wall

The Dead Plains

"Once in the lifespan of the universe, the element rhunite submerged into the 11th dimension and ceased to exist in time. Why? No one knew, not even the great elders ...."

– Tobin the Elder
"Lectures on Rhunite"

Introduction:

Tarina slipped on her robe and primped her still damp hair, having bathed from the day's labor. It was her best robe, gold with silver embroidery, and she donned her best earrings and necklace to match it. After a mist of perfume and a final check, she gathered up her oracle scroll and exited her residence.

The setting sun bathed Maywyn in crimson. The great towers, the many islands, and the expansive bridges assumed a regal aura, transforming the city of her birth into the land of kings. It was appropriate that such an atmosphere accompany the reading of the ancient stories, and she felt it a great honor to participate.

She strolled down that path from her home with a bounce in her step. When a pair of guards passed over the bridge, she greeted them with her hand to her chest and a nod. They replied in kind and continued on their way. She wound her way through the city and arrived at one of the many community lounges.

When she opened the door, she saw the teens, having taken part in the Ascension Ceremony, assembled and seated upon pillows on the floor. Annalee sat in the front, knees pressed to her chest, a radiant smile on her face. "Are we going to hear more about Rory and Christy? I want to find out what happened to the baby."

All eyes turned to Tarina as she walked through the midst of the youths. She sat on a high back chair, hand carved and ornate; she settled herself and then laid the oracle scroll on her lap. "All threads must be weaved in their proper time for the tapestry to take form. Tonight we will hear the story of Kelvin and Cody."

The smile vanished from Annalee's face. The elva pouted and stared at the floor. Tarina said, "You will hear more of Rory and Christy's tale another night. You need to have patience."

"I'm just worried about the baby," Annalee replied, peering up through her bangs.

"All will be made clear to you in time. Knowledge, like a home, must be built in its proper order." Tarina paused from her pontification. She could see that the girl would heed no logical argument, but Annalee would have to wait. She slid her finger across the surface, watching the text fly across the face of the leather scroll. When she found the proper story, she began to read. "We begin our tale in the most unlikely of places …."

Chapter 1

Kelvin Faroe lived far away from everything exciting or glamorous – the most remote locale in all of Asgard – or so it seemed to him. He often dreamt of the King's Mountain, with its majesty and grandeur, and he had every map of Kurio, the capital city, residing high upon the mountain's peaks. However, Kurio was over 350 miles away, hopelessly out of reach. Whenever his father went to town, he sprinted to the quay, which skirted the Middle Fork River, and watched the cogs sail along its length. He dreamed of sailing away on the flat bottom boats, seeking glory and adventure, perhaps a pirate or better yet a noble knight on a desperate mission. After he had returned home, his dreams evaporated into empty yearnings.

His family farm lay in the small town of Knob Oak, which was in the Palisade Province. Knob Oak offered a simple life, good earth, meandering brooks, and rolling hills. The great wars and turbulent events passed by the small town, and life remained as it had ever since the first explorers arrived, tranquil and predictable.

Kelvin was the youngest son of a peasant farmer. His family lived in the soggy bottom between two hills. Black Mud Creek cut right through their property and meandered in a lazy fashion. Kelvin's father, Joash, chose to appreciate the free water rather than brood about the frequent flooding. It also helped that their little farmhouse and barn were constructed upon a small knoll, thus afforded some protection from the annual floodwaters.

Night fell and quiet settled upon the farm. Kelvin washed his face in a pan of warm water and scrubbed behind his neck. He drew his cotton nightshirt over his head and dried his face with the shirttail. A fading blast of winter cast a chill over the house and covered the windows with frost. He had hurried across the wooden floor before it stole the warmth from his feet.

He slipped underneath the covers and drew them up to his neck. "I'm ready," he called out. He heard footsteps in the hallway and saw the flickering glow of a lantern through the crack. The door opened, and his mother entered.

His mother, Fiona, carried a thick leather bound volume. Its corners and bindings were worn, and the gold leaf lettering was all but gone. However, it was his favorite book, and after a hard day's work on the farm, he was rewarded with reading time before bed.

Fiona brushed the bangs from her teenage son's face and said, "Let me see."

"Aw mom, I'm not a baby. I know how to wash behind my ears," he protested.

"I suppose," she said with a trace sorrow. His father, Joash Faroe, complained that the boy was too old for fantasy books; Kelvin's nineteenth birthday was only two months away, and then he would be a man, at least in the eyes of the law – he needed to read practical books, books about farming … or perhaps welding – yes, welding was a good choice. But childhood endures in the rural countryside far longer than it does in the bustling cities, teeming with crime, vice, and violence.

Yet Kelvin was Fiona's last child, her baby. She could not help but treasure the last vestiges of his youth. Birthing became too difficult for her, and her womb rejected any child she tried to bear after Kelvin. No. Kelvin was the end of motherhood, and she knew it. Never again would she feel a new life growing within her. Cares and responsibilities would soon wash away the boy's footprints and replace them with that of a man. Yet tonight he was still her baby. She asked, "What are you going to read?"

"I'm going to read about 'Tobin the Elder,'" Kelvin replied.

"You've read that a thousand times," she replied. "Don't you want to read another?"

"No. I really like that one," Kelvin said with enthusiasm.

"Very well," she said. "It's your book."

She arose and walked softly from his room but lingered in the doorway and watched her son for a moment. Joash was right. The man had to replace the boy, but her heart ached – the world was such a dangerous place.

She closed the door and walked the hallway to their bedroom. When she entered their bedroom, she saw Joash already dressed in his nightshirt. It looked a bit silly. The towering man could never find a nightshirt large enough to fit him. The warrior turned to farming, and his muscles grew even larger with the daily toil of farm work. His hands were callused, and a healthy ring of fat circled his waist; but she could still see the warrior in the farmer, the man she fell in love with so many years ago. The corners of his slate gray eyes wrinkled when he saw her, adoration radiating from them. She was his world, and he was hers.

Yet Fiona could feel the season change. Their last boy was almost a man, and men faced many dangers. Peter was dead, lost to the eternal lands, taken from her too soon by yet another war. Her three oldest boys, who were still living, left the farm over 20 years ago. In her mind, she imagined them marrying and returning home in triumph. They would build houses next door and have lots of grandbabies. Joash could retire and sit on the porch with her. They would grow old and listen to the music of their laughing grandchildren at play.

The boys never visited and never wrote. Was farm life so awful or the work was hard? She knew that they were not farmers, but they were happy. Weren't they? She picked up the family portrait: taken when the three oldest boys were still young. It never even occurred to her that they might leave and never return.

The bed creaked and drew her attention. Joash was larger than most men. He stood head and shoulders above all his peers. He also took up most of the bed and covers. It never bothered her though. He was her rock, the great love of her life.

Kelvin turned a dog-eared page and smoothed the onionskin paper. "Earth is Eden's twin sister. She lies in a parallel dimension and orbits a yellow sun, a sun much like ours. For nearly 400 million years these sisters danced through the endless void of night. Energy ribbons bound them together and allowed the inhabitants to travel between these two worlds. It was the Fifth Age, the golden age."

"Humanity was but one member of a community, a single voice in a chorus. The ancient races traveled between our world and others. They viewed these new residents in a paternal fashion. Both older and wiser, they schooled humanity in the ancient and secret ways. 'Tobin the Elder' was one such wizard. He studied at the hands of the masters and learned how to control the elements at the quantum level, even able to reshape reality through the spirit world."

"Tobin was a kind and charitable man, a friend to all who walked in the light. However, the many deadly creatures that lurked in Eden distressed him. Mankind stood ever vigilant, protecting those they loved from ever-present death. While he appreciated all that the first races did for humanity, he chaffed at their domination. It was time for mankind to stand alone and demand the respect afforded other races."

"He spent many centuries studying Rhunite. This enigmatic metal was the bane of many wizards and scientists. Rhunite, a Dwarvish word meaning 'Black Star,' was a mineral. Humans called it 'white matter,' a leftover bit of the 'big bang,' as opposed to 'dark matter,' which caused the expansion of the universe. Rhunite could appear black as coal or medium gray, and it came in many grades, from large boulders to fine dust. It existed in various concentrations throughout Eden. It had a low specific gravity and crumbled like sandstone when crushed. While dark matter had a weak interaction with the physical universe, white matter was its polar opposite, dangerously reactive. If struck with a hammer, it would send out a shower of sparks and a multi-spectrum emission of energized particles. These particles caused ion storms in the upper atmosphere, appearing like the aurora borealis, starbursts like atomic bombs, and fierce lightning storms in the desert. These emissions ranged from gamma radiation to radiowaves."

"Rhunite did have benefits. The average farmer had two harvests a year, three if they properly fertilized the soil. In low doses, rhunite permeated food and extended life. It activated dormant portions of the DNA, which caused the regrowth of amputated limbs and extended human life span. In large doses, it imbued supernatural powers, but it demanded a terrible price, causing horrible mutations and insanity."

"This life extension might have been Shangri-La, if not for all the creatures trying to kill humanity. Tobin was sure, if humanity had a private world, a world for them alone, a world without terrifying predators, a world without rhunite, that mankind would surpass the achievements of their elders. Such was the hubris of the youth."

"'Once in the lifespan of the universe, the element rhunite submerged into the 11th dimension and ceased to exist in time. Why? No one knew, not even the great elders ….' Tobin could not control rhunite, for that was impossible, but he could put it to sleep. He found a means to catalyze the rhunite and cause this reaction."

"Working in secret, he urged his fellow humans to cross over to the promised land, Earth. Many joined him, but a few tribes remained. They loved Eden and could not bear to part with it. So he bid them farewell and crossed the portals to the magical realm of Earth. The Great Gate, the Lord of all the lesser gates, closed its eye the very next day – and Earth was never seen again."

Kelvin shook his head and smirked. "That's not true." People came from Earth to Eden all the time. They wandered through the lesser gates when they winked (temporarily opened), and Gleason was from Earth. It was an entire town from Earth, located in the middle of the Wolf's Maw Mountains. His friends thought that one could get to Earth from Gleason.

I'm going to Gleason someday.

Gleason was a part of the kingdom of Salvia, and Salvia was a dangerous place, filled with murder, dark magic, illegal arms trade, vice, and prostitution. Some of the elders said that the Great Spirit cast the people of Gleason out from the sacred world for some great sin: "whoring no doubt," but the elders blamed everything on sex. Kelvin was not certain, but he supposed that it might be true. Who could say?

Salvia was a harsh, mountain country, and the king was cruel. They never joined the Asgard Parliament to become a free land. His great aunt Helen said that it was a sign: "The Great Spirit was moving." He had only a vague idea what that meant. She was a priestess, and no two priests agreed upon anything.

Kelvin leaned over his bed and retrieved an encyclopedia from underneath it. It was out of date and dusty, but it was still useful. He wished his dad would let him use his oracle scroll to check the Asgard database, but Joash said, "There are things in it that young eyes should not see." So he found the listing in the glossary and leafed to the correct page. Gleason arrived on Eden 45 years ago. It would wait a few more years for him to become a warrior.

One day not too long ago, Kelvin asked his mother about Salvia. "Why didn't Salvia join the Asgard Republic? It's so much better than be a part of something big than a tiny kingdom in the middle of the mountains. I don't understand."

Her reply was pithy: "Kings hate to share power."

A smile appeared on her face and took on a distant look. "Our ancestors wished to stay here, on our home world. They doubted Tobin and his claims, but that was long ago. When I was a little girl, I imagined our cousins on Earth. They lived in golden castles and bathed in sparkling seas. It was a wonderful world filled with magic, and no one ever made them afraid. There were no haugrs, daemia, drathva, skree, or any other terrifying creatures. I crawled out of my window and lay on the roof. I stared at the twinkling stars for hours. I imagined myself on Earth and prayed to the Great Spirit that I would go there."

Chapter 2

Kelvin awoke before sunrise and threw off the covers. Possible adventures and discoveries created a maelstrom within his imagination. He had big plans for the day, but they depended upon avoiding his father. He stripped off his nightshirt and grabbed yesterday's trousers off a wooden chair. After jumping about while stuffing his leg into the trousers, he found a shirt on the top of the laundry pile. He pressed his face to it and took a whiff. It still smelled good enough. He buttoned up the shirt and drew up his bracer straps, and with a snap, they were in place over his shoulders. One boot lay near the foot of his bed, but where was the other? He searched the open space in the middle of the floor but saw only scattered clothes. He crawled about and looked under the bed, spotting it on the other side near the dresser. After putting on a pair of socks, he stuffed his feet into the boots and tied the laces.

Kelvin moved to the window and threw open the curtains. Frost still covered the windowpane and turned his breath to cloudy wisps. A few orange beams broke over the horizon and cut through the fog. He had to get moving.

After putting on a sweater and a jacket, he exited his room. Snores, like that of a grizzly bear, shook the walls of his parents' bedroom. While his father was a sound sleeper, a scurrying mouse could wake his mother. He crept past the door, each creak of the boards sounding like thunder; two steps at a time, he descended the stairs.

The few last embers of a fire still glowed in the hearth, but the night's chill took hold of the house. His bow, quiver, and dagger lay where he left them near the sofa. After retrieving them, he exited the house and softly closed the door. He crossed the porch and jumped off it. The day and adventure awaited him.

"Where do you think you're going, young man?"

Kelvin cringed and shrank like a turtle into his shell. He turned and saw his mother: arms crossed, lips pursed, and standing on the porch. She glared at the boy with hawk-like eyes. "I'm going over to Cody's house. We're going to practice up at the old fortress."

"Do your chores first," Fiona said. "Wait here a second." She returned carrying a biscuit and a slice of bacon. She handed them to him and tousled his hair. "Be home by supper, or you'll have your father to answer to." She smiled when Kelvin let out a jubilant shout and ran to feed the chickens.

Fiona returned inside the house and drew open the fireplace screen. She tossed two logs onto the fire and stirred the coals. Orange flames licked up around the logs, snaps and crackles coming from the wood, heat warming her calves. The dry wood from last fall was gone and only freshly cut wood remained. Coal and fuel oil were expensive possibilities, and modern rhunite based heating system was totally beyond their means. She chewed on her thumbnail; they could sell a pig, but she planned to use that money to buy new shoes.

Heavy creaks came from the wooden stairs. Joash yawned and rubbed his face. "What's happening? What was that shout?"

"I told Kelvin he could go play after he did his chores."

"The boy needs to think about his future. What trade is he going to apprentice? He needs to stay with me so he can sample the various trades. He's almost a man," Joash grumbled. He closed his eyes and paused in silence. "I'm sorry. I just think we coddle him too much." Joash rubbed his face and wandered into the kitchen. Fiona followed after him carrying a hot ember.

"You know the trade he wants. He has never wished another," Fiona replied with the sting of indictment.

"Oh … yes. I suppose so. Too many war stories I guess," Joash mumbled and turned away from her.

"Far too many," she agreed. She opened the lower door to the stove and inserted the ember. She placed kindling upon it and blew. A few little flames began to glow. "I wish we could afford a more modern stove. This thing is positively ancient. I almost forget what it was like to turn a knob and have the oven heat up by itself."

"Stoves like that cost money, money we don't have." He stretched and knocked the ceiling with his hands. "I'll go and get the scroll."

"We could sell a pig," she said.

"That money is buying us new winter clothes and shoes for next fall."

"I know. But how are we going to buy coal? All of the firewood is too green."

"I'll have to take on some welding work. Jasper has been after me to repair his combine. His idiot of a son ran it into a tree stump."

"I see," Fiona said and returned to her labors.

Joash exited the house with a heavy thump of his boots. He spotted Kelvin slopping the pigs and the piglets. The swine crowded up to the trough and gobbled down the spoiled food as though it was a feast. Joash lingered a moment in the middle of the yard and debated whether he should speak with the boy. How many times did they have that conversation? Too many, he concluded. The boy knew what Joash thought on the subject of trade work. He turned and strolled away on the dirt road.

The dirt road skirted along the edge of a thin grove of pines and Black Mud Creek. The open field and his cattle were on his right. The frost still clung to the grass, and a blanket of mist hovered low on the meadow. A cow paused from her morning meal and eyed him. Satisfied there was no danger, she continued dining on a delicious clump of grass.

Joash strolled along the driveway and hummed a merry tune. The fiery beams of dawn passed through the pines and cast long shadows over the field. His boots dug into the loose dirt and ground it with a loud crunch. He liked the sound. In times of war, the military forbade such sounds, and they stepped as if it was their last. Perhaps that was why he enjoyed it so much. Peace was a prize most men fail to appreciate. They imagine themselves victorious upon a field of battle, not writhing in agony, their life's blood spilling out onto the grass, never to see home and family again, realizing too late the great worth of a peaceful life. He had seen too much death, cradled too many dying friends, and wept too many tears.

Kelvin should be a welder. He has steady hands, and the pay is excellent. He could live in town and afford all the modern conveniences. Yes, a welder makes sense.

He crossed a small bridge over the creek. His boots beat out a noisy drum on the wooden planks. Looking over the railing, he saw fish swimming in search of a morning meal. He made a mental note to return later with a net. Fly fishing was for city folk. He needed free food.

The driveway intersected Jasper Road. Well worn and weathered by many storms, a small cask sat atop of a wooden pole, resembling a mailbox but lacking a door. It contained three leather sheets, an oracle scroll, rolled up into a tight bundle. Engineers modified the scrolls at the subatomic level. The entire knowledge of mankind could be contained in a single molecule. When a scroll touched another, the scrolls exchanged information, as if in a double relay race. He paid a local boy, Edgar, to touch his scroll and deliver the news.

Mail arrived in a diffused, obtuse fashion. It leaped from one scroll to the next until reaching the recipient. A DNA lock meant only the recipient could open it. This network functioned with surprising speed.

The Great Gate

He drew out the scrolls and put another set in the box. It was worth the price to have two sets and avoid a second trip to the mailbox later in the day. He unrolled his scrolls and held them before him. They read his DNA and activated; the icons and text blazed to life. He touched the mail symbol. Worthless advertisements of sex services filled his mail slot. He deleted the trash and brooded: the boys never wrote. *Damn them;* he snorted and twitched his nose. Their mother needed to hear from them, and he made a mental note to write to them.

He opened the news and leafed through to the sports section. Soccer, or football as they called it, topped the headlines. The Mantov Tigers defeated the Bentley Streaks in sudden death overtime. He grunted and nodded. That was little surprise. The Mantov Tigers came from a prosperous city, and they could afford the best players. When Joash wore a young man's clothes, he played rugby. He was too large and perhaps too slow for football. However, he made an excellent defender.

Back at the barn, Kelvin performed the last of his chores. He filled a cloth sling with firewood and carried it up to the house. When he opened the door, a blast of heat rushed over him and made his skin prickle. He lugged the wood into the kitchen, and with a grunt, heaving with all his might, he refilled the wood box across from the stove. Fiona set a kettle on the stove and eyed her son. "You stay safe and no going underground. I don't want you getting eaten by a haugr."

"Mom, there are no haugrs around here. The defenders killed them over a thousand years ago. The King's Guardians left none for the rest of us to kill," he said.

"Hmm," she said. "You stay away from caves anyway."

"See you at supper, mom," Kelvin said.

"Wait a second," she said and turned to him. "I want a hug." He gave her a quick squeeze and scurried from the room. Kelvin charged out the front door and slammed it. She shook her head and returned to her work.

Haugrs were the same size as a man, covered with black leathery skin and course hair, powerfully built like a bodybuilder, had fingers tipped by razor sharp claws, and had faces resembling that of a bat. People whispered that their blood red eyes could steal a man's soul. If her son ever saw one, he would soil himself. She wondered if that might not be a good thing — scare him a little. She repented of the thought. The haugr were a deadly plague, and they were better off without them.

Kelvin picked up his weapons and waved to his dad as he trudged up the road. Joash returned his son's wave as Kelvin sprinted away around the stables, causing the horses to scurry away in fright. A moment later, he disappeared from sight.

Kelvin charged into the woods and down a sloped bank. His feet found the stones as he pranced across the stream. He dodged around the ancient oak, which he imagined to be a sleeping Ent. The morning sun spread its warmth across the land and burnt away the mist, wooing the morning glories to open and bringing the meadow to life. He ran through the deepening grass, flowers snapping shut as he passed, charging up to the summit of a knoll, and through a rainbow assortment of wildflowers. The cows paused from their feeding, their ears turning toward him, large brown eyes fixed upon him, noting the boy's path as he crossed the field, trying to determine whether he was predator or prey, the calves hiding behind their mothers, and remained alert. Seeing and hearing nothing amiss, they resumed chewing their cud.

Cody's house lay 3 miles by road and a world away. Kelvin's legs flew and lungs burned as he sprinted through the rolling meadows and over the gentle hills. More trees lined Chelsea Creek, and he dodged around them, pretending they were giants, slashing at them as he ran. When he arrived at the creek, he grabbed a rope and swung across the water – almost – his left foot splashed in the frigid water, but he paid it little mind. He scrambled up a steep hill covered with trees. The thick layer of soggy leaves made it slippery, but he fought his way up the slope.

The last barrier lay ahead of him. Francis Douglas Moyer III Esquire, Cody's father, built a tall fence around his property. It was high, white, and bordered the rim of a flat top hill. However, Kelvin knew a secret way onto the property. He and Cody found it many summers ago. A drainage tunnel, made of concrete reinforced with steel, passed underneath the fence. He crawled through it and pushed up the grate. Seeing no one, he scrambled onto the property.

The Moyers must like flowers, Kelvin concluded because they had enough of them. Large flowerbeds provided a remarkable display around the thick pile lawn. Teenage boys have little use for such adornments, and he raced around them at pell-mell speed. He charged up a set of brownstone steps, across a large patio, and leaped around furniture.

The mansion soared up three stories before Kelvin. Its white and black face stared down at him with self-importance, disapproving of him and his reckless ways. Unlike Kelvin's home, it was a "state of the art" mansion, having all the modern luxuries: radiant heat, stainless steel kitchen appliances, indoor plumbing, hot showers, toilets, a water heater, and artificial lighting. But it was hot water that Kelvin envied the most; cold water made for a miserable bath.

Green ivy-covered a trellis and climbed the wall next to Cody's window. He scampered up it like a ranger taking a fortress. When he reached the second floor, he knocked on the window. A minute later, it slid open, and Cody leaned out. As beautiful as any flower in the garden, curly blonde hair framed a pair of sparkling blue eyes, cherry lips, and adorable button nose. Her lips curled into a smile, and a rosy hue adorned her cheeks.

"You're not dressed," Kelvin said and frowned. "We're going to practice at the old fortress today."

"I can't; my mom is making me go with my sister's to a recital." She sat down on the cushioned window seat, her hands pressing together, creasing her nightgown between her thighs. "It's not fair. All of Judith and Lila's friends will be there. I won't know anyone."

"I'm coming in," Kelvin said. Cody moved away from the window. Kelvin grabbed the window and tumbled into her room with a thump.

"Shh, my mom will hear you."

Kelvin rose to his feet and said, "Get dressed. We'll sneak off. It will be fun."

"Fun for you maybe," she replied. "I'll get punished."

"Aw come on, we need to practice. You promised."

"I know." She scrambled onto the bed and stuffed her feet underneath the white comforter. "My dad said, 'You need to start behaving like a young lady.'" She spat out the words as if they were sour. "All young ladies do is sit around and gossip. It's sssooo boring."

Kelvin slipped off his muddy boots and crawled onto the bed with her, which was more appropriate when they were young. He laid back and stared up at the white canopy looming above them. "Why do you have that? The bed is on the inside of the house. Why is there a canopy above it?"

Cody scooted next to him, resting her head on his shoulder, and gazed up at the white gauze. "I'm not sure. It's just something they put in girl's rooms."

"It's no fun without you. I can't practice by myself," Kelvin said. "Are you sure you can't get out of it?"

She rolled away and drew her knees. "My parents have my entire life planned. They've even picked out a husband for me, Stuart Grimsby."

The Great Gate

He was a sheepish boy who his family more than once caught him sampling his sister's clothes. "They want me to betroth him on my Ascension Day." Kelvin and Cody were born in the same town but into two very different worlds. "I'll be engaged for a year, and we will marry when he turns 19."

"That's awful," Kelvin replied.

"We won't be able to see each other anymore." Her face contorted, her eyes threatening to shed tears at any moment, and she shook her head. "My mom says it's not right for engaged women to be alone with other men." She rolled back toward him and clutched his arm. "I don't love him. I don't even like him."

"It's not going to happen," Kelvin replied, a matter of fact. "Stuart has a boyfriend."

"He does?" she said sniffling and moving up to a seated position.

"Yup," Kelvin replied. "I saw them kissing!"

"Who?" asked Cody with glee and jumped up to her knees. "I bet it's Joel Saffron. He's a real slut. He sleeps with all the boys, according to my sister."

"Nope, it's Albert Brown."

"No!"

"Yes."

"No."

"Stop that. Yes, it's Albert Brown," Kelvin huffed. Albert was 19 going on 20 and the mayor's son. Kelvin rose up to his knees and leaned forward; his voice lowered to a whisper, "I know a secret, but you can't tell anyone."

Cody scooted up close to him, leaning forward until their noses almost touched. "You can tell me. I won't tell anyone. I promise."

He leaned in close and whispered in her ear. "Albert and Stuart went to the wizards without their parent's permission. Albert bought a potion for Stuart. It causes 'nature's calling.' He's going to be a girl before too much longer. She might already be one."

"That's perfect." She threw her arms around him and kissed him. Heat flashed over Kelvin and turned his cheeks bright red. She scrambled off the bed and raced from the room.

"Mmmmoooommmm," she shouted.

His eyes went wide, and he chased after her. She sprinted through the house like a Valkyrie into battle and sped down the stairs to the first floor. Victoria, Cody's mother, sat in the breakfast nook, octagon shaped, white with yellow accent, with her husband and two oldest daughters. She was dressed in an antique white silk gown and a pair of stylish slippers.

One could always differentiate married women on Eden. On Earth, women wore wedding rings, but on Eden, women wore magical wedding rings. These rings included the family crest, embossed on the face of the ring. Having a murky past, most scholars linked its history to the Elven practice. However, like most traditions, the public accepted them without question.

Victoria's ring was silver, and it has the family crest embossed on the front, showing her to be of exceptional status. Tradition demanded that lesser women, like Kelvin's mother, who wore no ring, would remain servile. It was a matter of tradition for the ranking women to parade around a party, demonstrating their spouse's rank, and forming up into cliques. Each group dominated the lesser wives, requesting food or a beverage from them, or taking her chair. The ring-less women —

typically single, engaged, or widowed — avoided such functions if possible.

Joash could not afford such an expensive item, and he was too proud to let Fiona wear steel, which symbolizing low rank: maids, cooks, and nannies. Perhaps it was pride, maybe it was love, but he would rather people think Fiona unmarried than common.

Cody put her hands on her hips and leaned forward, as only a teenage girl can. "I don't have to marry Stuart. He's in love with Albert Brown, and he's going to be a girl." Kelvin stood at the foot of the stairs, frozen with fear, staring at Cody's family.

Her father lowered his oracle scroll and peered at her over the rim of his reading glasses. Her mother said, "Cordelia Anne Moyer, what's all this nonsense about? Stuart is not a girl. He's a fine, healthy boy."

"Oh mother," said Judith and rolled her eyes. "Everyone knows Stuart prefers boys. I thought you would have figured it out by now. Lila nodded and nibbled a muffin. "Pamela's father sold Albert the potion. Stuart took it a month ago. By this time he – I mean 'she' has probably had her first period."

Lila offered a non-sequitur comment. "I wish I was already 19 so I could take the 'Blue.' I hate having a period."

Victoria narrowed her eyes and glared at Kelvin. Husbands of quality were scarce and a precious commodity. She was sure the filthy farmer's son had something to do with this. "What are we going to do? This is scandalous."

Francis shrugged. "It's not our fault. Harriet and Richard will have to deal with their son … um, daughter. We'll just have to begin a new search." He paid little attention to his wife's obsession, but the crude telepathic link created by her ring made it clear that she was unhappy. Girls in the city of Solva never married until they were 21 years old, and many remained single until they were 25. He felt a girl of eighteen was too young to get married.

"Husband's are not so easy to find. If you joined me in the search, you would know it." She crossed her arms and legs, bouncing her right foot. "How are we going to find her a husband on such short notice?"

"Perhaps you could find her an older man to marry," Francis said.

"Be serious," Victoria said.

"It's not a bad idea," Judith said. She held up a butter knife with a slab of butter on the tip and a muffin poised. "I know several girls that are engaged to older men."

Lila said, "It's true. Maryann, Patricia, and Ashley are all engaged to men twice their age. When Ashley turned 19 last week, her father shipped her off to Solva. Some businessman was looking for a fourth wife." Asgard law allowed dominant spouses to have four submissive spouses, male or female. "From the way Ashley's father reacted, he must have been rich and powerful."

"Well, I suppose that is a possibility. I know of several widowers. Cody might marry a lawyer." She tapped her chin. "Yes, I think it will work. Don't worry sweetie. I'll find a nice businessman to marry."

"I don't want to marry an old man," Cody blurted and pouted. "I want to marry someone my age."

Victoria eyed her daughter's bare hand. She often argued with Francis; she wanted Cody controlled by a ring, but he refused. "Very well, I'll try and find you a boy your age, but you're going to have to compromise. Most parents have already seen to the engagement of their sons. Kurt Faber was my second choice for you. I'll talk to his mother. How old is he again?" asked Victoria.

The Great Gate

Cody understood why her mom stared at her ring finger and felt her stomach twist into a knot. The situation went from bad to worse. Now her mother was going to marry her off to a stranger.

"You know Conrad Peat has feelings for Cody," Lila said. "His father owns half of the Beltroze Valley. Whenever he sees Cody, he gets a hungry look in his eyes. I'm sure he would be open to marriage."

"He is a year older than Cody, he turned 19 last year," Judith stated and scrunched up her nose. "He's kind of a slob, stinks like salami, and no one really likes him, but he's available."

Francis placed his elbows on the table and leaned forward. "I don't want Cody getting married to anyone before she's 21-years-old. My family in Solva already thinks we are a bunch of hicks in a backward little town. No. I'm putting my foot down. She will be 21 and not a day younger," Francis insisted, but Victoria roundly ignored his declaration. He grumbled and returned to his news.

Victoria saw Kelvin lingering in the hallway. She ate a slice of buttered bread and pondered the best solution to rid herself of the little tramp. "Your father is right. After the engagement contract is completed, we can send Cody off to boarding school. They can always consummate the marriage later when she is older. She needs to be educated in ways of a young lady and to associate with young people of her own rank."

Kelvin recognized that the last remark was directed at him. His mother always said, "Victoria has her nose so high in the air it's a wonder she doesn't drown when it rains." He interpreted that to mean she thought she was better than everyone, especially him.

"What about you?" Victoria asked Lila. She thought a moment and looked up at the ceiling. "I know of three older men interested in you. Lewis Parker's father owns P&R Glass Manufacturing. He's really cute, and they have three homes. One is 20 minutes away from us; the other is on the coast near the Hampden ports, and the third one is a lovely chalet in the Regal Mountains. Of course, Lewis would be dominant. "What do you think?"

Dominance and submission were chiefly legal designations. The titles affected inheritance, business transactions, and legal representation in court. Informally, a submissive took care of the home, and in the case of a female, she bore the children.

Victoria was submissive to her husband, Francis, though she liked to pretend that she was not, and had more than once suggested that he should wear her ring. The practice of male submission was less common and typically performed where both parties were male. He ignored her, but Victoria had a determined nature that left him shaken and quite a bit nervous, concerned for his future.

"He's nice," Lila replied. Changing the subject, she said, "You know daddy is a hot property. I know of seven women who would pay real money to use him as a stud. Miss Fayote, the School Superintendant, has a thing for daddy. She would be interested in marriage. Her father is the lieutenant governor; her brother is the Assistant State Attorney for our region, and her sister is a commander in the military. She is thinking about running for mayor."

"That is something to think about," Victoria said.

Francis looked up from his news. Things had spun off in a very wrong direction. "I'm happy with your mother. I don't need a second wife." When they met, Victoria was 52, a youth by Eden standards, and Francis was just 24. He came from wealth and had a title, and when they married, he received a full third of the family's holdings, a living inheritance.

This new turn of events worked in Victoria's favor. The corners of her lips curled into an ever so subtle smile. She had it all planned: she secretly had herself declared a man by the court. All that remained was to obtain the proper leverage, and Cody's failed engagement was just what she needed. Francis collateralized a business loan with Cody's bridal price.

Now there would be no marriage and no bridal price. Victoria could file a petition with the court for ruling of "Failed Dominance." Therefore, she could take control of the family and have him wear her ring.

When Francis saw the predatory look in his wife's eyes, and he cleared his throat. "We need to take care of this Cody business." Victoria recognized the tactical diversion, but she let it pass.

Cody crossed her arms and pouted. "I don't want to go to the recital. I want to go out and have fun!"

"Oh very well," Victoria relented, "go and play with your friend." Cody marched past Kelvin, and he chased after her. Victoria could wait another two short months to pry the pair apart.

After Kelvin and Cody had departed, Judith and Lila left to dress for the recital. "You know Cody should be ringed. Every day she runs through the woods like a wild animal. She needs to be constrained for her own good. A ring would force her to act in a refined, ladylike manner. She is going to 'Ascend' soon. Then what will become of her? Would you see your daughter live in some ramshackle hut in the bottom region?"

Francis sighed and rubbed his face. He detested his wife's endless social ambition, greed, and divisiveness, but she had a point. Cody was getting too old to run through the woods with a boy. "Perhaps you have a point. But I want to wait until her Ascension Day. Then we will ring her and betroth her to an appropriate groom."

"It's for her own good," Victoria said with a nod. "I'll have a ring made for her, but we must keep it a secret. I don't want to upset her."

The pair ran up to her room, and Kelvin jumped on her bed, the soft mattress wooing him to rest. Cody moved behind her dressing blind, a white accordion panel with bright flowers painted on it, located in the far corner of the room. They had seen each other naked on many occasions while swimming in the creek, but she was getting older, and she wanted some privacy.

She reached for her play jeans and white panties but paused. She hated the idea of marrying Conrad. He was abusive, a bully, and ugly. However, if she refused him, then the only remaining choice was to marry an old man. She could not understand her mother's thinking. Kelvin was a perfectly nice boy, a fantastic choice – and she intended to do something about it.

She reached out and opened her top dresser drawer. When she noted that the soft mattress almost had Kelvin asleep, she picked out a pair of black satin panties and a matching satin bra. As she stepped into the panties and whisked them up her legs, she giggled. She had no idea why her mother couldn't see it. He was perfect.

The gates blinked, allowing ships and travelers to inadvertently switch worlds, finding themselves strangers on Eden. And in the case of Gleason, an entire town arrived on Eden. Thus much of native Eden and Earth populations mixed, bringing technology and culture with them. Such was the case with regard to names, architecture, and clothing.

Cody's lingerie was an Earth design, very popular with the ladies. The panties and the bra complemented her nubile figure. When Cody crossed the room, on her way to her walk-in closet, she passed by the foot of the bed. Kelvin rubbed his eyes, sat up, and watched Cody stride past him. Upon seeing Cody's blossoming body, he was both aroused and confused. He never saw her as anything more than a friend who happened to be a girl. Yet nature insinuated puberty between them, and he saw her in a new light, as she intended.

Cody returned from the closet carrying a black, patent leather ensemble. She disappeared behind the dressing blind, and Kelvin lay his head back down, pondering what it all meant. Cody slid her arms into a white silk blouse and buttoned it. After she stepped into her leather tights and whisked them up her legs, she tucked in her blouse and zipped up the

23

slacks. She sat down on a small bench and put on her knee-high boots, which were black patent leather and had a chunky heel, offering stable foot support. The waist jacket matched the tights, and both glistened, reflecting the light.

She left the changing blind and hurried to her cosmetic table. She sprayed some instant dye giving her blonde highlights, and then she set to work on makeup. It took her several minutes, but her crimson lips and blue eye shadow appeared wonton, just the way she wanted it. She secured the top blouse button and slid a black ribbon underneath the Peter Pan collar, which tied in a bow. After putting on a pair of black patent leather gloves, she rose to her feet.

Feeling beautiful and sexy, she hurried to the foot of the bed. Gleaming as though freshly painted, she put her hands on her hips and struck a pose. Kelvin was sound asleep. Cody furrowed her brow and pouted. She kicked the footboard and said, "Wake up!"

"Huh, what?" asked Kelvin as he rubbed his eyes.

She smiled and asked, "How do I look?"

"Um … nice are we still going out to practice?" asked Kelvin, perplexed by the female of the species.

"Of course," she replied. "I just want to look nice for a change."

Girls are weird, thought Kelvin.

He slid off the bed and put on his boots. "Okay, let's get going." The pair raced out of the house and slammed the front door. They shouted as they raced through the backyard. Francis stretched up and wished he could run off. He knew Victoria was planning something. What she planned both perplexed and frightened him.

The teens exited the rear gate and ran down the back road. They soon left the road for adventure in the wilds. Kelvin arrived first at the creek

24

and danced across on the stones. Cody, being far nimbler, sprinted across them, and she soon caught up with him. After they had climbed an embankment, they arrived at a meadow that ascended a gentle hill.

Cody sped past Kelvin with the swiftness of a doe and streaked across the field. Kelvin, being much slower, stomped the ground and struggled to keep pace with her. She leaped over a rock like a gazelle and then danced around an abandoned plow.

"Wait for me," Kelvin called out with a gasp.

He circled around the obstructions and searched for her, but she was already at the base of Little Round Top. He hated it when she did that. It made him feel as though his shoes were made of lead.

Sweat formed on his brow, and his lungs burned. He made it across the field and arrived at the gravel road. It wound its way around the hill in a corkscrew fashion. His boots crunched the rock as he circled around the hill. She was out of sight.

"Cody, wait," he gasped.

Cody arrived at her goal well ahead of Kelvin, and the final segment of the road ahead of her led to the flat hilltop. She often heard her sisters talk about boys and their preferences. Most boys stared at either a girl's chest or her bottom. Between the two, she thought that her bottom was sexier, but she had to make good use of it. The question was how?

From where she stood, she could see a pile of square stones spilled onto the ground, and a few miscellaneous blocks lay before her. She turned around, placed her right foot on a rock, and put her hands on her hips – a pose she observed in advertisements – making sure Kelvin would see her bottom first. She checked to make sure he would get a view: tugging on the hem of her tights, smoothed out a wrinkle, and waited.

When she heard footsteps and gasping, she stood still, holding her pose. Kelvin jogged up the road, his legs and lungs burned. "What's the hurry?" he gasped, beads of sweat forming on his forehead. He plodded past her by without giving a second glance. Cody tried to look around her waist, to see her bottom, but it was impossible. It was an absolutely nice bottom in her opinion, but his response, or lack thereof, made her question this assumption.

The weight of someone's stare intruded into her deliberations. Someone else was watching her. When she turned around, she saw Conrad Peat jogging up the road. "You look beautiful," he shouted. "I thought we were going to practice?"

"We are," Kelvin called back to him.

Cody's cheeks turned bright red, and she chewed on her index fingertip of her glove. She recalled her sister's comment. Conrad wanted to have sex with her, and that felt very strange. He focused on Cody's chest and grinned. "Hi Conrad," Cody muttered. She cringed and ran up the road, feeling Conrad's eyes upon her.

Reaching the top of the road, Kelvin gasped, "I win." He collapsed into the soft grass and stared up at the sky. A fluffy white cloud passed overhead. He was studying the rolling shape when a face blocked his view. Cody leaned over, blonde locks draped past her face, and she looked down at him. "Do you need glasses?"

"What? No." He rubbed his nose. "My eyes are fine."

"Are you okay? You're not feeling sick, are you?" she asked.

"I'm all right," he replied and rose to his feet. "Why did you run off like that?"

"I wasn't running that fast," she replied with a shrug.

"You must be part elf," he said. "I've never seen anyone run that fast."

When Cody turned around, she bumped into Conrad. An impish, threatening smile appeared on his cooked face. "You look beautiful today. What kind of sword practice did you have in mind?"

Cody's lip curled into a snarl and revulsion welled up within her. Although still young, the brooding disillusionment of an older man lingered behind Conrad's eyes. To squelch his anger, he ate and grew bulbous, developing a beer belly and heavy jowls, making him appear 40 rather than 19. Yet what bothered her most was how he ridiculed other people and bullied anyone smaller than him.

Conrad stared at Cody's hand, and she knew what he was thinking. He wanted to ring her, to possess her, to bend her to his will. He also made it clear on many occasions that girls were mere toys that one used and discarded, and unbeknownst to his father, he often frequented brothels. "You look nice," he said, but inwardly, he imagined her naked.

"Thank you," Cody said with a cringe and hurried away.

Piles of stones and jagged walls lay strewed about Little Round Top. It had once been a fortress of some kind. Who built it and why faded from living memory long ago. Kelvin liked to pretend that he was a commander, and they were fighting a desperate battle. They constructed enemies to battle, most made from burlap sacks, stuffed with straw, and sticks for bones.

Kelvin pulled an arrow from his quiver and fitted it into the bow. He took careful aim and then let it fly. The arrow flew through the air and hit the center of the target. "ATTACK!" he shouted and drew his dagger. It was a rusty, duller than a butter knife, having a blunt point, and salvaged from the trash heap, but it was his first sword: that made it special. He charged at another and ran it through. "Die," he said. When he attacked another straw man, he saw that Conrad followed Cody up the hill.

Kelvin asked, "What's the matter with you two? Aren't you going to practice?"

The Great Gate

Cody crossed a plateau and walked toward a fragment of a square block wall, having a rectangular window in the center. She looked through the window and saw the valley stretch out before her. Where rolling fields of wheat ended, the tree line skirting the creek began. She gazed as far as her vision allowed; the lush growth formed a blurred ribbon of green on the distant horizon.

"I heard about Albert Brown," Conrad said. Cody turned around and saw that he stood very close. "I hope you're not upset by it."

"No. I didn't even like Albert. He was too … girly: every time he came over to my house, my lingerie turned up missing. I guess we know why." Cody crossed her arms.

"I guess we do," he replied. "But your mother is pushing hard for you to get married. What is she going to do?"

"Find another boy." Cody brooded, turned, and leaned out the window, resting her elbows on the stone ledge, sculpting her slacks to her body, in a sexual position without knowing it. Conrad leered at Cody's ass and then leaned against the wall.

"You do have other options." Conrad shrugged. "There are plenty of guys who want you."

Cody cringed and moved away from the window. She wrung her hands and moved toward an L-section of the wall. "Yes, my sisters mentioned that. They said that … they said that you liked me."

"I do," Conrad said. "I've liked you ever since we were kids."

When Conrad took a step forward, Cody took a step back, and a protruding bit of rock poked her back. She surged forward, tripped, and stumbled into Conrad's arms. He bent over to kiss her as if in slow motion, Cody saw a pair of lips coming toward her. When their lips met, his hands circled her waist, holding her tight.

Cody squirmed for a few seconds, her heart beating in her throat, and Conrad's kiss silenced her mewling protest. Conrad's passionate kisses and powerful grip took control of her body. Cody's breathing quickened, and her body tingled. For the first time in her life, someone was kissing her, but she never imagined it would be Conrad.

Conrad lost control, relishing Cody's soft body, groping her. He smothered Cody's lips with a sloppy kiss as if to consume the girl. Cody felt his hand all over her. When his hands grew bolder, she began to struggle.

Kelvin stabbed at a few more dummies and slapped the sword on a wooden fence. His enthusiasm and interest, however, began to wane. He flopped down on the grass and stared at the passing clouds. He closed his eyes and imagined fighting in a glorious battle. It would be a close fight, but he would win.

When he grew lonely and curious, he rose to his feet and trudged across the knoll. "Conrad, Cody, where are you two?" When he rounded a curved section of wall, he saw that Cody was red-cheeked and pensive; her ribbon tie was loose, and the top blouse buttons were unfastened. Cody tucked her silk blouse and adjusted her tights.

Cody appeared as if she would burst into tears for a second or two. She tucked a blonde tress behind her left ear, lowered her gaze, and chewed on her lower lip. Fear welled up within her and demanded a reasonable and innocuous explanation. "We were just —" she stopped in mid-sentence, her mind a blank.

"We were just looking at the fields," Conrad said.

Kelvin strolled past them and looked out the window. It looked the same as ever, boring. "I don't see anything special."

Cody asked, "Kelvin, has your mother found a wife for you?"

He said, "My mom always says, 'You are too young to worry about such things. You have the rest of your life to fall in love and marry. You only get to be young once.'"

"Well … but have you ever thought about it? Are there any girls that you like?" asked Cody, feeling Conrad moving behind her, caressing her shoulders. His hands circled around Cody's waist and held her.

"Do you like any girls?" asked Cody, leaning forward and elbowing him, trying to break his grip.

"Me? Nah," he replied. "But there's a bunch of girls who like me though?"

"What? Who?" asked Cody, ignoring Conrad.

"Your sister, Judith, for one," he replied. "She's all the time giving me these strange looks. It's like she's hungry, and I have the last sandwich in town."

Cody frowned and narrowed her eyes. "I knew it. She was the one who wanted me to marry an old man."

"You should have a young man," Conrad said slid his hands around her. Cody bit her lower lip and wrung her hands. She pressed her chin to her chest and saw his hands.

"Last week, at the Spring Harvest Festival, she kept asking me to dance with her, and then Karina asked me to dance, and then the two of them got into a fight. They kept calling each other names like 'bitch' and 'slut' and stuff like that. Two other girls snuck over and asked me to dance while they were fighting. Girls are weird. Who cares about dancing anyway?"

"Dancing is fun," Cody said.

"I guess," Kelvin commented and circled around the wall.

30

When Cody saw Kelvin leaving, she said, "Kelvin where are you …
mmnn." She was cut off by Conrad's kiss. Once again, Conrad embraced
her, his hands exploring her.

Kelvin trudged down the knoll and through a small grove of wild apple
trees. He picked off a little green apple and bit it. The sour fragment
made his mouth pucker. He spat it out and hurled the apple fragment
into Rose Pond, named for the beautiful rose bushes that circled the
pond. Beside a collapsed shed, an old dock awaited him, glad to have
someone use it; its weary bones creaked and clunked beneath his
footsteps. When he sat down at the end, he saw tiny fish swarming in the
shallow waters. Everything was changing; he could feel it.

After a few minutes had passed, he glanced up the hill at the fort and
tossed a rock into the shrubs at water's edge. There was no trace of his
friends. *What are they doing up there?*

Cody burst forth from the shrubs, her clothing in a state of chaos. "What
the hell Kelvin! Why did you leave?" Conrad emerged from the bushes.
His hand was pressed to his face, and blood poured out from his nose.

At last, Kelvin understood the situation, and rage blazed within him. His
hands clenched into fists; his face turned red, and the veins in his neck
bulged. He strode down the dock, murder in his eyes. Cody hurried onto
the dock and blocked his path. He glanced at her and then glared at
Conrad.

"Why'm gwoing," he mumbled, pinching his nose to stop the bleeding.

"Please Kelvin, don't." Cody wrapped her arms around him and held on
tight. "I don't want you to get in trouble."

Kelvin wrapped his arms around Cody and held her; "Are you all right?"

"I'm okay now," she said. When she looked up at Kelvin, their eyes met.
As if in slow motion, he bent over and kissed her. A rush swept through
her, far different from what she felt with Conrad. He took her in his arms

31

and held her tight. She caressed the back of his neck and pressed up into him. Exhilaration surged within them both. A golden glow settled upon her mind, and she melted into him.

Chapter 3

Kelvin's eyes popped open wide, and he scrambled out of bed. He made it halfway across his room before the hardwood floor stole the warmth from his feet. A quick search of the floor revealed that his slippers lay underneath his bed. He rushed back and slipped them onto his feet.

It was his nineteenth birthday, the day of his ascension, the day he became a man. He rushed to the window and threw wide the tan drapes. Looking out from the second floor, he saw his father feeding the chickens. After releasing the latch, he heaved and pushed up the sturdy wooden window frame. It hit the top sill with a clunk, and a gust of chilly wind flapped the curtains, stealing the warmth from his bedroom.

"Father, are we going to town. It's my Ascension Day," he called out.

Joash paused from his work, a handful of seed sifted through his fingers. A pained expression took shape on his face. The chickens rushed about in a feeding frenzy, pecking at the ground and sometimes at each other. Deep in thought and brooding, he lingered in silence and cast his gaze to the ground. He tossed the remaining seed onto the ground and emptied the bowl. "I suppose," he replied.

"YES!" said Kelvin and then slammed the window shut.

Joash strolled to the barn and removed the lid from the feed barrel. The smell of grain displaced the stench of chicken manure for a moment or two. He dumped the bowl into the barrel, creating a cloud of dust, and replaced the lid. He walked to the gate and unhitched it. Making sure that no chickens made a break for freedom, he passed through and closed the gate behind him.

A loud "moo" passed through the open barn door. The last cow in a long line gazed back at Joash. The cow's udders were full and painful. It was past time for him to relieve her. She swatted a fly with her tail and returned her attention to the feed bucket.

Joash entered the barn and rubbed his aching back. He carried a milk bucket and stool to the cow. He sat down beside her and cleaned off her utters with a special solution. Grasping a pair of teats, he squeezed in alternating fashion; milk jetting from her teats splattered in the bottom of the bucket. Modern dairy farms had machines to perform this task, but modern farms had the money to buy them.

A door opened and then slammed shut back at the house. There was no need to look back. He knew what was coming. Fiona entered the barn and marched up behind him. Hard years caused streaks of gray through her chestnut brown tresses, and fine creases appeared at the corner of her eyes, but she was still the beautiful girl that stole his heart so long ago.

She dried her hands with a dishtowel, the worry evident on her face. "You said Kelvin could go into town?" She rubbed the gold locket that hung from her neck. A picture of Kelvin, her youngest, lay inside it.

"He's nineteen. It's his right. In the eyes of the law, he's a man now."

"He's no man," she said. "He's a boy. Lucinda Witney told me her youngest boy was twenty years old before he pledged a trade. He worked on the farm until he grew into his father's shoes."

Growing into "his father's shoes" was a common expression applied to young men. It meant a young man needed time to mature and be able to take care of himself. Kelvin was Fiona's last, her baby; he would never be old enough or safe enough for her. Still, he had to admit that the boy lagged behind his older brothers in many ways.

"He doesn't need my permission to join a trade. He could do it by mail if he wanted." His hands shifted to the other two teats and continued milking. "Here's what we'll do. We will take him to town and let him talk to a few folks; most of the recruiters are good people, and they know when a bird needs more time in the nest. Anyway, it will give him a goal while he grows into a man. If he's interested in welding or farming, he can do it around here. I could teach him."

"He wants to be a warrior like Joffre, Ben, Richard, and … well … like Peter," she replied with emotion choking her voice.

"Joffre's done well as a warrior. He's a second lieutenant now, and that's in the regular army, not one of those fighting guilds. It's a decent career. They give them discipline and skills for civilian life. He wrote to us six months ago about leaving the military and starting a law practice. That's an excellent paying career."

"What about Peter? What did it do for Peter … nothing; it led him to an early grave. We don't even know where he fell. He's lying in some forlorn killing field beyond the Hargal Wall. I won't lose Kelvin."

Joash sneezed away from the bucket. He retrieved a red bandana from his back pocket and wiped his nose. The stale odor of hay in the barn aggravated his sinus. He picked up the milk pail and poured it into the 5-gallon container, destined for the cheese barn. As he secured the lid, he said, "You're right. He's not ready to be a warrior." He sniffed again. "I hoped that he would see it, but he's got his head full of those stories, heroes and such. If it comes right down to it, I'd prefer a recruiter break his heart. He needs us to believe in him."

"Yes but –" she started to object.

"Are you ready," Kelvin shouted. The screen door slammed shut behind him. He sprinted across the wooden porch and leaped over the stairs, hitting the ground with a thump and a cloud of dust. Kelvin sprinted up to them. "I'm ready to go. Why isn't the wagon hooked up?" He searched his mind. "I want to get to the recruiter's offices when they open. Cody and I want to join the same guild. They may want to test us. I need to get my bow."

The young man dashed back to the house. Joash shouted, "Bring my sword and armor too. They may want to see you use them."

"Okay," Kelvin shouted and rushed into the house.

"Your sword? He can't even lift it," Fiona whispered, "and Cody is a girl. She's even smaller than he is. These children are too young. Kelvin stumbles when he picks up your sword and makes a constipated face."

"I know," Joash said with a smile. Comprehension lit up her face, and she smiled. Kelvin kicked the screen door open. He dragged the sheathed sword across the porch; it thumped as the tip impacted each step. "Lift that sword off the ground boy. I don't want it getting damaged or dull."

"Yes sir," Kelvin replied. He hugged the sheath and heaved it off the ground. Unfortunately, it was upside down. The blade slipped out of the sheath and fell onto the dirt and gravel. Kelvin looked about wondering why the blade became so light. When he saw the gleaming blade upon the ground, he laid the sheath on the ground and slipped it over the blade. Lifting the handle straight up, he picked it up again and carried it toward the barn. "Here it is," he huffed and dumped the blade onto the floor.

Joash reached down and grasped the handle. His large, meaty hand fit around the leather wrappings as though it was an extension of his arm. He unsheathed it and held the blade before him. Despite the many battles, the blade was perfect, without nicks and battle scars; modern weaponry included energized cores in the tang; although the reinforcement field that was invisible to the naked eye, it stabilized the metallic structure of the cutting edge, making it sharper than an ancient sword. It brought him safely through many battles. He held it straight out as though pointing off into the distance. He brought it over his head and assumed a fighting stance. "I fought with this blade for over 400 hundred years. It always brought me victory."

He returned it to its sheath and added, "That was a long time ago. I'm a farmer now. You'll need it more than me if you're going to be a warrior." He extended the handle toward the teen. "Take it and show me your fighting stance."

Kelvin gripped the handle with both hands and drew it from its scabbard. The heavy tip plummeted down and hit the barn floor. It penetrated the wood and became stuck. Kelvin grew red-faced as he fought to dislodge it. "It won't budge."

"Here, let me." Joash took the handle from his son and lifted it as if it was a feather. He laid the guard across his shoulder with the blade pointing up and back. He sighed. "Son, what is the blade telling you?"

Kelvin screwed up his face and pondered the question. "I need more practice. I've been using a dagger, but it's not the same. I'll use your sword to practice with from now on."

Fiona rolled her eyes and shook her head. She caressed the boy's cheek with her right hand. It was smooth as silk and ruddy, but his strong nose and square jaw reflected his father's face. He was a bit on the smaller size of average, ruddy and handsome, but he was a dwarf when compared to his gigantic father, as most teens his age would be. He would grow into a handsome man, if only he lived long enough.

Joash prepared for this moment as though going into battle. The best decision is typically the one which preserves the most tactical options. In this case, he needed to delay. He knew his son's weakness and used it to his advantage. "I wanted this to be a surprise, but I guess I'll have to tell you. We can't go into town because of the party."

"Party, what party?" asked Kelvin. Fiona cocked her head and listened with interest. He never said anything about a party to her.

"Your Ascension Party," he said and rubbed his back. "I invited everyone. All of your friends and their families are coming. We can't go to town today. It would ruin everything."

Chapter 4

"You can't do this," Francis said and rubbed his face. He paced back and forth, his mind groping for a solution. "It's not right."

"It's done." A white stripe around Victoria's finger replaced what had once been her ring. "I am dominant now."

His face red with rage, he glared at the ring. "This is ridiculous. I'm not doing it. What will all our friends say? We'll be humiliated."

"Our so-called friends will accept it because they have no choice. It's our relationship, not theirs." She rose to her feet and looked out the bay window. The garden dazzled the eye with a rainbow of new blooms, and birds darted through the trees, capturing a morning meal. She turned toward him and crossed her arms. "I'm the man now, I'm dominant. The court's approved my petition and certified your submission to me."

"You can't do this," he chanted like a mantra. His skin was blazing red, the arteries in his neck bulged, and a fine coat of perspiration made his forehead glisten. His stomach was upset, and he was light-headed. "I don't feel well." He tried to swallow, but his throat was dry. Clutching his left arm, he said, "I need a doctor."

Victoria smirked and shook her head. "You'll be fine. It's just an upset stomach." She circled around him, her boots clacking on the hardwood floor. "You're just acting dramatic."

Footsteps came from the stairs, and Cody appeared. She wore a white silk top, a cobalt blue accordion pleated skirt, and a pair of strappy high heels. Her golden blonde locks swirled around her neck and draped down the front of her blouse. "I'm leaving for Kelvin's birthday party." Victoria exited the breakfast nook and drew the yellow dividing doors shut. Cody saw her father bent over the table, holding his left arm, clenching his jaw; "Is daddy okay?"

"He's fine. He has an upset stomach. I'll get him to bed and tend to him." She held her daughter's hands and said, "My you look pretty."

"Thank you," Cody said, taken back a bit by the complement. Her mother seldom said anything nice to her. Seeing the contrasting white circle of flesh around her mother's ring finger, she asked, "What happened to your ring?"

"I'm having it cleaned," Victoria replied.

Cody said, "You said I could go to the party."

"Yes, that's fine." Victoria crossed her left arm and tapped her chin with her right index finger. "But you can't go traipsing through the woods in high heels. You had better take the Harbor Road. The blue gravel provides better footing, and you can hire a passing carriage. You don't want to walk in those heels all the way to Kelvin's house."

She held out her right foot; "I guess that makes sense."

"Go along," Victoria said. "You don't want to be late."

Wary of her mother's intentions but eager to get to the party, Cody exited the house. She passed through the gardens, circling around the planters, admiring the orange mums. When she passed through the oak and maple trees, she paused and looked back through the wrought iron gate and the rose bushes. Through the bay windows, she saw her mother in the breakfast nook, but her body blocked Cody's vision. Her mother helped her father rise to his feet and exited the room. With a shrug, Cody turned and passed through the gate, glad to leave her home behind.

Mill Road meandered through rolling green hills and by gentle streams. It was a peaceful trip and afforded her some time for introspection. Kelvin was her best friend, but she now felt awkward around him. Was he her boyfriend or still just a friend?

She gazed up at the apple trees. Birds flew between the branches, capturing bugs, assisting the farmers. Beyond the waving branches and green leaves, she saw a single fluffy white cloud passing through a clear blue sky. A cool breeze wafted up her miniskirt and between her thighs, making her feel naked. She would have worn jeans or slacks, but her mother confiscated them and insisted, "You are a lady, not some trampy warrior." All Cody could wear were skirts and dresses. It seemed strange that she would never again wear slacks.

Despite the chilly weather, she felt warm, and her thoughts appeared to be a bit scattered. She dismissed it as lack of sleep; she spent many nights worrying about her future. Where would she go? What career path would she take? Her mother wanted her to marry and have babies. This future made her feel trapped as if they had her entire life planned — not the one of her choosing.

She rounded a gentle curve in the road. Down the steep embankment, she saw blue water and heard a babbling brook. When she climbed the hill, she saw Conrad Peat and tension racked her body. She brushed a blonde tress behind her right ear and stared at the blue gravel that covered the road.

"Hello Cody," Conrad said, approaching her. "I was waiting for you. I thought we could walk together if you don't mind?"

"That's fine," he said, and he slipped his right hand into the pocket of his windbreaker. "You look beautiful."

"Thanks," she replied with a strained smile, looking for a carriage she could hire.

"Listen, things have been a little weird lately. I lost control back on Little Round Top. I apologize for that. I want you to feel comfortable around me."

"It's alright," Cody said with a shrug. She heard the clip-clop of a horse-drawn wagon filled with potatoes ascending the hill. Mr. Caster removed his hat when he saw them.

"Morning, it's a beautiful day," Mr. Caster said.

"Morning," she said with girlish intonation.

After the wagon had passed them on the hill, Conrad said, "Listen, I want to make it up to the both of you. I have some gifts for Kelvin stowed away on my family's boat. It's nautical stuff; I bought it at the harbor. I was wondering, could you help me carry them? We can be a few minutes late to Kelvin's party. It's going on all day."

Cody was reluctant to be alone with Conrad, but he seemed genuinely sincere. And his family was wealthy. Very wealthy. He could afford to buy some nice presents. Kelvin needed whatever Conrad had to give. "Your family owns a boat?"

"Yeah, it's on Cedar Lake. I go there from time to time when I want to be alone. Anyway, I stored the gifts in the lounge. "They're all wrapped and everything. I just don't want them to get ruined on the way to Kelvin's house. Cody nodded, and they made a left turn and headed away from Kelvin's house, toward the harbor.

———

Joash directed traffic as wagons arrived. They drove around the house and stopped in the grassy field behind it. White rails fenced it in, and the stream provided ample water. Scores of young men and women rushed across the field. Some of the adults dropped off tables and folding chairs, which they set up in the yard. The women prepared food and decorated.

Kelvin passed among his friends, welcoming them. Fiona was impressed. He was quite popular, and it seemed like everyone wanted to be his friend; and the girls adored him, staring at him and giggling. The boys formed teams and played a game of soccer.

During the halftime, the boys charged up to the refreshment tables, their sweaty clothes clinging to their young bodies. Kelvin chugged down a glass full of punch and wiped the sweat from his brow with a towel. He jogged up to his mother and asked, "Is Cody here?"

"Um … no. I don't think so." She rose to her tiptoes and looked about. "I'll ask some of the ladies. You go back to your game and have fun. I'm sure she will be here soon."

————

The pair passed through the woods and emerged into a crescent-shaped harbor. Tall-mast ships, schooners, houseboats, and powerboats clung to a maze of docks. Summerhouses and cottages climbed up the side of the wooded hill, each one clambering for the better view. The posh Mission Shopping District lay across the bay: miles of restaurants, shops, and bars. Tourists, weary from the hustle and bustle of city life, retreated to property along the lake and brought with them much needed revenue.

Gentle waters flowed under the dock, and an occasional trout burst up from the waters, capturing an unwary fly. A sea-hawk skimmed the waters looking for a quick meal and snagged a leaping trout. They walked side by side along the dock, Cody's high heels causing sharp clacks on the wooden planks, accordion pleats dancing around her thighs, drunken men on boats leering at her. Fishermen dressed in rough garb paused from their labor at the cleaning tables. Holding filet knives and fish intestines, they watched Cody walk by their shanty as if it was a parade. She never looked up at them, despite their course jokes and their many attempts to gain her attention. The pungent aroma of fish and the stench of raw sewerage made her nose twitch. Cody hated the docks.

The Great Gate

Amidst the proud ships and great sailboats, one yacht stood out from its peers, both elegant and sleek. Like all the properties the Peat family owned, it was impressive. The ship rose up two stories from the hull and had white, graceful lines. Large windows trimmed the sides like racing stripes, and through them, one could see lounges, bedrooms, and dining areas. It even had a large, tiled patio and hot tub on its roof. It was as beautiful as Cody's home and three times the cost.

"All aboard," Conrad said, gesturing with her right hand. Cody paused for a second and then moved past him, feeling his gaze linger on her bottom. She clutched the rope railing and ascended the gangplank, hearing the water lap against the yacht. She ducked, although it was not necessary, and entered through the side door, finding herself in a luxurious lounge. Like everything the Peats owned, opulence and beauty defined it. The interior space had blond wood flooring, hand-woven area rugs, plush tan sofas, mahogany tables, and recessed lights that provided soft illumination – most people dreamed of owning such an extravagant vessel. But the room was unused, factory new, a sterile space devoid of human warmth, as if it had been purchased and then forgotten.

"Where are the gifts?"

The ship lurched, threw her off balance, and she tumbled onto a love seat. Lying sprawled across the sofa, it took her a few seconds to recover. When she looked out the window at the deep blue waters, she noticed that they were moving. Cody rushed across the room, looked out the other window and knelt on a bucket shaped chair. The water glided past the hull, and the dock and the lakeshore shrank into the distance.

The water acted as an insulator and provided distance from Rhunite. Unlike land vehicles which were forced to traverse "safe roads," designated by a blue triangle, ships could travel any waterway, and they were the primary means of travel and shipping. In many areas where the foliage was especially dense, transport companies employed submarines to transport goods. The houseboat used a regenerative electric power supply that powered a jet prop; thus it could pass through the shallow channels and marshes.

Cody searched a connecting hallway, but all she found were staterooms. Where was Conrad, and where were they going? She navigated the hallway to the stern, entered a master suite, and hurried to an expansive glass window. The blue water, forming an ever-expanding gulf, separated her from the shore and escape. Cody chewed her fingernail and searched the ship. Like the lounge, the staterooms were an opulent void. She found an oak door leading to the second level, but Conrad locked it. She returned to the entry door, but the deck appeared too narrow, and she feared that she might fall in the water.

She settled onto a love seat and tugged the hem of her skirt. The accordion pleats draped over her thighs, and she wondered when the boat would stop and what would happen when it did. When she brushed back the curtains, the shore appeared as a razor thin strip of green on the far horizon, a vanishing point, and a few seconds later it disappeared, leaving her surrounded by dark blue water. She searched for some hint as to their destination, but the expansive blue waters gave away no secrets.

The Calen Islands, a series of 23 small islands, rose up out of the deep blue waters, and dense forests covered these volcanic islands like a toupee. Water cascaded from the peaks of dead volcanoes and leaped over cliffs, forming a dazzling array of waterfalls. Cody opened the door and settled down on the bow, resigning herself to go wherever Conrad led.

They passed through a channel between two islands. Lush forests climbed up steep cliffs and colorful birds winged between them, their cries lonesome and foreboding. She leaned upon the stainless steel railing at the prow of the ship, and locked eyes with a deer on the shore. They share a terrifying moment, and unlike Cody, the deer sprang free, disappearing into the dense foliage.

The Great Gate

She watched the rocky shore, festooned with sharp knife-like rocks and saw hidden peril, a reef, below the waterline, passing by on the port side, and heard shrill cries that penetrated the jungle. Where the lethal shore ended towering black walls began, vaulted and dangerous, overlooking the bone shattering rocks and drowning surf. Could a detachment of marines take such an island?

The island wall suddenly turned inward, forming a horseshoe-shaped cove, and at the apex of the cove, she spotted a small private dock, bare-boned and without embellishment. It traveled back to a set of stairs, the lower flights retractable as if a siege was imminent, and then they zigzagged up the face of the cliff. A high curtain wall skirted around the upper rim; sealing in or out, it was hard to determine. The top flight of stairs passed through an arched entryway. Her gaze fell upon a steel gate, left open for their arrival, yet with a promise of later closure. As her eyes beheld the fortress, she wondered, *Will I ever see the outside world again?*

The boat slowed and cruised up to the dock, and making a leisurely turn, it floated up to the port side mooring. The boat pressed against the rubber bumper and came to rest. Cody saw Conrad leap off the stern of the boat and run up the dock. "Throw me the bow line," he called out. Cody saw a coiled rope and assumed that it was what he meant. She tossed the line to him, and he tied it off to the cleat. He then tied off the stern line, securing the boat.

Cody made her way to the port side of the boat and leaped onto the dock. "What's going on? Where are we?"

"My parent's own a Villa up top. I thought we could go there and see it." Conrad ran down the wooden dock, ignoring Cody. "Come on. It's great."

Cody pranced a few steps and glanced back at the boat. "What about Kelvin's party? Where are the gifts? We have to go." Conrad ran down the dock either not hearing or not responding, the latter possibility twisting her stomach into a knot.

As if invading, Conrad sprinted to the end of the dock and charged up the stairs. His footfalls pounded like a drumbeat. "Hurry," he called out. Cody stripped off her shoes and hurried after him.

The waters fell below her, and the jungle drew closer as Cody climbed the stairs. When she reached the top platform and looked through the entryway, she saw a spectacular Spanish style villa. A portico led to a two-story, tan stucco mansion. Pillars and archways covered the first level, and each bedroom on the second floor had a private balcony; and red tiles covered the roof, protecting it from the fiercest storm. Cody chased after Conrad and ran up to a pair of thick wooden doors, supported by wrought iron hinges. At their approach, the doors opened automatically.

She chased him across the yard, passed through a hallway, and emerged into the center courtyard. It was paradise. Plants, lounges, and mosaic tiled patio skirted around a large swimming pool; a fountain of sparkling blue pool jetted into the air and splashed down into the crystal clear waters. Cody spun around in a circle and gazed at the structure. Every room, first and second floor, had a commanding view of the pool. She spotted Conrad on the second-floor walkway and chased after him.

Cody charged up the stairs in pursuit of her captor. She saw a set of open accordion hinged, brown frame glass doors, and when she passed through them, she found Conrad lying upon a brown leather sofa, his legs spread as an invitation. He slurped a beer and asked, "So what do you think? Isn't it great?"

"It's fantastic, amazing. I can't believe it. Now let's go." Cody wandered into the room; a warm breeze wafted the white gauze curtains and cooled the room to a perfect temperature. "We have to get back. Kelvin is expecting us at his Ascension Party."

The smile evaporated from Conrad's face, and he sat up straight. "Do you remember what it was like two years ago at one of his parties? We slept on the floor with him and his friends. When they weren't giggling

47

and farting, they were snoring. We spent three days sleeping on that floor. It was horrible."

Cody sat down cattycorner to Conrad. "Yes, I remember. My whole body ached for a week."

"We swore to never do that again." Conrad scurried over to Cody's sofa and jumped onto it beside her. "Besides, I have a better idea."

Cody knew what Conrad had in mind, and it distressed her. She rose up from the sofa and strolled across the room. She looked out the window, noted that the gate was still open, and spotted the ship in the harbor, and forming an improvised escape plan, she asked, "What is it?"

"They can come to us. I sent Kelvin a map with instructions on how to get to us. You know how he loves an adventure." He smiled and placed his hands behind his head. "They can get rowdy back at his rundown little farm house, sleep there a day or two, and then come here. It's perfect. The villa has plenty of rooms, and it is fully stocked with food. We can party for weeks if he wants."

Conrad jumped to his feet and rushed out of the room. He returned a few minutes later wearing swimming trunks. He tossed a Cody a black bikini and a towel. "We have to go swimming." He left the lounge without waiting for a reply. "Come on. Get on your swimsuit."

Cody looked at the swimsuit in her hand and slouched. She had little choice. There was no leaving the island without the boat. Of course, she could hide in the forest, but there were too many predators. Releasing a sigh, she decided to play along with his scheme and humor him. "Crap," Cody muttered and stepped into a small changing room. After locking the door, she stripped off her clothes and hung them up in the corner. She stabbed her feet into the bikini bottom and whisked them up in a hurry. She then put on the meager top, which covered only the essential parts.

Cody emerged from the room and gazed over the railing on the second level, chlorine stinging her nostrils and the tile floor stealing the warmth from her bare feet. Conrad dove into the pool, swam beneath its clear water, and emerged near an artificial boulder, positioned at the far end of the pool, serving as a wet bar and water slide. "Come on, the water's great!"

Chapter 5

Fiona carried an empty serving tray into the house. The raucous laughter of teens at play mixed with the sound of music. Adults lingered in the house and out in the yard. They sipped cups of ale and discussed topics of interest: politics, crop yields, the weather, and taxes. She passed through the crowd and entered the kitchen. When she rounded the corner, she saw waded paper covering the floor and Kelvin seated at the table. The young man grumbled and labored before a single lamp. Parchment sheets and open books lay scattered around him.

"Why aren't you out at the party celebrating?" asked Fiona.

"I need to solve this puzzle," he mumbled and returned to work, turning the page in a reference book. Fiona looked over his shoulder for a minute. The cryptic note they received from Conrad's messenger lay before him. The first page, which declared the Ascension Day Adventure, was written in the common tongue. However, the next page was written in gibberish, and the third page was blank.

She circled around the table and passed through the kitchen. Dirty dishes and empty platters covered the countertop. A pair of women set to work and began to wash them. Other people prepared more food.

Joash strolled into the room, a mug of ale in his hands. He slipped a strap over his left shoulder and let it snap. "What are you doing boy? Still working on that puzzle?"

"Yes." He threw down the pen and ran his fingers through his hair. "I just can't get it. It is like none of my ciphers. And I know all of them."

Joash sniffed and said, "Let me see it." The young man knew better than to rebel. He handed the note to his father and rose from the chair. He began picking up the discarded papers. "Hmm," he said and shook his head, a grin appearing on his face. "This is an old Elven trick."

50

Kelvin rushed to his father's side and inspected the paper once again as if some new insight would occur to him. "What do you mean? What kind of trick?"

"The elves are pretty clever." He handed the encrypted note to Kelvin. "This is gibberish. It's a diversion. The enemy would keep trying and trying to break a code that has no key. All the while they would ignore the real answer." He held the blank paper above the lamp, moving it about in the heat. As if by magic, words and a map appeared. "Conrad wrote the secret note in lemon juice. All you have to do is heat it to bring out the actual message." He laughed, "He's pretty clever."

When the map and text fully appeared, he handed it to Kelvin. "Here you go," he tousled Kelvin's hair, "one secret map. He used your cleverness and education against you. He knew you were stubborn and an expert code breaker, so he gave you an impossible puzzle to solve – it's a diversion. You've been out-witted."

Chapter 6

Victoria heard a knock at the door and opened it wide. "Melanie, Charles, what a pleasure to see you both." The Peats entered the house.

Charles cleared his throat and forced an unwilling smile. "It's good to see you too." After the pair had removed their coats, they handed it to the new maid that Victoria recently purchased, a slave girl, something Francis forbade. The girl curtsied and hurried to hang them up in the cloak closet.

"It is so unseasonably cold," Melanie complained. "I barely survived the walk from our carriage to the door." The trio laughed and lingered in the foyer.

"I see that it's true: you wear the dominant ring. Did your husband actually allow you to become dominant?" asked Melanie.

"Oh yes, he insisted. The poor dear has never felt at ease leading the family. I had myself declared a man, so I am able to carry out the negotiations."

"Will he be joining us?"

"No. He's not feeling well. I think it's the flu that has been going around," Victoria said. "He has complete confidence in my decisions."

Charles tried to smile, but it appeared as though he were sucking on lemons. He had business dealings with Frances, and Francis shared his concerns. She did not have his confidence, but he often called her an evil shrew, pompous, and devious. Charles quietly checked with his resources in the court and uncovered Victoria's plan, but it was too late: she filed the papers. He could do nothing. Charles brushed a few errant gray strands back over his balding head and then stroked his gray beard. He detested Victoria, but he was cornered. Conrad was smitten with Cody; the reason why escaped him.

"Why don't we relax in the parlor before dinner?" asked Victoria.

"An excellent idea," Charles said and guided his wife into the parlor.

They sat before the hearth, enjoying the simulated fire. "I have a lovely meal planned. Our new chef is a wonder with food."

Charles choked down his rage, growing red-faced. He was an abolitionist, a small but growing minority, and they considered the laws on involuntary servitude barbaric and immoral; but the crown supported the law, so he had to choose his words with care. "I hate to be blunt, but we really did want to get down to business." Charles retrieved a legal document from his pocket. "This is a bridal contract. We are prepared to pay 500,000 kronars for your daughter Cordelia Moyer. Our youngest son Conrad has his heart set on the girl."

Victoria's heart leaped when she heard the price, but she remained calm. "I see." She took the document from Charles. As she leafed through it, she said, "It is a fair price, but what about her care? Will Conrad be given a living inheritance?"

"Of course, you needn't worry about that. We are quite well off, and we've set aside a substantial inheritance for Conrad," he said.

Melanie added, "He is our youngest son, and we want to take care of him. We do have some questions about Cordelia. Does she want babies? We would like them to start a family as soon as possible. Conrad has agreed to join the family business and learn from his father."

"Cody … Cordelia loves babies. She can't wait to have one. Will you engage the services of a stud, or will Conrad father the child? The only reason I ask is that Cordelia would prefer to carry Conrad's baby." Victoria said.

"Yes. Our son will be fathering the child," Charles said with emphasis. He understood why some families hired studs, but the practice was too widely spread in his opinion, a symptom of Asgard's moral decay. "He has made that perfectly clear."

"Yes. We want it to be a shared baby," Melanie said, "a part of both of them."

"Wonderful," Victoria said. "She will be so excited to hear the news."

Chapter 7

The setting sun cast long shadows over the harbor. Cody lingered upon the landing at the top at the cliff. Still clad in her black bikini, her blonde locks danced around her bare shoulders. When she returned to the changing room, Conrad claimed that he was laundering her clothes. He then shoved a tropical drink in her hand, suggested it was a special cocktail that she would enjoy, and gazed at her with an impish, sideways stare. When he turned his back, she dropped the glass, causing it to shatter on the coral tile. As Conrad cleaned up the mess, she fled the mansion.

"Come on," she muttered, standing upon the platform at the top of the cliff, leaning to the left, trying to see around the thick vegetation at the end of the bay. The slamming doors boomed, and angry shouts escaped the mansion. She glanced over her shoulder and rushed down the stairs, fearful that he might discover her at any moment. When she reached the bottom, she ran barefoot down the dock and rushed up the gangplank to the houseboat. She frantically tugged on the door, but Conrad locked it.

"CODY!" Conrad called out with annoyance.

She chewed her fingernail and eyed the water. There were many dangerous creatures beneath the deep waters, any one of which could eat her whole. She hurried to the end of the dock and studied the water with frantic eyes. "Cody," Conrad shouted from the top of the cliff, "Get up here! You can't swim there. It's not safe."

She was about to dive into the water when she heard shouts. Hanging from the sides, crowding the decks, shouting at the top of their lungs, girls dancing, Kelvin captained the first of two vessels. She waved her arm and shouted. "Over here!"

"Cody, we found you," Kelvin shouted.

"Great," Conrad mumbled. He trudged down the stairs and watched the pair of sailing ships moor at the docks. Scads of teens tumbled onto the dock and ran pell-mell toward the stairs. He offered them a simple smile and waved as they passed him by. Kelvin leaped off the lead sailboat and onto the dock. Cody jumped into his arms and kissed him. At seeing this, Conrad's face grew red, and his mouth formed a deep frown, making him appear even uglier and menacing.

Cody hung onto Kelvin's arm as they strolled down the dock. Conrad watched them pass with a hateful glare. They could have their fun today, but soon Cody would belong to him. Then Kelvin would never see her again. Then he would tell Kelvin to "get lost" and slam the door in his face. He followed them and nurtured his wounded pride with all the things he would do to Cody.

Kelvin held open the door, and Cody entered the mansion. Conrad trudged behind them, grim-faced and brooding. Splashes and the gleeful shouts of teens at play came from the interior. Kelvin raised his eyes and gaped at the grandeur. Worthy of a king, the palatial interior dizzied him. Rows of high columns, like trees lining a street, supported the second level, and the rectangular interior had four sets of stairs, two at each end, coiling around and reaching up to the second level. Sharp light beamed in through lead crystal panes that trimmed the ceiling, and countless rainbows washed the interior with color. He ran his hand along the plush furnishings, feeling the richness of the water resistant fabric. A private café opened to the pool area, and some of the teens were cooking food on the grill, others seated at the counter, waiting for the food.

Cody squeezed Kelvin's hand, desire burning in her eyes. Kelvin replied with a quizzical gaze, mystified by the female mind; Conrad had so much, and he had so little. He never used the word "poor" to describe himself – until this moment. But he was poor, and he lived a hard life. What did he have to offer her?

Conrad wandered into the café, hands in his swim trunk pockets. Scores of teens crowded around circular tables, and they waited to eat; and they chatted, and they gossiped; and they laughed, and they tried to imagine the future. Ascension Day was pivotal. It steered the course of a young person's life, influenced their marital choices, and hinted at how they would live. Conrad avoided such discussions. His parents decided his future, determining every detail of his life. He would work with his father, managing and developing commercial and residential real estate. It would be a life filled with endless meetings, working from sunup to well past sunset, suffocated with quiet desperation, and empty, a life predestined for him since before he was born. And he would never achieve greatness: his five older brothers made that clear. They were already ensconced in the company, every bit of power in their hands and none for him. What would he do if given a chance? He had no clue, but he would like to find out. But it was meaningless to think about such things. His father and brothers controlled the family's wealth, and they made it clear: he would do as they told him.

When Kelvin embraced Cody, she melted into him. Her lips were so soft, her body so inviting. He withdrew and said, "I don't understand it."

"Understand what?" asked Cody.

"How you could want me. Conrad has so much. I mean, I knew he was rich, but I had no idea. He's got more money than the king."

She caressed his cheek with her right hand. "I don't care about those things. I want you, not Conrad's money."

He slid his arm around her waist and strolled around the pool. "My dad always says, "A man's life is measured by how many people he loves, not how much he owns. I guess I understand that now."

"You love me?" she asked, gazing up at him through her bangs.

"You know I do."

She grabbed his right hand and led him back to a private room. Kelvin closed and locked the door. Cody stood at the foot of a bed, arms tight to her side and her body stiff. When he moved to her, his arms encircling her waist, his lips meeting hers, she kissed him and wrapped her arms around his neck. His hands slid over her body and held her tight. His love ignited her passion and thawed her body.

He stripped off her bathing suit, and she removed his suit. They lay on the mattress together and intertwined, their bodies moving together. When at last she was ready, he moved between her thighs and slowly thrust his member inside her. She squeezed her eye shut, tilted her head backward, and gasped. He began to pump his hips, moving in and out of her, their bodies sliding against one another. She planted her feet on the bed and pumped her hips, their bodies meeting with a fleshy slap. Kelvin struggled for control, but there was a limit to how much his youthful, inexperience body could take. He thrust inside her and felt his fluid stream into her.

Some moments change our lives, watershed events: making love to Cody was one of them. Joash never told Kelvin the stories of their ancestors; his mother, Kelvin's grandmother, always said, "We are descended from a race of giants." Joash dismissed such stories as fables, the kind mothers tell children. Yet sexual contact with Cody and the surge of sensations within Kelvin activated hidden parts of his anatomy, bits of DNA, non-native to a human body, and they set to work, surging growth hormones through his system. His body had a single imperative – grow!

Cody walked with a skip in her step, and Kelvin strutted like a king entering his court. A few of the girls spoke in whispers and restrained giggles. The boys gawked as if viewing some fascinating spectacle. A few grinned and hurried over to them, eager to greet the happy couple.

But not everyone was happy.

Conrad lounged upon a submerged rock, and he scowled at the waters. His sister, Amanda, swam up to him, and she tried to talk with him; but he gave her one-word answers. She soon gave up and decided to enjoy herself, swimming away for a group of girls at the far end of the pool.

A circle of boys formed around Kelvin. They laughed and joked. The girls, however, formed around Cody. They wanted details. How was the kiss? How did she like it? When Cody leaned in to whisper, all the girls grew quiet and leaned in close to hear.

Chapter 8

The Ascension Day celebration ended after two days, and three ships sailed for home. The friends parted company, and even Kelvin kissed Cody goodbye and headed for home. Cody walked up the garden path to her home, and the floral perfume of the blossoms hung in the air. Upon hearing the parting calls from her friends, she turned and waved. "BYE!" She looked through the black iron gate with rose bushes on either side. The carriage, overloaded with riders, forced most passengers to stand. Tommy Munson slapped the reins, and the carriage lurched forward. The girls grabbed the seat to steady themselves.

She circled around the back of the house. Through the bay window, she searched for some sign of her father. It was late afternoon, the second edition of the news came out, and he was always eager to read the stock quotes. But the breakfast nook was empty, and the chairs were scooted up to the oval table; and his coffee cup lay between the porcelain figurines that adorned the lemon yellow walls. Off in the distance, she heard a dog; it had a lonesome, agonized howl.

Cody rounded the white corner of the house, and she observed the redwood deck. Their family spent many happy hours entertaining guests, but pine needles covered the outdoor furniture; and black ash still filled the bottom of the red brick barbecue. Through the crystal clear pool water, she saw leaves and debris covering the bottom, obscuring the blue tiles. That was peculiar: her father fussed about keeping the patio and pool clean, laboring daily on it and forcing them to help.

She circled the next corner and saw a host of E-cars, wagons, and carts. Was there a party? Men clothed in black congregated near the door, smoldering pipes hanging from their lips, and they spoke in reverent whispers. An uneasy look in their eyes, they paused and stared at her. She furrowed her brow and offered them a sideways glance, offended by their fixed gaze, and she entered the house, perplexed and a bit afraid.

When she entered through the front door, she encountered a host of people dressed in black. Judith and Lila sat across the room by the hearth, emptiness in their watering eyes. Victoria spoke with the local priest, Douglas Brothers. The priest stood close to her, nodded, and stroked his chin with his index finger.

"Where's daddy?" The crowd turned toward her but remained silent, as if afraid to speak. Strangers to her, some old women burst into tears and dried their tears with laced handkerchiefs. She took a few steps and saw the grief in her sister's eyes.

Victoria approached Cody and rubbed her shoulders. "I'm sorry sweetie. Your father …" she swallowed, paused, and set her face like stone. "You father died. Doctor Parsons thinks it was a heart attack. We will have the funeral pyre this afternoon —"

"NO!" Cody burst into tears. "You're lying."

"Cody," Victoria sighed, "he's gone."

Through the den doors, she saw a body wrapped in white linen, still, lifeless, shaped like a human body. She turned, fled the house, and ran down the driveway, her mother calling after her. She raced down the small hill and through the open gates. Black wreaths hung upon them, the mark of mourning. She ran through the gates and charged into the woods, her mother's voice fading into the distance.

Tears streaming down her cheeks, she sped down the path. It marked a well-worn route, but she had no destination in mind – she just ran. Kelvin emerged from the woods. "Cody!" he shouted and charged toward her. She flung herself into his arms, and holding him tight, she buried her face in his shoulder and sobbed. He said, "My mother told me when I got home. I had no idea he was sick."

She pushed away from him. "Daddy wasn't sick. She did it."

The Great Gate

"What? Who did what?" When he tried to caress her arm, she pulled away. "You're not making any sense."

"I can't. I just can't." She staggered for a second and then her eyes rolled back into her head. Kelvin caught her as she tumbled to the ground, unconscious. He picked her up in his arms and rushed back to the house.

————

Mourners clothed in black stood in a field of green, trees swaying off in the distance, a babbling brook winding its way around it. Spreading off into the distance, ostentatious marble mausoleums and simple headstones marked the final resting place for countless ossuaries. They climbed over the rolling hills and lay beside the quiet waters. Endless. Timeless grief surrounded them.

Black cloth wrapped tight around the body of Francis. The earthly remains of Cody's father lay atop a tall pile of wood, all set upon a block base. The priest stood between a pair of brass stands, flames burning in the conical, brass basins. He read from a book of common prayers, and quiet sobs arose from the assembled mourners. With hands upraised, he said, "We beseech the Great Spirit to accept Francis's spirit into the sacred dwelling place of the dead ...."

Black veils covered the ladies faces, and the men presented gifts for the afterlife: a beer mug, a weapon, a pair of shoes, and so forth; all were placed upon the altar beside the body. Cody was unmoved by their tribute and stared at the ground with empty eyes, the hired mourner's cries distant, as if miles away. Just last week her father was alive. They sat together in the garden and talked. How could he be dead? It was impossible. It had to be a mistake – yet she could not bring herself to look up at the proof lying atop the pyre. Kelvin stayed close by Cody's side, anxiously studying her every facial expression and body movement.

"… We now commit the body of our brother Francis Douglas Moyer III to the ages. Attendants, please come forth." Joash and Benjamin Moyer,

Francis's cousin, stepped forward. They picked up a pair of wooden torches, oil soaked rags wrapped around the tips, and they held the tips in flames, igniting them. "Send forth our brother to the afterlife."

Joash and Benjamin touched their torches to the dried wood. A small flame flickered to life, and it began to grow as the oil ignited. The men circled around the woodpile, touching the oil soaked wood at random intervals. The flames climbed up the woodpile, engulfed the body, and shot high into the air. Black smoke rose into the clear blue sky, marking Francis's path to the afterlife.

When Cody's legs began to weaken, Kelvin supported her, holding her by the side, and he helped her walk back to a stone bench. She sat next to the mausoleum that would be her father's final resting place. Kelvin tried to support Cody's heaving body as tears fell from her eyes. Off in the distance, the flames climbed high into the skies, and the mourners began to depart. They would return to the Moyer home and wait, for the next week ladies would prepare food and tend to the family's needs.

Victoria, Judith, and Lila clutched bouquets of flowers and walked single file toward the mausoleum, black veils over their faces. They placed the flowers in urns at the door, said a final prayer, and touched a drop of holy water to their foreheads. Even through her veil, Kelvin saw the smoldering resentment on Victoria's face. He could not fathom the wellspring of her hatred. What had he done to engender such venom? Their families were neighbors; his father and Francis were friends. Did she think he was somehow responsible?

Cody grew still and lapsed into vacuous silence, emotionally spent. She stared at the white marble steps leading into the mausoleum but could not bring herself to join her family inside the vault. She heard scraping stone as the door opened and a clunk from a box as it was placed on a marble table – her father's final resting place was prepared. How could it be? How could he become dust? She clung to Kelvin and tried to pretend it was all a lie. Francis was back home, smoking his pipe and reading his oracle scroll. Then a hiss came from the pyre, and the incendiary mixture, able to burn bone to ash, caught fire. She buried her face into Kelvin's neck and squeezed her eyes shut, clutching his jacket with white-knuckled intensity, wishing it to all go away – she wanted her father back.

Victoria paused in the doorway and spoke with the remaining mourners. It was then that Inspector Higgins passed between the structures. He was a portly man with a gleaming baldhead, trimmed on the sides by a semicircle of gray hair. His bulbous potbelly preceded him, hat tucked underneath his arm, and his gray vest struggled to maintain its grip; and a gold pocket watch chain, draped across the front, swayed as he walked. His eyes narrowed, and the corners of his mouth were pulled down into a deep frown, causing his many double chins to ripple. He charged up the steps and barked, "Mrs. Moyer, I sent you word."

"Yes I know," Victoria replied. "This is not the time."

"It must be the time." He waved his hand at the blazing fire. "I have a court order for an autopsy, and yet you deliberately defied it."

"I did not defy it." She crossed her arms and glared at the inspector. "I have a certificate of death from our family physician. My husband had a viral infection that caused myocarditis, succumbing to natural causes. Your disgusting autopsy was not necessary. I told this to your man."

"You defied a legal court order to surrender the body." Inspector Higgins began to pace and slap his arms against his sides. "I could have you arrested."

"The funeral was scheduled, and your court order was absent. Hinting that you might obtain one is not the same as having one. I was under no legal obligation to wait for you. My guests were here, and my husband was gone. We needed to lay him to rest. I can't believe you how you just show up here in our time of grief."

"And I can't believe you. You conspired behind your husband's back. You had yourself declared a man, took out a large life insurance policy and then thwarted a legal investigation." He thrust the documents in her hand and signaled his men. "Put out that fire. I want that body."

"I took out that policy to protect my family. We needed that money should anything happen to Francis. He incurred many debts when he led the family. You can't do this!" exclaimed Victoria.

"I can, and I am." The fire wagon pulled up to the pyre. While two men dragged the induction hoses down to the river, the others activated the pumps. It took three men, straining with all their might, to hold the hose as water jetted out the tip. The water and flame waged war for the body. Hisses and thick smoke issued from the conflict.

"Stop that!" Victoria shrieked and ran toward the blaze. Policemen intercepted her, and when she began to flail, they grabbed her arms and restrained her. "You can't. You can't do this!"

Chapter 9

Six months passed since Kelvin's Ascension Day, and his course remained fixed. Joash persuaded him to wait until the country fair: more guilds would attend. The young man grudgingly agreed, and Fiona had a temporary reprieve.

He leaped up from the wagon seat and stabbed his fists in the air. They passed up a muddy lane between narrow field stonewalls. Thatched roofs and chimneystacks loomed overhead. The heavy smell of smoke and baked goods hung in the air. A boy and a girl paused from their play to watch them pass. Farmers on Eden, as on most other worlds, were impoverished. They worked long hours by the sweat of their brows and have little to show for their efforts.

Dirt roads gave way to cobblestone, and wood frame homes with tile roofs began to appear. Manicured lawns took the place of crops; barbecues and patios sets, forgotten toys and bicycles, and flowerbeds and gazebos filled the backyards. Through bay windows, one could see modern lighting; self-sustaining rhunite based illumination, comfortable furnishing; soft curtains, rich grain wooden tables, and paintings adorned the interiors, and climate control systems; warming in the winter and cooling in the summer.

They passed through the residential section and merged into traffic. E-cars, E-trucks, personal wagons, hansom cabs, and merchant carts formed double lanes of traffic. Joash's frustration grew with each wagon that cut him off.

The county fair always included recruiters. They swarmed about like predators, taking the best and brightest. Young men and women provided brute labor for their trades, fodder for the machine. After endless months of back breaking work, the trades dismissed half of the applicants. Only a third of those who remained joined a guild:

construction, welding, farming, fighting, or otherwise. The rest went home with little to show for their years of labor but broken dreams.

Fiona surveyed the latest fashions displayed in shop windows. A lovely green gown made of pure silk and trimmed with gold braid caught her eye. For a moment, she imagined herself clad in the gown, dancing at a royal ball, a princess in a fairytale. She dismissed the idle notion. They had little money saved and none for such luxuries.

They passed by one shop and found another right next to it. Hardware, weapons, clothing, dry goods, feed, and other commodities abounded. Soon the store walls fused together, forming a never-ending row of shops. Where the cobblestone ended smooth slate began. They were in the heart of the commercial district. Black steel benches provided rest for weary shoppers. Trees and flowers were confined to planters, and the hand of mankind was all around them.

The clatter of dishes and the din of conversations came from patrons who dined al fresco. Many of those eating paused from their meal to gawk at the family, as though a specter emerged from the past. Joash slapped the reins and hurried his horse, growing red-faced at their unabated stares.

Joash remembered a day, not so long ago in the backwaters of his mind, when he slept in castles and dined with kings. He walked the halls of the high-born and served as a captain of the guard. One war merged into another, and one award followed another until his accomplishments merged together. He won "The Legion of Merit" medal, the highest award in the land, six times for bravery. However, his life was empty – a void of passionless sex, drunkenness, and endless debauchery. While away on a mission, he happened into The Green Peacock Restaurant and dined outdoors, al fresco fashion. Fiona was his waitress. When she asked to take his order, he said, "I'll have you."

She put her hands on her hips, leaned toward him, and said, "I'm not on the menu."

The Great Gate

"With a body like that, you should be," he replied with a laugh on his lips. After a loud slap, Fiona threw a glass of water into his lap. He chuckled as he replayed the scene. He always told her, "It was love at first slap." The memory warmed his soul.

The fairgrounds lay between three bordering schools: two for boys and one for girls. Most days the children used it as a playground. Their carriage cruised into a grassy field and passed by long rows of carriages. A man clad in a red hat waved at them and directed them down a narrow aisle. He followed the line of traffic and came to a stop in an empty slot. Joash dismounted and tied off the horse's reins to a hitching post. After giving the horse a pail of water and another of grain, he stretched and surveyed his surroundings. Fiona waited for him at the rear of the wagon, but Kelvin was long gone.

Kelvin sprinted past the ticket taker. The old man used a cane to rise on shaky legs and shouted in anger. He tried to chase after Kelvin, but his body ached, and the crowd was thick. In the end, he grumbled and returned to his stool. "No respect for the law," the man muttered.

———

The Moyer family arrived in town days before the fair. Lewis and Lila's wedding took place at the elegant Straightway Hotel, a premier hotel that bordered the fairgrounds. The next morning the two joined families met on the veranda. Lewis led his new bride about by the hand, introducing her to all of his friends and family.

They sat at six round tables with umbrella awnings above them. All of the tables had a prime view of the fairground. The waitresses hurried about and placed plates of food before each guest.

When all were present, Victoria arose and held up a glass of champagne. "I know it's morning, but I would like to propose a toast. I wish every joy to Lewis and Lila Parker. May their marriage be happy and days filled with joy." They all cheered and downed the entire flute of champagne.

Cody languished in grief. The Crown Attorney's Office declined to prosecute her mother, due to lack of evidence: Francis's body turned to ash, and the circumstantial evidence too thin. Although her mother was safe from prosecution, Victoria was a social pariah and so were her daughters. No one wanted them at their party; no one wanted Cody to join their conversation, and no one wanted to be Cody's friend. Except for Kelvin, she was alone – yet her greatest grief was the loss of her father. Every day she went to his den and sat behind his desk, wishing he would stroll in and say, "It was all a mistake. I'm alive."

Cody hated to admit it, but Lewis was a great catch. Even though he was an older man, he showed his virtue when he ignored all of their neighbors and professed his great love for Lila. And Lewis was quite handsome. He was a little taller than Lila, had a lean frame, and had piercing brown eyes. Lewis wore a navy suit, and Lila wore a white sundress with a floral print, her skin appearing radiant and eyes lit with love. She displayed the silver band that circled her ring finger, the band that bound her to Lewis, her husband.

The couple stood to their feet next to Cody. Lewis took Lila into her arms and gave her a passionate kiss. "Save some for the honeymoon," laughed Mr. Parker: parents always admonished, and children always ignored.

In the middle of this festive scene, she felt "the weight of someone's stare," and sudden heaviness pressed down upon Cody. When she caught Conrad staring at her, she snapped her gaze away from him, but they sat too close to one another to avoid all contact; and Conrad's gaze was unrelenting as if he was mesmerized by her. Cody's cheeks turned bright red, complementing her baby pink satin gown. She bowed her head, chewed her lower lip, and tucked her dress underneath her thighs, pretending to study the mosaic tile floor.

When Conrad approached, Cody grew stiff, sucked in her breath, and clasped her hands in her lap. He slid a chair next to Cody and sat cattycorner to her. "I like the way you look in that dress, not a nightmare of lace like all the other girls," he said, trying to complement her.

Not wishing to make a scene at her sister's wedding, she said, "Thank you. I guess." She looked adorable in a pink satin dress and white sweater. The princess-cut bodice, cleaving to her nubile frame, the accordion pleats, draped over her thighs, and the lustrous pink satin, complementing her skin, made her appear innocent and elegant. A half-circle hair comb, which grew hot in the sun, held back her blonde locks, and her sisters took personal charge of her makeup. Much to her annoyance, it made her look beautiful, and everyone felt the need to point it out as if it was some great revelation; a compliment or an insult, she was hard pressed to decide.

Like most humans on Eden, their skin tone adapted to suit the environment: summer, winter, and fall; their appearance altered. In the north, the humans tended to have white skin, light color hair, and blue eyes. In the desert, they tended to have brown skin, dark hair, and dark eyes. There were exceptions. They called those with constant body coloring "fixed." However, there was an opposite extreme, "Morphs": their bodies swiftly adapted to the environment, known to transform within hours, and for some, minutes. Traffickers considered morphs prime merchandise, highly prized, and sought out for marriage by most people on Asgard.

Cody was a morph.

When the happy couple insisted that everyone dance, Conrad rose to his feet and held out his hand. "Dance with me." Cody glanced up through her flaxen bangs and nodded. He led Cody between the round tables, to the dance floor; then with a sharp jerk, he snatched the girl into his arms.

He whispered in her ear, "Your mother spoke to my parents before your dad died. She told us that you were a morph. That's why she never let you travel to the southern lands. She said that this is your Ascension Day and she favored of our engagement. My dad never liked the idea of us getting married, but he signed our marriage contract anyway. There's nothing he can do about it now. Our families are here; the priest is here; your family is here, so we should get married."

"There is the happy couple. I have a surprise for you Cody." Victoria held up a rectangular, black velvet box and opened the lid. A gleaming silver ring lay flat in the box. Gemstones and adornments, signifying her families rank, embellished it, and the center oval bore the Peat family crest. Victoria said, "It was just delivered from the jewelers today. I helped Conrad pick it out. Isn't it beautiful? We're all set for the wedding."

The girl hid her hands, and she said, "I have to pee."

———

Rows of booths, stretching out of sight, offered countless games. Most were the usual sort: men threw smooth rocks at stacked bottles; others tried to toss coins into the open mouths of jars, and still others performed feats of strength. However, a few of the booths used bows and arrows. The archer shot at a hole cut in a rectangular tile, the name of prizes written above it. The smaller the arrow hole, the greater was the prize, and the smallest holes were called "threading a needle."

"Like to try your luck young man," an attendant shouted. "It's only one Kronar to try. You might win a new sword or new armor. The girls love a man in armor." Kelvin searched his pocket and found a brass Kronar. He handed it to the man. "Now take good aim son. You only get one … chance?" Kelvin's arrow whooshed through a hole no bigger than the pupil of a man's eye.

The attendant scratched the back of his neck. "That was lucky, son. Why don't you try again and double your prize." Kelvin retrieved an arrow from his quiver and fired; again the arrow passed through a tiny hole. A crowd began to gather behind him. "You have to use my arrows this time." The man handed Kelvin two arrows. Kelvin held them lengthwise and observed their curve. He fitted one of the arrows in his bow and let it fly. It passed through the tiniest hole. The crowd gasped and began to chatter, most lost their money in such games. If he refused to award the prize, the crowd would riot. The attendant removed a sword from the wall. It was one-handed, medium length, curved, and sharp as a razor. He gave it to Kelvin and said, "You be careful with that."

The man thought for a moment. "You seem like a sporting young man. Why don't we go for double or nothing?" At the crowd's applause, Kelvin agreed. The man watched in stunned silence as four more arrows whistled through the tiny hole. Cursing under his breath, he handed Kelvin the swords matching twin and said, "Go on. This game is closed to you." The amused crowd clapped as Kelvin jogged away, eager to find another game.

Kelvin dodged through the crowd. When someone shouted "Kelvin!" the young man came to an abrupt stop. He heard his name called and searched the crowd. He and Cody prearranged to meet in the booth area should she get any free time.

He spotted a girl in a pink dress sprinting toward him, appearing desperate and frightened, as though someone was chasing her. "Cody," Kelvin shouted with a wave. When she saw him, relief appeared on her face, and she raced to him, leaping into his arms and hugging him. She planted a hard kiss on his lips as if trying to consume him.

"I was hoping I would find you," she said and wiped away a tear. "Conrad showed up at my sister's wedding. My mom wants us to get married – today!" He could feel the welling panic within her.

"It's okay. We can go around the fair together. Conrad won't find us. It's too crowded," he said, putting his arm around Cody's shoulders. She sighed and nodded; he always made her feel safe. "Your mother is weird. Why would she want you to get married? You're only 19."

"I know," she said.

Kelvin gave her a sideways glance. "I didn't want to say anything, but you're not the first. He's proposed to three other girls, all on the first date, and then he tried to have sex with them. And Gloria Dent, he tried to pay her. She slapped him so hard. HA!"

"Why didn't you tell me?" Cody said and punched him in the arm.

"I don't know. It wasn't important." He rubbed his shoulder where her slender hand struck it. "You would think that your mother would be … well … careful. It sounds like she wants to get rid of you."

"Yes, I know," she groused. "Ever since my dad died, she's been impossible. Nothing is right. I'm not ladylike enough. Cody, sit with your thighs closed. Cody, don't get your dress dirty. Cody, your hair is a mess. Cody, come down from that tree this instant young lady."

"Sit with your thighs closed?" asked Kelvin.

She primped a blonde lock behind her right ear and blushed. She whispered, "You're supposed to do that when you wear a dress, so you don't flash everyone. I don't like dresses," she said as if spitting out something distasteful. "They make me feel naked."

"I wouldn't know," Kelvin replied.

Across the fair, Joash carried his armor in a large, worn sack and his sword strapped to his back. He and Fiona wandered through the crowd and searched for Kelvin. Dense crowds flowed around them, and everyone appeared to be eating, nibbling on sweet cakes or ripping the flesh off turkey legs. When they passed by the food vendors, Joash spotted his son. He waved and called out, "Kelvin, over here."

They looked about and spotted his parents. Kelvin and Cody raced through the crowds and ran up to his parents. "Look what I won. Isn't it great? It was so easy too."

Joash furrowed his brow and scanned the young man. Kelvin wore a new a small steel helmet, a thick leather tunic with bits of metal sewn onto it, matching gauntlets and greaves, a knife, and a pair of sabers, a little longer than a dagger by his reckoning. Of course, Kelvin wore his bow and arrows.

"You won all these things, boy?" asked Joash.

"Yup, the arrow games are real easy. I can hit a housefly at a hundred yards," Kelvin said. "They didn't have a chance."

Joash stroked the gray stubble that covered chin. He knew Kelvin practiced day and night with his bow. He was so good of a shot that he let Kelvin hunt for their dinner most nights. "Well, if you won them in a fair contest, I suppose it is okay."

"You look so cute," Fiona said to Cody. "That's such a lovely dress. I hope you don't get it dirty at the fair."

"My sister just got married," Cody said. "They are all eating breakfast back at the hotel." She failed to mention Conrad's impromptu marriage proposal.

Fiona cooed and commented about her son, "You look so cute, just like an elvan."

"Aw mom," Kelvin groaned. "I'm a warrior, not an elvan."

"The elves are great warriors," Joash corrected his son. "Never feel slighted if you're compared to one. I've known elves that could slice off two daemia heads with one chop." When Fiona glared at him with disapproval, he cleared his throat and ushered them through the fair.

"Yes father," the boy replied. He leaped about and asked, "Can we see the recruiters now? Can we?"

"I suppose." Joash shared skeptical glances with his wife. "They're over there past the farming tents." As they strolled past the hog tent, he commented, "I should have brought one of my pigs. Those sows are mighty fat. We should stop by the tent."

"We don't have time for that. I have to join the royal guard." Cody cocked her head and puzzled, always finding Kelvin's desire to be a warrior perplexing, which both confused and delighted her.

"Now honey, there are other occupations besides fighting. You could be a farmer like your father," Fiona said. "It's an honorable profession."

"Father is a warrior pretending to be a farmer." The boy's frankness took them both by surprise. Fiona wanted to correct Kelvin, but the truth of his words cut through their comfortable lies. After the death of Fiona's father, Joash took over the family farm. If left to his preferences, he would still be a part of the royal guard.

When they passed by the last tent, they came to an open arena. Young men and women practiced with wooden swords. A few recruiters strolled about the dueling youths and scribbled down notes on oracle pads. Every so often, they would confer and award a youngster a pledge pin. The agriculture, metalworking, and trade booths were ignored by all but a few.

Kelvin hurried into the midst of the brawling youths, looking for a fight. However, Cody waited with Fiona, patent leather shoes and a pink dress was not fighting gear. Battles raged all around Kelvin, but no one engaged him. There was no honor in fighting a scrawny teen. Joash released a heavy sigh and dropped his armor on the ground. He put his arm around his boy's shoulders and rubbed it. Kelvin's spirit faltered, and tears welled up in his eyes.

"Aren't you a little old to pledge?"

Joash searched the crowd for the source of the taunt. A young noble stared at him with crossed arms. He wore a royal blue tabard with the king's golden crest stitched upon it. Beneath the tabard, he wore silver chainmail and black leather trousers. With silver gauntlets and greaves strapped to his limbs, he held a helmet under his right arm. "Perhaps the king has an old man brigade … no, a grandfather brigade." The young men gathered around Cebus roared with laughter and groveled to curry his favor.

"Just ignore a bully, and he will go away," Fiona counseled Joash.

Joash snorted and crossed his arms, turning his back to the whelp. He searched the crowd for a recruiter. There was no right time to break a son's heart, but despite his wishes to the contrary, that moment had come. The matter dogged his steps for far too long, and he wanted it over with; there were chores to do, and he had no time for foolishness.

"Look, he is old and a coward," Cebus roared.

"Insubordinate whelp," Joash growled. "Go back to your mother's teat."

"What did you say, commoner?" Cebus drew a few inches his double edged sword, a clear challenge. "I would be within my rights to challenge you to a duel and cut you down."

Joash scanned the young man's sword. It was a crisp blade, but it was made of simple carbon steel and lacked a power core. Combat notched most swords; that meant the blade and the teen were combat virgins. "Take that virgin blade and go home to your comforts. You're nothing but haugr bait."

"That's it. I demand satisfaction." The teen drew his sword and doffed his helmet, covering his thick blonde locks. As he secured the chinstrap, he snarled, "I will cut you down." A clearing formed in the crowd around them, as he fitted his left arm through the strap of his heater shield. The shield was red with a diagonal white strip, and it had a gold encrusted crest emblazoned in the middle of the stripe. "Fight me, unless you are a coward."

"That's it." Joash dumped out the contents of his duffle bag. He donned his padded tunic and then grabbed his weathered chainmail; pulling it over his head, he worked it down his thick torso. After securing a leather belt around his waist, he stripped off his muddy work boots and put on his combat boots. Steel plated shanks, and greaves, having many cuts and abrasions, covered the front of his shins and extended up to his knees. Gauntlets protected his arms. He hoisted his cuirass over his head, and after closing the clamshell, he cinched it tight. Both the breastplate and backplate bore many battles scars. One could still make out the royal crest emblazoned on the breastplate. This caused a collective gasp to rise up from the crowd. Embellishments of gold and silver marked the crest. They testified to his many battles and medals for heroism.

"Now, Joash," said Fiona.

"Stand back woman," he barked. He put on his leather combat gloves — they were covered with overlapping metal scales, worn from years of combat, and donned his helmet. His armor gleamed in the sun, and he stood tall like a giant. Joash threw off the farmer and became the warrior. When he drew his blade, it appeared as long as a sign post.

"I am the conqueror of the Great Pass, The Bloody Fields, The Wolf's Maw War, The Defender of the Hargal Wall, The Emeritus Champion of the Royal Brigade, and scourge of the west. Arm yourself for battle, boy."

Cebus's lower lip began to quiver, and his eyes welled up with tears. He shrank down, and held out his trembling sword, appearing seconds away from dropping it and running. Joash hauled back and brought his sword down with a whistle. Cebus raised his shield to block the blow. The impact shattered his golden crest and creased the thin metal, useful only for ceremonial purposes. The boy hurtled backward and hit the ground with a heavy thud.

Gasping for air and wincing in pain, Cebus struggled to his feet and tossed away the shield. He held up his sword and readied himself for the next blow. Joash swept across at the teen's left side, and Cebus brought up his sword in a classic block. Steel sang when the swords met. Cebus' sword flew from his hand, and hurtled through the air, tumbling end over end, the sword plunged into the sod at the feet of the crowd, a deep notch testifying to the impact. Cebus stumbled and fell onto his back. He cringed and held up his arms in terror.

Joash hauled both hands above his head and pointed his sword down at Cebus. Cebus screamed "MOMMY!" Joash brought down his sword in a killing blow. Sobbing and trembling, Cebus lay upon the ground. When at last he dare open his eyes, he saw slate blue eyes inches from his and hot breath on his skin; Joash hovered over him and glared at the young man. His sword was plunged deep into the sod by Cebus' left side.

Joash's voice choked with emotion. "There was a time when I would have killed you for such an insult. Now I am a father, and I lost a son to war. I wish to God that I could have him back. I will not take another man's son from his arms." He stood up and yanked his blade from the thick grass. After flinging off a clod of mud, he walked away and sheathed his sword.

Cebus sniffled and fought to control his tears. When he noticed the crowd gawking at him, he scrambled to his feet. "Get out of my way!" He charged through the crowd and disappeared from sight.

Kelvin leaped and danced around his father. "That was awesome. I knew you could fight. My dad is the greatest warrior ever!" Kelvin suddenly stopped. He searched for some other opponent. Perhaps they could fight as father and son. "Where did he go?"

"To change his underwear no doubt," Joash said.

"That was quite a show." A recruiter strolled up to them. "My name is Milton Frish. I'm a recruiter for The Black Dragon Guild. The guild owns the Black Castle in the city of Solva as well as 14 other major fortifications and countless lesser ones." He stroked his chin and narrowed his eyes. "Are you here to pledge?"

Joash's face grew long, and he said, "Me … no. My son, he wants to be a warrior but —"

"Let's take a look at the warrior. If he's anything like you, we want him." Milton looked about for a strapping young man, but then he saw Kelvin. "This is your son?"

"I want to be a warrior," Kelvin said, jutting his chin.

Joash shared eye contact with the man and nodded. When Kelvin left to speak with a friend, Joash said, "My son's Ascension Day was months ago. I promised to bring him here to pledge, but he needs more time at home. His mother still tucks him in at night."

"You are a Captain of the Royal Guard. Your son is now a man. The law is clear. It is death to refuse such a legacy; I must accept his pledge."

"But he's just a boy," Fiona said. "Would your guild take a boy to war? Is this what the military of Asgard comes to? It's not right."

Milton held up the palms of his hands. "There are more occupations in our guild than just fighting. We train in everything from cobbling to medicine. Most of our tradesman wear their uniforms once a year and march in the Founder's Day Parade. Even if he does pledge, Mistress Sabrina established strict rules before she departed our lands. Our regulations require all pledges to attend college from the age of 19 to 21. After that, they may learn a trade or pledge as a warrior. Also, while still training, she allows all pledges to revoke their vow and depart the guild before the age of 21. Once they reach 21 and graduate, the competition is fierce, and only the best are selected for active combat duty. The rest serve in logistical support … an important duty mind you, but it lacks the glamor of combat."

His words failed to sooth Fiona. All parents imagined the worst and noted the worried expressions Joash's and Fiona's faces. He put his hand on Joash's shoulder. "You are an honorable man, and we are honorable men. We will not send a boy to war. Once he sees how much work is required of him, he may grow weary and resign."

Joash knew his son. Nothing would detour him once he made up his mind. He looked at Fiona, and he saw the pain in her eyes. "If my son goes with you, I will go too. Give us time to sell our farm, and we will both report for duty."

Milton nodded. "Of course, take all the time you need." He reached into his pocket and handed Milton a pledge pin. "Give this to your son. I will record his name as a recruit and your name as an active duty officer."

Joash signed Milton's oracle scroll and called for Kelvin to join him. Kelvin jogged back to his father and then signed the scroll. The teen put on his pledge pin and jumped for joy. The father tousled his son's hair and said, "We will go together."

Cody watched the entire proceedings with fascination. Most great houses only allowed their members to marry those within their guild and only then with command permission. Her father was of lesser royal lineage, a noble by rank of service to the crown, and her mother, a parchment male, did not have legal title to the family title.

Cody barged between Joash and Milton. The girl held up a delicate gold ring that bore the royal seal of Asgard. "I am of a lesser noble, and I wish to join your guild." If Cody joined the guild, she has to attended college, and the college did not permit to marry. In this way, she would avoid marrying Conrad and her mother's ambition.

Milton scanned the pretty teen in the pink dress and furrowed his brow. "This is warrior's guild. We stand and fight when other men run. You would have to battle haugrs and daemia. Are you sure you want to be a warrior?"

Cody crossed her arms and tightened her lips, "Yes. I want to join the guild. I heard you. You can't refuse me."

"Yes … um … you are right." He jotted down her name and address. Fiona grabbed Joash's arm and urged him to do something. He shook his head and patted her hands. He could do nothing. Milton gave the scroll to Cody, and she signed it.

A peal of thunder ripped through a clear blue sky. All heads turned toward the south and gazed up in terror. A second sun burned in the sky just above the southern horizon. Terrible whistling and deep throbbing made them cover their ears and cringe in pain. A moment later, the ball of fire imploded with a sharp crack. The air rushed into the void and then reflected back at them. The hurricane force wind knocked everyone off their feet and shattered windows. Even Joash sailed backward and hit the ground with a groan. A tremendous roar rolled over the land, and the ground convulsed beneath them.

Chapter 10

It would be convenient if trans-dimensional events occurred in a linear timeline, but that was seldom the case. Effect often preceded cause, much to the consternation of physicists. Such was the case with Sabrina's trans-dimensional event: it sent shockwaves through time-space. This might not have been a problem, except that she awoke the Beast, rhunite that slept in the Earth, and life on both worlds would never be the same.

The golden angel, Sabrina, soared through the dimensional vortex with the baby clutched in her arms, unaware of Gleason's tragic transition to Eden, and unaware of the starburst above Knob Oak, and unaware of the perilous path which lay ahead of her; all she thought of was the precious life snuggling at her breast and how much she loved Eliza.

The city of Miami and the sparkling Atlantic Ocean lay behind her; Sabrina flew from Earth's skies to Eden's skies, catching the scent of burning Ascarba leaves on the wind, an offering rite of spring. The distant clang of bells called the faithful to worship and give thanks. It was good to be home.

When she released her grip on the aperture, it slammed shut. She hid the baby in her arms as brilliant white light engulfed them. A shockwave spread out across the face of the land and the deep. Hurricane force winds blasted: knocking over trees, sweeping leaves into the air, and causing a tsunami that spread out in a great ring. An exasperated groan arose from Eden, and the world eyed her as if a fly flew before its face. The ground shuddered, and cattle stumbled as if drunk; and wild beasts fled from an unseen predator.

That was new.

In the past, when she opened portals within and between worlds, it took place without incident with a quiet sizzle and the smell of ozone.

Something tore the fabric of space-time, the greatest impact being on Earth. The weight of her actions pressed down on her, but she could do nothing now. All that remained was to take action.

She surveyed the ironwood and sequoia trees of the Deepwood Forest, towering above the land. Her elva eyes spotted the rolling hills to the northeast, farmland that stretched out in an endless horizon, and to the northwest, she saw the lofty spires of the Black Castle and the gleaming skyscrapers of Solva, Asgard's New York City. The large, towering city rivaled any city on Earth, but it was too soon the fly there. It had been 88 years since she last visited the great port city, and flying in without announcement would cause a tumult. She turned in mid-flight and gazed south. The white-capped peaks of the Clarion Mountains rose up above the plains, the wind whistling through them played trumpet flourishes; and she beheld the Arner Sea (Storm Water Sea), its white-capped blue waters shimmering in the noonday sun.

She turned toward the mountains and sailed through the skies. To a man on the ground, he would have mistaken her for a Great Eagle. The land passed far below her. Her shadow raced over the forest canopy and gleaming streams that wound through the land like a silver snake. The child stirred and then fell asleep in her arms. Little Eliza would awaken soon, hungry for a meal, and she had no milk.

Sabrina flew down to the Clarion Mountains, gray stone towering on her right and left, high cliffs and sheer walls foreboding even to the bold; and she passed through a deep ravine, its high walls set at odd angles and white water rapids roaring, jetting cool mist into the air. The water leaped over a ledge and fell 300 meters to the canyon floor, creating a roar that echoed off the walls like thunder.

Looking down on its peers, Storm Mountain, engulfed in the "Never Ending Storm," lingered between shadow and light. The two forever waging war, black clouds stabbed at the mountainside with lightning bolts, but the mountain remained resilient, implacable, and insolent. As Sabrina flew toward it, clouds turned the skies gray and then black;

twilight replaced noonday brilliance. A cool mist nipped at her nose and stung her cheeks, a welcome sensation, the greeting of an old friend, but the baby slept snug in her arms, unmoved by the tempest around her. Storm Mountain grew larger by the second, as though rising up to confront her. Ignoring its sharp spires and hard face, she navigated around it with winged skill and sailed to a stone ledge, which looked somewhat like a diving platform. Without railings or other safety structures, the open ledge looked down upon a deep canyon that faded into darkness and mist. Where the platform ended a single flight of stairs began, but they came to a steep archway that had an impenetrable wall set in the middle, barring entry to the lodging within it.

She moved the tips of her wings and adjusted her flight pattern. The gorge far beneath her sank into darkness, and only jagged spikes penetrated the veil. She gave no heed to such dire scenes, as winged creatures are oft to do, and sailed to her destination. She winged through turbulences with ease, and her toes touched down upon the ledge with the lightest pressure. She strolled away from the edge as though crossing a room, the brisk wind gusting through her hair and feathered wings. She adjusted her form, assuming a humanoid appearance. Except for her black wings, she appeared like any other beautiful brunette, which put the other races at ease.

She crossed the long platform and then scaled a set of stairs. At her approach, a seam formed in the rock and a pair of giant doors took shape. The rock groaned and scraped as the doors swung wide for her; torches flaming to life, darkness giving way to light, she passed through a long tunnel, striding into the Eagle's Nest.

The Eagle's Nest predated Asgard by a millennium. Sabrina arrived on the continent when the land was still wild, and the dwarves dug their first shaft into Scepter Mountain. The Elysian population lived in the treetops across the continent, peaceful and unaware of the many dangers about to fall upon them. She constructed the facility as a safeguard, a private retreat in the heart of the mountain.

Being a builder at heart, she included great halls, ballrooms, many suites, and even a great pool set in a cavern among stalactites and stalagmites. She constructed the landing pad high up Storm Mountain to deny access to all but the invited. As a last measure, she blackened the surrounding rocks with dragon fire, making it impenetrable, and then she placed many magical defenses throughout the facility, guarding it against all invaders. There was no spot on Eden, or any other world, as secure as the Eagle's Nest. Elisa was safe, but to what end. *A human baby requires humans to raise it.* She required friends, lovers, enemies, and family – she needed a community.

She contemplated Eliza's needs as she passed through the compound. A secret lair and private chambers waited in patience for her return. Her armor hung upon a wooden stand, and her weapons hung upon the walls, some forged by her hands, some forged by artisans, and some taken from the dead hands of defeated foes. Piled up against the opposite wall, gold and gems spilled out of chests. The flames leap to life in the hearth and cast a warm glow upon interior. She stacked furs upon the bed and gently laid the baby in the middle of them. Eliza stirred but then drifted off to sleep again.

Sabrina stripped off her white gown, and the firelight illuminated her naked, feminine curves, perfection incarnate. A chiffon robe adorned with a spring bouquet print lay near the bed, ready for her use, where she left it so many years ago. She ran her fingers along the wooden furnishings, handcrafted, masterpieces of elvish craftsmanship. Mementos of lost love, great victories, and absent friends drifted through her consciousness. She picked up a dried, flat daisy petal, given to her by a young girl so many centuries ago. The girl and everyone who knew her were dust, but within the recess of Sabrina's mind, the blonde girl would forever twirl with her arms extended in a field of daisies, laughing and innocent. If not for Eliza, Sabrina would have departed the temporal lands for the undying lands.

The baby cooed.

The Great Gate

Spurred to action, she opened the double doors of a chifferobe and perused the contents within it. Several "slip-suits" hung in the closet. A slip-suit resembled a catsuit or a full body suit that included booties. The seamless garment was composed of polysynthetic material (PSM) and was arguably practical. It would keep her cool in the hottest desert and warm in the coldest arctic wasteland. The material was both cut and abrasion resistant, soft silk, and elastic as spandex. It could be adjusted to any color, even complex camouflage. However, in its natural state, the material bore a black, high-gloss sheen.

She stretched open the banded collar and inserted her legs into it. With wiggles, pulls, and elastic snaps, the silky garment engulfed her body. The light danced off the glossy material and highlighted her curves: her breasts, her hourglass torso, and her round bottom. The gloves that came with it were long and extended all the way to the top of her biceps, just below the armpit, strapping down tight and forming an airtight seal.

Like the gloves, her boots extended to the top of her thighs and strapped tight. This provided extra thermal protection and cut resistance, a benefit for any warrior. The next garment, a vest, was sleeveless, circled around underneath her breasts and traveled up to a banded collar, teardrop fashion, in part to avoid irritation of the wearer's chest and in part to allow natural breathing. Like its corset twin, this served as a back brace and armor support.

A maiden's belt, also known as "woman's burden," hung in the place where she left it 88-years ago. It was mercifully unnecessary on Earth but a grudging requirement on Eden: because of the haugr biological imperative to reproduce by rape, and the daemia predilection to do likewise. The maiden's belt resembled a silver metal thong that attached at the hip to an ornate silver belt. The belt circled the waist, and the deep V-panel of the thong cleaved so tight to the smooth arc of her sex that nothing could pass underneath it. The back portion of the thong, a thin cable attached to a T-back clip, cleaved between her PSM covered derriere and disappeared from view. The sum total effect was a revealing display of her feminine gender.

A chainmail tunic protected the upper torso, and it offered a small degree of modesty. Sabrina unlaced the back and held the garment over her head. Made of fine metal, resembling fabric, it slid down her body like a dress and tightly conformed to her frame. Having long, fitted sleeves and a skirt that extended down to the apex of the bottom, making it appear as though she wore a silver micro mini-dress.

The cuirass, both back and chest metal plates, hinged at the top in a clamshell fashion. Unlike standard plate, Sabrina insisted that her armor had to be pure mithril, adorned with power gems, able to infuse her with emergency stores of magical power, and portrayed a black dragon, its wings spread and talons ready to strike. The clamshell plate included interior hooks, which required skill, but her fingers recalled countless practice, like hooking a bra strap behind one's back, and she fit the hooks through the chainmail with one try, nestling them into harness slots. Thus the thick plate could be worn for long periods without causing pressure sores, and any blow would be spread out over the entire vest; and it included a gorget, a narrow band like a shirt collar, to protect her neck.

Every piece of armor came with a price: protection versus a corresponding loss of mobility, some more than others, and each warrior had to choose what suited their style of combat best. For instance, some advocated the use of faulds, or hip guards, but she left them in the bottom of her closet, finding them too encumbering in tight spaces, and rather unflattering. Rather she chose to wear tassets, plates to cover the front of her thighs.

All of her armor was designed to afford maximum protection while affording great dexterity, a necessary compromise to avoid excessive encumbrance. Pauldrons draped over her shoulders, interlocking segments added to protection to the outside of her arms, and gauntlets protected her arms. Greaves protected her shins, and gauntlets protected her forearms and hands.

After grabbing a helmet from off a stand, she strolled over to her weapon wall. A pair of medium length Katanas hung in the center of the wall, her prized and favorite weapons. She strapped them to her back, the handles forming a "W" at her neck. A pair of daggers joined the swords, pointed down to her sides, ready for quick access. She secured a dozen silver throwing darts at her sides

A backpack lay beside the bed, where she dropped it so many years ago. Rifling through it, she found her magical plate, bowl, and a cup. It was easier to call them magical than to explain the means by which they translated dark energy through molecular pattern buffers. She could craft everything from potato chips to clothing, and in this situation, it made milk.

Eliza stirred, and tears flowed a moment later. Sabrina took the baby in her arms and filled a mug with warm milk. She used her plate to create a baby bottle and rubber nipple. Sabrina holding the filled bottle, the hungry infant took the nipple in her mouth and sucked in the nourishing milk. Sabrina caressed the baby's silky soft skin and inhaled her newborn freshness. After Eliza had a full belly, the baby girl fell fast asleep in Sabrina's arms.

Sabrina cradled the baby and sat by the fire, watching the flames dance upon the ceramic logs. Her mind drifted through the featureless landscape of her life. So many memories turned sepia and faded, but some, like this moment, endured.

Sabrina an Elven Maige, and unlike the woodland elves, had two primary forms. The first was that of an angel, and the second was that of a dragon, a fearsome sight with a body longer than six city buses, a wingspan wider than nine busses, and impenetrable interlocking plates; to see a dragon was to know terror. A blast of her breath melted stone, and her claws could shred steel. It was the heart of the dragon that lusted after the flames, and unlike mankind, the flames greeted her as a friend, for fire is a dragon's only friend.

She ruminated over Eliza's care. The baby required a human caretaker and siblings. Eliza cooed and rubbed her face with her tiny fist. She gazed at Sabrina, assuring herself that her new mother remained, and drifted off to sleep. Sabrina's gloved hand caressed the baby's silky smooth cheek. While the Eagle's Nest could provide all provisions a growing girl might require, it lacked human warmth. The decision was made; the girl required humans, so she would return to humanity.

Chapter 11

Sabrina passed through the Eagle's nest, feeling its loving caress in her mind. Like encountering an old friend in the middle of the street, they had to part too soon. She ran her right hand along the rough stonewall, a last caress. "Don't worry. I'm back to stay. I need to get Eliza situated first, and then I'll come back to visit you." She closed her eyes and listened. "Yes. I can do that. You should have people living in you ... I have no idea how I'm going to get them up here, but I'll see to it." The torches in the tunnel lowered, and peace settled over the structure.

She strode through the tunnel, and the exterior doors swung open for her. A frigid wind blasted Sabrina, fighting her, shoving her backward, stinging her cheeks and biting her nose. Eliza squirmed inside the carrier strapped to Sabrina's chest, and like a marsupial in its mother's pouch, the baby girl was safe and warm.

As Sabrina descended the stairs, she released her wings, which eased a muscle cramp; they shot out from her back, arched high in the air, and plunged to the stones beneath her feet. Thunder rolling like war drums, as she traversed the platform, the storm lashed at her with its fury. A battle Maige dressed for war, lightning flashing off her glossy black slip-suit, silver tunic, and silver armor; swords, backpack, and heater shield strapped to her back; her eyes sharp as an eagle's; her boots eating up the ground, Sabrina ignored the storm and leap off the edge.

Gale force winds rushed over her wings, as she sailed into the storm. She rose up through the turbulent skies; thunderheads to her right and left, attacking each other with lightning bolts, she flew through the midst of this war, her outstretched wings silhouetted against the rolling storm heads. All at once, she burst through the clouds and soared into the light, sunshine caressing her face. Storm Mountain's peak in the center, the clouds stretched beneath her like an ethereal landscape, and blue skies encompassing like an ocean, the sky island, a mystical vista, was a destination that only those with wings visited.

While she would love to have flown all the way to Solva, to fly over the city's walls was too provocative: causing the city's defenders to go on high alert. Also, the cold might get through to Eliza. She had a subtler entry in mind, so she began her gradual descent. With the Clarion Mountains behind her, she banked right and headed for gentle rolling, green hills.

At her approach, a herd of horses galloped with thundering hooves. A black stallion led the mares as they ate up the ground. Sabrina swept in front of them and landed upon the crest of a knoll. The horses stopped in the valley and gazed up at her, their ears turned toward her, ready to escape.

"I need someone to share my adventures, but you will have to leave your green fields and the life you know. Will any of you come with me?" She stood with her hands on her hips and waited. The black stallion trotted up the hill to her and tossed its head. She rubbed his neck and said, "I think I shall call you Midnight."

After using her plate to create a saddle and tack, she placed them upon the horse and mounted Midnight. The trio circled around north of the Clarion Mountains and found the trail leading through Deepwood Forest. She peeled down the upper flap and saw Eliza fast asleep. The baby girl yawned and stretched, and she soon drifted off to sleep. Sabrina caressed the girl's soft cheek with a gloved hand, but armor is a cold comfort.

The Maywyn and the May River lay behind her, and the trail settled into a comfortable pace. She gazed through the leaves, searching for a trace of the skies through the dense canopy, brindled sunlight upon her face, and she contemplated how different the world appeared while flying: open, expansive, and free. The air hung thick around her: the smell of fresh rain, the odor of earth, and decaying vegetation. She returned her attention to the road, and filtered through the forest canopy, she saw fragmented bits of golden sunlight scattered about. The trail weaved through the Deepwood Forest: snaking, rolling, dipping, and widening; transporting her to magnificent vistas. She climbed a steep ridge and circled around bare rock that protruded like an anvil. From the top of the sheer cliff, she viewed the fertile green lowlands and the Port of Elvmer.

The marshy plains, sopping wet, muddy, and alive, spread out across the horizon and ended at the Port of Elvmer. Tall ships, more than could be counted, lay anchored in the harbor, safe from the many storms of the Arner Sea, and longshoremen tended to their precious cargo, using the ports infrastructure; an extensive array of wharfs, jetties, quays, and floating warehouses serviced the merchant fleet. Catboats, gaff rigs, fishing smacks, and cogs sailed the river like minnows; they scurried around the enormous cargo ships that lumbered in the bay like whales, churning up brackish muck, engorging themselves upon the ports bounty, and then the small ships rushed away from these leviathans, eager to ferry their cargo up the river, many destined for the busy port of Solva and a quick profit.

Much of the cargo traveled by waterway, but some cargo traveled by land; many cities lacked waterways but still required transportation. Since air transport by dirigible was expensive, winged travel made impossible because of ion storms, the only solution was shipping by land.

There were two primary land routes. The first was ground transport shuttles, antigravity silver bullets shooting through magnetic induction eye-pillars, were the most technologically advanced and safest means of transportation aside from ships. A city with shuttles was prosperous; for by shuttle one could transport significant quantities of both passengers and merchandise; therefore, all cities craved shuttle lines. However, diesel locomotives, which used blue triangle lines, indicating that they were free from rhunite, transported bulk or heavy freight to the city.

Railroad transportation was expensive and limited, so most small to medium customers shipped their goods by wagon train. Whether because of geographical isolation, a meager economy, or xenophobia most small towns still received merchandise by wagon. Thus, goods flowed from ship to shuttle, and then by wagon, transportation arteries to rural capillaries, arriving in many small communities, and exported goods used by the same route.

Sabrina lingered upon the cliff, her gaze fixed on the wonder of human industry. Humans fashioned their transportation networks after their circulatory system, an incredible achievement of ingenuity and industry. She ignored the great ships, smaller sailing vessels, and transport shuttles. Her attention was fixed on the wagon trains fanning out across the plains, branching out into ever narrowing trails until the wagons rolled single file. One of these corridors moved to Solva's northeast, landlocked entrances, which carried lower import duties and storage costs.

These wagons formed a long line that followed the "Hooked Road." It was thus named because it hooked around the west end of the Deepwood Forest. The Hooked Road was well worn and marked by sporadic taverns and inns, towns that fed upon this life giving flow. However, Hooked Road would add over twenty miles on their trip to Solva, and Eliza would not sleep forever. Thus Sabrina opted to take Murk Road, the less traveled and more dangerous route through Deepwood.

The journey on Murk Road was quiet by her recollection, and it also spared Eliza the trail dust of Hooked Road. Thus, they turned away from the cliff and weaved toward the forest, passing through a small clearing. As she traversed the field, she spotted an enormous stone statue lying upon the ground, its round segments and stone face laying half-buried in the sod. The grim-faced statue wore a toupee of yellow flowers; its gaping mouth, and its empty eyes turned toward the sky as if in shock – its builders passed from memory before recorded time.

93

The Great Gate

Trees rose up from the ground like great pillars, upholding a dense canopy, that thin layer at the top of the forest where life abounded. The forest reminded her of the Parthenon and the halls of the Roman Republic, which remained intact on other worlds. How she longed to set foot on those shores and to travel forgotten roads, but her responsibility lay with Eliza. Those adventures would have to wait for another day.

The horse neighed and tossed its head, loose reins draped about its neck. Midnight gazed back at her, eager for direction but finding none. While this slackness might create angst in other equines, Midnight was a proud Shire horse, and he accepted it with poise and confidence. Once again, he surveyed the road ahead of him and moved along its length.

Sabrina gazed at the sleeping girl's face, her mind adrift on a sea of memories. Faces of friends and enemies, battles and vacations, and lovers and murderers emerged from the shadows of memory. They swirled about in her imagination and pricked her thoughts. What adventures lay in store for Eliza? Whom would she love? Would she have children? A world of possibilities lay before her.

The child stirred and yawned. Searching for a meal, her hand pressed against Sabrina's breastplate, Eliza looked for milk, and finding none, she cried. Sabrina removed a baby bottle from the saddlebag, filled with synthesized milk, but it was so much less nutritious than "mother's milk": milk that contained rich proteins, nutrients, and immunity. She slipped the rubber nipple into the girl's mouth and watched her nurse. Sabrina inserted her index finger into Eliza's tiny hand, and the baby grasped it. All of man's creations and all of his achievements were brutish by comparison; Sabrina marveled at each tiny finger, tipped by a little fingernail, so small and intricate, so perfect.

Her elva ears detected a faint noise in the woods, the crack of a dried twig followed by the crush of dried leaves. Her instincts flamed to life. She turned in the saddle and scanned the woods: darkness hung like a thick blanket before the dense undergrowth. Her gaze shifted from visible light to infrared. Through sharp thorns, twisted limbs, decomposing foliage, thick mud, and jagged stones she saw flashes of red – predators sprinted through the woods.

Her maternal instincts sounded the alarm: the baby was in danger. The weapons strapped to her back could deal with most creatures. They sliced through flesh, bone, and steel; and she moved like the wind – no one could best her. Yet the sleeping infant urged discretion. She dug her heels into Midnight's sides, and the stead broke into a gallop. She retrieved her bow and drew an arrow. Pulling the string back, she watched for a flash of red and then let an arrow fly. A shrill cry, like fingernails on a chalkboard, penetrated the undergrowth.

Haugrs!

His head bobbing, muscles flexing, hooves thundering, eating up the ground, great clods of dirt flying into the air behind him, Midnight charged through the forest. Sabrina stood in the saddle and fired at the flashes of red. The concealment that once benefitted now hindered the haugr. Piercing screeches, the kind that passed through flesh and bone, came from the undergrowth. The horse zigzagged around trees the size of office buildings, causing the creatures to abandon their stealth, and the flock of haugrs took to the trees.

Only a half-starved haugr would leave its holes and risk a daytime attack. Shrill squeals, audible only to elves, echoed through the tree. Their strong limbs propelling them, the haugr leap from tree to tree, their razor sharp claws ripping through the bark and shredding wood. A haugr launched at her, baring its needle-like fangs, its bat face snarling in rage. She fired an arrow and put it through the right eye. The dead haugr flew past her and somersaulted into the brush.

Sabrina gazed back and searched the thick undergrowth, her dragon's heart burning with rage. She wanted to rip them apart and hear them scream in agony as life departed their bodies. The infant stirred in her pouch. Brown eyes looked up at her, and the baby reached up toward her face. Eliza's smile calmed Sabrina and squelched her rage.

Three haugrs sped past them, bounding from tree to tree. Sabrina fired, but her arrow bounded off the haugr's armor, patches of rough plate stitched to heavy leather. The creatures turned and leaped at her. She fired again, catching it in the throat. It flew past her, almost hitting the baby.

They charged through the trail, the haugrs squealing and leaping at them. The horse snorted and ran for his life; the menace that filled its dreams, the dread in the darkness rushed after him, bounding from tree to tree around him. They circled around an ironwood tree and twilight gave way to day: the boundary of the Deepwood Forest came into view. Midnight charged toward the light. Brilliant sunshine reflected off shimmering blue waters and lush golden plains of wheat. The horse burst forth from the darkness and surged into the protective wall of light.

Sabrina turned in the saddle and fired a last arrow. It hit its mark, and a haugr tumbled out of the shadow, somersaulted, and skidded face-first into the sod. She pulled back on the reins, and Midnight slowed to a trot, heavy snorts coming from his nostrils, and terrible, angry shrieks still coming from the forest. Haugr tolerated shade, but open daylight pained them. It was similar to the way men are loath to stand in the rain; both species avoided that which amplified their weaknesses.

A peasant farmer pitched some hay into a stall and then paused from his work, standing upright and stretching. Pain recoiled through his lower back, and he leaned upon the wooden pitchfork for support. From his back pocket of his patched trousers, he retrieved a handkerchief and wiped the sweat from his brow. His eyes narrowed, and his old eyes saw a rider approaching from the south.

A warrior rode toward him. Light flashed off mithril armor adorned with gold and a glossy black slip-suit: this warrior had great wealth, for such armor could cost a king's ransom. He stood his ground and waited, as with any predator, running only encouraged an attack. When she neared, he made out hourglass curves; it was a female warrior! Such distinctions were small when one contemplated warriors, who were violent and deadly. However, no man enjoys being intimidated by a woman.

The farmer pushed back his weathered cap, stained with sweat and dirt, and scratched his graying beard. The door to his cottage flew open, causing his head to snap to the right. Imelda, his wife, emerged and rushed to him. Despite the façade of her plump body, sagging breasts, and weathered face; he still saw the willowy girl who stole his heart so many years ago. Her kind eyes reflected fear, and she twisted a dishtowel as if wringing it. He held out his hand and urged calm.

Doors flew open, and men swarmed from homes. Family members, immediate and distant, moved into defensive positions with round helmets upon their heads, resembling rusty wash pots, and cinched down patent leather armor. They drew swords, which so badly nicked that they appeared serrated, and formed into haphazard ranks.

Milton shook his head and urged calm. They were too ready for combat, too willing to spill blood. Young men sought glory, but old men desired peace. He opened the gate and moved ahead of them: urging them to stay back and to give him time to uncover the matter.

Sabrina saw thatch roofs and brown dauber huts. The stench from horse, pig, cattle dander, and manure stung her eyes. She twitched her nose and tried to repress her revulsion. Elves have a superior sense of sight and smell. While they might eat pork, they would never raise pigs, and chickens were worse, the stench of their manure-carrying for miles. Elves preferred a vegetarian diet with an occasional fish filet.

She slowed her horse to a walk and forced a smile. She fixed her gaze upon an old man preceded by a mob of armed men and women. They massed in the street, their voices rumbling louder by the second. "Who are you? State your business," asked Milton, his chin raised and clasping a pitchfork. He was, after all, the village mayor and worthy of respect.

Sabrina ignored his confrontational tone and manner. "I am returning home to Solva, to be with my people. Is it common to greet travelers with arms and calls for war?"

"No, it's not. I apologize for that. There have been mysterious doings as of late, and the people are afraid." He stroked his beard and mused. "You're an elva. Humans live in Solva, not elves. Well, there have been more elves as of late, but it's still not that common." Milton stroked his scruffy chin. "Even if there are a few of your kind in the city, we don't see many of them in these parts. They stay far to the west, well beyond the borders of Bruton."

"Yet I am here and traveling to, as you say, a human city. Will you not let me pass in peace?" She glanced down at the baby and peeled back the flap. "If not for my sake then at least that of the child, she is human, and humans need their own kind."

"Yes, very true." Milton looked back at his wife. The sight of a newborn baby melts the heart of every woman. "How did you come by her?"

These simple town folk had no way of understanding Earth or "the war on drugs." She opted for a simple explanation. "Thieves slaughtered her parents, and only she was left alive. Her mother covered her in blankets and hid her on a balcony."

"Couldn't they be saved?" Imelda asked. She moved alongside her husband. There was no holding women back when the safety of a child was concerned.

"No," Sabrina said and sighed. "The walls were stained with their blood and formed thick pools upon the floor. The squalling child, covered in blood, tumbled off the balcony. I caught her and rescued her. She is my daughter now and a part of my family. I am responsible for her."

"And what of the criminals?" asked Milton.

"Long departed," Sabrina replied. "I thought to give chase, but the needs of the child came first. The authorities will have to deal with them."

"Of course," Milton replied. The old man shook his head and removed his cap. He sighed. "There have been many deaths in these parts as of late. Bandits lurk behind every tree and under every rock. I can well understand your distress and need for armaments."

"Bandits or Haugr?" asked Sabrina. The old man cocked his head and raised an eyebrow; a critical look appeared in his eyes. She explained, "A group of haugr chased me back along the trail in the forest. If not for the light, they would still be in pursuit."

"Haugr you say? There haven't been haugr here since the War of Purging. Even during the 'Invasion from the Seas' we were bypassed." The men behind him began to speak in low rumbles.

"Well, they are here now, and haugr are very smart. A flock of them might well disguise themselves as bandits. While men search for thieves, the haugr eat the men and rape the captive females so they can implant their eggs."

"This is distressing news, most distressing." Milton looked back at the men and then back at her. "You're sure? You saw haugr?"

Sabrina restrained her annoyance. "I know a haugr when I see one. Ignore the danger if you wish, but don't question my senses."

"I meant no offense." Milton tightened his lips and twisted his cap as if wringing it out. He lapsed into silence and paused deep in thought. "We must notify the governor." Another deep sigh escaped his lips, and he turned toward his kinsmen. "Gather the horses. We will ride to Solva."

Sabrina cocked her head and adjusted the baby in the pouch. Apparently, she was to have company for the remainder of her trip. The men departed, and the women broke into small clusters. The conversations rose in volume, creating an angry din, and animated gestures soon followed. There was nothing more dangerous than a town of frightened peasants.

She dug in her spurs and attempted to ride through the crowd; however, a group of women blocked her path and shifted from their private conversations. "Don't kill the messenger," was an appropriate if unheeded axiom. Although elves, dwarves, and humans lived amicably with one another, some issues divided them.

The villagers viewed her with suspicious eyes and brooding faces. All nations have varying levels of xenophobia, but small towns revel in it; and a crowd of people began to form a human wall around her. They looked at her and spoke in quiet whispers. She pressed her lips tight and stared off at the horizon, not wishing heightened tensions. It was as though she was a new panda bear in the zoo; the few remaining young men leered at her, but the women scowled.

Hard work and long hours defined Farm life. The women cooked all the meals, cared for the children, and took care of the other household duties. This left little time or money for beauty treatments and expensive clothing. The mature, married women wore knee-length skirts and modest blouses. A few of the unmarried, young women wore tight skirts above the knee, fitted blouses, and fashionable shoes; but they were the exception.

The married women pressed in toward them and stared at the baby pressed to Sabrina's bosom. Their maternal instincts and their notions of decency were offended. An unmarried woman, a loathsome warrior, a stranger, and an elva held a human baby. It disgusted them. Sabrina tried to avoid their accusing stares, but her temper grew hotter by the second. Sabrina was an unmarried woman: the law required her to submit to them.

Provincial idiots, she brooded. *All you know is changing soiled diapers and spreading your legs for your husbands. You have never traveled beyond the border of your squalor festooned village.*

A matriarch, Jerlug, pushed through the crowd. She wore a silver ring adorned with fiery garnets, the highest-ranking women in the village. The woman glared at Sabrina with her hands on her hips, and Sabrina met the woman's gaze with raw hate. Given half the chance, Sabrina would have burned her and left her a sooty smudge upon the ground. However, Sabrina was holding a baby, and it was not the time for combat.

"Give us the child," Jerlug said, a scowl on her face. "You are not fit to hold her."

"I have sworn an oath to take care of the infant. If anyone tries to touch her, I will kill them." She dug her spurs into the horse and galloped through the astonished crowd of women. She passed through the village in no time at all. Soon the dirt road led her past the last thatched home and toward a small grassy ridge covered with oak trees. She was glad to have the village and danger behind her.

The thunder of hooves rumbled behind her. She turned in the saddle and searched for her pursuers. A dozen men charged up the road on horseback. Her right hand reached up to her neck and touched the handle of her sword. Even with one hand, she was more than a match for them.

The men began to slow as they approached. Milton scratched his scruffy beard and cleared his throat. "I apologize for what happened back there: women can be a bit peculiar where the welfare of a baby is concerned. I told them, 'It's none of our affair.'" He twirled the signet ring about on his left hand. "I hope you can forgive them."

That was the second philosophy of small towns. They cared little about the outside world: their concern ended with the town's border. Sabrina was glad for this fact. "I understand how women can be," she replied. Milton nodded and rode past her.

Sabrina shifted in the saddle. Once again twinged by the peculiar sensations of her female body, she tried to ignore the phantom aches between her thighs. In most of her dominant lives, she lived as a man, and her brain, perplexed at the loss of her male organs, struggled to comprehend the phantom sensations that lingered in her sense memory. Compounding this was the cacophony of new, female, bodily sensations, and upon taking her next breath, she felt the rise of her breasts and the curves of her armor.

Her creation, rather than birth, was singular. She awoke in the "afterlife" as an elva with complete amnesia. "The enlightenment," a ceremony of cleansing and renewal, caused the return all of her memories. Disoriented by her new gender and species, she fled the Elvin lands in the "undying lands" and returned to a temporal existence. She assumed a male identity. However, her true gender resurfaced in a million different ways: the sum total dogged her steps, and in the end, she was forced to embrace her true self or go insane.

Conflicting emotions and desires built up within her, and she longed for a friend to share her feelings. But who would that be? Milton's brow furrowed, his gaze fixed on the road ahead of him. He droned on about crop rotation versus crop yield, neither of which interested Sabrina. She looked at the other men behind her, but they stared at her as if mesmerized; it made a poor starting point for a conversation. She faced the road ahead and sighed.

Her thoughts returned to the trail, and they rode in silence, neither of them having anything to say that would interest the other. However, boredom soon overtook them, and Milton launched into a lengthy lecture cornering wheat production and crop rotation. When that topic grew thin, he shifted to the weather; the spring rains were overdue and much anticipated. Sabrina listened with polite interest, but her eyes glazed over. She resisted the urge to cut off his head and ride away at pell-mell speeds, but she restrained her darker impulses and sighed.

She looked up to the rolling hills. Rich green grass waved in the gentle winds. The yellow and blue butterfly took to flight and fluttered about in a whimsical dance.

"… So what is your position?"

She looked at Milton and then at the rest of the men. They all waited for her reply. "What was the question again?"

"Do you think it was an isolated haugr, or are there more flocks?"

"That question can only be answered by knowing how they gained access. Haugr hate the water, and it's unlikely that they traveled over Lortrid Bay. True, there are many islands, but that makes navigation hazardous. It's possible they came from the Dead Plains and the Cordon Forest to the east. They abound in the wilderness, but the Hargal Wall would have barred them."

"Very true," Milton replied. "The Hargal Wall has kept our enemies at bay for over 2,000 years. One of my ancestors worked on the wall. It stands 300 meters high and extends down to solid bedrock. There's no passing through it except by one of the 12 gates."

"Then we have two mysteries. The second will answer the first. The quantity of haugr will be decided by how they arrived. Does the Royal

The Great Gate

Governor have a strategic mind?" It was a long time since she visited Solva, and she was eager to hear about the political landscape.

Milton's back straightened, as though a ramrod replaced his spine. He pondered her question, weighing each word as though it were good. "He has a sound enough mind for commerce and political intrigues."

Sabrina smirked. Autocratic governments were notorious for two things: First, they often favored the wealthy. Second, they did not take criticism well. The Wolf's Head Peninsula had a peculiar mixture of representative democracy and autocratic rule.

"No, he's not. He is an idiot. He spends all day contemplating the color of his drapes or the tailoring of his clothes." Kendall shook his head and contorted up his face, clear contempt in his eyes. "Everyone says so."

Disapproval flashed on Milton's face. "It's best to keep such opinions to yourself. Otherwise, you might find yourself strapped to a post and your back laid open by the tormentor's whip."

Kendall raised his chin. "I'm not afraid of him. He's a fat old man with a double chin and a weak arm. He never leaves the city and carriages ferry his fat arse about. It's probably been years since he walked on his own feet."

Milton squeezed his eyes shut and rubbed his temples. "When we get to the city, why don't you and the others get yourself some ale? I'll speak to the governor about the haugr." Kendall considered arguing the point, but drinking and fornicating seemed better than talking to a fat governor.

A gray road of field stone cut a path through lush fields of waving grass and circled around the crystal clear water of Picnic Lake. Sabrina drew in a deep breath and absorbed the pastoral tranquility. When Eliza stirred in her arms, she caressed the baby's cheek, and Eliza awoke with a shriek, a putrid odor emanating from her diaper.

The party paused while Sabrina saw to the infant's needs. In the wilderness, dealing with a dirty diaper was a complicated affair. She had to clean the fecal matter off both the child and the soiled diaper, disposable diapers being a luxury of city life. While Sabrina was a great warrior and a consummate wizard, she lacked domestic skills, and her stomach lurched as she performed the task. The men stood well away and pretended not to notice and not even thinking to assist her. At the conclusion of the ordeal, she resolved to hire a nanny to tend to Eliza's needs.

They resumed their journey, and after a short distance, they emerged from a small grove of apple trees. The sun loomed overhead with fervent heat, ripening the fruit, scorching the pavers, heat shimmering in waves off the gray field stones, making the humid air a suffocating blanket – Sabrina wished she flew to Solva. The gray road climbed through the middle of a rolling hill, making it appear endless. Milton wiped his brow and took a swig of water from his flask. The baby stirred: they would have to stop soon.

When they topped the hill, the wind swept across the prairie grass, causing it to flow in waves, and the monolithic walls of Solva rose out of a sea of green. Stretching back all the way to the Merchant River and ahead to Solva; humans, elves, and dwarves trudged along the winding highway. Freighter wagons – both horse-drawn and electric, loaded with cargo – abounded, as did the dog carts, carriages, riders, pedestrians, wagons, E-cars, and heavy haulers. The traffic pressed together into a tight crush and came to a slow, painful crawl, reminding Sabrina of a Los Angeles traffic jam.

Sabrina wished to avoid the choked road, the suffocating cloud of dust raised by the traffic, but there was no choice: the thick prairie grass could impede an elephant and would take far longer than the established route. Yet someone in an E-car had to try. A man with a stupid look on his face removed his cap, scratched his head, and stared at the engine compartment of an aqua blue electric car. The small, aerodynamic city vehicle was stuck in the tall grass; black smoke billowed from its electric motor, causing a stench like burnt hair. The car passed over a low-grade, rhunite fieldstone, and it induced a surge of high amperage current, which burnt out the control system. The driver was lucky. If it was high-grade ore, the car would have burst into flames.

The road they traveled led them across the face of a hill and then merged into traffic. None of those on the main road wished to give way, and they were met with glares and scowls. Martin pushed into the fray without a thought, but Sabrina hesitated, having grown accustomed to the anonymity afforded by Earth automobiles. After forging her resolve, she pressed into a temporary void caused by travelers. She matched the slow pace of the traffic and moved toward the city.

Chapter 12

The Solva city walls appeared small at first, a sandcastle on the shore, but they grew larger with every step, soon looming high above them. The walls were fashioned from great stone blocks, conformed into a single smooth surface, so tight that a razor blade could not fit between them. They stretched out to the right and left as far as one could see.

There is something within a man that loves a wall. Build a wall and men will vie to live behind it; make the interior space behind the wall large enough, and men will build a city; place guards upon the wall and men will establish a kingdom. Solva was one such city. The interior spaces filled in, out, and then up. Those unable to live within the city built just outside the wall, and when these new settlements grew prosperous, they added more walls, joining the old to the new, much like segments of a cell. There were seven sections or districts, the new districts attaching to the old. The eighth district was still under construction and located on the opposite side of the city to the northwest, along with the prosperous riverfront.

Guards stood high upon the walls with their pikes pointed toward the skies, gusting wind flapping elegant pennants. The pennants bore the crest of great houses or guilds, and there were many guilds within the city. Each house competed with the other for rank within the national government and local community. Higher ranks brought financial gain, fame, and opportunity. Rank meant more members within parliament, and that meant more votes; and that meant more political sway. Thus the successful houses could obtain lucrative government contracts, entitlement to public lands, defense spending, and lower taxes. Their children attended the best schools, and their spouses were the most beautiful.

The Great Gate

The drawbridge lowered, and the portcullis rose. Horse hooves clomped and feet stamped in a mad rush over the wooden planks. A hoard of travelers hurried over the bridge, eager to be the first one into the city, but wagons loaded with small shipments of grain, sugar, and coffee beans slowed traffic, much to the chagrin of pedestrians. Merchants lingering just within the city gate further congested traffic, purchasing soaps, fabrics, spices, and other commodities as soon as they arrived.

The crowd pressed up against Midnight, and they traversed the bridge in a shuffle. Guards positioned on the other side at the entrance made a feeble attempt to scrutinize the crowd, but there were too many people. By the time Sabrina entered through the gate, Midnight had begun to snort in annoyance. The river of people gushed into the city and branched out like a delta, passing into a labyrinth of streets. Midnight broke into a trot, glad to be free from the claustrophobic crowd.

"Milton, I will take my leave of you. I need to tend to Eliza."

The old man nodded. "What if the governor wishes to speak with you? You were, after all, the sole witness."

"I will send word to him as to the location of my lodgings." She smirked and examined his face for recognition. "Tell him Sabrina March 'The Overlord of the Black Dragon' has returned and bids him greeting."

Milton raised his brow and gaped at her. "I had no idea that you returned from your long travels or that I was in such auspicious company. Thank you for your patience, Mistress Sabrina. I will tell him. We shall part ways for now until the trail brings us together again."

He and the other riders turned to the right, passing by rows of five-story buildings, each made of fieldstone, wood, and stucco. Signs advertising taverns hung above every doorway, and the sound of music flowed out into the streets. They joined together on the road and created a carnival cacophony. Bawdy women lingered on second-floor balconies, breasts displayed like ripe fruit, clad only in scant lingerie, and they called out to men and women on the street, advertising their service. Men leered at the women's breasts, but Sabrina noticed their choker necklaces. Black with a silver setting that bore a crest, this adornment marked them as property. Slavery had taken a firm root in the "free lands."

During war, economic collapse, and famine, the citizens of Asgard remained free. They guarded it like an only child, wrote songs about it, and wrote books praising it: it was the cornerstone society – or it was when Sabrina departed. She left Miami expecting to return home, but instead, she arrived in a strange land, tainted by growing evil. The Great Spirit created all beings equal: it was unthinkable for one man to own another. Yet the spectacle and tragedy of slavery existed all around her. Why? How?

Sabrina chose the straight road and headed away from the red light district. It cut its way through the heart of the district and would carry her deep into the city. The sun beamed over the hilltop and turned the street to luminescent gold. It seemed like a good sign.

She perused the merchandise in the shop windows. Women milled about and inspected various wares. In one store, a woman bartered over a cast iron pot, and in another shop, an elva set up a display featuring a sultry crimson gown. Unlike the village women, the city women paid her little attention, since female warriors were a common sight.

The streets wove around one another like piled spaghetti. Some of them traveled down into underground tunnels while others emerged from them, and still others used roads that passed overhead of brownstone houses, an ingenious solution to the crowded streets. Sabrina scanned the buildings for lodging that would meet her needs and that of the infant. The Black Castle – the greatest fortification in the world and considered one of the 12 ancient wonders – belonged to her, but the castle meant entanglements that she was not yet prepared to meet. Thus she continued her search, examining and rejecting each hotel for a variety of reasons.

The Great Gate

Sabrina passed through a gate that led into the fifth district. The buildings were a bit shabby and the infrastructure worn. Boards replaced many windows and shutters hung askew. White and tan, brick, and stone facades were soiled and crumbling with neglect. Human, Elven, and dwarf children played games in the streets. The aroma of freshly cooked meals wafted through the air and made her stomach grumble. She considered turning around when a strange sight caught her interest.

A little elva, Angelina, stood outside a home near a fieldstone wall. Gold blonde locks held behind her head by a clip, eyes a pair of radiant blue sapphires, ears jutting through her hair and forming a pair of points, wearing a little blue dress and a bright white apron, the elva child personified innocence. However, tears flowed over her little apple cheeks, and she sucked in her lower lip, her little body trembling as she sobbed. The girl held the hand of her little sister, Abby, and tried to protect her. Abby appeared to be just able to walk, and she sucked on her thumb, tears threatening to flow at any moment.

A man rushed out the open door with an elva in hot pursuit. Sabrina rode forward and listened to their conversation. "…Please, don't do this. The guild will pay us my husband's death benefit."

"Madam, we have extended three indulgences on your mortgage and unsecured loans. We can offer you no more …." No matter where in the world Sabrina traveled bankers were the same, profit margins replacing mercy and contracts replacing hearts. The man hitched his thumbs underneath the lapels of his black robes, which draped on either side of his considerable belly, and a flat black cap draped over his egg-shaped head.

"My husband was a good elvan. It's a lie. He would never have run from battle. We deserve his death benefit."

"That is irrelevant. Either you have the money, or you don't." He waved over two men, lingering a short distance away; vast and ugly, they were the type one uses to complete unpleasant tasks. When one of them seized the elva mother by the shoulders, she twisted to get away, kicking the man's partner in the shins. His partner grabbed a fistful of her blonde locks, yanking back her head back, and he began to wrap a slave choker necklace around her throat.

Sabrina dismounted her horse and approached them. The pair came to an abrupt halt and gazed back at her, assessing the threat. "I'll pay off her debt. How much does she owe?"

The banker gaped at her and furrowed his brow; "If this is a joke —"

"I assure you that I am serious. How much does she owe? Tell me now!"

"Ahem … this is quite unusual." He furrowed his brow and studied her, his face lighting up a moment later. "You're Overlord March. I had no idea you returned. Why would you be interested in this property?" Sabrina glared at the man and stood akimbo. He cleared his throat and opened a large leather bound book. Mumbling under his breath as he read, he searched for the debit entry. "Let me see. After we include six months of missed payments, earned interest, and penalties, she owes us 27,330 Kronar."

"How much is that in the current exchange for gold and silver?"

"Ah, well," he gazed up at the sky. The setting sun cast brilliant orange and red hues upon the cumulous clouds. "That would be 20 gold and 13 silver coins. The price of gold has gone up in recent years, due to economic turbulence."

"Very well, I will pay the bill in full." Sabrina untied her saddlebags and took out a coin purse. "But I will expect a receipt."

"Naturally, if you stop by the bank in the morning, I will provide you with the deed." The banker furrowed his brow and tried to look in her coin purse. "Um, are you any relation to widow Karalynn or the Arndis Family?"

"No. I'm taking her as my vamon," Sabrina said.

Vamon was a legal term, which had two uses. The first use was that of a "duty wife." A woman pledged to the Valkyrie could never legally marry; she was married to the Corps. However, the legal designation vamon allowed her to establish a relationship with a man without officially recognizing her as a legal wife. The second use, one most common with nobles, allowed men and women of status within the royal court to adopt a sibling. The king had thousands of vamon under his protection. The reasons for this designation were as varied as the people who held the title and solidified political relationships.

"I am a warrior; therefore, I have status as a parchment male, and I am of royal, noble status. It is within my rights to designate her as vamon to me."

"Very well, it's none of my concern. The relationship appears a bit abrupt," he chuckled. Looking back at his men, he signaled them to free the young mother. When they released the young elva, she staggered backward and fell to the ground. "It's a pity you know. She would have brought an excellent price at auction. I'd wager that a beautiful elva like her could sell for 50 gold, perhaps more – but I suppose that's why you bought her. Anyway, best wishes on your purchase." He took the money from Sabrina and scratched out a preliminary receipt. As he walked away from them, he waved for his men to follow.

The young elva, Karalynn, rose to her feet and looked upon Sabrina with curiosity. She gazed down at her feet. "I am grateful that you paid off my debt, but I do not understand. We have never met."

"It is within my legal rights to take you as vamon. As to the why … Eliza needs a home, and so do I." Sabrina handed Eliza to the elva, and then she examined the home's exterior, which was run down like the rest of the neighborhood. However, there were many shops within walking distance, and it seemed to be a quiet neighborhood. "Is there a livery in the neighborhood?"

"There are two stables. One is two blocks east and one block north. The other is five blocks south. They charge by the day, month, or year. One is as good as the other."

"I'm tired and hungry. Feed and change the baby. I'll be back in an hour for dinner." She handed Karalynn two silver coins. "After you get dressed, buy some supplies from the grocery. I will have him bill my account with the bank."

She grabbed Midnight's reins and walked a few paces; then stopping, she paused and drew in a deep breath. After slowly exhaling, she turned around to face Karalynn. "I apologize for being blunt, and I know you have been through an ordeal. But I am tired, and I need someone to wet-nurse the baby, cook my meals, and keep my home. Eliza is my adopted daughter, and since you are now my vamon sister, she belongs to you as well. Is that acceptable?"

"I was almost a slave and so were my children. I am grateful that you will be taking care of us. I lost my world when my husband, Maj, died." She looked off into the distance. "We grew up together. I never wanted to marry anyone but him."

"You're certain he is dead?"

"Yes. They brought Maj's body back to me. It was loaded on a cart with other bodies like cordwood. They told me, 'He died a coward's death.' 'The Proud Lion House' warriors are cowards and children playing at war. They hire brave men and elvan: they slaughter them in meaningless quests. When the casualty reports are gathered, they negate their losses by claiming that none of their dead died in battle. They either die as a coward, of sickness, or as an accident. That way they don't have to pay the bounty."

Sabrina dropped the horse's reins and walked back to Karalynn. She embraced the young woman and held her tight. The young mother buried her face in Sabrina's shoulder and let out heaving sobs. "It's okay. I'll take care of you."

Chapter 13

Sabrina awoke to the caress of a plush pillow and the heavy weight of a duvet. She snuggled into the soft mattress and savored the caress of a real bed. A golden ray of sunshine beamed in through the glass pane doors and fell upon her face. She took a deep breath and savored the feeling of home.

The bedroom door to her right opened a crack, and a pair of blue eyes peered up at her from the fissure. "Hello, I was already awake," Sabrina said. The girl chewed on her lower lip and debated whether or not to cry. "You can come in."

The girl pushed open the door and entered the room. She wore a linen nightgown covered with a floral pattern. "My name is Angelina. My little sister is Abby."

"Yes, I know. Your mother told me your names." Sabrina sat up in bed and peered down the hallway. Brown eyes, belonging to a rosy-cheeked girl, gazed back at her. Abby sucked on her index finger and gave Sabrina a little wave. "Why don't you climb up on the bed so we can talk?"

Angelina grabbed the covers and used them as a rope, scaling the side of the bed. After she had reached the top, she turned around and grabbed Abby's hands. Working as a team, Angelina assisted Abby as she climbed up the bed. Sabrina was impressed. It was an exercise in cooperation and dexterity worthy of a Valkyrie. The pair then crawled over the bed to her.

Sabrina scooted back and leaned against a headboard. She brushed Angelina's golden locks behind her pointed right ear. "Angelina is a very beautiful name. It means sunshine in old Elven." The girl nodded as if this was common knowledge; Abby sucked on a finger and stared at Sabrina as if trying to comprehend her.

"I'm sorry about that." Karalynn charged into the room. "I told them not to bother you." The young mother wore a baby pink satin corset, an underwire bra, and matching panties. Hand embroidered, dark pink roses adorned the corset, and it appeared expensive, an anniversary gift perhaps. "I told them to let you sleep."

"It's alright. I generally only sleep about three hours a night, but I was exhausted. I slept a full six hours." Sabrina sat up in bed and leaned against the headboard. "I always feel so refreshed after a long sleep."

"Six hours," Karalynn remarked. "You must have been tired. I wake up after two. Angelina sleeps only one. I scarcely put Angelina to bed, and she's up again. She plays for a few hours in her room and then gets another hour of sleep. It worries me: a young elva requires four hours of sleep a day. If I had any money, I would take her to the doctor."

"That's normal, given the turmoil." Sabrina picked up Angelina, and after setting the girl on her lap, she primped the girl's golden locks. "Elven children her age are telepathically attuned to their mothers. I think it is an evolved response. If the mother is in distress, then the child remains alert: in this way, they are kept safe."

Karalynn stared off into the distance, deep in thought. "I had no idea." She covered her mouth, and her eyes welled up with tears. "I should have known that. I was just too consumed with my own grief."

Sabrina slipped out of bed. She took Karalynn in her arms and held her. This time, however, her tears soon stopped. She sniffled and said, "I'll be okay now."

"Here, let me tighten your corset," said Sabrina and shifted the girl off her lap. Karalynn nodded and stood before a tall wooden bedpost; then holding onto it with both hands, she braced herself. Sabrina put her knee on the small of the young woman's back and pulled. The cords grew tight, and the pink satin garment grew constricted, causing Karalynn to draw in shallow breaths, her body conforming to the feminine ideal.

Karalynn winced and gazed up through her bangs. "You are my Mistress, and I am bound to your will. Command me, and I will obey."

"Well," Sabrina said and cleared her throat. She could see that Karalynn yearned for Sabrina's control and her strength: the young mother longed for safety, but no great commands came to mind. "I could use some breakfast."

"I will fix you breakfast right away." Karalynn chewed on her crimson lower lip and thought a moment. "Have you any other commands for me?"

"Um … yes. You should go shopping." Sabrina realized that the corset was probably the only nice piece of lingerie that Karalynn owned. Her deceased husband, Maj, probably spent a year's wages on it. "I'm sure times have been very hard for you, and that you need to have some fun. The worst of it is behind you. Buy some new dresses and shoes. They should cover a broad range of social functions. As my vamon, you will be required to be by my side, and rightly or wrongly, the public judges vamon more harshly than are dominants. Besides, it should make for a fun day of shopping."

"Yes, Mistress," Karalynn said with a nod.

"Also, this room needs some new curtains. Have some tradesmen come by the house and inspect it. I would rather get all the repairs completed at the same time. Um, I also entertain quite a bit. Are you a good cook?"

"Yes, Mistress."

The children lingered on the bed and watched them interchange with rapt interest. Eliza's cries penetrated the nursery door and echoed through the house. "I think Eliza needs you."

"Yes, Mistress." Karalynn rose to her feet and ushered the children from the room. They scampered down the stairs and returned to their bedrooms. Then she changed Eliza's soiled diaper. After settling the baby into the playpen, Karalynn entered the master bedroom but left the door open.

Sabrina recognized this as an invitation. She strolled through the hallway, the wooden floor chilling her feet, and then she lingered in the doorway, leaned against the frame, and arms crossed. Karalynn sat on the edge of her bed and wrung her hands.

Sabrina sighed. She strolled over to the bed and took Karalynn by the hand. She led the young woman to the bed and sat down next to her. "You don't need to be afraid. You are my sister now. I would never sell you or anyone else. I detest slavery: I am shocked that the free lands tolerate it. If this happened three hundred years ago, the warriors would have killed the perpetrators."

"That was a long time ago, and much has changed," Karalynn said. "Many of the warriors died of old age or were killed in useless battles. There are barely enough experienced soldiers to train the young."

"So I see," Sabrina replied. "I want us to be friends, so please, try and relax. Everything is going to be fine." Karalynn chewed on her lip and nodded. "And if your deceased husband ... what's his name?"

"His name was Amajalia."

"Isn't that a girl's name?"

"Yes. That's why he like to be called Maj."

"Anyway, if Maj returns from the afterlife, you will still be his. Don't worry. I would never stand in your way. Do you believe me?"

Karalynn nodded and combed a tress behind her left ear. She glanced at Sabrina: "You're stunning. In fact, I've never seen a more beautiful elva."

"Thank you. I hear that a lot. I don't mean to be boastful, but an awful lot of people try to seduce me. It's wearying. Men approach me with such hope and lust in their eyes, and then I send them away disappointed – I feel like a rainy day." Sabrina clasped her hands in her lap and sighed. "I'm glad to have someone to help me deflect some of my many suitors."

Sabrina rose to her feet, took Karalynn's hands, and drew her to her feet. "As I said, 'You should go shopping.' Have another lady tend to the children and take a friend shopping. Buy a new wardrobe, money is no object. Now get yourself dressed."

Karalynn hurried into the closet. She had returned before Sabrina had time to leave and held out two different dresses. One was a white sundress, accented with pink lace overlay. The other sundress was purple, having a scooped neckline and an accordion pleated skirt. "Which one do you like?"

"The white one," Sabrina replied.

Karalynn crinkled her nose and held out the dresses. "I don't know. I think I like the purple one." Sabrina chuckled; even as a woman she still did not understand women. The purple dress seemed a bit impractical for housework, but Karalynn wanted to dress nicely for her. Even so, why ask her opinion if she knew which one she wanted to wear? Karalynn held the dress up over her head and let it waft down her body. She maneuvered the princess-cut bodice in place and turned around. With her back to Sabrina, she asked, "Can you zip me up?"

"Sure," Sabina said, and grabbing the zipper tab, drew it up. Despite the corset, the princess-cut bodice grew very tight and required some effort to raise the zipper. The fitted taffeta dress complemented her upper torso and the pleated danced around her thighs. Karalynn then walked over to her makeup table and touched up her cosmetics.

"You said that other women were in your position. Their husbands had been killed, and no bounty was paid?"

"Many," Karalynn replied. "It never used to be like this. The guilds used to be noble; they took care of their own. All that changed: I'm not sure when it happened, but it did. The guilds are selfish and self-serving, without a hint of honor. I never wanted Maj to join them, but it was the only way he could find work, and we had babies to feed."

"How old are you?" asked Sabrina. Once elves reach adulthood, 21-years-old by human appraisal, they cease aging; in fact, many appeared younger, 19 perhaps. It was only after thousands of years that elves appeared mature. Thus the scant traces of age on an elve's face revealed much about his influence and magical power.

"24 years old," Karalynn replied. By elvish terms, she was a child, a mere toddler just out of the nursery. It was peculiar that she married and had babies so young.

"I take it then that your parents passed to the undying lands?" asked Sabrina.

"Yes, when I was 16-years-old, before my ascension day," Karalynn replied with a sad nod. "At first I thought of the guild as my new family, but the guilds are terrible: the sacrifice their own for empty ambition. The widows have nowhere to go, or any means to keep their homes. Some widows leave the city to live with their families. Other families share a home and pool their finances. A group of widows shares a house two doors down. I tried to stay with them, but they said that they didn't

120

have any room for us. I think they were just afraid of the bill collectors. Some debtor families are hiding there, and the floors are covered with bedrolls at night."

Karalynn glanced at Sabrina in the mirror. She found it curious that Sabrina wore a silk nightgown. She assumed warrior women wore leather to bed or men's pajamas. However, she dressed in a silk nightgown and robe that made her look feminine, as though she was one of Karalynn's girlfriends.

"I'm going to the bank to finalize yesterday's transaction. I will pick up the mortgage and submit the legal paperwork for your designation as a vamon. It will need your signature since there is no senior family member. We need it for legal purposes; otherwise, someone could claim you."

"Long ago slavers used that trick. They would marry several girls in different regions, unbeknownst to the girls, and transport them to the western islands. The girls would then find themselves far from home and in a foreign port. To their horror, their new husbands sold them at auction."

"I spent 50 long years hunting these vermin, but they still persisted; the money is just too good."

"That's awful." Karalynn turned around. "I don't know what's happening to society. When I was a girl, the warriors would have never put up with it. Now they just accept it like sheep. Can't the authorities do anything for these women?"

"I have been away for a very long time. I only know the way it used to be. Sometimes the bride's family found and rescued the girls. Slavers were very cunning, and most of them were never located. A slaver would work three or four different regions and collect as many as twenty wives. It breaks my heart to think about the pain and humiliation those women endured. After they had been sold, it was too late. Honeymoons tend to be long, and it took time for their families to discover that the women were missing."

Sabrina was eager to change the subject. "I want you to have the other women meet us here for dinner. I have a bit of business to discuss with them. I think they will be quite interested to hear what I have to say." She threw open the doors and wandered onto the balcony. The chilled morning air wafted over her. "Why don't you pick up some meat from the butcher? We can provide them with supper."

"Okay, I can get some of the others to help me. But there will be quite a few. It will take more money."

When Sabrina saw the eagerness in Karalynn's eyes, she smirked. She left the room and then returned from her bedroom. "Here's my coin purse. Take it and put it away for the household needs. Use it as you see fit."

Karalynn strolled over to the dresser. The brown satchel bulged with coins. She drew open the string and gazed inside it; her eyes went wide. Gold and silver coins, more than she had ever seen in her life, greeted her eager eyes; 50 years wages would not reap such a sum. "Are you sure?"

"Oh, I have much more than that. That's my traveling money. Take it and use it for the good of the household." Karalynn nodded and clutched the coin purse to her chest. She curtsied and then scampered away with the treasure, causing the children to chase after her. Sabrina shouted, "Oh, and hire an armored wagon for the day."

Sabrina wandered out onto her balcony and rested her elbows on the stone railing. The fifth district sat on a hill with a magnificent view. Red rooftops flowed down the hill toward the east wall where they stopped. The wall formed a wishbone; the sixth district lay to the north, and the fourth district lay in the south. Buildings resembling castles of steel and glass marked the sixth district, the banking district. If one is going to invest one's money, one wants the broker to be prosperous.

She furrowed her brow and scanned the horizon. The towering buildings of the sixth district dwarfed all others and reminded her of the New York City skyline. Some of the buildings were over 100 stories, but most of them were 30 stories or less.

———

Karalynn hurried into her bedroom with the girls on her heels. She considered her bed, dresser, and then her closet, but rejected each one. A thief would search those places first. When she turned around, Karalynn saw a pair of curious faces gazing up at her.

She ushered them from her room and escorted them downstairs to their bedroom. "I'll be back in a minute." She placed the children in Angelina's bedroom. The walls were pink, and a white canopy bed occupied the far portion of the room, leaving the floor area available for them to play. She sat them around a small table for tea time and handed each one a doll. "Be good girls, play with your toys." She closed the door, hoping that the assortment of dolls would occupy them.

Karalynn hurried down three more flights of stairs to the first floor. She circled around the banister, rushed through the dining room, and opened the door to the basement. Ten steps carried her down to a stone landing, and five more brought her down to the cellar.

The sidewalls and floor of the basement were made of solid granite, gray and cold. Wooden boxes lay in high piles in the corners, and many contained unfinished projects: dining room chairs, lamp stands, and bedroom sets – dust covered all of them.

She hurried through the piles of debris, not wishing to soil her dress. A shaft of light penetrated a filthy basement window and pointed, like the finger of God, at a wooden workbench. Clamps, planes, and chisels were scattered on it, and they lay amongst piles of curled wood shavings. It appeared as though Maj would return at any moment to resume his work.

Karalynn walked toward the bench and covered her mouth with her hand. Tears began to trickle down her cheeks, and she began to sob. She leaned over the bench and caressed a wooden mallet. "Why did you leave me?"

"Don't be afraid. You will be together again someday."

Karalynn jumped and spun around. She saw Sabrina standing on the stairs. "I didn't mean to spy on you. It's just that you left so quickly, I didn't think you heard me. I needed you to hire a wagon and a driver."

"I heard you." The young mother wiped the tears from her face and then languished in silence. "Do you believe that we will be together again someday?"

"Oh yes." Sabrina walked toward Karalynn. "You are both elves, and you have received 'The Rite of Inclusion.' That means you are both eternal. While it is true we can die like anyone else, we have the power to return from the afterlife. I've been there many times but not because I died. I was there on business."

"You could bring Maj back?"

"The answer is both yes and no. The High Council has placed a temporary ban on resurrection from the eternal lands. They have concerns about cross-boundary contamination. A few elves brought back forbidden objects from the afterlife. They meant no harm, but it caused harm. It took lots of effort to clean up the mess, and the scandal rocked the council. The various committees will take at least five hundred years, perhaps longer, to fully investigate the matter and make a recommendation to the legislature. I think the real constant of the universe is government bureaucracy."

124

"One day, it may be possible to deliver Maj a message via courier. The type of energy storage used for data is cross boundary compatible. The only other way is to give it to someone who is dying." She crossed her arms and shrugged. "You need to face the fact though that Maj is gone. He may marry someone else. It's very common."

"No. Maj would wait for me. We love each other," Karalynn replied.

The young elva's naivety was adorable, and Sabrina knew better than to argue with hope. "I'm glad to hear that. If it helps you, think of him as being away on a long journey. He will never return, but one day you will go to be with him." She rubbed Karalynn's shoulders. "In the meantime, you need to heal and take care of his children."

Karalynn sighed and nodded; "I will."

"Now hide the money, and let's get some breakfast," Sabrina said.

"I want to show you something." Karalynn navigated around some old rugs covered with dust. She brushed aside the cobwebs and headed toward the far corner. Sabrina stopped when they passed an old sheet metal box, rusted and covered with grime, setting upon a stone base; a smaller box attached to the front, and ducting connected to the top of it.

"What is this?" asked Sabrina.

"What?" Karalynn turned around and looked at the device. "It's the heater. The cooler is in the attic."

"It's ancient. Have it replaced with a new unit. The old units break down all the time."

"Yes, Mistress. I will." Karalynn slapped the dust off her hands. She turned to the right and entered a small alcove with a single door. When

125

she opened it, Sabrina saw a closet. Old blankets, towels, and discarded garments filled it.

Karalynn opened a hidden panel on the right of the closet wall. A circular crystal set in a metal frame sat inside a panel, and tab type buttons, with old Elvish script upon them, allowed one to enter a code. Karalynn pressed six tabs and then pressed the center crystal with her palm. It began to glow bright blue.

"Blue means the combination was right. You get three tries and then it locks you out for three days." The interior closet began to slide away from them, and it moved back two meters, revealing a set of dark stairs. When Karalynn placed her foot on the first step, lights illuminated the stairs.

The young mother held onto a wooden railing and walked down the stone steps. "Maj told me to hide down here if we were ever in danger. No one would ever find us."

Artificial lights blazed to life above them. A vast sub-basement opened before her. There were three long wooden benches, shelves on the walls, and wine racks. "Long ago this was a tavern and inn. That's why it has so many floors and rooms. They stored food and liquor in the subbasement. It's a bit chilly if you ask me." She rubbed her upper arms and shivered.

"Is there a restroom?"

"Yes. Over in the corner." She pointed at the far corner of the room. "There's also a sink and a stove. I guess they prepared food down here too."

"I think I'll use this as a lab to do my experiments if you don't mind."

"I don't mind. I never come down here anyway." She wrinkled her nose and snarled at all the cobwebs and dust.

"Yes. This is wonderful. I can make something out of this place."

Karalynn drew her index finger along the top of a bench. It cut a channel in the dust. "Will you need help cleaning it?"

Sabrina pondered the question a moment. "I think I can take care of it. I can just whip up a whirlwind spell and clean it up in a jiff."

"So you are a wizard?"

"Um … what? Oh yes, I suppose you could call it that. I really think of it as advanced science, but magic works too." Sabrina glanced down at her bedroom clothes. "I need to get changed."

Karalynn clutched the bag and screwed up her face. It was evident that she fretted over where to hide it. "Just leave it in that cupboard. No one besides us knows about this place," Sabrina said. "I'll install a safe down here at some point in the future."

The idea suited Karalynn, especially since Sabrina chose the hiding place. She walked over to the cupboard and opened a wooden door. After taking a couple of coins from the sack, she put the purse behind an old tankard and plate. She closed the door and chased after Sabrina, her skirt dancing around her knees as she charged up the stairs.

Sabrina ascended two stories to the main floor and then another five to the top floor, all the while brooding over what she would wear for the day. Female fashion was always involved no matter which world she visited, but men all dressed the same; there were some interesting variations in male clothing once in a while, but men dressed with predictable regularity on all worlds. Women, on the other hand, defied all boundaries and their fashions changed with astonishing volatility. A few wrong details – the wrong hairstyle or the wrong shoes – created an embarrassing fashion faux pas.

The Great Gate

She unpacked a gown, a purchase she made in New York City and never had the opportunity to wear. She hung the gown from a hook on the wall and let the scarlet silk flow over her hand like liquid. The bodice was sculpted, seamless, and a sweetheart neckline with side shoulder straps. It draped all the way to her ankles, had a slit up the right side, and came with a matching shrug.

Since she was well endowed, foundation lingerie was a necessity. For this gown, a black satin corset, a thong, and black nylons seemed suitable. She attached the garter straps to the corset and set the garments aside.

Satisfied with her selection, she circled around the bed and entered the bathroom. She brushed aside a white lace shower curtain and turned on the water. "I'm looking forward to a hot shower."

After a week of dusty trails and sponge baths, the hot water felt marvelous on her skin. She lingered, letting the water flow in channels over her body. After washing her hair, she turned off the water and dried off with a fluffy terry cloth towel. An array of perfumes was arranged on the sink with care. She sampled them and settled upon a rose scent.

Cosmetics were the bane of her existence. Picasso never worked so hard to paint a face, and a few of her early attempts reminded one of his paintings. However, over time and with practice, she mastered the art. Foundation, blush, blue eyeliner, mascara, and glossy crimson lip gloss adorned her face. As she pinned up her hair behind her head, she saw a pair of blue eyes gazing up at her from the door frame; Angelina stared at her and sucked on a finger.

"How did you get in here?" She ushered the little girl out of the bathroom. Looking across the bed, she noted the locked and bolted door. "Okay you little trickster, how did you do that?" She looked underneath the bed but saw no means of access. "I'll figure it out later."

She escorted the little elva around the bed and out of the room. The curious little girl waved her right hand as the door closed.

When Sabrina emerged from her bedroom, the children gathered around the table and waited. Karalynn set plates of eggs, bacon, and toast in front of Angelina and fruit puree in front of Abby. As to Eliza, she cradled the infant on her right hip, lowered her dress zipper, pulled down a bra cup, and moved the baby to her breast. Eliza needed no encouragement, moved the nipple into her mouth, and began to feed.

"What do you think?"

Karalynn turned around, saw Sabrina, and scrunched up her nose with a smile. "You look so beautiful. Where are you going? Is there a ball at the governor's mansion?"

"Well no, I was going to the bank." Sabrina's shoulders drooped, and her lips formed a pout. "Damn it! I'll never get used to women's fashions."

"Damn it," echoed a tiny voice. Angelina gazed up at Sabrina still clutching a piece of bacon in her right hand. She chanted, "Damn it, damn it, damn it."

"Only grownups can say 'damn it,'" said Sabrina.

The girl sang a merry "damn it" song. "It's okay," Karalynn said. "She just turned four. She has no idea what she's saying. I'll talk to her later about it."

Sabrina moved close to Karalynn and spoke in a quiet voice. "I got it wrong again. I thought I should dress formally; a bank is formal. Should I go change? I look ridiculous."

"No. You look beautiful." She shrugged. "You're rich and royalty. You should dress nicely."

129

The Great Gate

That was better than poor and a pariah. Sabrina shook her head and rubbed her temples. She loathed the idea of changing clothes. "I'll go like this, but I need to have some of my clothes shipped over from the Black Castle. Do you suppose they are still fashionable after 88 years?"

Karalynn's face lit up. "Oh, you're that Sabrina. I had no idea. You own most of Asgard. Where have you been? No one has seen you in over 80 years."

"The only thing I can say to the matter is that I was otherwise occupied off world. But I am back now, and it appears I have lots of work to do."

Karalynn strolled around Sabrina and scanned the gown. "It certainly is beautiful. Where did you get it?"

"New York City, I stored it and some other things in my secret storage chamber."

"Where?"

"My secret storage chamber is in New York City," Sabrina said.

"I've never heard of York City," Karalynn replied.

"New York City is on another world, Earth."

"You've been to the mythical lands?" she squealed. "You have to tell me all about it. I want to hear everything. How did you get there? Is the Great Gate open?"

Sabrina cleared her throat; "You see … that is … I'm a Maige."

Karalynn tilted her head to the side. "I knew you were wealthy and powerful and a great warrior, but I never knew you were a Maige. Where are your wings? Do you turn into a dragon much?" she asked with girlish curiosity.

"No. Dragons cause the local populace to panic," she replied. "Of course, it means that you're married to a dragon. Does that upset you?"

"No. It is fine with me. I don't judge." She paused for a second and then asked, "Can I see your wings? They must be breathtaking."

"Certainly," Sabrina said with a smile. She stripped off her shrug and turned away from Karalynn. A pair of wings, which resembled an intricate tattoo, covered the entirety of Sabrina's back. This tattoo could transform into flesh and feathers; wings shot up from behind her; they arched and then swept down to the floor, draping behind her like a train. She primped her raven black locks behind her pointed right ear. Her blue eyes shimmered like gems.

"You look amazing," Karalynn squealed and clapped. "I never thought anyone could be so beautiful. You should keep them out; they really set off your eyes and gown."

"Do you think so?" asked Sabrina. "I can't wear the jacket if I keep my wings out."

"Oh yes," Karalynn replied. "If I had wings, I would wear them all the time."

"I could wear the gloves." Sabrina retrieved a pair of long, black satin opera gloves from her clutch bag. After she had donned them, she put her hands on her hips. "What do you think? Too much?"

"No. You look beautiful." Karalynn shifted the baby and moved Eliza to the other breast. The dress was seamless, sculpting to Sabrina's amazing figure, and it was glossy like wet paint. Sabrina had the type of body of which most little girls dreamed. Karalynn had to look away, as though she stared at the sun too long. Needing to change the subject, she asked, "Do you fly much? Your wings must be very useful."

"They are handy when I'm off-world. Flying really speeds up travel." Sabrina cocked her head and asked, "Have you ever been off world?"

"I have only gone to one other world. Maj and I went there on our honeymoon. It's where I heard the name, Angelina. 'Such a beautiful name,' I thought. So when our daughter was born, I gave her that name."

Karalynn wiped a bit of egg off Angelina's face. "Every man would propose to you if you weren't dominant. That includes the married ones looking for more wives."

"Oh … um … thank you. I'm not really interested in romance. I tried speed dating, but it wasn't for me."

"What's speed dating?"

Sabrina shrugged; "Courtship I suppose. You get a 3-minute date with 50 men. I found it a bit abrupt."

"To say the least," Karalynn agreed. "Maj and I grew up together. His parents lived in the house next to ours. We had a secret passageway through the basement to see one another. It used to be an old coal shoot."

"Is the wagon ready?" asked Sabrina.

"Yes. I gave a neighbor boy a copper to take a message to a wagon rental service. The driver is waiting outside."

Sabrina exited the house and locked the door behind her. Wheels made of metal, heavy-duty leaf springs, a rectangular cabin, a step up in the back, and steel doors worth of a bank vault, the armored wagon awaited her. A key waited in the padlock – yet she was reluctant: the entire rig was made of rust, ready to collapse into a pile of dust at any moment. However, the banking district was only across the wall, and she had no time to hire another rig.

The driver squinted and stared at her with his one good eye. His weathered face was marked by deep furrows and covered with a scraggly gray beard. A shabby hat covered his thinning hair, and his brown coat faded long ago, appearing to be made of rust much like the wagon. The man held a whip and chomped on a cigar butt. Surveying her wings, he cocked his head and furrowed his brows; "Are you an impersonator?"

She had no idea what he was talking about; nor did she care. "No. We need to get going. I have lots of business to conduct, and daylight is burning."

He grunted and replied, "Do you need help loading the wagon ma'am?"

"No, I'll be fine. Why don't you go inside and have a cup of coffee? I'll take care of loading the wagon." Sabrina held the door open, and the driver shuffled past her. His stiff legs caused him to wobble as he entered the house. He was just about to ask another question when she closed the door on him.

After removing the padlock, she opened the carriage doors. The interior floor was scarred and soiled, a layer of fine dirt covering the metal floor. The rear of the wagon faced a corner and hid her from pedestrians on the street. Sabrina stood before a gray stonewall. The blocks were gray, square, and covered with black lichen. She held out her arms and chanted, "Agor efore santuario menol." Eng. – open the way to the inner sanctum.

The stone surface rippled like water; waves spread out from a central point and formed an ever-growing pattern. Brilliant light beamed through the center of these ripples, and it spread out in a swirling vortex of light

133

and darkness. A large round opening appeared as though cut through the stone.

A set of steps led down into a chamber, the likes of which stagger the imagination. Golden light bathed the cathedral ceilings in a luminescent glow, and the immense size stretched beyond the reach of sight; a palace could fit inside it with room to spare. Massive pillars launched to the arched ceiling, and secret enchantments, cut into the pillars, blazed with blue light, as if on fire. The magical spells recognized her and allowed her to enter.

Broad, curving steps led down to the main vault, and an expansive floor stretched out from them. As far as the eye could see, great piles of gold coins, bejeweled cups, gems, necklaces, furnishings, sculptures, and other precious items filled the interior space, some on shelves and some in great heaping piles. It was a great sea of treasure, unmatched, beyond human avarice; and any man would sell his soul to have it, but she was a dragon, and dragons jealously guard treasure.

She strolled down the steps to the main floor. Steel armor covered the bleached white bones of a gaping corpse, and another man – still wearing wore a wizard's robes and clutching a shattered staff – lay with his back up against a golden candelabrum; his empty eyes gazing out at the endless horizon of treasure. Sabrina placed many spells and bound many spirits to the sanctum to ward off intruders. The spirits stripped the flesh off the man like a pack of ravenous piranha, and the wizard was struck down by Hades fire, burning his flesh to ash and trapping his anguished soul in a white marble amphora.

Eight large treasure chests lay at the foot of the stairs, recent additions, gleaned from her trips off-world, not yet sorted. The vault was vast, but even so, it was filling up fast; and it was time to do a bit of spring cleaning. The bank seemed like a safe place to store some of the excess.

She flipped open two lids and inspected the contents. The treasure was all there; not a single gold coin was missing, and she knew every piece. Although the mammoth chamber might have seemed haphazard, she remembered the location and quantity of every item, and she would reap a bloody vengeance if any of it was missing.

Now Maiges are far stronger than men, elves, or dwarves combined, and they have been known to toss automobiles around like toys. Stretching out her arms, grabbing the handles on either side of the chest, she picked up the treasure chest and carried it up the stairs. She placed it inside the wagon, more concerned with soiling her gown than the chest's weight. Thirteen more chests followed, and the leaf springs gave way, causing it to sit upon the frame; this resulted in the team of horses to crane their necks, trying to see what was happening behind the wagon.

Sabrina stood at the top of the stairs and examined her treasure vault, making a mental note to return and clean up the skeletons. She faced the aperture, and chanting in Elvish, she summoned the gray mist; a moment later, it began to coalesce and form a thick curtain. The curtain turned to stone: the portal was gone.

Portals were a fast, efficient, and flexible way to travel; however, it took great power to create them, and they caused distortions in the eleventh dimension. This meant that there were some restrictions: First, she could not open one near a rhunite vein or near fissionable power source. Second, other wizards or those magically endowed would sense the portal. Third, and most important, she could open one only where she had traveled. Alternate dimensions were an exception, but the portal opened at random, requiring her to explore the new world.

She closed the wagon door just as the front door opened. The driver sipped a cup of coffee. "Thank you much, madam. I appreciate it." He came to a sudden stop and eyed his wagon. He scratched his scruffy beard and narrowed his eyes; "What do we have here?"

"I loaded the wagon. I hope your team is up to it. The load is quite heavy."

"They'll get it done." The man climbed up to his seat and picked up the whip. The wagon crushed the street, as though it would sink into the ground at any moment.

Drawn by a dappled white horse, a landau carriage rounded the corner of the street; it had four wheels, a convertible white leather top, and two swinging half-doors. The driver rode on a high seat; always exposed to the elements, he could quickly become wet and cold. Sabrina signaled him, and he slowed. "Are you for hire?"

"Yes Ma'am." He narrowed his eyes and studied her wings. But he said nothing. If she wanted to wear fake wings, what concern was it of his?

"Good. I will need your services for the entire day." The man scampered down from his perch. He opened the door and placed a footstool on the ground. She raised her skirt and climbed into the carriage, her wings trailing behind her like a train. After the driver had closed the door, she said, "I want to go to the banking district. I have to make a deposit."

"Any particular bank, ma'am?"

"Hinner and Slough," she replied. She then said to the armored wagon driver, "Follow us to the bank."

"Yes, ma'am," the wagon driver, Chauncey, replied.

People stopped to stare at the procession, sensing the historic nature of the event but unsure why; the carriages passed by these spectators at a leisurely pace. Sabrina kept her eyes fixed straight ahead, enjoying the brisk morning air and the rhythmic tapping of horse hooves on cobblestone. She missed that sound on Earth. The endless race of automobiles left her emotionally numb.

The road wound its way down a steep hill and passed into the mercantile district. Fresh baked bread and pastries tempted her stomach. She signaled a boy, and he ran over to the carriage with a butter roll in hand, then jumping onto the running board. After paying him, he scurried back to the bakery.

A butcher, clad in a bloody apron, paused from chopping raw meat to stare at them, and several street vendors joined him. Wagons filled with flowers, roasted chestnuts, and fresh fish waited to service her. Sabrina called over a man and handed him a list Karalynn complied. "Take these supplies to the indicated address."

"Yes, ma'am," he replied. The other merchants huddled around him, reading the list, searching for items they could fill. It was a long list, the neighborhood ladies were coming over for dinner, and there would be plenty of business for all.

When the carriage reached the bottom of the hill and the boundary of the district, they came upon an inner city dividing wall. An access road traced the inside perimeter, the dividing wall rose up above the house tops. Guards, standing sentry duty upon the wall, watched the commotion with fascination; but their captain then shooed them away, making them return to their posts. The day watch would come soon: they had to be alert.

As they passed through the archway, Sabrina gazed up at the wall. Smooth stones soared and formed an arch; at the apex, she saw several slots. A series of steel doors filled the slots in the upper arch, and once lowered formed baffles; they isolated the city districts, impeding the progress of invaders.

When they passed beyond the dividing of the wall, a rainbow of flowers greeted them, and rough cobblestone gave way to smooth slate. The carriage ceased bouncing, as its wheels rolled over the smooth road. They passed by fountains, jetting crystal water into the air, and the water splashed into the pools of clear blue water; the fountains lay before sumptuous entryways and regal buildings worthy of a king. The facades of these buildings were opulent, adorned with banking heroes, figures carved in white marble and placed upon pedestals; they also depicted scenes of old: men battling sea monsters, mermaids luring sailors, and fish bursting forth from waters.

Tall walls, bastions, jutting towers dazzled the eye. Flagpoles topped their conical red roofs. Banners of blue and gold, red and gold, and black and silver depicted crests of the various banks and industries, financial empires that were constantly at war with one another.

Sabrina inspected her gown, and she felt a flutter in her stomach – worsted wool, merino wool, linen; black, gray, brown, navy blue; single breasted, double breasted, long line, short line; wearing white cotton, silk, and nylon shirts – not a single woman wore a gown. Many of the women were clad in black leather pencil skirts and double-breasted waistcoats.

Then she spotted the slave choker necklaces circling the women's necks, and she knew. These women were slaves, the property of the bank. Her heart grew heavy and angry ruminations consumed her thoughts. Slavery was everywhere.

The business people stopped to stare at her; she avoided eye contact, not wishing to interact with zealous salesmen. She perused the various street level shops; shoe repair, executive accessories, clothiers, jewelry stores, and even luggage stores abounded, an upscale shopping district. The many guards made it clear that the poor and working class people were not invited.

Black marble pillars supported a white peaked roof. The morning light gleamed off the gold, silver, and bronze; carved figures of horses, men, and scales; a magnificent portico atop a broad set of stairs. Hinner and Slough stood above its peers. The bank greeted her like an old friend, yet even this storied institution had changed. The bank's crest emblazoned the front of the silver oval setting of the choker. Black comprised the standard employee's uniform: black leather pencil skirt, double-breasted leather jackets, stockings, and knee-high black boots. A scarlet silk blouse, having a T-shirt neckline, was the one splash of color. A throng of these involuntary employees hurried in and out of the portico and between the buildings, each on an important mission for the bank.

A man approached the carriage. A uniform both princely and gilded – including a black cap, a red uniform having gold lapels, and black boots – marked a special services officer, reminding her of a 17th-century officer. The officer waited while the driver placed a footstool and opened the carriage door. He then extended a gloved hand and assisted Sabrina as she exited the carriage. "How may I assist you today?"

"I wish to make a deposit in my bank account. The carriage behind us is carrying several chests, and I want them brought into the bank. Um … you will require assistance to lift them." She handed the officer the key to the armored wagon's lock.

Chauncey rubbed his belly and pondered the situation. He and the wagon driver formed a line behind the bank employee, appearing very comical as they walked in lockstep, marching to the rear of the wagon. The officer inserted the key and opened the heavy iron locks. The wagon driver opened the doors, and then he scratched his head. Eight trunks filled the interior vault. They were made of steel with large metal straps wrapped around them. Out of idle curiosity, the wagon driver grabbed a handle and pulled on a trunk; the trunk stayed in place, and the driver jerked forward.

The officer rubbed his chin and then waved for more bank associates to join him. "We're going to need help – lots of it." Scores of men dressed in lesser ranking uniforms hurried to assist them.

The Great Gate

"What the hell?" Pondering the situation, the armored car driver lit a pipe and puffed upon it. "How did she load them by herself. I've never seen a Sabrina impersonator do that."

"Don't be daft, man. There is no way one woman could have loaded them. They weigh a ton or more. She must have had help." Chauncey gave the trunk handle a tug, just to make sure it was heavy.

"If there was a crew loading them, I didn't see them. She was alone I tell you." He grumbled under his breath as he returned to his perch atop the wagon.

Five dwarves charged down the steps and gathered behind the wagon. Two of them grabbed a chest and heaved. They raised it only a little bit and then dropped it again. The senior dwarf ordered, "Get a hoist. We'll break our backs on these trunks."

A dwarf hurried down the steps toward Sabrina. His hair was speckled black, and a neatly trimmed goatee capped his chin. He wore an olive green, double-breasted coat, the hem extending down to his thighs, a cotton cream color shirt, and trousers with a crease so sharp it could cut. It seemed strange attire for a dwarf, yet dwarfs were the best bankers.

He bowed and removed his hat. "I'm sorry to keep you waiting. My name is Martin Stewart. I am an Executive Vice President of Executive Accounts with Hinner and Slough. Whom do I have the pleasure of addressing."

"I am Overlord Sabrina March."

The dwarf stared at her in wonder. "I-I-I am sorry Mistress Sabrina. It's been so long. I thought you were an impersonator. There are many such persons these days. We had no idea that you returned. How may I be of assistance?"

140

Sabrina glanced back at the crowd of men behind the second wagon. "I wish to make a deposit. You still accept gold and gems don't you?"

"Yes, we do. How much should we expect?" He joined her watching the dwarves struggle, and a cart with equipped with a hoist exited from a garage. After they had wheeled it up the street, they inserted a boom and set the strap. Two dwarves worked the crank and lifted a single trunk from the back of the armored wagon.

"I have 14 trunks." She turned to Martin. "Your name is a bit unusual for a dwarf."

"My adopted father gave it to me. He told me it was a noble name from the ancient homelands of his people. He traveled 500 miles to Asgard from one of a chain of islands to the south. Perhaps you've heard of them. They are called 'The British Isles'?"

"Yes. I have heard of them," Sabrina replied.

Martin said, "Over 300 years ago, history recorded that a fleet of British ships departed their new southern colonies on Earth. They encountered a severe storm: then they passed through a winking gate … Of course winking gates are lesser gates that open and close in a random fashion. They may open one time in a thousand years or once a day. Most winking gates, however, open about once every five to ten years, and they may stay a few minutes to a few days; one never knows —"

Sabrina listened patiently as Martin began an in-depth lecture on gates, but her patience began to grow thin. Sabrina said, "Yes. I'm aware of how gates work. I travel through them all the time."

"Yes, of course. Anyway, terrified and unsure of what transpired, they sailed for home. Of course, they had no way of knowing they were on a new planet, Eden. They searched for years before abandoning the search and settled in a new homeland."

Sabrina said, "May we go inside the bank? I'm getting rather hot in this sun."

"Of course," Martin said. The pair began the long ascent. As they neared the top pillars, she saw a pair of golden lions that were three times the size of a man and seated upon rectangular blocks; they loomed on either side of the stairs, great beasts ready to devour an intruder. She gazed up at the pillars holding up the towering roof high overhead and felt like a small child.

At their approach, four guards, clad in silver breastplates and black uniforms, snapped to attention. They stood guard before a pair of colossal doors. Made of bronze and standing 10 meters (32 ft) high, embossed with scenes upon four large panels, scenes on Eden and some on Earth, counter weights assisting its operation, the doors opened at their approach.

Black marble spreading out before them, vaulted ceilings soaring overhead; sunlight passing through crystal panes; rainbows splashing across the floors, everywhere the smell of old money, they entered the great bank. Teller booths, made of mahogany, having steel bars providing security, lined the walls, and a female employee waited, ready to service them.

More uniformed men stood at attention around the plaza. Their polished breastplates and helmets gleamed like chrome. Sabers hung from some of the men's sides, while the others held long halberds. Sabrina became accustomed to Earth, and on Earth, banks hired elderly men to act as security guards; these guards wore shabby blue uniforms and carried service revolvers. Eden had no firearms: rhunite caused gunpowder to explode.

––––––

This world had vast and varied deposits of Rhunite. Rhunite was called "White Matter," a mineralogical cousin to dark matter. As such, it emitted a broad spectrum of electromagnetic radiation, inducing powerful currents in loose pieces of steel, welding them together. The Rhunite axioms stated, "Anything that can explode will explode, and anything that can be jammed will jam." This made gunpowder, petroleum distillates, and many chemical compounds unstable and illegal to transport. The broad-spectrum radio emissions interfered with all radio transmissions, reducing them to static.

Therefore, weapons technology advanced differently from Earth. Many of the swords, axes, and halberds were enhanced by Magic. Magic to the citizens of one world was "the scientific study of Rhunite and its effect upon organic and inorganic materials" to other. It imbued the weapons with a variety of powers, some amplified telepathy and others telekinesis.

———

Martin Stewart escorted Sabrina across the lobby, and Sabrina noted all of the female tellers. They stood behind a long row of wood and steel cashier's cages. She expected him to stop at any one of the desks. However, he led her to a private office within the heart of the bank. As they entered the outer office, he said to his human secretary, Tamara, "I will be engaged for the next hour."

She jumped to her feet and said, "Yes sir. Would you care for some tea?"

"Yes, that would be fine." Martin opened his private office door and gestured with his outstretched arm. Sabrina passed him by and entered a spacious office that was dominated by a large mahogany desk; behind it, the exterior wall appeared to be made of glass. Blood red leather chairs, a matching loveseat, and a coffee table sat upon an expensive area rug. "Please have a seat. Tamara will return with tea. I wish to personally attend to your deposit."

The Great Gate

Martin passed Tamara by in the hallway. He saw her carrying a silver tea set and sugar cookies upon a beautiful bone plate. "If she's hungry, order her something from the kitchen; bill my account; get her anything she wants." He scurried away and then called back, "Within reason of course."

The vice president, Riyeb Hahir, approached a wood paneled wall; a wooden door blended into the wall, hiding it from view. He retrieved a keychain from his right hip and sorted through it until he found the correct one. The key resembled those from long ago and fit into a large keyhole. A twist of the mechanism caused a click of the lock. He pushed open the door and entered.

The rooms located behind the main hall were for employees. Humans and dwarves rushed from desk to desk. The clack of typewriters caused a noisy din; they them scanned these documents into oracle scrolls. A dwarf, appearing older than time, was seated behind a towering desk. He supervised the organized chaos. Upon seeing Martin, he asked, "Rumor has it a large deposit is incoming."

"So it would seem," Martin replied. "Shelgar, you should come with me. I need you to gauge what resources are required to evaluate it."

"Yes, sir." The pudgy old dwarf climbed down from his perch. His round body was unaccustomed to standing up straight. He groaned and stretched his back. Martin rushed by Shelgar's station, and the old dwarf chased after him.

The pair exited the accounting department and navigated a series of hallways. They were long and narrow. Checkered white and black tiles adorned the floor, and medium brown wood paneling covered the walls. Brass light fixtures provided ample illumination. They strode down a long, straight corridor and then made a sharp left. This passage opened into a wide service elevator. They were magnetic linear induction based as opposed to electrical.

144

Three trunks were already on the floor. Chauncey squatted before one of the trunks. "Ah good, you're here. I have to say that I'm dying to know what's in them."

Martin stood close with his hands clasped behind his back. "Don't keep us waiting. Open them!"

Riyeb squeezed a release mechanism on the front of the trunk. The magnetic lock released and the latch popped open. He peeled back the lid and rested it open wide. The dwarves formed a circled around the trunk, eyes opened wide, and a collective gasp hung on their lips.

Branigan said, "That's got to be all the gold in the world."

An enormous pile of gold and platinum coins bulged up from the chest. Mixed in with it were diamonds (white, blue, and red), rubies, emeralds, and garnets. Martin picked up a small leather satchel and opened the drawstring. A pile of sparkling diamonds spilled out onto his hand. He held one up to the light. "18 karats," he speculated. "Flawless perfection, they are exquisite."

Shelgar picked up a gold coin and held it in his palm. "A full ounce, perhaps two," he speculated. He then inspected the relief image upon the gold coin, and he saw an eagle on one side; and on the opposite side was a woman holding a torch. "What is 'The United States of America'?"

"Overlord Sabrina travels to other worlds all the time. It is some far off land no doubt," Martin said. He returned the diamonds to the pouch and picked up a coin. Three more trunk lids opened wide for them. They were equally filled with treasure.

Martin spotted a large fire diamond. He set down the contents of his hands and walked over to it. The diamond was circular and flat, about the size of a large coin. Fire danced in the heart of the diamond, mesmerizing, brimming with power. No larger fire diamond existed in the entire world: it alone was worth a king's ransom. More gems spilled haphazardly within the chest. Then he spotted a hint of blue, and his heart leaped, and he struggled to breathe. Reaching into the pile with trembling hands, he pulled out a blue fire diamond. He knew of only one in existence, and it was in the king's crown.

"Get everyone, get everyone down here NOW!"

Something happened, which had not occured in years: Shelgar ran. His bulbous old body bounded as he charged through the hallway, disappearing from sight. "Assistance, we require assistance," he shouted. "Everyone report to the counting floor."

Men and woman flooded into the room, everyone eager to discover the source of the commotion, and then the treasure transfixed them. The elevator door opened before them. Two more carts rolled into the room transporting trunks. "I need scales, gemologists, and guards." The treasure mesmerized the staff. "Hurry!"

The trance broke, and the staff launched into action. Accordion wooden doors opened wide; scales, tools, and counting tables rolled into the room. Guards entered the room, weapons in hand, and took up stations around the chest.

Meanwhile, back in the office, Sabrina forced a smiled and took a sip of tea. Tamara stared at Sabrina as if she was a new exhibit in the zoo. "Would you like another sugar cookie?" She held out the plate. "I just made them."

"No thank you. Do you think Mr. Stewart will be back soon? I was hoping to discuss some financial matters with him."

"I'm sure he will be along shortly." The girl's face contorted, and she chewed on her lower lip. "I could make breakfast."

146

"No thank you. I'm really not hungry." Sabrina leaned back and stared out the window, as though waiting in the doctor's office without a magazine to pass the time. A heavy sigh escaped her lips, and she jostled her wings, adjusting how they draped across the floor. She pondered the city; like termites building a mound, or moles creating a tunnel, human architecture followed a familiar pattern.

She endured Tamara's rambling discourse on cheese. Starting with cheddar, she covered the entire gamut of product available; her family owned a dairy farm. She even offered a few recipes. However, Sabrina's patience grew thin, and the fourth recipe for cheese bread pushed her to the edge. She was about to leave when Martin entered the room. He appeared haggard, rather than the dwarf of unflappable bearing she met earlier.

"I apologize for keeping you waiting. We are counting and valuing your deposit." He sat across from her on a loveseat, and Martin collected his thoughts. "It's an astonishing amount of treasure. Just one of the chests has more gold than the king's treasury. If I may be so bold, how did you obtain them?"

"I traveled to many worlds and fought in many battles. If one wins, then the rewards are considerable: I win a lot." Such explanations usually satiated curious minds.

"Ah I see," said Martin.

Looking at the door for someone's arrival, Martin moved to the edge of his chair. Sabrina said, "I have adopted an elva as my vamon sister. Her name is Karalynn Arndis." She retrieved a note from her purse. "That reminds me. I was supposed to pick up the deed for this property. I paid off the mortgage last night."

Martin took the folded paper from her. He read it and raised an eyebrow. "This is for one of our competitors. However, I will have one of our people retrieve the deed."

Martin handed the receipt to Tamara, and she jogged from the room as fast as a pencil skirt permitted. Sabrina said, "You employ a great many human females. Is it because of the slave choker necklaces and how they control the marked person?"

"Oh yes, but they are not slaves, no, not slaves. We do buy them on the slave market, but we set them free. We employ only free people. If they agree to serve us for 100 years, we will provide all their needs and pay them a small stipend. It's good for them, and their integrity is vouchsafed by the necklace. Many free people participate too. The bank profits from these marked men and women, and they profit from the employment. In fact, employees wore choker necklaces enjoyed greater privileges and faster promotions than their un-necklaced counterparts. Many of our marked employees are in top positions within the bank."

Sabrina was relieved to hear that not every person marked by a necklace was a slave. Many people might consider it an abuse of power, but it fell far short of slavery, which was important. "Are these marked employees married?"

"Most of them," Martin replied. "Once the men and women see the employee bearing our crest, they know he or she is a good earner." The statement offended Sabrina on many levels, but lecturing a bank representative on morality was useless. Sensing Sabrina's disapproval, Martin added, "Even after marriage and the exchanging of rings, their choker remains."

"Yes, but they should wear magic rings, indicating that they are free. Otherwise, people will get the wrong impression." Sabrina replied.

"I do you see your point," Martin replied. He rubbed his chin and stared at the floor, deep in thought. "Our bank has never participated in direct slave commerce. We could change it from necklaces to rings. Would I have your support in the matter if I approached The Board of Directors?"

"You would have my full support, and my participation if needed." Sabrina changed the subject. "I assume that the bank has investment opportunities? I have been off world for a while."

"We have a large number of investments." Martin opened a desk drawer and retrieved a stack of prospectuses. After putting on a pair of reading glasses, he sorted through them and handed them to Sabrina. "Many of the best investments are located in the Tressler Industrial District near the Cataract Foot Hills, and business opportunities within Elysium are always a sound investment. Tressler manufactures everything from dinnerware to magical talismans. If you're interested in the textile industry, most of them are located in the Roth District. That is in the center-north Midway City. They produce excellent materials and garments for export. We ship them down to the fashion capital Nouvelle Maison in the land of Liberté …."

She asked, "I can't actually travel to all these various regions. Do they have any offices here?"

"Yes they do; Solva is a major exporting city. I have to admit that recent legislation passed by Parliament baffles me. They centralized the port authority in Androth, citing the port of Kheltal (Ice City) to the north as our main import conduit. Madness." He stood up from his chair and circled around his desk. The dwarf used a wooden pointer and stood before a large relief map. "Androth, of course, is to the north in what comprises 'The Wolf's Head Peninsula.'"

She interrupted him, "I am aware of the Wolf Head Peninsula's geography and its history."

The Great Gate

———

A single king ruled Asgard, and then he fathered two sons by two different wives, Asher and Ari; and they were born at the same time on the stroke of midnight, 1146 CE. When they reached 30 years of age, 1176 CE, the king decided to retire and declared that he was giving both his sons a living inheritance. The law demanded that the eldest son inherited the kingdom, but both were born at the same moment. What to do? One of the Lords proposed a solution: divide the kingdom; he drew a horizontal line across the middle of Asgard, dividing the Wolf's Maw and Regal Mountains. Ari took the kingdom to the north and established his capital city in Parglos, meaning ever snow or snow without end, located on the Razell Mountain. Asher assumed control of the current capital city, Kurio, meaning "glorious home," located on the King's Mountain.

Ari hated his inheritance. The North lacked the robust economy of the southern kingdom, and it had fewer natural resources, other than timber and fruit. The two kings and their families despised one another and were on the verge of war. Parliament resolved their conflict and assumed control of the both kingdoms, leaving the two brothers as figureheads.

———

"Yes. Ahem, of course, their ports are blocked by ice for a significant part of the year. Nearly all shipping takes place on the Merchant River. I really can't understand why they would put such a minor port in charge of such a vital part of our economy. I have trouble understanding parliament these days …."

Sabrina's attention began to fade. Martin launched into a lengthy discussion of fiscal policy. "… I have never understood slavery. We dwarves have nothing like it."

"And yet I have been informed that dwarves subcontract to mining companies that own many slaves," Sabrina replied.

"Very true, hypocrisy on our part," he said. "My brothers won't own slaves, but they do hire people in distress; and they make these laborers work to remit the debt. After a successful term of service, these involuntary servants are free. The system started off with the best of intentions. Society needed to protect itself."

"Human government has always had 'pressed service' for debt remission or criminal prosecution. We can't put every petty thief in prison nor can we execute them. Working off their debt to society makes the most sense. Debtor remission was reserved for the most egregious cases. Everything is different now. Now every a pauper or an orphan is captured and sold on the open market. To make matters worse, many husbands outright sell their wives as slaves. It's shameful. Once again we have the Androth to thank for that travesty; their ministers pressed for the change 53 years ago. The Southern Elite Party opposes them, and they have pushed for reform."

"Reform?" asked Sabrina.

"They wanted to set limits for pressed service and restrict slave use. Androth rejected it and tabled the discussion. The more I study humans, the less I understand them; sometimes they act like daemia."

Chapter 14

Sabrina exited the bank's internal access to the subway system. After 200 years of labor, it was finally completed. The Black Castle always had a subway, but the city lacked the funds to install such a system. She was glad to see progress. Making a sharp left turn, she passed under the angular plate glass structure and descended into the depths of the city.

Her high heels echoed off the tiled structure. It had to be noisy during rush hour and peak shopping, yet it was durable and easily cleaned; she appreciated such qualities. Only when she reached the bottom did she see the elevators.

Pausing before a subway system map, she studied the layout of the city. The most exclusive shopping district was near the waterfront at new shopping malls. Wishing to change her out of her gown and into regular clothes, she made her way to one of the many tubes.

She strolled along a long platform that wrapped around a massive bronze pipe; these tubes accommodated drum shape cars, easily seating 16 people. While they were functional, they were also beautifully adorned artistic details, harkening to Earth's Victorian Era. When a shuttle whisked through the tube, it caused a sudden rush of air that flapped the side slit of her gown, exposing her black nylon sheathed legs. She strolled under a series of arched pillars that supported the immense weight of the city. Tan tiles covered the floors while brown and gold tiles adorned the arches. Light beamed overhead through synthetic skylights, conveying a sense of the outdoors.

The doors automatically slid aside and allowed riders to enter and exit. A man and a woman gave her curious stares but dismissed her with a shrug. Sabrina walked down the center aisle, the rubber mat providing a sure grip surface, and toward the rear of the car. She passed by several rows and settled upon the furthest seats in the back. The bench style seat allowed her to drape her wings over the seat cushion and dusted the floor behind it.

A bell chimed, and the doors slid shut; a sense of excitement welled up within Sabrina: she loved trying new things. A round light glowed next to the "Ashton Station" on the map and a blue map detailed the car's course. The car lurched and pushed her back into the seat. Looking through the windows, she saw the flash of lights and cross connecting tubes. One light extinguished and was replaced by the next, tracing her journey through Solva.

The subway car slowed and stopped at the midway station. When the doors slid open, a pair of teens entered, chatting about a concert. They sat near the door, ensuring easy exit upon reaching their destination. They did not see Sabrina, or they did not care; for the moment they departed the station, they embraced, and their lips crushed together in a passionate exchange.

When they approached the Mercantile Street, the young lovers hastily fixed their clothes and exited the car. He grabbed her, and she wiggled a little; but she allowed his hand to remain. He turned toward her and whispered something in her ear; she giggled, wrapped her arms around his neck, and kissed him.

A crowd of travelers entered the shuttle and took a seat. The doors closed, and she was off again. She wondered if people could see her. After 88 years, a "hello, nice to see you again," was warranted and even welcomed. Yet they ignored her and sat facing the front of the car.

When the shuttle stopped at the "Quay Shopping Mall," she rose to her feet and traversed the aisle. One young officer leered at her bottom, light dancing off her scarlet gown. Upon exiting the car, she turned and faced the riders, and no one acknowledged her.

The Great Gate

Most peculiar. Perhaps everyone has forgotten me. Rather than upset Sabrina, the notion pleased her. Public adulation came with a price: the loss of privacy, which she greatly valued.

She crossed the platform and scaled the steps to the upper landing. Upon reaching the top, she observed a rather spacious shopping plaza. She leaned over the railing and looked down three levels. Endless shops lined the walkways and cavities below her. The subtle din of conversations rose up from the bottom level.

This required further inspection.

A bank of four glass elevators formed a column in the center of the mall. Sabrina pressed the button, and the doors slid open before her. She pressed the button for the lowest level and watched the mall pass by outside the car.

When the doors slid open, she heard, "… Thank you all for attending the festivities today," a woman's voice echoed out of a public address system. Sabrina heard the applause of several hundred patrons in the food court, many of them dining upon a quick meal. She circled around the elevators and saw an audience seated before a stage at the bottom of the amphitheater.

A young officer held a corded microphone; radio frequency equipment had too much static. She was beautiful, 21-years-old perhaps, and certainly Nordic. She wore a smart dress uniform that had a tailored cut: gold buttons, piping that formed a V-pattern, adorning a navy waist jacket, and a black leather banded collar and leather cuffs added a dash of style. With it, she wore black, stretch leather tights.

The girl's flaxen hair dusted her shoulder, but Sabrina could still make out the girl's rank as that of a "Nobel Patrician Commander," a warrior family with lesser noble heritage and honorary rank in the royal army. However, the girl was without service ribbons and medals, untested in battle, a paper tiger. The public and private armies accumulated many such persons during times of peace.

"I see we have another last minute contestant. Don't keep us waiting. Come on down." Sabrina looked behind her and then at the commander. "Yes, we mean you. Let's give her some encouragement with a round of applause." The crowd turned toward her and began to clap.

Sabrina shrugged and descended the red carpet, which stretched in a straight line down the center aisle. It was then that she observed women dressed in strange costumes: all had wings, many made of dyed chicken feathers, combined with uniforms, cocktail dresses, and regal attire – a few wore Overlord Uniforms.

When she reached the bottom, the commander said, "Come on up so we can get a good look at you." The audience clapped for her. Sabrina ascended the stairs, making sure not to trip on her gown and crossed the stage. "You really went all out on your costume," the young officer said, her nose scrunched up in delight. "I love it. You look like you're ready for a grand ball at the palace."

Sabrina's shoulder's sagged, and her lips formed a pout. "Well, I saw the gown when I was shopping, and I thought it would be fun to wear. Women's fashion trends are so hard to master. Each world has its subtle nuances."

"A story too," the officer said. "What do you think, everyone?" A round of applause thundered. "I believe that we have our three finalists." She turned to Sabrina and said, "You stand over here." Sabrina took her place in the center of the stage. Two other women soon joined her. One wore a black lace gown and the other a uniform.

"What do you think of contestant number one?" The crowd applauded. They repeated the process for the uniform clad, chubby girl and then Sabrina. The officer turned to the girl in the lacy gown. "I think we have a winner." She picked up a bouquet of roses and a trophy; after handing them to her, she gave the girl a friendly shoulder hug. The chubby girl won second place, and Sabrina won third.

Sabrina held a small trophy with the golden figure of a winged woman standing upon it. It read "Second Place Runner Up." It took her a minute, but then Sabrina realized it was for a costume contest.

"If only those wings could actually work, eh girls?" The chubby girl moved her shoulders and wiggled her fake wings. The girl in the lace gown used her hands to spread her wings, and the audience then all looked to Sabrina. She used her powerful but hidden muscles to spread her wings, and they shot out to the far edges of the stage, five times the length of her body; the tips raised high in the air. Her eyes ignited, radiating blue fire.

The young officer gasped and lowered the microphone; a gasp came from the crowds. Now Sabrina chose to be a brunette with tanned skin, blue eyes, and black feathers, but it was not her natural coloring. She released this shading and assumed her true nature. Her hair and feathers turned to gold; her skin turned porcelain, and her eyes gleamed like polished sapphires. "Thank you for the trophy. It is my first costume contest, but this isn't a costume."

"Overlord March," the officer gasped, dropped down to one knee, and bowed her head. The crowd and the other contestants copied her and knelt before Sabrina. She was after all an adopted member of the royal family: a political ploy by the king to gain popularity with the people.

Seeing that the audience lingered on their knees, she said, "You may rise."

Tears streamed down the officer's cheeks. She rushed across the stage and stood before Sabrina. "I am so sorry Mistress – I had no idea you

156

returned – You were gone so long – No one knew – Oh my god, I can't believe this."

Sabrina wiped the tears from the girl's cheeks; "What's your name?"

"Nobel Patrician Commander Marla Thorsby," she replied. "I always imagined meeting you but not like this. I worked hard to honor you. We all have. I can't believe this. It is so humiliating."

"It's all right," Sabrina said. "I may be wildly overdressed, but I still have my sense of humor."

Marla covered her face with her hands and calmed her mind. "We are all glad that you have returned. How may I be of assistance to you, Overlord Sabrina?"

"We need to go to the Black Castle and meet with the general staff."

After summoning the carriage, which took a while to arrive, they rode through downtown traffic as though a part of some grand procession. Business people crowded the sidewalks, eager to see the source of the commotion, pausing to watch them pass, gawking at Sabrina and discovering her return.

She draped her wings on the seat beside her, absorbing that which was Solva: towers gleaming, bridges spanning, walkways weaving, shuttles passing; men congregating, women gossiping, children playing; meat cooking, almonds roasting, sauces simmering; horses neighing, sheep bleating, chicken clucking, dogs barking; banners advertising, V-billboards playing, signs announcing, merchants shouting, and merchandise teasing – it dizzied the senses and satiated her soul.

Police officers struggled to restrain the swelling throng, which flowed out of every doorway, and they forced the crowd to remain upon the sidewalks. Trolley cars passed, and their bells clanged, demanding a clear channel; an endless river of wagons, E-cars, and E-trucks flowed through the streets. It all added to the bedlam. The police efforts were in vain: the crowd gathered like a storm, threatening to burst forth from its constraints at any moment, desperate to see the hero of old, the mythical Elven Maige, Overlord Sabrina March.

She returned!

A silver shuttle passed overhead, racing through the eye-towers; its silver skin, needle-like tip, and slim body reminded her of a throwing bullet. These ultramodern transports shot through the city to destinations near and far, each on an important task, some ferrying passengers and others carrying cargo. There were so many, far more than she remembered.

They made a sharp right turn onto Market Street. Two squads of mounted patrol officers joined the procession. One led the carriage, and the other followed. The sweet perfume of apple and cherry blossoms hung in the air. Petals from the trees swirled about in the wind and danced all around her.

When they reached the foot of Prospect Hill, the wagon angled in a steep pitch. Five story businesses covered the hill, pressing shoulder to shoulder on both sides of the street. Off in the distance, she heard the clarion ring of bells calling the faithful to worship. The sweet chimes that echoed off the buildings harkened back to simpler days.

Solva greeted Sabrina like an old friend. It was one of the first cities settled when men stepped foot onto these shores over 3,000 years ago. In three millennia, it had been sacked by various armies, most of them daemia or haugr, but a few human armies took the city. However, the grandeur endured, and the Black Castle never fell. Never!

Sabrina exhaled the tension, pressure within her mind that took root long ago; she suffered with it for so long that it became normal. She was home. As they traveled through the first gate, the gray fortification cut off the clear blue skies and marked her passage onto the fortress grounds. They passed underneath the boundary wall that marked the first area, rode 100 meters to the right, and made a left through the second gate. Overhead, she saw the pointed staves of the portcullis. At the warning trumpet, the portcullis would crash down in the entrance; three gates then barred the entrance.

Four sentries stood to watch at the four corners of the gate. They clutched long halberds, topped with cutting axes and spikes. Of course, the halberd was only effective against mounted riders. They also wore daggers and swords for close quarter combat. They wore black and white uniforms and insignias designating them as city protectors; no one would miss them in a crowd; of course, that was the point. They acted as both security for the castle and auxiliary police for the city.

The sharp clack of the horse hooves echoed off the walls of the final gate. The carriage circled around the drive and came to a stop. Chauncey dismounted and placed a footstool on the ground, opening a half-door. Sabrina rose to her feet and wiggled her wings, straightening her feathers. As she exited the cab, she said, "I will be in the castle quite a while, but I would like you to wait for me."

"Yes ma'am," he said.

"Marla, don't dawdle," Sabrina said. Marla scurried out of the carriage and chased after Sabrina. Catching up with the legendary woman, she matched her pace and walked lockstep as they ascended the seven steps to the front portal. The moment they stepped through the doorway, a powerful wind propelled her through it, as though shoved by a giant's hand. Sabrina glided her hand over the bare stone, and like the Eagle's Nest, the ancient fortress greeted her with joy, celebrating her return. The foyer was stark and unappealing, by design, but it was better than a five-star hotel to Sabrina. The battlements, the guards, and the strength allowed her to breathe, and finally, to relax.

The Great Gate

A massive pillar dominated the room, but it served a purpose beyond mere structural support: arrow loops, cut into the pillar, allowed defenders to fire from relative safety. She moved close to the pillar and peered through a slot. The interior space was well lit and spartanly furnished. A lever jutted out from the wall, naked in its placement. It closed and opened the main door. Two levers in the center of the floor controlled two smaller doors, which allowed entry into the castle.

These dual secondary entryways led into a vast hall. A network of corridors funneled entrants into a cavernous hall, a chamber large enough to be considered an arena. Rafters, composed of ironwood, stretched across the ceiling in a high arc. Like its name, ironwood was as strong as steel and twice as flexible, immune to fire damage.

She passed through the great hall, memories thick in the air around her. She remembered the great warrior Roman; his laugh boomed through the corridor and echoed off the wall. It seemed only yesterday that Maillol whispered in Sabrina's ear, declaring her love for Bruin; a daemia's arrow took her life a week later. Bruin held her in his arms, weeping, as her life's blood flowed from a mortal wound. The universe can be cruel; Bruin lived a long life and survived all of his many battles. He died in his bed, an old man with a broken heart. Yet the story continued – death is a solitary journey, and one we all must take. Bruin left his life and ventured to the next.

Maillol stood on her tiptoes, scanning the eternal shores, and when she saw Bruin burst up from the water, she rushed into the water and leap into his arms, never more to be parted.

Chapter 15

One of the 12 wonders of the ancient world; the 'Black Castle' stood defiant against all who opposed it. The builders cleaved the top off Prospect Mountain and built the Black Castle upon it. The black monolithic structure loomed over the city, frowning upon the ways of men.

Sabrina first met the castle on the day of its birth, 750 CE (common era), and loved the castle from afar until 1223 CE. Upon a business trip to Solva, she heard that the castle had fallen into disrepair. The city fathers would have demolished it; however, blackening stone was a process perfected by the dwarves: impossible to destroy once created. Sabrina placed a strategic bid, hiding her eagerness, and purchased the castle at an unheard of low price. She spent a fortune to restore the castle because of what it represented: freedom, honor, duty, and service; rare qualities in any age.

Three separate curtain walls circled the castle, having gates offset to their corresponding gates in the other walls. This slowed invaders and caused high casualties before they reached the castle. The defenders would then find themselves facing burning oil; it flowed through channels cut into the surrounding paved surfaces, creating a firewall. Meanwhile, the defenders used ballista crossbows to fire heavy ordinance, rhunite tipped arrows that released powerful blasts of energy upon impact; and they used catapults to fire rhunite infused globes, exploding upon impact.

It surprised many visitors to find flowers, arrayed in a color explosion, before them. The flowerbeds hid a tactical advantage. Beyond aesthetical beauty, they divided avenues and courtyards; these planters blocked the path of siege weapons, and their slanted exterior walls prevented enemies from hiding behind them.

The Great Gate

The building grew larger as one traveled up the mountain, as though a giant might reside within it. The sights and sounds of the city were swallowed up by the structure. Once upon a time, the entire city's population fit inside the immense interior, long before urban sprawl, skyscrapers, and international commerce. Modern interior lighting replaced oil lamps, yet soot stains remained upon the walls. The new lighting was manufactured in Asgard, a product of the modern industrial base. Certain combinations of metals were modified and infused with Rhunite. They were then suspended in resin and juxtaposed next to other, interactive materials. Thus the lights continued without fault and supplied their own power.

A balcony stood high above the main door, the first of many defenses; known as a "murder hole," one could pour down boiling oil upon attackers; parapets lined the upper walls, and crenellations provided archers with ample firing positions; round towers, bastions, stood at every point of the buildings star.

In the center of this base stood a castle; it alone was formidable, but when combined with the base, impregnable. It too had walls, parapets, and fortifications that were lethal. Even if the outer walls were taken, even if the main structure fell, the central castle would never fall.

There were two types of access points to the base complex: First; roof dormers allowed freight and personnel to access the room, and elevators hung over the walls. All cargo traveled up and onto the roof; it then passed down through the dormer and was dispersed around the base compound. In case of attack, the elevators were retracted and moved out of the way.

Second, there were 12 main doors on walls perpendicular to the approach. The architects used a fortune in an exotic wolfram blend to cast the doors; measuring 8 meters in diameter and 3 meters thick; the circular doors bore the black dragon crest. The doors rolled on an encasement track, which used the blackened structure for support, and the perpendicular angle precluded the use of battering rams. Ten thousand daemia with battering rams the size of mountains could not break through the doors.

The footprint of the base structure of the castle covered 10 square city blocks, or 100 total blocks, and its shape was that of a 20-point star; the cattycorner walls allowed defenders cross-cover lines of fire. Its internal structure included segments that formed a labyrinth; thus it could mean a mile or more to any given destination, and many inhabitants cursed the architects as they wandered through the complex. As a result, a pneumatic tube system was adapted and then upgraded for modern use.

A full castle – including curtain walls, defenses, and living quarters – sat on top and in the middle of the base. Its high walls and towering spires were visible for 100 miles. Although many of the walls were black, many were normal; this allowed the internal structure some flexibility, allowing for limited building modifications. The castle was a complete city that included residential areas, retail shops, shopping malls, theaters, residences, offices, schools, academies, universities, manufacturing, military facilities, and governmental agencies.

The structure was a labyrinth worthy of an ant maze. While other floor plans might have made sense and eased traffic, the castle was constructed with other concerns in mind; every dead-end, corridor, bulkhead, and arrow loop increased the castles defensibility. Whether inside or out, the castle was an implacable barrier, a place where foes met death.

The main castle was officially reserved for guild officers and their families. However, certain powerful royals and influential members of parliament modified its charter and purchased residences within the castle. In a time of national crises, this ownership afforded nobles a place to hide. Sabrina permitted it because it tied their fate to that of the castle, thus aiding her efforts. It also generated quite a bit of revenue, which benefitted the operation. Units located within the castle were traded on the stock exchange and could be optioned, thus creating a thriving secondary market.

The lower structures, the many areas without a view, were occupied by members in good standing, officers near the top and enlisted near the bottom. This included barracks, various shops, a transit system, and such the like. Pledges and the enlisted languished in the tombs, a nickname given to the lowest levels.

There are three sublevels below the residential levels. The weapon forges, armories, and laboratories were located on the first sublevel. Supplies were kept in the second sublevel. They ranged from food to iron ore. The third level held treasure and other sensitive materials. Dumbwaiters and elevators allowed easy cargo movement from floor to floor.

Of course, the entire facility had gravity-impelled water pumped through it and running toilets. It was one of the building's luxuries, a necessity that Sabrina insisted upon. It also contained subway tubes, or "The Tube."

Chapter 16

When Sabrina exited the elevator, the conversations in the lobby slowed and came to a halt. Sabrina could read the confusion on the officer's faces. Who gave permission for a Sabrina impersonator to enter headquarters? It was only when a senior officer shouted, "ATTENTION!" that they understood the situation. All of the men and women snapped to attention, thumping their fists on their chest.

"As you were," Sabrina replied. The officers relaxed and pretended to resume their assigned tasks. However, they stole furtive glances at Sabrina as she strode through the complex. Sabrina hated these moments; she was on stage giving a performance, but a performance without a script.

News spread through the compound at a rate no technology could match. Officers, chiefs of staff down to lowly second lieutenants, poured out of every hallway and office. The junior staff lingered near the walls while the generals all vied to greet her. One might only have a single opportunity to encounter a living legend.

A Hispanic man emerged from the crowd and stood with the poise of nobility. Curly raven black tresses framed his delicate features. His eyes were dark as coal, and his skin was mocha colored. His "cat's eyes" fixed on Sabrina like a predator, and his lips curled into a slight sneer.

He wore the traditional uniform of the Spanish court; black trousers, white tunic, and a blood red jacket with gold braid and double-breasted brass buttons. Everything about his appearance was deliberate and presented with great care; such was the ways of the Spain Royal Court. Both personal attire and decorations were precise as calculus and showed true breeding.

The Great Gate

"I am Alexander Carlos Garcia Vargas de Nuevo Seville of the Españoles Corte Real."

Sabrina noticed the gold medallion draped over Alexander's black necktie. The medallion bore the crest of the Spanish Royal Court and indicated that he was a member in good standing. Moreover, it stated that he was a wizard and one of considerable accomplishment.

She raised an eyebrow and further considered this man. He was a slender man with a diminutive frame. Furthermore, he was attractive, perhaps a bit too pretty for a man. Apprehension hidden behind his polished façade was apparent, and she decided to put him at ease. "I am very pleased to meet you, and I apologize for not greeting you in person. We are very honored by your presence, and I am grateful for your service in defense of all free people."

Alexander faltered for a second, taken off guard by her generous reception. "It is no problem. I too know of travel difficulties. It was a long and arduous trip from Spain."

Like many of the humans in this world, their ancestors were transplants from Earth, passing through the "Winking Eye," an unstable portal. Spain, on the planet Eden, was an island nation located in the far southern waters near the equator. Wealthy nobles and patrons of the court often displayed their affluence by their lack of skin pigment. Alexander's swarthy complexion testified that his family had fallen on hard times, so they sent him out, one of their many children, to seek his fortune.

"Thank you for your gracious consideration," Sabrina said and clasped Alexander's hands. "I am so happy to have you here with us. Please let me know if there is anything I can do to assist you."

"Well, yes of course … I mean, thank you very much." As on Earth, tensions between Spanish and English speaking nations often flared into a hot-tempered rivalry. Then general staff and local nobles gave Spaniards a lukewarm reception.

Sabrina intertwined her arm with Alexander and walked with him. "I am sure that we will become superb friends. I would love to have dinner with you some evening. We can discuss our mutual travel woes and share a bottle of wine. I have some 500-year-old vintages in my personal cellar. I will have a secretary set up the time and have the page deliver you a personal invitation."

"I welcome the opportunity. I will have my maid put it on my calendar." He performed a slight blow and then kissed Sabrina's right hand. "I will wait with great expectancy until that time."

General Longstreet stepped forward; "Warlord Halfter is waiting in his study to greet you."

"Excellent, I'll go and meet him right away." As an afterthought, she said, "I would like Marla Thorsby assigned as my adjutant. Please have her calendar cleared, and her service made available to me." Marla's eyes went wide and all the blood drained from her face. When she opened her mouth to object, a single stern glance by General Longstreet silenced her.

"I will see to it," the general said.

Sabrina entered a private office, and a guard closed the doors. "I was informed that you had returned," said Warlord Edward Halfter. "It's been a very long time."

Sabrina walked toward him, her heels clicking on the black marble floor. The afternoon light beamed in through tall windows and made her glow with an ethereal radiance. She was more beautiful than he remembered.

The Great Gate

"I remember you," she said. "You were a Commander Warrior serving in 'Highland Legionnaires' based in the city of Phillipa in the eastern provinces, on the Hargal Wall."

"So I was," he said with a nod. They grasped each other's forearm by way of greeting. "But that was a long time ago. I moved to Central Command in Agama 32 years ago. It seems like ages ago. There are many times I wished to be back with my comrades in arms and grip my sword once again."

"And yet you have risen above your brothers in arms," Sabrina said. "Warlord of The Realm, it is a title of which few can claim."

"A title which should have been granted you," Edward said. "I remember the day when you saved the realm. Although it was noon, the skies were dark as night and the rain formed rivers at our feet. We stood in the breach, in the middle of the damaged section of the Hargal wall; our enemies outnumbered us by three times. You stood before us with a sword and shield, and you raised your battle cry. They came down upon us like crashing waves of the sea. We fought for six days without rest." He closed his eyes and drew in a breath through his nostrils. "I remember you standing upon a high stone. You shouted, 'I am weary of this rabble. I will take their heads and soak the ground with their blood.' You charged at them. When we saw you sprinting at them and slicing through them, we screamed in madness and burst forth from the wall. The terrified daemia fled before us, and most of them fell by our swords before they reached the Cordon Forest."

Edward opened his eyes. "You should have been made 'Supreme Warlord of The Realm.' Instead, Parliament admonished you. Damn them. Damn them to hell! The cowards criticized and accused you of risking the survival of the republic! Imbeciles, you saved the republic. Even a fool could see that."

Sabrina nodded and took a seat in a Roman style chair. "They saw it all too clearly, and they feared it. I had grown too popular, too rich, and too powerful. If I uttered a single word of contempt for the government, the people would have overthrown the government and made me queen."

"Would that have been so bad?" asked Edward. "Parliament is full of hucksters, deceivers, and narcissists. Noble Lords pander for bribes in the full light of day and fail to blush if observed. They pervert the law and overthrow our traditions for a few coins. The king has used his veto more in the past ten years than in the previous thousand. Every law handed down is worse than the one before it."

"Vacuous journalists sing whatever song their master's desire. They destroy the reputation and lives of good men and women. All the while, they hide behind the cloak of journalistic freedom and integrity. Proud, haughty, and without compassion, they shatter lives and puff up inferior men. These men, I know them well. Their eyes are ever searching for ways to do evil; the good is as unknown to them as daylight is to vermin."

Edward shook his head and returned his gaze to her. "Your return is most timely, welcome news to weary ears. I will dispatch a messenger to the king at once. He has long desired to hear of your return."

"Of course, you should inform the king." Sabrina crossed her legs and smoothed her gown. "However, our actions must be circumspect. We are behind enemy lines, and our foes are all about us. Some evil has stretched out its hand across these lands," she paused deep in thought, "for purposes I cannot yet fully discern. We can see the devastation all about us; slavery, oppression, and violence. Yet these are all distractions. They hid the darkness's real aim; we must use stealth and cunning to uncover it."

Chapter 17

Sabrina met with the chiefs of staff, The Royal Esquire for Solva, a host of royal dignitaries, and endless officials; the high-ranking officials gave long-winded speeches, and the mayor presented her with the key to the city. Even though she was an eternal being, the constant chaos wore out Sabrina. She lay back in the carriage and soaked in the last few rays of sunshine. The setting sun bathed the steel and glass city in fiery red light.

Her carriage rounded a corner, leaving the commercial district behind, and continued toward home. Birds winged their way to nests, and retail shops closed their doors. The horse trotted by street vendors closing up their wagons and rolling up awnings. Tavern doors lay opened wide, the sounds of music and laughter spilling out into the street. Through the tavern windows, she saw men and women hoisting mugs filled with ale.

The carriage came to a stop before Karalynn's home. The driver scurried down from his perch. He grabbed a footstool and opened the door. Sabrina arose and stepped down from the cab. "Will you need my services tomorrow?"

She considered the question and studied his eager eyes. The carriage needed repair, and the horses needed new shoes. Chauncey's long tail jacket was a bit shabby and his shoes scuffed. It had been too long since he had a steady source of income. She was not a charity, but she required transportation. "What is your name again?"

"Chauncey Timmons," he replied. "My father was British, and my mother was Nordic."

"Very well Chauncey. Consider yourself engaged. Where do you live, should I require your services at night?"

He pointed to his left to where Columbia Street ended. "I'm just one block over to the left on Barrel Lane. You can't miss my house. It's the red brick house with green shutters. I have a small stable attached for my horses and cab. Just call upon me, I'll be there night or day."

"Mr. Stewart is engaging a solicitor for me. Call upon him and arrange for a weekly draw of 770 Kronars a week. I need you here ready and waiting in the morning when the sun rises."

"Yes, ma'am." The man tipped his hat and picked up his stool. "I'll be here at first light."

"I'm not sure when I will be leaving in the morning, but I would like your services to be available."

"Yes ma'am," he said with a grin.

Weariness overshadowed Sabrina like a blanket. A day of walking in high heels caused her feet to ache, and the leering glances left her perpetually self-conscious. She wanted a hot meal, a tall glass of red wine, and pajamas. Culturally acceptable or not, she was going to wear fleece and settle down for the evening.

The carriage rolled away from behind her. "Night, ma'am," Timmons called out in a loud voice and tipped his hat. She rubbed her sides, bottom, and other aching body parts. She was too tired and too sore to care who saw her. The city grew still and night engulfed the street; rhunite powered street lamps illuminated and cast long shadows along the cobblestone street. She wandered toward the door of her new home as night took hold of the city; a sudden gust of frigid wind, a reminder of winter, urged her to seek out shelter from the chilly night air. The windows of her new home glowed brightly with warm, inviting light. She grasped the brass handle and opened the door.

"I am … ssssoooo … tired," she said and entered the house. A hundred female faces stared back at her. They filled up the living room and spilled out into the foyer. She passed through the mob, not understanding why they were in her home.

"I gathered the widows together just as you asked." Karalynn moved through a group of ladies and approached Sabrina. "We've been waiting for several hours."

"If you have some business, I'd like to be about it." A matriarch with gray hair stood to her feet, her face weathered by centuries of hard living. Her clothing was a study in black and gray, a widow no doubt. She had a look of steel in her eyes, smelted in the furnace of affliction. "I have a family to attend."

"And your name is?"

"Gertrude," she replied.

"I will be brief, Gertrude. It is my intent to pay all of the unpaid bounties for the loss of your loved ones. Martin Stewart with 'Hinner and Slough' is engaging a solicitor to service my account. He is the one who distributes the funds. Please have any documentation ready for submission."

"Why would you pay the bounty? It's not your responsibility." Gertrude crossed her arms and raised her chin. However, Sabrina looked past the woman's gruff exterior and saw a tender-hearted woman beneath it.

"I am a warrior of the light, and the death of a fellow warrior diminishes the light. With the loss of each light, the world grows a little bit darker. That affects me. These brave men and women, our honored dead, have the right to expect our gratitude, and I am honor-bound to take care of their families. I just returned to Eden from my travels abroad, and I am pleased that the Black Dragon Guild still conducts itself with honor."

"I know the warrior's creed as well as anyone. I understand your rhetoric but not your intent. Why are you paying the bounty? What is in it for you?" Gertrude stood defiantly and glared at Sabrina.

"Everywhere I look both men and women are deaf. Can't you hear the roars of your ancestors? Can't you see their hands are clenched with rage? Judgment is on their lips, and a sword is in their hand." Sabrina trembled with rage.

"Old men linger around money tables, counting out their profits. All the while, their spoiled whelps send brave men off to die. Why? It is so that they can brag over tankards of ale. They are drunken children, who linger before mirrors, and fall in love with their own reflection. Meanwhile, they deny the families of the dead justice and their bounty. Widows and children end up in the streets. The courts seize their homes and lands. Then these same depraved children buy the property of their slain troops at a discount. What could cause such depravity, you ask me? It is because their fathers will not increase their allowances. I tell you the truth. Unless this generation acts, the entire land will be drenched with blood. Its homes will burn, and its walls will crumble."

She began to pace before them. "Men and women of honor will rise up and demand justice. Slavery has come to the free lands. Is this the Western Isles? Do we now eat our own and crush the poor? When any man or woman suffers, it is my business! I will be damned if I see the families of brave men suffer such injustice. So yes, I will pay off every unpaid bounty in the city. I will hire men of war, and we will set this country aright. 'The House of the Black Dragon' will arise and take back the free lands from these interlopers."

Applause broke out from the assembled crowd; Gertrude faltered, and she uncrossed her arms, studying the faces of the other women. Karalynn said, "Tell everyone that the royal family is going to put the kingdom aright. The widow's bounties will be paid."

173

Sabrina sighed. "I'm sorry for losing my temper. Greedy men have worn me thing. They justify their crimes with moral pretense. Let me ask you a question: what is so fascinating about my bottom? Some of the men stared at it for a full hour. The other men could not take their eyes off my chest." All of the women let out a chuckle. "Then there are the double entendres. 'May I service you, madam?' 'Why don't we go into the back so I can show you my wares?' Then there is my personal favorite, 'Would you like sample my sweet sausage?'" Laughter filled the home.

A woman called out from the back. "I've been to see him. It is really quite a disappointment. It's only a mini-sausage." Roars of laughter broke out.

When the room quieted, Sabrina said, "I have returned to the Black Castle and taken command; we will address these matters with the King and Parliament. If you or your men need employment, go to the castle. I'll have the contractors interview them. I spoke with the mayor's aid, and we are making much-needed improvements to the newest city walls. If anyone feels they are due more than the bounty, have them see Gertrude. I will trust her judgment in the matter." She then said to the astonished woman, "All I ask is that you be fair but firm."

"I will see to it," Gertrude replied.

She turned to Karalynn; "Do we have any refreshments? I'm ravenous."

"Yes we do," Karalynn chirped. She hurried into the kitchen with three other women following after her. They returned carrying platters of food. It took them all day to prepare. "The napkins and silverware are over on the small table. We'll be back with beverages in just a minute."

"I'm famished." She approached the food, and the other ladies joined her. There were deviled eggs, cheese balls, spicy nuts, and cold cuts on crackers. She loaded down a plate with food. Karalynn set down a glass

174

punch bowl filled with a red fruit punch. She poured a glass and handed it to Sabrina.

Sabrina passed through a gauntlet of women. She sat in a cappuccino leather covered chair. A minute later, Marla, her aid, appeared and sat down beside her. "I just had to come and speak with you. I have always wanted to be a warrior my entire life. That's why I joined your guild. Everyone knows female warriors can earn the same promotions and respect as men."

Sabrina chewed a mouthful of food and glanced at Marla. She swallowed and crossed her legs. "So tell me about yourself. We will be working together; I should get to know you." She took a final bite of her hors d'oeuvre and a sip of punch.

Marla took a deep breath and said, "My father and brothers were all warriors. They died in honorable combat, despite 'The Proud Lion's' claims. I fought with my family since I was a little girl. I am proficient with the bow and the ax. My skills with a sword are excellent."

"Hand to hand?"

"I know some moves. I fought my brothers all the time. Little Jerrod and I were equals."

"Little Jerrod is dead too?"

"No. He joined the merchant fleet long ago. He had some terrible fights with my father. Jerrod preferred the company of men. My dad used to yell at him. 'If you like to sleep with men so much, you should take the serum and become a woman.' Jerrod did just that. He … she has long curly blonde hair, gorgeous blue eyes, and she is so beautiful. She is so beautiful that it makes men uncomfortable —"

The Great Gate

"Oh I see," was all Sabrina could manage to interject. The girl kept prattling on regarding her family. It was a constant litany of their royal lineage and battle achievements. She recounted each death and the pain it caused; their graves were located a few miles outside the city. Without a certificate of honorable death, their ashes were rejected for interment with those of the hallowed dead, and the Royal Crypts are close to Magmara; no one can venture there or risk joining the dead. Sabrina felt compassion for the young woman. The image of a young girl alone and crying in the wilderness appeared in her mind.

When Marla paused to take a breath, Sabrina interjected, "You are both beautiful and intelligent. You could have been a successful businesswoman, or you could have married and lived a prosperous life. Yet you chose to serve your country and do without the trappings of wealth. That impressed me, and that is why I wanted you to serve as my adjutant."

"Thank you," she squealed. The girl threw her arms around Sabrina and hugged her. Sabrina wondered whether she inducted a new warrior or adopted a new daughter. Marla remembered herself and then saluted Sabrina with her right fist pressed to her chest.

Wailing cries came from the upstairs. Karalynn excused herself. She entered the foyer and scaled the stairs to the second level. The joyful women wept and laughed about their great relief. Sabrina managed to excuse herself from the gregarious women. She followed Karalynn to the third-floor nursery.

Karalynn pinned a new diaper in place and then tickled Eliza's stomach. Sabrina lingered in the doorway. In part, she did not want to disturb the touching scene; the other part was from the stench of the soiled diaper. In many ways, mothers were still a mystery to her. They always loved, always hoped, and always endured for the love a child. No matter the cost, a mother would pay it to keep her baby safe.

She set the baby in a high chair and opened a jar of food. With the exception of the butcher, baker, and wine merchant, she made all the food by hand. It consumed much of her time. Karalynn said, "Oh hi, I didn't see you."

Sabrina entered the room; the lingering smell offended her nostrils. Karalynn fed a spoonful of fruit mash into Eliza's mouth, and the baby waved her arms in joy at the treat; Sabrina moved a wooden chair up beside them. How hard it was for mothers. They spent a lifetime of love and effort to raise a child only to have a daemia blade take it.

She caressed Eliza's cheek: no silk could have been softer. The baby's brown eyes gazed up at Sabrina as she savored another mouthful of food. Half went down her throat, and the other half oozed out her mouth; either way, she squealed with delight.

"The ladies seemed happy," Sabrina commented.

"They are thrilled. All of those women and their children are packed into two houses. Gertrude has eight families living with her. There's barely a place to walk at night. During the day, they usher all the children out of the house. It makes for bedlam in the streets." Karalynn wiped the baby's mouth.

"And increased crime no doubt," Sabrina replied.

"That too," Karalynn said. "It's hard to blame them. They are hungry most of the day and clothed in rags. The children of the rich stroll around in velour and complain about everything." She closed the jar and wiped her hands. "I once saw the cutest little girl with big brown eyes. She was dressed in a patched little dress. She walked up to a boy wearing a new suit; he was eating a treat from a local bakery, and she was so hungry that she asked for a bite. The boy threw the treat onto the ground; 'Now you can have it.' I was sickened when the girl picked it up and ate it."

Such stories abounded. Orphans scurried through the sewers and rooftop like rats. They lingered in every alleyway and shadow. They stole silk handkerchiefs and heavy purses, and if caught, the orphanages resembled prisons.

The revelers soon caught up with Sabrina and Karalynn. Karalynn put the baby down in her crib and tucked her in for the night. Abby, her other daughter, was out-growing the baby phase. The young mother enjoyed caring for babies.

Sabrina ushered the guests to the main floor once again. The festivities continued late into the evening. When the midnight chimes struck, Sabrina ushered the last of their guests to the front door. As Marla passed by, Sabrina said, "Report to my home at sunrise and wear your armor tomorrow. I want to review Guild troop strengths and logistical deployment plans."

"Yes, Mistress," Marla replied. The term "Master" or "Mistress" was used by the Army to recognize a superior officer. The Navy, however, used a unisex address of "Sir" when addressing a superior officer. This was because many of the commissioned officers on the ship carried Master or Mistress as a part of their title.

Sabrina added, "And bring your weapons. I want to gauge your fighting skills."

"Yes, Mistress." Marla quickened her pace and caught up with the departing women. The street lamps silhouetted the women in black and created a checkerboard glow on the cobblestone streets.

The last guest to leave, Tuva, was a short, cherub woman with rosy cheeks and piles of curls. She stroked Eliza's cheek and gushed over the baby. Sabrina said to Karalynn, "I forgot to mention it to you earlier. I stopped by the registrar's office and procured a 'Writ of Vamon.' All you have to do is sign it."

Tuva read the piece of paper and then studied Karalynn's face. "She's taking me as her adopted sister," Karalynn said. Tuva nodded but remained silent. "It's just a legal arrangement," Karalynn insisted. Tuva replied with a vigorous nod. "Sabrina wants to protect the children and me."

"I completely understand," Tuva giggled.

It was surprising how fast a short, plump woman could run. Her heels clicked on the pavers like a typewriter. When she caught up with the other women, they heard hushed conversations. Karalynn huffed and pouted.

"They would have found out sooner or later," Sabrina said.

"I would have preferred later." Karalynn frowned, turned on her heels, and marched away from the door. Sabrina closed the door and braced herself. Karalynn blurted, "They didn't have to know. We could have just told them that we were sharing the house. A lot of single women do that."

Sabrina strolled into the room. "Why? Are you embarrassed that I'm taking care of you?" Karalynn pouted and remained silent. "Many people are declared vamon by the royal family. There is no shame in it. To be honest, I fail to see why more widows don't seek out a vamon relationship. It saves taxes and prevents male heirs from usurping their property."

Karalynn set Eliza down in a bassinet and chewed her lower lip. A male heir could claim her, her children, and the home as property. His wife and children would assume dominant roles within the house. She knew of a few cases where the male heir forced the widow and her children out into the street.

Karalynn smoothed her dress with a rustle and sat down on a sofa chair. She clasped her hands in her lap and stared at the floor. "You're right. I'm safe; my children are safe. All of my fears vanished the moment you arrived. I owe you everything."

"It's been a long day." Sabrina slouched on the sofa and leaned her head back. "My feet hurt, and my thong is chafing. It's a great irony: the better looking the clothes, the more uncomfortable they feel. If only fleece wear was sexy, I'd be in heaven."

"Can I borrow some of your clothes?" asked Sabrina. Then she pressed her chin against her chest and considered her bulging breasts. "Never mind, I don't think we are the same size. I have some of my old clothes in the castle. We can have them shipped here. Those will do until I can purchase new ones. I'll just wear my armor for the time being."

Chapter 18

The magnetic eyelet stanchions snapped passed the window in shuttered fashion, causing the lights reflected off the Merchant River to strobe, blinking like stars in a field of black. The sound of rushing air over the shuttle's skin, the droning of the circulation vents, and the snores of sleeping passengers mixed together. Joash gazed upon his sleeping son and smiled. Kelvin snuggled with Cody as though she was a stuffed animal, and he dreamed of bold adventures.

Joash met Fiona's eyes. The farm, the animals, and the life they built receded into the backwaters of their minds. How? They were going to spend the rest of their lives in that home. They would grow old in the comfort of one another's arms, their hearts warmed by the sight of their grandchildren. How could it all be gone?

Fiona's eyes turned toward her baby, Kelvin. She looked at him with a mother's heart and boundless love. The city and the world were frightening places; young men lived with the illusion of immortality and invulnerability: delusions that led them into danger. When Peter died, it almost destroyed her. Losing Kelvin would be beyond her ability to bear.

Solva arose like an island of light in a black sea. Its gleaming towers rose up into the heights, and office lights marked the face like freckles. A bell dinged, and then a synthetic voice announced, "We will arrive in Solva Central Station in 15 minutes. Please return your chairs to their upright position, and stay seated until the shuttle comes to a full and complete stop. Thank you for choosing 'Gryphon Travel.'"

The cabin lights arose and roused the weary travelers. Kelvin sat upright and rubbed his eyes; leaning forward, he craned his neck to see out the window. He asked the universal question: "Are we there?"

The Great Gate

Joash rubbed his aching neck and said, "We will be there in a few minutes. Put your seat up." Cody yawned and then stretched; she drew up a gray wool blanket and hid from the chilled air blowing from the vents. When she saw the lights of the city, she shrank back and cringed. It was the first time Joash had ever seen the girl afraid.

"Don't worry. I spoke with your parents, and you will be staying with us. Solva is a big city, so stay close to us: don't go wandering off on your own."

"Okay," Cody replied with a yawn and a nod.

Kelvin strained against his seatbelt. The city rose up before him in all its panoramic glory; even in the middle of the night one could see crowded restaurants, alfresco dining upon terraces; V-billboards played fantastic advertisements; one was a commercial of a crystal bottle containing golden perfume, "Angel Essence." Another V-billboard advertised a musical drama and showed dancers upon a stage. Kelvin often wished it otherwise, but broadcast transmissions were impossible because rhunite caused massive ionization of the atmosphere and static on all radio frequencies.

Joash rubbed his face and snorted. What was the point in having defensive walls if the shuttles passed right over them? He argued against any breach in the defensive walls that put the city at risk, but his warnings went unheeded. The Hargal Wall, the eastern boundary that demarked the eastern border, blocked out the nightmarish creatures. It did its job too well and lulled the people into a false sense of security.

As they passed over the outer wall of the ninth ward, Kelvin tried to release his seat buckle. "Stay seated until we are stopped. I've seen these things stop suddenly and send people flying." Kelvin settled down and heeded his father's advice. Joash gazed through the window and down at the streets below them. A wagon, appearing the size of a child's toy, traveled a lonely road, and it passed underneath streetlights, lights that cast scalloped segments of light on the darkened street.

They shot over a series of office buildings and then between a pair of hotels. Kelvin saw a man and woman dining upon a private balcony. The man leaned upon the green railing with his left elbow, and the woman primped her blonde hair, laughing at a humorous anecdote. Cody noticed the woman's gown. The silk gown draped over her womanly curves, appearing both beautiful and expensive. She imagined herself wearing such a gown, dining with a handsome man, his hanging upon her every word.

Once past the hotels, the city opened up before them. Buildings, lights, music, parties, dining, operas, billboards, advertisements, and such the like spread out below them. The passengers all broke into conversation at once and filled the car's interior with the noisy din of conversations; travelers pointed at various points of interest and discussed their plans. Even Fiona lost herself in the excitement.

The shuttle slowed and slid into the station. The rings diverted it to platform 26A in the Solva Central Station. The shuttle stopped beside a platform, and the doors opened, allowing the city air to tease their noses. The passengers released their seatbelts and sprang to their feet. Businessmen snatched satchels from the overhead bins and pressed toward the exit; Fiona wrestled with her bag, which was jammed into the bin; but Joash came to her aid, jerking it out with a slight tug. They joined the line and walked single file toward the exit. An attendant stood near the exit and thanked them for using Gryphon Travel.

The roar of footsteps, shouts, and station calls echoed off the tiled walls. Kelvin and Cody stayed close to Joash. They gaped at the dizzying assortment of faces and the hustling mob. A short ways away, a group of dwarfs adjusted their load upon a rolling car and argued with a platform attendant. Just beyond them, a couple shared a passionate embrace, a last kiss goodbye. Cody imagined herself in a lover's embrace and chewed upon a fingernail, turning the points of her shoes toward one another.

"Let's go. We need to get checked into the hotel. It's not too far from here. I hate hailing a cab on a Friday evening," Joash said.

"What about our bags?" asked Fiona. "Shouldn't we collect them?"

"No. I paid a little extra to have them delivered to our hotel. That's another trick. It costs a few kronars, but it saves so much time." When he started to stride away, his family chased after him. Travelers parted and formed a corridor for them; there was no need to tell them that this was a warrior. It was more than his immense size; a confident swagger in his step, roll of his shoulders, eyes always searching for threats, and self-confidence declared that he was a man to be reckoned with. Kelvin fought off the urge to hold his father's hand; he was too old for that, but part of him longed to do it just the same.

Joash charged down a long set of stairs and led Fiona by the hand. She appeared as lost as the children. She was a small town girl, a fact he loved about her. They exited the terminal and passed around the queue of taxi carriages and e-cars. Several drivers tried to lure them with the promise of a cheap fair. Such drivers typically took the long route to gouge consumers.

"We're staying at the Randolph Hotel. It's a bit pricey, but you have to pay if you are going to stay near the terminal. It is only for the night though. We will report into the Black Dragon Guild tomorrow. They will provide us with accommodations." They hurried through the street amid the shouts of angry drivers. From Joash's point of view, it was as though he never left. The feel of the city soaked into his body like a healing balm.

The doorman stood in the open entry way and tipped his cap. They passed by him and found themselves in the center of a lobby. Ivory marble stretched out before them, and the hotel's trademark was inlaid in the center of the floor. If focused the eye across the expansive lobby and declared you were in the presence of the great. Fiona gaped in astonishment at the crystal chandeliers; there were so many of them as if every craftsman in Asgard labored upon them. She wondered how long it took and how hard it must be to clean them.

Joash crossed the lobby, ignoring the opulent furnishings and the busy restaurant. When they stood before the desk, the clerk offered them a smile and wondered if these simple peasant folk were lost. "My name is Jeremy. How may I be of assistance?"

"We have a reservation." Joash handed the clerk a reservation ticket. "It's for one night."

The clerk searched for the reservation number into his oracle scroll. "I have your reservation right here, Mr. Faroe. I have a luxury suite with two bedrooms. Your bags will be placed in the delivery port when they arrive." He handed them a pair of keys to the room. "Is there anything else I can assist you with?"

"Could you have a meal sent up to the room? It's late, and I just want to dine in the room …." He ordered a family meal from off the menu and a bottle of wine.

Now Kelvin had never been in an elevator, and he was quite excited about it. He felt a slight tug and then nothing; the numerical display began to change. It was all so … disappointing. He imagined rockets shooting him up to the highest floor. It was all so mundane.

When the elevator doors opened, Joash read the placard on the opposite wall and turned left toward their rooms. Red carpet covered the floors, and brass lamps provided subdued illumination. The hallways were quiet, for the most part. A few loud conversations managed to penetrate the doors, but what they were saying was unintelligible. Their suite was at the far end of the 48th floor. He inserted the key and entered the room.

They passed through a short hallway and found themselves in a small living room. Cream color sofas lay in a circle around a glass plate coffee table. A bowl of fresh fruit sat upon the pass-through counter to the kitchenette. "We'll be in the master suite, and you kids will be in the spare room."

Cody and Kelvin often slept over at one another's house. When they were children, Fiona often put Kelvin to bed at night only to find Cody and Kelvin sharing a bed in the morning. She had some reservations about it. However, they were best friends, and there was no keeping them apart.

Kelvin and Cody trudged into the bedroom. Kelvin collapsed onto the bed and closed his eyes. "Do you want to shower first or second?" asked Cody.

Kelvin opened one eye. "Neither. I'll shower in the morning."

"You stink. I'm not sleeping in the same bed with you." She crossed her arms and set her chin.

"Fine," he groaned. "I'll shower first. You take too long."

When Kelvin trudged into the bathroom, Cody rushed over to the sliding glass doors. She stepped onto the balcony, and a warm wind rushed over her. It carried the tantalizing aroma of cooking food. Her stomach rumbled, suggesting that she seek out sustenance, but she lounged and imbibed the wonder of it all – it was all as she imagined it would be. She almost had to pinch herself to make sure it was not a dream, yet anxiety lingered in the background. She wondered about academy life; would the other pledges like her? Was she smart enough for school work? What about combat? Did she have what it takes to fight? She drew up her knees to her chest and rested her chin upon them.

"All done," Kelvin shouted. He dumped a wet towel on the floor next to the bed. He fished around in his bag and found a clean pair of underwear. He stepped out onto the balcony still naked.

Cody glanced up at him and rolled her eyes. "Put on your underpants. We're in the city now. You can't go around naked like you did at the creek."

"Yeah, okay," he mumbled. He stepped into his shorts and drew them up around his waist. He then pulled over a chair and sat down next to Cody. "It's all so … big. I knew it was big, but not this big." Glass and steel towers abounded and extended into the murky depths of night. A dirigible glided overhead, the propellers silently slicing through the air. "I'm going to ride in one of those someday."

"What do you suppose it will be like?" asked Cody.

"Fun, I guess. I heard that they are pretty safe," Kelvin replied.

"Not the airship, our new school. We were home schooled. Being in a classroom is different; teachers can be mean. My friend Jenny told me so."

"Eh, my brothers all wrote me about it. It's hard, but you can do it. You're really smart, and you're good with a bow. Everyone makes it through school, but not everyone gets to pledge the guild. Many of the kids go on to trades and stuff like that. The worst is that you'll become a lawyer or something," he replied.

"You think I should become a lawyer?" asked Cody.

"Nah, I'm just saying. You are going to be fine. You have what it takes. Nobody in our town is smarter than you. You memorized that entire fishing poem. What do you call it?"

"The Sea of Tranquility?" asked Cody.

"That's it. The one about the fish and the fisherman," he said. "It was 50 pages long, and you memorized the whole thing. There aren't many people who can do that. Besides, we could always become mercenaries and hire ourselves out. That's where all the real money is."

She smiled and wrinkled her nose. Kelvin always knew how to make her feel better. Leaning against him, she laid her head on his shoulder, and he placed his hand on her thigh, starting to caress it. "We can make it together." He turned toward her and kissed her; his hand moved to the junction of her thighs and stroked her.

"Stop that," she giggled. "Your parents are in the next room."

"I know. That's what makes it so great," he said, exploring her body.

"Children, supper," Fiona called out.

"Just a minute," he shouted.

The pair rose up from the patio loveseat, and Cody went to the bathroom. They joined Joash and Fiona in the living room. A platter of fresh meat, bread, fruit, and vegetables lay in the center of the coffee table. Joash opened the wine bottle with a pop and poured two glasses of wine.

"I hope you two are hungry," Fiona said. "Where's Cody?"

Kelvin shrugged and said, "Taking a quick shower, she'll be right out." Cody emerged a few minutes later, drying her hair. The day was long, and they were hungry. The meal soon disappeared from the table, and all were satiated.

Joash and Fiona were only on their second glass of wine when Cody and Kelvin wandered over to the sofa. The decided to watch a play on their oracle scroll. However, a few minutes later, the young lovers lay fast asleep in each other's arms and dreamed of adventure. Kelvin's parents, however, were glad for the quiet moment before the upheaval.

"I'm going to register with the guild tomorrow. I'm not sure what kind of posting I will get. I hope it will be here in the city, but I can't guarantee that," Joash said. "It all depends upon need."

Fiona lowered her wine glass and stared into her lap. "I hate the idea of you going away. The whole point of us moving here was to stay together."

"Soldiers go where they are ordered. I have no say so in it. That said, I will probably be assigned to a support role. It has been 50 years since I fought in a battle. My skills have atrophied; that means warehouse duty. They always need strong backs."

"I guess," Fiona replied. "Still, it makes me nervous."

He pulled his wife close and held her. "There's no need. After I put in a year, I will have enough seniority to select my next posting. At the very worst, I would be away for a year." She snuggled against him and held him tight. Her mind accepted his logic, but her heart feared the worst.

The Great Gate

Chapter 19

S abrina opened her eyes, and she saw a pair of blue eyes staring back at her. Angelina lay upon her right side facing Sabrina. She seemed to be searching for something in Sabrina's face, a puzzle that required solving.

"How do you keep doing that?" She locked and bolted the door. Sabrina sat up in bed and let the covers slide onto her lap. The balcony doors were closed and locked.

"Angelina, where are you?"

"She's in here." Sabrina unlocked and opened the door. "I think she's been there all night."

Karalynn strode into the bedroom. "I've been looking all over the house. You need to have a bath and get dressed for the day." She picked the little girl up in her arms and groaned. "You're getting too big for me to carry."

Sabrina closed and locked the door, not that she thought it would do any good. She reckoned that Angelina could break into any bank vault and escape unseen. After bathing and drying, she retrieved her slip-suit and armor. She had enough of women's fashions. She wanted something simple and easy, something she understood.

She stepped into her slip-suit and drew it up to her neck. The PSM suit cleaved to every nook and cranny of her body, and it gleamed like liquid; but it felt as smooth as silk, a fact she appreciated. She wrapped the vest around her torso and cinched it tight. This supported and displayed her breasts all at the same time. A chainmail tunic came next; the mithril woven garment was beautiful and flat, long sleeves and a fitted bodice cleaving tight to the skin and stopping at her upper hips.

190

While putting on a pair of thigh-high, watertight boots, she sensed the weight of someone's stare. Looking over her shoulder, she saw Angelina. The golden-haired child sat on the edge of the bed and rested her chin on her kneecaps.

"You're back. You don't say very much." The girl screwed up her face as if to cry and refused to look up at her. Sabrina picked up the Angelina and held her in her arms. "Hey there, it's okay. I didn't mean to upset you." She caressed the girl's face. It was as soft as a summer breeze. "You can stay as long as you like, provided mommy approves."

"Angelina, where are you? Your breakfast is getting cold." Karalynn marched up the stairs and circled the railing. Sabrina strolled out of the room, carrying the girl on her right hip.

"It's okay. She can stay with me while I dress. We'll both be down for breakfast in a few minutes."

"Very well," Karalynn said. She wrung her hands and looked at them with eager eyes. "Come down when you're both ready."

Sabrina set the girl on the foot of the bed. "I need to finish getting dressed." She tested the fit of her armor and then picked up her maiden's belt. She wrapped it around her waist and cinched it tight. She reached around her right thigh and grabbed the crotch strap. Yanking it upward and situated the metal thong.

"What's that?"

Sabrina snapped the T-back into the back of the belt. "Well, you can speak after all. I was starting to have my doubts."

"What is it?" asked Angelina pointing at the belt.

"It's a 'maiden's belt.' Women wear them underneath their clothes, and warriors wear it on the outside. It keeps us safe."

"How?" The girl cocked her head and screwed up her face. "It looks weird."

"It's so daemia, and haugr can't do mean things to us." She neither could nor would explain rape to a little girl. Obfuscation was her best friend.

"What kind of mean things?"

Sabrina was starting to regret letting the girl stay. She sat down on the bed beside her and collected her thoughts. "Sometimes daemia hurt women in special ways. They want to make them have their babies, but it is a bad thing. It hurts the women."

"Oh, babies hurt women?"

"No sweetie. Only daemia and haugr babies hurt women. Normal babies are fine."

"Daemias hurt my daddy."

"I'm so sorry, sweetie." She pulled the girl close to her and held her tight. The girl's pain ran deep into the recesses of her soul. Elves possessed greater intelligence than humans and have varying degrees of telepathy. Elvish children could speak any language and had a clear recollection of early childhood memories; they formed a strong psychic bond with their parents, friends, and community; it traumatized Angelina when her father died.

She set the girl on her lap and raised the girl's chin with her index finger. "You don't need to be afraid. I'm never going to leave you. I can't die."

"You can't?"

"No. I'm a particular type of elve called a Maige. We can't die." That included dismemberment as well as being crushed alive, terrifying information that she withheld from the girl. "I'm always going to come back for you, no matter what. Do you believe me?" The girl nodded. "Good. I'm glad that you do." She set the girl down on the floor. She held the girl's hand with her right and her weapons bag with her left. The pair descended the stairs together.

A short while later a knock came from the front door. Karalynn arose from the table. She circled through the living room on her way to the foyer. She opened the front door and said, "Yes?" Marla and a stranger waited. A dwarf stood behind them.

"Sabrina told me to report here in the morning. I brought my friend Billy here to meet her, and this is Tormod. I told him that I was coming to see Sabrina, and he insisted upon joining us." The trio stood before her: a young woman, a boy, and a dwarf. The young woman wore ragged armor, soiled leather covered with rusty rectangular plates.

Billy was rather small. In fact, Karalynn could see the top of his head. He looked very much like a young boy who raided his father's wardrobe. He wore an oversized man's tunic, a rusty chain around his waist, and a dagger on his right hip. The young man fixed his gaze on the floor and chewed the right corner of his lower lip as if tears would flow at any moment.

Karalynn bent her knees and tilted her head to getter a better look at him. He parted his raven black locks in the middle and covered all but the bottom tips of his earlobes. These black locks framed a rather delicate, adorable face; his eyes were vibrant green, and his nose the cutest little button; and his lips formed a perfect Cupid's bow. In fact, he was the prettiest boy she had ever seen; pixie described both his face and body. She concluded that he had not yet reached puberty.

The Great Gate

Tormod, the dwarf, was Marla's kindred. Dwarves were half the size of men but thick as a tree trunk. They were also exceedingly strong, strong enough to move enormous boulders and split rock. The dwarves moved blocks that would give a man a hernia. The tips of his pointed ears drooped a bit, and his hard features appeared as weathered stone. Even if the dwarves were the same size as men – which they were not – there was something tangibly inhuman about them.

Tormod wore a steel helmet shaped like a metal band with a metal "X" covering the crown of his head. It had flaps on the side that protected his cheeks, and it had a guard that covered his broad nose. His deep brown eyes stared at her with unnerving intensity, and his lips stretched tight together. He brushed some caked on dirt off his armor and let it fall on the foyer floor. His armor was covered in the mud: cleanliness was a human obsession.

"Please come on in." Karalynn stood to one side and gestured. "I didn't mean to stare. It's just that I haven't seen many of your kind."

"Warriors?"

"No … um … dwarves."

"Just go to any bank, and you will see one," he grumbled and marched past her. Leather sheaths held a pair of war-hammers on his back-plate. The leather wrapped handles protruded well past the sides of his neck and connected to long steel shafts. They had a double head with a short spike at the end; the spike could punch through most armor.

"I'm sorry about that. Tormod's a little grumpy before his morning cup of coffee," Marla said as she passed by Karalynn. Billy lingered in the doorway a moment and rushed after the pair, like a child not wishing to be left behind. Sabrina looked up from the table and saw them round the corner. "This is Tormod, and this is my friend Billy. They want to join too."

194

Sabrina smiled and rose to her feet. "It's been too long. I saw you last at the Battle of Telemar Plains. You were chasing after that drathva with bloodlust in your eyes. Did you ever catch it?"

"I got a piece of it," Tormod said and stuck his thumbs into his belt. "One of its horns is mounted on my den wall. But what about you, where have you been? It's been … what, 90 years?"

"Eight-eight," she replied. "I needed a long vacation after that battle. I toured several worlds, and I had some fun along the way. I spent most of my time on Earth. But I see that you joined my guild. What prompted that? I thought you would never leave 'The Royal Mason Grenadiers.'"

"Ach, that's a long story." Tormod said and took a seat, "One best saved for another time." He poured a cup of coffee, clasped it between his calloused hands, and savored the aroma. He took a large gulp and let out a satisfied sigh.

"I will look forward to hearing it," Sabrina replied. She looked over at the young man. He stood near the china cabinet and scratched the back of his left calve with his right foot. "Have a seat," she said to Billy.

Tormod's feet dangled above the wooden floor, and his elbows rested on the wooden table. He took another gulp and closed his eyes. "That's better. I can't deal with people before my morning cup."

"Two in the morning, one more mid-morning, three at noon … let's just say I drink it all day long." He downed the entire cup and poured another. "This is good coffee."

"It's 'Red Ridge' coffee." Karalynn straightened her apron. "Could I cook you something for breakfast?"

"That would be good." Tormod scratched his nose. "I'll have three eggs – scrambled, four … no – five pieces of bacon, four slices of toast, hash brown potatoes – three pancakes dusted with powdered sugar, a ham steak, and a bowl of porridge."

Billy shook his head, stared at the table, and languished in silence. "What will you have?" Billy remained silent and shook his head. "Oh … ah … okay." Karalynn looked up at the ceiling and tried to remember the list. She pushed through the double swinging doors and hurried to the task.

As the group chatted, Sabrina surveyed Marla's attire. The young woman wore a patchwork of green leather armor, a hooded tunic, baggy slacks, oversized boots (still caked with mud), and a quiver strapped to her back. A bow draped sideways across her back, and a sword dangled from her left hip. The entire ensemble was a hand-me-down and passed along through several generations. Billy wore less armor than Marla.

Sabrina knew better than to question a dwarf about food. Such conversations could last for hours and usually included tirades, laughter, and tears. Food preparation was serious business and not a topic of idle chitchat. Rather, she scooped a forkful of food and held it to Angelina's mouth. The little elva parted her lips and accepted it. "I have a solicitor dropping by the house. We need to wait until he arrives. While we do, Tormod, tell me of your conquests."

"Hmm," Tormod took a sip of coffee. "I have fought in eight wars: five of them with the daemia and three with the skree. Of course, there have been many minor skirmishes." He stroked his scraggly beard. "Most of them were underground. Punch a hole into the wrong cavern and haugr flood the tunnel. Nowadays they would collapse the shaft, killing everyone inside it, rather than let the haugr gain a foothold. I'm looking forward to fighting above ground."

"So then you fought on the side of the dwarves?"

"Most of the time," Tormod said. "I fought for the humans a few times." Sabrina gave Abby a drink of juice and then wiped her mouth. He said, "I took a wife. Her name is Daphne. She's with child, and we are shopping for a home. It's all been rather exhausting. The real estate agent drags us from house to house. I have seen enough bathrooms to last me a lifetime. If I see another three-story duplex, I will run amuck."

"Your wife is human?"

"Partly, she's a halfling, but she looks like a dwarf. Most people think it's a good match. We do get along well."

"Yes, but are you in love?"

"Love?" He pondered the question. "I can't image life without her or how I existed before we met. She's my world. I suppose that is love."

All attention shifted to Billy. The young man was preoccupied with a sticky bun. He nibbled on it, not quite sure what to make of it, and noticed that all eyes looking upon him. "I come from Norwich located on Serenity Lake." The voice seemed high pitched, too lyrical, but puberty changes many things; she guessed.

"It's a woodland city," Tormod said. "Daphne and I lived there a long time. However, there are few opportunities to improve one's station. A lot of halflings live there,"

"Ooohhh, so you're a halfling," Sabrina replied with a nod. "So you're what mix?"

"I'm not a halfling. I'm all Giant Pigmy Insect Fae." Billy slapped his hands over his mouth. "That was a secret. I wasn't supposed to say anything."

A giant fae is a matter of perspective. Most insect fae are the size of one's thumb and live in hives. All insect fae, however, would choose death before disloyalty to the hive. Billy's eyes grew glassy and appeared on the verge of tears. Sabrina asked, "You don't need to be afraid. I will make sure you have plenty of work." That bit of news cheered up Billy. She then asked, "How old are you?"

"Nineteen," he replied. "I'm old enough to be a warrior, despite what my parents say."

A knock came from the front door. Sabrina excused herself and walked around the table; Tormod stole a furtive glance at her bottom; he saw many elvas wear a maiden's belt but none quite as well as her. Such thoughts, however, were not proper for a married dwarf, so he diverted his attention. Billy, on the other hand, never even noticed Sabrina or her bottom; rather, Billy's attention returned to the perplexing sticky bun situation.

Tormod moved the girl's plate and continued the task of feeding Angelina. The little elva was as fascinated by Tormod as she was by Sabrina. Another knock came from the door. "Just a second, I'll be right there." Sabrina navigated her way around the plush chair and the assortment of toys that littered the floor. When another knock sounded, she shouted, "Yes. I'm coming." She hurried through the foyer and reached for the door handle.

The man had his hand poised for another knock as the door whooshed open. He was a traditional man dressed in a traditional business suit: bowler hat, wool overcoat, dark blue coat, matching trousers, and patent leather shoes. Like all people of his ilk, he clutched a briefcase as though it contained the royal jewels. Although she was hard pressed to know why, all men of his type wore brush mustaches. "My name is John Mayhew." He retrieved a small brass case from his right pocket. He opened it and withdrew a business card. "Mr. Martin Stewart, employed by Hinner and Slough, requested that I pay you a visit. They informed me that you were in need of a solicitor."

"Yes, I am. Come in out of the morning air." She held the door open wide. As Mr. Mayhew passed her by, Sabrina saw Timmons. He stood by his carriage with a bowler cap in his hand. Unlike the previous day, he wore a gray suit, gold vest, and polished shoes. "Oh yes, Mr. Mayhew, this is Timmons. I've hired him as my driver. How much did we agree upon?"

"770 Kronars a week if it please you ma'am," Chauncey replied.

John Mayhew sniffed and raised an eyebrow. The black carriage showed signs of wear: scuffs around the bottom quarter and worn red leather seats. As to the horse, it was a bit long in the tooth. A woman of Sabrina's means could afford a solid gold carriage. However, it was not for him to judge. "Yes, well, I'll see to it then."

Timmons' face twisted into a frown, and he glared at the lawyer. Sensing the tension, Sabrina said, "We will be with you in a few minutes. Why don't you get yourself a cup of coffee?"

"Yes Ma'am." Timmons placed his hat upon his head and tugged on his lapels. He strutted around the wagon with his large belly jutting out.

Mr. Mayhew removed his hat and looked about the foyer. Hardwood floors, wood paneled walls, and even wooden beams above him. The builder certainly liked wood. The light fixtures, however, were made of brass and a bit tarnished. Through the archway, he saw the living room. A worn area rug covered the marred wooden floor. The sofa and chairs were frayed and showed a bit of their stuffing as if they had been used once too often. There was a large hearth, but it was covered with black soot. He wandered into the room and heard a squeak beneath his foot. He jerked up his foot and saw a squeak toy.

"We are all just getting started. Would you like something to eat? Karalynn could fix you some breakfast. She's an excellent cook."

"No thank you, ma'am. I've already had breakfast." He noted a rather old portrait of a man in armor wearing a broadsword. Such warriors were common in days gone by. Since the Hargal Wall was completed, the need for such armaments faded from memory or use.

"Welcome Mr. Mayhew, pull up a chair and have a seat at the table." Karalynn set down three plates in front of Tormod. She hurried back into the kitchen to retrieve the remaining dishes.

"Thank you," he said. He picked up a wooden chair and set it down beside Tormod. The dwarf twitched his nose and glared at him. As if reaching some unspoken conclusion, he returned to his meal. John held his briefcase in his lap and looked at Abby. The girl's face was smeared with a combination of jelly and egg; little Eliza squished her oatmeal through her fingers and reveled in the sensation. He then glanced at Billy; the youth seemed a bit too pretty for his liking. A hair cut and a few fist fights might toughen the boy up a bit. He decided to skip the conversation with them entirely.

Sabrina took a seat and asked, "You have some forms for me to sign?"

"Oh yes ma'am." John opened his briefcase and pulled out a contract. It was as thick as a chemistry text and bound together with brass rivets. He reached in front of Tormod and handed it to Sabrina. For a moment he feared the dwarf would bite into him, mistaking him for food.

Sabrina moved aside her plate and took a sip of coffee. She screwed up her face. "Karalynn, could I get some hot coffee. This is cold." She opened the first page of the document and began reading.

"Just a second," Karalynn set down several more dishes in front of Tormod. She then took the cup from Sabrina. She rushed back into the kitchen.

John had to admit that Karalynn was a striking young elva. One could see her royal heritage borne out in her features, and she was very fertile. As to Sabrina, she was exquisite, an astonishing beauty of rare quality. It was then that he noticed her flipping through the pages. For a moment, he thought she was just pretending to read them; great wealth does not always mean great education. However, he could see her eyes darting from page to page, and there was comprehension in her eyes, even though it lasted less than a second per page.

The kitchen door burst open. Karalynn set down a steaming mug of coffee in front of Sabrina. She then set one down before John. Although he had not asked for one, he was glad to have it. He took a sip and savored the bold flavor.

Sabrina paused from her reading and looked up at John. "You charge 550 basis points for an annual fee? Is that standard practice?"

"Oh, yes ma'am. There are additional charges for accounting, closing costs, and such the like. It's a very reasonable fee given the reputation of Mayhew, Barnes, and Kemp."

"Hmm, yes I see. Well, everything seems to be in order." When she opened her mouth to ask Karalynn for a pen, the young woman set the pen down before her. "Oh, thank you." She signed her name at the indicated mark and then blotted it with a roller. She then held up the pen and cocked her head. The technology of this culture seemed so strange after her time abroad, but it was this way every time she traveled; all culture seemed peculiar to outsiders; to the native born, it was normal.

John reached in front of Tormod again and took the document from Sabrina. "Very good," he said. "Martin informed me of your intended acquisitions. Do you, in fact, wish to purchase the Stinner Defense Industries?"

"Yes, I do. In fact, I would like to speak with an architect and contractor about its renovation. Could you arrange to have a man meet with me this afternoon?"

"Certainly," he replied. "Will you be looking for a house as well? There are some lovely homes just completed in the Third District."

"No. I'll be living here or in the castle. I have agreed to pay the bounty for the unpaid claims. You should expect … a great many inquires at your offices. I've asked a woman by the name of Gertrude to act as their representative. You should refer the women to her."

"Pay the bounty … for the death of warriors in battle?" He furrowed his brow. "That could add up to quite a lot of coin. Are you sure you wish to do that?"

Tormod snarled at John and pushed away from the table. "Suddenly, I've lost my appetite." He threw down his napkin and stomped away from the table.

"I don't mean to offend, but the liability belongs to others. I will admit that many guilds unduly withhold payment of such claims, but it is up to them to pay. Every time a man dies in their service, they will send the grieving widow to you."

Sabrina clasped her hands around the hot mug. "I suppose you do have a point, but I have my word of honor to them. I will see it fulfilled." She stared into the steaming coffee and paused deep in thought. "As to other matter, I want you to set up an insurance fund. Warriors, no matter their guild, are eligible. In exchange for a monthly fee, their families will be compensated for a specific amount. That way the risk is spread across the entire population. As to the guilds, you will find them eager to join. It will

202

lessen their costs and limit their liability. The manner of death, precluding suicide, would be irrelevant."

John's face lit up. "It is a very intriguing notion. It would be a sort of 'life insurance,' if you will."

"Yes, exactly," she replied and took a sip. "The fees and payout will vary. Mitigating factors would be age, skill, occupation, and medical history. We could charge additional fees for the high-risk professions, types of death, and even dismemberment. It would be a great challenge, but I have confidence that your office is up to the challenge."

John preened his mustache and stared at the table top. One could see the wheels turning inside his brain. In a quiet voice, he said, "The bounty payment would be excellent advertising. We could set up mortality charts and fee schedules. The fees paid could be invested in lieu of claims. We could incorporate and sell shares in the company. There could be significant profits." He looked up at Sabrina. "Brilliant, fantastic, I don't know why no one has ever thought of it."

"While on Earth, I was a temp worker from time to time. I once worked for as a secretary for a life insurance company." Sabrina shrugged and acted nonchalantly. "They are quite profitable if well managed."

He arose from the table and slid the chair along the floor. "If you will excuse me, I will begin work at once." He walked away from the table without waiting for a reply. He mumbled and stared at the floor as he walked.

"Lawyers love money like warriors love battle," Sabrina said.

Karalynn emerged from the kitchen holding a plate of food. She looked about the room. "Where is Mr. Mayhew? I fixed him breakfast."

"I'll take that." Tormod marched back into the room. "My appetite returned the moment that the lawyer left the house."

Karalynn shrugged and set down the plate before Tormod. She picked up Eliza from her high chair and sniffed her bottom. "It looks like someone needs changing." She carried the infant from the room and crossed through the living room. They heard her footsteps on the stairs as she climbed to the nursery.

Sabrina cleaned up Angelina's face and then picked her up from the chair. "Marla, pick up Abby for me. We need to take them up to the nursery for the day." The pair followed after Karalynn to the second floor.

They found Karalynn standing before the changing table. "We need to get going. I'll be home after dark. Keep a plate of food warm for me."

"Very well," Karalynn replied. She picked up the infant and drew down her blouse. She pressed the baby to her breast and began to nurse it. She sat down on a rocking chair and began to hum a lovely melody. Sabrina was glad to see that Karalynn's milk had not dried up. Different cultures vary on when a baby should be weaned, and Karalynn often found work as a wet nurse.

The pair left the room and met Tormod in the foyer. Tormod asked, "So where are we off too? Battle, I hope."

"I'm afraid not. We have to tour the Black Fortress and meet with recruits. Perhaps you'll get a chance to fight them, to see if they are battle worthy. Very first thing on our list is to get Marla and Billy some decent armor." Sabrina grabbed a small leather backpack she kept near the door and slung it over her shoulder. Skin tight PSM slip-suits have no pockets.

When they opened the door, they found Timmons, the carriage driver, waiting. He scanned their armor. "Are we off to somewhere dangerous?"

204

"Only for these two," Sabrina said. "They need new armor. Where is the best establishment in the city?"

"Oh well," Timmons said and scratched his lamb-chop sideburn. "That would be 'The Broken Lance.' It's been around for over 500 years. Can't say it's cheap though. There are other armories, and you might get a bargain. They don't look as fancy, but their armor works just as well."

"Take us to The Broken Lance. We need a little panache," Sabrina said.

Marla asked, "Panache?"

"Yes, panache," she replied. "I want your armor to be stylish, to let people know that you serve someone important."

Chapter 20

“I don't know.” Marla turned this way and that, fretting over the reflection in the mirror. The maiden's belt cleaved to her bottom in the most obscene fashion. It sculpted her slip-suit to her bottom in a very graphic, if not pornographic, way.

“Don't be silly. You have a very cute bottom.”

“Yes, but I don't want everyone to see it.” She tugged down on the hem of her silver metallic tunic, but it stopped at the top of her thighs. She wished it was longer, but that might give the enemy combatant something to grab while they fought, which would be fatal. No, it was long enough to cover her but not so long as to impede her movements.

Sabrina would not argue with the girl's insecurities. She rose to her feet and turned the young woman around, facing the mirror. With her arm around Marla's shoulder, she said, “You are a beautiful and powerful warrior. Now you look like what you are.”

It was Billy's turn next. Sabrina stood near the dressing room door and waited. “Are you ready yet?”

“No,” Billy whined.

“What's wrong?”

“I'm almost naked.”

Latimer, tailor and armorsmith, stood with his hands on his hips; “It's alright. A tailor is like a doctor. I've seen many a naked young boy. You needn't feel ashamed.”

"Okay," Billy groaned. He peeked through the curtains and peered into the room. A second later, he left his hiding place and shuffle stepped into the room. Sabrina cocked her head. The young man wore a diaphanous silk slip, and a bandage was wrapped tight around his chest.

"Are you injured?"

"No," he said and chewed his lip, his head bowed and eyes fixed on the floor.

"Let me see." He found the end of the bandage and began to unwrap it. After three loops, the bandage grew slack and unraveled. A pair of nubile breasts distended the slip. Latimer said, "Well I'll be, 'he' is a 'she.'"

It appeared as though she wore some brightly colored backpack, a dazzling collage of black, red, and orange. Billy cringed, and her cheeks flushed bright red. When she hiccupped, a pair of wings popped out behind her. At the same time, an antenna shot out from her black locks. The girl's butterfly vibrant blue wings were outlined with black. Her antennas were green and worked independently of each other, poking furiously in the air, and like a man with his blindfold removed, she took stock of her surroundings. Like breathing, they were autonomic, but they could be controlled by conscious thought. They searched the room for sound, shapes, light, radio waves, and life.

Tears began streaming down her rosy cheeks. "I'm sorry. I just want to be a warrior so much. I thought if I was a boy you might accept me."

Sabrina dried her tears and combed the girl's hair revealing her pointed ears. "I don't discriminate. I accept everyone regardless of species, race, or gender. Of course, you can serve in my guild."

Billy asked, "I can?"

The Great Gate

"Yes. However, all Giant Insect Fae are magical. It's nothing to be ashamed of. You can be quite an asset to us in battle."

"How? All my magic works on plants and trees. I'm excellent at pollinating fields, but I don't see how that helps."

"That is a failure of imagination; we'll have to see to that. Nature and the earth make powerful allies. You'll have to trust me on this matter." The girl nodded. She kept her head bowed but finally looked up at Sabrina. She sensed a kind soul behind Sabrina's eyes. Sabrina took the girl's hand and led her through the store. "Armor is a matter of perspective. Human armor is far too heavy for you. You require something more magical and light.

Sabrina sorted through the various outfits, and she examined and rejected each one. In the end, she selected three outfits. They were made of glittering mithril. The first outfit was a mini-dress. She held it up to Billy. The garment hung down to her hips and just reached her upper thighs. The body of the dress was shimmery dark blue, adorned with blue fire, and lighter than a feather. The woven mithril fabric appeared like a combination of satin and metallic cloth. An inch wide silver band trimmed the neckline and short sleeves. It came with a matching a pair of panties and a circular silver headband.

The second outfit was made of scarlet satin, or so it appeared. In other circumstances it would be called a panty set; the cups of the pushup bra appeared like crimson flames stretching over the breast. The panties were a cross between a thong and a panty. It came with a diaphanous crystal camisole that glittered like a rainbow when moved about in the light.

"I wanted to wear armor;" Billy pouted.

"This is armor; it is fae armor. It protects you and enhances your magical abilities." Sabrina held up the next outfit: it included a black halter-top, the front having a myriad of straps and silver buckles, and it included a pair of black shorts. The micro-shorts were made of treated patent leather, converting them to PSM, and appeared small enough to be panties, arching over the apex of the fae's bottom and formed a deep V-in front. It cleaved to the fae's body as if spray-painted on her.

"We recommend a black body stocking with that set." Latimer draped the sheer black material over his right hand. "It's color adjusting mithril. It's quite impervious to all cutting and stabbing weapons." He drew the fabric across Billy's shoulders. "Quite lovely, I would say."

He walked over to a wooden display case. Through the glass panels, one could see expensive jewelry. He unlocked the case and retrieved a diamond crusted, choker necklace, and an oval placed in the front reserved a place for her owner's crest. He held it up to Billy's neck and stroked his chin, contemplating the fit. "A fae's necklace includes a leash attachment. This collar is magically enhanced and attuned to Fae requirements: it amplifies a fae's natural talents, and it also protects them from most malevolent spells. They would deflect right off her, and it even provides a minimal energy barrier, combined with the outfit would make her a force to be reckoned with. We even have matching pearl earrings and a silver protective head circlet; the circlet extends the range of her antenna.

"Oh, I almost forgot. Shame on me," Latimer said. He went to the display case and returned with a pair of silver gauntlets, pauldrons, and knee-high boots. The boot shanks included ultra light plated greaves. "These are very useful in combat. They increase the fae's physical strength. It would enhance her to be equal to the average man. "Of course, the collar and armor can change color. They can adjust to red, black, green, or chrome, silver, and gold."

"Can the body stocking also change color?"

"Oh yes. The dress can be adjusted too. It can appear red with black trim, black with red trim, and other combinations such as blue, black, and silver. Some of our customers have adorned their fae with a prism effect, shimmering iridescent colors. That is my favorite."

"I have to wear a necklace?" Billy held the necklace with both hands; her antenna bent forward and scanned it. It seemed very scary.

"Yes. It's a matter of law and tradition; all fae must wear one. Most regions insist upon it, and don't get me started on the priests; they can go on for hours. It's a poor testament to the security of our city that she was able to enter without one. If they caught her, they would have arrested her, and I'm afraid, they would have sold her. A beautiful female fae such as Billy would have fetched a very high price. She is most valuable."

Billy's eyes opened wide, and her heart skipped a beat. She remembered her mother's admonishments not to enter the city. However, she never told the girl why.

"Will you be binding her to your house or someone else?"

"I will," Sabrina said. Billy stared at them with wide-eyes. "I am claiming her. She belongs to me."

"Excellent," he replied. He patted Billy on the head. "You are quite lucky. You will become property of the royal family. It's a real honor."

Billy asked, "Why does she have to own me?"

"The fae can be quite impulsive and volatile. There are many incidents of farms attacked by their crops and woodsmen harassed by trees. It's quite impossible for you to be independent, I'm afraid." A deep pout formed on Billy's face.

Sabrina squatted and held both of the fae's hands. "I am making you a part of my family, part of my hive. Do you want that? Because if you don't, I will escort you outside the city and set you free."

Billy thought for only a moment, and her eyes welled up with tears. "I've always dreamed of what it would be like, to grow up and join a hive. Yes, I want to join your family."

"Wonderful," Sabrina smiled and primped Billy's bangs, "Being part of my hive, my guild means being a person of honor, courage, and duty. You have to trust the people you serve with. Do you trust me?" The fae nodded and gazed up through her bangs. "I'm glad. You have nothing to be afraid of. I promise to always love and take care of you. We will take the necklace and the outfits."

Billy held out her arms, the various outfits draped across them. Sabrina said, "Put on the blue mini-dress. Latimer can adjust it for you."

"Very good ma'am, I will see to it right away. Right this way." He guided Billy and Sabrina into the fitting room.

Marla lingered before a set of three mirrors. She turned this way and that; contemplating every nuance of her new armor. Sabrina approached and smiled. "You look fantastic. I love the armor."

Sabrina turned Marla towards her. Having gleaming silver plate, black scrollwork, and gold accent panels, the cuirass provided style and protection. Of course, it bore a bold outline of a black dragon: mouth roaring, wings spread, and talons ready to strike. The chainmail, pauldrons, scaled arm-sheaths, gauntlets, shin guards, and boots were light and stylish – specially designed with a female warrior in mind. While the armor appeared solid, it was actually "liquid armor" or "liquid metal," crystalline based material referred to as "sheer thickening fluid." It was as flexible as cloth, but when impacted, the nano-particles interlocked, forming a barrier as hard as a diamond. It effectively blocked spikes, blades, and ballistic projectiles. Of course, it helped that the armor appeared outrageously sexy on her.

"Try on the helmet," Sabrina said and jumped with excitement. Marla removed the rigid helmet from underneath her left arm; it fit snug on her head and had a silicon fluid cushion that diffused blows; it also had a nose bridge, preventing one's nose from being sliced off, and it had cheek guards to protect one's face. The eye slots were angular, Y-shaped, like a Spartan helmet, allowing a wide viewing angle. "It fits well enough by itself, but you should try it on with the mask."

Marla removed the helmet and handed it to the tailor. She gathered her blonde locks up behind her head. The hood covered her head, pressing down her locks, and had a circular opening for the face. She then placed a mask over her face. It had angular lenses for her eyes that matched the holes in the helmet; the mask, resembling a black dust mask, covered both the nose and mouth, and it refreshed one's breath, scrubbing out the carbon, returning pure oxygen. She drew the web of straps behind her head and cinched them down tight. Sabrina handed Marla the helmet and helped her fit it over her head.

"It has a good snug fit." Sabrina cinched the chinstrap tight and perused the armor. She liked the panache. Ornate scrolling black lines and golden panels, matching the plate armor, adorned it. She circled around behind the girl and inspected the back-plate. It sculpted to Marla's back and hung well on her chest harness. She then lifted the girl's tunic and examined her maiden's belt. She wormed a finger underneath the garment and gave it a tug. "The maiden's belt requires tightening. It's far too loose."

"Twoo woose?" Marla replied. The girl raised her arms in the air and looked around her left side. "It feews oo ight ow."

"You don't want daemia able to worm fingers underneath it." Sabrina moved around before the girl. She once again wormed her finger underneath the V-shaped crotch piece. While beautiful, silver with black scrollwork and gold, it was too loose to be effective. "A daemia could

212

slip a tube underneath this and pump his semen into you. It has to be tight. You don't want a 'death pregnancy' do you?"

"But –"

"No 'buts,' it needs tightening."

Latimer busied himself with fitting Billy clothes, but he took a moment to explain something. He said, "Of course, all our armor has stealth capability." He tapped Marla's left forearm and tapped the gauntlet. "The armor has many colors and sheens programmed into it, and this includes camouflage, which is useful in combat. It samples the background environment and colors the armor accordingly." The gauntlet turned black and text illuminated on it. He tapped the "stealth" and then the "adaptive" mode. The armor reflected the shop interior behind Billy. It appeared as though his disembodied head floated about in the air. Two more taps and the entire ensemble appeared chromed.

"Very nice," Sabrina replied. Her armor had the same features. It demonstrated the quality of the goods and the expertise.

Tormod sniffed and said, "Dwarves don't hide." He then continued to read the morning news on his oracle scroll. The three large segments of leather were stitched together on the side, but it was possible to separate them; which he did, and he laid three sheets around him.

He enjoyed sports. Football, aka soccer, was very popular. As improbable as it might seem, the dwarves fielded a winning team. A black and white photo showed a dwarf charging a goal. When he touched the image, a short video played. The dwarf sped toward the goal and gave the ball a powerful kick. The human goalie leaped through the air, his arms outstretched. The ball sailed past his fingertips and into the net.

"Would you care for another cup of coffee sir?" asked Latimer.

The Great Gate

"Huh? Oh yes, that would be fine," Tormod replied.

The balding man stood while Tormod held out a coffee pot and filled the cup. Latimer was attired as what one might expect for his profession. A white shirt and black vest stretched around his bulbous belly. A yellow measuring tape draped around his neck and dangled free. A small leather kit hung from his right hip, and various tools of his trade hung on it.

Tormod took a sip of coffee, which was bitter, but it was hard to argue with free. He glanced over at the ladies. Sabrina continued to lecture the pair on self-confidence and willingness to stand out from the crowd. Tormod knew Marla since she was a little girl; she was a skilled warrior and hunter. However, she was insecure about her body, as were most young women her age.

He took another swig and surveyed the shop. A bay window divided into rectangular glass panes looked out upon the commercial district. It viewed the cobblestone street since it was a basement shop. The gray bark trunk of a tree sat off to the right, creating a shady spot on the grass. The legs of a man and woman strolled past the window. Beyond them, the brilliant sunlight hurt his eyes. It reflected off signs and windows of the various businesses. A carriage rolled past and broke up the light with a shutter effect.

"It's not fair. Men should have to wear them too." Marla glared at Tormod. Tormod, however, was preoccupied. He grunted and returned to his reading.

Sabrina reached behind the girl's back and squeezed the release mechanism. The device sensed her bio-signature and determined that she was authorized to unlock it. It released and the diamond shaped plate popped open. She removed the maiden's belt and handed the belt to Latimer who was fitting Billy. "It requires shortening."

She then asked Marla, "Have you taken 'the blue' to halt your period?"

Although covered by a slip-suit and armor, one could feel Marla blush. "No. I haven't." She crossed her arms, uncrossed them, fidgeted, and then crossed them again. "I thought it might be nice to have a baby some day."

"You can always take the red and restart your menstrual cycle. We will have to stop by the apothecary. It's all perfectly safe. Women have used it for several millenniums, and it has proved to be an effective means of family planning."

Latimer interrupted and said to Sabrina, "The binding ceremony is typically performed by the owner."

Sabrina held up the choker necklace, a rainbow shimmering on its surface. Billy lifted her chin and stretched her neck. She cringed as Sabrina wrapped it around her neck and set the clasp. Sabrina touched her signet ring to the front oval of the necklace. Sabrina read from a card. "I seal you as mine for now and all time." The flashed with power and then glowed with blinding light, binding it magically to Billy.

Billy's wings fluttered, and the girl hovered in the air. Her hands moved to her throat and examined about the necklace; it was part of her body. Like all collars, it could change color, and be removed for bathing. However, if left behind, after 100 paces, it would reappear around her neck. She flew over to a mirror and inspected her neck. "It feels so heavy." Tears trickled down her cheeks. "Why is it so tight?"

"Come here," Sabrina said and caressed her cheek. "I'm telepathic like you. You know that I love you. Don't you?"

"Yes, Mistress," Billy said and threw her arms around Sabrina. A moment later, she recovered and assumed a submissive posture, hands clasped behind the back, head bowed, and eyes fixed on the ground. "I am yours now and forever. I will serve you as my Mistress, my Queen. Speak the command, and I will obey."

Latimer said, "The ring has a particularly powerful effect on the fae. It harnesses their whimsical nature and bends it to your will. It's like bits and bridles for a horse. It's for the best. It keeps them out of trouble."

Sabrina ignored Latimer's comments. She lifted the girl's chin with her index finger and looked her in the eye. Billy's eyes turned deep blue when she surveyed her mistress. The fae said with great sincerity, "I love you, Mistress. I really do, with all my heart. I've never loved anyone as much as you. What do you wish from me?"

"I wish for you to be at peace," Sabrina said.

The fae sighed and relaxed her adorable face. "Thank you, Mistress. I feel much better. Is there anything else you wish?"

Latimer blurted, "I almost forgot. Dear me, I am getting forgetful in my old age. He spun Billy around by the shoulders. "Just touch your ring to the back of her panties." Sabrina touched the crest. "Her undergarments are now locked, acting as a combination chastity belt and maiden's belt – it keeps them safe and chaste. One doesn't want any unauthorized breeding."

Billy bent and inspected her black panties. She wiggled her hips and tugged at the waistband. The undergarment stayed in place and refused to budge. "I don't really like being locked in my underpants. What if I need to pee?"

"Have your Mistress unlock you," he replied.

"Every time I need to pee?" she whimpered.

"Yes, she is responsible for you now," Latimer stated. He then picked up a silver rod with a crystal at the tip and attached Sabrina's ring to the tip. "With the purchase of armor, you receive a complementary brand. Let me demonstrate." He drew up Billy's top, exposing her back flesh, and pointed the rod at the small of her back. "Now this will sting a little." A brilliant light shot out of the device. A perfect copy of the rings crest appeared on her back, scrolling silver lines grew up her back, glowing with bright light. When he removed the ring, Sabrina's crest indelibly tattooed to her flesh at the base of her spine and the scrolls work formed a beautiful silver pattern that appeared to luminesce. "There we go. Now she's marked. All fae have to be branded."

Billy once again rushed to the mirror. She turned her back toward it, and lifting up her dress, she examined the artwork adorning her back. She hissed and traced the lines with her fingers. Once again, her wings flapped and feet lifted off the floor. "It stings. It really does." She pondered it and asked. "Does it look lovely, Mistress? If you like it, then I like it too." She gazed at Sabrina's face in the mirror, hungering for Sabrina's approval.

"It is beautiful, very becoming."

Billy nodded; "I think it's beautiful too."

Marla watched the proceedings with a bit of dismay and worried that she was next. She had no ring, and it was within Sabrina's rights to claim her. Latimer looked at Sabrina and asked, "Would you like to claim the girl? She's very attractive." Tormod looked up from his reading.

"Marla is my ward," Tormod said. "I could offer you a good price. She's from excellent breeding stock. I'm sure she would bear you many strong babies."

"I'm not interested in a marriage contract, but a service contract does interest me. How much do you want for Marla?" Service contracts were common for engineers and warriors; this ensured that the servant would not depart after receiving advanced training.

Marla's face grew long, and her lips parted. Tormod set down his reading skins and walked over to Marla. "She is healthy and vigorous. She will give you at least 500 hundred years of service, perhaps more. She's at least worth 10 gold."

"Ten gold is fair," Sabrina replied. "Yes, she is well worth the price. I'll take her."

"Done!" Tormod held out his right hand. Sabrina placed 10 gold coins in his palm. "You've made an excellent purchase. She is a fine, fit young woman. I'm sure you will be pleased with her service."

Marla whispered to Billy, "I didn't know he was going to sell me."

"At least you didn't get collared, branded, and locked in your underpants." Billy hissed and rubbed the small of her back. "It hurts."

"Here," Sabrina huffed and pulled up the back of Billy's dress. She unlocked the undergarments. "I don't want you getting pregnant and to start building a nest."

"Yes, Mistress," Billy said, gazed at her feet, and blushed.

The doorbell chimed as they exited the Broken Lance. Tormod and Sabrina emerged from the shop, but Marla lingered in the doorway a second, fearing what strangers might say. Billy stood beside her and gazed out into the street; it was full of very scary humans. She scrambled out from the shop and pranced to Sabrina, holding a silver leash that attached to her choker. Billy handed Sabrina the leash and then hid behind her. Every so often, she leaned to the left and peered around Sabrina, stealing a furtive glance.

Men and women paused to stare at Billy since fae were an uncommon sight, and their gaze moved to her neck, hoping to have the good fortune to happen upon an un-collared fae, hungering to take her as their property. When they saw her collar, they continued on their way. When the young fae saw the crowd disperse, she sighed and relaxed her shoulders. She kept her head bowed and every so often she stole a furtive glance through her bangs. When Sabrina moved, Billy danced around pedestrians and stayed close behind her mistress, desperately wishing she could hold Sabrina's hand.

They stood in the center of a sunlit street, and Marla used her hand as a visor. Wagons rolled down the street, heavy laden with wooden crates, barrels, and wrapped parcels. Men and women hurried as if their business was the most important matter in the world.

Sabrina and Tormod turned to their right and began walking down the hill. Billy lagged behind a moment and then felt a tug on her leash. She scurried after her mistress, and tentatively grasped Sabrina's right hand. When her attempt to hold hands was accepted, joy spilled over from her heart, and she began to sing, as all fae do when they are truly happy; her soprano voice buzzed as it sang a merry melody.

When Marla noticed them leaving, she hurried after them. Every so often, she kicked out a leg, trying to ease the pinch of her maiden's belt, wishing she lived in a world where it was not necessary. She then tugged on her silver tunic, and suitably covered, she left the shop.

Marla fixed her gaze on the slate sidewalk beneath her. Every so often she stole a quick look around her. Men wore gray and black wool suits. Fresh carnations were pinned to their lapels, and a shine gleamed off their shoes. Likewise, the ladies wore dresses and skirt suits. Many were knee length, but a few wore miniskirts; all of them matched with an appropriate jacket and blouse. Most the women wore some sort of ring, which varied according to a complex matrix of wealth and social status.

The Great Gate

When they reached the bottom of the hill, they happened upon a small pond: jets of water pulsed and splashed into the pool, creating a cool gust of wind. Marla felt a wet spray upon her face but a scant sensation on her body. The water glistened on her armor and slip-suit, but she remained dry and warm. She glided a gloved hand over her west breastplate, and she sensed the cool water right through the PSM glove; the transmission of the tactile senses was fantastic.

Marla searched for Sabrina, Tormod, and Billy, but they were gone. A crowd of people blocked her line of sight. They swarmed past her and around the pond. She pushed through them and jumped, trying to spot them.

The three-story brick buildings might as well have been fortresses. They blocked her view, and endless display windows assaulted Marla's senses, insisting that she make a purchase. Dresses, dishware, furnishings, and lingerie screamed out sale bargains, belligerent and unyielding. Not content with this cacophony, sales people wandered the streets, shoving their wares in people's faces.

Marla's stomach became tight. She pushed through the crowd, causing angry glares, and whimpered. It was then that she noticed the pair walking up the next street over from her. They trekked up the hill and disappeared behind the corner of a cheese shop.

Marla dodged around a wagon and sprinted down the middle of the street. "Look out!" a driver called. She ran around it and between another. A man exited a shop carrying a cheese wheel, three wrapped packages, and a salami log. She ran into him, spilling all onto the ground.

"I'm so sorry." She helped him pick up his purchases. "I'm in kind of a hurry."

"I can see that." He snatched a package from her. "You need to be more careful. Just because you are a warrior does not give you the right to knock people down in the street. We have rules of proper conduct."

"Sorry," she said.

The plate glass to her left reflected her image. The silver armor gleamed in the sunlight, sculpted around her chest, and molded to her tiny waist. She was a young warrior woman, clad in armor worthy of a princess; the notion settled in her consciousness: *I'm a warrior.* It was an obvious conclusion, but one that failed to register in her consciousness. Oversized and shabby, the old hand-me-down armor made her feel like a small child playing dress up. The new armor made her feel like a professional warrior, a defender of Asgard.

Annoyed by the crowd, annoyed by the hectic pace, and mostly annoyed by Marla, the man scowled at her and hurried about his business. She dodged underneath a rectangular field stone column and rushed around the corner of the building. Sabrina and Tormod topped the hill, Billy prancing by Sabrina's side, clasping her hand and singing. Marla sprinted after them; her boots were so light and fit her feet so well, that she flew up the steep grade. When she caught up to them, she slowed to a walk.

"Try to stay with us," Sabrina scolded Marla. "It's annoying."

"Yes, Mistress," Marla replied. The young woman walked with a bounce in her step. She felt as if she was coming alive.

"We are heading toward 'The Courtyard.' Keep your sword in its sheath and say nothing." The Courtyard drew its name from the square parade grounds. The grounds stretched out before the governor's mansion. An array of government offices flanked it.

Weathered porticos, dreary windows, and stark columns marked the face of the buildings, making them appear like gray monoliths, tombs for men long dead. Men clothed in black, hooded robes, and somber vestments, wandered the streets, as if priests carrying out sacred rites: long faces, gray beards, joylessness, and pained expressions appeared mandatory.

Tormod saw his ward walk with a bounce in her steps. Her flaxen ponytail swished behind her head. "Try not to be so happy. It makes government officials nervous."

"Yes, sir." She tried to quell her smile, but it kept resurfacing, as did the spring in her step. Once again, she reminded him of a schoolgirl on her way to recess. Several officials furrowed their brows and glared at her, restraining the urge to fine her for some undefined civil infraction, perhaps disturbing the peace. All entrants were required to obtain a permit to enter "The Courtyard." Ordinary citizens were barred entry without just cause. Surely, this young warrior was a trespasser.

Sabrina stopped and whispered in a stern voice, "Stop bouncing."

"Yes, Mistress." Marla cringed and clasped her hands behind her back. She tried to copy them, but the spring kept returning to her steps. When she saw a childhood friend, she broke out into a squeal and sprinted toward her.

"Kayla," Marla said. A brunette young woman jerked her head to her left just as Marla collided and embraced her. "It's so good to see you." Kayla held out her hands, uncertain how to react, and then melted into the warm embrace of her friend.

As with all warrior women, Kayla wore armor and a slip-suit; her armor, however, was silver and embellished with many golden marks of her rank. Her armor bore the outline of a rearing horse.

"What are you doing here?" She clasped the sides of Marla's face. "It's been so long. How have you been?"

"I'm well. I just returned from the Cordon Forest," said Kayla. That news shook Marla. The Hargal Wall marked the boundary of their territory; where it ended, the Dead Plains began, the location where countless battles decided the fate of humanity, and there were so many bleached bones that they protruded from the soil as if growing from it. The fields gave way to the Cordon Forest, where death waited around every tree and every rock; few who entered ever returned to tell the tale, and those who whispered of nightmares beyond comprehension.

"What were you doing there?" Marla whispered and wrung her hands.

"The king commissioned a reconnaissance expedition to survey the forest. I'm one of the few who returned alive." Kayla asked, "Are you going to introduce me to your friends?"

"Oh, yes of course." Marla moved and used a broad gesture. "This is Tormod, my guardian. This is my new Mistress, Overlord Sabrina March." She searched her mind. "I'm not sure, but I think I belong to her."

"It is an honor," Kayla said with a fist thump to her chest. Billy hid behind Sabrina, and leaning to her right, peered around Sabrina's side. "Who is that behind you? Oh my god, it's Billy." She rushed over and gave the fae a hug. "Let me look at you. You're so cute, and you finally captured a Mistress. I always knew you would." While human girls dream about future lovers, fae children dream about their future asnalia (az – nul – e), meaning leader or ruler of the hive, and spend long hours imagining who they might be.

Billy gazed at Sabrina with dewy eyes. "I love her so much. We're going to go on adventures together; she's going to teach me how to fight; she's going to teach me all about magic. It's everything that I dreamed of." She grabbed Sabrina's side, squeezed her eyes shut, and hugged her.

The Great Gate

She noted the small gold sword hanging from Billy's left side. "I'm glad to hear that. You deserve to be happy." She looked over Billy's attire. "Your clothes are so beautiful."

"My Mistress bought them for me. They are exquisite. She trusts me too; she unlocked my shiny underpants." Billy ran her hands down the side of her shimmery dress and then resumed a submissive posture.

"You had trouble in the wilderness?" Sabrina asked, wishing to change the subject.

"Yes." Kayla crossed her arms, sighed, and shook her head. "We set out with 100 warriors and three times as many footmen. We were at the edge of the forest when they were upon us; the forest floor became black with our enemies. We set up a skirmish line and readied our lances, but it was like an avalanche fell upon us. Our flanks began to collapse, so we closed into a defensive circle; there were so many dead bodies that we had to stand upon them. The pressed us back and crushed us together; I could barely swing my sword – death came for us. For no reason, they fled."

"They pulled away from us and fled back into the woods. When I looked to the west, I saw a brilliant white light in the sky, like a star cutting through the blue skies, and peals of thunder rolled over us; and then the ground shook – it threw us around as if we were nothing; the ground split and bones pushed up from the soil, as if coming to life. A mist arose from the ground, and it enveloped us; and through it, we saw opaque scenes of past battles, warriors of old, men in heavy armor, horns mounted to their helms; they wielded deadly weapons, and they were locked in mortal combat with agents of death. I'm still not sure what happened. If I was not wide awake and gripping my sword, then I would have thought it was a dream."

"Anywhere else that story might seem strange but not in the Dead Plains. Tormod asked, "How many casualties were there?"

"36 warriors and 210 footmen died!" She shook her head and looked off into the distance. Her face quivered as sorrow broke through her emotional defenses. "I lost most of my friends that day. We rose up through the ranks together; we were closer than family."

"I'm sorry to hear that," Tormod said. "I've lost many comrades in battle."

Kayla scowled at the administrative building behind her. "They don't believe me. With a sniff and a wave of his hand, the Maven dismissed me. It was as though I was a child telling a wild fib. Damn it, 246 good soldiers died. What more proof does he need? One of the clerks actually suggested that the other warriors deserted during battle. It is disgraceful!"

"It's a standard practice these days. Our dead cover the battlefield, and the princes can't hear the cry of the dying, or see the corpses, or smell the stench of death." Tormod crossed his arms and glowered at the royal crest above the door. "Who needs an enemy when we kill our own?"

Sabrina raised an eyebrow and mused. The conversation continued, but she mulled over Tormod's words. "You're right." They stopped talking and turned toward her. "Who needs an enemy ... indeed? Or perhaps it is better to say that the enemy is already among us."

"You mean to say —"

When the doors to the building flew open and slammed into the exterior wall. A group of youths exited the building and cut Tormod off. They wore seamless satin tunics, velvet tights, and hats with long feathers, hand stitched by the finest tailors, vestments of the royal court, banned for all but those of noble blood. They hurried down the steps and whispered in hushed conversations; and then they broke out in laughter. The gaggle of young men strutted through the street toward the governor's mansion.

Kayla shouted, "Go home and feed upon your mother's teat." The insult was apparent to all. A blond, curly haired youth turned around and walked backward, formed a tube with his right hand, and pumped it at his hips. "I can't stand those stubs. They play at being men and form worthless guilds: The Proud Lion, The Striking Hawks, and The Silver-Glint ... you are all cowards!" Of course, the young men were too far away to hear her insult, but it was just as well; they would have been honor-bound to answer her challenge with a duel. In a prince's case, it meant hiring a champion.

"To what guild do you belong?" asked Sabrina.

Kayla winced, and she gestured at her breastplate. "I am ... or I was a member of 'The Emissaries.' After this disaster, Lord Mallory James IV withdrew his support. We failed to finish the probationary period." Noting Marla's questioning expression, she explained, "It takes two persons of royal registry to register a new guild. Then there is a very long process to become a recognized house."

"It's a timely meeting then," Tormod said. "Sabrina has just returned, and she is looking to supplement her ranks with experienced warriors."

"Sabrina is our sponsor and overlord. She has fought in many battles, and she is the wealthiest person in all Asgard. She's paying the bounty to all the widows, no matter which guild they joined."

"Yes, everyone has heard of her, and the bounties are beyond generous," Kayla said. "They say you have more gold than the king and dispense it with a liberality of a Dolomite priest." Kayla felt overshadowed by Sabrina, like a gangly youth when compared to a mature woman. Sabrina was more beautiful, and grander than described in the history books. "You are paying the bounty to all the widows. Why?"

"Because it is the right thing to do," Sabrina replied.

The hard edge that marred Kayla's beautiful features gave way to melancholy. She lapsed into a deep remorse and languished for a moment or two. The memories seemed thick in the air about her. Even Tormod slouched into a forlorn state. Sentiments such as honor appeared to die long ago.

Marla looked at her comrades seeking some explanation for the shift in mood. Kayla brushed away the phantoms as one would an annoying fly. She took a deep breath and returned to the moment. "I do like the idea of serving for an honorable guild."

"So then you are open to the notion?" asked Sabrina.

"I am," Kayla said.

Sabrina asked Kayla, "But I must also echo the question you asked me. Why?"

"Why?" Kayla searched her thoughts for a cohesive response. "My oldest sister was raped by a skree. Our guards managed to find and rescue her, but it was too late. That thing that grew in her womb took over her body. My parents were desperate; they hired every physician for a hundred miles, but no one could save her. That thing grew inside her and drove her to madness. She climbed up to the top of a tower and leap to her death."

"So you became a warrior for revenge?"

Kayla said, "No. That's not it at all. I never wanted to be a helpless damsel like my sister, Nora. I require no man to save me: I will save myself, not wait for someone else to do it. Of course, it also suits my temperament."

"Do you know of any other warriors looking to join a guild?" asked Sabrina.

"You already have the best. I heard Joash Faroe has re-emerged from the dead. He joined your guild along with his son Kelvin. He was Captain of the King's Guards, and he is, or was, the best warrior in the Wolf's Head Peninsula. You should speak with him."

Chapter 21

The group of comrades strolled toward the tavern. Marla paused and said to Sabrina, "Billy has to stay out here. They don't allow fae in a place like this."

Sabrina said, "I understand."

"I don't," Billy interjected. "Why can't I come in?"

"I wish I could clear it up for you Billy, but prejudice is illogical. Men enforce arbitrary rules of inclusion and exclusion: eye color, parentage, national birthplace, and such the like. It is tribal thinking and a vestige of a primitive past. We don't want to give offense, so you will have to wait out here." Sabrina searched the front porch of the bar. She saw what appeared to be coat hooks on the exterior wall. Two other fae were already tethered to it. Sabrina draped Billy's leash loop over an empty hook. "Wait here for me, Billy."

"Yes, Mistress," Billy replied. The other fae leaned forward and peered around Billy, fluttering their wings. One of the faes had long blonde curls and the other shoulder length chestnut brown hair. All of them were impossibly cute. When Sabrina looked directly at them, they scrambled into a line and assumed a submissive posture.

Sabrina entered the tavern first and lingered atop the stairs. Rough hued wood covered the interior, forming the support pillars and support beams. Large planks stretched out before them, and a well-worn track led to the bar. Square pillars held up the second floor, and reused boards from a barn composed the walls. Round tables, large enough to seat four, were scattered about the room and lacquered to a high sheen, easily clean with a damp cloth. Two barmaids hurried about with trays filled with beer, mugs filled with dark and others tan; all overflowed with a thick head of foam. Every so often, an inebriated patron reached up underneath a girl's skirt, and a sharp slap resulted. Cheers inevitably broke out from the male and female warriors. They drank beer, laughed hard, and fought. Instead of darts, they threw knives at a corkboard. Most warriors have few interests aside from combat skills.

Sabrina wandered through the bar, searching for threats. The last time she saw Joash, it was over a century ago. There were many warriors but none of his size and prowess. She spotted a mountain of a man with a bushy beard in the far right corner, but his armor was rusty armor and attached to worn leather. Joash kept his armor in much better condition: it had to be some other warrior. This stranger pulled a waitress into his lap and gave her a slathering beer kiss. Although she slapped him and squirmed, he smothered her with another kiss and began to grope her.

Joash emerged from the restroom, and roared, "HANDS OFF!" He grabbed a wooden club that hung near the end of the bar. It was a little smaller than a baseball bat and had a center plug of lead. The many scars along its length testified to its frequent and violent use.

Stifled squeals came from her smothered lips. Joash leaped over a bench and landed on the floor like a cat. "Get off her now," he bellowed. The redheaded man stood to his feet, and the girl rolled off his lap, hitting the floor with a fleshy thud. "Now get out!"

The redheaded warrior whipped out a dagger. When he lunged, Joash stepped aside and struck the man's wrist. The blade fell from his hand. He then twisted and pinioned the man's arm. It only took a gentle nudge to flip the man onto his back. The redhead rolled away and scrambled to his feet; he lunged at Joash with his hands outstretched. Once again Joash stepped aside like a bull fighter. Joash hit the man in the gut with the blunt tip of his club and then whacked him in the back of the head. The redheaded warrior collapsed to the floor with a heavy thud and groaned. Joash grabbed the back of the man's shirt and the man's belt. He frog-marched the man to the side door and tossed him out in the street. Applause and cheers broke out from the other patrons.

"Are you okay, Meja?" asked Joash. The girl sniffled and straightened her disheveled clothes. She then picked up her tray and went into the back of the bar.

"Joash, how are you doing? You tough old dog," Kayla said and threw her arms around him. "It's so good to see you." He gave her a bear hug and closed his eyes.

"It's good to see you too. The Wolf's Head Peninsula has been boring without you." He furrowed his brow, and the smile disappeared from his face. "I heard about the trouble in the wilds. I wish I could have been there."

"I wish you were too. We lost a lot of good men. Eljon and Norrad both fell in battle."

"Both of them?"

"Yes. But that's not what I came to talk to you about." She turned to the side and held out her hands. "This is Overlord Sabrina, Tormod, and Marla. I've known Marla ever since she was a little girl. Oh, um, and Billy is tethered outside. Sabrina captured her this morning."

"Overlord Sabrina, it is an honor to meet you. Give Billy my congratulations." He gave Marla a hug. "The last time I saw you, you were so little. You have grown into a fine young warrior. Tormod, it has been a long time. How long I can't quite remember."

"Too long," Sabrina said and gripped his forearm. "What brings you to this bar?"

"I actually pledged your guild. I came here to see an old friend." Joash sighed. "He died 20 years ago. His daughter Meja asked me to help out with the bar, and I can use the extra coins in my pocket."

They withdrew to a private booth in the back. Joash listened with rapt interest as Sabrina discussed her travels. When they finished, he asked, "And what is it you want from me? You have a castle full of warriors just waiting to serve you."

"I do, but I have a particular position in mind for you," Sabrina said. "I would like you to take over combat training for our junior cadets, senior cadets, and guild pledges. Your skills as a Master Warrior are in great need. You would train pledges and plan training missions, as time permits and necessity requires."

"The position pays 250,000 Kronar or 157,000 pounds per year," she said. "That does not include the rewards we might glean from quests."

The Elite Praetorian Guardians, the Immortals, had a separate system of ranks and compensation. Although Joash had the skill and experience to join the Immortals, it would mean divorcing Fiona, since Immortals can only marry other Immortals, preventing divided loyalties. In addition, Immortals could neither bear nor father children, which was not important in Joash's senior years.

The conversation bounced around the topic of income for a minute or two. The annual salary was generous. There could be no doubt of that. Years had not only given Joash experience as a fierce warrior but as a shrewd businessman, and he bartered for additional benefits. He insisted that the funds remain with a solicitor instead of the bounty paid to his relatives; he also wrangled for a housing allowance, outside the castle, and per diem rates while traveling.

Kayla retrieved a pitcher of ale for them as Joash continued. He insisted upon an expense account, travel allowances, armor repair, and weapon purchasing. Rather than annoy Sabrina, it encouraged her. It was a little-known fact by civilians, but logistics win or lose many battles: food, shelter, transportation and medical attention were essential. An army that fails to plan for such needs, fails to win the battle, and thus fails to win the war.

Tormod remained silent during the entire exercise. He puffed away on his pipe, filling the room with the sweet aroma of black cherry. Kayla set down the beers and explained the concept of per diem expenses to Marla; when they settled the matter, Joash said farewell to Meja and departed the bar.

They exited through the side door. As they neared the corner, they heard a furious debate. Pouting faces, angry glares, shrill indictments, crossed arms, pointing fingers, and red faces, the fae all spoke at once, none listening to the other. When they caught sight of the group, the fae all snapped into the submissive position and formed a row. Sabrina unhitched Billy and glanced at the other fae. The kept their heads bowed and eyes fixed on the ground.

When they walked away, Sabrina asked, "What was that all about?"

Billy's lips pressed tight and formed a frown; she glared at some invisible enemy. "They claimed their masters were greater than you. Aria said her master was best because he had a horse and five stupid soldiers following him. I told her that her necklace was too tight, and it was cutting off the blood to her brain." She thought a second and asked, "How many people are in our family?"

"Well, that's a good question; there are you, Karalynn, Angelina, Abby, Eliza and ... 4.3 million warriors, spread across many worlds." Sabrina was the richest person in the entire region, and her vast corporate holdings required a vast army to protect it. Such a large military consumed much of her profits, but there would be no profits without it. Bribery and thievery were common among civil authorities. Only the threat of force kept them at bay, and this was why most wealthy patrons created fighting guilds – they operated as a private security force and army.

Billy skipped and clapped. "I knew she was wrong. I just knew it." She pranced along beside Sabrina and fluttered her wings. She threw her arms around Sabrina and said, "I'm so glad you captured me, Mistress. I was so afraid without you."

"You're safe now." She stroked Billy's head and gave her a squeeze. When Billy released her, Sabrina gave her leash a slight tug. "Now let's get going. We have to meet with someone."

"Yes, Mistress." Billy flapped her butterfly wings and hovered in the air behind Sabrina like a kite. It was easier than trying to walk through the crowd.

Roadside vendors, midday traffic, carriages for hire, delivery wagons, and foot traffic congested the city streets. At a whim, merchants opened their carts and stalled traffic; passersby purchased a hot meal and cold drink. Of course, shop owners complained bitterly to the police about this breach of conduct, but stopping the vendors would be like stemming the tide. This caused pedestrian traffic to scramble around them or risk walking in the middle of the street.

Marla once again found herself lagging behind the group. An anonymous hand grabbed her ass; she yelped and spun around to identify her molester. Traffic merged, and this allowed the pervert blended into the press. Sabrina waded through the crowd and put her hand on Marla's shoulder. The girl spun around, fists ready to fight.

Sabrina asked, "What's the problem?"

"People keep touching me."

"I get that all the time. Some men get a thrill from groping a woman. In a crowd this thick, even noble women have to suffer through it. Just keep moving. If they get too aggressive, then deal with it." In Sabrina's case, it

234

was doubly difficult. She remembered her previous life as a man; never once did anyone grab, touch, or pinch her bottom. It was quite a shock when it happened to her for the first time.

The pair continued through the crowds to their destination; Marla jumped and danced away when a man touched her. However, the crowds began to thin when they departed the commercial district; it was there that they found Chauncey. The coachman was flirting with a matronly vendor. Upon seeing Sabrina, Chauncey said to the woman, "I have to go love, but I'll be back tomorrow for more of your excellent figs." He hurried over to them and removed his hat. "How did the shopping go, ma'am?"

"Very well, I made several purchases, and you need to pick them up from The Broken Lance and The Cutting Edge. In the meantime, we are going to meet Joash's wife and bring them to a house in the second district. I promised him a home, and I have a particular property in mind. It's located on 3413 Cold Water Lane."

"I know right where it is, Mistress." The wagon shifted and groaned as Joash climbed on board. Chauncey looked over his right shoulder as the big man took a seat. "Sir, could I trouble you to sit in the middle of the seat? You're making the wagon shift to one side."

"Oh, um, sure," Joash replied. He scooted into the middle of the bench with his back toward the front of the wagon. Kayla sat on one side of him and Marla on the other; Tormod and Sabrina sat facing the front; Billy folded up her wings and sat on the floor before Sabrina, her knees bent and legs curled underneath her. The fae laid her head on Sabrina's lap and began to purr like a kitten. When Sabrina stroked her head, the girl closed her eyes and reveled in Sabrina's affection.

Chauncey released the handbrake and snapped the whip. The horse struggled for a second and then leaned into it. The carriage rolled forward and merged into traffic. Five blocks later, they stopped by a market and picked up Fiona.

Cotton ball clouds parted, and sunshine beamed through the gap, shining upon them. The second district lay on a gentle slope, and since it was a planned community, the streets were laid out in a chessboard pattern. Each block had eight generous homes, and each home had a private garden set in the center of the structure. There were no front yards or backyards since the homes butted up against the city streets. Most of the homes were three stories and had a stucco exterior. The archways, red tiled roofs, and porticos with fountains reminded her of Spanish architecture. Like everything else Asgard, they were transplants from another culture, another world.

Paved streets, green lawns, lampposts, and benches marked the beginning of the suburbs. Grocery stores, clothing shops, pharmacies, and such the like provided retail merchandise to local residents. Every so often they passed by a professional office building; lawyer, accountant, and doctor offices were common occupants. When they passed by an elementary school, a children's choir penetrated the red brick walls.

Winding streets led them to the heart of the district and to the top of a steeply sloped hill. Off in the distance, Sabrina could see the outer boundary of the district. The city wall was so flimsy a herd of sheep could knock it over. She doubted that it could stop a single daemia let alone a besieging army. Yet beyond that wall, she saw new houses under construction. These homes were larger and sat on generous plots of land, having stables, patios, and swimming pools, a suburban paradise. There appeared to be no attempt to wall in this community, a fact which disturbed Sabrina.

They traveled up a small hill and went past an assortment of shops. When they reached the crest, they saw "Glenn Brook Estates." Tan brick walls formed a half-circle and funneled them into the housing complex. They passed through gorgeous green lawns that spread out like thick carpets. Two story homes sat on generous plots of land that came with lavish gardens.

The street swept in a lazy circle to the east and looped around grand residences. "There it is," Sabrina said. A ring of pink and white flowers circled around this island in an explosion of brilliant color. A white driveway circled around an island of green shrubs, expertly manicured, reminding Fiona of the public gardens back in Knob Oak.

The house astounded Fiona. It was two stories tall and wide enough for two homes. Burnt orange tiles capped the roof, and cream stucco adorned the walls. There were two verandas located on the second floor and set on either side and above the entryway. The iron railings of the terraces gave way to high, arched doorways made of glass. Four pillars supported the portico and sheltered the oak doors that gave entrance to the home.

The carriage came to a halt, and Chauncey scurried from his perch. He placed a footstool on the ground and opened the half-door. One by one he helped them exit the carriage. When Joash stepped out, the springs groaned, and the carriage rose. He worried about the stool collapsing under Joash's great bulk.

"Wait for us. I have a meeting this afternoon with an architect and contractor," Sabrina said. "I'm making some much-needed improvements to my off-campus home."

"Yes, ma'am."

Although she had only recently returned, Sabrina felt like a real estate agent. She knew of many properties built by her construction company and was eager to see one of them. Fiona smoothed down her dress and primped her hair. "I'm not really dressed to meet the lady of the house. What is her name?"

Sabrina cocked her head and raised her eyebrows. "Her name is Fiona Faroe." It took a few seconds for Fiona to process the information. Her eyes lit up and lips parted.

"This is my home?" She took a pensive step and turned to face them. "There must be some mistake. Are you sure this is the right place?"

"Yes," Sabrina chuckled. "Your last home was smaller?"

"Much smaller," Fiona said.

"Perhaps Joash is a better warrior than he was a farmer."

"Truer words were never spoken," Joash said. He lumbered past them and threw open the front doors. He marched into the foyer and stood with his hands on his hips. "This is more like it."

Fiona entered after him feeling like a child lost in a cathedral. Gleaming oak floors led to a spiral staircase that climbed to the second floor. To the right lay a lavish parlor filled with handmade furnishings, a great hearth, and paintings of pastoral scenes. "I don't believe it," she gasped. "It's a palace."

"No, a palace is where he used to live," Sabrina replied. "He never told you?"

"Told me what?" she asked him.

Joash turned toward Fiona and withdrew inside himself for a moment. Taking a deep breath, he looked into her eyes. "I never told you ... I meant to a thousand times, but the time was never right. As the years passed, it became harder to tell you the truth. Well, it is not the truth exactly, just a piece of my past."

"What?"

"My father is King Olaf Erickson III, the high king of Asgard." He rubbed his face and walked away from her. "My mother was Elsa Faroe, she was a concubine. My mom was a lesser royal of Thalwin. It's a small island kingdom to the west. I was there once when I was a boy. My mother passed away when I reached manhood."

"But you were the Captain of the Royal Guard," she replied.

"All sons of royal birth are titled Captain of the Guard. It was an honorary title, one which I spent my entire life trying to earn." He turned back toward her. My father never approved of me. He called me his '… a lumbering giant of a son.'"

"The king, my father, is a small, frail man, but he has a sharp mind for politics. I am a warrior: I am at home on a battlefield not in parliament. Every time I joined him in court, I embarrassed him. I spoke my mind; I go straight at a problem – no one in the legislature does that. I grew weary of their smirks and quiet whispers. So I just kept going from one battle to the next. When we met, you were the first girl who accepted me as I am, not because my father is the king. I just couldn't bring myself to tell you."

"When you wanted to move home to be near your parents and become farmers, I saw my way out. I would never have to tell you. You would always love me as I am." He rubbed his nose and gazed down at his feet.

She wrapped her arms around as much of him as she could and pressed her face to his chest. "I do love you as you are. That would never have made any difference to me."

He held her tight and closed his eyes. "I knew that, but I was so afraid. It made no sense, but there it is. I just wanted to forget the past."

She leaned back and asked, "Will you be king some day?"

"Me? No. Ascension to the throne is only for sons birthed by wives, not concubines, and my father decrees the order ascension. My brother Jonathan is just like our father, shrewd and calculating; he navigates those waters like a shark. I'm probably on the bottom of the list of 69 children."

"I've seen a picture of the king. He's small," she said.

"I take after my mother. The king prefers powerfully built women. My mom isn't the only concubine who fits that description. Most of them are built like her. I have quite a few large brothers and sisters."

Chapter 22

Nine months passed, and the summer sun scorched Eden; it blazed like a furnace from sunrise to sunset, and Eden cooled only when it sank behind the western sky. Sabrina rose while the city still slept, preparing for the day. Clad in her armor, she passed through the house like a ghost.

When she descended the first set of stairs, she paused at Angelina's room. Through the open door, she saw Billy and the little elva already at play. The fae knelt on the floor with Angelina and drank imaginary tea – Billy loved the game – it was so much more fun than drinking real tea. She spent hours with the little girl, relishing each improvised game.

Sabrina circled around the banister. Karalynn sat in a rocking chair within the nursery. She cradled Eliza at her breast and hummed a motherly melody. The pungent aroma of the diaper pail kept Sabrina from entering the room. She wished that Karalynn would clean it more often, but she was afraid to say anything; it might evoke a request for her to launder soiled diapers, a task she detested.

Sabrina jogged down the wooden steps and adjusted her swords. A curious thought emerged in her consciousness. Somehow, she was not sure when they became a family. The process mystified her. Familial bonds, whether good or ill, transcend even death. In the long expanses of eternity, they would still be her family, a bond that made her believe in the Great Spirit.

When her foot touched the foyer, a fist pounded the front door. "Hold on, I'll be right there." The pounding grew frantic at her reply. She unlatched the door. "What is …."

The door pushed back and hit Sabrina; a girl rushed past her and collapsed to the floor. "Shut it. Shut it quickly!" Sabrina furrowed her brow. The hysterical girl scrambled backward and hit the wall, rattling the pictures hanging upon it.

Hands on her hips, searching the street, her armor gleaming in the morning light, Sabrina lingered in the doorway. Three young women languished in the back of a flatbed wagon, covered in grime from head to toe, and the stink of the sewers hung upon them, making Sabrina's eyes water. Two of them sobbed and tried to hide the slave choker necklace around their necks, the third stared off into the distance with empty eyes.

A man skulked about in an alley across the street. He was a filthy man clothed in black and ominous: dark clothes, deep-set eyes, and his face frozen in a scowl, deep crevices that marred his cheeks, a twisted old tree having seen one too many storms. His left hand clutched leather straps, and his right hand held a stun stick; the glowing red tip of the stun stick delivered an agonizing shock. When touched to the flesh, it incapacitated the recipient for hours.

Sabrina stepped out into the street and closed the door behind her. She crossed her arms and watched the man skulk. When he spotted her, he emerged from the shadows and pointed his stun stick at her. "You there, have you seen a young woman. She is my property. Speak quickly, or I will have the law on you."

He was a "razzia."

————

"The Treaty of Kingdoms," 622CE established the modern penal system. Prisons cost a great deal to operate and maintain, providing little to benefit society. Rather than hang or imprison a petty theft, the courts sentenced the thief to involuntary servitude. Thus, he or she could pay off his or her debt both to the victim and to society. Thieves, tax cheats, and vagrants, once convicted, became "pressed servants" or involuntary servants, slavery by another name. The "Edict of the Palisade" expanded this practice in 1016 CE, which Parliament broadened to include those convicted of tax fraud, bankruptcy, and non-violent offenses. Violent offenders, deserters, or insurrectionists suffered death of personality, and then they sold the offenders.

Fifty-seven years ago, while Sabrina was on Earth, youth crime and rebellion reached an all-time high. Parliament handled the crisis by modifying "The Edict of the Palisade;" children were considered chattel, which is property; their nearest relative or guardian could compel the child to obey. The law was intended to promote responsible guardianship and stop substance abuse; however, by declaring children as chattel, they became transferable property, such as a wagon or a horse.

Many impoverished fathers abused the law and sold their daughters to depraved men known as "razzia." Once acquired, the razzia sold the girls in private auction houses. Infamous "Houses of Protocol" purchased and trained young women, which spoken of in whispers and always ended with a curse.

––––––––

"Why do you have those citizens imprisoned in your wagon?" Sabrina crossed her arms and returned the man's glare. "Free them at once!"

"They are not citizens: they are vermin. It took me weeks of effort to track these sewer imps. They scurry around like rats and steal from the marketplace. The Asgard Attorney's office issued a standing warrant for their arrest. I caught them, and they belong to me."

"These are children, and they are free." She strode up to the man. The razzia glared at her with his one good eye; a milky cataract-blinded the other eye. "They deserve a happy home and parents who love them. I have had enough. Either you release them, or I will take your head. You filthy little man."

The razzia gnashed at her and lunged with his stun baton. She reached behind her back and drew her dagger, blocking the stun baton with one

243

motion. With a fluid move, she drew her sword in the other hand. As he stumbled past, she decapitated him; the head rolled down the street, an expression of shock on its face. Blood spurted in pulses from his severed neck; the gushes arced high in the air and splattered on the cobblestone.

"You've been busy I see." Tormod drew his war-hammers from behind his back. "Are there any more to kill?"

"No. This one is it."

"Pity, I could use the action to limber up for today's training." Tormod assisted Joash with the training of recruits. All pledges were required to meet with him for assessment of their combat skills.

"Help me with the body." After removing a small satchel of gold from his side, Sabrina grabbed the razzia's hands and Tormod the feet. They dragged him over to a sewer drain; it took a bit of effort, but they stuffed his headless corpse through the narrow slot. A splash from deep in the sewer escaped the intake vent when his body hit the water. Tormod fetched the man's head and shoved it down the same slot as his body.

The house door opened a crack. Karalynn and Billy peered out onto the street. "Fetch me a bucket of water," Sabrina said. The door closed, and a minute later Billy returned with a wooden bucket filled with water. Karalynn emerged behind Billy, and Sabrina washed the blood from the street.

"What happened?" asked Karalynn.

"A razzia attacked me." Sabrina noticed that Karalynn winced. "You don't need to worry. No one will miss his kind. Besides, it was self-defense."

The sharp clip-clop of horse hoofs on stone echoed through the streets. Chauncey pulled back on the reins and stopped the carriage. He looked over the wagon and its cargo, and a deep frown formed on his face. "Filthy scum," he muttered, "kidnapper of children."

Sabrina pointed at the horse tethered to the prison wagon. It was a painted young stallion, dappled white and brown, matching Chauncey's mare. "Take the horse and attach it to your wagon. The owner met with a bad end. He will not seek it."

"Yes ma'am," Chauncey said. He set the handbrake and scrambled down from his perch. "He is a beautiful looking young colt. What should we do with the wagon?"

"Leave it. I'm sure it will be stripped down to its bolts within the hour." She walked around to the rear of the wagon and released the girls. "You ladies have two choices. You can rush back into the sewers, or you can come with me. If you come with me, you will have food and clothing. There will be hard work and school, but you will be free. If you stay in the sewer, another razzia will find you and press you into service. I can assure you that neither I nor anyone else will rush to your rescue."

One of them asked, "May I bring my little sister?"

"Yes. Find her and meet me at the black castle."

The girls ran off. She presumed in search of a friend or relative. Men exited their homes and milled toward the wagon. "Strip it gentleman, it's yours." Upon hearing this, they rushed back into their homes and emerged carrying wooden tool boxes. The furious activity reminded her of ants dissecting a grasshopper, and in just minutes, every part of the wagon was carried off. Nothing remained to tell the tale of what happened.

"What's happening?" Marla looked about for some explanation. Tormod grunted and entered the home. The aroma of coffee teased his nostrils. Sabrina gave the young woman a brief recount of the conflict. Marla said,

The Great Gate

"One of those people abducted me by mistake once. I was a little girl playing with a friend in an old coal shoot. Well, we were rather dirty, and when we emerged, this disgusting man grabbed us – he threw us in the back of a wagon. My mother heard our screams, and she rushed out and saved us. I still shudder when I think of what almost happened."

"Let's go inside and get some breakfast." Upon entering her home, Sabrina saw the young girl huddled up in a corner of the foyer. She was curled into a ball with her face pressed between her knees. "It's okay. The man is dead. You're safe." The girl raised her head and looked just over her kneecaps. Her dewy brown eyes welled up with tears and cut a channel through the soot as it ran across her cheek.

Sabrina squatted before the girl and combed her fingers through the girl's brunette locks. They were matted with filth and covered with waste oil. She stunk like excrement and ammonia. "What happened to you? How did you end up like this?"

Her name was Kay, and she relayed this tale. Two years ago she lived in a home not far from Karalynn's home. Her father was a stone mason and her mother a wash woman; they had enough to pay their debts and even had enough to buy her a new dress once a year. She lost both parents, one fateful day. She came home from a friend's house; the hour was late, and supper would be ready. When she rounded a corner, she saw flames leaping out from her home; water spewed from a fire engine and shot through open widows, but the flames leap out of the home like a hungry beast. She wept, hoping that her parents had somehow survived.

The fire burned most of the night. The next day, the fireman left, and the crowd dispersed. She was alone on the sidewalk with nowhere to go. She returned to her friend's home, and for a month everything was fine. Then one day her friend's father entered the home with a razzia. She sprinted to the bathroom and wriggled out a window; she fled and never returned.

"We used to be safe in the sewers," Kay said. "Then we started hearing things. Strange shrieks echoed throughout the tunnels. We saw scratches on the tunnel walls, and people began to go missing. One of them was Old Ben" He had a pretty nice home. He found an alcove used for a lunchroom when they were building the sewer lines. He had a nice room with furniture and everything. All of us used to love going to visit him and hear his story from the old days. One day, when we all went to visit him, we found his room destroyed. Someone ripped apart his furniture, and blood streaks stained the walls. Most of the other kids thought it was soldiers."

"But you thought differently," Sabrina replied.

"Yes. The soldiers never come down into the sewers. They don't want to get their uniforms dirty. Sure, there are thieves and cutthroats, but they liked Ben. He fenced their goods in the market, and they left behind his stuff. If thieves killed him, why wouldn't they take his wares? It makes no sense."

Sabrina pondered the girl's tale. "You're right. It does not make sense. So you and your friends have been all over the sewer, and you found nothing?"

"All but 'the down below,'" Kay replied. "It's the deepest part of the underground network. It links up to the old caverns. They were the primary source of water and sewer removal before the tunnel system. It is very easy to get lost in them. They go on forever."

Sabrina raised the girl's chin and looked into her eyes. "You're fine now. Karalynn will wash you and give you fresh clothes to wear. After that, you will come with me and live in the black castle. I run an academy for children, and there are plenty of beds and food for everyone. You'll be safe and live with other young people like yourself."

Chapter 23

Anewly constructed facility housed "The City of Solva Public Works," located in the second district. The nearby residents called it the giant spider: steel legs, an octagon of domes frames, and a roof of plate glass. The aristocrats heralded it as the first fruits of a new age in architecture; the common man called it pretentious and creepy.

"What a disaster," Sabrina grumbled. It used high strength steel and enough glass to make 100 homes, and yet it lacked any defensive capability; it was literally a glass house. A boy with a slingshot could break into the facility.

Chauncey Timmons stopped the carriage and scrambled down from his perch. He placed the stool before the carriage and opened the door. Sabrina, Kayla, Marla, Tormod, and Joash exited the carriage; the wagon springs jumped up the carriage when Joash stepped off. "We'll be occupied quite a while. You should find a shady spot to wait for us."

"Yes ma'am," he replied, with a tip of his hat.

They climbed up the stairs and strode between the spider legs. Passing underneath a canvas awning, they transitioned to the cool building interior. They entered a spacious atrium bathed in light: copper brown tile covered the floor; octagon planters contained small trees and flowers, and metal benches lined the outside perimeter of the planter. Within the center of the atrium, they saw a cafeteria. Employees dressed in professional garb milled about the lobby, carrying trays filled with steaming cups of coffee and pastries. The three inner rings housed the offices, allowing managers to view the atrium and verify the length of employee breaks.

Tormod twitched his nose and searched the overhead offices. "Which one do you suppose houses the head of this gilded cage?" Before receiving a reply, the tantalizing aroma of coffee wooed him into the cafeteria.

It was a reasonable question, and a nearby kiosk provided the answer. A receptionist worked behind the desk, distributing memos and documenting the visitor's log in an oracle scroll; she wore her hair in a tight ponytail and wore a smart, tight skirt suit. "May I help you?" When she saw Joash, she blushed. Although advanced in years, the ruggedly handsome man stole her breath away.

"We need to find the director's office. Where can we find it?"

The girl, Ashley, stood to her feet. She tugged at the hem of her skirt and smoothed it. Unfolding a brochure, she placed it on the countertop and opened it to an architectural layout of the building; "'The Managing Director's Office' is located up on the third level." She circled the location on the map. "If you'd like, I could show you."

"No. That's okay. I think we can find it."

"Okay, have a nice day." As they walked away, she stole a quick peek at him. She read the list of signatures until she found his name, hoping to make a later introduction.

The group strolled to an elevator bank, the doors sliding open at their approach. After entering and selecting the third floor, the elevator launched up three floors, and when the doors slid open before them, a beautiful foyer greeted them. Tan carpeting, French Pavilion furnishings, and evergreen shrub planters adorned the interior space. The even had a brass cappuccino maker, which lay atop a wooden bar.

Sabrina felt like she was back on Earth, and the comfortable lobby bid them to rest; but it was not to be; they had work to accomplish. After a brief stop at the secretary's desk, they were ushered into the director's office, Gregory Kent. He was a small man seated behind an enormous desk, and his high-back chair, worthy of a monarch, was turned with its back toward them, allowing him to look out upon the city.

The brilliant sunlight silhouetted him in black. He swung his chair around, stood up to his feet, and circled around the desk. "Hello, my name is Gregory Kent. I'm glad to see all of you. My men have been missing for three days now. I thought you would never come." He shook all of their hands. "Please, have a seat." They all sat on a leather sofa set.

"I'm not sure about the incident to which you refer …." Sabrina relayed Kay's story about the tunnels. "… She was quite insistent that there is something in the tunnels."

"A week ago, I would have argued the matter." He released a heavy sigh and rubbed his forehead. "Two men went missing four days ago. We thought they might be hurt or lost; it happens on occasion. So I sent four rescue parties, and one of the search parties never returned. Four more men vanished. Rather than sending down additional teams, I notified the authorities, and they sent a single safety inspector. He looked down the shaft and then certified it as safe. My superiors ordered me to resume operations, and then I lost two more men. I don't know what to do!"

"With your permission, we would like to explore this situation."

"That would be most welcome." Gregory slid to the edge of his seat. "What would you require?"

"A tour of the facility would be a good start," Sabrina said.

Mr. Kent gave them a guided tour ending with the pump house. It lay across a small parking lot. Men lingered before a pair of open garage doors. They spoke in whispers and pretended to work, but palpable fear permeated the group.

250

He introduced them to the supervisor; "This is Thomas Bing. He's our chief engineer in charge of our water and sewer treatment plant." A typical beer belly hanging from his midsection, a bald dome trimmed by a ring of red hair, a pair of lamb chop sideburns, grease that stained his hands, face, and even his teeth, Tom Bing appeared the quintessential engineering foreman.

The weary man set down a wrench and wiped his hands. "Are these the people you sent for?" asked Tom. "We need some answers. Those men might be injured and waiting for rescue."

"No, they aren't the ones we sent for, but they are willing to help; and they have some skill with these situations. I want you to assist them."

"Yes sir," Tom replied.

"I will speak with you later about what you find." Mr. Kent passed through the gauntlet of men and disappeared from sight. Tormod grumbled some dwarven slander about bureaucrats under his breath.

Sabrina gathered them around in a circle. "We are not asking you to fight. What we need from you is your expertise regarding the tunnels and the sewer system. Tormod will lead a group of men through the upper tunnels. I will lead two teams down to the old infrastructure. No one else should enter the system until we return." Sabrina scanned the faces of the men around her. "I don't need any heroes, just navigation. Leave the fighting to us." The men rumbled their approval.

Tom led them to the heart of the facility. A massive, steel-reinforced concrete lid covered the top of an immense shaft: the lid was 10 meters in diameter, weighed over 100 tons, and made of impregnable wolfram. Four impressive chains gripped the lid, and each link was as large as a shoebox, weighing more than a man could lift. These chains wrapped around a pulley system and then connected to counterweights. When the

251

counterweights filled with water, the mechanism raised the lid, and it exposed the access shaft.

They all watched as the lid rose into the air and grimaced when a blast of sewer gas billowed out of the shaft. Joash and Marla put on their rebreather masks before Sabrina could give the command. Tormod searched the room and saw spare masks hanging from hooks on the wall. Stretching the rubber strap over his head, he snugged the mask to his face, but his thick beard caused a poor fit. It would have to do. The methane and other gases were unsafe to breath.

"Isn't there a risk of explosion due to the Rhunite in the rock?" asked Sabrina.

"We mitigate that with pumps." Tom pointed to four elbow joints. They were large enough for a man to stand in with his arms raised. They pumped in clean air and when necessary, they washed out the system.

An elevator rose up out of the darkness. They climbed up a set of steps and peered down into the abyss. There were many times in Sabrina's life when she grudgingly ventured into spine-chilling places: this was one of them. Her instincts rang like an alarm bell, and they urged to stay out of the cavern. Rather than ignore her instincts, she expressed them. "Do you feel it? I've been in more shafts than I can count. None of them gave me such a sense of foreboding. There is something down there."

When they tried to hand her a rhunite lamp, she shook her head, her lenses possessed low light technology. The lamp would do more harm than good, but Tormod took one since his mask had simple glass lenses.

Sabrina secured her helmet and snugged down the chin strap. They climbed onto the platform, hanging over the yawning abyss beneath them. As the platform lowered, it seemed that they were descending into a giant throat, and all eyes gazed upward, lamenting the fading light and the shrinking exit, narrowing to a pinpoint of light.

After they had descended through the shaft for 20 minutes, the platform slowed and then stopped. Tormod and his team moved to the edge of the platform. He swung the guard rail out of the way, and a small gap lay between them and the platform. If one missed or slipped, then one would plummet into the darkness and meet certain death. Being surefooted, Tormod gave it little thought and leap over the gap to the ramp. He and his team entered the horizontal shaft, their light fading to a white dot and then all became darkness.

The counterweight passed them by on their journey into the depths. Water sprayed out from a small valve at the bottom of a copper tank; the water outflow regulated the speed of the descent. They watched the glistening shaft wall pass them by, growing wetter by the second, and in the end, a stream of water flowed down the sides of the shaft.

"We're at the bottom." The operator flipped up the rail and stood out of the way. "Signal me when you want to come out. I'll wait at the top of the shaft."

Sabrina exited the platform first and sank down into the knee-deep water. The swift current fought to drag her feet out from underneath her. When the city was first founded, the river was enough to supply all of their drinking water, and when flushed, it carried away the sewerage. They stood in the last level, the sewerage removal level, filled with contaminants and human excrement.

The swift current made walking difficult and running nearly impossible. As the city grew, the old systems could no longer accommodate the quantity of sewage, and new tunnels were constructed; both ancient and new systems flowed through a network of tunnels and then dumped into a treatment facility. They workers treated and packaged the sewerage. They then sold it to farmers who used it to fertilize their crops.

Four main access tunnels formed a four-way connection. The two lower main tunnels were flooded with a swift moving current of waste; therefore, it was impossible to explore them. However, the two overflow tunnels carried a minimum of waste and were passable. Sabrina and Kayla took one. Marla and Joash took the other.

Sabrina paused on a set of slick stairs at the far end of the shaft. She watched Joash and Marla ascend their stairs and disappear from sight. The feeling of dread grew stronger with each step taken and made her question the wisdom of entering this shaft.

———

Tormod gripped his war-hammers and crept through the tunnel. Whenever he moved his head, the lamplight reflected off the glistening round walls, creating a jigsaw portrait of the passage, but most of the tunnel remained a dark void. When he scanned the walls, he saw something out of the corner of his eyes and snapped his light back to it. Scratch marks, deep and long, marred the circular black walls, and they were fresh.

Dwarves are very sensitive to the soil, so Tormod removed his armored glove. Then touching the wall, he sensed the planet's heartbeat. Something was amiss. Like static on a radio, he sensed something nearby – something familiar, something deadly — but he could not discern it. A dwarf in the mines would smell the air and taste the ground, but here that would yield only sewerage. With two of his senses disabled, he relied upon sight and touch. Danger lurked ahead; he knew that, but he had to proceed. Lives were counting on him.

———

Despite the crosshatch pattern cut into the steps, Marla's and Joash's boots slipped on the slippery stairs, filth oozing out from underneath their boots. The flight of stairs led out of the tunnel and up a side passage. When they arrived at a small landing, they found yet another flight of stairs. Red with rust and stained with sediment, a steel railing provided meager support, and each handhold caused green fungus to squish through their fingers.

Joash reached the top of the stairs first and found himself at the entrance to a long tunnel. He paused near the side and waited for Marla. The low light lenses activated and transformed the dark tunnel to shades of green. Joash drew out his sword and strapped on his shield. Although he saw nothing, holding it made him feel better.

The tunnel walls were damp, slimy, and glistening. At first, Joash thought it was rubble, but there was something amiss, something wrong about its appearance. They tried to move with stealth, but one could still hear the squish of their steps; and a spongy substance covered the floor … rubber? He could not be sure. He glanced back at Marla. She too had her weapons drawn and ready.

The tunnel came to an abrupt end. A half circle barrier stood before them. Joash searched the wall: green light illuminating the surface. He saw structural supports and bolts pounded into the stone. Sweeping his gaze back and forth, he made out the form of a hatch.

He returned his sword to its sheath and then grabbed a circular wheel. Straining with all his might, he tried to turn the rusted gears, but they would not budge. Marla's hands joined his, and they heaved. The gears gave way, and the wheel turned, causing six large bolts to retract.

The vault door groaned and echoed on the tunnel walls. Joash ducked and passed through the opening with his sword ready. Although muscular and tall, he moved with the stealth of a jungle cat and crept to the edge of a concrete platform. He sensed Marla moving behind him, covering him from the rear.

The pair stood on a platform that overlooked an immense cavern. The natural cavern dome rose high and out of sight; however, they saw rooftops below them and counted six buildings; three were house size, and the other three were warehouses, and many little shacks were scattered among these buildings. Like everything within the sewer, a fine layer of muck and water covered the structures, leaving them dingy gray and glistening. Rust, like cancer, ate through the metal roofs, causing them to collapse into the center of the structures, rubble of a forgotten time. Broad streets passed between the large buildings, but debris blocked most. Machines dissolved into dark red rust, freezing in place like fossils, waiting for some future discovery by an archeologist.

They discovered the old public works.

Joash heard a click and paused on the steps; another three clicks echoed around him. When silence returned, he continued down the steps. A concrete wall rose up to the left, and the railing lay to his right. His steps placed with care, and he made his way down the stairs; after descending several flights of stairs, they arrived at the bottom of the cavern. The clicks grew louder and more frequent. Screeches like fingernails on a chalkboard set his nerves on edge and made his heart pound and ears alert to every sensation.

When Joash's foot touched the bottom of the cavern, it stepped into something sticky. Dread overwhelmed him like nausea. He resisted the urge to run and pressed forward.

They passed by a small building. The windows were broken long ago, and the wood rotted to a wispy covering. The mask's green light reflected off a thin film on the water. He looked behind him and saw Marla. She walked backward, covering their flank.

Joash evaluated and placed with caution. His senses screamed of danger, shouted for him to flee, but he saw nothing. The old streets were empty, but he was sure that something lingered in the darkness.

———

Scott Marcy

The void reached out and enveloped Sabrina, and each step escalated a sense of foreboding doom. The ground heated the water into a dense fog, but her starlight vision emitted pulses of high-frequency light; and after reflecting off a surface, it bounced back to the lenses. She saw scratch marks on the walls and heard shuffling noises up ahead. She paused and reached out with her mind. All elves are telepathic, but she was a Maige: her senses were more powerful. In ordinary circumstances, her telepathy extended for miles, yet her scans were blocked. By what? What could block the telepathic ability of a Maige? The list was short and terrifying.

Something lay on the floor. Sabrina took a few pensive steps, and the lenses illuminated irregular shapes, reminding her of crisscrossing gashes. She took another step, and the ground grew sticky. Her senses screamed in alarm as she approached the peculiar piles.

Sabrina squatted beside a pile and probed it with the tip of her sword; a chunk of flesh rolled down from the top and landed at her feet. Something fell past her eyes and hit the ground with a splat. She gazed straight up at the ceiling overhead. Gauged eye sockets, stripped flesh, blood oozing, bare bone exposed, a screaming skull gazed down at her. The mutilated corpse of a man hung above her, glued in place by slime. Her gaze darted to the right and saw another victim; intestines swelled out of an abdominal cavity, and terrible gashes ripped out chunks of flesh. Blood dripped onto her face. Sabrina heard rushing sounds, and she poised her weapons. They were under attack.

———

Tormod crept around the curved edge of the tunnel, but the smooth wall came to a jagged end; sharp pieces of concrete, jagged and irregular, steel reinforcement bars jutting like spiked teeth rimmed it. He examined the cuts, and no tool he knew of would create such an opening. Bits of rock and soil lay scattered about the ground. He set down a hammer, picked up a handful of earth, and squeezed it. The soil was still fresh.

Retrieving his hammers, he moved through the rupture. Swirling like a fibrous vortex, peculiar interwoven fibers formed a funnel, held in place by some type of resin, and lined the interior of a twisting shaft. All at once, his mind comprehended what his eyes beheld.

Skree!

The dwarf warrior readied his war-hammers; one poised above his head and the other before him. Over the long years of his life, he bashed skree, creating piles of bodies. Then he remembered those who stood behind him. The worker's trembling hands caused their lights to jostle, which created a strobe effect. Sabrina was right. This was no time for combat.

He recalled countless battles; the skree preferred concealed places deep within the earth – the other search parties were in danger. He spun around and sprinted past the men. The two workmen watched the dwarf sprint past them and looked at one another. They dropped their lamps and chased after him.

Tormod sprinted through the tunnel; his short, sturdy legs bounded, taking great strides. When he neared the tunnel exit, he saw two platforms. One was before him, and the other platform hovered in the air across the cave; and a thin ledge circled the shaft.

"Go up to the top. I'm taking the other lift to the bottom of the shaft." The men piled onto the lift and threw the lever. The platform soared out of sight. Tormod raced around a narrow ledge; his dwarven feet met the small ledge with the surefootedness of a mountain goat. The operator saw Tormod leap through the air and land on his platform. Tormod shouted, "Take us to the bottom. Now!"

————

Joash saw a single drop splash across his right lens, and another fell on his hand. Drops rained down upon him and splashed in the water around his feet. He gazed upward to find the source.

A scream ripped through his mind. Crawling, rubbing, swarming, glistening, squealing insects, millions of them hung upon the dome; some were twice the size of a man, others the size of hawks. A layer of slime made them shimmer, and they crawled in a boiling mass. He could not breathe – 400 million years of evolution screamed, "RUN!"

He fought his instincts and suppressed the urge to flee. When he looked back at Marla, she stared at the cavern dome as if frozen like a statue. He turned and walked around her with calm, deliberate steps, and on his way past, he gave her a slight nudge. Marla swung her blades at empty air. Her stomach lurched and threatened to vomit. She dry heaved and fought off the compulsion. Removing her mask in this environment would be fatal.

The pair reversed their path and stepped through each puddle as if it would break. Bits of flesh rained around them, splashing in the puddles, and as Joash gazed at the dancing waters, a horrible revelation occurred to him, a revelation hidden from his eyes by the green starlight amplification – the puddles were blood.

Joash hid this epiphany. Marla's mind was already at the breaking point. They climbed the steps, two at a time. Each step took them higher and closer to the chaos looming above them but also brought them closer to escape. When they reached the upper landing, they halted. Cockroaches the size of cats streamed through the open hatch.

———

"FASTER," Tormod shouted.

"We're going as fast as we can," the driver replied, the updraft swallowing his words. "If we go any faster, we won't have enough time to slow before we reach the bottom."

Tormod shoved the operator aside – he grabbed the lever and thrust it to maximum. The platform plummeted out from underneath their feet; they fell through the yawning darkness, the bottom and destruction rushing toward them. His dwarven instincts reached out and sensed the approaching bottom.

———

Horrible screeches, like fingernails on a blackboard, stung Sabrina's ears. Fragmented green images rushed at her from the darkness, and she slashed at mandibles and deflected pinchers. Sword-like legs thrust at her like spears. She deflected them and sliced off insect limbs; her blade chopped off a compound eye and then severed a torso. Insects flew at them in a wild frenzy.

Viscous fluid splattered them like paint. The toxic secretions, adhering to flesh and burning lungs, would paralyze them, but their masks and slip-suits protected them. Sabrina whirled, chopping at fragmented images; angry venom spewed in reply, coating her mask with thick green ooze.

Skree eat their victims alive.

Kayla slashed at bugs, out of control, her instincts going wild. Wings and bodies pelted her, and fluid sprayed all over her entire body until she dripped with it. Out of the corner of her eye, she saw Sabrina. The elva jumped and whirled; every slice of her blades hit the mark and cut through an insect exoskeleton. Flying limbs pelted her and deflected off her in a wild frenzy; it was as though the bugs were in a blender, issuing a spray of limbs and fluids.

All at once the attack stopped. Sabrina drew breathless heaves and searched the darkness. "RUN!"

The pair sprinted through the tunnel, shrill screeches chasing them. The insects filled the tunnel like a rushing torrent of water. Sabrina rushed past Kayla toward the end of the tunnel. When she came to the stairs, she leaped over the railing and fell into the darkness. She hit the sewer water with a splash and rolled. Kayla hit the water after her.

Sabrina jumped up out of the sewerage, her blades ready for combat; a moment later the platform hit the water, sending a tidal wave at them, throwing them backward in the filth.

Two figures leaped over a railing and plummeted through the darkness. Joash and Marla hit the water. Joash came up first, his blade ready for combat. "Skree are after us," Joash signaled.

"GET ON THE LIFT!"

The four warriors ran through the waters and tumbled onto the platform. The operator cowered in fear, but Tormod launched into action and threw the lever. The platform exploded out of the water, and the force slammed them onto the deck. They raced through the shaft, feeling the speed but unable to see a thing. In midflight, the copper counterweight plummeted past them and streaked to the bottom. The cable feeding through the pulley began to wind tight, rotating the platform in a clockwise direction. A pinhole of light appeared above them and grew larger by the second. The cable wound tight, and for a precious moment, the platform stopped rotating; it then began to spin in the other direction.

They could hear the rush of a million wings and countless screeches. Round and round they spun, barely holding onto the platform. The light grew larger and larger, rushing at them like a train.

Tormod fought the G-force, and his fingertips tickled the lever grip. With a final heave, he grabbed it and yanked it backward. The cable mechanism groaned; the armature strained against the load, and the cable threatened to snap. The platform slammed into the bumper rail, and they launched into the air, then striking the bottom of the plug. A second later gravity resumed, and they fell.

The armature hit Joash in the gut, and he doubled over it like a sack of potatoes. The others hit the platform with a loud bang and the groan of metal. Marla's thighs smacked the edge of the platform, her upper body swinging down into the void. At the last moment, somebody fell on her legs, pinning her. She dangled upside down in the inky void, staring into the abyss, watching her swords tumble into the darkness, barely able to breathe as they disappeared from sight.

Joash was the first to recover. He crawled off the armature and jumped onto the stairs, but Tormod was right behind him. A hand grabbed Marla's right arm and yanked her onto the platform. Sabrina planted her hand at the junction of Marla's thighs and heaved, launching the young woman into the air by her crotch. Marla flapped her arms and legs as if trying to fly. Hurtling through the air, she sailed up and out of the shaft, and remembering her training, she recovered and rolled, coming to a stop on the concrete floor. A moment later, she saw Kayla sail through the air; Kayla landed on top of Marla between her spread knees, her hands on Marla's breasts. The pair of women recovered and rolled out of the way. The lift operator fell toward them, and he hit the concrete with a meaty thud, a groan coming from him a moment later.

Sabrina leaped out of the shaft and ripped off her mask. "Shut the lid. SHUT IT NOW!" Tom hesitated a second and then ran for the emergency release. He grabbed a steel lever and slammed it. The counterweight buckets opened at the same time and dumped their contents. The lid fell and hit the shaft with a thunder clap. A moment later, insects impacted the 100-ton cap with an enormous explosion, causing the cover to jump and then fall with a rumbling crash.

"What is it?" yelled Tom.

"SKREE!"

Tom slammed down the emergency release arm. Three glass chambers lined the far wall. 1000 gallons of grayish yellow and brown inert chemicals filled each bottle; sitting upside upon metal stands, the fluid within the bottles began to bubble and mix in a single, larger container. They combined into a deadly pesticide and sprayed into the airflow ducts, filling the shaft with a lethal toxin.

They struggled to their feet and watched the fluid bubble and drain. The tumult in the chamber began to calm, and it became so quiet no one dared breathe. Sabrina was the first to move and crept over to the lid. Pressed her ear to the concrete lid, she said, "It's working. I can hear them falling."

Tom wiped the sweat from his brow with a red handkerchief. He let out a loud sigh and shook his head. "I'm glad the architects thought of everything. It paid off today."

Sabrina walked over to a bench and collapsed onto it. She rested her elbows on her knees and rubbed her face. "A vital question must be asked – who put the skree down there?"

Chapter 24

Cody curled into a ball on her bunk, her back to the wall. The laughter and joyous merriment of other teens penetrated her dorm door, but she was sullen, deep in thought. The exhilaration of the trip, adventure, and future glory came to an abrupt end, replaced by a continual academic grind.

A single overhead lamp beamed down upon her and the rough wooden furniture that filled her dorm room; it saw many generations of cadet warriors, and it showed it. The Spartan room provided shelter, but it lacked the warmth of her room back at home, a room decorated by the loving hand of a mother.

Adolescence gave way to adulthood, and the girl blossomed into a woman. Solva lay far to the south near the southern seas; its summers were hot and winters mild. Bathed in this temperate environment, her body adapted with stunning brevity, as was the nature of all morphs. Her flaxen hair turned raven black; her fair skin darkened to a deep bronze, and her blue eyes became so dark that they appeared black.

The door burst open and slammed against the interior wall. Kelvin strutted into the room and waved, laughter still hung on his lips. "I'll see you guys in a few minutes. I need to change my uniform and cleats."

After he had closed the door with his left foot, he stripped off his tan cotton tunic. "Oh, there you are. I was wondering where you got off to. I'm going to soccer practice. Would you like to come? I hear that the cheerleaders are having open tryouts. I bet you could make it."

"Master Tormod was here," she snapped. "He gave us five demerits. You can't leave your dirty laundry all over the floor." She flung the demerit slip at him by way of proof. "Now we have kitchen duty tonight."

"Yeah, okay," he grumbled. He scooped up his soiled clothes and stuffed them into a wooden hamper. "Everybody gets demerits. Running is a demerit. Talking loud is a demerit." When Cody failed to respond, he glanced back at her. Cody stayed curled up in a ball and kept her gaze fixed on the floor. "What's wrong with you?"

"Nothing, I'm fine," she said.

"No you are not," he replied. He crossed the room and scooted up next to Cody on the bed. "I've known you my entire life. I know when you are upset." He waited in silence, but she refused to answer. "Okay, let's play a guessing game. You're angry because I peed on the toilet seat?"

"No. Yes," Cody said. "I hate it when you do that. But that's not what's bothering me."

"Something is bothering you." When he tried to rub her shoulder, she pulled away from him. "Is it something I did? Is it something my dad did? Is it something our resident advisor did? I'm not going to leave you alone until you tell me."

Another long silence pause ensued. Finally, she forged her courage. "It's just that … well, it's just that we're so far away."

"'Far away,'" he echoed. "I know the cafeteria is way across the campus near the gym. I mean, they could have given us a closer room in the new dormitories. So what if the upper classman outranks us. We need to eat too."

"Not that," she huffed and scooted off the bed. She lifted up Kelvin's hamper lid and flipped the draped shirtsleeve inside it. She looked at a bookshelf with vacant eyes.

"Then what?" he said. "I'm not a wizard. I can't read your mind."

"It's my family." She turned to face him. "You have your mother and father near you. My dad is … he's dead; everyone thinks my mom is a murderer, and my family lives over a thousand miles away. We only get three weeks off for the winter celebration and another three weeks off for the summer festival. It would take me five days at a minimum to travel by shuttle and wagon to home. It's not enough time. We've been here six months, and I just realized that I'm never going to see my family." Tears welled up in her eyes.

"Oh, about that, I was supposed to give you a message, but I kind of forgot." He shrugged and rubbed the back of his neck. "You know how we found out that my dad is high royal?" She nodded. "Well, your mom found out too. How I have no idea. Your family lives so far away. She's scary. Anyway, it was probably because the Solva Journal wrote a story about him a couple of months ago. Anyway, the other news services picked it up and echoed it everywhere. I asked my dad if I was a prince. He said, 'No. You have to be officially registered to be a prince, and my grandmother was only a concubine.' My dad could register me. It would give me increased standing in class. I could have individual instruction —"

Cody crossed her arms and interrupted, "What was the message?"

"Oh yeah, your mom is coming to visit. 'She wants to be a part of our lives.'" He crossed his arms and frowned. "I'm not sure what that means, and I'm pretty sure I'm not going to like it. She hates me. Your mom contacted a realtor and bought a flat. Apparently, frequent visits are in our future. She has given up on Conrad, and I think she wants us to get married. I told my mom, 'We are only 19. I don't want to get married or even engaged.' We have plenty of time for that. It's insane. Who makes up the rules for these crazy traditions?"

Cody threw her arms around him and hugged him. He held her for a second, and she began to cry. "I thought having your mom visit would make you happy?"

"It does," she sniffled.

"You better tell your eyes because you're crying," he said.

She wiped the tears from her eyes and laughed, "Girls cry about everything."

He took her in his arms and kissed her. Soon they intertwined and made love. They began a physical relationship long ago, but now it was a regular part of their lives as if it always had been. As he stripped off her clothes, cares barged into her mind. Something about the journey from girl to woman that was so public, so humiliating. Cody hated it. Boys grew strong and tall; girls swelled up and bulged out. It was so unfair.

On Eden, when a girl became sexually active, her body developed the classic female shape. This generally occurred over months, perhaps years. However, for some girls, most notably morphs, it took place overnight. Everyone called it "the heat." Mothers and girlfriends were the first to notice the signals. They had visible proof that their daughter had become sexually active. The idea distressed Cody: everyone, including her mother, would know what she had been doing. There was no use denying it.

As they lay together, her mind began to wander. She wondered what life was like for a boy. She rolled onto her side, propping her head with her left arm, and asked, "Would ever you trade bodies with me? So I could see how sex is for a boy? I hear there are magical medallions that can do it. I just mean temporarily."

"No, I'm happy being a guy." He got out of bed and wandered into the bathroom. Cody heard the toilet flush and the water run.

"Why not," she whined. "It would be fun."

The Great Gate

He ignored her and strode from the room. She quickly threw on her clothes and chased after him. He was talking with three other boys: Calvin, Gerald, and Hugh. She jumped to a stop and stood at Kelvin's right hand.

Kelvin put his arm around Cody's shoulder and leaned against her. Cody saw his hand grasping her shoulder and wondered what it meant; he had never done that around other people. The other boys understood it – Kelvin laid claim to Cody – interlopers would be punished.

Another first occurred, Kelvin's hand slid down her back and glided over the swell of her bottom – and it stayed there. Cody's cheeks burned hot, and her body went stiff. His hand glided over the slopes of her cappuccino leather slacks. When he grabbed her bottom, she gasped and rose to the balls of her feet. All the boys were staring at her – she froze.

They chatted for a while, his hand lingering on her nether regions. When his hand departed her body and moved to her hand, she began to relax. He led her toward the cafeteria, and she shuffled stepped beside him. She released a tense breath and combed her fingers through her hair.

Boys passing them by in the opposite direction stared at her chest as they approached and then her bottom as she passed. The girls, however, looked at them holding hands and then at her breasts, by way of comparison. Girls were never happy with their bodies: if they had large breasts, then they wanted small ones, and if they had small breasts, they wanted large breasts. It was always something.

They walked through the dormitory hallway and entered the commissary. A throng of shouting, laughing, and playing cadets gathered around tables. Hungry youths crowded around food concessions, while others engaged in private conversations. Retail outlets lined the perimeter of the dining hall, filled with clothing, school supplies, shampoo, laundry soap, and other goods.

They merged into the crowd and became separated. Kelvin's arm slipped off Cody's shoulders when he spotted a gaggle of girls; they stole furtive glances, giggled, and spoke in whispers. Cody lagged behind him as he wandered toward the girls. They were so beautiful, and there were so many of them. As if in a trance, he walked toward them, unaware of his seething girlfriend behind him.

Cody crossed her arms and glared at the other girls, daring them to speak with Kelvin. The girls stared back at them like a group of curious owls. When Kelvin talked to the girls, they scattered. He gaped and scratched his head, and when he turned, he saw jealousy in her eyes.

"I need to get to practice. The coach will be angry if I am late again." Kelvin turned to flee, leaving a furious girlfriend behind. Fending off amorous females was a full-time activity. Kelvin grew at an astonishing rate. Every day, he grew a little taller and stronger than most of his peers. His thick black locks, broad nose, and square jaw reflected that of his father. In a land where 2 out of 3 babies were female, such young men were in high demand.

Chapter 25

Brilliant light beamed through the hall. Kelvin slung an equipment bag over his shoulders and hurried out to the practice fields. The freshly mowed grass and the dry summer heat begged her to come out and play. But Cody flopped onto a chair and moped.

All of the other girls belonged to a group, a clique. Some of the cliques were five and others as many as eight. While everyone else was forming friendships that would last a lifetime, she spent her time studying, exercising, or with Kelvin. That left little time for other girls her age. She considered joining the cheerleading squad, but they hated her. It might have had something to do with her constant insults.

A voice called out from above the crowd. "…We are the Dagger Guild. Our mission, our destiny is to become the greatest warriors in Asgard. We fight harder and endure longer than all others. If you are smart and tough, then pledge with us and join the future of the Black Dragon Guild …."

That was all that Cody needed to hear. She moved toward the registration table and picked up the stylus. She asked a boy seated at the registration table, "Do you take girls?"

"We sure do," Corbin Jones replied. "Sign up." When she signed her name, the boy used the opportunity to look down the neckline of her top. *Nice tits*, he thought. *I'd do her.* The fact that she would never "do him," never occurred to him.

"My name is Andrew Boylan," a boy said as he walked up to the table. "We don't get many female pledges. Most of them join the 'Slasher Guild.' That guild pledges the Valkyrie." He searched for some recognition of the group in her face. Seeing none, he took the stylus from her and said, "We have a pledge meeting outside on the athletic fields starting in 50 minutes. Be there on time or don't bother coming."

"I'll be there," Cody replied.

"Good, if you want to get a few paces ahead of the others read the pledge handbook; be ready to answer a few questions. You will have to memorize our code of conduct and our house history. The probationary period is one semester. At the end of the semester, we vote on where you can join. All it takes is one black mark, and you are out. Do you still want to pledge?"

"Yes," she said.

"Fine, we will see you then."

When she turned to walk away, a male voice said, "Excuse me." Cody turned around and saw a swarthy young man. "My name is Jedidiah Sansier. I'm the Dagger House Chapter Treasurer. Do you know Kelvin Faroe, the son of the new 'Battle Master' in charge of recruiting and training?"

"Yes. Kelvin's my ... well, he's my boyfriend." Cody cocked her head. "Why?"

"Nothing, I was just curious. His father's exploits are legendary. I wrote a paper about him in a course, "the History of Warfare." Do you think I might be able to speak with him about addressing our guild sometime?" asked Jedidiah.

"Sure. I go over to his house all the time." Cody cocked her head and screwed up her face in a question mark. Jedidiah's face lit up. What was the big deal? It was just Mr. Faroe.

The Great Gate

"I have to speak with some people," Jedidiah said as he backed away. "I'll stop by practice with some of my brother warriors." He then turned and disappeared into the crowd.

Cody flipped through the rulebook. All morphs have an eidetic memory, and she memorized it with a single scan, committing the entire book to remembrance. She sighed and rose to her feet, tossing the book back onto the signup table. "I've got it," she said to the astonished boy. "I'll be at practice."

The academy hallways teamed with students. They rushed around her without a single hint of recognition. She was a stranger, soon to be forgotten, but she would remember them in detail, the hint of a smile, a lustful gaze, a disapproving frown; the shape of a nose, the curve of their chin, and the color of their eyes; every detail was burned into her brain. Not one of them looked at her with affection or love.

While the standard cadet uniform; cappuccino leather slacks, matching jacket, and a tan silk blouse were excellent for studies, they were inadequate for exercise. She stripped off her jacket and then unbuttoned her blouse and stripped off her athletic bra, a bra designed for a less developed woman. Cody cringed and studied her reflection. How would she explain her body to her mother? Would the other girls tease her? Stupid question, of course they would, but unlike boys, girls criticized in private whispers, sharing veiled barbs, fighting with friends rather than fists.

The tiny nylon bra draped across her hand, insisting that she make a decision. If she kept wearing it, her secret would appear regular, no larger than any of the other girls, but the constriction would reduce her lung capacity, resulting in poor athletic performance. How long could she maintain the façade? Eventually, she would have to appear without it.

Summoning her courage, she tossed aside the undersized bra and accepted her fate. Her mom sent her a proper, sensible sports bra –

supportive but complementary according to her mom – but it remained unused, hidden in the bottom of her dresser. She opened the bottom drawer and fished around for it; seeing and then pulling on a black satin strap, the dreaded garment dangled from her pinched fingers, reminding her of some strange apparatus for an alien species.

The bra had a simple design; she worked it down her upraised arms and fed her head through it. The elastic material constricted around the top of her breasts like a cloth rope. Pinching, pulling, and cursing, she worked the elastic over her spongy breasts; the globes slipped into the cups and bulged.

She fussed and struggled, wondering if she had it on backward. Examining her back in the mirror, she noted how non-supportive the back appeared. A sigh escaped her lips. She tried to adjust the constrictive garment, but it was no use; it presented her breasts for all to admire.

She held out the matching panties and stabbed her feet into them. The garment had a wide, elastic waistband and arched high over her hips. When she saw herself in the mirror, it appeared as though she was wearing black satin lingerie, not the fashion statement she desired. What she wanted was rough, athletic, and dangerous, but what she got was sexy.

The workout uniform was little better. The boys wore athletic shoes, blue knee lengthy baggy shorts, and white cotton T-shirts. The girls, however, wore metallic gold shorts – short, shiny, and entirely too tight – called bloomers, they provided marginal covering. The matching crop-top left her midriff bare, and the neckline exposed a tantalizing bit of her bra cups.

Why do girls have to go around naked all the time?

The Great Gate

She spotted a pair of Kelvin's soiled gray sweat pants and a T-shirt. When she picked them up, his aroma drove her nostrils wild, and she pressed them to her face, imbibing his scent. Her mind floated upon the clouds for a second and peace settled over her like a warm blanket. She was tempted, but if she wore them, they would send her right back to change.

After putting on her running shoes and ankle socks, she took a breath and steeled herself. She left her dorm room with her head locked in a forward gaze, fists clenched, ready for the first rude comment. She refused to make eye contact and walked with swift steps, certain that people were pointing and giggling.

She made her way through the compound, certain that her breasts were bouncing like a pair of balls. After exiting a fire door, the black metal fire stairs rattled underneath her feet. She hopped past the last two steps and landed upon the thick sod. After sneaking up to the corner of the building, as if an enemy waited on the other side, she leaned around the corner and peered out at the athletic field.

Hopeful girls tried out for the cheerleading squad. Most of the girls floundered, flailing their arms and legs as if they had bug down their shirts. A few girls performed semi-erotic dances: bumps, grinds, pelvis thrusts, and undulations. The captain of the squad appreciated their performance a little too much, unmasking her sexual preference.

The boys raced about the athletic field. Cody left the protective cover and chewed on her index fingernail. Kelvin ran through the soccer field, kicking the ball and dodging opponents; his chiseled muscles, his sun bronzed skin, his raven-dark hair, his captivating brown eyes ensnared her imagination. She wandered to the edge of the field, and everything faded but him. When a defender stepped in his way, he bowled over the boy, resulting in a whistle blast from the referee.

The Dagger House banner was unimaginative and unattractive. A pair of black daggers was set on an azure field of blue. Above them were scrolls of knowledge, and below them was a white shield with a black dragon upon it. Battle Master Tormod stood before a group of students seated upon the ground. Cody hurried to the back and sat with the girls.

"Now that we are all here, we may begin." Tormod drew out his sword and recited the pledge with the cadets. "We pledge our fealty, our duty, and our sacred honor to the Dragon House and The Black Dragon which we serve, devotion in life, nobility in service, and courage in death."

"Now let's attend to the new matters. We have three new pledges to our guild; Roman Adams, Kari Stengle, and Cody Moyer. Please come up front and let us take a look at you." The three of them rose to their feet and passed through the seated cadets. They stood before the assembled group, and all eyes shifted to Cody, making her feel a bit conspicuous. Cody clasped her hands behind her back and stared at the ground, every so often stealing a furtive glance through her bangs. "Welcome to our group. Let's give them a hearty cheer." The group rose to their feet, thumped their right fist to their chest, and gave an exuberant shout.

For some peculiar reason, Cody felt like crying. She fought off the tears and let pride replace them. "Let's break up into pairs. We will practice our hand to hand combat drills."

Corbin and all the boys surged toward Cody. Corbin stood in the front of the crowd and reached her first. "We'll work out over here," he said. He placed his hand on the center of Cody's back and led her to a private corner beneath the shade of a leafy elm. She glanced back at him and then at his arm, wondering what kind of workout he had in mind.

"I'll go easy on you since it's your first time." Corbin crouched down in the ready position, feet and arms spread, eyes fixed on his opponent.

275

Cody stood upright and replied with curiosity. He said, "Get ready. I'm coming for you."

"I'm ready," she replied.

Corbin lunged at her and tried to grab her. She stepped aside, deflected his right hand, and tripped him with her foot. He stumbled and hit the ground, sliding face first on the grass. Peals of laughter broke out from the rest of the group.

The young man scrambled to his feet. He brushed off the grass and nursed his wounded pride. "You got lucky. Let's see if you can handle this." He spread his feet apart and poised his fists by his sides.

When Corbin thrust his right fist, she both deflected and grabbed it. She jumped up, grabbed his arm and head in a scissor lock, then twisted her body, and flipped him, Corbin's body hitting the ground with a fleshy thud, a pained groan arising from the young man. She squeezed her powerful thighs and twisted his arm, pinching the nerve in his wrist. "Do you yield?"

"No!" he shouted.

She squeezed harder and turned his arm. "I'll snap it if I twist any harder. Do you yield?"

Kelvin jogged over to the sidelines and took a drink from the tin water cup. He witnessed Cody's takedown maneuver. She was nimble and athletic, a dangerous combination. He often grimaced from the kick of her foot or groaned from the sting of her punch, both finding his nerve clusters. The girl did not know how to hold back.

The pair got up off the ground and brushed off the grass. Cody's opponent must have yielded, or he would have had a broken arm. He chuckled and shook his head. Then something happened which he did not expect.

Three boys, including Corbin, escorted her around the corner of a building. An instinctual sense of danger made Kelvin's hair stand on end, and something screamed for him to act. He threw down the cup and jogged around the bleachers. Master Tormod saw Kelvin race through the squad and watched him round the corner.

Kelvin lingered next to the brick equipment building. While Corbin talked to Cody, one of the other boys, Peter, walked behind her. Without warning, he dropped to his knees. Corbin shoved Cody; she tripped over Peter and fell backward into the bushes. While she lay there stunned, Peter grabbed her legs. She tried to wrestle free, but the other boy, Douglas, helped restrain her; the pair wrestled her onto her stomach.

Blood burned in Kelvin arteries when he saw Corbin reach into his shorts. He sprinted toward them and threw himself at Corbin, knocking him to the ground with a body blow. Corbin sailed through the air and hit the muddy sod, his hand still in his shorts.

Peter released Cody's legs and jumped to his feet, and he threw a punch at Kelvin. Kelvin deflected the blow and hit Peter on the right side. His other elbow swept down and hit the side of Peter's face. Peter spun, spitting blood and teeth, and hit the ground.

Douglas attacked from the rear. Kelvin leaped into the air, kicked, and spun around. His right foot struck Douglas's stomach. When Douglas doubled over, Kelvin kicked with his left foot, smacking Douglas in the face. The boy wilted.

Master Tormod ran to them. "What is going on here? Stop all this."

Cody jumped up from the ground, ready for battle; she danced about on her tiptoes, searching for someone to fight. When she noticed Master

The Great Gate

Tormod's angry expression, she cringed. "Corbin said that he wanted to show me a secret spot over here. He knocked me down, and these two grabbed me."

"And you, what's your story?"

"I walloped them," Kelvin replied.

"And?"

"And whatever he was going to pull out of his pants, Cody wasn't going to like it."

Tormod scratched his bearded chin and mused. "Ten strokes of the rod for the three of you. We are a fighting guild; your comrades in arms must be able to trust you with their lives. If you betrayed that trust, then you damage the group's unity. As to you young lady, ask more questions. Don't be so gullible." He turned to Kelvin; "You have one of two choices. Join the guild, and all will be well. We fight as a part of our training, and I could dismiss this as a part that mandate. If you refuse, then your actions will be reported to the headmaster. He will impose whatever discipline he deems best. Expulsion is a possibility."

"That's not fair. They were the ones acting like daemia," Kelvin whined.

"Perhaps, but you could have called for a school official or run for help. You chose to fight. Now you must live with the consequences. Besides, running around kicking a ball is no preparation for combat."

"But I already practice two hours every morning with my father."

"Who is your father?"

"Battle Master Joash Faroe," Kelvin sighed. "I have to practice every day and eight hours on Saturday. I hardly have time for anything else."

278

"We will join you." Tormod crossed his arms and tapped his chin with his index finger. "That is if your father has no objections. I fought against your father once in the 'Grim Wars.' As it turned out a nagual worked its way into our ranks and deceived us; your father exposed the creature. Quite a few wizards were embarrassed in the dwarf community. The next five wars I fought by his side. He's a great warrior and a great leader. Now that I know you are his son, you must join our guild."

"Fine, but I want to fight Corbin," Kelvin replied.

"Done," Tormod said. "He could use a good beating." He then turned to Corbin. "Keep your hand out of your pants, or I'll cut off whatever it's holding." He said to Cody, "You will administer the lashes."

Cody opened her mouth to object but thought better of it. "Yes sir," was all she said. The group followed Tormod back to the practice field.

The dwarf chose a switch from a pile of weapons and handed it to Cody. The boys took off their shirts and bared their backs to the girl. The switch was thin and light, stinging but causing no real injury, just red streaks. After she had lashed the boys, they returned to practice.

They broke up into pairs, and Corbin had a difficult afternoon. Tormod forbade broken bones or severe injuries, but bruises were acceptable. Corbin had them from head to toe.

The Great Gate

Chapter 26

The bells sounded, and the students shot up from their desks. Kelvin collected his oracle scrolls and stuffed them into his pack. He had every minute of his day accounted for – his father saw to that. He never pictured academy life as being so exhausting. He was tired and sore all the time.

Cody chatted away with some of the girls from their guild. When Kelvin trudged past her, she scampered up to his side and bounced as she walked. Kelvin grumbled. There was nothing as annoying as a cheerful person when one is exhausted.

"I never knew that about the Solva Range Wars. I heard about them of course, but I never knew the details. Who would think people could ever get so excited about cows?" asked Cody.

Kelvin grunted. When he took an unexpected left turn, she hesitated and stared at him as he walked away. "Where are you going? I thought we were going to the room." She chewed a fingernail and then hurried after him.

Kelvin ascended three floors of spiral mahogany stairs. Wooden framed doors held stained glass panels. He shoved them open and marched down the center aisle of the chapel. A wide band of gold, red, blue, and green stained glass stretched across the face of the chapel and tapered down to a point, much like a banner. A beam of light reached down like God's finger, and the tip touched the center of an altar placed upon a dais. He walked past the wooden pews, and the melodious sounds of a children's choir reverberated off the walls. Midway through the chapel, he slipped down onto a bench and leaned back.

Cody waited in the rear of the chapel and cocked her head. Many questions arose in her mind, but she voiced none of them. Instead, she approached him with timid steps and sat down beside him; he glanced at her and returned his focus to the empty altar. She waited in silence, pain filling the void.

Kelvin rubbed his face and rested his chin upon the pew before him. "I remember my first trip to a temple. It was so ... spectacular. The priests wore white robes with gold embroidery. Censers swung on golden chains, and the incense was so spicy. The high priest stood upon a high podium set at the end of a colonnade. He raised his hands, everyone went silent, and he chanted in elvish. I was afraid the Great Spirit would rush in and sweep us all away."

"Two days later we saw the high priest drinking whiskey at a hotel bar. He staggered around and groped barmaids. Every so often he let out a loud belch. I was so deflated," he said.

Cody puzzled over the enigmatic declaration. "We're not talking about a drunken priest. Are we?"

"I don't know," he said and shrugged. "I guess not."

"The academy is different from what you expected," she replied.

"No. Yes," Kelvin said. "The building and the people are what I thought they would be. I'm not. I imagined fighting heroic battles and planting my flag at the top of a hill. Most of war is just slogging through mud and going hungry. I'm working so hard I don't have five minutes to just relax."

"We don't?" asked Cody.

"No. We have to run, fight, or stab all the time. I just ... well ... I thought it was going to be more fun. The training is like doing my chores back home. They are just your daily duties, and the real work begins when they are finished."

The Great Gate

Joash lingered in the back of the chapel. When he heard his son's words, he gazed at the floor, and his mind swam in a sea of memories. Kelvin's words touched something deep within him. When he walked toward them, the boards creaked underneath his feet. Cody and Kelvin turned and saw him. "I couldn't help but hear you," Joash said. Kelvin frowned and shook his head. "Now don't be angry. I wasn't trying to spy on you."

The big man sat sideways before them on the pew. He looked his son in the eye. "I have lost many good friends in battle. Average warriors fill the graveyards. Their corpses litter the ground at the end of the battle. Imagine all of your new friends going into battle. Now imagine the battle won, but most of them are dead. That's what happens to the unprepared."

"Yes sir," Kelvin croaked.

Joash took a deep breath and restrained his impatience. "I never pushed your brother Peter. When I told him to practice with his sword, he snuck into town and met girls. I thought, 'He's only young once. Why not?' I went easy on him. When he asked me if he was doing well, I lied. I told him he would make an excellent warrior. After all, we were at peace. What did it matter?"

Kelvin saw tears in his father's eyes. "We … I lost him. You brother is in the grave because of me. I put him there as surely as the daemia that killed him. Night after night I dream of him. I see his terrified face as a daemia runs him through the heart. I run to him, but I can never reach him; and then I wake up in a sweat, and for a moment, I tell myself it was just a dream. Then I remember he's gone: no parent should lose a child."

He rose to his feet. "I am much harder on you than your older brothers. They settled for trade positions. Joffre is a lawyer and only plays warrior on weekends with his volunteer unit. Ben and Richard are leaving active duty to work at their in-law's arms factory. They're excited about armament production and shield crafting innovations. You are the only one of my sons that wants to be a real warrior. That means you will have to live while those you love die. As the years pass, more and more of them die until only a precious few remain."

"Tell me that you've changed your mind. Tell me that you want to be a lawyer or a sword maker, and we can end all this. I'll send you to a trade school, and you will have your weekends free. There will be plenty of time to drink and play darts with your friends. Otherwise, we will continue to train until you are the best warrior in Asgard. No one will be able to best you in battle. Men will utter your name with respect, and the enemy will fear it." He wiped the tears from his eyes and strode down the aisle. "Now get moving. You and your guild are going to the northern woods on maneuvers. Put on your gear, and get ready to move out."

Kelvin rose up from the pew and shrugged off the weariness. His twenty-first birthday was only a few months away, and it was the first time since his ascension that he had a choice. He gazed up at the stain glass windows high above him and contemplated his father's words. In his mind's eye, he could see two paths diverging in the woods. One led to the city and an ordinary life, a life of comfort and prosperity, a life filled with pleasures. The other path led into the wilds, through winding valleys skirting around rocky outcroppings; it led to danger and glory. It afforded few comforts and heartache. Yet destiny determined this path for him.

Cody rose to her feet and asked, "Are you coming?"

Chapter 27

Kelvin gazed through the leaves, dappled fragments of golden light upon his face. The sun rose late that morning, or so it seemed, forestalled by an early morning shower; but it now burned hot and brought the forest canopy to life. Birds darted about through the trees in search of a quick meal and then raced back to hungry chicks. The rich odor of wet earth still hung in the air, and the runoff lay in puddles, soon to be absorbed into the ground, nourishing the forest.

The comforts of Bruin, a Waypoint Town of the North Forests, lay behind them. Their destination was the seasonal camp known as "The Quarters," a destination point and haven for the migrant laborers each spring. It was a tradition that cadets traveled ahead of the main company and secured the camp.

A brown mustang swayed underneath him, and a gentle clip-clop of its hooves soothed him; books, study, battle practice, and assignments lay behind him; what lay ahead was an adventure, the type of adventure which prompted him to join the guild.

It felt strange to straddle the broad creature's back; its muscles flexed and released beneath him. The stable manager insisted that they learn their horse's name, which sounded very strange to him, but he complied with the man's request. His horse was named Chestnut. Why a horse needed a name still eluded him; it was a means of transportation, not a pet. Yet he understood the connection some men felt for their horses if he rode it for many years. This horse was still a stranger to him, a single choice presented by the stable manager.

Chestnut followed the trail with dull familiarity and careless indifference. The horse knew the trail to Silver River by heart and could navigate it blindfolded. For ten years Chestnut pulled wagons and bore riders over the same path; it was as familiar to him as was his stall in the barn. Even on the darkest night, he could follow its winding length. Kelvin's input as to his speed and destination was neither needed nor desired. Yet horses have no voice in such matters.

Kelvin studied the forest around him. Thick pines and majestic oaks hid the sky. Through the woods to his right, he saw a shimmer of light, and he heard the running water of the Silver River, thus named for the silver taken from it long ago.

The trees gave way to a small, horseshoe-shaped field, and ruins rose up from the prairie grass like a ghost; a single curved wall skirted along the tree line, and within its protection were piles of blocks, as if spilled upon the ground. Who built it and why was beyond living or written memory. Kelvin discerned one thing: the builders met a bad end. Most of the blocks and the wall still bore battle scars. It reminded him the Round Top Fortress and the lazy days of his childhood.

He snugged the straps that held his cuirass and took comfort from his armor. Most men, Kelvin included, wore PSM treated leather, eschewing the slip-suit, associating it with the female gender. The difference was one of aesthetic rather than function, as are many clothing choices.

Endless hours of tactical study, battle practice, and harsh discipline lay behind them; and yet something within him longed for the safety of school. However, 1,453 miles lay between him and the academy in Solva; they were alone, and everyone looked to him for command. He struggled to remember the many lessons on leadership, all became crowded together, becoming a mishmash of jumbled platitudes. When his stomach twisted into a knot, he tried to quiet his fears and not let the others see his apprehension.

Cody focused on practical issues: her bottom ached. Compounding this matter, her maiden's belt cleaved as though trying to cut her in two. Her hand rubbed her sore bottom and glided over her slip-suit smothering her body. She knew that warrior women appeared provocative, but she had no idea about the discomfort of a maiden's belt.

Corbin smirked and leered at her; "Having problems?"

"Yes, one of the idiots in our platoon is staring at me rather than keeping watch on the trail," she said. Cassie and Daphne suppressed a giggle. Corbin dug in his spurs and galloped up to Kelvin.

"Cody is treating me with disrespect. I am a senior cadet and a specialist 3rd class. I outrank her. Why don't you do something about it?" Corbin narrowed his eyes and glared back at Cody.

Without looking back, Kelvin shouted, "Cody, when you address a superior officer you must conclude that address with 'Sir, Master, or Mistress.'"

"Yes sir," she replied. "Specialist Third Class Corbin Jones, Sir, you're an idiot."

"Much better," Kelvin said. Corbin did not think it was much better. In fact, he thought it was disrespectful.

They wound around a Sawmill Trail that crept down a gradual slope. Wagon tracks carved parallel ruts in the dirt road. When they reached the bottom, they passed close by the Silver River; its frigid blue waters originated in the distant Regal Mountains glaciers.

Twice a year, crews descended upon the river camp facility. Some lived in tents, but most families maintained cabins; and generations participated in the harvest. Every year the cadets arrived in town first and secured it. There was no real danger: they provided traffic control. But it was a good chance to test their organizational skills and interact with the public as warrior pledges.

Scott Marcy

An orange bed of pine needles covered the forest floor in a thick mat. The immense pine trees lined the river's edge like a palisade, their branches extending far over the turbulent waters. Kelvin noticed a fallen oak, a victim of a winter gale, creating a gaping hole in the canopy. Exposing the roots thick with clods of rich brown earth, its broken body lay upon the forest floor, tracing up the face of the hill. The lumber crews would be busy; they would fashion the fallen tree into planks and for commercial use.

They passed through the thinning ranks of trees, a void created by the small seasonal community. Quaint cabins made of wood and fieldstone with shingled roofs lay between the remaining trees; thatch covered second-floor balconies, and shutters still guarded the windows.

Kelvin rose up in the saddle; he was a deputy, an enforcer, having the power to arrest or imprison men. The adult warriors would supervise, but he would still have the authority of law behind him. It was everything that he dreamed.

Kelvin and the group chatted, awestruck by the growing collection of buildings. The roads forked in every direction, and they found themselves lost in a small city. Buildings of fieldstone and timber rose up three stories and formed the entertainment district. He imagined himself drinking in a one of the countless pubs or gambling in one of the casinos, and the brothels ... they intrigued him; he imagined scantily clad women sashaying through gilded parlors. It struck him as peculiar how drinking, gambling, and prostitution went together. A grin appeared on his face as he contemplated enjoying all three activities. Then he noticed Cody gaze and wore a series expression.

"Okay, who has the town map displayed on their oracle scroll?" asked Kelvin.

"I do," said Crystal. She trotted her horse to his side and stopped by him. The buxom girl gazed up at him with dewy eyes, batted her eyelashes,

287

and smiled, but he pretended not to notice. This was a serious military operation; there was no time for infatuations, and yet his attention shifted to her alluring body. His gaze fixed on her a few seconds too long, and Cody noticed.

"I know where we are," Cody said and glared at Crystal. "The fort is that way, in the center of town." The girl wilted and returned to her place in the column.

"Let's keep moving," Kelvin ordered and rode away from the confrontation. "I'm eager to reach the fort and get working."

A crude palisade crafted from felled trees formed the walls, and rough-hewed buildings trimmed the parade ground. "We have a lot of work to do before the warriors arrive. After we stow our gear and bed down the horses, we need to get right to work." He reached back and patted his saddlebags. Hearing the metallic clank of the keys assuaged his angst and reassured him that he had not lost them.

When they reached the main gate, he dismounted and stretched. Cody walked past him and rubbed her derriere. "I'm sore, Sir," she said. "I bet maiden's belts were designed by a man." Kelvin knew better than to argue with a contentious woman.

Mushy brown sod slipped under his boots as Kelvin scaled the ramp to the front gate. The lock was an antique, black iron and handmade. He inserted the large key and turned; the lock groaned and gave way with a snap, releasing its bolt. He removed the chain and swung the gates open wide. His eyes watering, his nose burning, his lungs seizing, a terrible stench assaulted him. He turned his face this way and that, trying to escape the stench. "What is that? It smells like rotten chicken dung."

He pinched his nose and entered the fort. Chestnut, however, refused to follow. It reared up and skittered. His father often said, "Listen to an animal's instinct. They sense danger from afar and will inform you of it — if you have the ears to hear."

Kelvin drew his sword and studied the boarded buildings that trimmed the central parade ground. When the others saw him, they too drew their swords. "What is it?" asked Cody. "Did you see something?"

"No. I sense something." He backed down the ramp, keeping his face toward the compound; Chestnut was glad to follow his lead. When he was away from the gate, he mounted his horse and ordered, "Show me that map," and Crystal held her oracle scroll in the air. He glanced at it; "We're going to the secondary location. There's a newer fort up on the hill. The officers billet there. We will secure that first."

"But our orders were to secure the central fort," Corbin objected.

"I know what our orders are. We will secure the upper facility first, and then we will return after we are properly equipped. Now move! That's an order," he barked.

Corbin frowned. "Yes, sir." It was unfair: Command promoted Kelvin because of his high royal ancestry. *The fort is safe. He's just showing off.* This delay just meant working late into the night, yet Corbin had no choice in the matter. He turned his horse away from the gate and followed Kelvin.

Eyes peered out from the darkness through vertical gaps in the shutters. The creature's heavy breathing disturbed a cobweb and sent the spider scurrying. A gurgling growl and a wheezing squeal, like fingernails on a chalkboard, echoed off the walls. The haugr lowered its rusty blade and moved into the darkness, shunning the open light of day.

The squad galloped through the town and up a steep hill. The "Overlook Fortress" was a modern, comfortable complex that was placed atop a small hill, and a field stone wall protected its perimeter. Unlike the Old

The Great Gate

Fort, its gate was made of iron, and vibrant patina of orange rust covered the exterior.

Upon reaching the gate, Kelvin dismounted and stood before it. He searched through the keys, cursing each wrong selection. When he found the correct key, he twisted it in the lock and heard a metallic snick. "Help me," he ordered Corbin. The young man dismounted and assisted Kelvin as he dislodged the reluctant hinges. When the gate opened wide, they hurried into the fortress, each person fretting about possible danger.

"Is this one dangerous too, or shall we enter, sir?" asked Corbin.

"It feels safe," Kelvin replied.

They closed the gates behind them and secured the metal bolt. The gate was constructed like a vault door, and when secured, rods passed through holes and were lodged inside the metal frame; two metal bars, each larger than a man's arm stretched across the seam between the doors. "Okay, get the horses into the stalls. Daphne, Crystal, and Megan feed and water the horses, but don't remove their saddles. We may still need them. Corbin and Cody, you come with me. I want the rest of you on the wall with your bows at the ready. We are going back to investigate."

The three young warriors retrieved the rest of their combat gear off their horses. They donned hoods, masks, and supplemental armor; it was old, sacred, and tarnished; but it was sturdy, forged by the dwarves, as strong as the mountains, protecting them with a layer of steel. After they strapped circular shields to their left arms and drew their weapons, Daphne opened a lesser door at Kelvin's signal. The trio rushed through it and held their shields up in defense. The girls slammed the door shut and secured them.

Kelvin took the lead with Cody and Corbin on his right and left flank. He crouched down behind his shield and only exposed enough to peer over it. They walked down the hill, toward the shadows. The Old Fort gate yawned at them like a gaping maw. Kelvin's heart raced; he recalled the many horrors that might await them, terrified of what they might find and worried what they might not find. If it turned out to be nothing, the others would mercilessly tease him. Yet he esteemed it better to be prepared than to guard his pride.

They walked with a deliberate pace, searching for signs of danger. Cody had sharp eyes, and she spotted broken padlocks lying upon the ground. Using hand signals, she notified Kelvin. Kelvin's mouth went dry as the Thunder Desert, and his heart seemed to be beating in his throat.

When they passed through the gate, they formed a triad, each facing a different direction and trusting their back to the other two. They moved across the compound in tight formation. When Corbin set down his right foot, he felt a squish beneath it. He raised his foot and snarled; fresh dung covered the bottom of his shoe. He signaled Kelvin using his shield hand. Kelvin nodded and continued.

They approached the quartermaster building. It was a lonely wooden structure, often patched with wooden planks and weathered; each year required more mending until it was nothing but patches. The decaying roof allowed rain water to flow into it, and the walls appeared feeble, a weathered old man ready to collapse.

Kelvin stopped. The door creaked open and then shut again. Was it the wind?

For what seemed like an eternity, he kept watch on the door and tried to peer through the seam in the shutters. Nothing emerged from the darkness. He continued, and Corbin and Cody followed him. When he stepped upon the soiled walkway, he noticed fresh claw marks. They were wider than a man's hand and cut deep into the wood, a Great Mountain Tiger?

The Great Gate

He used the tip of his sword and opened the door. It creaked open and allowed unfamiliar sunlight to probe the murky interior. Kelvin saw dung and bones, lots and lots of bones, strewed about and heaped in high piles. The blood stained the walls, and claw marks abounded; he looked up and saw more on the ceiling.

A ramp located across the room led into the basement. Kelvin readied himself for the cat to leap out of the darkness. It would be a fight to the death, its death he hoped. Corbin stood by Kelvin's side, their shields forming a wall. Cody walked backward down the ramp, covering their rear.

The low-level ocular scanners activated when the light fell beneath a single candle and outlined the room in shades of green. They searched the darkness and poised their swords for combat. Broken pottery and crates littered the floor. A few coals from a smoldering fire lingered in the hearth. He elbowed Corbin and pointed at the coals. This was no tiger.

A second ramp led into the sub-basement. The Old Fort was constructed on the ruins of a dwarven outpost. The dwarves, of course, lived underground, but they abandoned the outpost before men set foot on the Wolf's Head Peninsula.

Shoulder to shoulder the pair descended the second ramp, Cody providing a rear guard. Rectangular slabs of stone, covered with runes, lay tilted against one another, but they still held back the loose soil. Kelvin opted to pry open his mask and sniffed. The moment the air reached his nostrils, he began to wretch. Cody turned to him and asked him with signals if he was okay; Kelvin nodded and fought to get control of his stomach.

Each step taken across the room came with squishes and slurps beneath their feet. Kelvin opted to risk a little light; he retrieved a glow bar from his equipment belt and shook it. The chemicals mixed and illuminated the room with a gentle yellow light. He tossed it across the chamber and dispelled the darkness.

A cache of weapons, appearing like machetes, covered with rust and blood, lay next to the carcass of a butchered buck, and the rotting corpse of a bear lay beside it. Something ripped the bear's fur from its ribcage, spilling entrails onto the floor. The poor creature's eyes were missing, a delicacy for many creatures. It was then that he spotted a single iron shield with haugr writing upon it.

It was a "hellhole."

He spotted a dark circle in the far corner wall. The tunnel mouth gave way to utter darkness, and fresh claw marks covered the wall. Kelvin recalled his biology lessons; a haugr's claws could slice through granite; their armor would stop a single blow, but it would fail upon the second.

Corbin's bladder released, issuing a stream of urine down the leg of his leather trousers. Kelvin signaled retreat, and they struggled to contain their urge to flee. Of all the scary stories recounted around the campfires, the hellhole frightened the most. It seized the imagination like the yawning gates of hell.

Kelvin and Corbin backed toward the ramp with their shields covering their retreat. Cody took the lead and guarded their path up the ramp. When they reached the main floor, Kelvin fought the urge to voice the alarm going off in his brain. *Stay in formation,* he growled inwardly. *Get control of yourself!* For what seemed like forever, they crossed the second level and backed up the ramp to the first.

After they had exited the quartermaster building, they resumed a triad formation and passed through the courtyard. They expected an attack at any moment, arrows swishing out from crevices and screaming haugrs falling upon them. Yet they passed through the gate without incident.

The Great Gate

Kelvin and Corbin pushed the gates shut and set the lock. This would delay the haugrs only a few seconds, but they still wanted those seconds. Their claws allowed them to race up vertical inclines with the speed of a tiger, but it would block most of their sonar; like bats, the haugr used a high-pitched squeal to navigate. Their eyes were weak and only useful in very low light, the bright light of day causing them searing pain.

Daphne signaled Crystal and Megan that the exploration team was returning. When they saw that the patrol was still in strategic formation, they realized that something was wrong. They poised their bows and scanned the hill for a threat.

When they reached the door, Megan rushed down to the gate and opened it. Kelvin stripped off his facemask; "It's a hellhole." The girl went ashen and sucked in a gasp. "Get the horse. We're retreating."

The squad exited Overlook Fortress at record speed. After they shut and locked the gate, they galloped down the hill at top speed. Making a sharp right turn, they swept past the Old Fort and thundered up the road. When Kelvin looked behind him, he saw haugrs in pursuit. Their claws dug into the earth, and they bounded in 20-foot leaps. The terrified horses sensed the danger and thundered at pell-mell speeds; their muscles flexed and hooves swept across the ground. Shrill cries erupted behind them, making their skin crawl, and their minds became paralyzed with fear. Some of the haugr climbed up a tree and bounded from tree to tree. Crystal turned in the saddle and released an arrow; it hit a haugr in the chest, finding the seam in its armor. The creature screamed and tumbled to the ground in a ball. Megan and Daphne also released their arrows, and two more haugr fell.

Kelvin's eyes focused on the trail; everything else became a blur – all that mattered was escape. A haugr leaped from a branch and sailed through the air at him. He slashed at it, hitting its throat. The haugr hit him, nearly knocking him out of the saddle, and smacked the sword from his hand. While he hung sideways on the saddle, the frenzied horse bounded in a desperate gallop. Cody rode to his side; she grabbed his right armpit. The slight leverage allowed him to right himself in the saddle.

With the loss of his sword, Kelvin grabbed a dagger from behind his back. It was little defense, but at least it was something. They charged past the bend on the trail and up the hill; Chestnut moved with the speed of a 3-year-old race horse.

The haugr chief scrambled up to the top of a ridge. The sun emerged out from behind a passing cloud and stabbed at the haugr's eyes. At its shriek, the others gave up the pursuit. The chief sniffed the air and forged a memory of this young human; he was cunning, well trained, a danger to the colony. If they met again, he would kill him. For now, he returned his sword to its sheath and returned to feast upon his fallen comrades.

Chapter 28

Joash and Tormod appeared comical when as they rode beside one another, a giant of a man next to a dwarf. The dwarf rode an equine mountain goat, powerfully built, light, and agile. They could leap from one slick rock to another at dizzying heights.

On the other hand, Joash stood just over seven feet tall and weighed 379 pounds, with only 3% body fat. A travel pony could never carry Joash and his armor; it would have collapsed in exhaustion after only a few miles. This is why he chose a destrier, a knight's horse: tall, sturdy, and weighing over 3,000 pounds. This allowed the horse to carry 30% of his body weight into battle, 900 pounds. Joash bore 110 pounds of armor, 30 pounds of weaponry, 20 pounds of leather clothing under his armor, and a 30-pound shield – all of which was rhunite forged and custom designed. Shiloh also wore armor; steel plate covered his head and chest while scaled armor covered his torso. It weighed another 70 pounds, not including the saddle; all of it was well within Shiloh's load bearing range.

The large man and dwarf emerged from a narrow strip of trees. The dirt road stretched diagonally across a field and carried them into the scorching midday sun; the air became a thick hot blanket, and a cloudless sky offered no relief. A column of men rode behind them; most of these warriors were veterans, their days of battle lay long behind them. These volunteers enjoyed wearing armor and forming ranks with their old comrades; it was a time to tell tall tales and recall desperate battles. Fading memory and ale made their stories grow grander with each passing year.

Joash enjoyed the comradeship, and their stories set his mind adrift: he recalled the faces of absent friends and times he would never see again. He wiped the sweat from his brow, wishing he wore only his light armor and not the heavy set. Joash commented to Tormod, "Did I tell you I met Thordal once?"

Tormod puffed his pipe. "No. I don't believe that you ever told me that one. When did you meet him?"

"It was when I was a young second lieutenant, my first command. The chief miner, Thordal, tasked with clearing the 'Rose Mines.' Wretched pests filled them and bred at incredible rates. Thordal was eager to reenter his mine and resume his work. He saw us bashing the rodents with our hammers and carrying them out by the wagon full."

"He told me, 'That's not how you kill glaggall.' The miners carried up three barrels of fuel oil and broke them. After the oil had flowed down into the mine, he set it on fire. Thick, black smoke billowed out of the tunnel entrance. A few minutes later, glaggalls exploded out of the mine like rushing water …."

Tormod cocked his head wondering why the story halted short of the ending. Joash rose up in the saddle and pointed across the field. "What's that? It looks as though someone's riding toward us."

"Indeed, and they appear to be in a great hurry." Tormod drew his weapon. "Sound formation. Prepare for battle." The trumpets blared, and formations of mounted cavalry stretched out on either side of them. "Archers hold until I give the command."

Joash said, "It's Kelvin, and he's riding as though hell itself was chasing him."

"His entire squad is with him. I wonder what got them spooked?" Tormod grabbed his spyglass from his saddlebag; looking past the field, he scanned the edge of the forest, but nothing was in pursuit. He stroked his beard and mused. Kelvin was sober-minded and a natural leader. This was not like him.

As they neared, Joash held up his hand. "Slow down," he shouted. "Make your report."

Kelvin drew in several gasps of air and glanced over his shoulder. "We went to the harvest camp, the Quarters, by the Silver River. When we opened the Old Fort, a terrible stench came from the interior ...." As Kelvin relayed his tale, Cody added in a few missing details.

When they finished, Joash pondered their report and took a drink from his water flask. "What do you make of this?" he asked Tormod. "There haven't been any verified haugr sightings on this side of the Hargal Wall since 'The War of Purging.'"

"I have proof," Cody said. She drew a small knife from her belt and handed to Joash; the warrior took the knife from her and examined it. He did not doubt them, but it was proper to ask questions regarding such a report. The black haugr blood splashed across his breastplate was proof enough. He handed the knife to Tormod.

The blade was curved and short, perfect for the skinning game. The black metal and the bone handle were of haugr construction. When Tormod moved the flat side of the blade toward the tip of his tongue, Corbin exclaimed, "You're not going to taste that? It smells like crap."

Tormod ignored Corbin and tasted it. He sampled the residue and then spit it out. "I detect 11 males and 4 captive beasts that are heavy with a death pregnancy, but they have not dropped the haugr young yet." He sniffed the blade and added, "I can detect fragmented scents of several more males and captive females, but I cannot identify the species. It's a full colony."

"Mistress Sabrina detected a colony near the town of Bruton, but no evidence was ever found. The governor referred it to a committee for study. It was his way of politely dropping the subject." Joash shook his head, "But we are too far north for it to be that colony. It must be another."

"Perhaps," Tormod said. He scanned the horizon with his spyglass again and saw nothing. "I recommend that we investigate and send riders back to notify command HQ in Bruin."

"Major Briggs, send a messenger back to Bruin and apprise them of our situation. We ride to the Quarters." Joash then said to Kelvin, "Take your warriors to the rear and join ranks." Joash prepared to lead the column of soldiers back along the trail that Kelvin just traveled, returning to the harvest village.

"Yes sir," Kelvin replied.

"Travel formation," Tormod ordered. The riders reformed the column. "Major Briggs, send word to the platoon commanders that we have encountered enemy haugr at the Quarters."

"Yes sir," he replied and rode back through the column.

As Kelvin led his squad to the rear of the company, the gray-haired veterans stared at them without expression. Kelvin sat up straight and kept his gaze fixed straight ahead. The warriors then adjusted their armor and prepared their weapons. They traveled up Sawmill Road every year and secured the camps; it was a cakewalk. They chased the occasional bandit and investigated burgled cabins. However, this was the first time that they faced combat. The warriors recalled lessons learned long ago and readied themselves for the carnage.

Kelvin and his squad joined the rear of the formation. The sweltering sun baked them with merciless cruelty. When the company began to move, clouds of dust billowed, choking them. They followed close behind the last platoon, awash in a sea of fine dust; the reddish brown powder soon turned their slip-suits hazy brown and covered their faces. He wet a rag and wiped his face, resisting the urge to wear his mask. None of the veterans wore their masks; masks cut of valuable odors carried by the wind and sense of the environment.

The slip-suits used either hot or cold as a power source. The composite material translated the thermal radiation into energy at a quantum level, maintaining precise environmental conditions. With their bodies completely covered by PSM, their bodies were kept cool and comfortable, as if reclining under a shade tree; but this did not completely cut the wearer off from the environment: they could sense basic hot and cold through the material.

Kelvin looked over to his right and saw Cody. Many times, he dreamed of this moment, and yet it seemed unreal. The grungy armor and slip-suit covered her head to toe, replacing the girl with a warrior woman. He said to her, "Can you believe this?"

"No," she replied. "It seems like a dream."

The academy had a limited stable of horses. This allowed them rare opportunities to train riding in battle formation. Kelvin recalled various textbooks and lessons. *In case of combat, we linger behind the formation and aid in tactical support. What does that mean? Do we provide medical evacuation, or do we fight? I hope its fighting. I am awful at first aid. Okay, no matter what happens I need a new sword.* Kelvin rode back to the supply wagon and requisitioned a new sword.

They passed through the field and reentered the forest. Once again they found themselves in the cool forest, sheltered from the blazing sun. He searched the trees and saw a hint of the Silver River. For some peculiar reason, he longed to strip naked and to dive into the frigid waters.

After an hour of riding, they began to near the quarters, the harvest campsite. The supply wagons stayed behind and began to erect medical tents in a small oval clearing. Two squads remained behind to provide tactical support. Kelvin and the cadets were surprised when command allowed them to continue.

Four squads rode ahead to appraise the situation. Kelvin searched the pine trees high above them. He spotted the carved bark and bare wood caused by haugr claws. The span of their leaps surprised him. It was then that he rode by his sword lying on the ground. He ignored it and stayed on his mount. It was no time to be on foot.

Kelvin detected a hint of smoke in the air as if a campfire burned upwind. The smoke grew into a thick, suffocating cloud. "Put on masks," he ordered. Masks covered their faces and cleansed air. A gray haze surrounded them and hid the forest in a dense fog; perhaps it hid the haugr. He searched the gray and brown stripes for haugr and battle.

Finally, Kelvin reached the outskirts of the town. The flicker of bright orange flames cut through the haze. After the windows shattered, the flames shot out from home interiors. As they passed by a store, the glass burst and flames leap into the sky. His horse shifted and whinnied. Kelvin moved Chestnut away from the flames and continued through town.

Kelvin saw squads of warriors, shields raised and weapons ready, entering the Old Fort. He and his squad dismounted and led their horses to an impromptu corral made of rope. He asked Master Tormod, "What can we do?"

"Assist the warriors with firefighting," he replied.

The warriors broke up into fire brigades. They dragged hoses down to the river and lay them in the water. They then activated the impeller pumps. Powerful jets of water streamed out of brass hose nozzles, requiring three men to hold and aim them.

While the others dragged a line to the water, Kelvin picked up the hose. "Give me a hand holding this." Corbin and Cody gripped the hose. The hose snapped like a snake, awakened and angry. Water jetted out of the firehose, and he swept the water through an open door, underneath the flames. The flames curled over the edge of the wooden porch and shot high into the sky. They pressed forward and moved into the home; the entire structure was ablaze. Furnishings, transported and collected over centuries, burned.

They doused a burning velvet sofa, exposing the white stuffing and inner springs. Kelvin gazed up at the ceiling; flames rippled across it as though alive. The rafters above them began to moan and sag. He signaled them to back out of the house. No sooner had they cleared the porch then the ceiling collapsed, and a gust doused them in burning embers.

A man tapped Kelvin's arm. "Forget the homes — wet the trees. If we lose them, the entire forest will be set ablaze." Kelvin and the others shifted the stream of water and jetted up three stories, soaking low hanging limbs. The flames from the burning homes shot high into the air. The heat began to melt glass, and gusts tried to suck them into the fire. If not for their protective clothing, they would have been consumed.

Groups of men began chopping down trees, forming a fire break. Great pine trees groaned and toppled through the air. They hit the ground with a crash and crushed burning homes. This shot burning embers high into the air. When several trees flamed, the fire teams shifted to the trees on the other side of the break. They danced back and forth, fighting both the flames and the self-willed hose. More trees groaned and fell to the ground with a thunderous boom. The logs rolled down the embankment and into the town.

The inferno turned night into day. Kelvin and his squad joined the shovel line. They dug away ground clutter that might fuel the fire. They also stamped out flames that tried to cross the fire break.

In the middle of the night, Cody tugged Kelvin's arm. She pointed up into the dark sky. They saw a winged figure silhouetted in black against orange flames and rolling columns of smoke. It glided out of the sky and fluttered when it met the ground. Sabrina approached Kelvin. Hands on her hips, she asked, "Where is Battle Master Joash?"

Kelvin stripped down his mask. Soot and sweat covered his youthful face. "He's at the command tent coordinating the activity." He pointed to his right toward a clearing well away from the fire.

Sabrina paused for a second and studied Kelvin's face. "You remind me of him. Are you any kin to him?"

"He's my father. I'm a student at your academy. I'm going to join the Black Dragon Guild some day."

A smiled brightened her face. "I look forward to the day when you join me in battle. I'm sure you will be an excellent warrior just like your father. Now I must go and meet with him. Perhaps we can speak later."

Kelvin saluted; "Yes, Mistress Sabrina." He lingered a moment and watched her walk away. She passed through the frenzied men fighting the fire.

She climbed a small hill and stood upon the crest. Lamps caused the tents to glow. There were makeshift infirmaries, which treated burns; others were hospitality tents, providing food and cots to rest, and the rest were command tents.

Sabrina walked down through the thick grass. When she passed by a sentry, he thumped his fist to his chest, saluting her. She reciprocated the salute and continued on her way. She walked by a campfire, an irony in the midst of a forest fire. When the men guarding the entryway to the command tent saw her, they snapped to attention. She passed by them and pushed open the flaps to the tent.

Joash, Tormod, and other warriors leaned over a table. Oracle maps and various papers lay scattered about it. An officer called out, "Attention!" The warriors all saluted her.

"What's the situation, Joash?" asked Sabrina.

He pointed to the Silver River; "We have reports of five separate fires along the river bank. Three of them are contained, but two are still burning out of control. I have five platoons searching for the haugrs, but they have thousands of square miles in which to hide; there is little hope we will find them."

"Yes. Haugrs move swiftly. I've seen them cover a hundred miles in a single night, and they always have an emergency burrow." She pointed to two uncontrolled fires; "I will dispatch wizards to those fires. They can create a rainstorm using the water from the river. That should extinguish them."

"Excellent," Joash replied. "As to the haugr, we will need trackers that are experienced with seismic detectors. I've seen haugr tunnels spread over a hundred square mile area. They could be right under our feet at this very moment, and we would never know it."

"We'll need tunnel rats," Tormod said. "Once we find their lair, someone will have to go down and kill the haugr."

"Very well," she said. "Give the orders." Tormod excused himself and left the tent. She took Joash aside. "I spoke with the provincial defense minister. Unless he has definitive proof of haugr activity, he won't declare a state of emergency. The word of a few cadets and a single knife is not enough. The Prime Minster is afraid of upsetting the financial markets."

"Damn fool," Joash sputtered. "By the time we have that sort of proof the war will be upon us. Now is the time to prepare."

"Yes, I told him as much, but he refuses to act. His advisers counseled him that the children must have mistaken a group of bandits for haugrs. That is what he told the national media." She crossed her arms and shook her head. "Unfortunately, most of your evidence went up in flames."

Chapter 29

Three years of peace lulled Asgard back to sleep. Most people dismissed Kelvin and his platoon's encounter as the product of an overly active imagination. After all, haugrs died off in Asgard long ago. When pressed, the skeptics concluded that Kelvin encountered a pride of panthers, and his fear transformed his perceptions, making them haugrs. Kelvin resented the skeptics; he knew what he saw, but his father and Overlord Sabrina believed him; that was enough.

With an alternative explanation posited, Asgard went back to sleep. The military and guilds changed from alert status to standby, and after three months, it changed to stand-down status. The media lost interest and returned to their two favorite subjects: murder trials and political intrigues. The public settled into its dull routine, assured that it was a false alarm and that everything was as it should be – normal. Two more years passed, and the incident became a forgotten footnote in Asgard history.

One day a rider charged through the city streets, the horse bounding in long strides; its horseshoes sparked on the cobblestone, and fierce snorts came from its nostrils, pedestrians scurrying out of the way; the stead's muscles strained, and his reflection blurred in shop windows. The rider's hat folded backward; and his jacket flapped, and his elbows stabbed the air behind him. He stood in the stirrups, and his legs flexed with the motion of the stead.

Sabrina spoke with Marla in the entrance to the Black Castle. The young woman discussed her swords. She retrieved them from the sewers and mounted them on a plaque hung on the wall. She obtained two new swords from the armory, both were curved Elven blades and leather grips provided a sure hold. However, they felt strange in her hand, and she was not certain if she would get used to them.

Upon reaching the castle, the rider dismounted his horse while it was still moving and ran toward the castle. He scrambled up the stairs as if fleeing from some unseen pursuer. Sabrina recognized Kendall, a young man she met in Bruton.

"Mistress Sabrina," he gasped, "we need your help." The young man appeared ready to pass out from exhaustion. "We searched all night. There's no sign."

"Catch your breath and calm yourself," Sabrina replied.

He took several deep breaths and collected himself. "I was away from our village on a midnight harvest. The glosser berries are best when picked by a full moon. When we returned, we saw fires blazing in the night. We dropped our bags and ran to the village. Our homes burned, and dead bodies littered the street. My wife and children are gone; all of our people are gone! We don't know what happened to them. Martin sent me to warn the governor and get help."

"Did you?" asked Marla.

"Yes. I left my horse behind and ran through the first district. I told my story to the governor's press secretary, Yost Struusan, but he didn't believe me. He waved his hand and dismissed it as the work of bandits. He told me to speak with the protectors." The young man scowled and shook his head. "The Protectors took a report and filed it in triplicate. An officer might stop by in the next few days. Please, we need your help."

"Gather our men," Sabrina said to Marla. "We ride at once."

An hour later 480 warriors and 12 cadets assembled in the courtyard before the castle. They strapped swords to the back and cinched down their armor. War dogs, great beasts covered with scaled armor danced and yapped with anticipation. Sabrina strode through their midst on her way to Midnight. She took the reins from the groom and mounted her stead. The horse snorted and shuffled, eager to throw off the confines of stable life, ready for action. The activity grew still, and all eyes looked to her. "We ride to Bruton. Bear no burden other than that which you will need for combat."

Fiona stood upon the hill that overlooked the cohort of men. A knot of fear formed in her heart and tears welled up in her eyes. She searched the mob until she found Joash; covered in steel armor, he appeared strong and powerful, a warrior of the ages. He stepped in his horse's stirrup and mounted it.

Like a swollen lake escaping its dam, the riders flooded out from the courtyard and swept through the streets. Fiona kept an eye on him until he disappeared between the nearby homes. A prayer for Joash and Kelvin left her lips.

Sabrina charged through the streets of the fifth district. Men and women hurried out of their way. Others opened windows and looked down from on them. The roar of hoofs on stone echoed through the streets like thunder. The guards at the city gates moved aside as the riders and war dogs charged past them. Their faces questioned the implications. Where did they ride? What was the tumult?

Midnight's hooves thundered upon the dirt road. Its powerful muscles flexed as it charged toward battle, and great clods of dirt flung up behind it. Sabrina stood in her stirrups and matched the horse's beat. The men raced behind her. Pennants flapped from pole arms that reached high into the sky.

Bruton lay 93 miles south of Solva. They charged through the countryside and reached the small farming community in record speed. As they topped a hill, the village came into sight. All that remained of the homes were bare walls stained black soot. The bodies of horses, pigs, and sheep lay scattered about the detritus; they were hacked and stripped of their meat. The stench of death was everywhere.

As they neared, they saw bodies wrapped like linen mummies, which were piled on wagons like cordwood. Axel staggered out of his scorched home. He bore the linen-wrapped body of Fenia, his wife, and tears streamed down his cheeks; his chest heaved, and he let out great sobs.

He carried it over to the wagon. Ever so gently he set the body amongst the other victims. Leaning over the wagon's side, he gazed at the corpse. His right hand gently caressed Fenia's cheek. "How can I go on without you? You can't be gone. Please don't be gone."

Sabrina rode up to the man and dismounted. "Nobody's dead until I say they are dead." Anger flashed in the man's eyes. "Move aside and do it quickly." She touched the wrapped body and closed her eyes. "Get these grave bindings off them. They're not dead."

"What do you mean they're not dead?" Axel demanded.

Sabrina drew a knife and cut through the linen cloth. She grabbed the material and pulled it apart with a rip of fabric. The ashen face of a young woman gazed up at the sky with empty eyes. "The haugr excrete paralytic agent from glands in their claws. It paralyzes the victim, but the heart remains beating: the haugr prefer their meat fresh." She held the side of her blade to the woman's lips. A moment later, a breath fogged the gleaming metal. "She's still breathing. Get these people out of the wagons."

Axel and the other men hurriedly removed the bodies from the wagon. Sabrina ran to her horse and retrieved a vial of anti-venom. "I hope this is enough. We have very limited supplies." She removed a glass stopper and let a single drop fall between Fenia's lips. A minute later, the woman gasped and arched her back. Her eyes blinked and searched the faces of the worried men."

Axel grabbed his wife and clutched her to his chest. "Praise the Great Spirit, you returned to me. I thought I lost you."

Sabrina touched his shoulder. "She's still weak. Get her into the house and let her rest. She will sleep for a long while." When she came to the third victim, she saw a gaping wound across the man's neck. Blood soaked into his hair and clothes. "I'm sorry. He is gone to the halls of your fathers." She looked up and saw tears trickling down a young man's face. "Was he any relation to you?"

"Yes. He is … was my father." He dropped and knelt in the mud. "We had a fight. I wanted to go to school in the city, but he wanted me to stay for one more harvest. I was so angry. I told him … I said that 'I hated him.' Now he's gone, and I can't take it back."

"You will see him again in the eternal lands. Trust me. I know of what I speak. I have been there and traveled back to the land of the living. You will see him one day. Get married and have children. Live a good life. That is all he could ask of you."

"I will," he said with a sniffle. Some men helped him pick up his father's body and lay it in the wagon again. He walked away as if the world pressed down upon his shoulders.

Sabrina saw an old man; he wandered out from charred ruins. She barely recognized Martin, the village elder. Soot covered his wrinkled face and clothes, making him appear like a walking corpse. He gazed at her with sorrowful eyes, full of pain and regret. He removed his cap and gathered what dignity he had left. He asked Sabrina, "Did the governor dispatch you?"

"The governor thinks this is the work of thieves. He did nothing." She touched him on the shoulder and asked Martin, "Have you tracked the haugr?"

He pointed to the southeast. "The trail ends at Deepwood Forest. Even a small child could follow it, but we dare not enter." The woods stood between The Port of Elvmer and The City of Solva. The local population would have deforested the region if it was within their power to do so, but many of the trees were ironwood, which dulled axes and saws with a few strokes. Felling them required special equipment, fire-lances, to cut through the trees. A single tree could take several months to process, and the lumber sold for a high price.

The survivors stumbled about through the ruins and called out the names of loved ones, but the restless wind was the one who replied. The sounds of hammers and saws came from all around; men searched through the debris for victims. Women gathered grains and vegetables; numb with grief, they prepared meals, even though their families were dead. The slightest sound made them scatter like a flock of birds, and all eyes looked to the surrounding hills. Not a single wall protected the village: they felt naked.

A single tear cut a channel through the black soot and rolled down Martin's cheek. "Please, if there is anything you can do, save my family. I'm an old man. They are all I have." He turned and wandered toward the rubble. He sat down on a charred wooden bench and picked up a scorched rag doll from the ground. He clutched it to his chest and wept bitter tears.

The Battle Maige mounted her horse and saw Axel emerge from his hut. He wore rusty and tarnished armor over thick leather and chainmail. He clutched a broad ax in his right hand. When he mounted his horse, there was no need to ask why.

She signaled the remaining half of the warriors, and they rode from the village in a two by two formation. The trail was as Martin described it: ragged and ripped sod torn into great clumps; clods tossed about, and claw marks all over the ground; no trail had ever been easier to follow.

The Great Gate

After only a few minutes of riding, the gorgeous green grass grew damp with blood, turning it scarlet, and a somber hush fell over the warriors; it was as if they entered a cemetery. Their war dogs sniffed at the trail of death and charged ahead of them, following it and searching out the enemy. They soon arrived at Deepwood Forest; the trail passed through a thicket and into the forest's dark heart.

They dismounted at the forest's edge. Joash ordered Kelvin and the recent war college graduates to guard the horses. Kelvin was the reflection of his father, and in fact, he was both larger and stronger than Joash. However, they lacked vital combat experience. When Kelvin glanced at Cody: he saw the fear and felt the same fear in his heart – no one complained about his father's orders. They knew that where these warriors tread men would die.

As they surveyed the various entry points, Sabrina could sense her warrior's angst, but she had no time for inspiring speeches, no time for reassuring gestures. Lives depended upon speed. She stepped across the seam from light to darkness and entered the forest. Her warriors took strength from her courage and followed after her. Gnarled trees and dense thickets of thorns blocked their path. She got down on her stomach and saw the path taken by the haugr. The thorns were twisted and bent to form a tunnel. Sabrina crawled forward and underneath the brush. Blood coated the thorns and soaked the ground wet; and soon glistening blood covered her from head to toe, making her appear as though she survived some horrible accident.

The tunnel snaked through the thorns in a winding path. Sabrina heard the quiet curses of her men as they became stuck in the dense undergrowth, and the blunt end of a spear poked Marla's backside. "Will you quit poking me with your spear, idiot." A twinkle of light shone up ahead, and the briar patch came to an abrupt end.

Sabrina rose to her feet and followed the tracks. Only a few meters away she came upon a gash in the earth, the yawning mouth of a cave. She moved between the towering trees and stood on the edge. Jagged boulders guarded the entrance to a gaping wound in the forest floor.

"Alexander, stay here and prepare our defense. We will most likely be returning in haste and disarray," ordered Sabrina.

"Yes, Mistress," he replied. "We will stop them." Fire burned in the young sorcerer's eyes. He ordered the archers, "Form up on either side of me and prepare your bows." The archer's bows were of little use in tunnels and the haugrs hellholes.

He set up a formation at the fallback point, located in an open area; it was still within arrow shot of enemy archers, but it was the best they could do. The sorcerer scanned the tree line and put on a jewel pendant. The pendant allowed him to see and hear far beyond human ability. He detected nothing, but that was to be expected. A peaceful forest could turn into a killing ground; haugrs could emerge from their holes and overwhelm an opponent; in mere seconds, the haugrs could surround and butcher men.

Sabrina climbed over a rock formed like a serrated shark's tooth and peered down into the dark throat of the yawning cavern. Glistening blood, shades of brilliant red, stained the rocks and made the entrance appear like a snapping maw. Dismembered limbs and half-gnawed skulls filled the gaps between the jagged teeth. She climbed over the rocks and slipped down into the entrance; squatting behind a rock, she sniffed the putrefied air, which stung her nostrils with a mixture of urine, excrement, soot, and sulfur.

"This is going to be a tight fit for you," she said to Joash.

"I can squeeze through that sphincter," he said. "I'd chase those things to hell itself." Chasing a haugr into its hole was the surest way to die, but she appreciated his enthusiasm. When Sabrina removed her helmet, putting on her hood, the other men did likewise. The air grew stagnant, and they plunged into darkness. Their night vision engaged and the cave light up before them. Deep within the bowels of the caves, they heard drums — and screams.

The caverns amplified the sound like a trumpet: sounds that traveled for miles. They could easily disorient a novice, causing them to stumble from one wrong path to another. Sabrina, however, understood haugr construction techniques and strategy. She searched the signs among the nexus of tunnels and marked false paths, many of which had false bottoms or deadly snares.

When a man stepped in a pile of haugr dung, he jerked out his foot and cursed. Sabrina signaled to him to be quiet, and Joash slapped the man on the back of his helmet. "This is the right path," she signaled. He nodded and spread the word back through the formation. Sabrina proceeded, but the walls narrowed, which forced to crawl.

The passage expanded and opened to a connective node. Five tunnels spread out from the central point. Sabrina took a step and felt her right boot sink into haugr excrement: haugr crawl on the walls and ceiling, eschewing the use of the floor. Removing her mask was impossible, due to the stench and the parasites that live in haugr dung. Once inhaled, they bored through the sinuses and made their way into the brain, causing insanity, convulsions, and death. The starlight vision illuminated the cavern but bathed it in green light. She could not distinguish the red trail of blood from the condensation that covered the walls.

She moved through the muck and examined each cave. A flicker of light penetrated the darkness, and Sabrina pressed toward it. She emerged into a cavern; a short ledge that formed a ring around the basin-shaped depression. She circled around the rim, allowing others to pass around the ledge.

Haugr filled the bottom of the depression, piled around one another like an orgy of snakes. They sat around fires, providing blue flame without smoke, and feasted upon flesh. Their great maws and razor like teeth ripped off chunks of raw, bloody meat from the bone. Others scooped out handfuls of blood matter and slathered it into their mouths. They washed it down with skulls filled with Gurt Ale, having the consistency and appearance of motor oil; the drink was a putrid mixture of black root, human blood, fermenting bacteria, harvested from their feces, and death of nightshade. When they tipped up the bottom of their mugs, the ale flowed in down their chins in rivers over their armor.

Sabrina crouched, and she saw something out of place; a man stood in the far corner of the chamber, a hooded black robe concealing his face. He spoke with the haugr colony leader; the haugr gripped a spiked club in his right hand, and his left hand gripped a bulging leather sack. He gave the bag to the man, but the feeding frenzy, which echoed off the walls, obscured their conversation.

Corpses lay strewed about the floor among the teaming haugr. It was then that Sabrina spotted a stainless steel ring adorned with fiery garnets – Jerlaug – the matriarch's ring remained on the hand, but the rest of the arm was missing. Not even an arrogant woman like Jerlaug deserved such a fate.

Sobs and whimpers rose above the din. Sabrina moved up to the edge and peered straight down over the ledge – some of the women and children were still alive. The women removed their maiden's belts in exchange for a few months of life. The haugrs would rape and brutalize the women, forcing them to bear haugr young, a death pregnancy. The women would remain unharmed while haugr spawn grew inside them, but upon birth, whether animal human, the young consumed the host. As to human children, the haugr considered them a delicacy and saved them for their chieftain: young man-flesh was highly prized.

The Great Gate

The warriors took up positions around the perimeter of the cave, crouching low and poised for action. The haugr reveled in a blood orgy, building into a frenzy, and anticipating the rapes to follow. Sabrina drew her sword and raised her right arm, extending the sword; she brought it down, and they all leap down into the midst of the haugr. Howls erupted; blades sliced through unguarded haugr necks; black blood sprayed like rain.

A frenzy of fighting erupted. Marla sliced through the arm of a haugr and then took his head. Kayla thrust her dagger deep into the chest of a haugr, and the sharp blade emerged out its back. Joash kicked one down and took off the head of another. He took a step back and let a leaping haugr jump by him. As it passed, he chopped along its back and cut it in two.

Tormod equaled all of them. He swung at the back of a haugr's knee, and he smashed its head as it fell. His war-hammers punched right through the haugr armor, and they spewed black blood and teeth. His hammers landed in repeated deathblows.

Sabrina appeared to dance: she spun and kicked; her blades whistled through the air. Haugr screamed in anger and then in agony; their bodies hit the cave floor with wet splats. She flipped backward and kicked another haugr as she did so. Her blades sliced through the haugr armor as if it was paper. Blood squirted through the air in long jets, and headless bodies tumbled to the ground. The remaining haugr drew away from her, opting to fight a less challenging foe.

The fighting ceased with the suddenness of a summer storm. The bodies of fifty-eight haugr lay at their feet. Black blood flowed in rivers over the rock and formed puddles, glistening like used motor oil. They cut through the bonds that bound the surviving women and children; they sobbed uncontrollably and clung to their rescuers for dear life. But there was no time to comfort them. The sound of the slaughter echoed through the caves; more haugr would come to investigate.

316

Marla escorted a woman to Joash; Sabrina and Joash formed a pair of stirrups with their hands. When the naked woman stepped into their hands, they hurled her into the air; hands reached out from the darkness and caught her. They hauled her up to the ledge. Other men formed a human ladder, standing on the shoulders of the man below them. The women and children crawled up their backs.

When the last victim exited the cavern, Sabrina climbed the wall and waited at the mouth of an adjoining a cave; shrill haugr cries echoed through the caves, attacking her nerves like fingernails on a chalkboard. Time was running out. "They're coming," she signaled.

She saw the last man climb up from the bottom of the basin. She lingered for a moment and surveyed the carnage; tangled human bodies and haugr lay mixed together in a horrible scene. She searched for the body of the hooded man, but he was gone.

Joash waited at the tunnel entrance. When the last man passed him by, he returned to check on Sabrina. He stared at Sabrina, wondering what she was doing. She then left her perch and scrambled around the perimeter of the cave. When they met, she entered first, and he followed her.

The men blocked the false passages, guiding the rescued people toward the proper tunnel. Screeches and drumming feet grew close. Sabrina stared back at the cave behind her and felt the haugr approaching; it made her nauseous and made her head hurt. If she was alone, she would have risked using magic to collapse the tunnel, but there was too great a risk of injury from falling debris.

"We have to go," Joash said. He squatted down by her side and stared into the abyss. "The women and children are out of the cave." She nodded and followed him to the cave entrance. They climbed up the bloody jagged rocks and hands reached down to them, assisting them out of the pit.

The Great Gate

The warriors assisted the survivors and showed them the safe passage through the thorny undergrowth. A large crowd of scared women and children formed at the end of the undergrowth. They trembled and cried as the shrill screams echoed out of the caves.

It was the first time Sabrina could risk using magic; the haugr would have sensed it. "I've had enough of this crawling." She released her wings from her back and summoned her power. The snarled vines ripped out of the ground and flew into the air. She walked among the prostrate men and survivors still crawling on the ground. She marched through the undergrowth ripping trees from the soil and tossing them aside. She cut a snaked path around the titan ironwood trees. The survivors rose up to their feet and followed behind her.

Alexander braced himself for the assault. The frenzied haugr exploded from the cave in a wild frenzy, like water jetting from a fire hose. The first wave rushed up the rocks with a wild look in their eyes, and the archers let fly. Arrows pierced bone and steel armor. Several arrows pierced through their skulls. The haugr fell back upon their comrades, and the dead formed a wall of flesh. The living crawled over the dead and renewed the attack. The archers fired at will. Any that got past the archers the swordsmen soon cut down. The dead choked off the mouth of the cave. There was no more room for a single haugr to crawl through the tangled pile of corpses.

Shrieks ripped through the forest, and Alexander searched the forest floor. It hung like a green curtain before him. However, his mind penetrated the undergrowth and searched, trying to see their arrival.

Terror gripped his warriors: their courage hung by a thread. "FORM RANKS!" Joash ordered and moved to Alexander's side. They formed a shield wall and pointed their spears in a phalanx formation. The archers took up position behind them. "READY!"

The first haugr burst through the foliage twenty meters from them. An archer released his arrow and cut the haugr down; fifty more exploded through the foliage, and when the haugr saw their dead comrades, they formed a shield wall. The archer's arrows stuck in the haugr's shields but failed to penetrate. This barrier allowed the other haugr to exit the forest in safety.

All fell silent. Beating hearts, frayed nerves, anxious glances, Joash and the warriors waited for the attack. The haugr's war cry cut through the air and made the warriors grimace in pain. Fifty haugr emerged from behind the shield wall; they stood in a tight square; half of their shields were raised above their head, and other half formed a barrier around them; a quill of spears then stuck out from between their shields, known as "the turtle formation," making them appear like some sort of bizarre animal.

The haugr chanted, their shrill voices making the warrior's skin crawl. The haugr moved in slow, tight ranks, and other haugr emerged from the forest. The first formation crossed the field, and the others followed. Alexander had no doubt that hundreds, perhaps a thousand, would follow.

It was then that a gust of wind wafted through his curly black locks. The breeze was to his back: the time was right. He pushed through the shield wall and stood before it. Joash furrowed his brow and narrowed his eyes.

What is he up to?

Alexander chanted in Elvish under his breath and then thrust out his hands; flames erupted from his hands like geysers, jetting across the field and igniting the dry thatch. Flames shot up into the air and were picked up by the winds; the swirling gusts whipped the flames into a firenado; the swirling vortex of flame rose high into the sky, creating an inferno. The first haugr formation was incinerated; they fled the flames like living torches and the collapsed to the ground, setting other areas ablaze. The remaining haugr broke ranks and retreated from the whirling flames.

319

The Great Gate

"Let fly," Alexander shouted to the archers. A hundred arrows sailed overhead and through the flames, igniting them. They struck the haugr on the back where their armor was the weakest and set them on fire. Their screams ripped through the forest.

When the last haugr fled into the woods, Alexander said, "We must go: the wind could shift at any time." When Alexander passed through them, the men lowered their lances and opened a hole. The warriors did not have to be told twice; the heat from the raging column of fire drove them away from the fire and through the new path cut by Sabrina.

"A handy trick," Joash said.

Alexander looked to his left and saw Joash standing beside him. "It is a secret best kept until needed." As he watched, Joash grabbed the greasy hair of a haugr and cut it off with a swift slice. "A trophy?" asked Alexander.

"Evidence," Joash replied.

The iron trees were fire resistant, and their seedpods required fire to germinate. Thus the forest protected the retreating troops from the inferno. When they emerged from the thicket, they saw the others already mounted and waiting. When Joash mounted his steed, he saw a sorrowful look in Kelvin's eyes. It was then that he saw the body of a cadet draped over a saddle. "What happened?"

"A cloud of haugr attacked from the rear; they were returning from a hunt. We never saw them until it was too late. Corbin took three arrows to the back. He fell into my arms. There was such fear and pain in his eyes. I saw him die." Kelvin fought back the tears.

Joash remained silent. What could he say to ease his son's grief? He allowed for a moment of silent reflection and then said, "Did you kill the haugrs?"

"Some of them," Kelvin replied and wiped away a tear. "The others scattered when Overlord Sabrina emerged from the forest."

Sabrina took the head from Joash and shoved it in a sack. They galloped away from the woods as fast as the horses could run. Sabrina glanced over her shoulder. She saw billowing smoke rise above treetops, and bits of ash wafted down to the field.

The horses thundered over the green hilltop. The warriors left behind readied themselves for pursuers. The men broke ranks long enough to let them pass. When they entered the town, the group came to a halt. "Shore up the defenses around town."

Martin hurried to Sabrina. "So few," he said and searched the faces of the rescued. "Are there more coming?" Sabrina tried to speak but could only shake her head. Martin's granddaughters and great-grandchildren ran up and embraced him. No one even questioned why they were clad in bloody rags; their families were just glad that some of them returned alive. However, tears of joy turned to tears of sorrow for many were lost.

It was a paltry sum compared to what was lost, but it was the best she could do. Unable to bear the sobbing laments, Sabrina passed between a pair of burned houses and climbed a grassy hill. She stood, shoulder to shoulder with her men and scanned the horizon. The haugr wait until dark to attack.

She then looked back at the town. It sat in a valley between rolling hills. A small stream trickled through it and turned a water wheel. It powered both a flourmill and a sawmill. In other circumstances, the town would have been picturesque. The times, however, were dire. She walked along

321

the line until she located Marla. "The haugr will come during the night and attack our flanks. We must evacuate the town. To stay here is to die."

"Yes, Mistress," Marla replied.

When Sabrina turned, she saw Tormod staring at her. She lost track of him in the battle. He clutched a pipe between his teeth and sent out puffs of smoke. "I fear the battle has just begun." He glanced up at the brown wall with a charred black top. "There are many such villages and towns such as this. None of them have walls. What can we do?"

"I am going to see the governor," she replied.

Chapter 30

A hawk, perched atop the governor's mansion, spotted a winged figure silhouetted against fluffy white clouds. The figure flew at a brisk pace. Where was the predator, where was the prey? Seeing neither, the hawk raised its wings and decided upon a hasty retreat. It leaped off the spire and winged away to a private, safe perch.

Sabrina stretched her wings wide and descended in a slow spiral. The governor's mansion grew larger by the moment. A gold-domed building gleamed as if polished, looming over the city of Solva as a sovereign ruler. It sat high upon a hill, looking down at the complex, and broad, curved stairs led up to it. Four silver spires, appearing like rockets ready for launch, stood at the four corners of the dome. The entire structure shone in the sunlight after a gentle rain, the golden sun breaking through a crack in the clouds above it.

Gracious white balconies adorned the face of the building and afforded the occupants an outstanding view of the city. Two administrative buildings lay on either side of the main complex. Their roofs were slanted, and they stretched around the main entry stairs like a pair of enfolding arms.

The architecture made entrants feel small – children entering the house of a god. The archway loomed over one's heads, and the doors grew larger with every step. Male and female guards were stationed on either side of the doors; clothed in regal splendor, they wore gleaming silver armor, and their silver slip-suits made them appear like statues: masks and helmets hiding their faces. They wore gold and silver shields strapped to their left arms, and they clutched double-bladed swords in their right hands, ready to strike at a moment's notice.

Sabrina cruised to the stairs, made a sudden upsweep, stalled, and touched down lightly upon the stairs. She marched up the broad, semi-circular steps. Several men, clad in regal robes, paused from the discussion and watched Sabrina approach them. A battle Maige, clad in full armor and a slip-suit, was a rare sight and worthy of a few stares.

Sabrina raised her left arm and tapped the gauntlet with her right hand. She accessed the armor's and slip-suit's appearance settings. Chrome flowed over her as if pouring from a bucket, replacing the glossy black, and the sunlight gleamed off her silver-mirrored body; and the king's red lion crest appeared on her armor. Decadent fantasies filled the lobbyist's imaginations as they leered at her. Sabrina perceived their imaginings, as all women do, and shook her head. They should have been wondering why an armed warrior entered the Governor's Mansion. The law prohibited even a woman of Sabrina's rank from entering the mansion so armed.

Sabrina marched up the steps and glared at the residence as if it was an enemy. The guards kept their gaze fixed straight, unflinching and resolute, but they accepted her as one of her their own and permitted her to pass. Rumor suggested that the guard's minds were altered by a combination of drugs and magic, magic that changed the guard's minds at a neurological level; they were little better than soulless machines, machines that would die without a qualm. Sabrina was not impressed. A machine, even a human one, was easily defeated. They operated on strict rules of engagement: thus, they were predictable. Such enemies failed when confronted by the uncertainties of a real battlefield.

A great arch dominated the entryway, and successively smaller arches stretched to the right and left beside it. Underneath the central arch were two doors that were so large a giant could pass through them without ducking. Smaller, manageable doors were cut into the bottom of the large doors, and it was through these that Sabrina entered. The vast foyer stretched out before her. Black and white checkerboard tiles covered the floor and surrounded massive marble pillars, pillars which soared up high as though reaching to heaven; they supported white arches which in turn supported a high white ceiling. A set of grand stairs lay at the end of the foyer; they were broad enough to allow ten men to walk abreast, and a luxurious red carpet covered them. The stairs rose up two stories and ended on a wide landing, and then forming, the twin set of side stairs continued up to the next upper chambers. At that landing, a three-story set of crystal windows that overlooked the royal gardens.

The interior of the building was truly expansive. The mansion alone had 750 rooms, 15 staterooms, 40 grand bedrooms, and 5 royal bedrooms. Below these rooms were 158 staff bedrooms and 92 offices. The administrative buildings housed another 540 offices, 48 conference rooms, and 10 stadium-style auditoriums.

Sabrina strode across the foyer and scaled the grand staircase. The governor's personal assistant, Moyer Trimble, a heavy-set man with a double chin, was an unsympathetic and persnickety bureaucrat. Waiting at the top of the stairs, a foreboding scowl on his face, he glared at Sabrina over the brim of his reading glasses, which hung upon the tip of his thin nose, and he crossed his arms over his small frame, trying to appear menacing.

"Do you have an appointment?"

This was the death knell for most petitioners. Forms had to be completed in triplicate. Committees must review the pertinent data, and a tight schedule must be agreed upon by all. Thus high hopes ended in frustration.

Sabrina strode past the man without acknowledging him. He turned and gazed at her with a stricken expression on his face. "No, no, no," he said. "The governor has no time to meet with petitioners. He is a very busy man." Moyer rushed up the steps in hot pursuit, his feet drumming out a quick beat. She strode up three steps at a time with great speed. In other circumstances, the encounter might have appeared comical.

"I am of the royal family. He will make time to see me," she said.

The Great Gate

Upon reaching the upper landing, she looked out the window and observed the governor's private gardens. It was a lavish paradise far removed from the meager accommodations of the average man. Lush grass stretched out in a long rectangle like a great carpet. Flowers bordered it on either side in an explosion of color. In the center of the lawn lay a fountain; its waters jetted high in the air and collapsed into the pool with great splashes.

When she turned to ascend the second flight of stairs, Moyer snapped, "You must stop, or I will summon the guards."

"Why can't I see the governor?" While Moyer explained the intricacies of the government review process, Sabrina strode past him and threw open the doors to the private office. Upon hearing the doors open with a thud, Moyer rushed after her. Sabrina's cleats on the bottom of her boots clicked and clacked on the marble floor.

A grand chandelier hung overhead, and purple curtains adorned two story windows. The governor and another man stood before his gilded, golden desk. Rich cherry wood paneling covered the wall behind the bureau. Affixed in the center was a two-meter tall, embossed plaque. It bore the royal crest and scrollwork upon it.

Governor Henrik Alexander Sanderson was easy enough to spot. He had gray hair and a wrinkled face. A pair of reading glasses hung on the tip of his nose, and he wore a royal blue jacket with long tails and a pair of white slacks.

The man standing before the governor was a bit more enigmatic. A ring of graying trimmed hair circled the top of his balding head. A pointed goatee accented his narrow face and pointed chin. The man wore a dark blue suit trimmed with gold braid, and he kept his trousers tucked into knee-length black boots. Over the top of the jacket, he wore a gleaming silver breastplate and clutched a helmet. A sword draped from his right side. Its gleaming silver sheath and golden handle had the look of a ceremonial sword.

Sabrina opened the sack and reached inside it. She grabbed a fistful of the haugr's slimy locks and yanked out the severed head. She hurled it across the marble floor. It bounced as it rolled an uneven path, splattering black blood. "You wanted proof. Here it is? The citizens of Bruton paid with their lives."

The uniformed man walked from the governor and moved to the head. Using his right foot, he tipped up the contorted face so he could observe it. "A providential coincidence," the man said.

"So it would appear," the governor sighed.

Sabrina stood before them with her arms crossed. She glared at them demanding some explanation. The man said, "I am The Commander of the King's Royal Guard, Overlord Cameron Thrasher. You, however, need no introduction, Overlord Sabrina March of 'The Black Dragon Guild.' Where did you obtain this?"

Sabrina said, "I have just come from battle in the Deepwood Forest next to the town of Bruton, or should I say the former town of Bruton? More than 500 more of this haugr's comrades are now dead, but much more remain, perhaps an army. They are hidden in the woods and live underground."

Cameron turned toward the governor and put his hand on his right hip. "The armies of Solva must be activated. You must make a defense of the city."

"Can't the king's guard assist us? We have lost so many warriors to battles in the Cordon Wilderness, and we have no budget for such an extravagant expense. We barely have enough to guard our streets."

"You have a province to defend, but my thoughts are for the kingdom. The king's armies will march, but we have yet to determine the strength and location of our enemies." Cameron walked over to a large map hanging on the wall. "Solva is an important port city. That's true. However, attacks are taking taken place in all over the kingdom. Granton and Hampden are already burning. As you are aware, Hampden River and Greenwater River are also two main arteries for shipping. Merchandise flows up the King's Way River to the Glorloch Lake. If these arteries are cut off, the entire kingdom will fall."

The governor rubbed his chin, removed his glasses, and pinched the bridge of his nose. "Yes, I see. Haugr and Skrees litter the kingdom, and we have no indication of how or where they obtained entry. We will activate what troops we can. However, our sea lanes of commerce must be kept open. Will the royal navy assist us?"

Cameron replied, "Haugr hate the water almost as much as the light. The navy is patrolling the sea-lanes, but they have found little evidence of the haugr. They caught a few ships smuggling herbs and black ale favored by haugr. I would ignore the sea and look to the land. The haugr are here, outside your very walls. What need have they for ships?"

"Another salient point," the governor sighed. He returned to his desk and picked up some papers, and then handed them to Edward. "This is the complete listing of our guilds and their strengths."

Edward rifled through the papers. He seemed to be searching for something. "I don't see 'The Black Dragon Guild' listed. Where is it?"

"It's in a special volume. It's too large to fit in the ordinary listing. These are the oldest and best-equipped guilds." The governor said to Sabrina, "Refresh my memory. How many are in your guild and are based in Solva?"

The governor knew the answer, and Sabrina knew it. It was a diversionary tactic that would have her expend her resources instead of his. "We are housed in The Black Castle. As to our numbers, we have pledged 3,503 Mercenaries, 37,520 footmen of various ranks and specialties, 3,022 Overseers of different ranks, 485 artisans, 1,052 accomplished warriors, 527 ballistas, and 38 noble warrants."

"So many?" said the governor and looked above the rim of his glasses. "Well, we have our solution at hand. You and your guild can take up defense of the city."

"You cannot ask a single guild to bear the responsibility for the defense of the entire city and region," Cameron said, trembling with rage.

"Yes, of course," the governor replied with a sigh. "Still, the funding will be difficult. If we could count on your support with parliament for a special grant, then it would be much easier."

"We are under attack now. Parliament has the entire kingdom to consider." Cameron rubbed his temples and squeezed his eyes shut. "Budgetary overruns and wasteful projects have dissipated last year's bond issue. If we raise taxes, then production will slow, and businesses will relocate to other lands, lands without the threat of death. We must make do with our current resources."

The governor stared at his desk. "I thought you might say that. If we activate our defense forces, then our local economy will suffer. Importers will shift to other port cities. Why should we be the only state to bear this burden?"

"It is not a matter of fair. It is a question of necessity. You must protect your people." Cameron began to pace and rub his face. "You must act."

"The battle we fought will not be the last. I guarantee that. How will the fortunes of your city fair when your ports are under attack and cargo vessels refuse to navigate the Merchant River and the King's River?" Sabrina added, "Also consider this, if you act now and purge the haugr from your territory, then all will know that your sea lanes are safe. Can the other ports make such a claim? Attacks are occurring all over the Wolf's Head Peninsula. Surely there will be attacks on their ports."

Cameron said to Sabrina, "It is good to have you by my side again, Princess March. I have not seen you since 'The Edgewater Campaign.' Our lands are safer with you once again bearing the sword." He then cast a jaundiced eye toward the governor. "I will inform the king of these developments."

"Yes. I'm sure you will." The governor collapsed into his chair and let his hands hang limp. He then looked up at his aid Moyer. "Get someone to clean that thing off the floor."

"Yes sir," Moyer said and hurried from the office.

Cameron directed his attention toward Sabrina. "You have accomplished much since your return. We must see to the defense of the city. I fear war is upon us, and we are not prepared."

Chapter 31

S abrina soared over the rooftops, and the whirr of sirens stabbed at her ears. Merchants closed their shops, and wagons charged through the streets at pell-mell speeds. Men and women piled up at transit stations, eager to return home to their families. Mothers snatched up children and hurried through the streets, terrified by their imaginings. City defenders struggled in vain to bring order to the chaos.

She swept her wings in several powerful thrusts and rose up to the spires of the black castle. Looking down at the castle, she saw the dormers and the gates close. Defenders took up stations around the wall, ready to repulse all invaders. Sabrina touched down upon the balcony of her suite and passed through the curtains.

Karalynn fretted and stared at the door. When she heard movement behind her, she turned and saw Sabrina. She ran to Sabrina, threw her arms around her, and gave her a passionate kiss.

Sabrina was surprised. The intimacy in their relationship grew a little, but there always seemed to be a barrier between them. She assumed that it was Karalynn's sexual orientation, preferring to share a man's bed. However, the young elva's right hand dispelled that notion as it slid down to her bottom and squeezed, and she kissed Sabrina, mashing their lips together, as if trying to consume her, pressing up against Sabrina. Kissing the left side of Sabrina's neck, she nibbled on Sabrina's ear and then whispered, "I love you. I'm ready to be with you. You have to come back to me."

"It's okay. Nothing is going to happen to me. Haugr are attacking outlying villages. I have to return and take charge of the city's defense."

"Please, you can't go." Karalynn moved away from Sabrina and took two steps, her eyes cast down and heart heavy, tears welling up in her eyes. "I couldn't take it if you were to leave me."

Sabrina moved behind the elva and turned her around by the shoulders. She lifted Karalynn's chin with her index finger and gazed into her watering blue eyes. "Nothing is going to happen to me. I'm a Battle Maige. Fighting is what I do best. You trust me, don't you?"

Karalynn nodded and cringed. "Yes, I trust you. I just keep thinking about Maj. He said the same things."

"Remember, I am half dragon. It would take a lot more than a few haugr to kill me." Sabrina smiled and caressed Karalynn's shoulders. "When I come back, we will go on vacation, just the two of us. Billy and Tia can tend to the girls." With Billy's assistance, Tia was one of the many fae Sabrina gathered near Picnic Lake. She walked with Karalynn's to the balcony. "I need you to be strong. I can't focus on the battle if I'm worried about you and the girls."

"I'll be okay. You don't need to worry about me," Karalynn said.

Sabrina gave Karalynn a last kiss, then stretched her wings wide, and leap. Karalynn ran to the railing and leaned against it. She watched Sabrina soar away from the castle until she disappeared from sight. Karalynn offered a whispered prayer for Sabrina's safe return.

Chapter 32

Joash charged through the city of Westland, his horse racing down the cobblestone streets. Glass shards littered the road from shattered display windows and flames leap out of burning stores. Haugr bounded from rooftop to rooftop of two-story brick buildings, eschewing the ground and frustrating defenders. When the haugr smashed through windows, screams erupted, and desperate men fought for their lives.

A terrified woman burst out from a doorway, covering her head with her hands. "Help me," she screamed. A haugr leaped out from the stairwell and knocked her to the ground. Pinning her to the street, the haugr forced its hips between her thighs and ripped at her skirt. She tried to push the repulsive creature off her, but it was too powerful. The creature pressed back her knees and prepared to rape her. "No," she groaned, her eyes squeezed shut, still trying to dislodge it.

A moment later, hot blood splattered her face and hooves thundered past her. When she opened her eyes, she saw a stream of black blood squirting from a severed neck. The decapitated haugr convulsed and then collapsed on her.

Joash had no time to comfort the woman. He dug in his spurs and set out after three haugr devouring the mangled corpse. When he raced up the narrow avenue, one of the haugr turned its head and screeched. Sounding like fingernails on a chalkboard, the shrill cry made Joash's skin crawl and provoked instinctual aggression. Two of the haugr leaped at the red brick wall and scrambled up it as if it was level to the ground. The third haugr was a bit slow, and Joash's blade cut through the haugr's neck. The mortally wounded attacker flopped to the ground and screamed a death cry. Its brethren peered over the building's ledge and hissed at Joash.

The Great Gate

"Come down here and fight me!"

An arrow shaft shot out through one of the haugr's eyes. It collapsed over the ledge and hit the street with a wet splat. The last haugr gazed up at the sky and hissed. An arrow punched through its throat. The creature gurgled and collapsed backward, its arms and head draped over the ledge, black blood flowing over the red brick.

Joash searched the sky, his old eyes straining to see this new participant. He saw a glint of silver and then winged figures diving down from gray, cloudy skies. "Valkyrie," he whispered like an answered prayer.

Sabrina led the winged warrior women. They swept fast and low over the city. Their arrows hurtled through the air and stabbed through haugr necks. Racing over the rooftops, a thousand haugr scrambled in every direction. The Valkyrie split off after them, their arrows cutting down the haugr. When a haugr leap over a wide alley, Sabrina's arrow hit it in mid-flight. The stricken haugr hit the wall head first and tumbled to the ground.

Tormod rode up to Kelvin and brought his mountain goat to a stop. "The Valkyrie are forcing the haugr down to the streets. The east side of the city is thick with them."

The pair linked up with several other warriors and rode east. Haugr scrambled down the face of the buildings and began charging through the streets. Joash's steed overtook them, and he cut them down, his sword cutting through their plate and leather armor.

———

Kelvin, Cody, and the cadets retreated to Sentinel Hill. They stood with their backs to a tarnished bronze statue and were hard pressed on every side. Fighting for their lives, they swung and hacked at the frenzied creatures. When Cody thrust her blade through a haugr, two others seized her. She bucked and kicked as they pinned her legs. Hands covering her mouth, they carried the girl through the mob and took her into the woods.

Her armor made using their poison impossible. So while one haugr bound her arms behind her back, the other bound her legs, the leather cord creasing into her glistening black slip-suit. "No, no ... www mmnn," she mewed as a haugr pressed a leather ball through her teeth. When it popped into her mouth, they wrapped the strap around her head and tied it tight, creasing the corners of her lips. Her heart pounding, her muffled screams cut off by the gag, she watched a black leather hood stretch over her face. The slick material cleaved to her features and stretched over her head. She snorted gasps through nostril holes as the hood laced tight.

Submerged in darkness, she felt a haugr sling her over its shoulder. Draped over the haugr's back with her bottom thrust into the air, she felt each bound of the creature's legs. She struggled to free her arms and legs, but it was no use. She was tightly bound.

She felt the haugr jump and floated in the air for a second. When the haugr's feet hit the ground, his shoulder pressed into her gut. Cody drew in a desperate gasp and smelled raw sewerage. They were carrying her off through the city sewers.

———

Joash fought his way up Sentinel Hill. The haugr were everywhere, darting in every direction, leaping and slashing, and knocking defenders from their horses. He rode up the central concrete sidewalk, slashing and stabbing at Haugr. In the midst of the pandemonium, he saw Kelvin. The young warrior stood alone, his dead comrades at his feet. Black blood mixed with the red as he fought for his life. His blade deflected blow after blow, slashing as it swept. The haugr leaped about and screeched at him in rage. Joash charged through their midst and cut off two heads with one swipe. Kelvin grabbed Joash's right hip and swung him onto the horse. The pair charged through the mob, returning to their lines.

The Great Gate

Chapter 33

Cody lost track of time. The haugr had been carrying her for hours, perhaps a day or more. Amidst the shrill squeals, she heard the stifled cries of other women. She bounced on the haugr's shoulder, terrified what would happen to her when it stopped. Every so often, the haugr's fingers explored between her thighs and tried to access her sex, but the maiden's belt kept them at bay.

She wished for a single blade so that she could cut her throat, but it was an impossible dream. The haugr bound her limbs and seized her weapons. Her captor climbed out of the tunnel and scampered up a tree. She flew through the air and landed hard when the haugr found the next tree. Branches and twigs slapped at her as it sprinted from limb to limb. She kicked her bound legs, trying to throw off its balance. If she was lucky, the fall might kill her.

But the creature was far too nimble.

They traveled several more hours through Deepwood Forest. Finally, they descended to the ground. From the fresh blast of air, they were near the Clarion Mountains. A moment later, she felt the haugr's feet slap at rocks as it raced down into the subterranean passages. The haugr took one last leap and came to a stop.

Cody released muffled cries as a hand grasped her. She snorted in gasps, kicked her legs, and squirmed. A smooth wooden spike passed through her right armpit, and when it departed, she sensed rope pass between her arm and side. The spike then passed through the back of her left armpit, drawing the rope across her back. It looped three more times, forming a tight coil, an eyelet dangling from the front. A hook connected to a cable passed through the eyelet and cinched down tight, stretching her up in the air. She felt a cord move between her bound ankles and draw them part. Once they spread her legs wide, the haugr bound them to an inverted Y-frame. The entire frame tilted backward, locking in place at a 45-degree angle.

Cody heard the cries of other women as the haugr bound them. She lost count as to the number of the echoing caverns, but it had to be thousands. Terror swept away her control, and she wildly thrashed, straining against her body. She screamed into her gag as her mind collapsed.

She heard footsteps to her left, claws scraping upon a rock. A sharp hiss, steady and familiar caught her attention. What was it? A familiar whiff of chemicals mixed with the stench. It was a cutting lance.

Then Cody felt movement behind her. A crimson dwarf moved the bright orange lance to her side. He touched the tip to the strap stretching over the girl's right hip, and soon the metal glowed white-hot. The girl only vaguely sensed what was happening. Her slip-suit protected her from the flame. She wriggled and squirmed, crying out for help. When the right strap broke, she came to a sudden stop. When she sensed movement at her left hip, she thrashed about in an animal frenzy. The strap grew white hot and broke free. A second later, the maiden's belt pulled free from her body.

Cody braced herself for the coming rape. At a shrill squeal, the haugr's hand jerked away, and it moved to the next girl. Only captains and chiefs had the right to inseminate captive females and thus ensured the strength of the species.

She drew in a tremulous breath and tried to gather her wits. She recalled her training. After they had raped her, she had to focus on escape. She had two weeks to receive medical help and remove the growing fetus. After two weeks, she had another month where they could still remove it, but they would have to remove her uterus. When six weeks passed, the growing fetus extended a tendril that made its way to the mother's spinal cord and attached. Each day that passed, the growing haugr fetus would

338

take over a little more of her nervous system. When it reached her vagus nerve, it was too late. They would offer her poison, for a peaceful death, and after she was dead, they would cut out the haugr and kill it.

She tried to take deep breaths and remain calm, but then she heard the muffled cries to her left. They were drawing close. She lost control again and began to thrash, fighting to stop the inevitable.

Chapter 34

Joash and Kelvin rode through the chaos. When Kelvin spotted a riderless horse, he tapped on his father's right arm. Joash nodded and steered his horse across an intersection where a wagon burned. Kelvin jumped off as Joash pulled back on the reins. He sprinted to the animal and leap onto its back. A moment later, the pair galloped their horses toward the heart of the city.

They raced from Third Street to Fourth Street on Spring Avenue. One block to the East, they spotted three haugr. They sprang from a building with bound women over their shoulders. Before they could intervene, the haugr leaped down a manhole and disappeared into the sewers. Then to their left, they saw a pitched battle, five warriors fought eight haugr. The haugr scrambled up the red brick walls, shattered store windows as they leap, and sprang out of upper story windows.

They were about to ride to the warrior's aid when they spotted another battle east on the road ahead of them. Terrified women and children huddled behind three desperate men. The men fought to save their families, but haugr attacked them with reckless abandon, bouncing through the air in blurred streaks.

The sound of battle also came from above them. Valkyrie dove down and hurled javelins at haugrs on the rooftops. The haugr launched ballistas as the Valkyries and hit one of them in her right wing. She circled in a death spiral toward the roof, where the gnashing haugr waited to battle her.

Trumpet blasts arose from the north at the Access Canal. The clear call echoed through the city and called them to regroup. Joash ignored the call and rode toward surrounded families. They stormed up to the men and cut down the haugr as they leap. "Go north!" he shouted. "Flee the city." The men snatched up their children, and they sprinted away on foot.

When the trumpet call resumed, Joash said, "We have to regroup."

"No," Kelvin shouted. "Cody is back in the park. We have to save her."

"There's too many." Joash spun his horse around and galloped toward the trumpet calls. "We have to regroup."

Kelvin clenched his jaw and glared at the chaotic street leading into the city's heart. Hundreds of haugr sprang between buildings, scrambled across walls, and crashed down on warriors; defenders fired arrows in all directions; a woman leaped out of a fifth story window, waving her arms and plummeted, then disappearing behind a building. Flaming blue rhunite balls, launched from linear inductance cannons, hurtled over the city, slamming into the buildings, setting them ablaze. Kelvin cursed and rode north, away from the park.

He chased after his father, determined to form a recon squad and return to the park. They turned east on Second Street and left onto Park Avenue. They merged into a group of mounted cavalry. Their troop numbers grew thick while the haugr grew thin. Warehouses burned all about them, showering the streets with burning embers.

After they had passed through the smoke, they saw the quay. At least a dozen barges, most half filled awaited them. Kelvin pulled back on the reins and dismounted his horse. He ran up to Tormod and said, "I need a squad to return to the Sentinel Park. The haugr separated me from my unit. They could still be up there."

"No." Tormod waved troops toward the barges. "The city is lost. We have orders to burn it. We are evacuating across the river."

"There are survivors still in the city. Our people are in the city." He grabbed the dwarves arm. "We have to return!"

Tormod glared at the young man and jerked his arm free. "Don't you think I know that? They've overrun they city. Our troops and survivors are scattered along the length of the river. If your squad lives, they are on one of the barges. If they are dead, your death will avail them nothing. Now get on a barge. You have your orders."

Kelvin threw down his helmet and turned toward the city. Cannons launched volley after volley from across the river. The burning oil splattered buildings setting them ablaze. Engineering crews hurtled flasks filled with chemicals through open winds, setting them ablaze with Greek fire. They mixed more chemicals into the town's water supply, and when it erupted through broken water mains, upon contacting the air, it exploded into flaming jets, a geyser of fire. Clouds made of thick black, a suffocating chemical smoke, rose up from the dying city; buildings groaned and collapsed; horses leaped into the river to escape the flames, and screams filled the dying city.

Kelvin dropped to his knees and wept.

———

"We have to save her!" Kelvin's trembling hands combed through his thick black locks. "You know what they are doing to her." He grabbed his head and collapsed to his knees.

Joash stood upon a hill on the north side of Access Canal and surveyed the destruction. Unable to stop the rampaging haugr and fearing for his own safety, the governor ordered the city burned. The troops enforced a scorched earth policy and burned Westland, Meadowton, Appleport, Edge Hollow, and eight other cities. Joash took a swig from his canteen and washed the grime from his face. The haugr took all the land south of the river.

Tormod moved to Joash's side, and Joash offered Tormod his canteen. The dwarf took a swig and wet his parched throat. "How many did we lose?"

"The population of Westland is well over 250,000 adults. I was told that 46,000 survivors reached this side of the river, but they are scattered along the canal, making an accurate count difficult." He wiped the tears from his eyes.

The dwarf performed a quick calculation and said, "Haugr have multiple liters from a single female. That means half a million pups. But their young will need food."

"They have it. The pups will feed off the carrion the haugr set aside." A bracing cool breeze swept across his face. "And a single female can birth multiple litters, and when she dies of exhaustion, they will feed upon her corpse. That means 1 to 2 million."

Kelvin sat with his head between his knees and sobbed. Cody was one of the kidnapped females. She was not a statistic; she was his best friend. He wanted to scream for them to stop, but all he could do was weep.

"What about the elves?" asked Joash.

Tormod screwed up his face and spit. "They are too busy defending Maywyn. They will send no help. We are on our own."

"Will Overlord March burn the forest?"

"It's no use. The haugr holes are too deep underground."

"What then?"

"She's going to summon a great storm from the Arner Sea."

The Great Gate

"I see. Sabrina's going to drown the haugr."

Kelvin ran down the hill to the amassed warriors. He strode through their midst, not caring who saw him cry. In truth, most of them were also crying. They lost half of their comrades in combat.

Joash turned back toward his exhausted troops. Off in the distance, he heard war drums and a column of warriors snaking through the rolling hills. "At long last Solva's forces arrive, after the battle is lost."

"We can still achieve victory, but not for those who are held prisoner. We can cleanse the land of these evil haugrs," Tormod said.

Chapter 35

Cody jerked and struggled in mid-air. She grew still and listened as the haugr secured the next female in line. In a hall constructed like an amphitheater, over a thousand women hung in the air, legs spread, facing the stage, as if waiting for a performance to begin. A lone human rushed down the steps and chased after a dwarf.

"No, no, no," a man shouted. "It wasn't supposed to be like this."

"You were paid," a crimson dwarf said. "Now take your money and leave while you are still able."

"I was supposed to rule over Solva and the surrounding lands. But you're killing everyone." Moyer Trimble gazed up at the scores of women hanging overhead. They were beyond count and disappeared into the darkness. "It wasn't supposed to be like this."

"You still have a task to perform, or should we tell the humans what you did? Would you prefer that?" The Crimson Dwarf's face contorted into a dark scowl.

Moyer collapsed onto a rock, his mind a void. "No," he muttered and hung his head. "No. I don't want that."

"Then open the city gates," the dwarf snapped.

"How?"

"That's your problem, but you had better get them open. Or I will personally tell every human who will listen about your treachery. There won't be a world on which you can hide." He tossed another coin purse into Moyer's hand. "This gold should buy some cooperation."

"Yes, of course. I'll see to it." He rose to his feet and took one last look at the women hanging around them. "I need someone to show me the way out. I am turned around."

When Cody heard this, rage welled up within her soul. She tried to break free, but all she did was jerk the line. The other women languished in silence and prayed for death.

Hours later, she felt activity at her left nostril, and a tube slid through it. She shook her head and gurgled as a tube snaked down her throat. A minute later she sensed fluid filling her stomach. It was a mixture of drugs and nourishment. Warmth spread over her, and her thoughts became vapid, floating free upon a tranquil sea. Her loins began to burn and then ache. She drew in rapid breaths as the drugs insured her fertility.

But Cody was a morph.

Her body had enough of the situation. As if a separate entity, it quickly compensated for the drugs and eliminated them. It examined the ropes and rejected them: primal instinct insisted that she had to be free to live. Adrenaline surged through her system, and in a sudden burst of strength, she cried out and snapped the rope. A scream of agony followed a moment later, both of her wrists broke and her arms broke in three places. Sobbing and fighting to regain control, she snorted in great gasps of air. In less time than it takes to stretch out a muscle cramp, her bones pulled together and mended. She then lifted herself off the frame and dropped to the floor.

Her trembling hands searched the back of the hood and fumbled with the laces. In the end, she ripped the laces as if they were made of string, and yanked the hood from her head. She then untied the gag and stripped it out of her mouth.

Haugr have no use for torches or lamps. They perceive their world by echolocation. Her eyes searched but saw only darkness. Yet her body adapted once again and made use of the meager scraps of light. Although monochrome, the cavern illuminated. As one might see in an amphitheater, rows of captive women, stretched up and legs spread, filled it; both bound and hooded, they waited for the assaults to begin.

Regaining her impetus to escape, she set to work on freeing her legs. Once again, the knot frustrated her. She pulled with all her might, snapped the cord that bound her ankles, and released them. She staggered away from the rig and collapsed to her knees. She gasped in putrid air, but her lungs absorbed only the oxygen.

When her strength returned, she rose up to her feet and placed her left hand upon a rough outcropping in the cave wall. It was slippery and wet. Water dripped and formed a stream. She scooped up some of the water and gulped it.

At the sound of screeches and approaching steps, she ran back to the rig and pretended to be bound, drawing the hood once again over her head. She took several breaths and relaxed, slowing her heartbeat.

The haugr carried in several more bound women. They walked past her with the women slumped over their shoulders, two guards followed after them. One paused and turned toward Cody. It moved close, its foul breath hot on her neck. It studied her a moment and then continued on its way. Whereas the human eye would have detected the missing ropes, the haugr weak eyes failed to perceive it, and its echolocation worked best when moving. At the call of its superior, it hurried to join the others.

After the haugr had departed, she removed the hood. She saw several captured cadets, female Praetorian Guardians, and Valkyrie. Snapping all the ropes was too much to ask from her exhausted body, and the haugr had stripped her of all weapons and armor, leaving her clad only in her slip-suit and vest harness. She dropped to her knees and searched the floor. Her left hand bumped into a loose rock. It had a sharp enough edge to cut.

Cody moved to a Valkyrie, Marissa, and when she touched her, the woman let out a shrill cry. "Shh, I'm trying to free you. Stay quiet, even if I cut you." The Valkyrie nodded and braced herself. Cody moved around behind the bound young woman and felt the ropes on her wrists. She grasped the rock and began to cut. Although she injured Marissa's wrists, she managed to sever the cord. Like Cody, Marissa jerked her arms free, and Cody cut through the strings, and then she ripped off the hood. Cody said, "Free your legs. Then free the others. Start with the warriors."

Moving with the stealth, Cody crept to the exit tunnel. She peered around the corner and fragments of the shaft. Footfalls sounded as the haugr walked away from the amphitheater, and a moment later, they vanished. She snuck down the tunnel, staying close to the wall. When she rounded a corner, a brilliant light, as if coming from a spotlight, temporarily blinded her. When her eyes adjusted, she saw a warm light beaming out through a rough rock doorway. Her heart pounded so hard, she was sure they would hear it. She snuck up to the doorway and stole a quick glance in the room. A pair of crimson dwarves stood in the center of four rough tables. The confiscated weapons were stacked so high that they spilled onto the ground.

"These should bring a fair price." Riller stroked his long white beard. "Some of these weapons were made by the Carbon Mountain Dwarves." He then spat as if the words were distasteful. "May they rot in the grave."

Dal licked the side of a sword. "It is of excellent quality. These are powerful weapons. Their capture testifies to the weakness and stupidity of the humans. May they forever be in chains!" He sniffed the air. "These haugrs stink of excrement, urine, and vomit. Is there any filth they avoid?"

"No." Riller tossed aside a dagger. The weapon slid off the pile, and it fell on the floor with a metallic rattle. He looked around the room and snarled. "Where is the gold, where are the gems? We were promised wealth beyond our greatest dreams."

"We still have to take Solva. The Maige's fortune lies with the vaults of Hinner and Slough. My sources informed me that it includes at least two dozen fire diamonds. Some of them are as large as my fist. We will have the prize, even if we have to kill every human in the city …."

Cody moved away from the door and hid in a narrow slot. She hoped it was enough to hide her from a dwarf's gaze. The pair exited the room, carrying torches. She tensed her muscles, ready to kill them with her bare hands. When they turned to the left, walking away from Cody, she relaxed and drew in a deep breath.

After piling swords in a soiled canvas sack, she grabbed a torch and returned to the amphitheater. When she entered the room, she saw a dozen warrior women gazing back at her, crouching, ready to strike. "Hurry," she whispered. She handed the sack to one of the women. "There are more weapons down the hall to the right. Get them and bring them back, but watch out for the Crimson Dwarves." Four of the woman moved past her. "We need to free the other captives."

There had to be at least a thousand bound and gagged women. Cody was determined to leave none behind. As they freed each woman, she picked up a weapon and assisted freeing the others.

"I don't know about all of you, but I would rather die fighting than be raped by a haugr." Cody saw agreement and ferocity in the women's eyes. "Now let's go free our sisters."

———

Sabrina flew into the sky and hovered with great flaps of her wings. She shouted with a voice of thunder, her cry breaking over the Arner Sea. West winds swept over the sea, tempest tossing the waters, high waves rising like angry mountains. Boiling clouds rose up from the chaos, black as a drathva's soul, lighting stabbing them in their heart. She shouted with a voice that made the ground shudder and mountains stagger. Dark clouds, rising up like a continent in the sky, moved toward the land. Ships danced about and sank beneath the waves. Men and beasts fled the assailing storm.

"I declare a day of suffering, a day of pain, and a day of death. Death to haugr. DEATH to the haugr! DEATH TO THE HAUGR!"

———

Cody staggered as the rock shifted underneath her feet. The haugr bound last coffle of women in place. "Hurry! Something is happening. I can feel it." She ran to the entrance and waited with her weapon poised. When a pair of haugr entered, she chopped one at the neck and shoulders, nearly decapitating it. The second haugr tried to spring away. She slashed its leg, severing the muscle, crippling it. Marissa swept her sword and took its head.

"How do we get out of here?" asked Marissa, her voice betraying her panic.

"There's a fresh air intake across the cavern. Have the civilians escape through the tunnel. I'm going to search for more survivors," Cody ordered.

"We're coming too," Marissa replied. The other warrior women amassed to Cody's left. "Our sisters, mothers, and daughters are out there."

"Fine, we move in squads of five. Archers take up the rear." Cody saw a steady stream of water flowing into the cavern. "We need to get moving. Something is happening up above." She exited the cavern with four women following her.

Cody heard the stifled cries of women. She sprinted down the tunnel, abandoning caution. When they emerged at the cavern, the archers took up position on a narrow ledge. "Death," the women screamed with rage and tears as if going insane. They rushed at the startled haugrs. Cody slashed the body of a haugr chieftain, and the creature's intestines burst out from its body, falling upon the ground. The haugrs were naked, having discarded their armor to ease their movement while performing the rapes. Arrows cut down those who ran, and the sword cut down those who fought.

Cody slashed a haugr's abdomen and then its neck. When it fell to the ground, she hacked at it until black blood sprayed all around her. She cursed and brought down her blade in wide-eyed madness. She stopped when her arms grew too weary to lift. She drew in heavy gasps, black blood covering her face and armor.

"We need to hurry." Marissa ran past Cody. "I think that one is dead. We need to free the captives." Cody nodded and joined the other warriors. When a terrified woman held onto Marissa, she broke the woman's grasp. "We don't have time. We have to get out of here. Help us."

Cody moved to the opposite end of the chamber and peered down the tunnel. Somehow, it was still empty. Why? There was no time to question their good fortune. She and two other warriors moved through the tunnel.

It was then that Cody's heart skipped a beat. Terrified children, most under the age of seven, huddled together and gazed at her in terror. "Get the freed women to help. We need to evacuate these children. The other warriors returned to the chamber, but Cody pushed ahead. When she came to a T-junction, she paused and deliberated. She might find more survivors, or stumble into the midst of the haugr, bringing a ferocious attack down upon them. She drew in a tremulous breath, and her hands began to shake; and her vision narrowed; and her heart hammered, and her mouth went dry; and her courage fled.

We saved enough people. We have to go. We can't save everyone.

She turned to leave. After three steps, she stopped and drew in a deep breath. She closed her eyes and exhaled, forging her courage, summoning her strength of will. She turned around and explored the right passage. After only a short way, the tunnel came to an abrupt end: rubble and boulders piled up before her, the result of a cave-in. She returned to the junction and took the other passage, but it too was blocked.

The adjoining tunnel nexus collapsed. This isolated the survivors from the rest of the compound, perhaps sparing them from attack, possibly saving them. No doubt, laborers: the haugr lived in a complex society with divisions of labor. They were clearing the debris from the tunnel, and if her education was correct — and it had been brutally accurate — the haugr would work with swift hands, returning at any time. She turned around and ran.

When she reached the rape cavern, she discovered that all the women were free. The warriors assisted the freed captives as they exited the cave. Cody said to Marissa, "The connecting nexus is blocked, but they could unblock it at any time. We need to go."

Chapter 36

Torrents dumped out of the sky as if emptied from a great basin, flowing across the land in swollen rivers. Streams swept around Midnight's feet and carried away dark topsoil; the muddy waters joined into a single river and leaped over the sharp edge of the cliff, plunging into a ravine, exploding against the jagged rocks, and flowing down to the tempest-tossed Arner Sea. The water leap in a wild frenzy, whitecaps riding the crest of liquid mountains; and the driving wind attacked all who opposed it.

Sabrina gazed up at the pitch-black skies and felt as though she were underwater, swimming in a murky sea. However, her slip-suit kept her dry and toasty warm, as though seated before a comforting hearth. It was not so for Midnight. The great steed shivered as the frigid water stole his warmth, leaving him miserable.

She pulled the reins to the right and dug in her spurs. Midnight drew up his feet, but sucking slurps came from his hooves: a slow walk was the best he could manage. To go faster would mean disaster; a hidden rock could wrench a leg or break an ankle; so the horse placed each step with care. Upon reaching a rocky outcropping, he scaled a small hill.

Sabrina pushed forward toward the congregated group of warriors. All at once, mounted riders emerged from the darkness. Kayla and Marla rode toward her. Their mask impeded speech, rhunite making radio communication impossible, and the roar of the storm created a near-deafening noise. Kayla stripped off her masks and shouted, "The caverns are flooding. It is as you predicted."

A sharp pain stabbed Sabrina's soul. She envisioned the women and children struggling against the rising water and desperate for a last gasp of air. Her tears mixed with the rain, and she stared at the swirling waters with empty eyes.

The bodies of frantic haugr floated on the water and washed over the cliff. Given time, the haugr could construct an intricate tunnel system that would withstand such deluges, but the tunnels were of hasty construction, lacking adequate safeguards.

"Notify the others. We are returning to the city." She locked eyes with Kayla and shared a pained moment. "Tell them that there are no survivors."

"Yes, Mistress," Kayla replied.

Hit and run attacks took place all over Asgard: the media whipped the public into a terrified frenzy, fearful that the next attack would come by sea. It defied logic. Neither daemia nor haugrs were seafaring. They hated open water, ensuring that the Western Islands remained infestation free. The gorgons, amphibias reptiles, sailed the Arner Sea, but the Asgard navy found no violations of the peace accord. However, fear has a logic all its own – the public insisted, the courts mandated, and the politicians acquiesced – their best warriors served on crowded ships waiting an attack that would never come. The people of the southern shores died without hope of rescue, abandoned to their fate.

Upon reaching the crest, Sabrina saw Tormod. His eyes fixed on the black skies and flooded ground, the dwarf stood resolute upon a large rock, as if becoming one with the stone. Sabrina removed her helmet and mask. The frigid water stung her flesh, like a slap in the face. She shouted, "Our duty is fulfilled."

"So many lost," Tormod hung his head and streaming floodwaters. "I thought we could save a few."

"It's time to go, my friend. We'll find only the dead here." Sabrina looked to her right and saw Joash riding toward her. Great splashes of water came from his horse's hoofs. When he neared her, he removed his mask.

"I heard we are withdrawing," said Joash. Sabrina nodded. "It's just as well. I think my horse is about to grow flippers." When he saw the pain in her eyes, he said, "At least they had a swift death."

"We were just talking about that." Sabrina looked past the Clarion Mountains to the river flowing to the sea. "I fear this is but a taste of the suffering to come."

"You suspect they came by land?" asked Marla.

"I do. These attacks are minor harassments, probing attacks. They are gauging our troop strengths, our defenses, and our response times. They know everything about us, and we know little or nothing about them. As a great general would theorize, 'The best we can hope for is a stalemate.' We cannot win."

"Then what do we do?" asked Marla "This is ridiculous. Our best warriors guard the least tactical positions. It is insane."

"Insane? Politicians have a logic all their own, and the public cares only about their safety. Yet this is peculiar even for them. Corruption has taken hold of the government. It betrays itself and its people." Sabrina paused to collect her thoughts. "We can talk later, we ride for home." She raised her arm to give the signal, but she saw something peculiar. A small figure crawled over the edge of a tunnel and struggled through the rushing water. It was a human child. She dug in her spurs and raced toward him.

Dismounting Midnight, she ran to the shivering child and embraced him. "O-o-others," he stammered. Sabrina handed him to Marla and ran to the yawning cavern, the water sloshing about her knee. She stood upon the precipice, water pushing upon her feet, trying to drag them out from underneath her and wash her into the yawning mouth of the shaft. When she spotted a woman climbing over the ledge, she raced to her and grabbed her arm.

"How many more survivors are there?" asked Sabrina.

"Thousands," the woman said, her entire body trembling.

A pair of hands raised a howling infant through the floodwaters. She picked up the baby, and then she grabbed the woman's arm and hauled her up to the ledge with one pull. "I want rescue teams right away." Marla sprinted through the waters and informed Joash.

Teams of warriors attached ropes to rocky outcroppings and leap over the sides. They waited at the ledge staring into the inky void. A minute later, they began hauling up survivors. "We need more teams. Get more rope." Tormod scrambled over the side without a safety line and descended into the shaft.

When Tormod reached the bottom of the shaft, he scrambled across jagged rocks, sheets of water falling upon his head. He saw terrified woman and children, huddling together for warmth. After warriors had tied ropes around a woman's waist, she shot up into the darkness. He pushed through the desperate survivors, women eager to escape the hell chasing after them. He passed through their midst and saw Valkyrie and female Praetorian Guards holding torches. Their distraught faces reminding him of a funeral, and their eyes betrayed the suffering of their soul, the nightmare they endured.

He descended a corkscrew access tunnel, its design familiar and disturbing, wrong for haugrs. He passed through the terrified women, each looking to him for comfort. "Rescuers are busy at work. You'll be out of here soon. Everyone stay calm."

The line of women extended deep into the bowels of the complex. Finally, he reached the end. To his great joy, he spotted Cody, but there was terror in her eyes; and her right hand reached for its weapon. He furrowed his thick brows and then asked, "Is everything well?"

"Crimson dwarves," she blurted. "They were behind the attack. They constructed these tunnels."

Tormod's face flushed with anger and shame. It was a despicable thing, but so were the Crimson Dwarves. They were sociopaths who hated all intelligent beings. Seduced by the dark forces, it took them and turned into something altogether evil. Pushing down his rage, he asked, "Are these all the survivors? Is there anyone else coming?"

"No," Cody said. "It's all we could do. The collapse cut us off."

"You did well." He moved past her. "Help me now. We have to collapse the remaining tunnel behind us." She nodded and followed him back into the caverns. He could see the terror in her eyes, and it pained him, knowing that his kind was responsible. When they came to a four-way junction, he stopped and surveyed the supporting beams. "This is the place. We bring it down here."

"What do you need me to do?"

"Get some rope or cord, anything we can pull on." Tormod removed his war-hammers from their sheaths. He brought them down upon the stones around the beam footings, sparks flying from the impact. Cody sprinted past him and ventured deep into the tunnel. He watched her disappear into the darkness, never more proud of her than at that moment.

It seemed only a few minutes to him when she returned. She dumped an armful of tattered rags. She picked up a slashed pink skirt. "I'll tie them into a rope."

The Great Gate

Tormod stared at the shredded clothing, and its pain twinged his soul. Somehow, he hoped that all the women escaped, but the evidence demanded otherwise. They drowned in the tunnels. Then he noticed that Cody wore only her slip-suit and harness: her armor and maiden's belt were missing. He wondered if they raped her, but he remained silent.

"Yes, that should do fine. Make sure that the rope is strong and long enough. We want to be well away when the ceiling collapses."

Cody nodded and set to work. She weaved the garments into an impromptu rope. It would suffice for the task. When Cody picked up an ivory silk blouse, a baby shoe fell out and tumbled to Tormod's feet. He fought to contain his emotions as he struck the last blow.

Needing the distraction, he said, "Mine engineering is a difficult science to master. In many cases, you have to support a half a kilometer or more of rock and debris. Making a shaft fall in the right way is as difficult as making it stay up if you want it to fall in the correct manner." When Cody handed him one end of the rope, he tied it around the base of the central support pillar. He followed the line back to Cody. "Go to the next shaft. I'll be right behind you." When he saw Cody scurry around the corner, he took the slack out of the rope. Shrieks and howls echoed through the cavern. The Haugr broke through the previous collapse, and a swell of haugr rushed through the tunnel at him.

"Burn in hell!"

He gave the rope a power yank, and the support slipped out from its anchor. The structural supports, wooden beams thicker than a man's abdomen, creaked and groaned. The haugr rushed underneath them just as they gave way. Tons of dirt and debris slammed down upon them, billowing dust in a thick cloud.

Holding a torch in one hand and a sword the other, ready to fight to the death, Cody returned around the corner. By the torchlight, she saw

358

Tormod and the collapsed shaft. "It would take them a week to dig out that cave-in. We need to go."

As they ran through the spiral shaft, the floodwaters trickled past their feet, resulting in wet splashes. It grew deeper by the moment until they struggled to walk. The rushing water leaped and roared, shoving them backward. When Cody tried to grab the side of the cave, her hands slipped on the wet rock. The water rose up to her waist and Tormod's chin.

"Grab the rope," a distant voice shouted. The pair grabbed the rope and held on tight. The line heaved them forward and grew slack. Tormod struggled to keep his head above water, but seconds later the tunnel was completely flooded: a side wall collapsed, resulting in a flood. Holding their breath, they held on as the line dragged them forward.

They burst through the waters and sucked in a desperate gasp of air. Rain splashing upon their faces, flashes of lightning silhouetted a giant of a man. At first, Cody thought that it was Joash, but then Kelvin jumped into the water. He threw his arms around Cody and hugged her. "I thought I lost you."

"Can't breathe," she gasped.

He clasped her face and kissed her, the floodwaters flowing over them. Tormod said, "You have time for that later. Are all the women out?"

Still gazing into Cody's eyes, Kelvin said, "Yes. We got them all. You two are the last." He brushed a wet tress from her face and stared at her as if to memorize every nuance of her features. There was so much to say, but he could not draw the words from his heart. When she caressed his cheek, he knew there was no need.

Tormod ascended, and then another rope dropped near them, smacking Kelvin's right shoulder. As he tied it around Cody's waist, she said, "We collapsed the nearest junction, and the passageway is flooded. There's nothing you can do."

He gave her a quick kiss and smiled. "Thanks to you, there will be other days to fight. Today we escape." The lightning flashed, reflecting off her glistening slip-suit and armor, and she scrambled up through the pouring rain. He never saw a more beautiful sight in his life.

Chapter 37

Carrying soaking wet and bone weary survivors, the Black Dragon warriors trudged through the rain like a defeated army. Somewhere in the night, they arrived at the outer boundary of Solva. The pennants hung limply upon the staffs; the riders bent forward in the saddle, and the footmen struggled to take each step. The column slogged along the muddy road. It weaved along the foothills and at last came upon the city gate. The guards kept it closed and locked. If they did not open soon, the soldiers might rebel and attack their own city.

A guard, high upon the wall, signaled, and Sabrina signaled a proper reply. A few minutes later the gate began to rise, and a sigh of relief came from all. She led her troops through the gate and entered the Fifth District. When Midnight's hoofs met the solid ground, he tossed his head in celebration. Walking upon stone was a treat compared to the muck.

The spires of the Black Castle were set against the luminescent backdrop of Solva, above the roofs of the nighttime city. Midnight quickened his steps: food, warmth, and sleep awaited him. It became hard to restrain the warhorse, but it turned out to be unnecessary. The troops were just as eager. They marched fast, some jogging, and a few sprinting.

When they arrived at The Black Castle, the footmen headed for shelter and the horses headed for the stables, regardless of what the riders wanted. They entered the barn and passed through the curtain of rain. Midnight snorted and tossed his head, eager to eat a meal and to wear his warm blanket. Sabrina dismounted Midnight and led him to the tack area. She drew up the stirrups and released the girth. Since Midnight was a shire horse, she had to use a small set of stairs. Lifting high, she removed the saddle and carried it into a tack storage room. The blanket, as well as everything else, was soaking wet; water poured off of it and flowed between the boards.

The Great Gate

A pair of cadets hurried to their assigned tasks. Suzanne Chi gave them grain to eat and applied ointment to their aching limbs. Midnight always seemed appreciative of the care. This time it was doubly so. After throwing a warm blanket over him, Suzanne led him to a stall and closed the gate. Although horses only sleep three hours a night, Midnight's eyes closed the moment he entered the stall.

Sabrina stood at the edge of the barn and watched the rain fall in a sheet. Kayla and Marla stood by her side; they hated the idea of getting wet, even if their suits protected them. Joash and Tormod marched past them and strode into the rain, eager for a hot brew and a warm hearth. The girls looked at one another and chased after them. Their feet splashed deep in rivers cascading down the stone steps. "All sunshine makes a desert," but all rain makes a swamp; or as the locals said, "The greener the land the more the rain." Sabrina would have gladly killed anyone who offered such a platitude.

They entered the castle through the main door and broke through the wall of water. The rain came to an abrupt halt, and a rush of moist air propelled them into the castle as if the great castle breathed. A great din arose from the banquet hall. The men had already changed into dry clothes and enjoyed pitchers of hot toddies. It was tempting to flop down onto a chair and join them. However, fraternization broke down the chain of command. She strode through the hall with the others close behind. The men paused from their celebration and watched the women walk by them, the water making their slip-suits glisten. When some of the female warriors observed the men, they gave their men a sharp jab in the ribs.

They hurried up the stone steps on the left side of the hall. After they had passed through a set of burgundy curtains, she let out a sigh and released the tension from her shoulders. The mood lightened, and the girls resumed chatting.

362

"I hate that. I felt like a piece of fresh meat before a pack of hungry wolves. I almost expected them to jump us as we passed by them." Marla contorted her face and rubbed where her maiden's belt circled her hips. "I'll be glad to get out of this thing."

"I know what you mean." Sabrina rolled her eyes and shook her head. "Like men staring at me, it leaves me feeling a bit chaffed." Marla and Kayla laughed at the notion.

"I like it," Kayla said. Marla screwed up her face and wondered if her friend had lost her mind. "You should try growing up with three brothers that call you ugly all the time."

"I remember the way your brother, Mathias, used to taunt you." Marla rubbed her bottom, which was sore from days of riding. "He ridiculed you like it was a sport. Night and day, he never got enough of it. I wanted to punch him in the face, but I don't see why you put up with him."

"I didn't. I never told you, but I used to put Billbay leaves in his mead." Billbay leaves were a powerful laxative. "He would run through the house on his way to the toilet. There were a few times that my father was in the bathroom, and he did not quite make it."

Marla covered her mouth and burst into laughter. "You're terrible. Your mother took him to every doctor in the city trying to treat him. He had to drink all this awful medicine." The laughter faded when they realized that they were speaking of the dead. He died in battle three years ago in the Dead Plains.

The ladies strode through the station; their heels caused a click-clack that echoed off the tile walls. To their right and left they saw notices posted by the transit authority. They hurried down two flights of stairs to the platform floor. A uniformed security officer nodded at them. "Good evening ladies." Marla's cheeks grew rosy, and she paused for a second. She then hurried to catch up with her friends.

The Great Gate

Security officers were a part of the civilian support infrastructure and not required to salute. The castle had its own fire, police, and medical staffs. This was in addition to a complex bureaucratic infrastructure.

The ladies had lingered before the circular doorway cut into the brass tube. An iris opened when the car was ready for loading and unloading. Arrival and departure times varied depending on the time of day and use. At this hour of the night, the cars arrived every five minutes. They heard footsteps to their right, and the guard strolled over toward them. Marla restrained the urge to giggle. "My name is Jarrod. What's your name?"

"Marla," she replied. The girl looked down at her feet, clasped her hands behind her back, and chewed her lip. "It's pretty lonely here this time of night."

"It's not so bad. Things are quiet this time of day. Most days everyone is asleep. I can walk my rounds in no time at all." Of course, he recognized Sabrina and Marla, but he could not take his eyes off Marla. "Say … um, I was wondering if you would like to have supper some evening. The castle has some excellent restaurants."

"That'd be great." They heard the rush of air as the car entered the station. The iris opened before them. "I am Mistress Sabrina's adjutant. I live in the main complex in the central tower."

"Excellent, I'll stop by and see you. We can set up a time to have dinner." He nodded at them as they entered the car. Marla hurried to a padded leather bench and took a seat. She clasped her hands between her thighs and stared at her knees.

Sabrina held onto a stainless steel pole. Out of the corner of her eye, she watched Jarrod as the door closed. When they felt the tug of inertia as the car left the station, they all let out a burst of laughter.

Sabrina sat down and crossed her legs. "I am so tired," she said as the laughter faded from her lips. "Even I am surprised how much rain fell."

Kayla sat next to Sabrina and said, "I know what you mean. For a while there, I was sure we were underwater." She looked at Sabrina and asked, "So what about you? Are there any men who prick your imagination?"

"Oh … um … no," Sabrina said. She bounced her right foot and crossed her hands in her lap. "I don't need romantic distractions."

"You can still have three more spouses. Besides, who said anything about romance?" asked Kayla. The ladies began to laugh once again. She said to Marla, "I know I don't need to urge you to seek male companionship."

Marla turned to her right and faced the pair. "You're a fine one to talk. I remember you at boarding school. The headmistress kept chasing you out of the boy's dormitory. You got in so much trouble."

"True, but I had a lot of fun too," Kayla replied. They all chuckled. "There was this one boy, Edgar Winthrop. God, I wish he was here." And she went on to describe his prowess in bed.

"Alright ladies, let's not get crude," Sabrina said.

When the car stopped, the doors opened, and a group of men entered. Sabrina was glad the conversation ended. Even though she was a woman, and had been one for a long time, she found it embarrassing to admit that she had sex with men; a slight sense of panic welled up inside her when she admitted to it. Memories of her male sexuality still lingered in her thoughts.

Sabrina said, "I hear that you have another dinner date. Alexander is interested in you."

"He is?" Marla exclaimed with alarm. She appeared stricken, as though someone had challenged her to mortal combat. She gaped at her friends looking for the laughter, indicating that it was all a joke.

"Yes. Why else would he invite you for a private dinner?" asked Sabrina

Marla cringed and wrung her hands. "I have dinner with lots of people. I didn't think he meant it like that. What am I going to do?"

"Don't be such a prude. It would do you good to enjoy the embrace of a man for the night," Kayla said. "You're not a priestess."

"Just be sure of what your partner wants. If he's noble, he can compel you to marry, but I admit, most men want sex without commitment," Sabrina said. "Yet it is still worth an awkward conversation."

The elevator display declared that they reached the central tower. The girls exited the car and the station. Marla and Sabrina chatted about the agenda for the next week: the endless meetings, the governmental inquiries, and the press conferences. But Kayla lapsed into silence, the sum total of their efforts catching up with her. And soon, as they rode up the elevator, fatigue overtook them all.

When they reached the 52nd floor, they exited the elevator and turned to their right. The officers' housing was luxurious, far better than those of the enlisted men. Even the hallways reminded one of a five-star hotel complete with plush carpeting, subdued lighting, gracious adornments, and handcrafted doors. And the blessed silence, resulting from noise canceling materials, was salve to a troubled mind.

The ladies stopped by the armory, each floor having its own, and each person had a private locker. Sabrina reached behind, to the small of her back, and released her maiden's belt T-lock; and it open with a mechanical click. As she removed the protective garment, she said, "I hate these things, yet I would hate it more not to have one. Marla, I want you to investigate how Crimson Dwarves removed the maiden belts. I know the dwarves have advanced cutting tech, but the belts should have resisted it. We need to know how, and how to avoid it. I don't care if we have to replace all of our maiden's belts. We need armor we can depend upon."

"Yes, Mistress," Marla said. They placed their weapons and armor in the appropriate spot. When they were naked, they took a long hot shower and toweled dry. After putting on their civilian clothes, they closed and secured their lockers.

They exited the armory and walked down the hallway. Marla lingered behind Sabrina and Kayla. The gap began to widen between them. A door suddenly opened, cutting off Marla from the others. Alexander emerged from his quarters wearing black satin pajamas with gold monogrammed initials. "Marla, I was thinking. We should have that drink tonight."

"Well, I don't know. I'm exhausted."

"Nonsense, I insist." He extended his left arm and placed it on the small of Marla's back. He guided the girl into his room. As Marla entered, he stared at Marla's body. "I have the perfect thing in mind to help us relax."

"Do you think we should rescue her?" asked Kayla.

"No. She needs to fight some battles on her own. If she doesn't make a choice, others will make it for her." Sabrina turned and strolled away. Kayla lingered for a second or two and then hurried after Sabrina.

Chapter 38

Kayla yawned and stretched. She wandered through the hallway, lured by the rich aromatic aroma of coffee. She wore her silver silk nightgown; since warriors lived nearby, they observed an informal dress code when on base. Everyone considered bedclothes normal attire for breakfast. When she passed by Alexander's bedroom door, it opened, Marla hurried out and bumped into Kayla.

They stood face to face, trying to comprehend the moment. Marla wore black satin panties, a surprised expression, and nothing else. At seeing Marla, her cheeks flushed to a shade of crimson. She stared at the floor and covered her chest with her arms.

"Where are you going in such a hurry? We're not even close to being finished." Alexander pushed the door open and stood behind Marla. He wore a pair of black boxer briefs and had an impish smile. He stood close behind Marla and guided the girl back into his room. As Alexander closed the door, he said to Kayla, "Don't expect us for breakfast."

Kayla looked at him in astonishment for a moment and watched the door shut. When the lock clicked, it broke her trance. She clucked her tongue and crossed her arms. She hurried through the hallway taking rapid, short steps. She rushed into the dining room, leaving the door open. Kayla rushed over to the table and jumped into the seat. "You're never going to believe what I saw."

"The ghost of Good King Ferdinand IV," quipped Sabrina.

"What? No. I saw Marla coming out of Alexander's bedroom. She was naked, except for her panties."

"Where is she now?"

"He ushered Marla back into the room. He closed and locked the door."
Kayla rushed over and retrieved a cup of coffee. She hurried back and sat
with her left ankle underneath her right knee. "I can't believe it. Marla
slept with him." She looked back at the door.

Sabrina shook her head and took another sip of coffee. "She's a grown
woman. She can have sex with anyone she wishes."

Kayla shook her head. "I don't see how she can do it. I can't stand him.
He's so superior."

"It's still her choice. It will help her mature a little bit. Besides, sometimes
we choose our love and other times it chooses us."

Tormod took a seat and cradled a cup of coffee between his hands.
Kelvin sat opposite him; the large man wore pajama bottoms and a tank
top. The thin cotton top cleaved to his bulging muscles, worthy of the
most developed body builder, and six-pack abs drew the attention of
most women around him; they gazed at him with dreamy stares,
captivated by his rugged features and smiling eyes.

Cody hurried to Kelvin's side, eager to fend off these female interlopers.
Through her white gauze robe, one could see her gold metallic bra and
panties. She passed by Kelvin with a deliberate sway of her hips, her
perfume lingering in the air, guaranteed to gain male attention. The large
man watched her walk away from him and toward the serving line. He
rose up and followed her like a lost puppy. They chatted for a few
seconds and then Cody helped him carry five plates, piled high with
breakfast food, and she took a bran muffin for herself. He placed a plate
piled high with food on the table. "Did you all have a good night's
sleep?" asked Kelvin.

"Some of us hardly slept at all," Kayla replied. She sipped her coffee and
then preened her brown locks. She spoke to Tormod. "Have you seen
your ward this morning?"

The Great Gate

Tormod twitched his nose and grunted, "No."

A girl entered the dining hall. She was an adorable little thing. She had blue eyes, a button nose, and sunshine blonde hair that flowed over her shoulders. She wore only a diaphanous chemise, somewhat inappropriate since it exposed a vague hint of her breasts; Sabrina was relieved to see that the girl wore a thong. The girl rushed over to Peter, another warrior of the guild, and dragged over a chair. She wrapped her arms around his thick left arm and laid her head on his shoulder.

Peter said, "Oh … um, I should introduce you to Amy. She's a serving girl I met last night."

"He said that he loved me." Amy's girlish naivety forced a laugh to burst from Sabrina's lips, but she disguised it as a cough. "We're going to live together."

Kayla coughed and wheezed. After clearing her throat, she said, "How wonderful. You really should redecorate. His quarters are so bleak. He leaves his clothing and armor everywhere."

"Um hmm," Amy said. "I'm going to get started cleaning right away. I'll move my things in afterward."

This was too much fun for Kayla to pass up. "Have you discussed starting a family? I know his mother wants lots of grandbabies."

"We're going to have 5 boys and 5 girls. That's one more boy and girl than my mom had. It's going to be so much fun, changing diapers and feeding the babies." Amy wore an irrepressible grin, but Peter appeared stricken. "I'm not on the blue so I might already be pregnant."

Peter snapped his head toward her and blurted, "You're not?"

"No. My mother said that I was too young to start. I'm glad I listened to her now. This is going to be great."

Sabrina asked, "How old are you?"

"Sixteen," she replied. "My mother was sixteen when she got married." The legal age of consent, with a parent's permission, was fourteen years old in Asgard. Of course, this law stipulated that a man had to marry the girl in question. A woman of nineteen, in a modern city such as Solva, might have many lovers before marrying. However, traditional families still relied on the old code. If a man took the virginity of a girl and refused to marry her, then the male heirs would swear a blood oath to kill him.

It just so happened, that Judith Benhaus, Peter's mother, entered the dining hall. After the King of Salvia executed her husband, Herb, Bill Kendal risked his life and smuggled her out of Gleason. Peter later enlisted the Black Dragon Guild and joined her in Solva. Their sister, Stacy, remained in Gleason. She worked in a brothel by night and fought for the resistance by day.

Any mother would want to check up on her son after such a rigorous posting. When Kayla pointed her out, Amy jumped to her feet and scurried over to Judith. She held the slender woman's hands and jumped up and down. A look of astonishment appeared on Judith's face when she heard the news.

"You're deep in the muck now, boy," Tormod said and took another sip of coffee. "I told you not to have that last ale."

"It was never like this back on Earth," Peter said. "People have sex all the time without getting married."

"You're from Earth?" asked Kelvin.

"Yeah, I was a boy when Gleason moved from Earth to Eden. What a nightmare. Salvia took over, and they are true monarchy, not part of the Asgard Parliament. You can forget about civil rights and justice. Of course, on Earth, you didn't have to marry a girl if you had sex with her."

Sabrina raised an eyebrow and asked, "Even if she was only 16?"

"Yeah, I guess you have a point," he mumbled. "I'd be in prison back home."

Amy rushed back over to Peter. She jumped onto his lap and wrapped her arms around his neck. She nestled her head against his chest and purred like a kitten. Sabrina watched Peter with a cat-like gaze. "Have you set a date for the wedding?"

The girl looked upon Peter with dewy eyes and said, "It will take me at least a month to get all of my family here. I can hardly wait."

Judith said, "Six weeks it is."

"We have many chapels and reception halls here in the castle. You can get started decorating right away. I doubt that anyone else will use them. Most of the other men are happy with their lazy days of bachelorhood." Sabrina then said, "I'll have Marla put it on my calendar. What was your last name, Amy?"

"Pumpkin," Amy replied.

"Your last name is Pumpkin?"

"Yes. Why?"

"No reason. It's just such an unusual name. Your extended family, they're all farmers?"

"Yes. How did you guess?"

Tormod looked about the room and asked, "Where is Marla?" Kayla and Sabrina looked at one another but remained silent. His voice broke into a low rumble asking, "What?"

"Well, Alexander and Marla had a date last night, but Marla didn't know it was a date until later …." Tormod listened to Kayla's abridged story. She tried to put a positive spin on it, but Tormod's mood darkened with each new revelation.

Sabrina rose from the table and walked over to the French doors. She opened one and slipped out onto the balcony. The white marble chilled her feet, and a gust wrapped her nightgown around her legs. Needing relief from a cramp in her back, she released her wings, letting them shoot out from her back and drape on the floor behind her. She kept her elbows close to her side and cradled the coffee mug in her hands. A red sun arose on the horizon, and its beams set the sky ablaze – the storm was past. She drew in a cleansing breath and savored the aroma of the city. Merchants opened shops and prepared for the day's chaos.

Kayla hurried out onto the balcony and stood by Sabrina's side. "Tormod is so angry. I thought the veins in his head were going to burst." She glanced over her shoulder and looked through the glass doors. Tormod scowled at the tabletop. As for Peter, his new bride-to-be clung to him and purred. "I did not see any of this coming."

Sabrina arched an eyebrow and pondered the point. She had the gift of foresight, but its application was involved. The future was like a great tree; as she traveled from branch to branch, all other paths were pruned, leaving a single trail to the past; however, the path to the future included many paths, paths once taken steered the course of one's life. Compounding this, each person's path was interwoven with countless other lives, and each decision affected countless other lives – and all destinies were intertwined like a great tapestry.

The Great Gate

In one of these untaken paths, Marla remained in the great hall and wound up sleeping with Peter. This led to a torrid love affair that ended in sorrow. This path was gone, pruned away by fate, with a little help from Sabrina. The alternate path had Marla spending the night with Alexander.

Sabrina felt a little arms wrap around her right leg. She looked down and saw blue eyes gazing up at her. Angelina sucked her thumb and clung to her. Sabrina squatted and scooped up the little girl. Together they watched the sun turn from orange to yellow, and the city abounded with life.

"There you are," Karalynn said. She took the little girl from Sabrina and groaned. "I don't know how she does it, but she can sense you from a mile away. She runs right straight to you."

"She really is a cutie." Sabrina brushed a golden tress from the girl's face, and she gave Angelina a gentle caress. "It's good to see you and mommy."

Kayla scooped up the little elva and carried her back into the dining hall, wishing to give the couple a private moment. Karalynn held up a large black velvet box. "It was finished while you were away fighting the haugr." She pried open the lid and showed it to Sabrina. A mithril ring gleamed in a black velvet setting.

Sabrina picked it out and examined it. The ring bore the royal crest. It displayed a black dragon and symbols of royalty set on a field of blue. Its eyes blazed with fiery red rubies. Its upper right claw clutched a sword, and its upper left clasped an olive branch. Its lower claws gripped a banner that read "Yeste' E' Ohato – Yeste' E' Seere," which translated from Elvish means "First in War – First in Peace."

Sabrina hesitated a second. They discussed Karalynn wearing her ring, but they left the issued undecided. A ring suggested an intimate relationship, transitioning from adopted sister to that of a wife. The court had no interest in the nature of the relationship. Its only concern was the legal implication: Karalynn would belong to Sabrina. It was a big step, one that Karalynn seemed intent on taking.

Stealing a furtive glance through her bangs, Karalynn said, "If you still want me, I'll wear your ring."

"Of course I still want you," Sabrina said and caressed the elva's cheek. "I love you."

Karalynn slipped down to her knees, bowed her head, and clutched her hands behind her back. "I am yours, for now, and for all time. I present myself to you with all my heart. You have captured me with your love, so seal me now with your ring."

"I loved you from the first day we met, so I accept your pledge to be my bride." Sabrina opened the ring and inspected it. The ring connected to Karalynn's nervous system as Sabrina slid it up her ring finger. "This ring is a visible symbol of my great love for you. I take you as my wife, my lover, and my best friend." Sabrina touched her signet ring to the emblem on Karalynn's ring. "With this ring, I seal you for all time as my wife."

Karalynn winced and closed her eyes as the ring became bound to her. Karalynn's lips parted, drawing in a tiny gasp, and an ephemeral glow radiated in her eye, illuminated with Sabrina's power, bathing her in Sabrina's love.

"I had no idea —" Karalynn gasped, her words fading to silence "So wondrous." The new bride admired her wedding ring. "You are my Mistress: command and I will obey."

The Great Gate

Sabrina held out her hand and assisted Karalynn rising to her feet. She lifted Karalynn's chin with her index finger, and ever so gently, kissed her. "I had no idea how much I would come to love you. You are my wife, my beloved. I accept your submission, and I promise to love you with all my heart, protect you with all my might, and care for you all of my life."

Tears flowed from Karalynn's eyes, and she leaped into Sabrina's arm. Their lips pressed together in a passionate kiss, and cheers erupted from the spectators in the dining hall. Karalynn hurried into the hall and retrieved a compact; she gazed at her reflection and sighed. "Maj could never afford a nice ring. We had to make do without one, but he planned to buy me a stainless steel ring." Karalynn's mithril and gold ring denoted her rank as a member of the high royal family; there was no higher rank among women.

Karalynn gazed at the beautiful band. The other women flocked to her and formed a circle around her. She held out her hand so that they could all get a clear view of it. The other women sighed and drifted into fond imaginings. When they beheld the ornate design, its many jewels — sapphires, rubies, and blue diamonds, each stone supercharged with a different protecting power — dazzled them. The gemstones blocked magical attacks, physical assaults, and biological attacks – ensuring both her safety and her obedience.

Many of the unmarried women began to congregate around Sabrina. Since she was a warrior and carried the rank of a "man," she could legally have 4 wives. It was true that Karalynn would always outrank them: she was Sabrina's "first wife." But they would outrank all the other women in the castle and the women in the city.

A group of women congregated around Sabrina, ambition hidden behind their eyes. When a woman offered to care for Abby, another woman butted in, and a quarrel broke out. One of the ladies snatched up Angelina as she licked a spoonful of applesauce. The other women formed a circle around the confused girl. One complimented Angelina on her beauty, and the others all joined the tumult. A few declared that they loved babies and wanted to bear a dozen. Karalynn would never have to lift a finger if they were around. Senior wives often selected subordinate wives for their Master or Mistress. Karalynn remained aloof to their overtures.

Amy laid her head upon Peter's shoulder. She whined, "I want a ring. All the other serving women make me stand up to eat. When can we get one?"

Peter shrugged and said, "I suppose we can go shopping for one."

"That would be great." The smile returned to Amy's face, and she squeezed his neck. "I bet we can at least qualify for a silver ring."

"Well, actually, I'm of the lesser royal line. My family is of Danish Royalty, and my father paid to have our name registered so we can get a gold band." A platinum band required official recognition of the royal court.

"Yes, yes, yes," Amy said and bounced in his lap. "I'm going to get a gold ring." All of the other women pretended to be happy, but jealousy hid behind their affirmations. No one wanted to be outranked by this bouncy little blonde.

Eliza sucked on her finger and tried to understand the tumult. She was sure it was awful and screwed up her face; tears threatened to follow. Sabrina scooped the girl up in her arms, carried her over to the table, and handed her to Karalynn.

A serving girl brought over bowls of oatmeal and a bottle of syrup. She set them before Abby and Eliza and poured the syrup onto the oatmeal. Karalynn scooped up a spoonful of mush and fed it into Eliza's mouth. The young girl swallowed it with one gulp and giggled.

The Great Gate

Sabrina said, "Karalynn, stop by my suite after the children finish breakfast. We need to get you moved into my bedroom."

The young elva gaze up at Sabrina through her bangs with dewy eyes. "Yes Mistress, I'll see to it." She pondered a moment and then asked, "You won't be long, will you?"

"No. I just need to discuss some pressing business. I'll see you in a bit." Sabrina arose from the table and strolled away. As Tormod and Sabrina exited the dining hall, the woman all gathered around an oracle scroll and suggested lingerie Karalynn could wear for her honeymoon.

As they strolled side by side, Tormod stroked his scraggly beard. "You're in for it now. I bet you have three more wives and fifty concubines by the end of the year."

"Fifty?"

"Oh yes," Tormod said. "I knew this one fellow. He owned a quartz mine and discovered gold in it. Before he knew it, he was living in a mansion on a vast estate. His wife was an ambitious woman and very strategic. She negotiated 3 wives from various influential families. On top of that, she obtained 522 concubines. True, the concubines had a lesser rank than that of wife, but they still outranked most other commoner women. The poor man was dizzy with female intrigues, backbiting, and power plays. Every woman, including the concubines, wanted a baby. Most of them wanted more than one. It was pandemonium; children ran around the estate like rats. They got into everything. It was so bad that he had to hire an army of nannies to take care of them, and then he had more children by the nannies. It was chaos."

"Your friend needed to get a vasectomy. I am not going to have fifty concubines, and I don't want three more wives." Sabrina wrung her hands and screwed up her face.

378

"That's good because you're much richer than my friend. Given your status, I would say you would have 1,000 to 2,000 concubines. Look on the bright side; you can hire sires to inseminate the women. Of course, that is another problematic issue. The better the sire, the higher her rank is in the family." He strolled in silence for a moment and let Sabrina absorb the news.

"You have the status of a man, but you are still female. If you act as a surrogate for a wife or concubine, by that I mean carrying her fertilized egg, her child would rank higher than all the others, even if she was of lesser status. You are the Mistress of the house, and the child technically came from your body. He or she would legally be entitled to a significant share of your estate and would carry your name in the royal court."

"I'm not having a thousand babies." Sabrina crossed her arms and pouted. "I'm a warrior."

Tormod smirked. "You may have the master ring, but they have the power. Never forget that. They can drive you mad with incessant whining and bickering. They instinctively know how to twist and bend us into anything they want." He paused at Alexander's door. "One question though, why didn't you two have a church wedding?"

"I'm of the royal house. I would take years to invite all the guests and plan the wedding. Karalynn didn't want to wait that long for me to marry her," Sabrina said. "I'm having only one wife, just one, and I am not getting pregnant."

"Your adopted father, the king, may have some opinion about the matter. Now that you are married, you opened the door. Most royal marriages are based on political strategy, not love. In addition, you left Eden for 88 years. Wives, concubines, handmaidens, nannies, guards, servants, and children have a habit of keeping the most independent person home. The king knows this, and keeping you tied to one locale will enhance his political influence."

The smile vanished from Tormod's face, and a troubled expression replaced it. She respected his need for intellectual privacy and walked in silence. When they arrived at Alexander's suite, he said. "I will join you later. I need to speak with my ward."

"I need to discuss something with Alexander," Sabrina said and waited with Tormod.

Tormod raised his hand to knock on the door. It opened and struck him. He took a step back and gave way to the door. Bella, Alexander's maid, stood in the doorway, but the dwarf strode past her and stormed into the room. Sabrina strolled in and surveyed the disheveled room. Alexander lounged behind a small table on the balcony, his legs crossed and a cool, catlike expression on his face.

Tormod strode through the living room and came to an abrupt stop. He gaped at what he saw. Marla was on her knees. Gold shackles bound her ankles, wrists, and, neck golden chains connecting them. The bound girl wore a black leather thong, a typical slave garment, and nothing else.

Upon hearing footsteps, she turned her head to the right and gazed up from the floor. A black leather panel gag muzzled the girl and dug into her white cheeks, parting her short blonde locks. Upon seeing him, her face grew red, and she averted her eyes and tried to cover her breasts with her shackled arms.

Alexander was of the lesser Royal Spanish Court; as such, Marla could not refuse his proposal of marriage. All rational thought drained from Tormod's brain. No dwarf ever treated a female in such a fashion – he was outraged. He tried to speak, but no words came out of his mouth. Sabrina shook her head and sighed.

Tormod broke the silence. "You have every right to press my ward into marriage, but not to treat her like a prize pig. She is an honorable warrior and a sentient being. My wife and I cared for her as our own. You have no right to do this to her. Release her at once!"

"We can discuss the matter over breakfast. Bella, bring enough food for three," Alexander ordered.

"Yes, Master," Bella replied. The girl curtsied and hurried away. Sabrina and Tormod sat across from Alexander.

"She's a beautiful girl. You and your wife did an excellent job of raising her. I think she will make a good wife. I thought she should have three babies to start, perhaps more if the mood strikes me. As to her predicament, I prefer to keep my wives in this fashion. It keeps them out of trouble."

Tormod recovered his wits, and he cared deeply for his ward; but the couple was betrothed. If he wanted to bind her, he could do about it. These were humans, and only human law applied. All he could do was cement a fair deal for her purchase. Alexander was playing a game to throw him off, of that he was sure.

Alexander could pay a single copper for her, and he could not refuse. However, it would reflect poorly upon her house. If Tormod flew into a rage and insulted Alexander, then he would be justified in his actions.

Tormod said, "So you wish a large family. That is admirable. Children are a blessing. Who were you thinking of to sire the children?"

"Oh I don't know. I won't have her sullied by the touch of another man. I suppose that I will have to do it, although I find such activities commonplace and boring," Alexander replied.

Tormod glanced at the tousled bed, and the clothes strewed about the floor – this was no accident. Alexander did this to inflame his passions and diminish his wits. "As you wish, you are the girl's betrothed. Yet there are many formalities to consider. You must register her with the royal court. You must register her family name and rank. Otherwise, your children will lose their status within the court."

"I think everyone is getting ahead of themselves," Sabrina said. Tormod cocked his head, and Alexander paused from spreading jelly upon a cracker. "I paid Tormod 10 gold coins for Marla's service contract, and I am exercising it right now. I am pledging her service to the Valkyries, and she is vamon to me."

Vamon had three meanings: First, it could mean duty wife or full marriage. This was the common use. Second and less common, it could mean an adopted, dependant, and subordinate sibling. This is a case where a child, not the parent, chooses to adopt a brother or sister. Corporations most often used the third option, which was a service contract. Sabrina had the second and third use in mind.

Tormod's face lit up. "That's right. You paid for her option. She does belong to you by law."

She gazed down at the helpless girl and said, "Have those ridiculous bonds removed."

Alexander set down his knife and cracker. One could see his mind working on the problem. In the end, he said, "Very well. I was not informed of your prior arrangement; she should have made this clear to me." He signaled Bella and said, "Free the girl."

Belle rushed over and released Marla's gag. "Www mmmnn pphhh," Marla mewed. When the gag pulled free from her mouth, she exclaimed, "Son of a bitch, get these chains off me!" When Bella released Marla's bonds, Marla rose to her feet and threw down the shackles, making them

382

clatter on the marble floor. Her face burned red, and her eyes narrowed in rage. Mortal combat was seconds away.

"Don't think I'm going to rescue the two of you again. I expect the both of you to have more sense," Sabrina said.

Sabrina's chastisement took Marla by surprise. She cringed, and Alexander's back grew stiff and straight. He crossed his arms and legs. "I don't know what you mean."

"Don't you," Sabrina said. "I know how your parents goad you. They compare you to your older brothers and sisters. 'Why can't you cast spells like Maria?' 'Why don't you have standing in the royal court like your brother Pablo?' It was they who pushed you to take this abrupt and ill-considered action."

"I don't think it was ill-considered," Alexander replied and crossed his arms.

"Oh no? First, you do not love Marla. In fact, you do not even like her. You are refined and catlike. She is a warrior woman, a she-wolf. You did this to impress your parents and embarrass the 'Asgard Royal Court,' something that your father has been laboring to do for years. His approval would be momentary and fleeting. After that, you would be trapped in a miserable marriage, or would you care to argue the point?"

"No. She is rather annoying." Alexander took a sip of orange juice and eyed her. "It would be a very awkward marriage."

"As to you Marla, from the moment I saw you up on that stage, I knew that you would one day be a great warrior. However, you have a lot of growing up to do. You should have said, 'No,' to Alexander's dinner invitation. When he tried to seduce you, you should have pushed him away. You created the imperative for him to propose marriage when the two of you made love. If you walked out, it would have been inappropriate for him to force marriage upon you."

Marla said, "I'm sorry. I guess I just liked the attention."

Sabrina shook her head and sighed, "The bedroom is no place to build a relationship. I expect better of you than this. I have made my decision. You are forever pledged to the Valkyrie."

Chapter 39

S abrina stretched out her arm and drew Karalynn close to her side, caressing the elva's side. Her wings draped over the back of the carriage, the warm sun drying her feathers after a recent bath, and savoring the cloudless sky – stretched from horizon to horizon, so vivid, so blue and so expansive – the tranquility soothed her soul. The warm air, the sweetness of the blossoming trees, and the blooming flowers complemented a near perfect day.

Billy lay curled up in a ball at Sabrina's feet, her wings folded like a resplendent backpack. The fae basked in the sunshine and slept peacefully on the maroon plush carpet. She dreamed of an abundant harvest and endless labor. Every so often, she purred and whispered soft blessings to the maker of all things. Tia attended to the children back at home, giving Karalynn a chance to relax, but it seemed strange to Karalynn, as though she was missing an appendage.

Sabrina's love and compassion challenged Karalynn's assumptions: lessons and subtle hints gleaned over a lifetime. Elves whispered stories about Maiges around campfires. The Maige raised armies of haugr, daemia, and drathva, and then they slaughtered entire cities and burned continents. The priests wrote lengthy prayers to fend off such evil, and yet Sabrina was as kind and as loving as one could hope. Perhaps William Blake in his poem, "The Tiger," summed up Karalynn's questions when he asked:

TIGER, tiger, burning bright
In the forest of the night
What immortal hand or eye
Could frame thy fearful symmetry

In what distant deeps or skies
Burnt the fire of thine eyes?

The Great Gate

On what wings dare he aspire?
What the hand dare seize the fire?

And what shoulder and what art
Could test the sinews of thy heart?
And when thy heart began to beat,
What dread hand and what dread feet?

What the hammer? What the chain?
In what furnace was thy brain?
What the anvil? What dread grasp
Dare its deadly terror clasp?

When the stars threw down their spears,
And water'd heaven with their tears,
Did He smile His work to see?
Did He who made the lamb make thee?

Tiger, tiger, burning bright
In the forests of the night,
What immortal hand or eye
Dare frame thy fearful symmetry?

How does one reconcile the tigress – she cares for her loved ones with tender mercies, yet she kills prey with merciless savagery – and how do those who witness such ferocity quell their fears and cease their endless nightmares? How do you return to peace once you have seen the blazing heart of a dragon?

But not all contemplated such questions. Tormod brooded over processed rhunite, categories of crushed stone to powder, which traded on the Solva Stock Exchange. His finger traced over the various quotes; silver was up by an eighth, but gold was down by two, a surprising inversion of prices. He draped another leather scroll over his lap and pulled up his issue of "Mine and Mineral's Quarterly." There had to be some explanation for this dichotomy.

Marla languished in silence. The circumstances of her inducting into the Valkyrie were not what she imagined when she was a little girl. Her hand fluttered around her neck, and her thoughts lingered on her choker necklace. Her fingers explored the necklace that bore Black Dragon crest: the mark of royalty, wings that stretched around her neck, confirming that she was part of a religious order – a Valkyrie, a warrior maiden, a sacred sister – part priestess and part warrior, a mythical being that terrified all. The sisterhood's devotion to the Valkyrie and to Sabrina was absolute and fanatical.

Although the rolling green hills and the forests, both conifer and deciduous trees, inspired artists, they were lost on Marla. She chaffed at Sabrina's scolding, and lamented her unexpected and shameful induction into the sisterhood, more punishment than reward. Most women competed for years for the honor; only a few receiving the prized invitation; a select few were appointed by royal decree as a reward for meritorious service; but her acceptance was by relationship, a vamon, void of achievement.

As is the case on most worlds, the law confused the average citizen. Sabrina thought of Marla as her little sister, solidifying their relationship as a family. However, in the eyes of the law, Marla and all Valkyrie were Sabrina's family, and since Marla was an adopted sister, she was now of high noble status, second only to Sabrina.

Marla understood only bits and pieces of the law, but she understood that she was bound to Sabrina both body and soul; and the weight of it pressed down upon her. Despite her draftee status into the Valkyrie, she had to rule over them. Warriors with hundreds, perhaps thousands of years of experience, distinguished in battle, awarded medals of valor would have to salute her and obey her command. She was without recourse: she was bound to her vows and bound to her sister, Overlord

The Great Gate

Sabrina March: an eternal union, neither in life nor in death would it end, an eternal conjoining of souls.

Marla shifted between despair and anger. All guild pledges imagine glorious victories and overwhelming praise. She hoped to fight in a desperate battle and win the victory, achieving her rank through accomplishment, but her status included a promotion to the rank of Meritorious Warrior. Never once did it occur to her that she might achieve it all by adoption into the royal family, given all she desired without achievement. Her wounded pride rushed into this painful void and sought to defend her.

It's not my fault. He seduced me. Kayla is right. I'm not a priestess. I can have sex with whomever I choose. These thin mental defenses left her feeling naked and raw. She gazed up through her bangs with melancholy eyes. She searched for some hint of comfort or reassurance in Sabrina's face. Finding none, she sank back into despair.

A cool breeze ruffled her white feathers. When she shifted in the seat, Marla's wings moved at her sides. These new appendages were difficult to manage. As with an infant learning to walk, her mind struggled to perform the simplest tasks. For the moment, keeping her wings pressed tight to her side was the best she could manage. The white wings rose up high above her head and draped over the maroon leather seat beside her.

A sigh escaped her lips as she stroked the soft white feathers. Only the most senior, the most honored Valkyrie received their winged necklace. Recruits, warriors, and artisan warriors dreamed of that day. It marked their journey as a battle-mage, a warrior who fought with the blade and magic. They were influential, respected, and lethal, living legends. Marla appeared like one of them: her gleaming armor, her many blades, and her wings. But Marla was terrified, a scared child trying to walk in her mother's shoes.

Sabrina was telepathic and could sense the girl's pain. She wanted nothing more than to throw her arm around Marla and comfort her.

However, that would abort the life lesson before she learned it, but it would be unwise to push the girl beyond her ability to bear.

There were benefits, even if Marla failed to appreciate them. Her choker necklace bound Marla to Sabrina, her Mistress, and Sabrina was a Maige. As such, the girl's peaches and cream complexion would last forever – ageless. Maige were also impervious to most magical incantations and potions. They healed quickly and were hard to kill, if one could kill them at all, in the sense we understand it. Even after ten thousand years, Marla would appear to be the same 21-year-old girl when Sabrina inducted her. However, such eternal youth and beauty came with a price: the magic prevented her from bearing children. She would never know what it was like to have life grow inside her and never know the joy of giving birth.

Sabrina smile at Marla.

Marla noticed the smile and at first wondered if someone was riding behind her. When she realized that those caring eyes gazed at her, a shiver rushed up her spine. She returned the smiled and then averted her gaze. After a few minutes she dared steal a furtive glance at Sabrina, her Mistress looked at her with compassion.

Sabrina sighed and patted her right thigh. "Come here, Marla." Marla slipped off the bench and scooted across the carpeted floor of the carriage. She sat at Sabrina's feet and laid her head on Sabrina's thighs. Sabrina stroked the girl's short platinum locks. "It's going to be alright. I'm going to take good care of you. You are my little sister. You know why I chose you, don't you?" Marla gazed up into her Mistress's eyes, cringed, and shook her head. "I chose you because I love you."

"You love me?" asked Marla.

"Yes, of course I love you. I knew I loved you from the moment I saw you hosting that silly contest in the shopping mall. You, Karalynn, the girls, Billy, Tia, and I are a family. You are my little sister, and you always will be. As to your Valkyrie, you may marry another Immortal Warrior, but you can never give birth. Giving birth, motherhood, and grandbabies are for mortals."

"I understand, and I love you too." Marla rested her head on Sabrina's lap. "I'm glad to be part of your family and your sister. It's more than I could ever have imagined."

"Then let yourself be happy. You may love any man you wish, but there is always a price to pay. You will never give birth, and you cannot marry him: a Valkyrie is bound to your vows. Your first loyalty, your first love will always be to your sisters, the Valkyrie and to me."

Marla threw her arms around Sabrina, and she buried her face in Sabrina's neck. She sobbed saying, "Thank you so much." Billy awoke from her nap, and when she saw them embrace, she sprang to her feet and joined the hug. Tears rolled down her cheeks, whether of joy or sorrow, she was not sure, but she wanted to be a part of it. Karalynn wiped a tear from her cheek and caressed the girl's arm. Tormod rolled his eyes and wished women were less emotional, and that female relationships were less complicated. He harrumphed and returned to the news.

"Does this mean Karalynn and Billy are my sisters?" asked Marla.

Sabrina was about to reply, but then she paused; and she gazed at Billy's dewy brown eyes. The fae was lost in her love for Sabrina. This fact never occurred to her, yet the implication was clear: when she collared Billy, she became part of Sabrina's family, making Billy the matriarch of the fae; and by rank, she was Sabrina's sister. "Um … yes, they are your family." Sabrina furrowed her brow and tapped her chin. The whole matter crept up on her.

Marla returned to her seat, feeling a great deal lighter and purged, like the fertile ground after a spring rain – joy replaced sorrow – Sabrina loved her! She was, by proxy, a high royal daughter, a ruler of Asgard, an Overlord, and founder of The Black Dragon Guild, and a member of the White Council. Her authority outstripped all she knew or would ever know, but somehow it all seemed tolerable knowing that Sabrina was her big sister; and that she would take care of her.

The young warrior sat up straight and tightened the closing links between the plates of her cuirass. Since becoming Sabrina's adjutant, her sister, and a Valkyrie, she wore a mithril breastplate — overlaid with the golden image of a dragon, wings spread and talons bared — polished to a high gloss and shone brightly in the midday sun.

She adjusted her weapons and cinched down the securing straps. All the while, she fought off the urge to strip off her maiden's belt and hurl it away. She hated it, but it was the lesser of two evils when weighed against a very great evil of a death pregnancy. The updated model was impervious to the Crimson Dwarf's lances. She wiggled her bottom on the seat, trying somehow to ease her discomfort.

Marla's thoughts returned to her choker necklace and the way it marked her. For some reason, it felt quite comfortable and made her feel safe. In the reflection of the wagon's stainless steel, she observed it. The choker's oval front bore the crest of the Black Dragon, and the necklace's silver wings stretched around her throat, which clasped behind her neck. She could remove it to bathe or sleep, but if she moved more than a hundred paces, magic would cause it to reappear around her neck. This magic bound her both to the Black Dragon and her Valkyrie sisters.

Her right hand then slid around her side to her back. Although covered by her maiden's belt, she sensed the second mithril tattoo stretched across the small of her back, Sabrina's crest in the middle of the scrolls, and when she learned how to alter her form, withdrawing her wings into her back, which made the wings appear like tattoos.

391

The Great Gate

Tormod patted Marla's right knee saying, "I'm proud of you, girl. You've joined the greatest house in all of Asgard, and you are sister to the greatest warrior I have ever known; and you are a member of the high royal family." When he saw Marla's blue eyes begin to water, he said, "Now don't start crying." She threw her arms around him and hugged him, burying her face in his neck.

The dirt road weaved through the rolling green hills like a thin ribbon and wrapped around the flourishing countryside, presenting it like a gift. The road sloped into a fertile valley, the kind where lush grass and rolling hills seemed to go on forever.

Far off in the distance, they saw the May River surge off the Clarion Mountains and plummet into the finger lake city of Maywyn. The cataracts rumbled, the sound rolling across the valley like thunder, a plume of mist spread across the sky, causing a million rainbow splinters to shimmer. The river flowed toward the northeast where it wound around the Deepwood Hills, and from there it fed into Picnic Lake, cobalt blue and shimmering in the sun.

Twelve white pinnacles rose up from the forest and stabbed at the sky like needles; the morning sun reflected off them, reminding one of mother of pearl. From the base of each tower, twelve bridges extended like the spokes of a wheel, broad at the base, but so thin in the middle they almost disappeared. They reached out to a myriad of islands, a small community on each island; more bridges extended to other islands in an interconnecting network.

Stone monuments hewed from the Clarion Mountain — titans, stern sentinels, fortresses of Elven might, and keepers of the way — stood guard around a circular white building. Black stones carved to resemble spreading trees supported an oculus made of crystal – a great eye, eternally gazing upon the stars.

They passed shallow boats punting through narrow canals. Elves cast nets seeking a late morning catch. Most elvan boats were already in port, trading in their catch; a few vessels ferried passengers to a thousand splintered islands. Families labored to harvest fruit trees: apple, cherry, boysenberry, and pear; regarded as the best in Asgard, the harvested exported around the nation and between worlds.

The road transformed from ruddy brown soil to cobblestones, and the horse hooves clacked out a quick beat. They circled in front of a small visitor's center. The entire building was made of glass, including a blue tinted glass roof; one could see through it and view the entire city. Chauncey slowed the carriage and stopped in front of the main entryway.

"Welcome to paradise," Chauncey said.

The world burst into happy song around them. Birds darted through the air and lighted in trees. Billy squealed with delight and clapped her hands. She fluttered into the air, lost in the wonder. They walked up white stone steps, joy filling their hearts, and they passed through the portal, entering the welcome center. An intricate mural adorned the floor; tan, brown, and gray tiles formed a directional compass; Elven script, beautiful and mysterious, was written in circles around this compass.

An elva turned to greet them. The elva's eyes were so brown they appeared black; her smile warmed the heart; her tresses flowed like water, cascading over her shoulders; her pointed ears emerged from these silky locks, declaring her as an elva, and her face radiated beauty like the dawn. A long black velour robe, embroidered with silver thread, hung down to her ankles, but it remained open in front; and with it, she wore a cobalt blue dress, embroidered with crawling ivy and blooming red flowers. It was as though she embodied the gardens and stepped out of a dream.

With a mythical voice, heralding back to the first age, she said, "Welcome to Maywyn, home of the Cilien Elven Clan."

"Elen sila lumen' omentielvo," Sabrina replied.

"Le suilion," she replied.

"I am Sabrina, and this is my wife Karalynn Arndis, and this is my sister Marla Thorsby; and lingering near the door is Tormod son, of Glistad." She searched for Billy. "Where is she?" Billy hovered above the bountiful garden and broke out into a song; her quavering voice caused the flowers and trees to bloom. "That is Billy, and she will busy for quite a while."

"Billy is also our sister," Karalynn added. Sabrina twitched her nose, not quite settled with the idea. However, the words were true, so she let them stand.

"Welcome all, my name is Aranel. How may I assist you?"

"I was summoned by Lord Thalvon. He sent me an urgent message." She moved close and whispered, "I andon pantaie."

The smile evaporated from Aranel's face. "I see. You must speak with him at once then."

"Thank you for the carriage ride, Chauncey. We will send word when we are ready to return," Sabrina said. "Take Marla with you and go to an inn just up the road. Make lodgings for yourself and us. Of course, I will cover all expenses. Have a pitcher of ale on my account. I'm told it is the best in these parts."

"I will at that," he replied and walked away.

"Actually, it would be proper for at least one human to represent their people, and the matter is most urgent. We have no time to find another," said Aranel.

"You need what?" asked Marla.

"I know this must seem strange to you," Aranel replied, "but all will be made clear. Would you come with us so that we can discuss a matter of some importance?"

"I suppose I could," Marla replied and wrung her hands.

Aranel smiled. "We will try and keep it as brief as possible. Thank you for your patience."

"Certainly."

Tormod rubbed his nose and strolled to the glass wall, and he gazed out into the valley. "It's an excellent home you've built here. It must have taken you a long time."

"Thank you for the compliment, but there is more behind your words than praise." She crossed her arms and moved to the door, disapproval clear on her face. The dwarves mined the Clarion Mountains, and the Elves heavily taxed them for mineral rights. "We should be on our way to speak with Thalvon."

Tormod grunted.

They exited the structure and descended a set of stairs. A rainbow collection of flowers surrounded them. A spray of white Queen Anne's lace was mixed with blue pansies, and to the right were blue delphinium; next to it was vibrant yellow and orange marigolds. A thick green carpet of grass lay between these flowering islands; in the next island were red, yellow, and white flowers; white jasmine lay between towering red tulips; beds of red roses, lilacs, blue daze, and creeping vines crested a small hill. Interspersed in this splendor were pink magnolias trees, cherry trees, and purple crape myrtles.

"It's wonderful, Mistress," Billy squealed and soared.

Marla squatted before an orchid; the flower peddles were white with a hint of pink. She caressed the flower as if touching the face of a lover. It was magnificent, a plant unknown to the mountainous regions of her childhood. The prairie flowers bloomed in the spring but died with a single touch of frost.

The weight of someone's stare interrupted her. She saw the others stopped upon the stone path, and they waited for her with questioning eyes. "I always wanted a greenhouse back home. After my parents had died, I lived in the mines with Tormod, and it was impossible. Sorry."

"No apologies are required. Many walk past the beauty of life in a dull haze. Your admiration is appreciated," Aranel said.

"Um … you're welcome."

They came to a small white wooden bridge that stretched over a lazy stream, and she leaned over the railing; a blazing fish, as if on fire, swam through the crystal waters; and then a yellow fish, its fins tipped orange joined the first fish. A moment later a school of brilliantly colored fish, slivers of the rainbow, swam out from underneath the bridge.

Music hung in the air like perfume. Marla wandered along the path as if in a dream. Her hand brushed delicate flowers and fluffy reeds. Red cardinals and blue jays hopped about, and a flock of doves winged into the air before her. Nature, in all its glory, celebrated life. It overwhelmed.

A hand touched Marla's shoulder, and a soft voice asked, "Are you all right?"

Marla looked upon Aranel and shook her head. "I'm fine," she replied, but it was far from her; pain burned within her heart; disappointments and conflicts vexed her soul. "It's just so … so amazing. It's like my entire life has been in the shadows."

Even Tormod deflated: his rage dissipated into a vague sense of peace. On the border between laughter and tears, he searched for some respite, but the blue skies and amazing surroundings offered none. "It's not fair. We should have met them back at the inn," he mumbled. "Damn elves always do this sort of thing."

Aranel's encouragement made Marla's heart grow lighter. Aranel's bright face and sparkling eyes made them feel at home. Marla's heart soared with the birds. They followed a lazy, winding path through gardens and over bridges. Elves punted flat bottom boats. Their smiles warmed her heart and eyes bid her welcome. Light flowed from her heart like liquid, dispelling the darkness. It beamed out from within her and blazed like the paradise around her.

A song grew in Sabrina's heart, and it flowed out from her lips. She sang the classic Christmas hymn "I heard the bells on Christmas day." Aranel said, "That's a beautiful song. Did you write it?"

"Me? No. Henry Wadsworth Longfellow wrote it after his son was gravely injured in the American Civil War. The poem became a song, and the song is sung at Christmas."

"That's an interesting story. What is Christmas?"

"It is a religious holiday … or at least it used to be. Now it is a secular holiday; it has Santa Claus, reindeer, and tiny elves that make toys. The faithful eschew the secularism and maintain its true meaning – the birth of Jesus Christ who came to save people from their sins and give them eternal life. The religious people go on for hours complaining about empty consumerism and vacuous celebration. I consider the holiday to be about home, family, and love. To me, this place feels like Christmas morning."

Aranel listened with interest, but it all sounded so foreign. Yet the light in Sabrina's eyes reminded her of "The Spring Rite." The harsh winter lay behind them and rebirth took place. Sprouts pushed up from muddy ground and leaves unfurled on every twig. Songs filled the air: they celebrated life. Spring was her favorite time of year.

They strolled through the gardens. Kelvin and Marla gazed up at one of the spires and commented on the skillful artisanship. Only Sabrina acted impatient. "The gardens are pleasant, but our business is urgent. We must press on to meet with Thalvon."

The Great Gate

"Very true," Aranel agreed. "We should ride a launch to speed our arrival. The city is vast and the gardens complex." After passing tall hedges, flowerbeds, orchards, regal buildings, and a lakeside community, a white boat awaited them at the dock; its rows of seats and white awning provided comfortable accommodations. After they climbed into the ship and took a seat, the captain gripped the rudder and stepped on the control. A pressure wave impeller activated. These fields of energy squeezed the water, jetting it out the back of the device, and the boat surged through the water.

As they moved away from the docks, swans and ducks paddled out of the way. The narrow channel wound between sod and mud riverbanks, green sloping hills, and lakeside villas. They passed underneath a small foot bridge and into an open expanse of water. A grand bridge, which stretched across the channel, arched overhead, appearing like a bow stretched across the water. Once in open water, the boat increased speed and skimmed over the glassy surface.

Towers stretched toward the heavens, and trees, tall and proud, skirted the lake. The skies were bluer than Marla imagined possible. When they passed by a few boats, several elvan paused and watched them with interest. The elvan wore loose cotton shorts and a cloth tightly wrapped around their waists. They drew in fishing nets laden with fish and dumped their cargo into the boat's hold; the fisherman laughed and chatted as if they were recreating. Marla realized that all work is pleasant when it meets one's needs. Even the elvan at the bottom of Elven society enjoyed comfortable accommodations and prosperity. In this way, they performed that basest task with joy and skill.

Children played along a distant shore. They squealed with joy as they jumped into the water and played a game. An elva kept watch on them as she swept a patio. The elves bore fewer children, and they spread these births over vast expanses of time. Thus, the community celebrated and treated each child with great care.

398

The boat sped toward a stone pier. The pylons rose high out of the water, a residual stain marking the peak of spring flooding. Most elves milled about the docks, performing various tasks, but some wore armor. They grasped spears and swords, but what trouble could there be in paradise? They won the Battle of Deepwood, and the corpses of the haugr rotted in the holes. What new danger kept them vigilant?

Just on shore, they saw their destination. Great pillars upheld a domed glass roof with a round oculus in the center. The building was beautiful, but Marla questioned the use. What would one do in such a structure? The rain would fall through the hole in the roof, and the gap between the pillars allowed the wind to gust through it.

The boat slowed and turned. It drifted up to the dock. A dockhand wrapped a rope around a cleat and caught the bow. The stern drifted toward the dock, and it too was tied off. They stepped out of the boat and onto the solid surface of the dock.

They strolled along the pier, and a flight of stairs transported them to the main quay. A few crates and other supplies lay scattered about. Tormod marched ahead, leaving the others behind. He jogged up a set of steps and entered the building.

A set of pillars soared to the heights. They were so vast and so magnificent as to make one feel like ants. They passed through these titans with their heads gazing upward, trying to absorb the grandeur of it all. Marble floors stretched out before them as if going on to eternity. Mosaics of ancient lore were set in white marble: they passed another ring containing power-words written in the Elvish script, the penmanship style as important to the meaning as the words; and the next ring had strange markings that made the air shimmer, like a fervent heat rising on a desert highway. When they passed through this magical barrier, it took their breath away; and they saw constellations inlaid into the marble floor, but to their wonder, the celestial bodies moved.

The Great Gate

When Tormod reached the center of the structure, he snapped, "Thalvon, you knew about the Great Gate. You knew the gate would open the way to the ancient lands. You knew about the growing menaces that took many lives, and yet you said nothing to us. We have a right to know the truth! Earth is as much our home as it is yours. This is a clear breach of the treaty between our peoples. The Dorvkrack Accord clearly states, 'The sister worlds belong to all peoples … the Dwarven and Elven peoples shall share all resources and access to these lands.' Never trust an elve."

The dwarf stormed about and threw his hands up into the air. "My people see this as a serious violation. The Dwarven kings and lords may even vote for war. How could you do this?"

Thalvon, Lord of the Elves, interlaced his fingers and restrained his anger. "I believe introductions are in order. Tormod and Sabrina I know, but who are the others?"

"Marla Thorsby is my sister, and Karalynn, of the Arndis Highlands Clan, is my wife," Sabrina said, "and that is Billy fluttering around. She is also my sister. We are family."

"Marla is the human representative," Aranel said.

Thalvon arched an eyebrow. "Mae g'ovannen. Welcome to our home. It is a pleasure to meet you. Karalynn Arndis, your name means 'royal bride.' You are of the high-born elvish clans. Are you not?"

"I am," Karalynn replied.

"Yes, well if introductions are concluded then I demand an answer. Why have you violated the treaty?" Tormod glared at Thalvon as if his thoughts could kill.

Thalvon held out his arms and gazed upward; he spoke with a voice of thunder that echoed within the great structure. The Elven words plunged into their minds. Marla covered her ears and grimaced. The blue skies overhead began to swirl like waters; the sky spun in a swift ring and parted; stars appeared and shimmered like diamonds set in black velvet; the stars stretched down as if falling from the heavens and filled the air around them.

The floor dissolved away beneath their feet. Stars twinkled; red nebulas hung low, and a great nebula cat's eye gazed back at them; it stared at them – somber and unblinking – as if looking into their souls. They stood like giants among the galaxies, looking down upon the speck that was Eden. The pillars of heaven surrounded them.

"Long ago," Thalvon began, "the twin heavens were one: united by a common thread, one that stitched them together. Gemini planets appeared like blue diamonds in the vast void of night. Rhunite – the ancient power of the universe – linked them together by a myriad of portals. These portals connected both these worlds and countless other worlds in the multiverse. The Great Gate stood above all others; it could connect to the twin worlds and all others. A high council, established long ago at the beginning of 'The Fifth Age,' the Elves, the Dwarves, the Fae, the Ents, the Ferla, the Glavnors, and the Saurens, ruled over the Great Gate. This council ruled over the gate and maintained peace, but a new power arose from the eternal womb, humanity. They too joined the council as a young but important race."

Thalvon's face took on a somber expression: "One day the Great Gate disappeared, and Earth, our second home, was lost."

"Ever since that dark day, the beginning of the 'Sixth Age,' the council lingered in the sacred city of the north, Alkval. But the sixth lingered and stretched out over the long expanse of time. One by one each of the ancient races departed until only the elves remained. We watched and longed for the return of the Great Gate, the portal to our ancestral lands. Once a year we performed the reunification ritual."

The Great Gate

"You must have known that it would open," Tormod insisted. "Otherwise, why would your people have passed through the gate? We should have been invited."

"Long ago humans from Earth appeared on our shores. Your people and the other races knew this. They passed through the lesser portals when they blinked. The evidence was clear to anyone who had eyes to see it. The time of darkness was drawing to a close," Thalvon said.

"Fifty years ago the human city of Gleason, Kansas transitioned from Earth to Eden. At the same time, the Elven city of Lantele vanished. We presumed it transitioned to Earth, but we had no way of being certain. The Mentra Andon, or temporary gate, opened three year ago and emissaries from Lantele returned to Eden."

"The Mentra Andon has never reopened. It disappeared without a trace. We believe, as does our enemy, that the Great Gate is due to return. So you see, we have fulfilled the treaty and informed you of the gates opening."

Tormod said, "Don't you play games with me. You knew that the reunion was at hand and you waited one year – the elves have once again take the best of the land for themselves …."

A sharp disagreement broke out between them. Voices grew loud and tempers hot. "GENTLEMAN," Marla shouted, "this arguing is pointless." Both Thalvon and Tormod looked at her with an air of surprise. "I would be lying if I said I understood the emergence of the gate. I do know this. Both of you share some blame, but it is not as bad as the other might portray it. Enormous conflicts may ignite from a tiny spark. Our leaders fought in long wars when they arrived on Eden. We should have found a way to make peace, but they failed. Don't be like us. Forgive one another, and find a way to make peace."

Tormod said, "We weren't going to go to war."

402

"No. We were just … passionately debating," Thalvon agreed.

"I'm glad to hear it." Marla gathered her composure. "This gate, if I understand it correctly, heralds the beginning of the 'Seventh Age.' Why not start it with cooperation? Why not consider this the first day and that the gate belongs to everyone?"

"Your words have wisdom." Thalvon took in a deep breath and released it. "The current warfare across Asgard makes it clear that we should have notified the other races. We waited too long, and lives have been lost."

Tormod rubbed the back of his neck. "I suppose we were too caught up in our own affairs to notice. We've suspected that the gate would open for over a thousand years. We became complacent when it lingered."

Sabrina said, "I share part of the blame. When I transitioned from Earth to Eden, I awakened the gate. Ever since then, the enemy has been escalating his efforts to take Asgard and the Great Gate. Every time I read about a battle or lives lost, I feel stinging indictments. What if I stayed on Earth? What if I went to another world? What if … the recriminations and second-guessing are endless and useless. One question remains: where is the Great Gate?"

Chapter 40

Sabrina had a heart of magic and the cunning of a dragon – such is the nature of a Maige. Her raven black wings arched high in the air above her head and draped across the floor like the train of a gown. She strolled through her quarters and paused before the hearth; flickering flames danced upon the logs. The soft light reflected off her chrome gown, making it appear as though she was on fire. Unlike human eyes, she beheld the flames with fondness, as though greeting an old friend.

The genus Elven had many subclasses, woodland elves being the most prevalent, but there were house elves, mountain elves, sea elves, and other varieties. One of the least common but of the most powerful class was the Maige. Their ears were pointed and their beauty beyond compare. All Elven cardiovascular systems included a peristalsis nexus instead of a heart. However, that is where the similarity between ordinary elves and Maiges ended.

A Maige child of five is stronger and more magically powerful than a full grown elvan, a male elve. By ten-years-old, a Maige could defeat a company of warriors, and by twenty a Maige could defeat a battalion. A peculiarity of the Maige was that they had two forms: The first form appeared like an angel descended from heaven. The second, however, was that of a war dragon. Both of them were a mortal threat to their enemies, and only a fool provoked a Maige.

Sabrina wanted to save the world, but she also wanted it to burn. She gazed upon the fire with a lover's passion and imagined herself dancing in the flames of destruction. The screams of the dying and the wail of the mourning were a symphony, music only a Maige could hear. Her human allies ignored this half of her nature, but she never did; and neither did the elves. The great beast, hidden within, slept for the moment. The elves were confident that it could awaken one day and do so with disastrous results. At moments like this, she wondered if they were right.

She stirred the logs and let the cinders fly up the chimney. She closed her eyes and drew in a deep breath. The smoke intoxicated her and stirred her soul. A gentle arm encircled her side, and a head lay on her shoulder. She turned toward her wife, her lover, Karalynn. She took the elva in her arms, wrapped her wings around the elva, and gently kissed her, her hand sliding down the back of Karalynn's silk gown, finding the swell of her bottom.

"It's been good having you here," Sabrina said. "You keep me sane."

Karalynn caressed her Mistress's cheek. "I always feel so safe when I'm with you. Can't you come back to bed? We could spend the day under the covers, Billy and Tia can take care of the girls."

"I wish I could. There's too much to do." Sabrina put on a robe and exited the bedroom. Tormod already sat in the living room sipping a cup of coffee, his feet up on an ottoman, reading the oracle scroll news. "You live in grand fashion these days," Tormod said and puffed on his pipe. "I doubt that a royal prince could afford such opulence."

Maige were the most cunning of any species. Their minds found patterns in chaos and weighed each action against their goals. "I am an Overlord – and the richest person in Asgard." She sat down next to him and interlaced her fingers. "It would be unseemly if I slept in a hovel."

He chuckled and said, "That's as good a rationalization as any. It's been my experience that women and Maiges never say what they're actually thinking." He slid his finger across the scroll and turned the page. "It says here that the Parliament awarded another defense contract to Cavalry Enterprises. You own that company. Don't you?"

"I am a majority stockholder." Sabrina strolled across the room. Her wings dusted across the marble floor. "But you knew that."

"Did I? Oh yes," he replied and looked up from the news. "You let that rotund senator stay here. What was his name – oh yes, Gilpin. The man was fat as a pumpkin and had more chins than I could count."

Sabrina slid out a chair from the table. The chair was white with a crushed red velvet seat cushions. "I do recall that. He hates the Wolf's Maw Mountains. In fact, he hates most places except his palatial estate on the shores of Glorloch Lake. Why?"

Tormod looked over the rim of his reading glasses and scanned the room. "This place reminds me of his estate. Opulent to the point of gilded, a bit garish for my tastes."

"One has to admire the dwarven commitment to bare rock and rough wood. One dwarven home looks like any other dwarven home. What harm would a splash of red do?" asked Sabrina and picked at a muffin. Her blue eyes glowed with power, and she searched the face of her comrade for a hint of his real purpose. Dwarves were also very tactical, despite evidence to the contrary. Perhaps that's why they got along as well as they did.

"The only splash of blood red you will find in a dwarven home is that of an enemy. After disposing of the body, we clean it right up. Brown, tan, and green are the proper colors for a residence." He sniffed and set down his pipe.

"You think we linger here too long?" asked Sabrina.

"Too little or too much time depends upon one's objective. Our goals appear a bit obtuse these days. Every day we marched out of Winter Pass Fortress and return with little to show for our efforts. One might conclude that you had no idea where the gate is to be found." He slurped some coffee and sampled a pastry.

Sabrina asked, "The warriors are complaining?"

"No," he replied. "They would never complain about the accommodations. Even a bare rack used by a recruit is better than sleeping upon some ice field. However, our ratio of male to female warriors is dangerously low. They fear 'nature's calling' and that fear grows stronger with each passing day."

Nature's calling was the evolutionary adaptation whereby one gender would transform into another. On Earth, this adaptation was limited to lower species such as clownfish, wrasses, moray eels, and the black swallowtail. However, on Eden, this gender transition was widespread and included humanity. This occurred so that the population ratios of males to females would be balanced. For the most part, this meant that males would transform to female, but it did work the other way as well. The greater the skewing of the gender ratio, the greater was the speed and number of those who transitioned. Since most males do not wish to become female, commanders maintained minimum gender composition 40% female to 50% male.

"Yes. In retrospect, it was unwise dividing the battalion based upon gender. The female warriors of the Praetorian Guard were caught in a time vortex. What should have been a two-week march has dragged into nine months. The commander responsible for the division has been disciplined and demoted. I sent Marla to locate and return with the Valkyries. They should arrive today." Sabrina crossed her legs and feigned disinterest in his response.

"Hmm, it is welcome news both for the male warriors and their wives back at home." Tormod was a dwarf, and dwarven DNA had a 2% difference when compared to human DNA. This meant that Dwarves were immune from nature's calling, but they did have a greater instinctual drive to maintain a balanced population. "But what of the Great Gate?"

"What of it?" Sabrina echoed.

The Great Gate

"If the damn Elves would have included the other races, we would have troops on Earth by now. Instead, we chase every gleam of sunshine upon the snow. Damn them," he sputtered.

"Hmm, Elves love secrets as much as others enjoy telling them," she replied.

"So they do," he chuckled. "These vortices plague everyone in the Wolf's Head Peninsula. How long will they endure?"

"Until the gate stabilizes," she replied. "Then time will synchronize. The time fractures here are a nuisance, but on Earth, they will be much worse. We should be glad of that."

"I suppose ... but I don't understand why you won't open a passage to Earth. We could arrive there in minutes." He poured another cup of steaming hot coffee, and he savored the aroma with a sigh. "I always found your ability to create these shortcuts between worlds and within worlds as a great advantage."

"Yes, as do I. However, if I create a bridge between Eden and Earth, I would force open all the gates. Who knows what might pass between our worlds. I have lived on many versions of Earths in many dimensions. None of them would fare well with the horrors that live on Eden."

"I see," he replied. "You know the humans of such worlds better than me. Humans are a strange lot: sometimes they act as pious as elves, and at other times they are loathsome as daemia. One never knows which one you will meet."

"Both and neither," she replied. "They are something new. They look like elves but act like men. Remember the old saying, 'Humans are like packages, you never know what is inside them."

"I should be going," he said and slipped off his chair. "I have an inspection tour planned for the armory."

She stood to her feet and escorted Tormod to the door. "I think I will go for an early morning flight. I want to see if there is any sign of the gate."

Chapter 41

The admonishment "sleep tight" was appropriate where Kelvin was concerned. The crisscrossing ropes that supported his mattress often became slack, causing several deep depressions into which his great bulk seeped, and he often became stuck in this depression, which inevitably led to grizzly bear snoring. His wool blankets provided little warmth, and if he moved too close to the castle wall, cold radiated from the stone and bit his nose.

He had just about fallen back to sleep again when the pressure in his bladder roused him. *I don't have to piss,* he decided. *I can wait until morning.* With that settled, he closed his eyes. He sputtered and fought his way out the hole that was his bed.

He worked his feet into a pair of slippers and drew up his flannel pajamas. Yawning and weary, he shuffled across the room. Cody, his roommate, mumbled something and rolled away from him. Kelvin's cotton tunic provided little thermal protection, and the frigid air soon stole away his slumber, leaving him fatigued and frustrated – a perpetual state these days.

A generous man would describe their toilet facilities as small. The hulking young man bent over so as to not hit his head on the door frame, his broad shoulders and muscular frame proving a challenge to the bathroom's narrow width. He lifted up the seat, which Cody insisted upon, not wishing to find his urine on the seat. A great wooden plug lay in the bottom of the toilet, which had a rope connect to it by an eyebolt. He grabbed the rope and pulled the plug out of the hole. The reek of raw sewerage stung his nostrils, making him turn his head this way and that, and after he had fished his manhood out of his underwear, he relaxed his bladder, allowing the urine to flow out of him.

I'd kill for a room in the warrior's barracks and a real toilet. Such was the musing of every new recruit. The officers and senior warriors resided in the best rooms. They had real toilets, hot baths, and warmth; they also slept upon soft mattresses and lay their heads on feather pillows. Their rooms were well appointed, and an assigned pledge attended them. How he envied them these small luxuries. *It must be nice to be a pampered officer.*

With his bladder empty, he replaced the plug and cut off the noxious gas. A sudden frigid gust blew in the vent above his head. It swept out the methane gas and vented it into the atmosphere. He was convinced that a sadist designed the pledge residences. When he turned to leave, he remembered to lower the seat, a lesson reinforced by Cody; one night he awoke to find Cody beating him with a stick and cursing after she sat on the toilet only to find the seat raised.

The castle took over 723 years to construct. Summer was only 3 months long in the Wolf's Maw Mountains, and even then it was filled with hardships; ravenous flies and mosquitoes formed dark clouds – flying up one's nose, biting one's private parts, and spreading disease – everything was wet, and mold grew everywhere. The architects completed the outer walls first and lived in tents during the winter, and upon completion of the barracks, the officers lived in them, even though it seemed hard to fathom; but that was over two millennia ago, and since then, the luxury accommodations and the infrastructure were completed.

Of course, the pledges spent a week in an igloo, one of their own making. While the snow shelter kept them from freezing, their chamber pot turned the contents to ice. Each day a different recruit had to start the fire and then thaw the fecal matter, a miserable job by anyone's standards.

Kelvin exited the lavatory and shut the door with a thump. The frigid air stung his flesh, leaving him wide awake. Once back to his bed, he slipped underneath the covers and closed his eyes. Sleep, however, refused to follow.

"Crap!" he sputtered.

"Not in here," Cody mumbled, still asleep.

Kelvin got out of bed and turned up the lights a little; modern lights were a small luxury afforded them. Cody pulled her pillow over her head and groaned. Kelvin did his best to quietly dress, but he was a large man; and he often bumped into things, and he stomped about like an elephant.

The teen grew into a man that filled out his father's shadow. His arms were as big as most men's thighs, and his legs were a pair of tree trunks. Muscles rippled across his back, and his chest brimmed with power. He stood "treetop tall" and lumbered when he walked. At this precise moment, he jumped around and held his foot, after stubbing his toe on his footlocker.

After stripping off his bedclothes, he searched for a change of clothes. Cody opened her eyes and saw the giant of a man standing in the center of their room, clad only in his underwear. His hulking body, bulging muscles, and rugged features seduced many women, but all she wanted was sleep. "A little modesty would be nice." When Kelvin cocked his head, Cody added, "Close the curtains when you bathe. That's why we have them."

"You've seen me naked more times than I can count."

"I'm so sick of hearing that," she said and rolled over to sleep. "We aren't dating anymore. Close the curtains!"

Their relationship had cooled off like passing of summer to fall, and an icy chill replaced burning passion. Kelvin had wandering eyes, and he flirted with most women; and Cody struggled to fend off other females: this was more stress than she needed during candidate life. She gave him little choice when she declared that they were just friends and no longer lovers.

Kelvin sifted through an enormous pile of laundry and tried to pick out the least soiled item to wear. Despite all the snow, liquid water was a precious commodity, and they could only wash clothes once a week; and they were often the last in a long line. After he had selected a tunic and clean underwear, he opted to take a cold sponge bath.

The rather frigid water urged speed and soon he was clean. He scrambled into his leather trousers and tunic. While males could wear slip-suits, they preferred male attire, in this case, PSM treated leather, just as effective as thermal protection.

After putting on his other garb, he hurried to his bed and put on a pair of clean socks. His father always said, "Fresh socks are as essential to a warrior as his shield and armor." Those who ignored their feet often wound up with trench foot and amputated limbs. However, subtle differences in their active DNA, and amputated limbs, in time, would regrow.

Cody grumbled and left the warm comfort of her bed. She stripped off her nightshirt and tossed it aside. Clad only in her underwear, she strolled across the room. Kelvin swore she was turning into one of the mysterious Ice-dwellers that lived in the frozen wastelands.

As a morph, her body adapted to the environment: her skin turned indigo; her lips turned dark blue, and her hair turned brilliant white, with the roots and tips medium blue. But it was her eyes – pools of frozen ice, dark and mysterious – that captivated him. Kelvin often gazed as if in a trance, sure she was a wispy cloud that would disappear at any moment.

"Stop staring," she said and entered the restroom. "I swear we could hang meat in that room. It would never thaw until spring."

"There is an appetizing thought," Kelvin remarked. A few minutes later Cody exited the restroom. She crossed the room as if it was a warm summer's day, and the sight of her scantily clad body made Kelvin shiver. When Cody slipped underneath the covers, Kelvin asked, "You had another rough night, huh?"

"I guess," Cody mumbled.

"Those must be some awful nightmares you're having. You woke me up three times, once you were shouting," Kelvin said.

"You're complaining about me?" Cody snapped. "You snore like a grizzly bear. You're so loud that you shake the walls. I bet the entire fortress can hear you." Cody pulled a pillow over her head and tried to force herself to sleep.

"I never used to snore. It's this stupid bed. I swear my butt sags down to the floor; we need to do something about it," he replied.

"I suppose," she agreed. "We could replace the ropes with boards. There is plenty of wood in the scrap pile."

"That might work," Kelvin agreed and kicked the side of Cody's bed. "Get up. Let's go get some breakfast."

"Breakfast? It's before the day watch. All of the cooks are still asleep," Cody replied. "Why go there?"

"The great room is warm, and the leather sofas are soft," Kelvin replied. Tapestries covered the great room's walls and a roaring fire burned in the hearth. Many of the pledges slept on plush furnishings instead of in their rooms. That was all he needed to say. Cody worried that she might stay blue, never to be normal again.

"Okay," Cody mumbled. She left her bed and began her morning ablutions. She then began to stretch, and when she was limber, she started calisthenics. Hot breath jetted past her lips, turning to fog, and her skin began to glisten with sweat. Jogging in place was interspersed with pushups and jumping jacks. She then performed stomach crunches and then returned to jogging. It was hard for Kelvin not to stare at this mysterious blue woman, especially since her bare breasts heaved. Was she really his childhood friend?

"Stop staring," she snapped, turning away from him.

He mumbled, "Guys like to stare at girls." This bit of news came as no surprise to Cody, and she drew the curtains close. A moment later, she tossed out a pair of white panties, made of a synthetic wicking material. "No peeking," she said.

"What am I, six?" Kelvin then added, "Like I keep saying, I've seen you naked. We've had sex."

"Not lately," she replied, "and not ever again."

Armor is a soldier's greatest friend and a maddening bane. If one wears too much, it encumbers them man, and he becomes slow moving; but if he wears too little, then he is vulnerable. The Praetors varied their armor depending upon the engagement and the warrior. Kevin's great size, his stature, and his great strength made him a natural fit for the Rampart Division: soldiers stationed at the front of the line, an implacable wall of flesh and steel.

Kelvin donned a chest harness and cinched it tight. The leather harness cleaved to his massive torso and covered his chest up to his neck and arms. After drawing a heavy chainmail tunic over his head, bulky like a cable knit sweater, he donned his cuirass, a clamshell of breastplates and backplates. The harness served as an anchor for the metal plate, but it allowed a certain level of flexibility as the overlapping plates slid upon one another. A gorget protected his neck; pauldrons protected his shoulders; couters protected his elbows; vambraces protected his forearms; gauntlets protected his hands; cuisses protected his thighs; poleyns protected his knees; greaves protected his shins, and sabatons protected his feet – appearing more of metal than man.

Kelvin found his fur liner, but his helmet was missing. He looked around the room and spotted it. His face stretched into a deep frown. Cody used it as a wash basin for her laundry – again. Kelvin snarled, "My helmet is not your washpot." He fished out sopping wet underwear, wrung it out, and tossed out the water.

"It is the only metal pot big enough to hold water, and I don't want the water to freeze with my underwear in it," Cody replied. She used a single candle to warm the frigid water for bathing. She tried to obtain a cooking pot, but the kitchen staff knew all the recruit's tricks.

"I'll be outside on the wall." After Kelvin donned his mask and helmet, he strapped on a claymore — a sword as long as some men are tall, which he wielded with the ease of a stick, one handed, able to cut a tree in half — a pair of medium length swords, daggers, knives, axes, throwing stars, and a warhammer. In the end, he appeared as a statue dedicated to war, too large and too massive to be real, and when he moved, men scurried out of his path, counting themselves lucky that he was not after them. Lastly, he picked up his long shield that was the size of a door: curved, covered with oiled leather, and a curved steel dome in the center, too heavy for most men but perfect for his massive frame.

When Kelvin opened the door, the arctic wind blasted him in vain, striding through the blustering currents with ease, and he slammed the door shut behind him. Cody failed to notice and wandered around the room wearing nothing but a towel.

Victoria, her mother, purchased for her the finest slip-suit, able to keep the wearer warm in a frigid winter and cool in a burning desert, but she adapted too quickly to either environment and had little need for thermal protection. Yet it was standard practice to wear one. It was a bit shiny and emphasized her womanly figure. At first, she was reluctant to wear it, but fear of what she might become caused her to relent.

Many a girl made the mistake of living in their slips-suit. After all, it was warm and soft as silk. Pledges had to undergo many training exercises. One such training exercise required the pledges to run 3 miles through deep powder snow, cross an icy stream, and scale a small cliff, having plenty of hand and footholds. At the end of the course, the recruits had to locate their clothing and dress. The recruits who slept in their slip-suits never acclimated to the frigid environment and often failed the exercise.

These types of exercises maximized Cody's adaptive DNA, and although naked and waist deep in the snow, she felt quite toasty, as one might feel on a sandy beach. While the other girls trembled and shivered, she took her time and thrived. She could sprint, climb, and fight all day and not grow weary. Her body was a marvel of efficiency. The trainers were impressed with her great feats, but the other recruits criticized her and ostracized her.

She stretched open the neck, and then she worked the elastic garment up her legs, over her arms, and up her torso. She slipped on a pair of booties and gloves. She was ice water in a thermos bottle and felt the same as before she donned it.

A leather body harness was next, and it resembled a vest. However, in the case of females, a teardrop neckline circled around and underneath the wearer's breasts; thus it avoided irritation and restricted breathing. She reached around her back and drew the laces tight. The garment constricted as tight around her abdomen, feeling snug but flexible.

What came next was the part she hated the most. She found her "maiden's belt" where she left it the previous night. She held it up before her for a second and snarled. It resembled a silver metal thong attached at the hips to a wide silver belt. Not every maiden's belt was as extravagant as hers. Civilian women wore a simple leather belt with a padlock. But Cody's belt had a single V-panel – adorned with mother of pearl set in silver, and elaborate scrollwork silver circled her hips, and it came with the latest bio lock that allowed one to release it at a moment's notice.

She drew in a deep breath and then exhaled, sucking in her stomach, and she kept her lungs empty while she wrapped the belt around her waist. When she heard the locking clicks, she drew in a gasp.

The Great Gate

Cody checked the door to make sure Kelvin would not return. She hated it when men watched. It always evoked leering and snickers. She reached around her right thigh, and after grabbing the crotch strap, she drew it back. When a click came from the T-lock, she released the cable. An experienced female warrior once told her, "I'm so used to it that I feel naked without it." She very much doubted that she would ever get used to the inconvenience of a maiden's belt.

There were good reasons to wear a maiden's belt. In the caves at the foot of the Clarion Mountains, Cody experienced every woman's nightmare. The haugr captured her and cut off her maiden's belt using a dwarven cutting lance. Horror and helplessness tormented her. She escaped before the rapes began, but the terror of a "death pregnancy" gave her nightmares. Like the senior warriors, she took comfort in its tight embrace: horrors that lurked in the shadows.

After donning her chainmail tunic, which gleamed like silver metal and cleaved to her body, she picked at the hem, but it only reached the swell of her bottom. She found her cuirass and opened the clamshell armor; she attached bars on the harness to the hooks on the sides of the cuirass. Once drawn tight, if the plates sustained a blow, the force of the blow would be diffuse across her entire torso.

Much to her embarrassment, her armor was worthy of a princess. Reinforced mother of pearl, ornate mithril embellishments adorned her armor plate. It was shatter-proof and energy defusing, the qualities of top armor. When the light struck it, the iridescent pearl produced an ethereal luminescence. Of course, the pauldrons, the gauntlets, and greaves complemented the cuirass. The armor came with a white coat with fur trim, which she never wore.

She reached into her jacket pocket and found a piece of Monk's Root. The brown root tasted like liquorice and provided more energy than three cups of coffee. She then slid up the left coat sleeve and tapped her gauntlet. The silver faded and gold Elvish symbols displayed on a field of black. The slip-suit, the armor plate, and her helmet included adaptive camouflage to match the environment. While she debated whether or not to alter her appearance, a vague sense of danger, as though someone was watching her returned – it crept into her mind and stole her peace. By day and night, she kept watch, but all she saw were fleeting shadows and only heard quiet taps on stone.

Kelvin trudged up the stairs, his boots scraping stone stairs, winding in a spiral fashion around the inside of the tower. When he passed by a shuttered arrow slot, the icy wind stabbed at him, but he was too well insulated to notice. Once at the top of the stairs, he arrived at the watch command post, a square stone box, reminding him of a refrigerator. A scrap of stale bread lay on a rough wooden table, and a rat scurried away with a quick morsel and disappeared into a hole in the wall.

A row of backpacks waited in a wooden holder, and although they all held the same contents – survival, combat, magical, and scientific gear – some were larger than others; and he required the largest pack. He strapped on his backpack, its 200 lbs. (91 kg.) weight barely noticed; and he was tempted to snack on the energy bars, but they were needed for combat.

He checked his gear and exited the watch room, a powerful gust of wind shoved against the door, but he put his shoulder against the heavy wooden door and pushed it open. Once open, the wind tried to rip it from his hands, and he struggled to close it again.

Powder snow gusted in swirls before him, as though dancing in some winter ballet. He trudged through the wind and stood by the parapets of the Winter Pass Fortress. The sun broke over the horizon in the eastern sky. The warm, golden beams stretched across the mountains and softened the icy tempest. The mask scrubbed the carbon from his breath and returned fresh air to his lungs. Through the angular lens slits, which fitted neatly in his helmet, he surveyed the Wolf's Maw Mountains, the Sundering Glacier, the expanse of the Great Pass, and the Regal Mountains off in the far distance. Their white bodies reflecting the morning light and glowing in a dazzling spectacle or red and orange hues, appearing as if on fire, the peaks surrounded him like titans, unimpressed by his massive bulk. He swore that they looked upon him like brooding gods from the ancient days.

He stood at the top of the world, or so it seemed. He peered over the wall's edge and looked down to the Sundering Glacier, lying so far below him that it appeared he was flying. He saw a great frozen river of ice that gouged its way through the valley on its endless drive south.

Kelvin heard Cody curse and battle with the door. He lumbered over and grabbed it. With a single shove, he slammed the door shut. The power sent Cody tumbling forward into the door. "Here, get up," Kelvin signaled and took his friend's hand. He yanked Cody to her feet and almost sent her sprawling in the other direction.

The pair navigated their way around the outer wall. Every so often Kelvin peered over the icy wall and stared into the ravine. It stretched down into murky shadows and black fissures. Jagged spires, covered with ice, emerged from the shadows and pointed up at him in defiance. He wondered what it would be like to fall from such a great height and what it would be like to hit bottom. He tried to imagine those few seconds before an inevitable end. Last year, a pledge jumped from the wall. They searched for weeks, but they never recovered it. Rumor had it that he failed to meet his recruitment requirements and command was going to discharge him for incompatibility.

Kelvin wondered what he would do under those circumstances. He never imagined any life but that of a warrior. He considered other occupations, but they all left him empty. Suicide was not an option. He could always become a mercenary in the Western Islands: pirate ships still roamed those waters around the island kingdoms, and they were always looking for warriors. It sounded exciting. Even if it was boring, it would be warm, and that suited him fine for now.

A curtain of fine white powder gusted before them. They thought that their eyes played a trick on them, and they saw a phantom in the drifting snow. An angel – her wings arched high above her head and curled in upon themselves – stood upon the outside wall. Her wings and hair were white as freshly fallen snow and her skin was alabaster, altered to offer camouflage to match the environment.

The morning light often played tricks on the eyes. Yet as they neared, her form emerged from the white background and came into focus. The light gleamed off her slip-suit and armor. Her wings hung down to her feet and framed her body. The material conformed to her with such precision that it cleaved to every nuance of her body, melding to her in lustrous perfection. It was as though one of the many heroic statues came to life, an ethereal beauty too wondrous for reality.

When she turned toward them, they saw the rest of her armor. Sabrina's boots, greaves, and gauntlets were custom made. Black inlay adorned silver metal plate. Her gauntlets and armor extended all the way up and underneath her pauldrons. Silver cuisses sheathed her legs. The flat links formed a steel belt that wrapped around her thighs like chaps. It covered all but the crease of her thighs.

The breastplate plate molded over what was an impressive pair of breasts, the size of cantaloupes, jutting out from her chest in an impressive display. The image of a winged dragon adorned the breastplate of the silver cuirass, its wings outstretched and mouth opened in a roar.

She stepped down from the parapet wall and onto the walkway. The pair saluted with a fist thump to their chest and snapped to attention. She returned their salute and approached them with a sultry sway of her hips. A pair of sapphire blue eyes gazed out from the dark of her Spartan style helmet.

Neither of them could move. They saw the jutting grips of her swords at either side of her neck and wondered if they were going to die. It was a ridiculous notion. They were, after all, recruits in her guild. Yet they were raised upon a steady stream of bedtime stories about Battle Maiges: in most of them, death and destruction followed such an encounter. Their weapons, though impressive, were futile against her. Her weapons were charged with magical power, and all of her armor, including the maiden's belt, were made from liquid metal, a type of synthetic nanocrystals; and under normal uses they were flexible, but when impacted the crystals interlocked and they became stronger than steel.

When she removed her helmet, a few strands of hair wafted about in the icy breeze. As if poured from a jar, the raven black color poured down her hair and wings, giving her a more familiar and safe appearance. Her vibrant blue eyes looked upon them with unexpected kindness, and her crimson, Cupid's bow lips formed a smile. For a moment, they thought they were bound in a dream.

"Quel amrun," she said in a voice that seemed to echo in their mind, as smooth as silk and as sweet as honey. "Are you on guard duty?" When they failed to respond, she cocked her head and asked with curiosity, "Are you well?"

"No. I mean yes, Overlord Sabrina," Kelvin replied. "We were just going to the great hall. Can we assist you in any way?"

"I'm going for a morning flight. Inform the captain on duty," she said.

"Yes, Overlord," they both replied.

When Sabrina stepped back onto the wall, Kelvin gawked at the beauty; Cody would have elbowed him, but armor plate covered him. Sabrina spread her wings and leap, falling out of sight. They hurried to the wall, and a second later, she soared up into the air; and watching in rapt fascination, mesmerized by the spectacle, they watched Sabrina rise ever higher into the sky. The winds carried her southeast, toward Midway City, and when she disappeared from sight, it broke their trance. Cody nudged Kelvin, which was like pushing on a boulder, and hurried toward the stairs.

It was fortunate that they wore hobnail boots. The stairs leading to the parade grounds had perpetual covering of ice, and every so often, a squad of recruits had to chip away the accumulated ice, by hand. When Cody reached the bottom of the stairs, she struggled against the mighty wind, a feather caught up in a whirlwind.

"You look like you're going to blow away," Kelvin said as he passed by Cody, a thin layer of ice crunching, snapped, and broke into shards underneath Kelvin's boots. Cody leaned into the wind, as though clawing at some beast, and fought her way across the ice; her light frame failing to make her cleats provide solid footing, white scratch marks raked across the ice, the wind pushed her backward. Kelvin paused and gazed back at Cody. Snorting in frustration, he marched back and grabbed her hand.

Snow for hair, ice for a beard, and two high windows for eyes, the ancient hall looked down upon them. The sunrise cast long shadows across the courtyard, and Cody pranced up the steps trying to keep up with Kelvin. She lost her footing and would have tumbled down the ice, if not for Kelvin. He squatted and threw her over his shoulder, leaving her dangling. After Kelvin had closed the double doors behind him, he walked over to the worn wooden equipment racks that lay on either side of the mudroom. He set his shield, backpack, and claymore in an empty slot. After he had stripped off his mask, he walked toward the inner doors.

"Hey," Cody whimpered, still hanging over his shoulder, "are you going to let me down now?"

"Yeah, fine," he said and set her down.

Cody scampered over to place her equipment in the rack. White clouds accumulated before their faces. Cody hurried through the second set of doors. When she entered the interior hall, a blast of hot air washed over her, and she wondered if dwarfs were smelting iron. This was another reason she wore a slip-suit: the interior was more uncomfortable than the exterior.

The vast hall stretched out before them. The square hearth lay in the center of the hall, viewable from all directions. Glowing orange flames danced atop a log and cast a gentle glow over the room. Several recruits were fast sleep on leather lounges, blankets covering them. One of them was a Valkyrie, a maiden warrior; the female regiment arrived during the night. She rested on her left side, facing the sofa back.

It had been nine long months since he had seen a woman other than Cody, and he needed a woman. He stood there transfixed by the ethereal image, but the moment passed all too soon; and the girl reached behind her, drawing a wool blanket up to her neck. It mystified him why girls used a blanket when they slept in their slip-suits, the garment providing ample thermal protection.

Alexander lounged a short distance away, and with the grace of a cat, he watched the pair enter the hall. The young sorcerer had an Elven like quality to him, piercing brown eyes, striking features, and a delicate frame, and speed that few could match. He appeared preoccupied, staring at the burning logs and the dancing flames. Kelvin lumbered over to him and asked, "Who is the captain of the guard this watch?"

The question broke the spell, and Alexander shook his head. He nodded at a figure across the room and said, "Marla Thorsby." Kelvin weaved his way around the furnishings. The blonde woman spoke with one of her female recruits.

Although Sabrina chose to give Marla her wings, the young woman kept them hidden, adjusting her form, the wings appearing as tattoos upon her back. She wore the uniform of a Valkyrie officer. A pair of dark black leather slacks molded to her curves like a second skin. She retied the strings of her black waist cincher, having tucked in her gold metallic blouse, the garment sculpting to her frame, which emphasized her breasts. Over this she wore a black leather waist jacket, having a T-shirt neckline. Her rank indicated on her choker necklace, and her service ribbons were pinned to the upper left front of the jacket. She flicked a blonde tress over her shoulder and felt someone staring at her, and when she glanced over her shoulder, a giant of a man was lingering behind her.

Kelvin stared at longer than was appropriate. Her arms crossed, she frowned and said, "When you're finished, be about your business." When he continued staring, she turned around to face him. "Recruit, stop staring!"

"I'm sorry, Commander," Kelvin said. "It's just that you're such an amazing warrior." She shook her head and rolled her eyes. He then relayed Sabrina's message to her.

"Very well, be about your business," she said, "or I'll find something for you to do."

Kelvin wandered across the room toward the cafeteria, still wondering what it would be like to bed her. There was an array of beautiful girls congregated in the hall. Then he recognized a girl. "Crystal, is that you?"

"I'm sorry but … Kelvin … that is you." She jumped up and threw her arms around him. "It's been a long time since I last saw you. How are you?

"Great," he replied. "When did you get here? I never heard the trumpet call declaring your entrance?"

"We arrived in the middle of the night. Mistress Sabrina wanted to let the troops get their rest. Have you been here long?"

"Long enough," he said without thinking. "I mean, we have been at this fortification for 9 months. Before that, we hiked 3 months through the mountains. Before that, we were stationed a year at the Akagos Castle. It's been one fight after another. Between the daemia and haugr we haven't got a moment's rest."

He asked, "What have you been doing?"

The Great Gate

"We've been riding everywhere from the Regal Mountains, to Midway City, through the Ferngal Pass, and nowhere. It's been two years for us too. I almost forgot what it was like to be warm. She cocked her head and asked, "Would you like to go up to my room?"

He thought about her offer and puzzled for a second. What was in her room? Then his face lit up, and comprehension dawned upon him. "Oh sure," he said. She giggled and led him by the hand from the hall.

Cody wandered out of the dining room with two flagons of cider, one hot and one cold. Cody preferred it cold, naturally. Kelvin was an easy man to spot, but she could not seem to find him. She set down the flagons. Putting her hands on her hips, she rose to her tiptoes and looked about. *He was here a second ago.* She sat down on a sofa and took a sip of cider. *Where did he go?*

Amanda slipped onto the sofa beside Cody and flicked a brown lock over her shoulder. She smirked and leaned over to Cody. She cupped her hand and whispered in Cody's ear. Cody's eyes went wide, and then her lips curled into a frown. "That bitch!"

Chapter 42

J oash stood with his hands on his hips and searched the dining hall. The clatter of dishes and din of conversation radiated out through the doors. The delicious aroma of bacon and coffee beckoned him. He shook his head and walked into the hall. He spotted Marla and Kayla seated with a few Valkyrie.

After filling up a tray, he carried it over to their table. "May I join you?" asked Joash. Chewing a mouth full of food, Kayla gestured for him to sit. "I heard you arrived during the night. Have you had any luck finding the Great Gate?"

"None. We looked under every rock, in every cave, and in every ice flow. We even contacted the Dwarves. They charged us five gold coins to say that they hadn't seen it." Kayla took a sip of coffee and shivered.

"Same for us," Joash replied. He counted only four other Valkyrie seated with her. "Is this all that you brought with you?"

"No. There are 130 in my company." Kayla shrugged and said, "Those warriors care for the company of other women."

"Ah, I see. I was wondering where all my recruits were off to. It appears some things are more important that food." He took a sip of coffee and ate a sausage link. "Some of my men are the same sort as these Valkyrie. That is, they care only for the company of other men. This type of assignment is ideal for them."

"I don't understand. Forty percent of The Praetorian Guard is composed of female warriors. Why do you risk 'nature's calling'? Such a large company of men puts them at greater risk," asked Kayla.

"We weren't supposed to be here without female warriors. One of our former commanders separated our males and females into different battalions. Most of our females took another route and were cut off by a time vortex and winter. The only female that came with us was Cody. She is my aid when we are out on maneuvers. I am surprised that you made it here."

"It takes more than a little snow and ice to stop a Valkyrie," she said with a smile.

"So I see," he replied, "and I'm relieved that you made it."

"Who is your senior commander by the way?" asked Marla.

"Sir Cornelius Van der Haas III, he's of Androth aristocracy." Joash spat out the words as if distasteful. "We seldom see him. He stays in his private quarters for the most part."

She sampled a bit of hot oatmeal and pondered the condition of the garrison. "We noticed few guards on watch last night and no roving patrols. Has there been an outbreak of illness? If there is, we travel with a skilled physician."

"No. No, illness," he grumbled. "Commander Van der Haas concluded that inclement weather precludes an attack. He scaled back our watches and ready reserve until the weather warms."

Peter took a seat next to Joash. He combed his fingers through his thick locks. "Can you believe this? We've been here 9 months, and not one of our missions has gone as planned. They were one miserable failure after another. Five recruits got lost in a whiteout. So we had to find them. Then 4 of our recruits got sick. So what do we do? We abandon our objective because someone else might get sick. We are warriors! Our mission to contact the dwarves should go as planned. I'm so frustrated that I could bludgeon someone to death."

"I see." Marla nibbled on a sweet roll. "Overlord Sabrina will be disturbed to hear about this. She expects all her commanders to maintain a combat-ready status while deployed and carry out their missions." Joash grunted and nodded. Peter paused to chew a mouthful of food and then continued his diatribe.

When the first bell of the morning sounded, Joash gobbled down the last bit of food on his tray. After his tray was cleared, he passed through the dining hall and then the great room. The second he opened the inner door the cold bit at his face. He threw on his coat and helmet, and after putting on his gloves, he grabbed his weapons, pack, and other items and exited the building.

Ice and snow danced about in swirls on the parade ground, making the parade ground as slick as an ice skating rink. A wooden platform lay near the wall, and he climbed onto it. After drawing his sword, he grasped the handle, pointed it down, and rested the sharp tip in a wooden plank. The sharp wind cut across his face, turning his skin red. He fixed his eyes on the assembly area and waited.

The outer doors opened, and the veterans exited the hall. They carried shields, swords, and spears. They moved into their respective squads and waited. A few recruits trickled out the door, and they hurried to their assigned marks. Rather than wait in silence, they tried to engage the veterans in friendly banter. Grunts and rude comments resulted. A mob of recruits and Valkyrie exited the great hall.

Marla led her warriors to their assigned section on the parade ground, forming them up in ranks, but there were several empty holes in the rows of soldiers. A few recruits rushed out of the building, still dressing after furious sex, and hurried to their assigned place, wondering if they were too late. Joash saw two, very noticeable, empty slots – Kelvin and Crystal. Kelvin was the type of man people noticed by his presence or absence. Marla walked up the stairs and across the platform, the impotent sunlight reflecting off her glossy black slip-suit and silver armor. She stood by Joash's side.

The doors flew open with a loud bang. Kelvin and Crystal rushed from the building, half dressed and in a hurry; they made it to their assigned

429

slots just as the final bell rang. Kelvin cinched down his armor and then snapped to attention.

"Are you cold? Well, that's a shame. This weather is beautiful if you ask me." He stripped off his fur coat and gloves, taking in a deep breath. "In fact, it's such a wonderful day that I want to go for a leisurely run. I want each squad to run double time around the inner grounds and then on the upper wall. The last squad here is on kitchen duty tonight. Get moving – double time – march!"

Those warriors who wore coats stripped them off but retained their essential equipment. The squads turned to the right and began to run. The heavy equipment bounced on their back, and their hands gripped their weapons. The total circumference of the inner grounds was a complex maze of 10 miles that weaved between buildings in a zigzag and skirted the parade grounds; and the upper wall was another 16. The recruits broke into a sprint and raced passed the veterans. They charged around the wall and behind the buildings. Those in better condition began to pull ahead and left their comrades behind. The veterans, however, stayed in ranks as they ran. Their shields were strapped to their left arm, a sling supporting it around their opposite shoulder, and their right hands clasped their swords.

Joash led the veterans. They ran in tight formation and each person in their unit. They had just finished their first lap when three recruits swept passed them. "What the hell do you think you're doing," Joash bellowed. "We are running by squad today. Where is your goddamn squad?" The recruits came to a halt, steaming breaths jetting out from their mouths. "Find your squad and get in it." The recruits turned about and scurried about trying to find their squad members.

The elder commander saw something out of the corner of his eye. Kelvin's squad passed them by. They ran in perfect formation with their weapons in hand. Kelvin bellowed out orders, and the men ran in lockstep. Pride swelled within Joash's heart when he saw Kelvin lead his squad. The warriors moved as a single entity around the walls.

Now Joash was a cunning man and crafted his orders with care. As he suspected, Kelvin ran the upper wall, which included the annex. Joash said nothing about the annex and took a shortcut. When he saw Kelvin's men round the corner and discover their mistake, they set out in pursuit. Joash quickened the pace. The men and women matched him. Soon his lungs burned, and legs ached. He sprinted around the wall and charged down the steps. Out of the corner of his eye, he saw his son scramble down the steps. He charged after Joash's squad like a raging bull; hot breaths snorted from his nostrils.

Joash's squad made it to the parade ground just ahead of Kelvin's squad and assumed their marks. Joash and Marla assumed their places on the platform. The warriors donned their coats and gloves again. The anger on his son's face caused a smile to appear on Joash's face. *You will win someday my son, but not today.*

Fragmented squads approached the parade ground, stretched out and lacking members. They took up the marks and gasped in gulps of air. A few stragglers descended the stairs and hurried to take a place with their peers.

"Those of you who did not arrive as a unit get a special treat. You get to run the entire course – again! This time stay in proper formation. Go!" Six squads left the formation and ran the course again. "For those who remain, we will begin drills."

The warriors drew their weapons and started to drill. Joash milled through the sparing warriors. Swords thumped on shields and sang when they met one another. He barked out instruction to the soldiers, and the veterans moved with machine-like efficiency. Each blow was calculated and exercised with care. The recruits were far less efficient: using their swords as clubs, they tried to overpower their opponent.

When he came to Kelvin, he stopped to observe. The big man's movements belied his bulk, moving about like a dancer on a stage. He swept and hit his partner's shield; he blocked; he thrust; he deflected; he spun, and he threw the man off balance. Joash could tell Kelvin was taking it easy on his opponent, but even so, Kelvin's blows nearly sent the man tumbling to the ground.

"Not like that," Joash said. "Watch me." He drew his sword and stood before Kelvin. Tapping his sword to his shield, he said, "Begin."

Kelvin hauled his sword high and brought it down with all his might. Joash raised his shield. "Don't try to stop his blows, deflect them." The sword glanced off his shield, causing a shower of sparks, and Joash thrust at Kelvin as if to impale him. Kelvin blocked the blow and spun; his sword whistled through the air. Joash recovered and deflected the blow. He then brought down his sword, and Kelvin deflected it. A circle formed around them; some cheered for Kelvin and others for Joash. The father and son traded withering blows as if two giants sparred – their swords sang; their shields thumped, and bodies strained. They pushed against one another, each digging in their heels, snorting in rage and fighting with all their might. When Joash felt his footing give way, he stepped aside, releasing potential energy and turned it into kinetic. Kelvin launched forward and hit the ground with a loud bang. Joash touched the tip of his sword to his son's back.

"You are dead."

Kelvin brushed aside the sword and scrambled to his feet. His eyes were wide, face bright red, and his hands trembled with rage. He raised his sword to continue the attack.

"Hold," Joash ordered. When Kelvin hesitated, Joash roared, "I said, 'HOLD'!" Kelvin lowered his weapon and thumped his weapon to his chest in a salute. Joash responded and circled the assembled warriors. "Power and youth are not enough. The bones of young soldiers lie scattered across the Wolf's Head Peninsula. You must battle with skill; deceive your enemy – let him think he is the more powerful, and you are feeble, a coward. Then, when you choose the time, unleash your attack and kill him. Now continue to practice."

Joash strolled through between the battling warriors. His knees ached as he climbed the stairs to the stage. Had it really been so long? Had he really gotten so old? The aches and pains of his old body combined with the terrible weariness in his soul. He recalled the offer to join the Elite Praetorian Guardians, the Immortals, and the promise of eternal youth, but it would mean divorcing Fiona, since the Immortals required absolute fealty. His love for her burned hotter than the pain and strengthened him.

Marla moved to Joash's side and turned to face him. She said with a quiet voice, "I have seen few matches to equal that contest. Your son is a great warrior."

"'Great' is not good enough. I promised his mother that I would keep him alive. To do that, he has to be the best." Marla nodded and returned to her recruits.

Joash wished he could throw his arms around his son and congratulate him. His soul ached because he still saw the boy hidden within the man. It was the boy that Joash told bedtime stories; it was the boy that he tucked in bed; it was the boy that hid from the monsters in his closet; and it was the boy that would become puffed up with pride and then die on a battlefield. The boy had to give way to the man, and Joash labored tirelessly to see it done.

Joash flexed his right hand. Arthritis made his joints sting. A lifetime of powerful blows weathered his body and left it aching. But he had to keep going. If he failed, his son would die; he just could not face that again.

When practice concluded, they reformed ranks. "Remove your clothing. Leave on only your underwear." The warriors began to strip, and their gear gathered in piles at their feet. Men and women stood before him, naked before the icy wind and snow. Many of them began to shiver, their limbs convulsed. "The coldest snowstorm is but a breeze. The hottest desert is but a warm beach. To gain victory, you will swim icy rivers and fight in burning buildings. Nothing can stop you. You are Praetorian

Guard, and you are Valkyrie." The warriors let out a deep grunt. "You may get dressed."

As they dressed, he said, "I want to meet with all the recruits in the lecture hall in the educational building. We will cover Roger's Battle Tactics when he fought the haugr in the Ice Caves. I hope all of you completed your assigned reading."

Joash watched his son stomp across the courtyard. Kelvin threw open the doors with a loud crash and marched into the hall. Joash rubbed his face and fought the heaviness of his heart. Marla patted him on his broad shoulder and then hurried after her girls. He strolled over to a stone block and took a seat. He did not know how long he could keep up the pace.

Chapter 43

S abrina soared through the crisp blue skies, the air under her wings, flowing over her contoured body. She passed through a wispy cloud, bathed in white for a moment and then broke through to clear sky; she scanned the ground, her eyes sharp as that of a Great Eagle, and searched for The Great Gate. The Wolf's Maw Mountains, the Sundering Glacier, the Great Pass, and the Regal Mountains appeared nothing more than impressions on a relief map, so small and insignificant; the curvature of Eden and the black rim of space stretched out like a curved lens around her, beyond the accusing eyes of the elves, she winged through the heavens.

It's hiding from me, damn it! I can just feel it. It is smirking at me with contempt, daring me to find it.

Sabrina's heart grew heavy as her search brought little success. The great Sundering Glaciers – 326 miles of irresistible force, carving their way through mountains, carrying away rocks the size of office buildings, and digging a trench deeper than the Grand Canyon – flowed in a relentless march to the plains. The ice field hid a secret: she could feel it. The glaciers gashed so deep into Eden's mantle that magma oozed out through the wound, glowing orange blood. Every so often a geyser erupted, and explosions of jagged ice, boiling water, and rock jetted so high that it stabbed at the jet stream. The water froze, and igneous rock rained down with merciless brutality. Thus was born the saying, "I'm hard pressed between fire and ice."

Although unseen, the dwarves labored beneath Eden's surface and endlessly worked their mines – groping, searching, and praying for the mother lode. The lava-fueled their great engines and smelted their hard earned bounty into precious metals: gold, silver, mithril, and other precious metals to finance their great cities. The haugr – a nightmare resembling a bat, a man, and a panther – also lived beneath the ground on which men walked. The haugr and dwarves, hidden from the eyes of men and elves, waged endless war, bloody battles, fighting in a mortal struggle, miles of ice above and blazing fire below. Their battles, measured in misery, raged for centuries, the bones of dwarves and haugr entombed within the rock, forever locked in mortal conflict.

Sabrina bent her knees and used her calves to tilt down toward Eden. If she flew too high, too long, she might lose herself, flying for centuries, never craving the grounds welcoming embrace; so she forced herself to begin her long descent although her soul longed to stay in the sky.

Her wings were outstretched, and she circled in a lazy spiral. A rare sight caught her attention. A group of dwarves trekked across the face of the ice flow; they raced as if pursued by some unseen menace. She wondered at the conditions which could force them above ground.

Thirty miles away, she saw a pack of dire wolves, hot breath jetting from the gaping maws. They chased a herd of white-back deer across the frozen wilderness, robbing them of precious energy, a marathon of death. The deer had little energy to spare: the evergreens provided meager nutrition. But the wolves cared nothing for the suffering they inflicted; their bellies were empty, and their young craved meat. They would chase prey for 30 to 40 miles, across deep snow, treacherous terrain, and a trackless wilderness. In the end, a terrified deer would succumb – its life ending in terror and crying for help. But the wolves would eat, and the pack would survive, thus ensuring the health of both species; but it was cold arithmetic. To save one was to kill the other.

Sabrina's heart was both immune and tortured by the struggle of life and death. A white-back doe lost the race, and a dire wolf grabbed its hind leg tripping it, causing the pair to tumble in the powdery snow. When the deer arose, it was surrounded by snarling teeth; urine dumped from doe, and her legs began to tremble as death moved in for the kill.

Sabrina saw three bucks lying frozen in the snow a half mile away, killed in an avalanche. She used her telekinetic powers to hurtle the corpses into the midst of this tragedy. The wolves scattered when the dead bodies hit the snow, and the doe sped through the gap. When the wolves regrouped, they sniffed at the dead deer and a moment later ripped flesh from bone. No act of kindness is ever wasted, and mercy is an end unto itself.

She winged down to the Winter Pass Fortress and circled it. The stone fortress appeared so small and pitiful, a stone lifeboat in a sea of white. Its spires and battlements appeared tiny, like that of a toy, a toy abandoned by a child and long forgotten. She soared down in a steep pitch, the outer wall rushing toward her, the ground a passing blur, the sun dancing on the ice. The wall grew larger by the second and loomed before her, implacable. The wind pressure pushed her up as she raced past it. She swept up in a critical angle of attack, her momentum stalled and lift faltered. She dropped to her feet, like a snowflake upon the earth, and drew in her wings.

Twenty-three mountain goats lingered inside their stalls, avoiding the bitter chill, the cold too sharp even for them. They fed upon fresh hay and drank warm water. They were dwarven mounts, creatures of the mountains, nimble beyond comparison, and the fastest means of transport. A delegation arrived. Was there news?

Sabrina rushed down the stairs and jogged crossed the courtyard. The last slice of icy wind lashed at her as she entered the building, but she paid it little heed, continuing on her business. Upon passing through the inner doors, hot air blasted her, burning her face, searing the flesh, melting steel … or so it seemed. Her body adjusted a moment later, color returning to her cheeks. She spotted a group of dwarves across the vast hall, huddled together, their voices kept low and sharing quiet confidences.

Several of the recruits gawked at Sabrina, their minds filled with lustful imaginings and their bodies yearning to express them. Veterans joined them and paused from their conversation. It was as she hoped. Tormod, Master Dwarf, met with Garak, another master dwarf. Sabrina entered the conversation and said, "It's good to see you, you old tunnel rat." Garak turned and looked to see who was addressing him.

"It's good to see you too," Garak said with a grin. "I have news for you. We should find a private room where we can speak."

"Yes. There are rooms in the next building." They passed through the great hall, passing warriors on rows of sofas, arrayed around tables, and loitering near barrels of ale. The soldiers paused from their conversations and watched the procession pass them by, all minds craving to hear the news.

Sabrina commented, "I see that the missing female warriors of the Praetorian Guard arrived."

"I met them in the East/West Pass near at Petitioner's city near Alkval. They were looking for a way up to the Winter Pass Fortress. I gave them safe passage through the Vonval mines to the city of Garduer and then up through the Edban Maze. Mind you, the passage over Daria (Ice Ordeal) was wearing, but they kept up with us."

"I'm glad to hear it." They burst through a set of double doors and charged up several flights of stairs, the dwarves breaking out into a jog to keep up with her. Their path carried them into the lesser halls, boardrooms with 20 chairs and freshly brewed coffee. These facilitities housed planning sessions and facilitated instruction. Private meetings kept most of the doors shut, but muffled voices escaped through the cracks. She marched up to the administrator's desk and said, "We need a room."

Douglas peered over his reading glasses. Dwarves leaned around Sabrina, all staring at him with eager eyes. "Of course," he said, tracing his finger down the logbook. "Room 51 is available and freshly provisioned." The punchy man slipped off his chair and plodded toward the room, his belly swinging from side to side. He led them through the labyrinth of halls, hallways branching off into different directions, kitchenettes filled with supplies, voices spilling out into the hallway. They passed by heavy wooden doors with round tops and wrought iron hinges. The man stroked his graying red beard and unlocked the door with his ring of keys. "This should meet your need."

The room was well appointed. Ancient tapestries covered split log walls and a roaring fire burned in the hearth. A set of high back, red leather chairs sat in a semi-circle around the fireplace. They took a seat, and the attendant returned a minute later carrying a tray. Upon it was a thermos filled with hot coffee and some pastries.

Garak filled up a mug and took a satisfying swig. "That is wondrous. I'd march all day for coffee this good."

Tormod sipped the brew. "We import it from the southern islands in the Spotted Sea. Now you were saying something about news? We've been searching for the Great Gate for years." Sabrina sat down in a low-backed leather chair, her wings draped on the floor behind her, legs crossed and hands placed in her lap.

Garak said, "Yes, of course. I forget myself. We dwarves relish a fine cup of coffee. It's the best thing the humans ever invented." He inhaled the rich, aromatic scent of the coffee and then took a sip. "I happened to be in Trinar six months ago." The dwarven capital city was located under the Carbon Mountains. "King Aglar summoned me for a private audience. He too has been searching for the Great Gate. He's sure that the damned Elven Council knows of its location, not that they would ever admit to it. They're as skittish as a Prancer Cat. Anyway, he has been searching south as far as Solva and south-east to the Hargal Wall. His emissaries discovered little but legend and myth. However, after I left the city and traveled north, an aurora storm ignited the skies above me. It was south-east of Turin but west of the great Ferngal Pass, in the vicinity of the Miller's Way through the Amphitheater Mountain Range. If I was a betting man, I would say that the Great Gate would appear there …."

Garak was a dwarf of few words until he was a dwarf of many words. She halfway listened to him, but his revelation weighed heavy in her thoughts. Finding and safeguarding the gate dominated her thoughts, an obsession and a goal. For so long, she could think of little else. "… So what do you think?" she asked Tormod.

"An interesting hypothesis," Tormod replied and then slurped his coffee. "The signs are favorable. It is worth a look-see."

"My thoughts exactly," Sabrina said and tapped her index finger on her chin.

"There is great excitement in the dwarven community," Garak said. "My brother thinks there will be significant profit. Humans have no instincts or love of mining. Many dwarves are preparing for a land rush. Imagine that, wide-open land as far as the eye can see, virgin territory just waiting for the right dwarf. Of course, the elves will probably lay claim to some of the land."

"Perhaps, but only surface territory," she replied. "The elves prefer an above-ground existence. However, mankind can be quite territorial, laying claim both to the surface and subterranean. Consider Asgard: the humans claim in all of the Wolf's Head Peninsula, even the lands held by the other races. The human's on Earth may not be so eager to relinquish their claim without due compensation."

"Well, I'm sure a deal can be struck if some piece of land is in question. But they cannot claim unused mines or vacant land. That is absurd. Yet it would be good to start off with the proper foundation. We could give them a few trinkets, some baubles to appease them." Garak looked to his brothers and heard rumbles of agreement.

Sabrina was a conglomerate being and was born at the moment of death. She lived many lives, most of them human. The division between her female and male lives was approximately 60/40. Thus, she knew a great deal about human worlds. She very much doubted that any human nation on Earth would be eager to sell off its sovereign territory. Land, above all else, is a symbol of a country's status and wealth, yet there was no point in addressing an issue before its time: Earth would never be the same after the gates opened, for better or worse.

A knock came from the door. "Enter," she replied.

Joash opened the door and said, "Good morning Tormod. I heard you were here. We have much to discuss. How is that wife of yours doing?" The marriage of a halfling dwarf and a full blooded dwarf was controversial among the dwarves. Most of the dissenting opinions felt human blood would dilute the purer dwarven race. Of course, love knows no boundaries and recognizes no constraints. The heart, human or otherwise, will have the object of its desire.

"Why don't you two talk for a while?" Sabrina rose to her feet. "There are a few matters which require my attention." She left the room and closed the door behind her. When she turned around, Marla walked down the hallway toward her. "I was just going to look for you. What is your report?"

Marla crossed her arms and shifted to one hip. "It's not good I'm afraid. Your suspicions were correct regarding Sir Cornelius Van der Haas III. Even in this wilderness, he manages to obstruct our progress …." She told Sabrina all that Joash and the other officers reported to her. Each indictment was weightier than its predecessor.

"I see." The weight of Marla's revelations weighed down upon Sabrina. "I will tend to the matter."

"Yes, Mistress," Marla replied and saluted.

"The Valkyrie and the Praetorian Guard will leave Winter Pass Fortress soon on a mission. I want to organize our logistical support and map our route. We will be leaving for the southern route and the Ferngal Pass."

"Yes, Mistress, I will see to the details at once."

The Great Gate

Sabrina left Marla and exited the lesser hall. The moment she stepped into the courtyard, the storm resumed its attack, wind gusted, and ice slashed. Frigid blasts pushed against her and swept her hair into the wind, tousling her feathers. She marched with bold steps, defiant of the wind and the gusting snow about her.

The Commandant's Residence lay in the center of the facility, and it grew in an organic fashion over the centuries, small houses gobbled up by larger additions, outer walls becoming inner walls, roofs connected to one another, and stain glass windows separating rooms. The outcome reminded visitors of a cathedral, spires appearing like rockets ready to blast off into the sky, and the building's face beset by heroic scenes carved in stone. They inspired entrants and warned that this was a hall of power.

Sabrina charged up a set of semi-circular, timeworn stairs. The guards snapped to attention at her approach, hands gripping weapons and eyes fixed ahead. She rushed up the stairs, white powder swirling around her feet and then formed a vortex around her body. Her boots clacked on the marble entryway, metal and rubber cleats providing sure footing. She marched past the pillars with resolute intent, and then she passed through four pillars, standing before two giant doors. The guards opened a lesser door, more manageable than their titan brothers in which they were set.

After passing through the doorway, the long central hall, a nave, opened up before her, reminding one of a great cathedral, giant twisting pillars rising and separating in fanning ribs that upheld a vaulted ceiling; stained glass bathed the floor in a rainbow collage, and she tread upon a red carpet that traced a straight line down the middle of the hall. Each archway opened up a little wider than the last and brought her into a circular room. Doors mounted on the wall, between the pillars, that led to separate narthexes. Gardens, chapels, private libraries and other facilities dazzled the eye with possibilities and wealth.

Her feet tapped out a quick beat as she passed through the long hallway. A loud sneeze echoed off the stone building, and Sir Cornelius Van der Haas III shivered, a blanket wrapped around his frail body, his face pale as death. The emaciated man curled into a small ball, like a withered corpse, seated upon a great stone throne, seated on a high dais.

"Send for the physician. This medicine is of no use." He shoved a glass vial into Atherton's, his assistant, hands. The balding man hurried down the carpeted steps and turned right toward the private clinic.

Cornelius squinted when he saw a figure approaching him. As Sabrina charged up the steps, he rose to his feet. "Overlord Sabrina, I am so pleased to see that you survived in this God forsaken place. No, one of the demi-gods, which serve the Great Spirit, loves this place. Albius, god of the north, reigns here. He is a cruelest master. He blasts us with his icy knives." He sneezed again, "What a vengeful god. How may I be of service to you?"

Great King Gunner Juhani Thorbrand the Righteous died in 1281CE, and he was poisoned by one of his sons, either Vomla or Shalva – but which one? Asgard established Parliament only 78 years before this event and charging one or both of the sons might cause a civil war. To prevent the murder from ruling over the entire kingdom, Parliament divided the kingdom between the two sons, an act that the news media criticized.

Volma ruled the north in the city of Parglos on Razell Mountain, to the northwest of the lost city of Magmara, and Shalva ruled in the south in the grand city of Kurios. Volma was unhappy with his lot on the icy mountain, ruling over Androth, lands of the north; the real economic power and temperate environment lay in the south in Shalva's domain; so Vomla decided to take all of the lands, waging a war of assassination and intrigue.

The contest between the brothers became so fierce that Parliament feared all out war between the great houses, so they devised a cunning plan – they offered the kingdom to Volma's daughter, Velna, and

443

Shalva's son, Aleksi, if they married and disavowed their fathers. It was immaterial that they were first cousins or that their parents were still living.

Also in exchange for relinquishment over titles for specific lands, Parliament appointed them rulers over both Asgard and Earth. No one cared that Parliament never consulted the people of Earth. It was one of the ancient worlds; therefore, it fell under their domain. Velna and Aleksi agreed; Parliament stripped Vomla and Shalva of power, and their family line now ruled over Asgard and Earth.

Cornelius was descendant of the Velna and Aleksi, and because Sabrina was an adopted member of the royal family, he was part of her family. Sabrina understood the ancient Roman admonition: "Promote the man up and out."

"I have good news," Sabrina said. "I have promoted you as Special Envoy to Parliament on behalf of The Black Dragon House. Of course, this will come with a generous expense account and accommodations within the capital city. I do not need to tell you of all the intrigues of the royal court. It will take a man of your cunning to ferret them out."

"Yes, that it true." Cornelius sneezed and drew up his blanket. "The royal court is beset with dangers. It takes wisdom and tact to discover them. I accept." He looked about the great hall. "It will be good to leave this ghastly place. It is freezing cold even in the summer. I feel like I am entombed here. You know I swear that the spirits of our ancestors watch me day and night. It troubles my sleep. They come to me in the darkness and whisper dreadful things."

She put her arm around his shoulder and led him down the stairs. "You should pack at once. Your health requires a temperate climate. Perhaps you should go south to Glorloch Lake and recuperate with your family. I'm told they just finished building a new mansion in the Trammel Estates. It's quite exclusive and would make an excellent place to begin your efforts. Let the dead trouble you no more and take your rest."

"I'll do that at once." Cornelius hurried down the steps. "Timmons, pack our bags. We are leaving."

Chapter 44

Kelvin trudged up the stairs to the great hall. As punishment for his defiance after the contest with his father, Joash assigned Kelvin an additional night of sentry duty. Not even the cold could keep the great man's eyes open, raw hunger gnawed his belly, and fatigue pulled at his limbs. The dawn broke in the east and crept over the wall, golden beams falling upon the veins of ice upon the stonewall. He was too tired to take comfort in it. After a meal, he was required to participate in the morning training regimen; only then, the leaders permit a few precious hours of sleep.

He entered through the outer doors and spotted an empty slot in the rows of wooden racks. He stripped off his pack and shield, feeling much lighter for it, and placed his equipment on a rack. When he passed through to the inner hall, a girl shivered and yelled for him to shut the doors. He passed her by without a second look: hunger alone drove him. The aroma of freshly baked bread wafted out from the dining hall.

Kelvin lumbered through the building and searched for Cody, a sea of people swarmed around him, some familiar and some not. There were far too many people to pick out one person. He moved through the crowd, entered the breakfast line, and grabbed a tray. The kitchen staff unceremoniously slapped the food on his plate. After filling a mug with hot cider, he searched for a table to sit. It was then that he spotted Cody. His friend sat on a lounge in a far corner, all alone. He turned to his right and passed through the hall. The clatter of dishes and din of conversations reached a fever pitch.

He sat down on a leather lounge with a sigh. "It's so good to sit. There's one good thing about the cold. My feet went numb an hour ago so I couldn't feel them ache." He took a swig of hot cider and looked to his friend for some response. Cody sat in the corner and stared off into space. In between swigs of icy ale, she mumbled. Kelvin asked, "It's a bit early for ale; don't you think?"

"I don't need your permission," Cody said and fidgeted as if sitting on a hot plate. "It's my breakfast, and I'll do as I wish."

"Alright Cody, there's no need to get angry. I was just commenting," Kelvin replied. "It's just that ... well, you can't live on ale."

"You can't live at all around here," Cody said took a swig. "This place is a dump, no it's a mausoleum. We're all buried here."

Kelvin placed a slab of ham and a layer of eggs in a roll. He took a large bite and spoke with his mouth full. "What do you think of Crystal?"

"I don't know. I tried talking to her. She kept going on and on about her family. She explained to me every little detail about eggplant and squash farming. The longer she spoke, the worse it got. Then one of her friends tripped and spilled her wine all over me, the stupid cow! I can't believe her," Cody hissed and began to rock, chewing on her fingernail. "Tamara made an ugly face at me. I got up and left."

"I'm sorry to hear that. She seemed nice." Kelvin ate a cinnamon roll in three bites and took a slurp of cider. "I hear we're going on another exploratory mission soon."

Cody's eyes locked on a royal blue tunic, her body stiffened and lungs seized. Her mind instantly traveled back in time to a day when she was in ice caves. The ice caves were located in the Sundering Glacier to the east of the castle. Her platoon was on a routine patrol. When she entered the cave, she saw the richest and deepest blues imaginable; its smooth contours forming a narrowing funnel. It amplified the screeches. They made her nerves tingle and skin crawl.

The haugr rushed out from the darkness. They filled the ice tunnel to overflowing, crawling on the floor, walls, and ceiling – gushing forth from the dark void like rushing waters. For a moment, she thought she was dead. Kelvin hurtled two vials containing Greek Fire, and it exploded before them, tongues of fire licking up around the ice, forming flaming vortexes; heat gusted over them and burning her flesh. The chemical reagents burned hotter than a blast furnace and incinerated the rushing flock.

"Are you okay?" asked Kelvin.

"What? I'm fine. Don't worry about me. I can take care of myself." Cody gulped down her ale and slammed down the cup. She jumped up to her feet. "Just take care of yourself. That's what you're best at." She turned and marched away. Kelvin lingered in astonished silence, gaping at the stranger who attacked him. Cody shoved another recruit out of the way and marched away. Cody glanced back at Kelvin and then sat down with a new recruit. Her face tightened, and hands waved as she railed.

When Kelvin ate the last bite, he carried his tray over to the cleaning station. He placed his tray and silverware into the receptacles. A voice broke through the noise and caused a hush. Cody shouted, "… You're an idiot. We could all die. This fortress is no defense; the haugr could climb right over the walls. We need to be prepared!" Everyone stared at Cody for a moment and then returned to their affairs.

Kelvin strolled through the cafeteria, and he saw the recruit make a hasty retreat. Cody sat alone, bent over, and gazed at the empty table. Now he needed the drink and filled his mug with ale. He wandered over and sat down next to Cody. She held a knife in her right hand. She turned the blade, using the polished surface like a mirror; her eyes traced the razor sharp edge. Without looking up, she asked Kelvin, "Have you thought of killing yourself. Just a quick cut and it's all over."

"What? No. I've thought about cutting other people's throats, not my own. Are you serious?" asked Kelvin and put his hand on her shoulder. "Are you okay? You've been tense lately."

Scott Marcy

"I'm fine. I guess." Cody returned her blade to its sheath. "I just wonder what it is like to die. What happens?"

"The priests say we pass through the great light on our journey to the eternal lands," Kelvin said.

"How would he know? Has he ever died? This life might be all there is. We just end and face eternal night." Cody rubbed her nose and pushed away the welling tears.

"Now I know that is untrue. Overlord Sabrina has traveled back and forth from the afterlife. She brings news with her, news she would only know if she talked to the dead. There is an afterlife. You can be sure of that," Kelvin said and straightened his back.

"It's probably as miserable as this life," Cody grumbled.

"Can I speak with you a moment, Cody?" asked Marla.

"Of course, Mistress, it's not as if I was already doing something," she said sarcastically. She rose to her feet and followed her from the hall. Kelvin picked up Cody's mug and carried it to the dish trays. He refilled his mug with hot cider and joined another group. They chatted about home and read the news in their oracle scrolls. Kelvin's thoughts lingered on Cody.

Cody burst into tears and ran from a room and sprinted across the dining hall. Tears streamed down her cheeks. Kelvin rose to his feet and opened his mouth to call out to Cody. It was too late. Cody rushed out of the room.

Fear arose within him like vomit. Kelvin passed through the hall and the separating doors. He saw his father, Marla, and Tormod. They spoke to one another in hushed voices. "What is it? What happened?"

Joash rubbed the back of his neck and shook his head; "It's for her own good."

449

"What's for her own good?" demanded Kelvin.

"We ordered Cody to report to the infirmary. I've seen recruits like her before, battle fatigue overwhelms the mind. We want her to recover, but if she can't, she will be sent back to the rear. For a pledge that means she will be cut from the corps," Joash said.

"She's fine. It's just exhaustion. Our room is cold and drafty: no one is getting a good night's sleep. All she needs is rest," Kelvin said.

Marla touched Kelvin's massive arm, "I hope you are right. She does need rest. That is why we are sending her to the hospital. She will get rest and the treatment she needs."

Kelvin wiped the tears from his cheeks. "You can't send her away. She doesn't deserve this. She's my friend." He pulled away from Marla and charged through the exterior doors.

He exited the great hall without collecting his gear, risking expulsion. The wind broke on Kelvin's barrel chest and gusted through his black hair, white snowflakes blowing about and soaring into the air. The parade ground was empty except for the ever present ice. He charged up the steps and turned toward their residence. It was then that his worst fears were realized, and his face contorted in horror.

Cody stood upon the wall. She gazed off at the distant Regal Mountains as if in a dream. "I wish I could fly," Cody said and closed her eyes. The icy winds swept across fields of white and cut them with bitter cold. When Kelvin took a step toward him, Cody said, "Don't come near me." She gazed down into the abyss and felt the void tug at her body. "I hope you're right. I hope there is an afterlife."

"Wait! I know everything seems hopeless. You just need a good night's rest. After that, you'll be good as new." Kelvin struggled to find the right words. Cody lingered in silence, waiting for a last goodbye. The ice spires pointed up at her as though beckoning her, growing larger somehow as she stared at them. Kelvin broke the trance saying "We'll go to the hospital together. When you're better, you will be back on duty. I need the best warrior in E-company by my side."

"I don't need empty praise," Cody snapped. "Save it for a green recruit."

"It's not 'empty praise.' You saved my life back in the ice fields. That daemia was going to spear me through the back. You stopped him." Kelvin's eyes watered and tears flowed down his cheeks. "You're my best friend. Don't leave me."

Cody glanced over her shoulder and saw the tears trickle down Kelvin's cheeks. Her eyes welled up with blue tears that formed tracks as they trickled down her cheeks. "You're my best friend too."

"Please, come back to me. Don't leave me," he said. "I need you."

"Okay," she said and climbed down from the wall. Kelvin rushed over and threw his massive arms around Cody. "You're crushing me," she groaned. Kelvin released her for just a second but then took her in his arms again. He leaned over and kissed her. She rose up into him and mashed her lips to his. Her lips turned from blue to crimson, and for a second, she appeared human. When they moved apart, the blue tint returned.

"I can't believe I almost lost you. Don't ever do that to me again," he said. She nodded and pressed her face against him. He then took her by the hand, and the pair walked to the hospital. "No matter what happens we will stay together."

Chapter 45

Asunray warmed Cody's face and roused her from a deep sleep. She yawned and scratched her nose. For a moment, she wondered if it all had been a dream. Then she saw the white, antiseptic hospital room, sterile tiles, and blinking medical equipment. She drew up the clean white sheets and thick blankets. Sounds of the hospital penetrated her door, and the odor of disinfectant stung her nostrils.

Through the crevice between the door and frame, she saw the black shadow of feet as they passed through the golden light. She swung out her legs and stepped down into a pair of slippers. After putting on her robe, she walked toward the door. It opened before she could reach it.

"I see that you're awake." Doctor Morton slid his glasses up his nose and carried a chart in his other hand. "Have a seat, please. I would like to go over your findings."

A feeling of doom settled over Cody. She shuffled back to bed and took a seat. The doctor dragged over a chair and sat down before her. He flipped through the patient charts and notes, often pushing a pair of black-rimmed glasses up his thin nose. After reading in silence, he said, "You have a high level of amphetamines and psychotropic drugs in your system." He closed the chart, and his face lost all expression, a clinical look that only doctors present to patients. "Have you been using Monk's Root?"

"Well, yes. A veteran told me it would give me energy. It really helped on the march to Bendalli Pass," Cody replied. "But that much —"

"I'm sure," he said, cutting her off. "Everyone thinks they are the exception to the rule. Amphetamines are a double-edged sword: they borrow tomorrow's energy for today's use – the problem is that the bill always comes due. The longer one uses the drug, the worse the effect.

You had ten times the allowable levels in your system. It's wonder you didn't have hallucinations or go into convulsions. Just a little bit more of the drug and your heart would have stopped. If you weren't a morph, it would have arrested a month ago."

Cody searched her mind. She used the drug, but that was only on a few occasions. "I don't understand," she replied. "How could it still be in my system?"

The doctor sighed and rubbed his stubble covered chin. All drug addicts deny their habit; he wished one, just one, would admit it and come clean. They all denied it until faced with absolute proof. By then their careers and lives were a shambles, friendships destroyed and vocational ambitions derailed. But there was a slim possibility that she was telling the truth.

He removed his glasses and cleaned them. "It's possible … just possible that your body stored the drug. Morphs aren't like the rest of us. Your body has reserves other than fat. It can store antibiotics and anesthetics and use them when needed. However, even a body as amazing as yours has limits." It was then that she noticed her reflection in the glass. The night in a warm bed made her appear human. He retrieved two containers of pills out of his jacket pocket. "I have a couple of prescriptions for you, Xiomin and Clemndia. They will cleanse your system and put your feet on solid ground again."

A knock came from the hospital room door. "Come in," Cody called out. The door opened. Kelvin ducked into the room and stood near the door, fearful the staff would eject him at any moment. "They said she could have visitors. I've been waiting for hours."

"We're almost done," Doc Morton said.

Kelvin lumbered across the room, his body covered in heavy plate armor and leather. He appeared to have emptied the armory, a broadsword strapped to his right hip, two swords strapped to his back, multiple daggers and knives, throwing bullets, and even a pair of battle axes. He removed some of his gear as a grudging acquiescence to hospital policy, his steel helmet under his left arm and a shield strapped to his back, making him appear like a turtle, a turtle ready for combat. His hobnail boots clacked as he crossed the tiled floor, but the rubber studs provided sure grip on hard surfaces.

The doctor once again pushed his glasses up the bridge of his nose and cleared his throat. The giant of a man appeared to be a different species, a throwback to prehistoric times. "Yes, I suppose we are done." He slipped the two bottles of pills back into his jacket pocket. "You can pick these up later. They may make you drowsy. Pick them up from the pharmacy."

Kelvin held out a black duffle bag. "I brought you some clothes. I wasn't sure what you should wear. So I bought your new uniforms." He twitched his nose and sniffed. "Hospitals smell weird."

"They think I have some issues with post-traumatic stress made worse by drugs," she said. "My weird body stores up drugs like a squirrel stores acorns. The psychiatrist told me that, 'All the veterans know that post action recovery is an imperative. They deal with their issues in less formally structured groups, but they do deal with them.' He wanted the pledges to learn some mental coping skills from them. He assigned me to a recovery group. I feel like a mental patient."

"You need to get dressed for duty," Kelvin said and dodged the entire subject.

"Does that mean I'm going to rejoin the platoon?" asked Cody.

"Yes it does," the Kelvin said with a grin.

"YES!"

"They assigned you to light duty for the next week," he said.

"I'll get dressed right now." Cody stripped off her hospital gown and wore only a pair of white satin panties. Whether on Earth or Eden, hospital gowns were uncomfortable and awkward, and people hated to wear them. "Did you get in trouble because of me?"

"I'd like to say no, but the answer is yes. I'm responsible for everyone in my training unit. Marla said, 'If you are going to lead a group of warriors, you have to know how to spot mental and physical illness.' I suppose she's right. I had no idea that you were using Monk's Root. I almost got you killed."

"It wasn't your fault. It was six months ago. I thought I was safe. It's not fair." She set aside the top and stared at the floor. "I'll go and talk with them. You're a good sergeant. You shouldn't be punished because of me."

"It is my fault. The health and safety of the warriors underneath my command are my responsibility. I told them that it should be me who gets punished, no one else, and they agreed," Kelvin said.

"What did they do?" asked Cody.

"They promoted me. I am a Warrior First Class, a second lieutenant. Okay, Marla did give me 10 demerits and signed me up for a bunch of courses, but they promoted me anyway. It's all really confusing. I guess they appreciated how I handled the situation. Anyway, I'm now in charge of 4th platoon, assigned to the 2nd Death Dealer Battalion – Eagle Company," Kelvin said.

"That's wonderful," Cody said and beamed with joy. She threw her arms around Kelvin's great bulk and hugged him. Still clad in his armor, it was like hugging a steel statue. "I knew you could do it."

"I guess, but I never pictured myself as an officer. I always pictured myself rising up to a battalion sergeant. Still, I do get to wear my rampart armor, and I did jump ahead to a class 1. Classes 2 and 3 are reserved for

The Great Gate

advanced degree university graduates. They know how to command but not to fight. If you ask me, it is a dangerous combination."

Cody could not contain herself. She jumped a little and clapped her hands. Kelvin set down a duffle bag on her bed and unzipped it. Cody drew out a crimson metallic top. It confused her. The duty uniform for the Death Dealers was black with a crimson tunic. Then she saw the insignias on the banded collar. "This is Valkyrie."

"That's the other news. Command assigned you to Valkyrie, Special Operations. You'll still be assigned to my platoon but serving in intelligence gathering operations. They think it will suit you. I guess they are right. You always have been fast and sneaky."

"After they talked to the doctor, my dad said something about having a better support structure and training. Anyway, he said it was a promotion of sorts." He glanced out at the rising sun. "You need to get dressed. You'll be meeting with other the Valkyries."

"Okay," Cody said with a nod. She stood to her feet and rummaged around in the duffle bag. She pulled out a black satin thong and a matching bra. She then carried the duffle bag into the bathroom. "I'll be out in a couple of minutes."

She stepped into the thong and whisked them up her legs. She wrinkled her nose when the string nestled into place. She never much cared for thongs; they felt weird. After putting on her bra and adjusting her breasts in the cups, she stepped into the black leather slacks. The elastic garment was buttery soft and molded to her body, gleaming as if someone dipped her in liquid black. Likewise, the top seemed cleaved to her arms, torso, and breasts as if shrunk wrapped. It would take a little getting used to.

Kelvin wandered about the room, stared out the windows, grew bored, began to pace, grew tired of pacing, and returned to the window. Fat, wet snowflakes plummeted toward the ground and hit with a splat. The skies turned dark gray and cut off all trace of the sun, turning the slush to ice.

456

He wondered if he was command material. It was more than just failing to detect Cody's addiction; she seemed normal to him – how could he miss it? Command responsibility meant sending warriors to their death, yet losing Cody was beyond what he could endure. Every time he closed his eyes, he saw her standing on the wall and staring down into the abyss. He almost lost her, and he was not sure if he could take that. It left him shaken, and the entire world went out of focus.

The door opened behind him. Cody smoothed the material over her bottom, picking at the taut material, cleaving like a second skin; she screwed up her face saying, "Their duty uniforms are really ... body conforming ... and shiny. It feels like they are painted on me." The crimson top gleamed as if made of liquid metal and adhered to her as if wet.

She approached him and wrapped a black leather cincher around her waist. The many silver buckles in front proved a bit time-consuming. She slipped her arms into the sleeves of a black leather jacket, tugged on the lapels, but left it unzipped. "I've never been so conscious of my body. Apparently, everyone wants to see it."

"Well, you do have a great body," he replied

She ignored him since he meant it as a compliment. "Can you lace up my cincher?" asked Cody and lifted up the back of her jacket. His meaty hands grabbed the laces and pulled. The cincher constricted and compressed Cody's waist. "This thing is tight," she complained. "Why do the Valkyrie wear these things."

"It's tradition," he replied. "The first Valkyrie had no uniforms. They had to wear men's clothing, which included oversized tunics, and so they used cinchers to keep their tunics tight around their abdomens."

Cody glided her hands over her thighs and around her bottom. "These slacks are anything but loose." She fidgeted, unsuccessfully trying to loosen the garments. "I guess I'll have to get used to it. What is the dress uniform like?"

"That depends on whether you are designated as engagement, support, officer, enlisted, dominant, submissive, vamon, or Elite," he said.

"Dominant or submissive?" asked Cody.

"The Valkyrie served alongside men, but they are all female. If two of them are in a relationship, one is the dominant and the other submissive. It is kind of like the husband and the wife. It's a duty marriage, the submissive is vamon to the dominant."

"I had no idea, so many of them were like that." She winced and wrung her hands. "I'm not interested in girls."

"Most of them sleep with men, but they also enjoy female companionship. It's not required though. Just tell them you're not interested." He lumbered around her and picked up her duffle bag. "Oh, and stay away from the spiced wine. My dad told me about that one. It has some herbs that get girls all worked up if you know what I mean. Some of the male and female veterans use it to seduce the recruits."

All the girls in boarding school whispered about the Valkyrie. Some of the veterans would go to extremes to bed a girl. Kelvin knew all of Cody's expressions, and he said, "Calm down. They are not going to rape you: they are some of the most honorable warriors in our guild. Just say no! And be firm."

She nodded and breathed. "You're right. I'm worrying about nothing. Plenty of the girls at our school had boyfriends and girlfriends. Some had both at the same time."

"Yeah well, like I said, 'Stay away from the spiced wine.'"

They exited the bedroom and found the nearest stairwell. The white, antiseptic corridor gave way to dark stone. Kelvin held the door open to the stairwell door and let her pass him. The dim glow of a light cast long shadows on the stone stairs. After a brief visit to the pharmacy, they left the clean, bright hospital and emerged into the dank stairwell, feeling as if they entered another world, submerging into the depths of Eden.

Cody hurried down the stairs and jumped down the last step with girlish enthusiasm. She put her hands on her hips and turned her right leg to the side. "These boots are comfortable." The boots certainly had sculpted lines and a heel that melded comfort with fashion; the patent leather material blended seamlessly to her slacks and made them appear as one garment. "What do you think?"

"I like them. I can't wait to see what other clothes they have. I bet they have a lot of different dress uniforms since all of them are girls." She turned and walked away without waiting for a reply.

Every man in the fortress will try and seduce her.

"What did you say?" she asked and looked back at him.

He thought it but never voiced it. "Nothing, I was just thinking how much I liked your uniform." He hurried up to her side and walked next to her. "You know what? We should go to the entertainment complex tomorrow night. We need to have some fun."

She looked at him out of the corners of her eye, gazing at him in a way that only a woman can. "That sounds fun. We could go dancing." Dancing, of course, was a test. Kelvin hated to dance, and she knew it. He reminded everyone of a tree swaying, ready to fall, and the other dancers gave him plenty of clearance, not wishing him to topple over on them. If this was a date, and if he was serious about their relations, and not just two friends going out on a lark, he would say, "Yes."

"I suppose that would be fun," Kelvin said. What he pictured in his mind was stomping around the dance floor as though putting out fires or killing rats. Seeking to minimize the humiliation, he added, "Then we can take in a show at the theater. I hear they are performing a new comedy."

She grabbed his arm and gave it a squeeze. "Great! I have just the dress in mind. It's perfect. It is made of gold silk and has a very short skirt. I can wear my matching shoes with it."

A series of underground tunnels connected most of the buildings. They were dark, glistening, and smelled of mold, but they were below the permafrost, well out of the bitter cold. Water dripped from the ceiling, splashed onto the floor, gathered into channels, and flowed into gray water cisterns. It flowed through a series of sewers and dumped over the ledge, freezing before it hit the ground, raining down icy shards.

They passed through connecting tunnels and arrived at the Valkyrie barracks. "Here you go," he said handing her the bag. "You'll be barracked with them during your training but on maneuvers with us. I'll meet with you and your squad leader this afternoon."

When Kelvin bent over toward her, Cody started to take a step back. His powerful right arm circled around her waist and brought her to a sudden halt, then sweeping her back toward him. Her eyes closed when his face moved toward hers; and their lips met, causing a rush through her body. Her mind vapid, heart pounding, and blood coursing – she rose up to her toes and pressed into him; arms wrapped around his thick neck, she surrendered to him and mashed her lips to his. When his right hand grabbed her, a surge rushed through her and stole away her breath.

A chorus of heavy footfalls echoed off the stone tunnel, and Kelvin released her, letting her descend to her feet. Their lips lingered for a moment, unwilling to part and then separated. Her blue eyes gazed at him with adoration, and her soul sang with joy. "So you do like my boots?" Cody asked with a giggle.

"And everything else," he replied. He gave Cody a last quick peck and a squeeze. "I'll see you later." He turned and walked away. His heart urged him to rush back into her arms and never release her. Sheer strength of will propelled his steps and forced him to part from her.

Cody watched Kelvin lumber away. The urge to jump and shout "YES!" exploded within her. Once out of his view, within the dark stairwell, she did just that. She danced about and pumped her arms in the air. The steps grew close and forced her to hide her joy. She charged up the stairs feeling as though she won a great battle.

By the time she reached the eighth floor, anxiety had replaced joy and fear crept back into her consciousness. Who were the girls in her platoon? Would they like her? Would she like them? Did she know them?

She wandered through the hallway, reading the brass numbers above the doors until she found the correct barracks. When she pushed open the door, she saw a group of women, some sitting on sofas and chairs, quite a few sitting on the floor around a fire pit, a flicking glow making them appear ghostly and ominous.

A thin blonde clad in a slip-suit approached. "Hello, I'm First Lieutenant Gwen Cross. How can I help you?" She wore the choker necklace of an Elite Valkyrie, an Immortal.

"I'm Cody. I was assigned to this barracks," she said.

"I was told that you would be arriving. Let me show you to your bunk." Cody struggled to keep up with Gwen. The light flashed off her uniform as she strode through a narrow corridor, wide enough for only one person, suffocating and tall. She made a quick left, strode through a short corridor, and entered a long rectangular room with tall ceilings that disappeared into the darkness. The bunks were stacked four high in five rows. Each bunk had a single footlocker and a small rod to hang up clothes. "Pledges get the top bunks. The veterans get the bottom. A word of advice: pee before you go to bed. You don't want to wake up a veteran. They've been known to make pledges with bladder control issues spend the night on their feet."

Cody followed Gwen to the far left corner. "I'm the company warrant officer for this company of Valkyrie. If you have any problems, see me." She pointed up at the top bunk. "That's your rack."

"We sit together as a unit during all meals, and you are expected to participate in all unit activities. No excuses. The Elite Valkyries have separate facilities and formations. Any questions?"

Cody blurted, "I prefer men." She cocked her head and added, "It's not that there is anything wrong with girls. It's just not for me."

"Acknowledged," Gwen said and stiffened. "I know about the rumors. Civilians whisper that we are all 'sex-crazed degenerates.' It's not true. Most Valkyries have families: partners and children waiting for them. Although they don't look it, some of these warriors are old enough to be your grandmother. They take care of young warriors. As to sex, you are free to enjoy the company of another woman or a man if you wish. If you wish for them to leave you alone, say 'no' and everything stops. That said: some warriors are eager for a duty wife, so they may try to romance you. I can't stop people from being nice to you or giving you gifts; that kind of problem is up to you. The senior warriors can be a great source of help where this is concerned. Are we clear?"

"Yes, Mistress," Cody said in a quiet voice.

"Get your gear stowed away. Command sent over your armor on ahead of you. But we will be in training seminars for the next three days, so wear our duty uniform, and we will sit together at all conferences. The first meeting is in two hours, so you have plenty of time to store your gear." Gwen strode away, and the darkness engulfed her.

Chapter 46

"Hello, I'm Kira Lyra, your platoon sergeant, and orientation supervisor."

Cody spun around and blurted, "I like boys."

"I like boys … and girls," Kira replied, a bit uncertain as to the topic. "Why don't you like girls? Did your mother beat you?"

"No. My mom did not beat me … sergeant. I only meant to say that I only am interested in sleeping with boys," Cody replied. "Not that there is anything wrong with girls."

"So you had a bad experience with a woman. A friend of mine went through a bad breakup. She swore off girls, but she met someone who made her happy —"

"I didn't have a bad breakup," Cody interrupted. "I've never … you know … been with a girl."

Kira cocked her head and furrowed her brow. "Then how would you know you don't like being with a girl? You should try it at least once."

The question took Cody by surprise, which caused her mind a blank, and she had no real reply. She spent four long years in school belonging to the Black Dragon House. Males comprised most of those who joined the guild. As a result, she had very few girlfriends. "Well, I guess I don't really know what it would be like. I suppose it must be okay, but I have always wanted to marry a boy."

"Why?" asked Kira.

"'Why' what?" echoed Cody.

"Why marry all boys? You're allowed up to four spouses if you're dominant. Will they all be men? The only reason I ask is that men can get possessive. Some men don't want to share their wife with other men, but they will share her with another woman. My father has four wives, and Adeline is my birth mother. Technically, she is married to two females and my dad. It's kind of confusing, admittedly. You should see the house around the holidays, all of the children and grandchildren crowded into a small home. We get along, most of the time. Sometimes momma Nina can be a bit selfish. That always upset momma Marie and my mom. But they still love her."

"Your mother has sex with all of them?" asked Cody.

Kira snarled. "I don't know – and I don't want to know. I know she had sex with my father, but I don't want to know the details."

"I guess you have a point." Cody snorted and crossed her arms. "If I don't find someone soon, or if I'm not exempted because of enlisted status, my mother is going to make me marry Conrad Peat. He just finished prelaw, and he is on his way to law school. His family owns a lot of land back in our hometown. The man is relentless. I'm sure he doesn't love me: I think he's looking for a trophy wife."

"Why would you be a trophy wife? I mean, you are beautiful, and you have a great body; but there are a lot of available women," asked Kira.

"I'm a morph. When I get older, I'm supposed to be able to reshape my body, you know, my hair, my eyes, my skin color and my other part," Cody whispered. "Men have a lot of fantasies about that kind of thing."

"That's great," Kira said. "I wish I could do that." Kira tossed her chestnut brown locks over her shoulder and crossed her arms. "I joined the Corps when I was seventeen. I attended the Black Dragon Boarding School, and then I pledged when I turned 21. I never gave marriage a second thought or girls a second thought."

"My boyfriend Tory and I joined on the buddy plan for the Praetorian Guard. He had it all planned out: after he became an officer, we would marry. I loved him so much," she sighed. "We were recruits in the same company, and we even served in the same platoon. We did everything together, and I was sure he was the one, and I was going to get my happy ending – then he broke up with me and proposed to someone else. A month later, they left the Corps and returned home to get married. I was devastated."

Cody cocked her head and studied Kira's choker necklace, which designated her as vamon to an Elite Valkyrie. She had never seen Valkyrie necklace up close. It included a discreet and swinging D-ring, held by a clip on the right side of the oval crest. In addition to the D-ring, it included a special mark that designated her as Vamon. "You're a Valkyrie and a vamon?"

Kira crossed her arms and legs. She averted her gaze and stared at the fire burning in the hearth. "I was assigned as adjutant for Major Claudia Turner. It was wonderful serving with her. We came to know each other over the next year. Then one night she invited me to her quarters for supper. After dinner, she and I … well, it was my first time with a girl. A month later, we moved in together, and six months later, she took me as her duty wife, her vamon. It's not the same thing as regular marriage: I'm still a Valkyrie, but I'm bound to her. We share the same quarters, and I take care of her." Kira's hand circled around her neck and fluttered around her choker. "Being a vamon means that I clean her clothes, cook for her, and … well, I take care of her."

"Claudia and I really love each other. I'm sorry to hear that your mother might force you to marry someone," Kira said. "Being a vamon is better than I thought it would be. Claudia takes good care of me. Many of the Elite Valkyrie officers are looking for duty wives. I could arrange for an introduction if you are interested. You would automatically be accepted into the Valkyrie, and your mother would have no voice in your future."

"No thanks," Cody replied. "But I may not have an option about getting married. Conrad already has the wedding planned, and he asked for my measurements. Conrad's father is going through the process of becoming a lesser noble with standing above that of my family. Once that happens, I'll have to marry him, unless I'm inducted into the Valkyrie."

"Like I said, he may not get the chance. Many of the veterans will try to seduce you. They can be very persuasive if you know what I mean." Kira's hand returned to her throat and circled it.

"I kind of have a boyfriend here," Cody said. "His name is Kelvin Faroe. I've known him ever since I was a little girl. We broke up for a while, but I think we are getting back together again," she said with a girlish smile.

"Kelvin? Are we talking about the same person? Our platoon commander?" asked Kira.

"Yes. Why?" asked Cody.

"Crystal rrreeeaaalllllllyyy wants him. She keeps showing up at his room and sitting by him in the great hall. I saw her getting awful friendly with him just last night," Kira said.

Cody's face grew red, and she said, "I can't believe it. He slept with her ... again?"

"I don't know. They went off together, but I have no idea what they did. I do know that Crystal wants him, and that she will do anything to get him."

"I hate her," Cody huffed. She crossed her arms and pouted. "What does he need her for?"

Kira said, "Tory loved me, but he couldn't keep his hands off other girls. He cheated on me all the time. Does that sound familiar?"

"No." A moment later, Cody said with a lament, "Yes." Kira sat on the bed next to Cody and crossed her legs. Cody sat down and slouched. "It sounds just like Kelvin. We dated all during our academy days – girls kept throwing themselves at him: I hated it!" She showed him Kelvin's photo. "Whatever happened to Tory?" asked Cody. "Did he get married?"

"Funny story about that," Kira said with a smirk. "I heard about what happened to Tory through a friend. Tory and Melanie set sail for the western aisles. They stopped at Dalton's Cove, on the Cardiff Isle. All of the ladies went on shore to shop, and all the men stayed on the boat. A sudden squall hit the island and drove the ship into the southern seas. They ran aground in the De Garcia island chain. There were 68 men in the isle and no women …."

"You're kidding," Cody gasped.

"Oh yes," Kira said. "Tory transformed into a girl, an exquisite girl with long blonde hair and blue eyes. The captain was of a lesser noble family."

"No," Cody gasped.

"Oh yes. He forced her to marry him. When a ship finally rescued them, she had given birth to three babies. Their supply of blue was lost in the shipwreck." Kira wrinkled her nose and giggled.

"I can't believe it," Cody said and covered her mouth as she laughed.

"I saw Tory last year, and she introduced me to her three little girls. Anyway, I'm not sure what my point is: I suppose that it's just that life never turns out like you expect." Kira stood to her feet. "We need to get back to your training. You need more than one duty and dress uniform. In addition, the Valkyrie use custom designed armor. I think it looks better than the Praetorian Guard equipment. I'll get it for you from the equipment room."

"Think about what we talked about. The heart can love as many people as it wishes." She turned and walked away. "Be right back."

As Cody watched Kira walk away, she tried to imagine kissing another woman. The idea seemed peculiar. As time passed, she began to pace and looked around. The bottom rack had extra locker space. She bent over at the hips and placed her hands on her knees. The locker had small drawers that would be perfect for her jewelry and cosmetics, but senior warriors used the bottom bunks.

Cody felt the weight of someone's stare. When she looked around her right thigh, she noticed a handsome man, almost elvish in appearance leering at her. Cody sprang up and spun around. She thumped her right fist to her chest and stood at attention.

"I am Alexander Carlos Garcia Vargas de Nuevo Seville, and I am responsible for all wizards for the Black Dragon Guild. I am training officer for this company." He began to stroll around Cody, while Cody remained at attention, hands pressed to her sides, back straight. "The bottom racks are reserved for veterans. It would take decades for you to earn that rack." He lingered behind Cody and surveyed the girl's bottom. "But there are other possibilities." He moved around to Cody's right side and studied her profile. "Yes, it's decided. You'll be my adjutant."

Alexander crossed his arms and tapped his chin with his index finger. "Yes, I think we will get along together." Cody noticed Alexander's signet ring. The crest of the Spanish Royal Court indicated that he was a lesser noble and could compel Cody to marry him. She wanted to reply, but she was still at attention. Gather your gear and report to my quarter in the officer's barracks."

Cody watched Alexander stride away and disappear into the shadows. Only then did she sigh and slouch. She wrung her hands and began to fret. She began to pace and tried to think of a way out of this predicament. Then she remembered Kira: perhaps she could help.

It sure is taking a long time. Cody rose to her feet and crossed her arms. She tilted her head back and gazed up at the top bunk. It was twice her height, almost to the ceiling. Rails on the side of the bed prevented the girls from rolling out during their sleep. Gwen was right about peeing before she went to bed.

Gwen happened to pass by Cody. "Excuse me, Mistress," Cody said. "Kira went to get me some equipment and uniforms from storage. That was a long time ago. Is there some sort of problem?"

"Ah … I'm not sure," Gwen replied. "The storage room is just across the chamber." Cody followed Gwen across the barracks and around several racks. The storage room door was ajar, and light beamed out through the crevice. "Kira?" called Gwen. She pushed open the door and saw gray metal racks filled with equipment. A pile of uniforms lay on the floor as if dropped by someone. A well-worn booklet, a new recruit's guide, lay a short distance away.

Gwen drew a dagger out from behind her back. She passed by four rows of racks, the fifth being against the far wall. Equipment filled the rows and nothing else; the room was clear. She scanned the ceiling and then stored equipment. "What's this?" asked Cody. Gwen turned and saw Cody squatting down behind her. "It looks like blood."

A drop of blood, the size of a fat raindrop, lay on the wooden floor in the middle of the aisle. Gwen ran her index finger through it and rubbed it between her fingers. "It's fresh." A thin layer of dust covered the shelves around her, the contents undisturbed for a long time. Then she saw an access panel located in the corner behind Cody.

Gwen inspected the panel. The slightest touch of her index finger caused the metal panel to fall into the service duct with a noisy clatter. The Valkyrie peered into the dark service conduit, knife poised for self-defense. Bloody smears replaced the dust and lead into darkness. "Summon the guard. Quick!"

Cody sprang to her feet and sprinted through the facility. She found a pair of warriors stationed in the outer hallway. "Gwen needs you in the equipment room. Hurry!" The Valkyrie guards charged past her and through the barracks. The lounging Valkyrie rose to their feet, curious as to the cause of the alarm.

When they reached Gwen, she said, "One of our sisters is missing. I want a full search of the facility and the connecting service tunnels."

Chapter 47

S abrina had a problem. The Winter Pass Fortress required a new commander, but who to appoint? There were many candidates, some better and some worse, and many political appointees: each one thought that he or she deserved the promotion, and each one would protest if not selected. Sabrina proclaimed her independence from politics and stated, "I will appoint the best candidate, based on merit alone." However, the various considerations pressed in on her and troubled her.

She spent the night without sleep, examining and re-examining each candidate's qualities. She prioritized and sorted the resumes; then she shuffled them again and reprioritized. When morning arrived, Sabrina was no closer to a decision than when she started, and the decision hour was upon her. She combed her fingers through her hair and sighed. No clear decision presented itself.

Karalynn yawned and stretched, entering the kitchen, looking to start her preparations for the day. Documents, photos, and lists covered every surface. If she approached a pile, Sabrina barked at her saying, "Leave it alone. I don't want my work being scattered."

Karalynn sat cattycorner to Sabrina, trying not to disturb any of the towering piles. She combed a blonde tress behind her right ear, crossed her legs, and tugged on the hem of her silk nightgown. "How is it going?"

Aggravation twisted Sabrina's face. She mumbled a rude reply and continued reading. She read the same page, shifted it to another pile, and shifted it back a minute later. A timid hand entered her field of vision and ever so cautiously touched her right arm. "You need a break from all this. You're too focused. You can't see clearly anymore; you need time and distance."

The Great Gate

"But I don't have —"

"But you need to. You're an Overlord and head of the Black Dragon Guild. They will wait." Karalynn clasped Sabrina's hands and helped her rise from the uncomfortable, L-shaped wooden chair. Aches and spasms recoiled through Sabrina's back. "Here, let me." Karalynn pushed on Sabrina's back and had her bend over the table, Sabrina's palms resting on the flat surface. She began to knead and stroke her back. "You're so tense. Your back is as tight as a piano string."

When Sabrina turned around, they locked eyes for a moment. When Karalynn bowed her head, Sabrina used her index finger to raise Karalynn's chin. She drew the lovely elva into her arms and kissed.

Sabrina drew her lips away and whispered, "Dragor."

"What was that? What's the matter?" Karalynn cocked her head and studied her lover's face.

"Dragor is the right candidate; he's not the perfect candidate, but he will do right by the posting if we structure it correctly," Sabrina said.

"What are you doing?" asked Abby, yawning and rubbing her eyes.

Karalynn tilted her head back and gazed upside down at the girl. "Mistress Sabrina and I were wrestling. She won."

"Oh," Abby said with a nod. She entered the kitchen with Angelina leading little Eliza. The girls uneasily stepped on the papers, as if made of glass that would break under their feet. "The floor is messy."

"You're right," Karalynn said, moving out from underneath Sabrina. She gave Sabrina a quick kiss. "We can finish our wrestling match tonight after the girls go to bed." As Sabrina exited the room, she heard Karalynn say to the girls, "Let's pick up all these papers and make it neat."

After closing the bedroom door, Sabrina sat on her bed and worked her slip-suit up her legs; little by little, she sheathed in glossy black PSM. She stood upright and continued working the garment over her hips, situating the body conforming fabric into every nook and cranny. After stuffing her arms into the sleeves, she drew it up and around her neck.

The door opened, and Marla entered. "Have you settled on a final candidate," she asked, trying to pretend that Karalynn had not already informed her. She picked up the leather harness and carried over to Sabrina, then sliding it up Sabrina's arms, and she added, "It's a critical posting."

Sabrina secured the hooks and situated her breasts through the teardrop neckline, circling underneath them. "You're correct. It is essential." Looking over her shoulder, she said to Marla, "Lace me up please."

"Yes, Mistress." Marla placed her knee on the small of Sabrina's back, grabbed the laces, and pulled – the leather garment sculpting Sabrina's hourglass figure. "So have you … made a decision, that is?" asked Marla, wounded that Sabrina had not chosen to share the secret with her.

After tying the laces, Sabrina raised an eyebrow toward Marla, and then she grabbed her boots. She slipped her right leg down the boot's throat, and it extended all the way to the top of her thigh. After the second boot had sheathed her left leg, she laced the boots, covered the laces with a flap, and cinched tight the straps around her thighs. Marla watched this common task with a deep pout on her face, her eyes glassy, and her head bowed.

"Dragor is my choice," Sabrina said.

A smile brightened Marla's face. "He's an excellent warrior. He has served our house with honor for many centuries."

"I'm glad you approve," Sabrina said, situating the crotch strap, and inserting the tab into the T-back slot, a click coming from the lock. She squatted a bit and tugged on the flesh of her inner thighs, situating the protecting V-panel for comfort.

Marla carried over the cuirass and chainmail tunic. The chainmail fabric was stronger than steel but light as a feather. After helping Sabrina slide her arms through the long sleeves, she held the cuirass Sabrina's head and carefully lowered it. Sabrina flicked her hair free and held up her arms; after connecting the cuirass to the vest, Marla closed and locked it. Sabrina asked, "Have you taken a lover yet? Many men would welcome the chance to share your bed."

Marla's cheeks grew rosy, and she said, "No, there are lots of wonderful men, but I always feel strange since I have authority over them."

"There are tradesmen and adjunct personnel within our fortress. Surely one of them has the ability to satisfy you," Sabrina said, donning her pauldrons, outer herringbone linked arm-plates, and gauntlets. Marla squatted before Sabrina, strapped on her Mistress's greaves and ignored her question. "Very well, keep your secret, but I will worm it out of you."

"I don't know what you're talking about," Marla said. She rose and retrieved Sabrina's weapons. "I'm dedicated to serving you."

"And your service is appreciated," Sabrina said, "but I know you favor someone."

After Sabrina dressed, the pair exited the bedroom. Angelina sprinted over to Sabrina and leap into her arms; Sabrina swung the girl in a circle and then kissed her cheek, making the girl squirm and giggle. "You are getting so big. Before you know it, you'll be all grown up and looking for a husband."

"I've already found one," Angelina said innocent enthusiasm. "Thomas Quimsby and I cut the passion fruit, and Carrie read the core. The core indicated that we would marry. He's my true love."

"Oh … um … that's wonderful. Shall we start planning the wedding?" asked Sabrina. Angelina opened her wedding journal. Sabrina took the book and leafed through it. "I see. Yes. This is very detailed." There were drawings of the church, the reception, and the wedding dance. "You even designed your own wedding gown. This Thomas sounds like a very lucky boy."

"I see you've been informed of the coming wedding." Karalynn entered the room and took the girl by the hand. "You need to eat breakfast and then get dressed for the day."

"But mommy, I have more work to do on my wedding," Angelina objected.

"You have another decade to plan it. Right now you need to eat." She dragged the girl into the kitchen, ignoring the girl objections and whines. Sabrina and Marla followed them into the kitchen.

Tormod sat at the kitchen table; he stabbed a forkful of pancake and egg, and then he dipped it all into syrup; and after stuffing it in his mouth, he said, "Good to see you finished dressing." He took a slurp of coffee and then wiped his mouth. Eliza sat next to him and squished pancake through her fingers. He cleaned her fingers and proceeded to feed her.

"What will you have?" Karalynn asked Sabrina.

"Just coffee," she replied. Karalynn put her hands on her hips and narrowed her eyes. "Fine," Sabrina relented. "Give me some pancakes."

Karalynn set a plate of food before Sabrina and Abby. "You need to keep up your strength." She licked her thumb and cleaned some jelly off Angelina's cheek; the girl squirmed and shrank like a turtle into its shell. When Karalynn returned from the stove, she set a heaping plate before Marla, overflowing with egg, sausage, bacon, pancakes, muffins, and hash browns.

Marla pouted and said, "I can't eat all this. I still have to fit into my maiden's belt. I'm going to get fat."

That was when Joash entered. "Mm, it smells wonderful. Do I still have time to get a plate?"

"Here, take mine," Marla jumped up and gave him her seat. The chair groaned as it struggled to support Joash's great bulk. He dug a fork into the pile and stuffed it into his mouth. "Cwaffee," he mumbled with a full mouth, and Tormod passed him the coffee pot. Joash poured a cup, steam rising from the black brew, and he gulped it down. "Ah … delicious."

Karalynn handed Marla a bran muffin. "This will keep you slim and regular." Marla's cheeks turned bright red, and she picked at the muffin, trying to ignore the reference to her bowel health. "Are you still having problems with constipation?" asked Karalynn. "I know how bound up you get. I think it's all the stress."

Marla shrank and said, "I'm all right."

"When was the last time you had a bowel movement," asked Karalynn. "You don't want to get hemorrhoids when you have to wear a maiden's belt. Your days of going on missions would be over before they really got started."

"She's right," Joash mumbled through a mouthful of food. "You should never neglect your health. You should go to the clinic and get a stool softener."

Marla twisted her nose to one side and turned in revulsion. "I said, 'I'm all right.' I've been doing better since I started eating more roughage." She set aside the half-eaten muffin and crossed her arms. "It's nice that everyone is so concerned about my bowel movements, but can we talk about something else?"

Billy and Tia arrived, pretending to be innocent but looking very guilty. The fae scurried over to a plate of sweet rolls and began picking at them, each nibble savored with happy purrs and a little dance. Between bites, they sipped on red berry fruit juice, which would have been appropriate for a hummingbird. Giggles and whispers erupted as the fae energized for the day. The three girls hadn't quite finished their breakfast when Billy and Tia decided playtime had begun. They ushered the giggling girls from the room, intent on having a grand adventure.

"We have to be going too," Sabrina said. "We have much to accomplish." When she arose, the others did too. Tormod swallowed the last gulp of coffee and wiped his lips.

Karalynn called out as they left saying, "I'll see you tonight at dinner."

As they exited the residence, Sabrina said, "We will stop by the clinic and get you a colonic. Good health is dependent upon a healthy colon …."

Chapter 48

D ragor was a short, thin man; his pinched face and his nose reminded one of a bird's beak. His combat skills were average, and most of his performance reviews ranked him as adequate. He was a good tactician, but he was a brilliant administrator, and more importantly, the troops respected him. He could organize any facility so that it operated with the efficiency of an ant colony."

He was surprised when Sabrina summoned him and even more so when she offered him command of The Winter Pass Fortress. She described the strategic importance of the facility – the fortress provided strategic support for the Fergal Pass and served as a waypoint for northern travelers on their way to Alkval – and the disarray left behind by his predecessor. He pondered the matter in silence, his hawk-like eyes fixed on flames dancing on the fireplace log, his mind sorting the relevant issues.

"It is a great challenge," Dragor said. "I have commanded warehouses and supervised logistical supply chains. However, the Winter Pass Fortress is of strategic value. It is centrally located between the Dwarves and the Elves. During the lesser months, a significant amount of commerce passes through its boundaries."

Sabrina took a seat and crossed her legs. "The operation of the fortress and the safeguarding of the civilian population would be yours. If some conflict arose, we would dispatch a commander to lead our troops into combat. Your roles would be complementary. Your chief function would still be that of logistical support and governmental coordination."

"Ah, I see. Yes, that does make sense. I've always felt that a man should know his limits and his best place of service." He slipped from his chair and dropped to one knee, holding out his weapon with both hands. With his head bowed, he said, "I do then pledge my service to The House of the Black Dragon as Master of Winter Pass Fortress."

She stood to her feet and took his sword from his hands. She touched it to each of his shoulders and passed it over his head. "I accept your pledge of service and appoint you commander over the Winter Pass Fortress and the surrounding territory. Arise, Protector of the Free Lands." When he arose, she returned his sword.

Those assembled congratulated him. They patted him on the back and shook his hand. Sabrina moved away and spoke softly to Marla saying, "Make preparations for our departure. We ride south toward the narrow pass to the city of Turin when the weather clears."

"The female warriors of the Praetorian Guard will be displeased to hear that. They only just arrived," Marla responded.

"Their pleasure is of little concern. What I desire is obedience," Sabrina said.

"Yes Overlord," Marla replied. "We still haven't located the missing warrior. The problem is that the service ducts and tunnels go on for miles. We are still operating under the assumption that Kira is missing and injured. But our hope grows thin with each passing hour. Claudia is beside herself with worry."

"Excuse Claudia from the mission and allow her to remain while the search continues; the permanently stationed troops can take up the task. We can't stay to solve this mystery," Sabrina replied.

"Yes, Mistress," Marla said. She moved through the crowded room, men and women still congratulating Dragor, sipping wine and eating hors d'oeuvres, and she had a quiet exchange with Joash. He nodded and departed with her. Sabrina then returned and congratulated Dragor.

There is but one true way to remove a bandage, swiftly. Marla marched into the great hall and climbed on top of a table. "Everybody pay attention. I have an announcement. The 7th Battle Regiment will depart Storm Mountain when the weather clears. Make all necessary preparations and be ready to deploy." A groan arose from many of the female warriors.

Marla climbed down from her perch, and Adrianna said, "It's been months since I've been with a man and slept in bed. Now we have to deploy when the weather changes? It's not fair."

"Enjoy both a man and a bed tonight. There is no time to waste," Marla responded.

"You Valkyrie have used up all the men. Look at them. They are all placid sheep, and I need a man."

Marla searched the room and saw many men lounging about. An unusually large man, a rampart warrior, chugged a tankard of ale and joked with his friends. She asked, "What's your name?"

"Gustavo," he replied with a Latin accent.

"I'm giving you an order. Throw her over your shoulder; carry her up to your room, and make love to her. Is that clear?"

"Yes, very clear," he replied.

"Hey!" Adrianna said, gaping in astonishment. Gustavo threw her over his shoulder, giving her bottom a loud slap, and she let out a girlish yelp. She hung down over his shoulder as he carried her from the hall.

"What are you men waiting for? These ladies need entertainment. Get busy, warriors." The men approached the women like an invading army. They broke off into pairs and hurried up to their rooms. Even the pledges helped out with the task and ran off with a girl.

"An impressive improvisation," Tormod said and puffed on his pipe. "I shall have to remember that. It will make an excellent story to tell around the hearth."

Marla flopped down on the sofa next to Tormod and Alexander. She groaned and ran her fingers through her blonde locks. "I know what they mean. I need to share my bed with someone."

"Don't look at me," said Joash as he crossed his legs. "I'm a married man, and I'm old. The only thing I think about these days is food."

"I'm married too," Tormod agree. "However, 823 years is not so old for a dwarf."

"I wish I had dwarven longevity." Joash swallowed a gulp of ale from his flagon.

"Perhaps you could concoct a potion for me?"

"If I could do that, I would retire a wealthy dwarf. Every magical bonus comes with a unique minus." Tormod puffed on his pipe and let the smoke sooth away his cares. "One never knows what it is, but one is certain not to like it."

Marla brooded about her lack of companionship and stared at the fire in the hearth. It had been a long time since she felt a lover between her thighs. She enjoyed a life of service and duty, but she needed passion. She longed for a lover.

Not every man ran off with a girl. Alexander lingered in the shadows, observing the actions of his northern comrades. He found their military approach to lovemaking peculiar, but the men of the north were as mysterious and cold minded as the glaciers they climbed.

It was then that Alexander caught sight of Cody, his new adjutant. Cody scurried down the steps and entered the hall. Her white and blue tinted locks cascaded over her shoulders and flowed down her back. The bounce in her step and the youthful innocence in her eyes appealed to him. When she neared the center of the hall, she looked about.

His eyes locked on Cody'. The light gleamed off the girl's curves. Cody was innocent, "cute as a button," naive, and had many suitors. In other words, she was irresistible.

Alexander arose and strolled across the room to her. When Cody saw him, she turned with a slight hop to him. She clasped her hands behind her back and asked with girlish innocence, "Where is everyone?"

"They … found partners and are sharing one another's bed," Alexander replied.

"Oh," Cody said with a shrug. "I was hoping we could play a game. I brought my falling tower game with me."

"I'm not doing anything. We could go up to my room and talk." Alexander shrugged and feigned innocence. "You are going to be my adjutant; you should see my quarters. You haven't seen them. Have you?"

"No, I'd love to see them," Cody replied. She looked about for the right door. "How do we get to it?"

"Right this way," Alexander said with a gesture. The pair weaved their way through the vast hall. "The officer's quarters are up those stairs." Cody seemed to bounce up the stairs ahead of Alexander: she was young, a Valkyrie candidate, and unclaimed. Cody had no way to know it, but she was Alexander's new project.

After they had scaled ten flights of stairs, they arrived at the officer's quarters. Unlike the enlisted warrior's barracks, it was well furnished and comfortable. Thick red pile carpeting covered the hallway floor, brass lights illuminated tan walls, and cherry wood doors passed on their right and left. The sweet smell of incense hung in the air, having escaped from a private chapel.

"I'm in one of the grand suites down to the left." Cody almost seemed to run she was so excited, but Alexander lingered behind, consumed with making love to her. "It's 522, down at the corner." Cody jumped to the side, stood up straight, and clasped her hands before her. When Alex unlocked the door, Cody waited for an invitation. "Come right on in." Cody scrunched up her nose and smiled. Alexander smiled but with a far different intent. After Cody had entered, Alexander closed and locked the door.

Cody marveled at the opulence. Two story windows, red walls between, towered to her right; a staircase led up to the second floor to her right. Plush loveseats, sofas, and chairs lay atop a handcrafted area rug; and the expansive bed sat on a dais in the back half of the room. There was even a small dining area. The opulence was worthy of the best resorts.

"It's so big," Cody said. "The barracks is smaller than this and has 30 other girls in it." She rolled her eyes and huffed. "Paige uses up the hot water. Other people need to use it too."

"That's no problem here. Take a look." She followed him into the gilded bathroom of white and gold. A round, white marble tub, which was big enough for four people, sat in the center of the room. To the left, she saw a private commode and a bidet. A full shower was in the right corner of the chamber, and a massage table lay across the chamber.

"I never imagined," she gasped. "This is great," she squealed, jumped, and clapped. "I could get lost in here."

"Why don't we go back to the lounge and relax?" He touched the middle of the girl's back and guided her back to the bedroom. He led her to the sofa, and Cody sat with her hands clasped between her thighs. Alexander ignited a log in the fireplace and adjusted the flame.

"I thought we could have some spiced wine? Have you ever tried it?" asked Alexander.

"No. I don't think so," Cody replied. She recalled Kelvin's warnings but dismissed them; Alexander was a nice guy – he wouldn't do that sort of thing. "Normally, I don't drink spiced wine. They say it can do weird things to you."

"I drink it all the time. It's perfectly safe," Alex replied with a chuckle. He picked up a large glass decanter and two glasses, and after he had handed a glass to the girl, he filled them with rehearsed grace. "It makes you feel all warm … on the inside." What Alex left out was the aphrodisiac spices enhanced beverage.

Cody took a dainty sip and smiled. "It's wonderful." She took a larger sip and then a gulp. Alexander joined her and took a sip. "So tell me about yourself."

"Well, I grew up in a small town just west of Greenvale, in a small town by the name of Knob Oak. I have two older sisters and no brothers; my father died several years ago …."

Alexander refilled Cody's glass each time it emptied and listened with rapt interest. He rested his elbow on the sofa back, his chin upon his palm, and he crossed his legs while gazing into Cody's eyes, which reminded him of deep blue ice. Cody took another gulp of wine between breaths. "… My father wanted me to be a boy. Mom said he was so disappointed … I was supposed to marry this boy, but he changed into a girl. My mother was so angry. His family had money, a lot of it and …." Cody shivered a little and said, "Whew, I'm sweltering."

"I am also," Alexander agreed. "Let me help you off with that corset. I am told that those things are very uncomfortable. Turn around." Cody paused for a second and continued prattling on as he moved close. After loosening the laces, he then reached around to Cody's right side and released the hooks. "Here we go," he said and unwrapped the girl's waist.

He refilled Cody's glass as it emptied and took a large gulp of his own cup. Cody's cheeks grew rosy, and she combed her fingers through her locks. "This is excellent," she chirped. "I could drink this all night."

"Well, I … we were going to … um … put off getting engaged. I think … that …. I forgot what I was … Oh yes … he and I never," Cody began to grow hot. Her heart sped, and her throat became dry. This made her gulp down more wine. "I … did … I mean … we," Cody rambled.

Alexander bent his head, moved his lips to Cody, and gave it a tender kiss. The glass slipped from Cody's hand and dropped onto the throw rug. She gasped and closed her eyes. His kisses grew hungry, and he felt the girl's heart beat. Cody squirmed a little but then melted into Alexander's arms.

Chapter 49

The door to Alexander's suite opened a crack, and Cody peered through the opening. The hallway was quiet, and more importantly, it was empty. Cody hurried out the door in a half-dressed state and closed the door behind her with a soft click. She tugged up the waistband of her stretch slacks – the supple leather cleaved to her like a second skin – and then she reached behind her back and finding the laces, she began to pull, compressing the garment around her abdomen. The cincher grew tight with each pull and squeezed her abdomen. This prevented her leather slacks from slipping and supported her back.

She hurried through the hallway with swift, short steps. The clatter of dishes and din of conversations echoed up the stairway. She slowed as she drew near the bottom of the stairs. She took a deep breath and slowly exhaled. Taking calm, deliberate steps, she strolled toward the serving line and picked up a tray. Other girls began to line up behind her.

Cody turned and caught sight of April out of the corner of her eye. The two girls and nine others met when they were hiking patrol around the Winter Pass Fortress. The winter storms had finally broken, and the sun made the snow gleam. It all felt so much like a thrilling adventure she heard so much about when she was a girl.

"I didn't see you last night. Where were you?" asked April. "I thought we were going to play tower fall."

"Well, I … I spent the night talking with some of the other warriors. It got very late, and I slept in their room." She tried to ignore the loose feeling between her thighs. "What did you do?"

"Nothing much," April said. "A bunch of the girls was playing cards and making a lot of noise. I had to sleep in the great hall."

The pair set down their trays and slid them before the serving line. Cody selected hot cider, eggs, toast, and a single piece of sausage. April copied her and did the same. They chatted as the crossed the vast hall. Cody's mood began to lighten as the normalcy of the previous night began to fade. She decided to pretend that it never happened. If anyone asked, she was playing cards.

Alexander waved to her from across the dining hall, and her heart sank. April cocked her head and studied the officer seated around the table. Apparently, they wanted them both to come over. April had no idea why – but Cody knew why – and it twisted her stomach into a knot. Cody cringed and shrank down like a turtle, feeling like a condemned prisoner.

Alexander slid back an empty chair to her right; "I saved a seat for you."

"Thank you," Cody said with a quiet voice. She set down her tray and sat in the chair. April sat down to Cody's right, next to Kayla. Cody lost her appetite. She scanned the faces of the women and men seated around her. *Do they know what we did?* She nibbled on a piece of toast hoping that the answer was "no."

"I was just telling everyone that I've picked you to be my new adjutant." Alexander rested his elbow on the table and his chin upon her palm. He smiled and added, "As my adjutant, you will clean my room, cook for me when we are on maneuvers, clean and polish my armor, and do my laundry. Basically, you'll be doing all the little domestic chores for me. Of course, you will move into the service room which connects to my quarters."

"You can get started now." Alexander held his hands out on either side of the empty table before him. "You're required to go get my breakfast and clean up afterward."

"Now?" asked Cody and took another nibble.

"Yes, of course," Alex replied.

"Yes, Sir," she said. She rose up from the table and walked away with quick, mincing steps. All of them, except April, watched her walk away.

Kayla combed her fingers through her brunette locks and then leaned up on her elbow. "Why can't I find a girl like that? She's so cute it hurts." Alexander glanced over at April in silent answer to Kayla's question. Trimming the fat from her bacon consumed April. The girl's fiery red hair reached her collar, covered her ears, and a swath of freckles spread across her cheeks. Her sparkling green eyes complemented her adorable button nose. Pink lipstick covered her small, Cupid's bow lips. She was small framed and delicate, just the way the more warrior women preferred. "Say April, tell me all about yourself. Do you have a boyfriend back home?"

The girl cocked her head and paused from dissecting her bacon. "Yes. His name is Doug Capple. I wanted to get married, but he wasn't ready to settle down." She twitched her nose. "I guess I got angry with him, so I pledged with the Valkyrie …."

Kayla scrunched up her nose and smiled. "That was bad for him and good for us. Please continue."

Cody filled a tray with an assortment of food. She forgot to ask what Alexander wanted. When she carried it back, she asked, "Is this okay … Sir? I can get another plate if it's not."

"That is fine," he replied. Cody set down the tray before Alexander and slid up her chair. When she stabbed a bit of egg, something touched her left thigh. Fork and egg in poised in midair, she looked down and saw Alexander's hand on the top of left thigh. It moved up and down her leg in slow strokes. She stuffed the food into her mouth and chewed. Without looking down, her mind traced the movement of Alexander's hand. She took a gulp of coffee, burning her throat, and hurriedly ate her breakfast.

"I'm not sure that's the best tactic ...." Alexander said and leaned back. They chatted on about combat strategy for the upcoming maneuvers. Cody began to waggle her left thigh, hoping Alexander would take the hint and remove his hand. It worked, sort of. Her eyes went wide when his hand slid around her waist and caressed her bottom.

"... Say April, I have a bottle of spiced wine up in my room. Why don't we go up to it and chat?" asked Kayla. "We could get to know each other better."

"Okay," April chirped. Cody's lips parted, as if to say something to April, but she remained silent, not wishing to incur Kayla's wrath. She watched them rise up from the table and carried their trays over to the cleaning stations. Cody agonized over what to do. Was it her place to say something? Before she could take action, they were gone.

Do they know what we did? Of course, they know, she chided herself. *I'm such an idiot.*

Alexander removed his hand from around Cody's waist, and he gave the girl's thigh a pat. "We need to over your duties and responsibilities. We will go up to my quarters."

Chapter 50

I n the midst of their rapture, Cody heard Alexander say, "… I'm going to claim you." Her addled mind replayed the comment, trying to grasp the meaning. Now most men say, "I love you, or you are so beautiful," during sex. Alexander said, "You're mine."

Her passion evaporated, and pending doom replaced it. Alexander lay on top of her, exhausted and satiated. She stared at the ceiling, barely able to breathe, agonized over what to do. One question burned in her mind – "Do you love me?"

He rolled over to his side of the bed and sipped spiced wine. "Love is a hormonal response. I am of the royal family, and I am claiming you. In time, we may develop some warm feelings for one another, a sense of comfort and familiarity. Are you betrothed?"

As the saying goes in Asgard, "Lesser nobles are still nobles." By common law, a noble could claim a peasant as a spouse, if she had intimate relations with him or if he had a legal claim. There was only one way she could escape his proposal if she was betrothed – and she was not. The question hung in the air like the ring of a bell, she was afraid to speak or even look at him, and when the silence grew long, and when his patience began to grow thing, she said, "Well no. But …."

"Then the matter is settled."

He scrambled off the bed and entered a closet. Cody sat up and curled her legs beneath her. A dull hum reverberated in her ears as she struggled to comprehend the events that overtook her. He returned carrying an ornately carved wooden box. "Of course you would be a subordinate wife. I will marry a woman of noble standing, and you would be subject to her will. However, I think this will be a profitable union. You are a rare beauty, a morph; you will complement my power."

He crawled onto the bed and sat before her. Alexander opened the box and removed a subordinate ring. "You will, of course, wear my ring for the rest of your life."

He leaned in close and slipped the ring onto her finger. "With this ring and by this sealing, I take you as my wife." Cody winced and squeezed her eyes shut. Her ring finger burned as the ring fused to her flesh.

Cody's eyes welled up, and a tear trickled down her cheek. Her heart ached, and her mind became vapid as she gazed at the ring on her right hand. How she wished she said, "No," no to him, no to the wine, no to his kisses, and no to making love. Now his ring adorned her hand, his seal of ownership, a subordinate wife, his property. Her dreams, her future, were gone.

The Great Gate

Chapter 51

Only now did Cody start to suspect the implications and limitations that Alexander's ring imposed on her. When he bound her to himself, she immediately transferred from warrior status to that of vamon, a duty wife: duty wives lived to serve their Master or Mistress, and if requested, they bore their children. Precious few ever transitioned back from vamon status to that of a warrior, and most of those cases occurred posthumously for heroic acts.

Since Cody changed to permanent status, her duty period began. This changed her life forever. As Alexander's wife, Cody was obligated to a term of service for no less than 50 years. Furthermore, since Alexander, her master and spouse made all the decisions; Cody would be automatically re-enlisted unless her master deemed otherwise.

Vamon wore decidedly different uniforms, distinguishing them from dominant warriors. The implications of her new role started to dawn on her as she zipped up the navy blue skirt: only warriors wore slacks. The synthetic microfiber skirt was complimentary to her figure, having a satin-like sheen and texture, and it was stain resistant, a useful attribute when cleaning; and its elasticity allowed for ease of movement.

Cody studied her reflection in the mirror. She drew a wrinkle out of her silk half-slip and tugged at the hem of her skirt, well above the knee, and made sure there were no wrinkles in her stocking. Her eyes traced the golden ring around her throat; and her fingers glided over the back of the skirt, pausing at the small of her back. Through the lustrous material, her fingers detected the metallic T-back of her maiden's belt. Vamon wore their maiden's belt at all times, and in most cases, it was locked by their dominant partner. Although her clothing concealed her belt, she could sense it and the ring on her left hand at all times.

Her fingers moved around her side, gliding over her chrome blouse. The gleaming fabric sculpted to her figure and hid a secret: beneath it, she wore a locked corset. A flap covered the laces, and only her master's ring could release it. Whenever she drew in a breath, the restriction reminded her of what her life had become. Four years of education, equivalent to a college degree, two years of hardship on the battlefield was for nothing. Alexander made it clear that her primary duties were cooking, cleaning, entertaining, and sharing his bed. As a vamon Valkyrie, she would never be his or any man's wife; her children would be little better than bastards, and her standing in the community was that of a concubine.

She sat on the edge of the bed, bent over at the hips, due to the rigid corset, and picked up the boot. Like the skirt, it was attractive but functional. It had a chunky heel and supported the feet with comfort: serving women spent most of their time on their feet, only allowed sit with permission. She pointed her toes and forced her foot into the boot. It had a pointed toe and stiletto heels, impractical for a warrior but acceptable for support personnel. She drew up the boot throat, which extended to her knee.

The navy blue jacket, which matched the skirt, lay draped across the bed. She dreaded this garment. She picked it up and slid her arms through the satin lined sleeves. All of her service ribbons and her rank were gone. The ring marked her status as vamon. She understood the implications: she was part of the support staff for the Valkyrie, which the sisters often referred to as "Seska": Elvish for a lover who is not a wife. Since Alexander was auxiliary support, Cody would never wear a Valkyrie collar.

Cody fought back the tears. She would never be an honored warrior or an officer. Her career was ended before it began.

Although Cody's hair only extended to her collar, she wore a black semi-circular hair comb, the tips nestled behind her ears. A pair of silver stud earrings, embossed with the Royal blue and gold family crest, adorned her ears. After misting herself with perfume, she put on a pair of black gloves and steeled herself. There was no hiding what happened, no evading the truth, and no shelter from the humiliation. She would eventually have to face her peers – and Kelvin.

A thousand excuses swirled about in a self-justifying tornado within Cody's mind. All of them had a single goal: to protect her fragile ego. Her career as a warrior was over before it began, her dreams of glory and battle vanishing like a dream. Years of education, combat training, and hard work meant nothing: a chambermaid could perform her duties.

She marched up to the door and grasped the knob. She closed her eyes and paused. After taking a deep breath, she jerked open the door and exited the room. *I am a warrior despite this ring.* Her fierce determination faded at the sound of echoing voices. She shrank down and tried to cover her neck, and her heart began to race. She fled into the darkness to escape curious eyes.

When she reached the bottom of the stairs, the noise echoed off the walls and up the stairwell. It was breakfast, a day passed. She took a step out of the darkness and stopped. Her legs grew weak and tears formed in her eyes. It was then that she saw April.

April sat by herself in the great hall, eyes fixed on the flickering flame in the hearth. The redheaded girl also wore a subservient ring and a vamon uniform. She gazed at the floor, thighs pressed tight together and sitting on her hands.

Cody sat on the sofa next to April. April looked at Cody with glassy eyes. "She said that she 'loved me,' and then she proposed. I can't believe it; I froze, and then I said 'Yes.' Why did I say 'yes?' I'm such an idiot; she claimed me. I always dreamed of a great wedding in a temple. My parents would be there, and my mother would cry."

"Alexander claimed me like I was a prize filly he bought at auction," Cody replied. "I'm not sure he even likes me."

rcy*nt>

April crossed her arms and gazed down at her knees. "Kayla wants me to have her baby. She's going to hire a doctor to have me inseminated with the DNA from her egg. She wants the child to be part of both of us. It's going to happen as soon as we get back to civilization."

"At least Kayla cares about you. I can see it in her eyes. She loves you. To Alexander, I'm just a prize." Cody crossed her arms and pursed her lips. "All I'm good for is cleaning up after him and sharing his bed."

"There you are," Kayla said. She strolled over to the girls. She took April by the hand and helped her rise. "I want to show you off to all my friends."

Looking up through her red bangs, she saw the adoration in Kayla's eyes. "Yes Mistress, if you wish it." April followed by Kayla's side with quick, mincing steps, as her Mistress led her into the cafeteria. A thunderous round of applause erupted from the hall.

Kelvin appeared to Cody's left. He gaped at her and stared at the ring. When she caught a glimpse of him out of the corner of her eye, she leaped to her feet and turned to face him. He snapped at her saying, "So it's true. You did marry him."

"I didn't marry him. He claimed me. He doesn't love me, and I don't love him. I belong to him. I'm his property, and it is your fault. You had five years to ask me to marry you. You pushed the subject and me away." Tears streamed down her cheeks. "He asked me if I was betrothed, and I told him 'No'; so it is your fault; you lost me. I never want to see you again." She turned and ran away from him, tears streaming down her cheeks.

Kelvin's legs gave out, and he slipped down onto the sofa. His hands lay limp in his lap, and all of his will seeped out of him. He gazed down at the floor. He could not believe it. She was gone. They met as small children. When he pulled her braids, she chased after him, and even though she was only half his size, she caught up to him and tackled him

495

in the grass of rolling hill. They wrestled and laughed, and when they were done, they were best friends. They spent the rest of the day lying side by side, watching fluffy white clouds float in an endless vivid blue sky.

He swallowed hard and tried to push down the sorrow. It flowed up through him and washed away hope. Nothing mattered, neither promotions, neither battle, neither vacations nor anything else. Without her, the world ebbed into dull shades of gray.

How could it have happened? He knew many others pursued her, but she left all them behind. He was going to propose to her some day – after they had a few more adventures – when they settled. She was gone. How? How can someone just leave? It was like losing his soul: he needed her, he loved her.

Maybe he will let us serve together. That would be at least some consolation. It was a frail and feeble hope - men like Alexander kept their possessions in gilded cages. He would place her in a large mansion set on a vast estate. Commoners such as Kelvin would only see her from afar, a rare gem too valuable for the likes of him. The years of her life would wear away, isolated and lonely, without love. One day they would meet, strangers, and go their separate ways wondering what might have been.

Joash searched the interior of the great hall; although the castle was large, news spread fast, and he heard about Cody. He spotted his son far to the left. Kelvin had the same look on his face the day that his dog, White Paws, died. There was little he could do for his son but help him bury the animal. When the last shovel full of dirt fell on the grave, Kelvin broke down and cried, sobbing for days. He longed for some way to make it all better, but there was none. Only time would heal the wound, but this time there would be no healing.

He marched across the hall, dodging around the furniture. He marched up to his son and stood with his hands on his hips. Kelvin glanced up at Joash. "Not now."

"Yes now," Joash said. "Get off your fat ass and do something. Another man has the woman you love. Will you surrender before the battle has begun?"

"There is nothing I can do. Alexandar is noble, so he claimed Cody. If we run off together, they will find us. The authorities will put me to death, and they will return her to him. I can't even speak to her; I'll never hear her voice again."

"You have planned very well for defeat; now find a path to victory. Get up and FIGHT, damn you. Don't just let the woman you love walk away." Joash paced back and forth. "It would be better to die in battle for the woman you love, than live a lifetime without her."

"Don't you think I thought of that? He is a noble, and I never registered. I cannot challenge him. Our family is of the Royal Guard. We swore to protect the nobles. What am I to do? Tell me how?"

Joash arched away, "Useless. You never listen. Figure it out for yourself, but do not sit there and languish like some sad poet."

Chapter 52

Cody stood at the far end of the barracks. She could not face returning to Alexander or his quarter. She leaned against the bunk beds and sobbed. Her life, her dreams were over, snatched away, and each new day would tear them apart. They would see each other in passing and exchange warm greetings. The gulf would push them apart. She was married to another man, his property. She would sleep in his bed and care for him. One day she would bear his child, a child not of love but an obligation. She wanted to see Kelvin's face in her son, not Alexander's.

She unsheathed a small dagger from her right boot. The blade gleamed, and she turned it in the light. The edge was sharp enough for surgery, but it had other uses. It would make quick work of the arteries in her neck; a quick slice and it would be over.

Clicking drew her attention. The familiar feeling of eyes watching her from the darkness returned, but the Monk's Root was out of her system. "Who is it? Come out and face me." She stood to her feet and gripped her blade. "I am sick of this game."

A tall, black figure moved from shadow to shadow. It walked toward her almost as if floating – Kelvin emerged from the edge of the darkness. Her arm relaxed, and she sat on the bunk. "Oh, it's you. What do you want? It's not proper for us to be alone. I'm a married woman."

"Married? You are bound but not married. We are going to run away together, just you and I. We will sail over the vast sea to the western islands. The pirates care little for Asgard law." He grabbed her wrists and helped her stand to her feet; then he pulled the knife from her hand and tossed it aside.

When she gazed up into his eyes, he appeared different, as though from a dream. "Nothing can come between us. I will have you." When he touched her cheek, revulsion caused her to recoil. There was something wrong: something that made her skin crawl.

Kelvin's hand moved around behind Cody's neck. He drew Cody's head toward him. Cody closed her eyes and felt the soft lips touch of his lips. The girl then threw herself against him and crushed her lips to his; powerful tingles swept over her. Rather than pleasant, his touch felt obscene, vile.

"Nnn, nnn, nnn," Cody whimpered.

Kelvin moved Cody backward and laid the girl on the lowest bunk. Disgust, not pleasure, made Cody gasped. To her amazement, somehow, she was naked and the chastity belt unlocked; only Alexander's ring could disengage it. He peeled the device off her and tossed it aside with a metallic clatter.

Brilliant colors and flashes of light shower down her. Her eyed dilated as gazed in wonder at the brilliant white light beaming down upon her. Icy fingers wormed into her mind, cruel as the grave and painful as slashing knives, gripping and squeezing her mind, plunging her in a black void. Her lungs refused to breath; her blood turned to ice; her heart slowed, and her body went limp. Slimy tentacles slithered around her, coils after coil encircled her arms and legs, crushing her body.

"Get off her," Kelvin roared. The powerful man grabbed the creature and hurled it across the room; a crash arose from where it impacted. Cody drew in a sharp gasp of air and passed out. Kelvin drew his daggers, crouched, and poised for action. He stood guard over Cody's limp body and refused to give way.

The Reaper spread out its 13 tentacles, each one tipped with a bone blade. A foul hiss came from its gaping maw. Its breath smelled like rotting flesh and brimstone. Its clawed feet grabbed the wall, and it scrambled up the wall. It raced into to the dark corner of the room like a cockroach, its infrared vision seeing the world in sickly shades of red. It scurried across the ceiling, safe from human eyes. It examined the young woman on the bed; her heart beat once again, and the spark of life returned to her.

The Reaper hissed with rage and launched down at them. Kelvin deflected the creature toward the sofa, tentacles slashing at him, sparks flying in the darkness, stony claws impacting at steel armor. It crashed on the couch, and Kelvin threw it against the wall. He leaped at the creature, slashed and stabbed, cutting deep into the Reaper. The creature struck back at him, razor sharp slashes cutting through exposed flesh. He recoiled for a second and grimaced in pain. The Reaper broke free from his grasps and scrambled up the wall. He surged up at it; his blade plunged into its back, between its exoskeleton plates. It threw back its head and screeched – the shrill sound made Kelvin stagger and grimace in pain.

The Valkyrie guards raced to the battle. Gwen hurled a javelin at the Reaper and pinned it to the wall. The others slashed at it with swords, but the Reaper blocked their blows. Gwen hurtled another javelin at the Reaper, and this time it skewered the creature's neck, pinning it like a lab specimen to the wall. Alexander held his palms facing one another before him. A spark of blue light appeared and began to grow. A moment later it began to swirl and grow bright. The Reaper yanked out the javelins that pierced it. It turned, hissed, and launched at them. Alexander hurtled the plasma ball at the Reaper. The energy ball impacted the Reaper; it exploded and showered them with slimy bits.

Kelvin struggled to his feet. Blood flowed from his many wounds. Gwen examined him and then ordered, "Sound the alarm! Alert the guards. Reapers have penetrated the fortress."

"Yes, Mistress," they replied and sprinted away.

When Gwen saw Cody and Kelvin's wounds, she said, "Get a stretcher for her, and help him report to the infirmary."

"I can fight." Kelvin stood up straight. The firelight cast shadows upon his strong features and made him appear like a warrior of old. "I will kill them all."

"You heard my orders. Take Cody to the infirmary and protect her," Gwen ordered.

Kelvin saw Cody placed on the stretcher, and his heart ached – she was so pale, so near death. "Yes, Mistress." He followed the stretcher-bearers as they left the barracks. He searched the ceiling and the dark, hidden places around them. Every so often he stole a furtive glimpse at Cody and offered a prayer to the Great Spirit. She had to live.

Chapter 53

"I cannot believe this," Sabrina said. "A Reaper loose here – right under my nose. How the hell did this happen?"

Dragor tapped his chin with his index finger. "Commander Cornelius was lax; his security measures were meager; patrols were infrequent and set at regular intervals. One could set one's watch by them, a poor security methodology." They stood around a rectangular table, and a holographic image of the entire fortress beamed to life.

Marla placed one of her hands for support on the edge of the table and pointed at the other at the sewer outlets. "We found damage to the steel grate on the southeast sewer covering. Engineering teams found a series of broken and picked locks. It would appear that it used the sewer system as a conduit to reach every area of the compound. We killed three more of them at strategic places around the compound."

"So they climbed up the sewer and roamed about at will," Tormod said. "How do we deal with that? Patrol the sewers?"

Joash scratched his scruffy beard and said, "Sewer security is only the lesser half of the question. The real important issue is what did it want?"

"Beyond feeding and mayhem?" asked Tormod.

"Yes. I have encountered many Reapers. I fought them in the 'Devil's Caverns.' They may be disgusting bottom feeders and soul thieves, but they are not stupid. That Reaper came here on a mission. Why?" asked Joash.

Kayla strode into the room, smelling like raw sewerage. "We found the bodies of Doctor Morton and three more guards in the southwest infirmary service duct. Kira Lyra was gravely injured but alive. It appears as though the creature followed pledge Cody Moyer about the complex, killing or injuring those about her as though playing a game of chess."

Sabrina straightened her back and drew in a deep breath. "All of the deaths, from the guards to the doctor, were aimed at one person. Why would anyone want to go to so much trouble to kill a recruit?"

Kayla asked, "Who is this recruit again?"

"Cody Moyer, she's a pledge, 2 years out of the academy. She was recently attached to the Valkyrie for training, but she has yet to pledge. She's taken part in a few assignments, none of any real consequence." Marla crossed her arms and shifted to one hip. "She's also a morph, a pretty valuable team member, but not vital. She has no access to sensitive intelligence."

The Reapers offered their services as information brokers as well as assassins. Sabrina was interested in the latter service. "What is her family's occupation?"

"Her father is deceased, but he was a lawyer. Her mother is of lesser noble status. She holds a few titles, but nothing of importance. The Peat family keeps petitioning headquarters to reassign her to Solva. Their son, Conrad Peat, wants to marry Cody. The Peats are very involved in politics, and the marriage would increase their standing with the nobles. Thomas Peat is rumored to have an eyed on a seat in The House of Commons. I'm not sure how killing Cody would affect that situation."

"Still, the girl is the key." Sabrina dipped her hand into the display screen and enlarged the sewer map, and she then traced the Reapers path. "That creature had intimate knowledge of our security measures and an architectural map. That means we have a traitor in our midst."

"A traitor working for whom?" asked Tormod.

"I don't know, but they are well connected, tactical, and wealthy. The Reapers are expensive, and they do not take the death of one of their own lightly. We are facing a very grave but anonymous foe."

"Agreed," Joash replied. "It feels like that icy hand of a drathva, but I have no proof."

"Who is the girl's platoon leader and company commander?" asked Sabrina.

"Warrior Kelvin Faroe, Joash's son, is the platoon leader, and Gwen Alcott is the company commander. She's a trainer for magic craft, beginner level," Marla said. "She has a short but impressive record." After few moments of silence, she said, "Quite unexpectedly, Alexander claimed Cody and became a vamon."

"I need answers," Sabrina said. "Post guards at her hospital room and make sure they are psy-trained." Psy-trained warriors were able to both attack and defend using telepathic and telekinetic abilities.

Chapter 54

Cody drew in a deep breath and snuggled into a pillow. Warm sunlight caressed her cheek like the loving hand of a mother. She snuggled into the soft pillow and pulled up the covers, but disorientation troubled her a moment later. *Why is everything so nice?* She rubbed her eyes and sat upright, took note of her surroundings and reached a conclusion. *I'm in a hospital room … again. Crap!* The crisp white walls were a decorative void, and the windows looked out upon the fortress complex. Beside her, the relentless machines measured her vital statistics.

Missing someone as large as Kelvin was impossible. Clad in full armor and bristling with weapons, he reclined in a salmon colored lounge, his bulk spilled over the chair. A pair or reading glasses hung from the tip of his nose, making him look very much like his father.

"What happened?" croaked Cody.

Kelvin set his scroll on his lap and removed the glasses. When he saw Cody awaken from her slumber, joy filled his eyes, but pain lurked beneath it. "Good. You're finally awake. I thought I lost you there for a while." He rose to his feet and lumbered over to her bed; and he sat down next to her, causing the mattress to tilt, and a groan came from the bed. "You were attacked by a reaper after you left me. You were in the Valkyrie barracks. When I found you, I saw that thing draining your life force."

"A Reaper attacked me?" Cody gaped and searched her mind. "Then none of it was real." She touched her hand and felt Alexander's ring. Some of it was real. She sighed and slouched into the bed.

Kelvin arched an eyebrow and asked, "None of what was real?"

Cody's opened her mouth to speak, but no words came out. She tried to tell him, but there was too much pain in her heart. "Nothing," she replied and looked away from him. Kelvin held her hand; it was as cold as death and lay limp. He agonized hoping for a miracle.

The door opened behind them. A female doctor entered the room, notepad clutched underneath her arm, stethoscope pinching her neck, an array of pens filling her jacket pocket. Joash, Sabrina, and Alexander entered after her. Kayla entered a moment later.

"I'm glad to see that you're awake. You gave us quite a scare. I'm Doctor Karen Phillips."

"What happened to Doctor Morton?" asked Cody.

"Well … Doctor Morton was killed several days ago. We suspect the Reaper replaced him."

"You mean that I spoke to a Reaper when I was discharged?" asked Cody.

"So it would appear. The drugs the Reaper prescribed would have pushed you into a psychotic break. That's how the Reapers operate. To obtain the most nourishment, Reapers excite their victim's mind and drive them into a delusional state; most of the time it means uncovering deeply hidden desires and fulfilling them, forbidden passions as some might say," the doctor said.

"Oh I see," she replied in a small voice.

"What did you experience?" asked Kelvin.

Drawing up the blankets, cringing at the question, searching the faces gathered around her, everyone expecting her to speak, filling the silent void, the room closed in around Cody. She glanced at Kelvin and then at Alexander. "You can tell me later. We need to give her some time to rest and privacy," Doctor Phillips said. "Revelations of this sort can be very personal. If you want to speak more about some of the things you went through, I can recommend a good counselor. It would help you process what you experienced."

Several questions popped into Cody's mind. "How long has it been inside the fortress? Why did it pick on me? How many people did it kill?"

"We don't know how long, but we suspect two months. The creature kept dosing your food with Monk's Root, to drive you into a delusional state so it could feed. It killed three people, including Doctor Morton, trying to get access to you. As to why if focused on you, we have no idea." The doctor combed a tress behind her right ear. "They generally prefer to attack when the victim is asleep, but first you bunked with Kelvin. Then you slept in the barracks; both precluded that form of attack. When you were alone in the barracks, it seized the opportunity and struck. The ring saved your life. The elves crafted the rings to protect their wives from such menaces."

"Yes, but it acted a bit too soon," Marla added. "It wasn't counting on Kelvin discovering it ...." Cody struggled to pay attention to what Marla said, but her heart was in agony. Each moment made her spirit grow heavier – there was nothing left to live for, and part of her wished the creature killed her.

Marla sat on the side of the bed and touched Cody's left arm. "I hope you don't mind. I volunteered to be your counselor. We will be spending an awful lot of time together on assignments, and I thought it help us work better as a team."

"That sounds okay," Cody agreed with empty affirmation.

Kelvin rose from the chair and walked across the room to Alexander. The young wizard took a step back and furrowed his brow; the room grew silent, and Joash stood ready to restrain his son. When Kelvin dropped down to his knees, it took everyone by surprise.

The Great Gate

Although kneeling, the big man still looked eye to eye with Alexander. "Please," he begged. "Don't take her from me. She is everything to me. I want nothing in life but her – she is my world. I was a fool: I took her for granted. I never knew how much I needed her. I love her. My heart is aching without her; please, I'm begging you – don't take her from me."

Alexander crossed his arms and huffed. "Wonderful, you had years to propose to her, and now I must give up my rights?" He saw tears forming in the big man's eyes and sensed his agony. A strange emotion – compassion – twinged his heart, and lit a small fire within his soul. "Fine, do you even have a signet ring to seal her?"

"Yes. Yes, I do." He stripped the ring off his finger. "We are Guardians of the Court and related to the king. The seal is recognized."

"She is yours, but you have to seal her right now, this moment! Otherwise, I am keeping her." He frowned, crossed his arms, and averted his gaze.

"I will. I am." He scrambled to his feet and moved to the side of the bed. The doctor left and returned with a fire diamond. Alexander inserted the diamond into his ring and touched her ring. "I release you." He then handed the fire diamond to Kelvin.

Kelvin removed his ring. The ring was much larger than the ring he had to hold it in place. He then asked her, "Will you marry me?" Alexander shook his head and rolled his eyes.

"Yes," Cody said. "I will. I do!"

He then touched the ring to her ring. She gritted her teeth and threw back her head. The fire burned her flesh and mind, but this time its light was that of joy. She embraced the flame, binding her body and soul to Kelvin. When he removed the ring, she blinked her eyes open and gazed up at him. "It is done?"

He brushed her silken locks with his right hand. "Yes. It's done." He leaned over and gave her a gentle kiss. Tears filled the eyes of all those present, even Alexander, although he tried to pretend otherwise. "I want you with me for the rest of my life."

"As your adjutant," she laughed.

"As my lover, my best friend, and my warrior wife," he said. His hand caressed her cheek and admired her wedding ring. "We will fight by each other's side and love each other for as long as the Great Spirit permits." A moment later, he took her into his arms and kissed her.

"We should give them some privacy," Sabrina said. After they had left the hospital room, Sabrina said to Alexander, "That was a magnificent gesture."

Alexander shuffled his feet and scratched the back of his neck. "It seemed the proper thing to do. They are in love. I still think it is just a hormonal response … but some people – so it would seem – are meant to be together."

Chapter 55

"I'm so sorry," Sabrina said. "I can't imagine your pain."

Claudia nodded, her face was ashen and long, her heart an aching wound. "She's severely injured and needs to be evacuated. Her necklace tried to protect her, but every time it healed her, the reaper tortured her again for information. I … I just don't know how to go on without her – she is everything to me. We are going to have a baby together."

"Bear your wife home to your family and see to her wounds," Sabrina said. "Take as much time as you need. I will have you reassigned to the local garrison."

"But my warriors are counting on me," Claudia replied.

"Take care of your lover and heal: this is the only service I require. Your unit will accompany you as an honor guard on the journey home. All of you will be missed, but your need is greater than ours." When Sabrina rose to her feet, Claudia joined her. She escorted the distraught warrior to the door. "Know that our hearts and prayers go with you."

"Yes, Mistress," Claudia said trying to be strong, but anxiety for Kira lingered in her heart. She exited the room, fighting the terror that rose up within her. Sabrina closed the door and sighed.

"Mistress, tell Alexander that I am not his maid and that I don't have to sleep with him," Marla said, her hands on her hips and feet spread. A private door joined Alexander's suite to their home.

"Excuse me, what?" asked Sabrina. Billy and Tia paused from playing with the children and cocked their heads, their antennae poking toward

Marla, wondering if this was some sort of new game. Alexander lingered in the back – arms crossed, gazing away from them. "What are you talking about?"

"Alexander says that he outranks me. So he gets to tell me what to do." Marla cringed and wrung her hands. "He's not right. Is he?"

"First, Alexander does outrank you only in so far as sorcerers are concerned: he's the expert. As such, he is responsible for the management of 'The Black Dragon House Wizards.' Second, you have authority over your body and your personal possessions. In other words, you can say 'No.' Also, you should never obey an immoral order. Immoral orders are forbidden by law and by me."

Marla marched past Alexander, her hands clenched in fists, her jaw set, her eyes narrowed. "See, I told you." Alexander followed as Marla stormed from the room.

"What was all that about?" asked Karalynn.

"It's just a spat between Marla and Alexander. They are getting to know one another." Sabrina took Karalynn in her arms. She held the elva tight and gently kissed her. Brushing a platinum tress from Karalynn's face, she said, "It's been glorious to have you and the other officer's wives here, but the time will soon be upon us to part. My heart aches at the thought. I will miss you."

Karalynn lowered her gaze and nodded. "I will miss you too." She paused a moment, a question taking shape in her mind. "Why does Alexander keep forcing women to marry him?"

"Like most people, Alexander suffers from the pains of his youth, so he makes poor choices. However, his strength and aristocratic nature hides a very gentle person. He cares more than he would like others to see, and he will make an excellent friend and commander, once his heart heals from the pain of his youth."

As they strolled past Alexander's quarters, they heard, "… But I can show you how to cast some fun spells. They might help you in battle."

"No. I don't want to sleep with you," Marla hissed.

Sabrina smiled and shook her head. "It's going to take us some time to get to know one another. It may be a challenge in the meantime."

"Um hmm," Karalynn said with a nod.

Alexander hurried from his bedroom, passed through the connecting hallway, and caught up with them. "Mistress, can we buy some concubines. It would be fun."

"Of course we can, but they also would have authority over their bodies and belongings," Sabrina commented.

Alexander twitched his nose and pondered for a moment. "I see." He returned to the bedroom. "I could present you to 'The Royal Spanish Court.' It would be very impressive. I guarantee it."

"I said, 'No!'"

Chapter 56

S abrina rolled over and opened her eyes. Angelina's blue eyes gazed back at her. The girl crawled into their bed during the night and slept between them. "I see you're still my best recon ranger," Sabrina said.

"Yes," Angelina said with a happy nod. The elva squealed when Sabrina began to tickle her. She thrashed about, kicked up the sheets, and laughed.

Karalynn awoke and brushed a tress from her eyes. "Are you two at it again?" She slipped out of bed, yawned, and rubbed her aching back. "We need to get you some breakfast." She led the girl by the hand and exited the room.

Sabrina also scooted out of bed, her scarlet silk gown wafting down around her legs. She yawned and stretched her arms and wings. There was no time to linger. She exited the bedroom, the cool caress of her silk gown, the chill of the hardwood floor, and the brisk early morning air making her come alive. When Billy and Tia passed her by in the hallway, she said to them, "We are leaving today, so assist Karalynn with packing. We are headed for the lower camp in the canyon, near the pass."

"Yes, Mistress," they said in unison.

"Have you seen Marla?" asked Sabrina as the fae scurried away.

"She spent the night with Alexander," Billy called back.

Sabrina knocked on the door but heard no reply. She then opened the door to Alexander's quarters. "Are you awake?" Marla lay face down on the bed; the covers draped across her lower back, and her face buried in a pillow. She lifted her head and looked over her shoulder. When she saw Sabrina, she blushed.

The Great Gate

"I guess he talked you into it after all," Sabrina said and crossed her arms. She heard the water running. "When Alexander gets out of the shower, tell him that we have work to do. Oh, and by the way, we have children present. Lock your bedroom door if you're going to have a romantic encounter."

Marla clutched the pillow to her chest. "Yes, Mistress. It's just that we got to talking, and he told me all about how sad he was as a boy. I don't know why. We just fell into each other's arms."

"As I said, 'Make love to whomever you wish,' but be sure to lock your door." Sabrina closed the door before Marla could reply. She navigated the hallways and made her way to the kitchen.

Breakfast was short, messy, and chaotic. The girls did more playing than eating; Billy and Tia joined in the games until Karalynn grew cross. Everyone returned to the table and behaved for a minute or two. Then the chaos resumed.

Sabrina returned to the bedroom and dressed in her armor. When she drew the cuirass over her head, she saw Angelina. The elva rested her chin on her knees and watched Sabrina secure it to the harness as if it was the most fascinating thing in the world.

"You should be getting dressed," Sabrina said. "We have a long journey ahead of us."

"There she is," Karalynn sighed. "I should have known she would be with you." The exasperated mother grabbed the girl's hand and led the protesting elva from the bedroom. "You need to put on your clothes."

Marla rushed into the room, still cinching down her cuirass. Her hands glided over her glossy black slip-suit, smoothing out a wrinkle on her thighs. "I'm sorry I was late. I was delayed."

"Yes, I saw." Sabrina turned her back to Marla; she began strapping the various weapons to Sabrina's back. "Did you enjoy yourself?"

"Um … well, I'm embarrassed to admit it, but yes. I did. It was a lot more fun that I thought it would be." Marla said.

"Sex is fun?" asked Billy, Tia standing behind her in the doorway. "Why?"

"Um … you'll see … it just is," Marla replied.

"Why?" asked Billy.

"You do fun things," Marla said.

"What kind of things?" Billy cocked her head and directed her antenna at Marla. Humans gave off many peculiar biological signals, which were ill-defined. Also eager to hear the explanation, Tia moved to Billy's side.

"I've never had sex." Tia asked, "How do you do it?"

"It's not … you know … complicated. I mean it's easy, but it can take years to master. You just do it," Marla stammered.

"How?" asked Tia, scanning Marla with her antennae. Billy and Tia leaned in close hoping for a detailed answer. "Alexander had sex with you. Are you going to have a baby?"

"Well yes … I mean no. I'm not going to have a baby, and yes, we had sex." Marla replied. "Humans have sex for fun aside from having babies."

Sabrina let Marla suffer a minute or two and then rescued her. "If you two are interested in sex, you should go to the infirmary and ask the medical staff. After all, it is a biological act, and you two should be on the blue. We don't want you getting pregnant."

"Yes, Mistress." Billy said to Tia, "Let's go and ask." Tia tittered and pranced after Billy. The pair giggled and disappeared around the corner.

"I would love to see the doctor's face when those two ask about sex," Sabrina chuckled.

Alexander swept into the room, his black velvet robe flowing behind him, ankle length and included a hood, embroidered with golden stitching, designating his status as a senior sorcerer and a member of the Wizard's Council. "Where were they going?"

"To ask the doctors about sex," Marla replied.

"After last night, I'm sure you could explain it to them," Alexander smirked and crossed his arms. "You did well for a beginner."

"I am not a beginner," Marla hissed. "I've had sex with plenty of people."

"Don't worry, Mistress. I will work with her to improve her skills in bed. I have some creative positions in mind for next time. You may have to stretch first though," Alexander said and sat on a high-back chair as if taking a throne.

"Don't forget," Marla said with crossed arms. "I let you use my best sword in exchange for you taking my night watch duty."

"Of course, that was our agreement." Alexander crossed his legs and tapped his chin. "Or we could make another wager. If you win, I will perform your watch duty for two months. If I win, I get to keep the sword. That's fair, no?"

"What kind of wager?" asked Marla.

Sabrina rolled her eyes and exited the room. She passed through the house and called out to Karalynn. "Some men will be coming to pick up our gear. Can you wait for them?"

"Yes, Mistress," Karalynn called, as she wrestled Eliza into her travel jumper.

Sabrina's personal residence was a mansion by anyone's standards. Like most mansions, it housed a large staff dedicated to the smooth functioning of her domestic needs. The staff hurried about, making final preparations for her departure. They would follow in two weeks, taking the time to close up the facility, and they would then rendezvous at Midway City.

At her approach, a pair of guards opened a pair of doors for her. A gust of frigid wind rushed through her hair and feathers. She stood upon a high balcony and gazed down upon the parade grounds. Wagons, hundreds of them, were scattered about the yard. Laborers hurried about their tasks, some carrying boxes, some hitching horses, and others assembling their troops – but what caught her eyes was the children; they ran around, heedless of the cold, and played a game of tag, as if this was some sort of grand celebration. Their mothers inspected the contents of their wagon, making sure all needful things were packed and loaded.

Sabrina idly strolled down the stone stairs that traced the outskirt of her residence. Guards snapped to attention at her approach and saluted with a thump to the chest; she returned their salute, and they resumed their duties. She made her way to the parade grounds; ice covered the cobblestones, making them appear like a skating rink; a fresh coat of white covered every roof, and long icicles hung like daggers from the eaves. The north wind blasted the parade ground and turned all noses red. She had to admit that she was looking forward to going south. It would be good to see golden fields and endless forests.

Tormod said, "It's been wonderful having our families stationed with us. I had almost forgotten my Daphne's face. I just wish we had longer to be with them."

"Yes. I will miss Karalynn and the girls. I'll even miss Tia and Billy." She drew her wings in tight and surveyed the bedlam around her. "Anyway, we will have a little more time with them at the lower camp."

The Great Gate

They heard a dwarven female shouting obscenities at a cargo hauler. The dwarven woman waved her arms and stormed around the freight wagon. "That would be my cue. I'll go see what's bothering my Daphne."

Sabrina met with the officers and provided them with the departure schedule. It took quite a bit of logistics to properly supply and move over a thousand warriors and their families. It was then that Marla appeared at Sabrina's side. "I met with the haulers. We are all ready to move out."

"Just out of curiosity, how did the bet go," asked Sabrina and raised an eyebrow.

"Alexander won," Marla mumbled.

"What did he win?" asked Sabrina.

"I have to clean his room and wait on him," Marla replied and pouted "And I have to polish his armor for six months. He even took my measurements and mumbled something about buying me a maid's uniform. What does he mean by that?"

"I think it means never wager with a sorcerer," Sabrina replied.

"Words to live by," Marla huffed.

"Hello," Alexander said. The wind caused his baby-fine black locks to fly in the wind. His silver cuirass, reminding one of a gem-encrusted goblet, protected his upper torso, and magical stones to increase his power. "I'm very much looking forward to the trip south." He said to Marla, "I found the perfect maid's uniform. It has a very short skirt."

"That brings up a good point." Sabrina turned and addressed them. "What happens in our home stays in our home. I don't want the troops or the media getting involved in our personal affairs."

"Yes, Mistress," they replied.

They watched Karalynn, Billy, Tia, and the girls exit the mansion. Karalynn hurried through the bitter cold, eager to be safe and warm inside their custom carriage. If the fae noticed the cold, they hid it well. They both wore skimpy outfits, as was typical, and fluttered about in the wind like kites, Karalynn barely able to keep a hold on their leashes. She scolded the fae and made them land; she then hurried the group into the carriage.

All eyes turned toward the East; Kelvin and Cody appeared on the outer wall. Dressed in armor and carrying weapons of war, they descended the wall. He lumbered down the stairs, while Cody scurried and pranced on the ice to keep up with him, fighting the icy winds. He was a warrior of the north, a giant among men, and she was his only love. Everyone could sense that they were witnessing the birth of a legend.

The lovers crossed the compound, the crowd parting to let them pass, honoring them as heroes of old emerging from the pages of history. Their adventures were yet to be written; their days had just begun, but everyone was sure they were witnessing living history. He took up position at the lead of the Garrison Division, a giant of a man among titans, ready for whatever the future held – his love for Cody shining like the true north star, blazing in his heart, giving him strength to face whatever challenge lay ahead of them. She was all he needed and all he would ever need.

Sabrina mounted Midnight and made her way to the main gate. "LET'S MOVE OUT. WE HAVE A LONG WAY TO GO BY NIGHTFALL!" The officers echoed her orders, and the column set out for the lower camp.

Chapter 57

Marla ascended the gentle slope of the hill with the sunset to her back, the sun having lingered in the sky, after it set hours ago in the southern regions: outcrops that cast long shadows stretched the face of the land, stretching into distorted shapes, like devouring monsters, and a thousand fragments of ice reflected the crimson sun, like some shattered mirror, luminescent splinters strewed upon the ground. Her cleats gripped the black volcanic gravel and ice, causing a plume of choking dust, and she slid backward, silently cursing the treacherous footing, making her journey twice as long; and her lungs drew in the frigid air and let out jets of steam. The patrol's midpoint lay a kilometer ahead and straight uphill, of course, and she was determined to reach it, anxious for the return trip and the reward at the end: hot food, a warm bath, and a soft bed.

The recruits trailed behind her, their arms and legs heavy, the thin air robbing them of energy, weary to the point of collapse, the endless trail weaving through the Wolf's Maw Mountains. They began the trip excited to serve. Service to the Black Dragon Guild would be a grand adventure, and there were so many warrior women, all clad in attire their mothers and sisters would never wear. At first, they were aroused by the scantily clad warrior woman, the glossy sheen of her slip-suit, the flash of light off her curves; but that entertainment wore thin long ago. Now they wanted her to lead them back to camp: their bodies cried out for sleep.

Marla allowed them to take a five-minute break. Although she served Sabrina for four years, her duties were primarily administrative, and this was her first independent patrol; and the recruits were green, juveniles that just departed their mother's arms. She wished that veterans comprised her patrol.

The sun collapsed behind the mountains, and the crimson light turned to darkness; the sudden blackness plunged them into night, and although it deceived her eyes, her muscles knew the truth: midnight was upon them. Everything within her cried out for sleep, but rest was ten hours away.

She took a gulp of water from her canteen and then rubbed her face. When a young man began to wash the black soot from his face, she barked, "Stow that water. It's for drinking, not bathing." The girls returned around the boulders, nonchalant as if they were enjoying the view and not relieving themselves.

Marla rose to her feet and stretched, as the dull ache of her limbs returned. "Let's get moving! We have ground to cover." The recruits groaned as their legs once again supported them. "Move out!" she ordered and continued up the hill. She considered using her mask, which had starlight vision, but the mask's power source was limited, best saved for an emergency. "Torches," she ordered, and the patrol broke out their hand-held lights.

When she reached the top of the hill, she stood with her hands on her hips. Her breath formed wispy clouds that seconds later faded. She swept her light across the face of the frozen slope; the brindle patches of snow and black rubble flowed into the valley.

Destruction lay all about them. The Wolf's Maw Mountains saw battles since the beginning of time, and every step one took was on the grave of a fallen warrior. Snapped spears, crushed shields, and bent swords jutted out of the ground, slowly sinking into the ground and the grave. Empty eye sockets gazed back at her – human bones, dwarf bones, haugr bones, daemia bones, and animal bones, were mixed together: the dead waged eternal war, locked in their grim tombs.

"Do I look fat?" Garret held up a bleached white skull. He moved the toothless jaw as if speaking. "I've been on a diet, but I think I have another few pounds to go."

The girls giggled, and Julia picked up a male skull. "Hey baby, you want to go back to my tent and have some fun? I have an awesome pelvic bone."

Jonas used the toe of his boot to kick back the rubble from around a dwarf skull. "Losers," he muttered. "They must have been terrible warriors to end up like this." He was going to be an overlord, maybe even a warlord, and they would bury his body in a grand tomb – no one will forget him. He kicked the skull down the hill and shook his head as it tumbled. "Pathetic."

"Is this a daemia skull?" asked Aija. She held up the specimen, turning it this way and that. Marla took the skull from the girl and examined it. Tumors and infections marred the skull, twisting it into unnatural shapes.

"No. This is human. This warrior died from a biological attack. The daemia love to infect their enemies with plagues. It's a slow, tormented death. Despite being sick, this man joined the battle," Marla said.

"And got himself and others killed," Jonas said. "Someone who was that sick should have been sent home to die. He didn't care about his fellow warriors; he wanted a glorious death, despite who got killed because of it."

"What's that?" Julia asked and shone her light on dozens of fire scorched carts. The most recent cart testified to a failed passing. "Let check it out on our way back to camp." She started down the hill, without waiting for permission. Marla followed after the girl, trying to appear in command. The recruits followed after them, ignoring the death and destruction all around them, kicking up a volcanic rock and black grit with every step. They used their pikes as a walking stick and steadied themselves on the uneven surface.

April hurried up to Marla's side and displayed her left hand. Kayla married April, enlisting her in the Valkyrie, designating her as a vamon.

The girl stole two quick glances at Marla's ring and asked, "How long have you been vamon?"

"Huh, what?" She noticed the girl's gaze fixed on her neck and remembered her choker necklace. "I'm not a vamon. Well, I am a vamon but not a duty wife. Sabrina adopted me and made me her sister ... I still don't really understand it: I really am her sister now. I even have wings. I don't know how to fly, but I do have wings. Since Kayla married you, have you made any plans?"

April gazed down at her feet and combed a red lock behind her right ear. "Kayla wants to start a family. She's going to hire a stud when we return to Solva. I'm not sure if I'm ready to be a mother. I'm only 21. My mom didn't have me until she was 123-years-old. What should I do?"

Marla tightened the chinstrap on her helmet and pondered the question. When the light failed, the cold whipped into a frenzied dance, lashed at them, like some cruel taskmaster. She was glad for the PSM suit, but it still stung her exposed face, turning the tip of her nose and cheeks ruddy, flaxen tresses dancing about her neck. They walked around a pair of jutting spears that formed an "X," both of which still bore shredded red and gold pennants, the tendrils flapping in the ever present wind. "Kayla is your Mistress. If she wants you to have a baby, then you have to do it. But I've known her for years, and she is reasonable. If you're not ready, just tell her. I know she loves you."

"I suppose," April said with a shrug. "Do you want to have a baby some day?"

"I've thought about it, but Sabrina wants me to wait until I'm 150. I still have a lot to learn as her adjutant. When I'm experienced enough, then I can take time off to have a baby." Marla drew her swords and squatted into a ready stance. The warriors drew their weapons and prepared themselves for combat. Marla crept up to the charred wagons; the icy wind gusted around a large rock outcropping, its jagged spires reminding one of knife blades, poised around a black hole.

The Great Gate

An eyeless corpse gazed up at them from its tomb in the ice, the exposed soft flesh pecked by ravens. Its skin was dried like leather and drawn tight, pulling away from the ivory white cheekbones. The corpse's mouth gaped as if screaming in agony – its withered lips stretched in a wide "O" – as if still crying out from the grave. A few strands of blonde hair still adhered to the rotting scalp, a testimony that he had once been a living creature. April looked away in revulsion, but Marla studied the corpse.

The small skeletal frame and delicate features belonged to a woman. Skeletal hands and withered sleeves reached up through the ice, still searching for rescue. She appeared to be clawing her way out from the icy tomb. April squatted down next to Marla and asked, "I wonder who she was?"

"From her tan cotton dress and tattered coat, I would say she was a farmer's wife. They often make the trek through the mountains and delivered produce to remote areas, which earns triple the price." Marla's tone was clinical and as cold as ice, yet her heart agonized: in her mind's eyes, she imagined this woman surrounded by a loving husband, siblings, parents, and children; gathered around the hearth in her home. Her loving arms embraced those dearest to her, and her eyes looked upon them with adoration. Did she ever imagine she would end like this? Marla wondered if some icy tomb awaited her, a prison for her remains and if strangers would look at her with revulsion, curious as to the identity of this fallen warrior maiden.

She swept her light and caught a hint of red: crimson ice surrounding an orifice leading into the outcropping. Although her mouth gaped in silence, a scream ripped through her mind. "Spread the word, we found a hellhole." April nodded and hurried to tell the warriors.

Marla crept toward the hole, her heart pounded in her throat. Every sound was cataloged for danger, and her gaze fixed on the approaching nightmare. The wind carried the stench emanating from the abyss, and as excrement, sulfur, and rotting flesh made her wretch, she resisted the urge to vomit, fighting for control of her body.

524

What appeared to be a doll lay face down on the ice. Its blonde hair was sparse, and a floral cotton dress covered what remained of its body. When Marla saw a hint of bone and leathery flesh, she recoiled in horror. It was a dead little girl, a 6-year-old, a deep gash in her neck, her throat cut.

When Marla's eyes traced up the side of the rock orifice that was beside her, she saw a dismembered hand. Skin and bone still clutched a rusty sword. At that moment, the horror of the situation dawned on her. The family became lost in a storm and wandered too near a hellhole. The haugr attacked and slaughtered the father. The terrified mother was beset by haugr. She cut the girl's throat, to spare her the agony of a haugr death, and then cut her own throat. But why did the haugr leave the bodies for the ice to claim? That was peculiar. The corpses were fresh meat, a rare treat for haugr in the frozen wasteland.

Marla crept back to Mathias. "The smell of death will cover our scent. We need to mark this on a map and then backtrack our steps. We can return later with reinforcements." The warrior nodded and used hand signals to communicate with the others.

They followed their tracks up the hill, trying to minimize their presence. Alerting a colony of unknown size and strength would be unwise. She chided herself for letting the men and women urinate on the ground. Human scent could linger for months; they should have packed it out.

When they reached the top of the hill, Marla sucked in gasps of thin air, anxious to the point of panic. She shone her light down the hill and inspected the hellhole. It appeared a tiny black dot, harmless from this distance. She scanned the adjacent slopes, and she spotted 13 more pinholes encircling the base of the mountain. The evidence fell into place within her mind: the bones, shattered spears, scattered armor, and rusted swords forced a conclusion; the entire mountain hid a mammoth colony. 30 to 50 thousand haugr might be underneath their feet.

The Great Gate

Marla swallowed and tried to push down the welling fear. Although she tried to steel her nerves, her right hand began to tremble. Few people who wandered into such peril lived to talk about it, and there was no safe path of retreat. "Lights out!" she ordered and night engulfed them

Okay, don't panic. The sun has just risen. You have 8 hours, maybe 9 before twilight.

It was a 4-mile hike to the base of the hill, and if they ran, the haugr would detect the vibrations of footfalls through the rock. That was how they tracked their prey. Her eyes began to well up with tears. *I've led them to their death. God, please help me!* She saw the worried faces of her warriors and her heart ached for them - they were dead. The recruits appeared worried but hopeful: not realizing their doom was assured.

The air became electric; their skin crawled as if covered with ants, and glowing wisps arose from the troubled earth; the fog grew dense, covered the hill in white, creeping up their legs, immersing them, drowning them. A sickly glow grew brighter with each passing second until the very air luminesced.

Marla saw a figure taking shape in the fog, and it strode toward her, body covered in armor, its war-axe ready for combat. She held out her sword, ready for battle. Shadows of men, elves, and dwarves marched toward them like an invading army. Their visage filled her with terror: hollow eye sockets, shredded clothing draped over rotten flesh, armor covered with grime, and dead hands still clenching rusted swords. The platoon went back up to the peak and stood back to back, their courage hung by a thread, their bodies trembled. The dead surrounded them, accusation in their empty eyes, outraged by the dishonor heaped upon their graves.

Marla's sword wagged like a dog's tail; her heart beat in her throat; her knees became weak, and her mind became vapid. They stared at the great army of the dead, their outraged ancestors, poised to avenge themselves. Something swept out of the sky, and Mathias shouted, "Look!"

All eyes gazed at the top of a jagged rock. Sabrina stood on the rock with her hands on her hips and a scowl on her face. "Impudent whelps! I heard your thoughtless and ungrateful accusations. You scorn the dead, those who suffered endless agony and gave their lives so you could live. You treat the sacred as profane and fill up the full measure of your ignorance. These people were … are my friends, my comrades in arms. Their devotion and sacrifice made me weep, and dare to treat them like filth? Then to fill up the measure of your infamy, you stagger around a massive haugr colony like drunks."

"I'm so sorry," Marla replied, tears trickling down her cheeks. "I am responsible. It is my fault, not theirs."

"Yes. It is your fault, and you will be punished for it; but not now." Sabrina turned her attention to the dead and flew down from the rock. "My brothers and sisters, be at peace once more. Forgive the words of these spoiled children. I honor your dedication and sacrifice. I know why you linger here, rather than crossing over to the undying lands, sleeping in Eden's soil; you are as dedicated to Eden in death as you were in life, and you linger here to watch over your beloved homeland." She reached out and touched the vaporous faces of the dead. "If you will not pass to the undying lands, then at least be at peace and sleep. This is a dead hole, and your service is complete. Rest now. Go to sleep."

The dead warriors lay down upon the ground as if lying in bed and dissolved into the ground at their feet. The last dead soldier was a giant of a man, clutching a broad ax and bearing a heavy shield, and raising them toward the dark skies, he released a mighty war cry; Marla and the patrol covered their ears and recoiled in pain. The cry echoed off the mountains, sending birds to flight and deer fleeing, declaring: "Beware, the dead watch over Asgard." He then faded, like wisps of fog in the swirling wind.

Marla collapsed to her knees and dropped her weapon. "I'm so sorry," she repeated. The other recruits copied her; some prayed while others lingered in reverent silence. She grasped Marla's hands and helped her rise to her feet. After removing the girl's helmet, she gave her a hug and dried her tears. "You are young and inexperienced; so I too forgive the offense."

"This is a dead hole. These warriors gave their lives to kill it. After the haugr were dead, we poisoned the interior tunnels with cyanide dust to ensure that they would never return."

"This was a training exercise?" asked Marla. Her tone betrayed her frustration and relief. "I thought we were going to die."

Lifting up Marla's chin, she gazed into the girl's watery blue eyes. "You were never in danger. I'm not going to let anything happen to you. Do you trust me?" When Marla nodded, she said, "Good. I'm glad that you do. Now, you were careless most of the way. You should have taken it slower and searched for haugr signs. Also, your warriors need to pack out their waste. However, when you discovered your mistake, you didn't give in to panic; you didn't fly away and leave your troops: you stayed still with them. Any direction you walked would have taken you further into danger. The only solution once you are on top of a haugr hill is to stay put and stay still. If they don't know that you are here, you might last the night. When you failed to return, reinforcements would have come."

"Yes, Mistress. I realize my mistake." She rubbed the back of her neck and puzzled for a moment. "If this is a dead colony, then where did the fresh corpses come from?"

Sabrina cocked her head and asked, "Fresh corpses?" After hearing Marla's description, Sabrina flew down the hill and settled near the wagon. Marla and the troops hurried down the hill after her.

Sabrina squatted down next to the mother's body. Marla joined Sabrina and said, "The mother slit the daughter's throat and then her throat. I can't believe it."

"I don't believe it," Sabrina replied. "Take a look at the left hand. The joints show more wear than that of the right hand. Also, there is quite a bit of wear on the vertebra, osteoporosis. This woman is about 750-years-old, and the girl is only 5. The girl might have been her granddaughter. Also, the woman's throat was cut left to right, indicating a right-handed attacker, and the same applies to the girl. You can see cuts on both of their vertebra. A left-handed woman would not kill in this manner, and most merchants who travel this region carry poison vials around their necks for a quick suicide."

Marla asked, "What about the severed hand near the entrance?"

"The haugr wield crude machete-like blades, and more often though, they use their claws. The bones in the hand were shattered and the flesh scorched. Besides, the haugr would never leave the meat behind." Sabrina scratched her nose and mused. "No. This family was murdered. The killer left the remains near a haugr hole hoping the creatures would consume the evidence. Even if they didn't, one would wrongly conclude that the haugr killed these people."

Sabrina rose to her feet and approached a wagon, its wheels and sides burnt black with fire, and Marla was close behind her. "The most curious thing is the wagon. Why burn it? That would send up a column of smoke that would be seen for miles. Besides, it contradicts the murders: the haugr never burn a wagon or the contents. They would use it as bait to lure in unsuspecting looters."

She leaned in close and sniffed the wood. "I'm picking up the aroma of …" and drawing in a deep breath she declared, "black powder. Idiots! What kind of fool transports gunpowder through these mountains?"

"What's black powder?" asked Marla.

"It's a primitive explosive compound used in munitions. It is widely employed on worlds without rhunite." She snorted and rubbed her face. "It is insanity to manufacture or transported it on Eden. The severed hand belongs to a man who was blown apart. The victims are probably his family."

"But why endanger his family?" asked Marla.

"I'm sure someone forced the family to transport the gun powder, from a safe distance no doubt. When the shipment was lost, they killed the grandmother and little girl. They were witnesses." She rubbed her neck and said, "Have the men gather the bodies in canvas and transport them back to camp. I'm going to search this hellhole and make sure nothing is hidden within it."

Marla said, "I should go with you. You don't know what you might find? The haugr may have returned."

"There is cyanide powder everywhere: this hole is dead; they did not return. But, it may be instructional for you to see a hellhole leading to a larger colony. Relay my orders to the men. Then put on your hood and mask. You'll need to stay covered the entire time. You would be poisoned otherwise." Sabrina retracted her wings into her body and walked toward the gaping maw of the hole. After donning her hood and mask, she entered with Marla close behind her.

Chapter 58

The hellhole loomed before Marla like a snarling maw. Stalactites and stalagmites, covered with frozen blood, appeared like gnashing teeth. She descended into the black mouth, trailing behind Sabrina, swords drawn, feeling safer with them in hand, but Sabrina's swords remained in their scabbards.

Sabrina strolled into the shaft with little concern, the gravel sliding underneath her boots. She recalled the battle, pressing into the hole, the blood and the screams, their dead littering the ground. The haugr tried to collapse the shaft, but archers killed them. Haugr reinforcements arrived moments later, and the battle raged – forward and back inside the tunnels. Bodies of comrades and haugr piled up underneath their feet; there so many and were so deep that one could not find the tunnel floor.

The Maige ran her gloved hand along a rock and rubbed white powder between her fingers, turned muddied gray by the black stone. The cyanide poison would remain potent for several millennia; the spring rains would dissolve it into the rock – the haugr would never reclaim this colony. Such lethal poisons were the last resort and precluded human use. If it leached into the ground water, it would kill everything for miles around – there was no choice – this colony killed 100,000 humans, elves, and dwarves; it had to be destroyed.

The victory was temporary. The haugr found a new home, and with few humans and no resistance, the haugr multiplied once again. The Great Mine War between the dwarves and the haugr flared every so often. Under the great sheet of ice and above the rivers of lava the war raged with endless bloodshed and horrible violence, death and destruction becoming a way of life.

Marla hurried to catch up with Sabrina, feeling like a small child, the black walls closing in on her, trying to crush her. The tunnel funneled to a narrow passage that allowed them to walk single file. It circled around and around in a spiral. All at once they broke free from the tight space and emerged into a sweeping cavern.

They stood on the precipice of a sheer cliff that looked out over a great expanse. Phosphorescent ore caused the ceilings to glow with a dark blue hue, and as if sprayed by a shotgun blast, bright blue spots twinkled like stars. The haugr used high-frequency sound to see and had little use for light. Dwarven miners constructed the luminescent ceiling. Shattered walls, collapsed rubble, and splintered furniture marked what had once been dwarven homes. They crept up a conical hill in the center of the cavern, and a once proud citadel lay in ruins, only shattered columns remaining upright. When the haugr took the hole, they slaughtered the dwarves, but that was long ago, beyond living memory. Not even a single record remained to document the apocalypse or the lives of the lost. The ruins were the only witnesses, and they lingered forever in horrified silence.

Sabrina spotted something at the bottom of the cavern. Black soot stained the walls, and new, shattered rock lay in a blast pattern around a jagged hole in the wall. She descended the spiral path that led to the bottom with Marla close behind her. Bleached bones of men, dwarves, and haugr were still clad in their armor and clutching weapons. There was no time to remove the dead: the hellhole had to die. As soon as they took the main complex, they engaged the blowers, spreading the poison dust, killing anything with unprotected flesh.

Marla saw the skull of a young dwarven boy. A hole punched in the center of his skull, and a fractured ribcage testified to the violence of the boy's death. At least it had been a quick death, she hoped. When she leaned close, she saw teeth and claw marks gouged into bone; and when she looked at her, she saw that Sabrina strode away, so she hurried after her.

They navigated around the piles of shattered timber and stone. It was then that they came upon an unusually large pile. It was four times as tall as a man and wide across the base. Bleached bones leaped out of the darkness and made her heart flutter: skulls, femurs, ribcages, and other bones forming the high mound, a nightmare, a horror. When a hand touched her shoulder, she jumped and let out a muffled scream.

Sabrina signaled, "Are you okay? Do you need to leave?"

"I'll be fine," Marla replied. She squatted down a little and placed her hands on her knees. She struggled to regain her composure.

"They are safe in the afterlife with their loved ones and friends. There is no need to grieve for them. Their suffering is complete," Sabrina said. Marla nodded and rose to her feet. The pair of warrior women circled around the pile of bones toward the damaged wall.

Sabrina stood in the center of the opening of the wall. Just beyond the collapsed rock, she saw a tunnel. Dark black charring and soot covered the tunnel's interior. Fragments of wood lay scattered about on the floor. Sabrina picked up a fragment and examined it. "This was a wooden stave for a barrel. They detonated the black powder here and knocked down the wall," Sabrina signed.

Why? There was no reason for it. The hole was dead and black powder was far too dangerous. It made no sense.

Sabrina climbed up into the tunnel and walked through the blast site. Her right foot struck more broken staves and a metal hoop. They followed a black, burnt line that traced up the tunnel floor, no doubt a fuse, and came up an old table with a lantern upon it. The lantern glass wore a thin layer of dust. The detonation was recent, within the past six months.

Marla saw a bit of white. She kicked it and uncovered a fragment of paper. She picked it up and handed it to Sabrina. Although most of the paper was burnt, a small portion of the document could be discerned. It was a shipping manifest from the Manitol Shipping Company, based in Gleason, located in the Trader's Harbor. They shipped a broad range of products around the Wolf's Head Peninsula by the Arner Sea. The black powder came from the Western Island Nations that supplied a wide variety of contraband, which now included unstable explosive compounds.

Chapter 59

Cody straddled Kelvin, her knees on either side of his hips, furs beneath them, and moans upon their lips. His massive girth filling her, enraptured by his touch, stroking her breasts, teasing her, she rode him. She tilted her head back and closed her eyes, a lifetime of desire fulfilled at this moment. His hands intertwined with her hands. It proved that she belonged to him: his lover, his wife.

Her hands moved down to his torso. They glided over his rippling abs and grazed his chiseled chest. His body was thick as an ironwood tree and powerful as the storms that swept across the face of the sky. The cold wind gusted through the tent closure and wafted over her hot skin.

He rolled her onto her back, and when she opened her eyes, she saw his brown eyes look down at her. She raised her hips, pushing him deep inside her. Her right hand traced the square line of his chiseled jaw, while her left hand combed through his dark locks. He raised his bulk between her thighs. Their lips neared, his breath burning her cheek; they kissed, ever so gently, like morning dew upon the tender leaf.

Kelvin's powerful arms wrapped around her and held her like iron bands. He rolled over; engulfing her, his massive bulk overshadowed her, his thrusts like a mighty beast. His manhood twitched inside her like a third person. Her body tensed and then quaked. She gritted her teeth and groaned. An orgasm shot through her and rocked her body.

Through the canvas tent, they heard Crystal's voices. "I know it's your honeymoon, but could you two stop for a few minutes? The platoon leaders are assembling for a meeting. There's something big happening."

"I'll be there," Kelvin said. The giant of a man rolled off Cody and lay back on the bed, his oiled body glistening in the early morning light. Cody marveled at the power of the male body, and a shiver coursed through her. "Well wife, we have done it now," That first bit he said to try it on for size. It felt comfortable and warm, like a soft sweater.

"Well husband," she replied and scrunched up her nose with delight, "we certainly have." She scooted out of bed and crossed the tent. A sudden gust flapped the tent closure and snapped at her bare flesh. Fending off the cold, her skin turned blue, and after recovering her warmth, she then turned pale white again. She stretched open the neck of her slip-suit and drew it up her body, sliding her arms in the silky sleeves and pulling closed the crotch seam.

"Turning blue like that is a neat trick," he said and supported his head with his hands. "I wish you could teach it to me."

"My reflex reactions are getting stronger. Doctor Phillips warned me that they might once I was married. The ring's Elven magic complements my nature morph. They are paxa, whatever that means," she said drawing up her slip-suit.

"It's the strongest type of nature magic. According to the elves, it's the source of all natural life that flows out of the eternal light. You just need to be careful, or you can lose yourself in it," he said.

"Lose myself?" she asked.

"You know, go crazy and think you're a snow woman or a gorgon. You might lose touch with your humanity, the source of your being." He paused from dressing and watched her for a moment; the thought sent a shiver through his soul: it was as if his heart left his body and walked beside him. She was more valuable than all the gold in the seven continents. She was the great love of his life, the only woman he would ever love, but she was a warrior; and death waited for them, patient, ever watchful, devouring all that drew breath.

He rolled onto his back and draped his forearm over his eyes. His thoughts shifted to the funeral procession for those killed by the reaper.

The Valkyrie captain that led the carriage carrying her wounded wife and the honor guard that escorted the funeral wagons. Through the wagon's glass panes one could see the honored dead on their last journey.

He felt Cody sit on the fur-covered bed beside him. Her hand glided up his chest and caressed his cheek. He removed his arm and saw the light of his love burning in her eyes. It was peculiar: she was still a vamon, still regarded as mere support staff, still without rank, and still just a Seska, but somehow none of that mattered. She was loved, and she served by his side; and that was enough.

"I almost lost you, twice. Wait. It's three times if you count Alexander … um … marrying you." He sat up letting the furs slid down his muscular chest. "Now that I know how much you mean to me, it's crushing me. Every minute I worry about losing you."

She leaned forward and gave him a gentle kiss. "You know I'll never leave you. Even if I die, I'll wait for you in the eternal lands. You are mine, now and forever. Don't be afraid. I have my feet underneath me, and I'm ready for battle."

Her words gave him strength, and he caressed her cheek and kissed her. "Good, that makes me feel better." His hand glided over the glossy black material and then squeezed her bottom. "But if you stay on this bed, I'm going to strip off all that armor and make love to you."

"We don't have time," she said with a laugh. She rose to her feet and scurried out of arms reach. "I just hope the information I gave the Overlord is enough. I tried my best to remember when we were lost in the fire caves. I think I caught a glimpse of the Great Gate, but it's all so fragmented. It is like my memory is shattered into a million pieces."

"Hey, you did the best you could. That is all anyone could ask." He chased after her and pulled her into his arms. He leaned over and smothered her with a kiss. Cody felt engulfed by the powerful man, and when their lips parted, caressed by his hand, gazing deep into his eyes, she melted into him. He wanted to say something romantic but had no words adequate for his love. His fingers traced the embossed symbols on her ring. "Stay close to me," was all he could manage.

"Okay," she replied with girlish sincerity.

He reached down and drew her up into his arms. She jumped up and wrapped her legs, mashing her lips to his. His hand held her body tight, causing tingles to rush through her. She smothered his mouth with hungry kisses.

Crystal burst in through the tent flaps and came to a sudden stop. Her eyes locked on Kelvin's hand exploring Cody, and her upper lips curled into a snarl. "Oh cut it out. We need to meet with Marla." She pouted and crossed her arms. When they continued to kiss, she rolled her eyes and left the tent. "I'll wait for you outside."

He lowered her to her feet and gave her a last kiss. "If we're going where I think we are going, you will need this." He picked up her maiden's belt and handed it to her. "Cinch this down tight. Where we are going there will be lots of things eager to rape you."

Kelvin strapped on the last his armor and weapons. He threw open the tent flaps, a frigid gust past him, eager to explore the interior of the warm tent. Cody hurried to the opening and watched Kelvin lumber away. "Bye," she said with a longing wave. He looked over his shoulder and waved back at her.

"Please," Crystal groused, "You're going to see him again in an hour." She marched away and joined some other Valkyrie. Cody hurried after Crystal and cinched down the double swords strapped to her back.

Kelvin stole one last look and saw the ladies walk away through the camp. He hated to be apart from her for even a minute. However, duty demanded his obedience.

Cream color tents were placed in a matrix upon a broad field. They stretched out as far as the eye and the ground fog permitted. The red banners attached to the central pole flapped in the unceasing wind. Naked granite rose up around them and soared high in the sky; these jagged, snow-covered peaks, scraped the gray clouds that passed slowly overhead. Even the ground beneath his boots was hard and unforgiving.

When he passed by the horse pens, they shifted about. The smell of horse manure hung in the air and offended his nostrils. A blacksmith bent over and lifted a horse's rear leg. He clipped a horse's hoof and nailed a new shoe in place.

After issuing orders to some recruits, Kelvin continued his trek to the command tent. A blue pennant marked it in the center of camp. He did not really see why they needed a pennant to mark it. The tent rose up higher and was wider than all of its peers. It could hold a small assembly with room to spare. He soon joined the river of platoon leaders walking toward it.

The tent adjacent to the command tent belonged to Sabrina. It was rather luxurious by comparison to the others. A rug covered the floor, and furs covered a double bed that included a mattress. Several trunks opened up and formed dressers. A writing desk allowed her to review and reply to correspondence. At the moment, she stood before the dressing mirror and examined her reflection.

Sabrina received a package from Dwarf Armor Master Kreag. He was an armor maker that owned and operated the Amor Artisan. As any woman would, she had to try on the new armor set. Of course, she wore a traditional slip-suit, but the new armor included a black mithril cat-suit, which was worn over top of it. This chainmail was made of flat links that formed an interlocking pattern, impervious to most weapons. They conformed to her curves in perfect unity as if the metal had been melted on her. Her right hand glided over the smooth, cold surface, and her eyes admired the beautiful pattern.

539

The Great Gate

The accompanying cuirass and maiden's belt was also black, but they were decorated with glittery silver, mithril embellishments. She admired the fine lines and intricate pattern that displayed the black dragon crest. Across the tent, Karalynn lingered in bed, exhausted from a night of lovemaking. She reclined and admired Sabrina's powerful, feminine body. The mail gleamed, armor plate protected, and weapons threatened: crisscrossed swords, daggers, knives, and throwing bullets provided ample offensive hardware – a panoply of lethal armament. Sabrina was powerful but feminine, and best of all she was Karalynn's.

Karalynn rose from the bed and strolled over to Sabrina. She ran her hand around Sabrina's sides and moved close, examining her armor. "You look so beautiful," she purred. "It must have been expensive." Her lips neared Sabrina's lips.

"Are we interrupting something?" asked Marla with Alexander standing by her side. "We could always come back later."

Billy stuck her head through the tent flaps and asked, "What's happening?" Four-year-old Eliza burst into the tent with Abby in hot pursuit. The girls squealed and hopped onto the bed. Angelina stood next to Billy and held her hand. She contorted her face in a worried expression. It was then that Sabrina noticed Billy.

Billy wore her fae armor. To a stranger, it would appear little more than lingerie. A red mithril bodysuit cleaved to Billy's diminutive torso, appearing very much like satin, and a black miniskirt wrapped around her hips. Both garments gleamed and sparkled with the rainbow of a million diamonds. Her legs were sheathed in a pair of black nylons, and Roman style sandals weaved up her calves.

The fae wore a silver helmet that reminded one of three pointed silver leaves, two serving as cheek guards and the third covering her head. Her antenna emerged up through a pair of holes in the top of it. She had a small dagger strapped to her hip and her wings folded up on her back. "I want to go with you and stop those haugrs," Billy said, with her face contorted in a scowl.

There were few things more dangerous than an angry fae. However, where they were going, Billy would be out of her element. Sabrina said, "The spouses are leaving today. I need you to make sure Karalynn and the children get to safety. Can I count on you to do that for me?"

Billy appeared a bit deflated and shrugged. "You can, Mistress. I'll defend them with my life. Nothing will happen to them." She then scurried over and threw her arms around Sabrina's waist. "Please come back safe to us. I just couldn't go on living if anything happened to you."

Sabrina raised Billy's chin and looked into her eyes. "Nothing is going to happen to me. I promise. You believe me, don't you?" Billy nodded and hugged Sabrina again. "Good, then no more worry. You just make sure my children and Karalynn get down the mountains safe. If anything tries to harm them, I expect you to tear them apart, no mercy."

"No mercy," Billy echoed with a stern expression.

Tia hurried into the tent, dressed in a cobalt blue version of the same fashion. "Well, what did she say? Are we going with her?" The blonde fae wrung her hands and cringed.

"We're going to show 'no mercy,'" Billy replied and march out of the tent.

"'No mercy,' to who?" asked Tia and scurried after Billy.

"I guess that the children and I will be going soon. We'll wait for you in Midway City," said Karalynn. Heaviness fell over her like a shroud, and her eyes were downcast. When Sabrina raised her chin, Karalynn looked upon Sabrina with glassy eyes, tears soon to follow.

"What's the matter?" asked Sabrina. "Why is your heart so heavy?"

"I remember the day Maj left. He was so happy as he strapped on his armor and picked up his pack. He kissed me and hugged me. I can still see him walking out the door. I lingered in the doorway and watched him stride up the street. The sun was so bright and the city so full of life. He joined some comrades and waved to me as they disappeared from sight."

Sabrina combed a golden tress Karalynn's pointed ear. "I know you're afraid for me, and promises of safety are foolish when going to a battle; so won't promise you I will be safe; I'll promise you that I will be dangerous. Trust in my skill as a warrior. I've been fighting in the land of the living thousands of years and in the land of the dead, longer than that. When I go into battle, it is my enemies that should worry."

"You don't want to be cocky," Karalynn replied.

A hearty laugh exploded from Sabrina's lips. She leaned her forehead against Karalynn's forehead. "Know that I will come back you." Karalynn tilted her head to the side and pressed in toward Sabrina. Her lips touched Sabrina, and her arms slid around her. She felt the steel plate, the Maige's powerful body, and her soft wings. Sabrina kissed her back and held Karalynn tight.

"I'll wait outside if you two want a few minutes," Marla said.

When Marla grabbed Alexander's hand and dragged him from the tent, he said, "But I want to stay and watch."

With their foreheads once again touching, Sabrina said, "We will have to continue this later." She kissed Karalynn's neck and whispered in her ear. "When I see you in Midway, we will continue where we left off."

Marla and Alexander lingered before the tent, Alexander pouting. Sabrina exited and strode toward the meeting tent. The pair chased after Sabrina. She watched them marched toward the gathering, shoulder to shoulder, warriors prepared for battle. Karalynn then felt a little arm wrapped around her thigh. Abby leaned against her leg and squeezed it. She leaned over and scooped up the girl, returning to the tent.

The sun contended with the north wind over the fate of the land. Sunshine warmed Marla's face while the wind tried to steal it away. They walked between the tents and saw lovers exchanging farewell kisses. It was hard for husbands and wives to be left behind. The husbands of female Praetorian Guardians struggled more with this. The male inclination was to protect their spouse, yet these warrior women had no need of protection.

A pair of squealing children, engaged in a game of tag, ran across their path. Their mother scolded them and hurried them into the tent. All over the camp, the families were gathering up their possessions. They would depart together later that morning, and a contingent of recruits would escort them.

"I have the information you provided. I'll go address the Valkyrie. Do you have any last minute instructions?" asked Marla.

"Yes. Light packs only, the mines are no place for encumbering loads. That also applies to shields. Tell them to bring their smaller heater shields. Any larger and they will be worse than useless, that goes for medium and short swords too." Sabrina stopped and faced Marla. "I can't tell you how many times I have seen a warrior bring a claymore to fight in a cave. It smacks of the walls and clangs against the ceiling. All the warrior can do is point it straight out and waggle it about."

Marla chuckled and said, "I'll make sure they are properly equipped for tunnel combat."

"Good, I will see you in the war counsel." They embraced and parted. Sabrina and Alexander then walked toward the gathered assembly.

Joash stood upon a small wooden platform and addressed the men. He explained the equipment and weapons provisioning. Tormod sat on a chair behind him, puffing away on a pipe. The aroma of cherry tobacco wafted through the air, Sabrina's favorite.

Sabrina crossed the stage and met with her commanders. Joash said, "We sent a team to investigate the evidence of an explosion in the hellhole, but they were attacked before they could reach it. Daemia came at them from a haugr hole."

"Daemia, in a haugr hole?" asked Sabrina. While not strictly enemies, the two groups often fought over territory, but on a rare occasion, the two groups aligned themselves for select objectives: it was only, however, for a specific, short-term engagement. Attacking a forensic patrol did not qualify.

"It's a mystery," Tormod agreed. "It is compounded if you consider that someone was foolish enough to use exothermic explosives. But King Leopold Justinian the IV of Salvia has made it a regular practice to ship illegal arms and contraband through his kingdom. The man is a tyrant and a menace."

"He's a dead tyrant," Joash said. "The Petitioner City Herald reported that Prince Gregory murdered him and fled the kingdom. The new Prime Minster sent diplomats to the Asgard Parliament. He wants to join the rest of the human kingdoms on the Wolf's Head Peninsula and form a representative democracy."

"Even so, there's still a lot of arms trafficking going through Gleason," Tormod countered.

"Yes, I've had operatives conduct an audit of Gleason. Anything is available, and that includes the black magic. They must be supplying the daemia and haugrs."

"To what end?" asked Marla. "Why would any human help them?"

"The Great Gate must be closer than we suspect." Sabrina furrowed her brow and took a step toward the edge of the platform, her gaze fixed upon the horizon. Thunder rolled across the brooding skies, and angry clouds raced over the mountain tops. The leading edge formed a dark cloud wall that rose straight up into the heavens, as though a great glacier engulfed the land, and lightning flashes struck the mountains, made to seem small by comparison to the storm above them. This was no ordinary storm: magical power rode on the storm, invisible to the human eyes but not to Sabrina – she felt its power charging at them like a foe.

"We lingered too long," she whispered. When she looked down at her warriors, she saw that they were all gazing up at the skies in awe. "We are under attack. That storm is of supernatural creation. A dark power is bearing down upon us. It will kill our families before they have time to flee the mountains. They must come with us. Get them into the caves. NOW!"

The men broke formation and sprinted back into the camp. Frantic cries came from the terrified women and children. They fled for the caves in a stampede. Sabrina rushed for her tent with Alexander in hot pursuit. Men and women passed her by on both sides. When she reached the tent, a warrior asked, "What do we do with the horses and dogs?"

"Bring them, or they will die in the storm. We can bed the horses down just inside the caves and protect them from the cold. See to it," she ordered. The man nodded and ran toward the stables.

Sabrina burst into the tent. Karalynn knelt before a steamer trunk; Billy and Tia knelt by her, and the three of them gaped at her in astonishment. "There's no time to pack. Put on your armor and grab a sack of food. Take the children and run to the caves. Leave everything else. Billy, lead the fae into the tunnels. Not even the fae would survive this storm. Do it now!"

This snapped them into action. Karalynn said, "Tia, get the children. Billy, you pack us some provisions. Hurry!" Alexander rushed to gather supplies.

The Great Gate

"I have to find Marla. We will both be back." She scrambled out of the tent and called out, "For god's sake, hurry."

When Sabrina exited the tent, powerful gusts of wind ripped through the camp. Tent poles cracked, and tent pegs ripped out of the ground. Tents snapped free from their moorings and sailed into the air like kites, swallowed by the storm. Baskets tumbled along the ground, spilling their cargo.

Sabrina ran to a gaping soldier. "Get moving. Gather supplies." A tent right beside her shot into the air like a giant tan umbrella, leaving behind a terrified woman holding her children. "Hurry, get them into the caves." She called over a soldier to assist them.

Hail began to smite the ground. It bounced off her armor and the remaining tents. Sabrina sprinted through the camp toward the Valkyrie assembly. When she was halfway there, she came upon Marla running toward her. The pair stopped and shouted above the storm. "What happened?" shouted Marla.

"A demon storm is upon us. Help get the families into the caves," Sabrina said, her hair whipping across her face. The wind howled like a leviathan and lightning stabbed at the plateau like pikemen. The looming storm moved toward them and covered the ground with suffocating snow. Even at its edge, the wind whipped dense flurries, cutting off sight.

Sabrina ran back to the assembly ground. Tormod issued orders to scrambling warriors. "We need the maps," Sabrina said. Tormod grabbed some soldiers and moved into the command tent. The canvas tent drummed and shook. They gathered up their maps in great armfuls and stuffed them into sacks.

"Leave the furnishings," Tormod ordered. "Just grab the maps and equipment. Run for the caves, and keep the wind at your backs, so you don't get lost in the storm. The men grabbed the sacks and hurried out of the tent."

Sabrina rushed into the tent, but it was empty. "Joash and the warriors are grabbing what provisions they can. We need to be off to the caves before we are buried."

"Right." Tormod used his sword to slice through the side of the tent, and the men exited after him. They only went a few paces when the main tent pole snapped and collapsed like a broken tree, hitting the ground with a great crash. Thunderous booms and lightning flashes stabbed all around them.

They pushed through hurricane force winds. Tents and debris whipped past them and disappeared into "white out" snow. They pressed toward the caves, fighting to remain on their feet. When Tormod fell, Sabrina grabbed him and helped him struggle to his feet. A horse bolted past them in a wild frenzy and disappeared into the swirling snow.

As they neared the cliff, the wind began to buffet them. Sabrina was knocked back and forth, her wings acting as a sail. When a micro lull occurred, she raised them and drew them into her body. The pair leaned into the wind, but they slid backward on the slick ice.

"Take the rope," a voice called out.

Sabrina tied off Tormod and then held on tight. The rope jerked forward and then stopped. It jerked them again and dragged them through the blinding white snow. Ice and rock emerged out of the white, and they passed through the mouth of a cave. The wind hurtled them forward into the cave, causing them to tumble to the ground.

Hands reached out and grabbed Sabrina. She rose to her feet and saw Joash. "I hope you are the last of it, because no one can survive that storm," he said.

"Block the entrance," she ordered. "The ice and snow will then seal it." As she entered the cave, Joash and Tormod strode along beside her. White snow and blue ice gave way to gray rock. She saw the worried faces of women and children still searching for loved ones. "Move away from the entrance. That way is blocked, probably for the next thousand years."

The warriors congregated around her, but they formed a corridor so that she could pass through their midst. Sabrina took note of the cavern; they stood upon an expansive shelf. She spoke with Tormod a few seconds, then climbed up on a large rock and addressed the assembled warriors.

Glowing red light radiated around them and carried with it heatwaves; it attacked the glacial dome over their heads, and this, in turn, melted the ice, which caused never ending rain. It splashed down onto the lava and instantly turned into steam; humidity, thick and choking – it enveloped them like a wet blanket. Rivers of water flowed into ancient pools and continued through stone conduits, worn into deep channels over the expanses of time. The combined effect of these two warring foes was relentless heat, suffocating humidity, and raging rivers.

Sabrina addressed her warriors saying, "That was no ordinary storm. It was a demon storm, and there is only one demon I know powerful enough to cause it, Moloch. He made the first move and forced our families in here with us. He expects us to react without a strategy. He wants us to fear for our families, thus leaving them behind, guarded by half our forces. The other half, enraged by his actions, will pursue the prize, The Great Gate. Once we are away, he will attack our families with overwhelming force. We will be compelled to return to assist them. Our divided forces will be outmatched and slaughtered."

"I will not play his game. We are going to guide our families to safety to the dwarven city of Urzak," she said.

"That will take us weeks out of our way," a voice called out from the crowd.

"I don't like the idea any better than you do. As to the time, Tormod knows of a more direct route. It should only take us a few days out of our way. It is worth the time to know that our families are safe. I would hasten to add, that it is our only option. Now let's get moving; every minute we delay puts us in jeopardy."

The warriors returned to the caves where their families waited. They wrapped rags over the horse's eyes to keep them calm and loaded the children onto their backs. Husbands shared a fretful glance with their wives and exited the sheltering caverns.

The continuous rain covered Sabrina; it soaked her hair, splashed around her feet, flowed in small rivers, and dumped over the sides of the causeway, falling upon the burning lava. Hissing vents of steam jetted up on either side of the causeway, forming curtains of white, cooling when it reached the ice and fell as rain. The humidity made them feel as though they were drinking the air. It was peculiar, but the glacier above them was radiant blue, that bathed the crisscrossing causeways in a gentle glow, lighting their way, the effect from rhunite dust in the ice.

Karalynn hurried up to Sabrina's side. She and the children wore waterproof coats, retrieved from the hastily gathered supplies. Billy and Tia did their best to make the journey a game, but the children fretted over the strange environment. Such was true of everyone who traveled through the Fire Caves, a wonder of fire and ice, a marvel and a horror.

The path led them ever higher until the curtains of mist gave way to cool air. The ice ceiling grew nearer with every step taken until it was an arrow shot above them. Looking past the sides of the causeway, one could see flowing red lava crusted over with fragments of black rock.

The magma flowed in a never-ending circuit. It rose up from the depths, was cooled by the ice, flowed into a second shaft, and plunged into the core. Once again, it became superheated. This cyclical action provided the dwarves with a never-ending supply of metals, both precious and common.

The Great Gate

The trail grew wider until four men could ride abreast. Groups of dwarves passed them by, some on higher causeways and some below them. They chatted about a variety of subjects, most of them mining related. When they met a cross path, the dwarves gave them curious stares. Humans seldom ventured below the ice.

Every so often, they came upon a circle of light. Sunshine beamed down ventilation holes cut in the ice. It allowed toxic gases to vent and fresh air to enter. Sabrina heard a crew of dwarves chipping away at the ice. Long ropes descended from the ceiling, and they sat on padded boards. Their hammers and picks worked on the ice, and every so often, a large block would come crashing down to the magma. It would hit the superheated rock and explode like a bomb; fragments of ice and snow filled the air.

Marla had no fear of heights and no love of them either. When she looked up at the dwarves, she could not help but feel tingling in her feet. The dwarves were up so high, the fall would be fatal, yet the dwarves chatted away as if seated around a table, and sang as if on an outing in the country. She had to remind herself that this was their home and natural environment.

The slow procession headed north, and the shafts of light gave way to darkness. However, the radiant blue glow persisted. It must be night, they reminded themselves, but such distinctions were lost in the Fire Caverns. The trek continued, only the tug of sleep reminded them that night had fallen. Sabrina carried Eliza, and Alexander carried Abby. Angelina draped over the horse's neck, fast asleep; Billy made sure that she did not fall.

The next day, they fed the children with what little provisions remained; however, it was the thirst that frustrated the adults, not hunger; despite the never ending rain, the water was non-potable, being unfit for human consumption because of heavy metals and rhunite contamination. Sabrina gazed up at the ice; the Winter Pass Fortress lay 1,000 feet above the ice, and in it were warm beds and provisions. They would have to begin their ascent and travel one more day north to the city of Urzak.

Once at the city, they would move south a half-day and emerge on the Winter Pass Trail. It would then be a half-day trek back to the fortress.

Night fell upon them again, and the endless trail continued. Their footsteps became weary and plodding, compounded by holding a sleeping child in their arms. Sabrina wanted to halt the procession and let everyone rest, but their enemy never slept, and death lurked around every turn at the Fire Caves. Their best defense was to keep moving, and everyone knew it, but she was the one who had to make the decision.

Marla moved to Sabrina's side. She took Abby from Sabrina's arms and gave the little elva a rest. Sabrina was glad for it. It afforded her time to read her maps and reconnoiter their position. Tormod strolled before them like Moses leading the children of Israel through the Red Sea. His spirit grew light and mood jovial, feeling happy to be home once again. He saluted other dwarves as they passed them by.

When the first rays of fiery red light beamed down the air shafts, Sabrina knew the end of their trek neared. The entire column got their "second wind" and roused. Urzak was a sight to behold.

When Urzak came into view, all became silent. The great city looked down upon them from the top of a sheer rock wall; grand and ancient, the city represented the finest craftsmanship the dwarves had to offer: towers, balconies, and bulwarks abounded; and opulence lay around every corner. Thousands of lights illuminated curtained windows, and dwarves hurried about the tiered defensive outer walls, inspecting the advancing column.

When they turned left and passed onto the main entryway, they moved underneath a colossus, a status that towered over them like the mountains. The likeness was that of Dwarven heroes, carved from stone, as hard as the mountains. These brooding giants upheld the cathedral ceiling with their upraised weapons. Their names were the stuff of legends, names that were still spoken of in hushed reverence, carved bold letters, their names blazed upon the pedestals underneath their feet.

The Great Gate

The door was large enough for a giant to enter, which perplexed when one considered the dwarf size; but the dwarves thought in grand terms, and that filled in the gap. Guards with pikes lined both sides of the boulevard. When they passed over the steel grate drawbridge, Sabrina looked through the grating: a red ribbon of molten metal snaked through a valley over a thousand feet below them. Wastewater from the city spilled out of culverts and dumped down into the river of molten rock, creating a stench that hung thick in the air.

They passed through the entry gate and found themselves on a crowded thoroughfare, in a crowded market, buyers and sellers sparring over prices, dwarves spilling out of taverns, mugs filled with ale. Geysers shot into the air and splashed in sparkling fountains. The road was paved with red tiles, and huge towers stretched up on either side of them. The ever-present blue glow made the city appear ghostly, an ancient land shrouded in mystery.

"I'll speak with the city officials," Tormod said. "You take them to the Proud Spire Towers. They have rooms large enough to accommodate humans."

Sabrina was glad for that. She hated crawling about dwarven accommodations hunched over like an old woman, hitting her head on door jambs, knocking over knickknacks like some oafish brute. "As I recall, the towers are down to the right on Garnet Avenue?"

"Yes, two blocks to the north," he replied.

Fatigue returned to the column of weary travelers, and they trudged through the avenues like a defeated army. Dwarves paused from work, and while watching them pass, discussed the implications, and debated the business opportunities. Dwarves hurried out from the stables, eager for the business, and attended to their horses. Sabrina entered the hotel and arranged for accommodations.

Karalynn, Marla, and Alexander plopped onto the lobby sofas and closed their eyes. The children lay scattered about the floor near the hearth, only the fae were wide-awake and ready to work. They looked about at the exhausted company, puzzled by their sleep; there was so much to see and do, but humans understood the human need for sleep; and soon the children dreamt of feather beds and endless tables of food.

Sabrina hated to do it, but she nudged Karalynn. "Wake up. I've arranged for rooms."

"Alright," Karalynn said with a yawn. Billy and Tia carried the sleeping children across the lobby. Three large brass elevators with curved doors opened before them. Cherry wood, brass light fixtures, and thick carpet adorned the inside of the elevator. When they were all loaded, the Dwarven operator twisted the control, and they rocketed up to the 101 floor.

When they exited the elevator, they found themselves in plush hallways. It had thick pile carpeting, and tapestries hung on the walls, done so to reduce noise. "I rented a suite adequate for all of us."

The living room was spacious and well appointed: sofas, chairs, and love seats – arranged around a hearth, the central feature of most dwarven homes. The hearth was round with glowing faux logs inside it, fueled by a natural gas derivative, and the chimney was funnel shaped and made of hammered copper. There were adequate safeguards to prevent the gas from exploding due to rhunite, but even so, it made some people nervous.

Billy and Tia passed through the living room and carried the girls into their bedrooms. They slipped the girls underneath the covers and tucked them in for the night. Tia and Billy shared a room with two queen size beds, but they slept together in a single bed since fae preferred to sleep as a group. Marla collapsed into bed still dressed in her armor, but Alexander took the time to prepare for bed – bathing, unpacking his gear, and selecting the proper attire for sleep in a dwarven hotel.

Fully-grown elves need far less sleep, but Karalynn and Sabrina were also exhausted. They slept a little while in the camp: there was too much to do and see —every night they found some new entertainment or discussion group. Musicians played merry tunes, and actors put on productions of famous plays. The sum total of the events caught up with them, and they were almost asleep on their feet.

Karalynn helped Sabrina remove her armor. Karalynn yawned and gazed at her lover through weary eyes, much like an exhausted child. Clad only in their panties, they stripped back the covers and slipped between the cool sheets. Sabrina cuddled up behind Karalynn and snuggled next to her. A moment later they both fell fast asleep.

Somewhere in the night, the Maige awoke and could not fall back asleep. Her mind replayed the approaching storm and the fear for her family that stole her peace. The chaos of screams and flying debris swirled about in her thoughts like the storm that fell upon them. A million details fought for her attention: tactics, objectives, strengths, weaknesses, provisions, troop strength, shopping lists, cleaning chores, and bills – they crowded in her mind and prevented her rest.

She rose out of bed, being sure not to wake Karalynn, and slipped out of the room. Clad only in a black satin thong, the Maige emerged from the hallway and strolled into the living room. A half-naked female, in a house full of women, was all too common; most nights, she struggled to get Billy and Tia to wear anything but panties. She released her wings, and they shot out from her back; and she strolled with a train of black feathers, dusting the floor behind her.

A crystal decanter of ambrosia wine awaited her use on the marble wet bar. She filled up a wine glass and took a long slurp. If only alcohol affected her, it might have calmed her, but she settled for the delicious flavor and curled up on a reclining chair, the legs extended. She watched the flames dance upon the lava stones and sipped her wine. The flickering light danced upon her bare body.

Sabrina chided herself for being so slack. Their families should have evacuated as soon as they left the fortress. She became comfortable. After thousands of years, she had a family … a home, and up until that moment of their imminent loss, she never knew how much she craved it. They were a happy family; she wanted to spend every minute with them.

She put the family she loved and her troops in danger. If anyone else did it, she would have convened a military court martial. She shook her head: recriminations were useless and self-defeating. She loved all of them and wanted to share their lives, a fate that she could not escape, nor did she wish to.

Moloch was a demon of the ancient world, void of love or honor. He, no doubt, perceived such feelings as weakness, yet they made her strong. She would fight with every fiber of her being to save them. There was, however, a lesson she needed to learn. She needed to know that her family was safe. Karalynn and the girls would return to the Black Castle and safety.

Having resolved her course of action, fatigue and sleep came swiftly. She rose up to her feet and set aside the glass. Wings trailing behind her, the angelic Maige returned to the bedroom. When she slipped under the covers, Karalynn scooted up to her and lay her head on Sabrina's chest, whimpering in her sleep. Sabrina wrapped her arms and wings around the elva, and after closing her eyes, the pair fell into a deep slumber. Sabrina dreamed of battles past and present, friends dead and living, and enemies vanquished and threatening.

Chapter 60

Cody awoke to an empty bed. The sun rose over the Wolf's Maw Mountains hours ago, but they could not see it because of the city is underground. Instead, she saw the same, relentless blue glow, merging day into night. She rolled over and tried to go back to sleep, but her mind switched on like a light. It began reviewing the day's events: a thousand details flowing through her consciousness.

Uttering a heavy sigh, she slipped out of bed and stripped off her nightgown. A hot shower would soothe her aching muscles. When she turned on the water, cold water gushed out of the nozzle. Cursing and dancing about, she washed in record time and then leap out of the shower.

She wrapped a towel around her and exited the bathroom. She sucked in a gasp and came to an abrupt stop. A dwarf wearing a tool belt stood in the hallway facing her. "I'm with maintenance. Your hot water isn't working?"

"No. No, it's not," she said.

"I'll have it repaired in a few minutes. The valves get stuck sometimes. I'm sure that's the problem." He entered the bathroom and closed the door. Cody heard the rattling of tools and scraping sounds. She walked around her bed and picked up her swords. Her encounter with a Reaper left her shaken and distrustful.

A knock came from the door. She hurried past the bathroom and then opened the door: two more dwarves waited in the hallway. "Building maintenance," the elder of them said.

"Yes I know, you're here about the hot water. The other workman is already on the job, and I would appreciate it if he knocked before entering my room," she snapped.

"He didn't knock?" asked the younger dwarf.

"There's another repair crew already on the job?" asked the elder dwarf. "We have the repair ticket. That's not proper. We will see about this." They pushed past her and threw open the bathroom door. The elder dwarf's eyes went wide, and his lips parted in a silent gasp. He slammed the door, ran toward Cody, and shoved her into the hallway, causing her to land with a grunt.

"Run!" yelled the dwarf and slammed the door.

The dwarves sprinted through the hallway, and Cody chased after them. Somewhere in the process, her towel slipped off and fell on the floor. A tremendous crash came from her hotel room door behind them. A Reaper exploded from the room and raced after them. The elder dwarf swerved toward a large red button and pounded it with his fist. A bell rang so loud it hurt their ears. The Reaper came to a halt and scanned the doors opening all around it, then plunged through a trash shoot, disappearing from sight.

Sabrina burst from her suite, swords in hand and wearing only her black silk thong. She searched the hallway, ready for combat. Cody sprinted through the corridor, naked as the day she was born. The two dwarves, on either side of her, brandished their wrenches like weapons.

"Report!" said Sabrina.

"Overlord March, a dwarf entered my room. Well, it wasn't a dwarf; it was a Reaper. The repair crew interrupted him ... before it could strike. It escaped down the garbage shoot."

The dwarven security force burst through the fire door, weapons in hand. "A Reaper is loose in the building. Send for a wizard and a tracking team. We have to find it." Sabrina then turned to Cody and said, "We need to get dressed in our armor. We will grab your equipment, and you can dress in my room. I don't want you alone."

557

It was only then that Cody realized that she was naked. She hurried through the hallway, now filled with frightened guests. The dwarves tried to calm the guests and have them return to their rooms. However, many fled the area, not knowing where they fled to or if they would be safe.

Cody grabbed her gear and carried it to Sabrina's suite. After answering a barrage of questions, they all dressed in their gear. Cody snugged down her armor when Kelvin burst into the room. He rushed over to her and threw his arms around her. He then turned to Sabrina. "Thank you so much for saving her."

"Don't thank me. The quick thinking of the dwarf repair crew saved her. When they sounded the alarm, it forced the reaper to flee."

"How did he get in here?" asked Kelvin.

"He just appeared," Cody replied.

"I doubt that. Your ring serves as a barrier to many types of magic. The spell he cast to conceal himself failed when he neared your ring. We need to inspect your room." The group followed Sabrina, and they made their way to Cody's room. Using her sword, Sabrina pushed open the bathroom door. Chains and hooks hung from the ceiling above the bathtub; meat cleavers, knives, spikes, and other torture instruments lay in an orderly array on the bathroom countertop.

Kelvin moved to Sabrina's side, and then Cody joined him. Cody's face went ashen, and her hands began to tremble. Kelvin helped Cody over to the bed and had her sit. Sabrina picked up a bottle of whiskey from off the wet bar, an expensive beverage in any world, and poured two glasses. She handed them to Kelvin and Cody. "Drink it down in one gulp." Cody stared at the amber liquid and then gulped it down. She screwed up her face, shivered, and grimaced. Sabrina then refilled Cody's glass.

"We need to put this to rest." Sabrina leaned against the dresser and crossed her arms. She studied Cody for a minute. "I was wrong for a second time. Moloch was never trying to beat us to the Great Gate. He has no idea where it is. He engineered this whole situation to drive you into the hands of his operative. The Reaper was waiting for you here in the city. Moloch is convinced that you know where the gate is located, and he is desperate to get his hands on it."

"But I don't know," Cody replied. "What makes him think that I do?"

"You have a detectable energy residue. I had the doctor measure your levels back at the Winter Pass Fortress. Somehow, Moloch found out about it before us." She tapped her chin with her index finger. "I know what we have to do. We need to bring in a Dreamer. He can rebuild, or assemble, your memories during guided dreaming. There are some risks to the procedure. That is why I avoided it. But I don't think we have a choice anymore. Of course, it is up to you. What do you say?"

Cody crossed her arms and set her chin. "I'll do anything. I want this finished."

The Great Gate

Chapter 61

"I thought we were going to trace my steps to the gate?" asked Cody.

"The mind is not so linear," Nikolai replied. "Information is fragmented and stored throughout the brain. It's decentralized, organic."

"But why are we here?" asked Cody.

Nikolai slid his index finger down the ice wall. "This is the blocking point. It's the nexus of your memory failure." He inspected it and strolled around it. "I do love the various shades of blue. The dark blue of glacial ice is particularly striking. It's funny how the ice tunnel forms, a scallop dip here and a rise there. If it wasn't so cold, I might like to live in such a place."

Cody crossed her arms and shivered. The loose gravel slid underneath her feet as she walked down the passage. "The battle took place right down there. The haugr rushed at us. They reminded me of rats streaming out of a sewer drain.

"A terrifying memory to be sure," Nikolai replied. "I can see why you brought me here. It's a very convincing deception."

"'Deception,' I'm not trying to trick you," she replied. "I have a nightmare about this place every night."

"I'm sure. It is the stuff of nightmares." He turned to face her and interlaced his fingers. "It is still a deception." He held up his hand in a stop motion and said, "Let me explain."

"The human mind is very complex. What we call 'conscious' is but a part of the brain, a small sliver of the total mind. Your brain is made up of wondrous layers starting with the primal and ending with the higher brain. Then there is the subconscious: it is like a second person residing within the same body. It has its own set of goals and motivations. Interwoven throughout this is the spirit, your eternal essence, your animal consciousness, that which is most primitive about you. One of them is distracting us, much like a magician."

Nikolai waved his hand about in the air and produced a dove. It fluttered away and flew out of the cave. "You are so distracted by this scene of horror that you ignore the real source of your problem." She then saw a knife clutched in the opposite hand. "You were so distracted by the dove that you never noticed the actual threat."

Cody crossed her arms and wanted to argue, but her mind was a blank. "If this isn't it then what is it? I have no idea what you want."

"Hmm," he said and pressed his index finger to his lips. "But you do. You're trying to decide whether or not you can trust me. The answer to the question is, you can." He put his arm around her, and they began to walk. "Now let's begin our journey to the truth."

When they reached the mouth of the cave, they saw a forest bathed in light by a silvery moon. It took Cody by surprise since the real cave exited into the Wolf's Maw Mountains. Nikolai strolled out and took a deep breath. "Ah, I do love spring when the land is perfumed, and life bursts from the barren earth." He raised his hand, and aspen leaves brushed against it.

They passed through the dense undergrowth and found themselves in a small clearing. Seven boulders, like round molars, broke through the ground and formed a circle. The soft glow of a campfire illuminated their faces and cast long shadows. There were blankets on the ground and warm food by the fire.

Nikolai sat down upon a blanket with a groan. "It's very kind of you to supply an old man with a soft bed." He stroked his white beard and crossed his legs; he then handed Cody a plate and retrieved some blackened trout from a pan; and after breaking bread, he thanked the Great Spirit.

"It's not real food," she interjected.

"What is real?" he replied.

"Real is real," she replied.

"Is it?" The sound of a horker echoed through the trees. The moon illuminated rolling hills covered with trees. They flowed down toward a great rolling meadow. A herd of horses grazed upon the grass and lingered near the top of a hill. He took a bite of fish and washed it down with some white wine. "A man sees a shadow cast upon a wall. It has to be a huge monster with terrible fangs. His heart beats and blood surges in his ears. Death is moments away."

"I've been there," she said with a shiver.

"A few seconds later the shadow begins to shrink and becomes distorted. The man takes a step forward to see what it could be. He sees a tiny mouse crossing his dinner table. It passed in front of the candle, casting a long shadow. Reality is a matter of perception."

She set aside the plate and drew close to the fire. She held out her hands, fending off the building cold. "Some things are real whether or not we believe in them."

"Well, yes," she replied.

"Except that this is a shared dream, and there is no horker. It is only your mind's construction or interpretation of a horker. If we were to find it, kill it, and slice it open, we would find many irregularities. You have only a passing knowledge of their biology. So your mind would omit important details, details that, if you knew them, would alter your perception of a horker and its behavior. So you see that reality is malleable. Its flows like water around the details of our life."

She rested her chin on her knees and stared into the fire. The flames danced and leap into the air as though in a ballet. "Some details are final."

"You mean like death?" asked Nikolai.

She rose to her feet, crossed her arms, and strolled toward a boulder. She gazed up at the night sky. Stars like diamonds sparkled in an endless sea of night, expansive and engulfing. "Everything dies, even stars."

"Even the universe itself," Nikolai added. "Birth and death are inexorably bound to this existence. Just the same as eternal life is linked to the undying lands. There one will never grow old and never die: there can be no birth where there is no death; these two forces are bound together. It is as impossible to die on the eternal shores as it is to live forever on this side of the grave. One may be tempted to say that the eternal lands are better, but one would be wrong – the miracle of birth is well worth the price of admission in this life."

"Have you been to the undying lands?" she asked and returned to the fire.

"Me? Well yes I have, many times. At the time of my illumination, I recalled all of my past lives and deaths … and life after death. It's quite a heady thing to have lived so many times … and very confusing. I have had so many loving mothers and fathers. I have been both mother and father, and I have bore many children … none of them remain in this lifetime though. A daemia killed my family. I was away on a mission for The Great Counsel, but I can't even remember what it was about. What I do remember is returning home and finding a charred ruin. Mounds of soil marked the places where the bodies of my family lay; one day I will go to be with them. I doubt that I will ever return to the temporal plain of existence. This is my last trip to this life: I will stay in the undying lands next time I return there."

"Do you miss them?" asked Cody.

"Every day of my life, and I am a very old man," he replied. "Love of that sort comes only to a lucky few and very seldom twice."

The skies suddenly blazed with light, and Nikolai shielded his eyes for a second and then rose to his feet. The campfire was gone, and they now stood upon the rolling plains. He turned to his right and saw the tree covered ridges off in the distance. "It would appear that our journey is to continue. Do you know where we are now?"

Cody smiled. "Yes. This is a field near my home. Kelvin and I played here all the time."

A boy rushed through the grass and ran past them. "Wait for me," a girl shouted. The pair held wooden swords and wore cooking pots on their head for helmets. The boy slashed his wooden sword in the air, vanquishing some pretend foes.

"Take that. I'll get you too."

"That's Kelvin and me when we were young. We played all day long out here. We even made a fort just over that hill." Cody smiled at the memory.

Nikolai opened the sash to his robe; "It's rather hot."

"Midsummer was the best time to play. It was between harvest, and we were off from school for the summer. I wish I could have just one more of those summers. I never worried about anything. I just enjoyed myself."

"Kelvin," the young girl screamed. She backed up and dropped her wooden sword. Kelvin rushed to her and looked to see what she stared at. A sow horker huffed, snorted, and dug its cloven hoofs into the black sod. The creature bared its tusks and let out a screech. Kelvin stood in front of her and waved his wooden sword about in the air. When the horker charged, he brought the sword down upon the creature's snout with all his might. The stunned animal backed away from them but stood its ground.

A pair of piglets emerged from the tall grass. They stood on either side of their mother, wishing to see what the commotion was all about. Kelvin backed away from the sow; the sow's mate, the boar, could not be far away. They retreated from the wild pigs, and the sow, for her part, was glad to be rid of them. When they were far enough away, the children turned and fled.

Nikolai picked a few calamous leaves. The green shoots had beautiful buds upon them. He walked up to the horkers and began to feed them. "It's alright. Your younger self just surprised them. The female was only defending her babies. Presenting calamous leaves is a signal of peace and good intentions, as far as this species of pig is concerned. Wandering males present them to sows: it is like a written invitation - it says, 'I'm friendly, and I want to spend some time with you.'"

He patted the sow on the head and then returned to Cody. "This dream is not just your mind but mine as well. If it was just your dream, the pig would have attacked me when I approached, since you knew nothing of calamous leaves. But I do, so the pig responded."

"What if there are no calamous leaves?" asked Cody.

"Then the visiting pig turns his buttocks toward the herd and flings his poop about. It is an invitation for them to smell his excrement and sample the menu on which he dines. He is saying, "If you let me stay with you, I'll show you were we can find tasty food."

"I prefer a menu," Cody replied.

Nikolai threw back his head and laughed. "Me too." The dream weaver then stroked his beard and mused. "It's strange that you brought us here. If I were to guess, I would say it is the first time you were confronted with your mortality. Without Kelvin's swift action, you might have been killed." zx

The world melted around them and transformed into a chapel. Rows of pews lay on either side of them. Stained glass cast dazzling colors upon the ornate wooden carvings. Cody and Kelvin stood up on the dais before the priest. She wore a white wedding gown, and Kelvin wore his dress uniform. A few guests, one of them Joash, were seated in the front pews. The priest read from the book of rituals. He then gazed heavenward and offered a prayer to the Almighty Spirit. Kelvin placed a ring on Cody's hand, "With this ring I take you as my bride, to love through all eternity."

Cody walked toward the wedding, tears trickling down her alabaster cheeks. She stopped at the head pew and gazed at the floor. Nikolai joined her and stood by her side. "I was wrong earlier. You were not afraid of losing your life that day. It was his." He turned and faced her. "You're terrified that he will be killed and leave you." Cody wrapped her arms around him and heaved as great sobs flowed out of her. Nikolai stroked her head and soothed her fears.

When she began to grow still, he raised her chin with his bony index finger. "I would not give you some empty counsel and tell you not to be afraid. Death waits for all of us, and you two are warriors. Death is imminent for you, more so than for the rest of us. However, this is also true. Death will not find you until the Great Spirit wills it. Pray and ask that it will be a long life."

The scene changed around them, and they stood between two columns of basalt rock. A landslide of powder and rubble stretched up before them to a hole in the wall. Cody burst feet first through the opening, and she tumbled, end over end, kicking up great clouds of dust. She slid to a stop at the bottom, like a runner sliding into home plate. Dirt caked her face, her eyes and mouth appearing two pink slits. She spat out the dust and rose to her feet. She grabbed her sword from the dust and brushed the dirt off her.

"Are you okay?" Kelvin called out.

"Yes. This is sssooo not the way out. Next time you get to explore the spooky tunnel," she replied.

"Just wait there. I'll lower a rope down to you. I think I can pull you out," he said.

Cody leaned to one side and craned her neck. A long, vertical slit was cut into the wall to her right. The pair turned to see what Cody stared at. They saw brilliant light emanating from a giant pearl, the kaleidoscope of colors stung their eyes, its brilliance greater than the phosphorescent ice above the. This light sliced through the break in the wall, a horizontal gash, and they saw a massive orb, glowing like a giant pearl. It hovered above a cauldron of lava. A rope emerged from the dark opening above the bygone Cody and descended toward her. She wrapped it around her waist around Kelvin began hoisting her out of the hole.

"I recognize this pool. It is a smaller chamber that lies near the great cauldron. It is only a short trip from the city." He put his hand on her shoulder and said, "I'm glad you trusted me with this dream. It is now time for you to wake."

Cody yawned and opened her eyes. She took a deep breath and roused. Nikolai lay on the fainting sofa across the room. He roused and opened his eyes. After a great yawn, he said, "You have the answer which you sought."

"Thank you so much." She rose to her feet and ran from the room. "I know where it is." The old man lay back down and closed his eyes. He wanted to dream of home and to hold his beloved Lenore, even if it was only a dream.

The Great Gate

Chapter 62

Between the tall spires of the hotel, the warriors and families gathered in a plaza. They shared a last embrace and tearful farewells. Kelvin cinched down Cody's pack and then adjusted her shield. Her examined the ring that twice saved her life; it seemed like it was part of her, an arm or finger; its power grew stronger each day and filtered through every fiber of her being, a warm embrace for her spirit combined with the radiance of the soul.

Cody tested drawing her weapons, positioned in a "V" on either of her neck. She reached around her sides and tested drawing her knives. Her maiden's belt pinched a bit, so she kicked out a leg and tugged on her slip-suit. A quick back-flip tested her and their balance.

Kelvin picked up his massive shield, a door of steel by most standards. He chatted with the other warriors of The Rampart Division. They were all large and muscular. Their armor made them appear to be made out of steel, only the gap in their helmets exposing their mouths and eyes. The dwarves scurried around them and joined their respective divisions.

A few other Valkyrie wandered to Cody and chatted with her. They shared a laugh and examined Chrisandra's new archery set, admiring the bow in particular. Cody made due with the same set she received as a gift while in the academy. It hit the mark well enough, and that was what a bow is for, but the fine Elven detail, the ornate carvings, the superior distance, and accuracy left her envious.

It was strange: she felt the presence of her Valkyrie sisters – the elvish power bound them together as a family, and when she closed her eyes, they blazed within her mind like torches on a starless night. Across the lobby she saw flashes of gold and Mithril, marking them, setting them apart. The Light of the Elven bound the Valkyrie together, but it also separated, creating an ever-expanding gulf between them and the rest of humanity. The Praetorian Guard, while comrades in arms, was a different organization: warriors, friends, and associates – others.

The ring also created an ache in her soul, a yearning that only her sisters could satisfy. She loved Kelvin with all her heart, but he would grow old … and then depart for the eternal lands. Her sisters would remain, frozen in the flower of youth, bound to the will of their Mistress.

Cody had felt Marla before she emerged through the lobby doors. Marla joined their group and shared a laugh. Like Cody, she reveled in the growing bond with her sisters. The notion of children, hearth, and home faded. Only the love of her sisters remained.

The female warriors of the Praetorian Guard looked upon the Valkyrie with a certain degree of envy. The Valkyrie were the best humanity had to offer: Olympians, warriors, scholars, and artists. Many hoped to one day join their ranks, but admittance was only by invitation.

Normalcy was the female Praetorian sole comfort. They could marry, bear children, and grow old with their husbands. Valkyrie sisterhood had no such respite. They remained ever vigilant, faithful, and true to their vows. This precluded many distractions that most took for granted. Cody understood why Sabrina permitted marriage only to warriors of Praetorian Guard or other women within their order: only they understood a soldier's burden.

Sabrina climbed onto the shoulders of a statue pedestal that stood in the center of the plaza. "We will be departing in 15 minutes. Please say goodbye to your loved ones and then form ranks." She jumped down from the pedestal and then walked over to Karalynn. She gave Karalynn a last hug and then a kiss. "The dwarves are going to escort you back to the fortress. A company of soldiers will escort you down to Midway City …."

"Yes, I know," Karalynn said. "I hate the idea of traveling all the way south without you. It's so far away. I'll never get to see you."

Sabrina held Karalynn's hands. "I know. I hate the idea too, but the future is hidden from me, and my every instinct screams that dangerous times lay ahead. I need to know that you and the children are safe."

"What about you staying safe?" asked Karalynn. "Who is going to take care of you?"

"That's Marla's and Alexander's job," Sabrina replied.

Billy fluttered down from her aerial tour of the city. "I've never flown around a Dwarven city. There's an awful lot of rock. I mean lots and lots of rock, really weird types of rock, some that look like huge ferns and stone trees."

"Then I'm sure you and Tia will be glad to be south again. You need to make sure that our fae family is diligent in their care of my gardens. Also, I have so many orchards and fields that need tending. I'm afraid you will be working night and day," Sabrina said. Billy clapped with glee and hopped. She then hurried over to tell Tia the good news. The pair held hands and began to dance in a circle, singing a happy fae tune.

Sabrina gave Karalynn a last kiss and left her embrace. She strode across the plaza and stood at the head of the column. Joash walked up and down the line of warriors, barking orders. Kelvin stood in front of his platoon, and Cody joined the Valkyrie and stood by Kelly's side.

Tormod hurried to them. "A company of 100 Dwarven warriors has agreed to join us. They are going to lead us to The Great Cauldron." The dwarven company took up position before the battalion of human warriors. Drums beat echoed like rolling thunder, and the procession began. The dwarf column began to march, and Sabrina followed behind them.

Dwarves ceased their commerce and began to congregate on the sidewalks. Children sat on the curbs before their elders, curious as to the meaning of these events. The warriors kept their eyes fixed straight ahead and walked in lockstep formation. The white petals of winter daisies filled the air above them like confetti. The mayor and city council stood by and made it seem as if it was all their doing. Sabrina saluted them as she passed, paying homage to her dwarven hosts. The mayor returned her salute and nodded.

When they passed through the city gates, the guards snapped to attention. "Stagger step," Tormod ordered. The warriors broke into alternating steps as they passed over the drawbridge. Once they were on the causeway again, they returned to lockstep formation.

Heaviness settled into their hearts and weighed down their feet. Bed, hearth, and comfort remained behind in the great city. Cold stone and comfortless nights lay ahead. They recalled the faces of loved ones and wagered their lives against an uncertain future. Where would the trail lead? Would they return or perish in a barren tomb of stone?

Winston Churchill's counsel came to mind, for Sabrina was familiar with Earth history. "If you're going through hell, keep going." Or to paraphrase what a Marine once said, "As I walk through the valley of the shadow of the death I will fear no evil because I am the baddest warrior in the valley." She donned her helmet, cinched down the strap, and grabbed the handle of her sword. She set her heart like flint and marched toward battle.

The Great Gate

Chapter 63

Gehenna, or The Accursed World, once had lush fields, deciduous forests, rich blue oceans, and crisp, clean air. That was long ago … before Moloch killed the trees, before he killed the fish before he killed the insects, and before he even killed every single cell organism – before he killed the planet. There was no one to bury or even digest the dead. All plants and animals appeared as mummies, an eternal tomb of unburied corpse circling the sun.

How did this abomination happen? Moloch captured Gehenna's Great Gate. He used it to cut off aid and gave his armies free access. Slowly, relentlessly, he slaughtered the living and scorched the earth. Hope became a vice as humanity lingered in misery and doubt. In the end, all life ordained by the Great Spirit was extinguished.

After Gehenna died, perversion remained. Moloch strode across his world as a god, a god of ugliness and hate, a god of vile abominations. In the middle of bloody seas, on the Island of Pain, he established his throne. The burning island was the capital of the damned, a hellish vision and a curse on the lips of men. The very air was poison, choking sulfur and toxic gases. Its borders were broad, and the scorching ground made the air shimmer and warp. Only a fool or a man would set foot upon its burning shores.

Flames erupted from the ground, and lava plumes sprayed miles into the air. Rivers of molten rock, glowing red and scorching the earth, weaved through the land and dumped over high cliffs. This burning discharge flowed into the sea, causing it to boil and splash as in torment. But life finds a way even in a hellish environment. Various forms of bacteria fed upon the sulfurous gasses and acidic rain. They formed twisted and gnarled limbs, like that of a tree burnt in a fire. Without comfort or coolness, the island vexed the good earth in an obscene display. Creatures with a twisted form and lethal abilities slithered about.

Amon, a drathva of the ancient days, strode between the black trees. A pair of curled horns emerged from his temples, and 13 blood red eyes gazed upon the hellish domain. These eyes were set on a grimacing face, twisted and marred in a permanent expression of hate – and hate defined him. He hated the rocks, hated the trees, hated the creatures, hated the lesser imps, and hated Moloch. But he feared Moloch and fear is a potent motivator.

The imps were pathetic weaklings that scurried away when he approached. They should run away. He was magnificent, and he knew it. They feared him, and they should. He would destroy them if they got in his way. His hooves dug into the burning sands and tread on the burning coals. His hooves must crush all, and fire must purify the world of life.

He was tired of the Accursed Island, the Island of Pain. He wanted to emerge from it and cleanse a new world with the purging flame. His red hand, tipped with black nails, gripped his blood ax. A dread sword swung from his right hip, a myriad of lesser blades strapped to his back. They would soon taste the blood of men and cleave spirit from flesh. Plates made of pure carbon, black as night and hard as diamonds, covered his muscular red body. Whenever his goat-like legs took a step, the ground trembled beneath him.

The screams of the damned filled his ears. Black warlocks and witches, failures all, were chained to rocks – nightmarish creatures slowly consuming their flesh in an orgy of pain. Moloch would not let them die. Their suffering both amused and fed him. He condemned them to forever burn in molten flame, pleading for death but living on. Their screams were music to him, and their torment his meat. Such was the way of all creatures of the underworld. They fed upon the dark pulse of the universe.

These prisoners would never taste bread, feel the cool of the wind, or feel the softness of the earth. They longed for a drop of water on their tongues, a single drop to ease their pain, but they committed the unpardonable sin, the only sin forbidden by the dark powers – they

573

failed. Amon hated them for their weakness. They deserved neither
respite nor mercy, and they got what they deserved. He would never fail.
He was Amon the Merciless, undefeated drathva and warrior god. He
would consume the free worlds and then defecate them onto the burning
ground.

Amon joined the parade of demons, drathva, and imps as they trudged
toward the great tower. They were a hideous congregation, vile and ugly.
These creatures snapped and snarled at one another as they marched.
The only love they knew was for themselves and no one else.

The tower stood on the rim of the great volcano, high and proud. Imps
labored a thousand years upon it. Great curved blades covered the
exterior and served as flying buttresses. Between these supports were
endless twisted thorns and jutting daggers. All sorts of blasphemies and
dark incantations were carved upon its face.

Moloch ruled over the Accursed Island. His body was bloody crimson,
and darkness hung about his shoulders like a cloak. His hands and feet
were tipped with razor-like claws, dripping with venom. Leathery wings
stretched out from his sides, ugly and bony like the wings of a bat. Jagged
bone spikes jutted out from his skull, circling it like a crown, and
traversed the length of his back. But it was those eyes, those damned
blasphemous eyes that defined him: they were raw, unquenchable,
forever fueled by hate.

Ruler of the accursed, god of the insolent, specter of death, he sat upon
the throne of pain in the center of the tower. It was made of the crushed
skulls and bones of his many victims. Their bones adorned his hall and
made up the frame for the chairs, and their tanned skins stretched over
the top. Lava, fiery red and blazing hot, flowed down the walls, oozing
and bubbling around his throne. It spewed out from the base of a
festering wound and flowed in anguish toward the sea.

To Moloch's right lay the Gehenna's, the Accursed World's Great Gate.
It was spherical, the size of a water tower, a beautiful pearl, iridescent and

beautiful in a world of ugliness. He used this gate that he controlled all the lesser gates and access to his world. He captured it in the great battle for Gehenna. The day he won, hope failed, and all races were doomed.

The army of the damned assembled before him on the burning plains, and his captains gathered around his throne. "We must control the Earth's Great Gate. The path to the ancient world is opening once again. We must have it. I will have it. I will control it." A roar broke out from the assembled mob.

"My spies inform me that it lies somewhere to the far north, beneath the Sundering Glacier. They encountered a filthy Valkyrie beneath the great ice in the Fire Caves and were about to kill her, but when they sensed the Great Gate's residue upon her, its energy signature, they followed her, intent on locating the gate – but they failed, frustrating our efforts to take what we deserve. Who will go out for me? Who is strong enough to take it?"

Amon thrust out his arms and knocked aside his peers. He marched forward and said, "I will get it for you, my king. My blades long for the blood of men and thirst for their misery. I have never failed you. I am the best of your army." At hearing this, the other drathva howled in protest. "I will get it for you. I never fail."

Moloch leaned forward on his throne. A deep rumble emanated out his throat and shook the tower. His fire eyes fixed on the drathva lord. He raised his great, jagged blade toward Amon. "Do this for me, and you will rule over Earth in my stead. Fail me, and I will have you skinned and torn limb from limb." Moloch unsealed the gate, and Amon led his daemon troops through it.

The Great Gate

Chapter 64

Sabrina slowed and then stopped, bringing the troop progress to a halt. She stared into the darkness as if searching for something; her face became ashen, and her right hand moved to her sword. Marla and Alexander moved to her sides. "Is everything alright, Mistress? You look pale," asked Marla.

"Something hit me: it was like a shockwave – a drathva arrived on Eden." She took a few steps toward the edge of the precipice, kicking off several small stones; the stones plummeted from the dizzying heights, falling to the rivers of lava that coursed through meandering tributaries. She searched the veil of darkness and probed it with her mind. Spirit darkness blocked her vision.

Marla wrung her hands and cringed. Every child grows up hearing terrifying stories told around campfires. They recount the nightmarish drathva and their unspeakable atrocities, leaving the children quaking with fear. Sabrina caressed Marla's left arm, and the girl took courage from the knowledge of who stood by her side. She then whispered something in Marla's ear, and she sped down an adjoining path and circled around a bulwark of stone.

Alexander joined Sabrina on the edge of the stone bridge. He joined Sabrina in staring off into the darkness. He asked, "A drathva, are you sure? I feel evil, but I cannot be certain what it is."

"You will after today. A drathva leaves a strange bad taste in one's mouth, like biting into an apple and finding that the core is rotten. This type of evil is unmistakable. It is a drathva, and he's not alone," she replied and turned toward Joash. "It's a race to the finish." They broke out into a run and cast aside caution, for running in a cavern was a dangerous business; false floors, frail walls, and collapsing tunnels abounded. Their footfalls now drummed out a beat upon the igneous rock. The dwarves led the way, being familiar with the passages.

Brilliant white light dispelled the darkness and shone ahead of them, but it was on the other side of the Great Cauldron. Their steps faltered, captivated by the crisp rainbow of light, recovering a moment later. The dwarves charged through a narrow passage, and they emerged into the Stadium.

The name Stadium was appropriate. Several large and irregular columns lined the perimeter and supported an enormous domed ceiling. Jagged rocks, jutting in every conceivable direction marked the first ring of the interior space. Obsidian, extruded glass from igneous rock, sharper than a surgeon's scalpel, jutted in a chaotic array – the slightest brush would tear cloth and slice flesh. Narrow paths of orange and blood red sand marked the safe trail and weaved through these deadly sculptures, leading one to an immense oval expanse. In the center of the burnt red sand, the glowing gate floated in the air like a great pearl; iridescent ribbons, a rainbow of light flowed across its surface. It marked the place where they would decide Earth's fate.

Amon assembled his forces on the other side of the Stadium. He and Sabrina locked eyes and both drew their weapons. Daemia and imps formed ranks around him, piercing shrieks, monstrous roars, and blasphemous wails coming from their lips. There was no time to discuss strategy, no time to hone a formation, and no time for inspirational speeches. The fate of Earth hung in the balance: the battle of the ages was upon them.

"ATTACK!" shouted Sabrina. Sabrina drew her swords and released her rage. Her blue eyes transformed to fiery blue diamonds, sparkling and shimmering; and her wings shot out from her back. Wings extended and swords raised, she cried, "TO BATTLE!" with the voice of a dragon, shaking the interior walls, and a thousand voices joined her battle cry.

The two forces sprinted toward one another in reckless abandon. Sabrina and Amon charged at one another, their armies stretched out on either side of them. Their feet sped over the sand, and their blades were poised in deadly purpose.

The Great Gate

The battle lines collided, like two waves crashing; clanging metal, meaty thuds, groans, and singing swords came from the impact. The warriors of both sides were enraged beasts, slashing and hacking in a crazed frenzy. Red and black blood streamed into the air from mortal wounds. Screams and cries of victory mingled together.

Sabrina deflected Amon's blow and brought down her blades. The drathva leap aside rolled and recovered. Sabrina knew to fight strategically, matching and besting each thrust of Amon's axes. All around them warriors and daemia clashed, red and black blood covered the sands. Sabrina and Amon surged at one another. Their blades sang, and armor clanged as they collided.

"I will eat your flesh," said Amon.

"I would mount your head on my wall if it was not so ugly," Sabrina replied.

Sabrina blocked a chop with her left sword and slashed with her right. Amon blocked the slash and kicked at her with his hoof. She spun to the left and swept her blades at him. He blocked them, but the force threw him backward, knocking the weapon from his hand. Amon retrieved his blood ax and then leap into the air, roaring like a wild beast. He brought down his ax with a great chop. Deflecting the blow was impossible, due to Amon's powerful blow; so Sabrina formed an "X" with her swords, and the force of the blow drove her down to her knees. Her blades cut through Amon's ax handle, and the ax head tumbled through the air, embedding in the sand behind her. The daemia looked upon the stump of his broad ax and roared with rage. He threw it aside and returned to his blades.

"I will cut off your wings and roast them for my supper," Amon raged.

"That's going to be hard to do when you're dead." They blades met and issued sparks, flashes of light, and peals of thunder. The angel and the demon dug in their feet. Their blades pressed together and their faces inches apart. The drathva's foul breath stunk of sickness and death.

When a daemia tried to intervene, Amon bellowed, "She's mine." He swung his right arm and knocked the daemia backward. The creatures rolled end over end and lay flat upon the ground.

Alexander climbed upon a column of stone, shield maidens gathered around him. He pointed his staff at the enemy lines. The fire diamond flashed and sizzling energy, raw and burning, leap from the tip. It cut through the enemy line, cutting daemia in half and setting others ablaze. A daemia warlock countered and fired back at her. Alexander ducked, and the energy blast slammed into the obsidian boundary, showering the warring factions with razor-sharp fragments. He returned fire and nailed the warlock in the chest; it flipped backward and landed upon obsidian daggers, impaling it.

At the same time, Joash and Kelvin fought side by side. The Rampart warriors formed a shield wall. Fierce blows rained down upon their metal sheathed bodies. The warriors dug in their boots and pushed back the raging mob, flashes of light and explosions above their heads.

Pikemen extended their telescopic weapons. They plunged their pikes into the daemia. Gushes of black blood and shrill cries arose from the enemy line. The daemia flew into a wild frenzy and beat upon the wall of metal. Others stationed behind them swung boleros, rusted cables attached to glass orbs. The orbs circled above their heads in faster circles, and then they released them, letting them sail through the air. The glass vials shattered on the warrior's shields, spraying poisonous acid. It burned into their shield and armor, stripping away any exposed flesh.

Valkyrie arrows sailed overhead in a continuous volley, passing through the powerful explosion from the sorcerer's weapons. Arrows found flesh and mortally wounded daemia, causing them to collapse onto the ground. The daemia returned fire and let fly their poison tipped arrows fly. "Shields up!" Joash bellowed. The secondary row of sword-wielding warriors raised their smaller, heater shields above their heads. The enemy arrows bounced off, but a few hit their marks. Poisoned warriors dropped to their feet as blackened arteries crisscrossed their flesh and faces. A medic dragged them out from the battle lines and treated them with antitoxin.

The dwarven warriors were not going to be outdone by the humans. They swung their war-hammers and axes at the enemy. They aimed for the knees first. When the daemia fell, they cleaved its neck or bashed its head. The war-hammer punched right through the daemias helmets. The dwarves followed behind Tormod in an arrow formation. They punched through the enemy lines and cut around behind them.

"Pivot," Tormod shouted.

They cut along the back of the enemy formation. This created havoc in the daemia lines as dwarves attacked them from the rear, a classic hammer and anvil attack formation. Half of the daemia warriors spun around to fend off the attack from the rear, dividing their forces.

A violent blow sent Sabrina hurtling backward and onto the sand. Amon leaped at her with his blades bared to kill. She kicked him with both legs and sent him sailing backward through the air. He hit the ground and rolled, landing face down in the sand. Sabrina kicked her legs and sprang to her feet, her blades ready for combat.

"I will consume your flesh," shrieked Amon.

"Less talking, more fighting," Sabrina gasped.

Amon bellowed in rage and swung his blade at her in a furious assault. She let him drive her backward. Thinking he had the upper hand, he lunged at her, as if to run her through. She deflected his blow and kicked out his front leg. Amon stumbled and fought to regain his balance. His eyes went wide when he saw the spike of his severed ax head sticking out of the sand. He threw out his arms, tossing away his blades, but Sabrina brought down the hilt of her sword on his back. He fell onto the black spike, causing it to pass through his right shoulder.

Amon howled in agony and scrambled away, the ax spike still piercing his shoulder. Dark red blood gushed from the wound and flowed over his black armor. "You will not win the day. I will return and run you through. You will die a horrible death at my hand." He turned and fled through the midst of his troops. Two lesser imps seized his blades and chased after their lord.

Another enemy warlock lost his focus, just for a second. Alexander fired at him, the beam cutting the creature in two, the halves splat on the rock which he stood. The warlock screamed in agony, and his upper body tried to crawl away. The warlock's body flashed as fire burnt every cell in his body, and he exploded with a tremendous blast, killing the daemia near him.

The daemia troops staggered backward, fear replaced rage, and they staggered back toward the jagged rocks. A few turned to flee, but Valkyrie arrows cut them down. The cursed army faltered and then broke ranks; they fled the battle, arrows cutting them down as they passed through the jagged stones. Before her troops could chase after them, Sabrina shouted, "Form ranks. Secure the gate!"

The warriors snapped into formation, creating a ring around the rotating ball. They searched the Stadium perimeter for a sign of an attack. "Now we have the damn thing. What do we do with it?" asked Tormod. "The gate is unstable, and the Accursed World can still tie into it. If they send any reinforcements through, we are finished."

"We need to seal the gate," Sabrina said. No sooner had the words left her lips than Elven warriors emerged. They rushed down the wall and hurried to the stadium floor.

"That figures," Tormod muttered and crossed his arms. "As soon as the fighting is done, the elves arrive to take the glory."

The Great Gate

The Elven warriors parted. Lord Thalvon and Marla emerged. Thalvon scanned the ground. Bodies of men, dwarves, imps, drathva, and daemia lay all around them. Black and red blood covered rocks and soaked into the sand, but one stain caught his eye. The dark crimson blood, almost black, stained a circular area. He raised an eyebrow. "I see a drathva was here. Is it dead?"

"No, but it is gravely injured," she replied. "We secured this gate, but the Accursed World can still tie into it. We need to seal it. It must be done before others can pass through and attack."

Thalvon waved his hand and priests passed through the guard. Clothed in gold robes, wearing breastplates of precious gems, which denoted their rank and tribe, the priests entered. They carried long poles, and a fire diamond capped the end which was secured in a gold setting. They circled around the lesser gate and took up positions. At the high priest's command, they thrust in their control rods. The gate began to shimmer and flash; its dazzling display of color faded to white, and then the entire sphere turned black. Four priests carried a pedestal underneath the sphere and set it up directly beneath it. The pedestal was made of mithril and was capped by a golden water lily, its petals forming a reflective dish, and a fire diamond was set upon the stalk of the stamen. The diamond burned hot and bright and beamed up into the sphere.

"The way is shut." Thalvon turned back toward Sabrina. "It is done."

Tormod twitched his nose and asked, "How the hell are we going to get that thing out of here?"

"Once our control rods are in place, we will relocate it to Alkval. The holy city will once again burn bright with its dazzling light," Thalvon said.

"It must make it hard to get any sleep." Tormod rubbed his itchy nose. "It seems to ripple with vibrant colors."

"The gate is still unstable. It may take a thousand years for it to rest. Once it does, we will be able to control access to the lesser gates. It is a control nexus which all other gates must pass through. Until it stabilizes, the lesser gates will wink." Thalvon signaled the priests and had them circle the rim of the chamber.

"Wink?" asked Marla.

"The lesser gates wink when they open and close at random. Their location may shift was much as a hundred miles. We will ultimately control the path to Earth, but each time a gate winks one may pass between worlds. This winking process will allow creatures from Eden to travel to Earth." Thalvon's eyes gazed off into the distance, his brows furrowed, and he touched his index finger to his lips. "I wonder if Earth will be ready."

Epilogue

Tarina lifted her eyes from the scroll. The teen's eyes were heavy, but they listened to the entire tale. "Rest yourselves now. Our story will continue another night."

"I'm glad Kelvin and Cody got together. I wondered if they were ever going to," Telis said. "Why is love so complicated?"

"Many scholars and poets have tried to answer that question, without success," Tarina said. "But they did consummate their love, and we will hear more about them in the future."

"We will hear about Rory and Christy too?" asked Annalee.

"Who?" asked Tarina with a yawn.

"They were in the first story we heard last night, 'The Seventh Age.'"

"Yes. We will hear about Rory and Christy … and we will hear more about the baby, Michael's fate," Tarina said. Annalee nodded and yawned. She snuggled into her pillow and drew that blanket. "But the question of the Great Gate is far from settled. We will hear more of its fate in future stories."

"You're obsessed with that baby," Telis mumbled.

"You're obsessed with sports," Annalee replied, but the comment failed to have the stinging indictment that she intended.

"No fighting," Tarina replied. "You are adults now. You must act with decorum and dignity …." When she looked around the floor, all of the teens were fast asleep. She clutched her scroll to her side and weaved her way through the midst of them. The hour grew late, and even she was weary.

Scott Marcy

A full moon beamed down upon the city and reflected off the lakes and tributaries. Golden light escaped the temple; the elders gazed at the stars and studied the mysteries of the universe. From their perspective, she was but a child. She took comfort in that: there was still so much to learn, so much to see. The world was full of wonder, and she wanted to see it all. She puzzled over the ways of men and pondered whether she might ever pass through the "Great Gate" and see Eden's sister world, Earth.

The End

www.ingramcontent.com/pod-product-compliance
Lightning Source LLC
Chambersburg PA
CBHW030840030726
47495CB00005B/1305

* 9 7 8 0 6 9 2 2 4 2 3 2 2 *